Do ye not travel through the land,
and see what was the end of those who came before?
They were many then, greater in strength
and mightier in the monuments they left behind,
Yet all they accomplished was no profit to them.

The Holy Koran

Robert Carter was born in Staffordshire and educated in England, Australia and Texas. Formerly with an American oil exploration company and then with the BBC, he has taught, worked in and travelled wilder places of the earth. His love for India has sent him there four times. Robert Carter now lives principally in London.

BY THE SAME AUTHOR

Armada

TALWAR

Robert Carter

ORION

An Orion paperback
First published in Great Britain by Orion in 1993
This paperback edition published in 1994 by Orion Books Ltd,
Orion House, 5 Upper St Martin's Lane, London WC2H 9EA

A CIP catalogue record for this book is available from the
British Library.

ISBN 1 85797 434 4

Typeset by Deltatype Ltd, Ellesmere Port, Cheshire
Printed in England by Clays Ltd, St Ives plc

For Mary, my own Indian princess

ACKNOWLEDGEMENTS

This work of four years has been materially aided by several people to whom credit is due. Principally, my thanks go to Toby Eady, a man who really knows writers; to James Clavell whose encouragement started everything; to Susan Watt who caused the tale to be written; to Rosemary Cheetham who caused the book to be realized; to Lynn Curtis, whose editing was essential; to Caroleen Conquest and Katie Pope; to David Wingrove, colleague and true friend, whose unstinting support and insight over the years have been richer than gold; and to Tom Robinson, brother and fellow traveller, in whose company I roamed Hindostan from end to end.

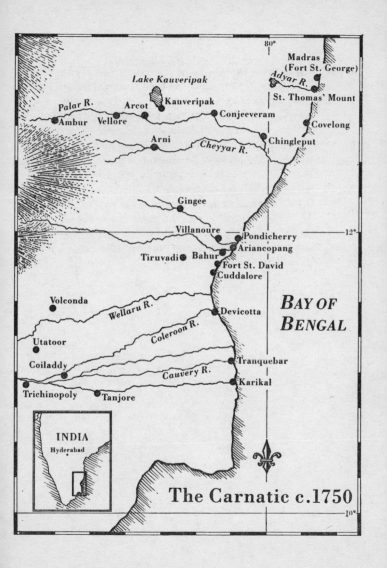

The Carnatic c.1750

Relationship of the Heirs of the Nizam of Hyderabad

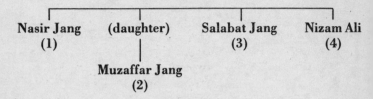

Qamar-ud-Din, Nizam-ul-Mulk, Asaf Jah

Nasir Jang   (daughter)   Salabat Jang   Nizam Ali
(1)   (3)   (4)

Muzaffar Jang
(2)

THE CARNATIC (1740–50)
Chief Political Players

Anwar-ud-Din   Nawab of the Carnatic, the Moghul province in which the English and French trade leases of Madras and Pondicherry stand. He was appointed in 1740 by Asaf Jah, the Nizam, to replace Safdar Ali and quell unrest.

Safdar Ali   Anwar-ud-Din's predecessor. His nawabship was unconfirmed by the Nizam. Ruled for just one year, leaving a five-year-old heir.

Muhammad Ali Khan   Second son of Anwar-ud-Din. His elder brother Mahfuz is Anwar-ud-Din's favoured heir.

Chanda Sahib   Brother-in-law of Safdar Ali. Governor of southern fortress-city of Trichinopoly. Pretender to the nawabship of the Carnatic. He was captured and held for ransom by the Marathas.

Asaf Jah (Nizam-ul-Mulk)   The Nizam of Hyderabad. Subahdar of the Deccan. Nominally the Moghul Emperor's viceroy, but in reality the absolute ruler of all the provinces of southern India since 1725.

Murtaza Ali   Lord of Vellore, a small part of the Carnatic, around the town

	and fortress of that name. First cousin (and also brother-in-law) of Anwar-ud-Din's predecessor, Safdar Ali.
Nasir Jang	Asaf Jah's second son. Contender for the Nizamat on the death of his ageing father.
Muzaffar Jang	Son of one of Asaf Jah's daughters. Nasir Jang's nephew and most deadly rival.
Joseph Dupleix	(Pronounced Doo-pleyks.) French Governor of Pondicherry. Politicard and would-be architect of a French empire in India.
Robert Clive	A twenty-one-year-old English 'writer' (indentured clerk) of the Honourable East India Company at Fort St George, Madras.

PROLOGUE

THE MOUNTAIN OF LIGHT

And so it was written in ancient scripture that the Syamantaka came down from heaven in a time beyond memory, and that this was the same jewel that hung about the neck of the sun god to give him his brilliance. But he gave it to Ushas, Daughter of the Dawn, and from her it passed to the Lord Krishna himself, who spoke unto the world, telling that henceforth the gem would belong to the Kingdom of Men.

And so Lord Krishna said that only those without stain might wear it, the virtuous and the pure in spirit, and that whatsoever impure man took it would surely die. Lord Krishna gave the perfect jewel to Akura, and Akura put it on a cord about his neck that it might garland him with light. Thus the stone remained in the South until the days of the fathers' fathers' time, when the seed of Tamerlane and of Ghengis Khan was united, and the power of the world moved North.

And so it came to pass that this peerless diamond was given to Babur, the Founder, and he took it to himself with an oath that it would be a sign of unity and power and of eternity. And all at Delhi who heard the oath drew in their breath and said it was rare as unity, clear as power and hard as eternity, and they called it Koh-i-Noor – the Mountain of Light.

And so the matchless stone passed undiminished and in this time all the world bowed down before the Great Moghul and paid tribute to his power, even the feringhee who came to Hindostan in their tall ships, and it seemed that the radiant power of the Peacock Throne would shine for ten thousand years. But, alas! The radiance dimmed, and the time of the diamond's passing was at hand.

And so on the night when Nadir Shah, the Persian Butcher, whose name be forever spat upon, brought the Armies of the

North to stand before the walls of Delhi it was decided that the jewel should be cursed afresh, that the words of the Lord Krishna should be renewed strongly, that the Butcher might take the jewel and so die in torment. So it was that the diamond was brought to a holy Brahmin who had been blinded by the Butcher, but the Brahmin stumbled as he invoked the words, and the curse was altered so that any man, pure or impure, should die in torment if he possessed the stone, and that henceforth it should leave a wake of blood.

The next day, ruin came upon the land of the Moghuls, and the Butcher raged through the city of Delhi, and all there fled or were blinded or were burned alive, and the Peacock Throne was carried off to Persia. But the Koh-i-Noor was hidden in a body-servant's turban and smuggled into the South in great secrecy, to the lands of the Nizam, its ancient home. And a lesser stone, the Darya-i-Noor, the Ocean of Light, was taken by the Butcher in its stead, and Nadir Shah knew not the deception all the days of his life.

At this time, the Nizam of the South was Asaf Jah, a Blessing be upon his Name, a great and cunning lord who even then had ruled the people of the South for many long years. And Asaf Jah had as his sceptre a mighty sword, the Talwar-i-Jang, the Sword of War, the Sword of Islam. And those among his subjects that were Muslims saw the sword and drew in their breath for they knew of its power, and these devout knew they must obey its possessor in all earthly matters. Asaf Jah consulted his advisers and his astrologers and those who were wise said he must throw the stone into the sea, but those who were corrupt said he must fix the diamond to the hilt of his sword that both Muslim and Hindu would know him as lord.

But Asaf Jah, the cunning man, the clever man, knew of the curse that any man who possessed the Koh-i-Noor would die in torment, and thus he drew aside the body-servant and bade him give the gem to his foremost wife, and when this was done the body-servant's limbs were struck off one by one, for did not the curse apply to him also? And therefore was it not inevitable that his death be lingering? And when this was done, Asaf Jah was content for he knew that all must now believe his wife's husband was lord, but that she, being no man at all, would not die in torment . . .

4

BOOK ONE

ONE

August 1746

It was the break of a day of ill omen, a day when evil gusted in the heavy monsoon air and sea-demons clung to the ship's rigging and squatted on the yards, howling. Indra, god of warriors, god of Nature, was triumphing in the storm, and surely every man on watch could feel his presence.

His name was Hayden Flint, *na-khuda* – captain – of the *Chance*, a five-hundred-ton country trader, belonging to the House of Flint. Two lascars – native seamen – scrubbed the planking at his feet. He braced himself against the weather rail as the deck pitched further over, and looked to the mainmast and along the bare lower yards, at the straining storm topsails, at the way the wake churned through the wine-dark sea.

It's war, he thought grimly. War, on what should have been my wedding day, and the French are coming to take Madras and all we own, and now the makings of a Bay of Bengal typhoon. The saddhu are right: what sour fate attends the man who misses his way in this life. My father should never have pressed this command upon me.

He cast an eye over the watch as the lascars huddled in the lee. The decks were squared away, guns lashed securely, port-lids closed. The fact remained: he was made captain of this jewel of his father's fleet, and as such, he would do his duty.

He listened to the creaking complaints of the stays, and could feel the mercury falling in the barometer. He was a tall man. A Yankee, conceived and born in the town of New

7

Haven in the English colony of Connecticut, but raised up in Calcutta and aboard his father's vessels wherever they sailed throughout the East. Sparely built, in his mid-twenties, hatless now because of the wind, and wearing a well-cut maroon coat, long-frocked, with cream facings and silver buttons over tight breeches and white silk stockings. He raised a slender brass telescope to his eye. He had a face the Calcutta ladies liked, fine and regular features, a golden complexion made by the sea and the sun on young skin; long dark hair, combed fashionably back and tied in a queue. He carried no sword, but a heavy flintlock pistol jammed incongruously in his belt.

'*Sab admi ko upar ana hoga,*' he shouted, looking about him. All hands on deck.

The serang – native boatswain – repeated the order to his mates and the men scampered to his command.

A shoal of flying fish stippled the sea on the ship's beam; they soared, glided, fell back, bemusing the predator that had frightened them. One swooped in through the rail, lay gasping on his quarterdeck, and he bent to pick it up and cast it back. The old grizzle-haired sailmaker sitting by the gratings put his hands together and grinned a respectful *namaste*, a blessing for the captain who had condescended to preserve a worthless fish's life.

Hayden Flint thought again of the fabulous worth of cargo the *Chance* carried. Normally the Flint holds would be filled with Indian saltpetre, cakes of raw Malay opium from Penang, and the products of Chinese silk winders – goods with a high trade value, with broad margins of profit and the whiff of illegality. They lived by base trade but could only grow by challenging the Honourable East India Company monopolies, breaking into their lucrative and jealously guarded markets. But this trip was different. The holds contained cardamoms and Siam gambodge and other goods of middling worth, a nondescript cargo, some of it contraband, carried north from the isle of Ceylon to the mainland port of Madras, on the south-east coast of Hindostan. But also aboard was the single most valuable item ever to come out of that paradise island. A thing so rich and rare that it might yet buy peace where war seemed certain: a secret present destined for the Lord of the Carnatic, the land in which Madras stood.

It had been his father Stratford Flint's idea to buy the cooperation of the Nawab, or overlord, of the Carnatic. Stratford had put it to Governor Morse's Council at Madras: 'If the offering's good enough, we might persuade Anwar-ud-Din to issue a proclamation that forbids the French to bring their goddamned wars to Madras. Only with the nawab's protection will the neutrality of the Coromandel Coast be assured, and I know of óne thing Anwar-ud-Din Muhammad covets – the Eye of Naga. It's a ruby that's to be had at Trincomalee, a large pigeon's-blood, a Mogok stone, from Burma. The finest.'

'A ruby, eh?' Morse smiled. 'And the price?'

'Fifty lakhs.'

One lakh – one hundred thousand. There were twenty rupees to the Sterling pound. Horror turned to anger on Morse's face. 'Impossible! A quarter of a million pounds, Sterling? The Company will not bear half the cost of such a bribe!'

'Ah, let the Company bear half, and I shall carry the rest, by God! I hate the French filth. And the trading house of Flint needs peace as much as the Company.' Stratford paused, readying himself as if for a killing blow. 'And I want trading rights for Flint and Savage to take effect after the war. Ye'll use yer influence t'get me permits for my ships to trade round the Cape.'

'No, Flint. The Company has a monopoly. You know that. Only an Act of Parliament – '

'Aye, a monopoly on trade with Europe. What I want is a permit to trade tea from Canton to Boston in Massachusetts.'

'You want to ship tea direct to the American colonies?'

'Aye. And without excise duty. No warehousing in London. I want a permit to do that in perpetuity. And ye'll promise it to me if ye want to keep Madras.'

The argument had been furious, but when Stratford Flint threatened to withdraw his offer, the Governor had no alternative but to agree, and that was the tacit deal the Council had finally accepted. Horse messengers sped to the Moghul capital at Arcot, and Anwar-ud-Din sent his younger son, Muhammad Ali, back with them to see the stone assayed, brought into Hindostan and carried safely inland to his citadel. At Trincomalee there had been delay and further news of the war between England and France: a powerful French squadron was to be sent to the Bay of Bengal, while the only British flotilla east of the Cape of Good Hope numbered five weary, disease-ridden ships under Commodore Barnett, last reported at Mergui, far away on the Burma coast.

Hayden Flint walked back abaft the mizzen mast, where the native seamen could not go. Here was Cully, the sailing master, young Quinn at the wheel just seventeen years old, and the two Indian passengers, one man, one woman, man and wife. He glanced in their direction, knowing their persons would be worth more to the French than the prize they carried. They were not merely high-born Muslims, they were Moghuls, the Persian-speaking invader-conquerors of feudal India. A princeling. And by his side, his black-cowled female property.

He was Muhammad Ali Khan, rose-turbaned, thick-limbed, powerful, cruel, infinitely arrogant, but sick-faced now despite his early-morning bowing and scraping to Allah. He was wrapped in a borrowed boat-cloak against the wind, vain and stiff with pride, impassive at the sight of the French. His father was Anwar-ud-Din, the ruler of the Carnatic, the most important province of southern India, and the man from whom the English and the French leased the land on which their vital trading ports of Madras and Pondicherry were built.

Hayden Flint's eyes moved to the silent noblewoman – the begum. He did not know her name. She was swathed from sole to crown in black against the stares of the seamen. In the whole voyage he had known nothing of her but her soft voice and a pair of extraordinary eyes. She was a lady, refined and aloof, exotic, mysterious, untouchable. Her brown eyes danced away from contact with his own; they were limned with black kohl, which made their whites appear very large and clear. Those eyes had plagued his sleep every night of the voyage. They were calm now, calm and unafraid, and he could feel them searching him.

He glanced down at the thick, almost opaque skylight that was set into the deck. Below it his father lay in his cot, asleep – if ever a devil truly slept. Stratford Flint owned the *Chance* and three lesser ships which ploughed the trade routes of the Indian Ocean. He had made his son captain of the *Chance* three weeks before. Pridefully, Stratford Flint had done that. Triumphantly. Angrily. Insistent.

The sailing master climbed down from the maintop. 'What's your reckoning, Mr Cully?'

'French Comp'ny ships,' the sailing master growled. He was a strong-built Virginian of forty, closed as a clam, heavily tattooed and pitted by the smallpox. He answered to no name other than Cully.

'And the flagship?'

'She's a King's ship, the whore. French-built, and French-manned, if I be any judge. Second rate ship-o'-the-line. Plenty guns, maybes a seventy-two. Guess she'll be La Bourdonnais's flag, *Achille*, out of Ile de France.'

'Helmsman, what's your bearing?'

'Still running afore, nor'-nor-east, Capt'n.'

'Bring her head round a point off the wind.'

Cully's pocked face was suddenly loaded with suspicion. 'You're going to heave-to? With the sky black as Whitby jet, an' all? How about I wake your father, and we crack on sail and outrun the French and the storm both.'

Hayden Flint turned to face the sailing master, anger seizing his chest. 'You'll please carry out my orders, Mr Cully.'

Cully hesitated, then backed, nodded. 'Aye, sir.'

Quinn put the helm amidships. Behind them, the wake that was curved like a sword had begun to straighten. The newly risen sun steadied on the horizon. Then a roar came from below, galvanizing everyone on deck.

'What's this? *What's this*?'

Hayden Flint turned at the commotion, crushing down his telescope, hating what had to come.

'You! Get out of His Honour's path there!'

The mate's shouts brought Stratford Flint pushing up the companionway. He was in his fiftieth year, powerful as a bull, brooding, corpulent, buckling his belt round his girth and the gold-embroidered tailcoat he always wore aboard his ships. A black cheroot was clamped in his teeth, half-smoked but unlit. He was foremost of the free Indiamen, a man who had fought to build his fortune in the East as an independent trader, the only man who had dared openly challenge the dominating monopoly of the East India Company.

He knuckled sleep from his eyes and glanced at the sun. It was a golden furnace trapped between the horizon and a swirling, leaden cloud base, and Stratford's huge shadow was cast long across the deck planks towards his son. Then he fixed his stare briefly astern.

'What's the meaning of this?' he demanded in the gritty Yorkshire accent he had never lost despite his years in the colony. 'Helmsman! I'll have my ship's head nor'-nor-east, as I told ye.'

'But, Mr Flint, it were the capt'n said – '

'Mr Cully, replace this man at the helm immediately!'

Steeling himself, Hayden Flint stepped in. 'Father, Quinn's quite correct I gave him that order, as *na-khuda*.'

'Did ye, now, *Na-khuda*?' The cheroot jutted. 'Well, Captain, what were ye about? Are ye lame in the head? Do yer duty, Mr Cully, before I desire t'see the whites of somebody's backbone. Bend more canvas. And smartly.'

'Aye, sir, Mr Flint.'

The starboard watch scrambled under the mates' rattan canes as Cully shouted orders in Hindostani. They jumped for the ratlines, climbing like monkeys.

'*Jage-jage!*' Ready about!

Stratford Flint strode over to his son, taking the telescope from him. 'Well, lad? I'm waiting f'yer explanation.'

'I thought it best to – '

'God damn yer thinking.' He lifted the heavy brass tube to his eye. 'The more a man clogs his brains with thinking the less he understands. So ye edged my ship about, hoping I wouldn't wake, did ye? Panicked by the sight of the French filth? Damn me, but ye're a fool.'

Hayden Flint bit back his reply, feeling cold anger. 'I'm no fool, and I'll not have you countermand me.'

Stratford grunted and shouted an order into the teeth of the gale. '*Istinge muro aur daman!*' Raise tacks and sheets!

Angrily Hayden yelled out, 'Belay that order!'

The watch ignored him. Stratford shouted, 'Let go and haul!'

'*Bharo argey!*' the native boatswain bawled out, echoing the order.

As the *Chance* heeled Hayden Flint could feel his father's eyes looking through him, stripping his soul, laying bare his lack of courage. The electric air was dense, thunder-choked as the tropical storm gathered, oppressing the humid sky until the atmosphere was unbearable.

'Take the wheel from Quinn, and do as I bid ye.'

'I'm ordering you below!'

'Take the wheel, before I knock ye down!'

'I'm *na-khuda*! And I say you'll go below!'

'So, *Na-khuda*, tell me, what's it to be?' Stratford squared himself, pulled the cheroot from his mouth and spat disgustedly.

Hayden Flint shook his head silently, burningly. He saw Cully mutely turn away. The Muslims watched closely, fascinated by the older man's violence.

'Ye bloody hobbledehoy! Take the wheel!'

Hayden Flint's rage welled up unstoppably at the humiliation. For the first time he raised a hand to his father's face in anger, his finger a dagger, his voice barely under control. 'You made me *na-khuda*, by God! Yet now you step on this deck and shove me aside like I'm nobody! I'll not – '

Without warning, fireworks exploded in Hayden Flint's eyes. He reeled back and found himself sprawled on the deck, on his back. His thoughts were all confusion for a moment, then he tried to speak, and could not, and he understood that he had been punched in the jaw.

'Get up, lad! Get up!'

His father's hand hauled on his sleeve, and he staggered to his knees groggily. Every time it had ended like this, his fight knocked clear from him by an iron-hard fist. But not this time. Not this time, by God!

Six feet away his father had turned his back on him, laughing. He put his fingers to his bloodied mouth, his head ringing with anger that blinded him. His red-slicked fingers grabbed the brass knob of his pistol grip, ripping it from his coat. He saw Cully turn, notice too late. Then his father's tricorn hat was flying into the sea, the grey wig still jammed inside it, and he felt to his shoulder the jar of his father's skull as the pistol butt slammed down into it.

The cheroot fell to the deck, then Stratford Flint crashed to his knees and pitched grotesquely forward on to his face. The wound in his bald pate was deep and white where the edge of the grip had cut into it. As Hayden Flint watched, it began to well with dark blood, and the sight of it stayed his terrible fury.

Cully's eyes were wide. 'Jesus, God . . . You've kilt him!' He went to turn the body over.

'Leave him be, Cully!'

'But he's – '

'*I said leave him be!*' He cocked the pistol menacingly. Cully backed off.

Suddenly the orders he must make were clear in Hayden Flint's mind. 'Stand by to clew-up topsails.'

He saw Prince Muhammad watching him with astonishment, the woman clinging to the rail beside him, those extraordinary eyes staring at the blood. Cully was shaking his head.

'God damn ye man, repeat my order to the lascars, or I'll do for you!'

14

'*Gavi istingi taiyar karo!*'

Hand over hand the lascars went aloft in the tearing wind. He saw Daniel Quinn in the ship's waist and ordered him back to the helm. 'Hard a-larboard!'

'Aye, sir.'

'Clew-up topsails.'

'*Istingi gavi ser,*' Cully shouted, his voice hoarse.

Hayden Flint pushed his pistol back in his belt and said, 'Sway out the longboat.' His veins were on fire, but he knew he must carry his actions through and impose his will. A wave smashed into the bows, and, as the *Chance* sheered off, she bucked in the following swell, then the foretopsail bellied and the teeth of the wind caught in her jib and she sliced through the waves, making for the coast.

Hayden Flint saw blood running across the tilted quarterdeck, but his father's massive chest was rising and falling. Thank God, he prayed. Don't let him die. Dear sweet Lord, don't let me be a murderer.

Hardening his face he spoke to his father's steward who had appeared. 'Get his coat off, and give it to me.'

Aji looked on, wide-eyed, aghast. He and two others rolled the master out of his coat.

'Now get him below. Gently, Aji. You're to mind him, and to tell me if he speaks, d'you hear?'

'*Achcha!*' The steward wagged his head in assent.

Half a dozen hands jumped to the order. The sun's disc was suddenly extinguished, blotted out by dense grey cloud. Another wave shivered the side, sending up a fountain of spray, swinging the longboat wildly on the tackles rigged from the mainyard. The rain blasted them in a driving flurry and hope deserted him. Rain drummed into the sails, filled the space above them, making mirrors of the decks. The wind howled, a terrible sustained force behind it, heaving the ship nauseatingly as she lost steerageway and began to wallow in the swell.

Huge drops of rain began to pelt the deck as he cradled his father's bloody head; he parted the eyelids and saw a naked eyeball roll up white. He tore off his own coat and shirt and set himself to staunch and bind the wound with cotton. Then he put on his father's coat and felt inside the deep, broad-flapped pockets. Nothing. Where did you put it, you bastard? Sweet Jesus, what if he'd hid it in his hat? he thought. The one that's flown overboard?

Frantically redoubling his efforts he lifted the coat's hem and his fingers felt a hard round object the size of a peach stone; he knew he had found what he was looking for. He ripped the lining and pulled it out. The ruby was in his hand. The Eye of Naga.

He studied it, gasping with relief, turned it over in his bloodied fingers. It was polished, not cut, like melted scarlet glass, but clear and hard and a deep malevolent red. He held it tight in his fist, knowing he must find the most secure place to hide it. A place so secluded that no one could find it.

I must get the Moghuls and the ruby to Arcot. I have to, or Madras will fall to the French, and never be retaken.

There was only one way.

'Lower the boat!'

Cully did not move. His eyes strayed towards the Moghuls.

'I said lower the boat. Trail it by the larboard quarter, damn you!' Hayden Flint's hand gripped the handle of his pistol, until Cully snapped the order to the men. Blocks squealed as the ropes snaked through, then the lascars struggled to bring the boat to the lee side, and rig climbing nets.

'Sah! Sah! The master, he's stirring now!'

He saw Aji coming up the gangway steps. The distant boom of cannon sounded: French warning shots; they had seen her heave-to. The sailing master backed away a step. 'I been to hell and back a dozen times for your father, Hayden Flint! You ain't half the man he is, and you never will be, y'hear me!'

But Hayden Flint was already up the companionway and on deck. 'You! Take the helm!' he told the mate. 'Quinn, get two men and follow me!' He turned to the Moghul, and shouted above the rising wind in the man's own language, 'If Your Highness would please get down into the boat.'

Muhammad Ali Khan's eyes slitted and his squat, muscular body resisted. Rain slashed at his face. '*Bismillah!* You are asking me to get into that? Now? When the seas are heaving like so?'

'Highness, I must recommend that you do. As you see, the shore is close by. No more than a mile away.'

'You're mad. I shall be drowned!'

'Does not Allah protect His own?' Hayden Flint drew on his determination, knowing he must go through with it, at pistol-point if necessary. 'Your Highness, as captain of this vessel, I promise you, the boat is quite safe.'

As the prince opened his mouth to speak again another shot from the closest French ship buried itself soundlessly in a wave half a cable's length to starboard, throwing up a dazzling plume of white spray; a second later the sound of the cannon struggled to them on the wind.

'Your Highness, they mean to sink us. According to our maritime custom, as captain I have the right to insist you obey me. I will not subject you or your lady to the dangers of a bombardment by the French. Therefore I order you to get into the boat with all haste.'

Muhammad Ali met his eyes challengingly, spindrift bedewing his face. 'Such words, Captain, are easily spoken by a man who does not have to go.'

'You mistake me, Your Highness, I intend to come with you.'

The Moghul stood aghast, holding to the rail as the *Chance* tossed. 'You will get off your ship? Abandon her in this, her hour of need? Did you not just proclaim yourself her captain?'

Hayden Flint shouted above the wind. 'It's true that a captain is responsible for his ship, but he must also take care of his cargo and his passengers. Since the value of these far exceed the value of my vessel, it follows that it is my first duty to see you safe to shore!'

'But your ship? Your crew? What of them?'

'The ship is sound, and the crew are capable sailors to a man. They must take their chance as must we all.' He took Muhammad Ali by the arm. 'Your Highness, I must insist! There is no other way.'

The prince was outraged at the touch. He drew back, his hand chopping out his words. 'Your first duty is to your ship! And to your father! The ship is the safer place.'

'You have no conception what their guns can do to this ship – and to you, if you remain aboard!'

'If you truly fear for our lives, then you will surrender to them!'

Hayden Flint's mouth set hard; water streamed from the driver sail above, drenching him. 'I will never surrender this ship to the French, sir! And I will never surrender you to them either! Do you understand that?'

The Moghul turned away, seemingly entranced by the huge waves. Then he drew close, the admission coming hard from him. 'I cannot go into the boat! I do not swim!'

'Nor do I, sir.'

Another French shot screamed at them. They ducked but it passed high, puncturing a neat hole in their main topsail.

'Quickly! I beg you, sir! Do as I say!'

Muhammad Ali was jolted from his paralysis. He looked privately to his woman. Hayden Flint saw her nod and then the lascars were watching them climb over the gunwale and on to the nets.

In an instant they were drenched. The sea, spuming madly, rose and fell away, and the boat with it. Quinn waited anxiously below, steadying himself. One moment he was up almost level with the *Chance*'s scuppers, the next he was carried far below under the curve of her stern quarter, the boat's top strake grinding and rasping against razor-sharp barnacles.

'Now! Jump!'

Muhammad Ali pushed his sword to the side of his sashed waist, and judged the next rise of the boat with a horseman's instincts. He landed upright in it, turned and immediately readied himself to receive his lady. But the moment had passed, the boat was falling away now, and in sudden fear her hand groped out for help that was not there. For an awesome moment she dangled, blinded by her veil and unable to locate her feet in the climbing net. When the ship rolled she swung out from the side; she threw her head back and the veil was plucked off by the wind.

Hayden Flint gasped. He signalled urgently to the two lascars attending the net.

'*Jaldi!*' Quickly!

But instead of making a grab for her hand, the men shied away from her. They were low-caste Carnatic Hindus and he saw the horror in their faces. On shore, a disrespectful comment made within earshot of a Moghul lady's palanquin was sufficient cause for instant execution. They dared not touch her.

'Grab ahold of her, damn you!'

Despite the order both lascars remained rooted. Her grip began to fail dangerously, and, careless of the stone in his keeping, Hayden Flint lunged forward over the rail, caught her above the elbow. She clung to his huge braided cuff, and he pulled with all his strength. For a moment their faces were pressed cheek to cheek, then the boat was rising again and he released her into it.

Quickly, she buried her head in Muhammad Ali's cloak and drew a fold across her nose and mouth. She had been disgraced in the eyes of her husband: a dozen men had seen her face and hair, and he – a total stranger and, worse, an infidel feringhee – had touched her bare upper arms. He had saved her life, but her embarrassment would far outweigh her gratitude.

He climbed over the gunwale and dropped into the boat, landing heavily, aware that Muhammad Ali Khan was staring furiously at him. He grabbed the rudder – the boat needed four oarsmen, so he shouted to three lascars to hurry down. '*Nazdik ao! Jaldi!*' Come here! Quickly!

Quinn drew his knife and severed the line that secured

19

the prow. They pushed off, and the boat drew away, he and Quinn heaving at the oars in unison. The sea was mountainous, waves of sapphire blue and churning white, vast rollers that had travelled up out of the uncharted immensity of the southern ocean. They were thrust deep into its pits where they lost sight of everything, where threatening bluffs of water towered twenty feet above them. Then their tiny boat was tossed up, as on a whale's back, and they saw the Frenchmen and the *Chance* and the storm-shattered coast.

Each time the boat sank into a trough, he prayed that they would not be swamped; he heaved at his oar until his arms ached and the skin of his hands tore. Each time they were lifted up the gale slammed them and he snatched a breathless glance about him, until the *Chance* and her French pursuers were small and far away. No shot would sink them now, no ship would come for them, French or English. And soon there was another sound soaring higher above the wind.

'The shore! God be praised!'

But the thanks died on his lips. He saw where the furious power of the sea met solid earth, where its fury was dissipated in wild breakers. The coast was long and die-straight, shallow shelving white sand, fringed with swaying palms and, beyond that, lagoons of safety. But the typhoon had set a triple barrier of shark's teeth between them and the land.

'What'll we do?' Quinn asked, horrified by the pounding.

Now the boat was awash shin-deep, despite the woman's frantic baling. Hayden Flint tore his salt-blinded eyes away from the curling crests ahead. The wind shed manes of pure white spume from their tops, and it seemed they were horse-heads charging for shore. The magnificent deadly beauty of it all but paralysed him. He fought the numbness in his arms. His breath came in gasps, his words almost lost in the roar.

'Keep stroke!'

20

He committed them to the tide, praying that his timing was good, believing that somehow he could keep the prow square to the enormous breakers. Then they ploughed into a hell of water.

Once – twice – three times they were carried forward on the surges. Each time, when the boat crashed down again, both oars were miraculously still in their hands and the sucking, twisting wall of water had missed them. The thundering sea was deafening, its grip irresistible. Thirty, forty yards and they would beach, but the boat was dragged back as the sea gathered for another smashing blow.

Again they were raised up, but the sea caught them in a rip current and threw them sideways. The oars were flung up out of their rowlocks and away. The fearsome wave arched over them and hung as they wallowed broadside to it, then a hundred tons of water fell on them and the world turned upside down.

He choked, broke into air, fought for breath. When his sight cleared he saw Quinn was gone. The boat was an eye-shaped rim of wood around him, barely visible above a boiling white maelstrom, the prince and his lady a struggling black mass, trapped within. Then Daniel Quinn's head burst from the water ten feet away.

'Help me! God, help me!'

A gasping scream bubbled in his throat, and the terror of drowning made his face a taut mask. He disappeared, and Hayden Flint knew that he could not help him, nor could any man; the next wave would overturn them and dash them all to their deaths.

In a rage of despair he stood upright, defying the sea. All his life he had lived on it and beside it. He thought he knew it; he knew he hated it. He had foolishly gambled all upon it, and now, in one savage strike, it had robbed him of his fortune, his honour and his life.

'Swim for it!' he shouted in Persian. 'Swim, or die!'

Then he threw off the sodden weight of his father's monstrous coat and flung it at the sea before abandoning himself to the waters.

TWO

A huge Union flag tore madly in the black sky above Madras. Throughout the summer months it had hung limp, bleached to pink and pale blue under the burning glass of the sky, while beneath it the crumbling ramparts of Fort St George had sweltered in tropical heat. Now the monsoon gales had come, and the rotted fabric was being torn to ribbons by the typhoon's fury.

Arkali Savage smoothed the front of her wedding dress of white lace, and examined her face again in the huge gilt-framed mirror. Grey-green eyes stared back at her, wide and clear; red ringlets hung in bunches at her temples, and a tress of hair fell across shoulders that were chalk-white. Her carefully preserved pallor remained intact, an achievement after so long a sea voyage through the tropics and the three months she had spent living within the Madras presidency. But as she looked at her delicate features, she saw that the events of the day had left their mark around her eyes.

The Savage mansion stood apart from the other, lesser merchants' residences at Triplicane. It rose amid watered lawns and lush formal gardens, a pillared palace of fifty rooms, stolen from Sir John Vanbrugh's architectural copybooks, with everything an equivalent English house possessed, everything except window glass, which could not be had here at any cost, and which would in any case have been an impediment in the climate. That grand mansion had been the sign and symbol of Charles Savage, his pride, his joy, the vain expression of his pre-eminent wealth and power.

She looked round the palatial bedroom. The monsoon gale was howling, making the chandelier tinkle and swing and the velvet draperies billow like sails. Overhead, a green lizard clung sinuously to the high ceiling, still as a jewelled brooch, tropical and alien and a reminder that although the fake chimney breast showed off a Hubert Gravelot engraving, and the wallpaper was *à la mode*, this was not the drawing room of some Great Marlborough Street salon; this was the other side of the world: a place where windows had no glass, where garden parties were destroyed by sudden storms, where weddings had no grooms.

She would have begun to cry again if it had not been for her father.

'Will you come down now, my dear?'

'Yes, Father. In a little while.'

She saw him surveying the garden from the balcony. Houseboys were going from room to room, shuttering and barring the tall windows. Heavy rain was sweeping the lawns; tables were overturned and tablecloths blowing away. Servants were carrying what they could of the marriage feast inside. She felt her stomach turn over at the sight of it. Her father had promised her the finest wedding Madras had ever seen. Now the hundreds of guests were sheltering miserably in the darkened ballroom. Everything was ruined.

Sir Charles Savage was forty-five years old, slight of build, elegant of manner and of speech, reputedly ice-hearted in all matters of business, yet now his fists gripped the rail of the balcony and his jaw clenched convulsively. Though his grey-blue eyes were open, their gaze was fixed, as if he was silently damning the gods of this faithless land for defying him.

'Father?'

A moment passed, then he broke off his staring. 'I'm so sorry. So sorry.'

Despite her terrible disappointment she tried to sound brave. 'It's not so bad. Perhaps now you'll walk me down?'

'Yes.' He paused, as if distracted by his inner vision again. After a moment he added, still without looking up, 'Take my arm.'

As they emerged at the top of the stair, one of the houseboys stopped and stared. There was something fearful in his expression, as if he had heard awful news.

'Why does he look so terrified?' she asked.

'It's only the lightning. It always upsets them.'

Since the day three months ago when she had stepped ashore at Madras, she had been accorded the highest degree of respect by her father's staff, given every attention by his two hundred household servants. On the day the *Bombay Castle* dropped anchor in the Madras Roads, a train of attendants waited to escort the Savage heiress ashore. And her fears had melted away when she met her intended husband. Hayden Flint had proved to be as fine a man as any woman might desire, tall and tender, softly spoken and handsome of face. She had fallen in love with him completely during those first embarrassed meetings when they took tea together.

We should have been married today, she thought, her eyes filling as she descended the vast stair. I should be a lawfully wedded woman by now, brought to bed and taken carnally, but instead the storm has come, and I remain *virgo intacta*. Has there ever been a more cruel travesty of a wedding day?

Below, the guests were milling in semi-darkness, their dresses and jackets drenched. The Hindu servants were struggling to light candles now the shutters were secured, but the draughts admitted by the louvres made the flames gutter.

'Father, what has happened to Hayden?'

'I don't know, child.'

'But the storm is so violent, and my Hayden at sea.'

'The typhoon will pass.'

'Is he safe, Father? I could be easy if I knew my beloved was safe.' She closed her eyes. 'Oh, please tell me so.'

The keen edge in her voice seemed to touch Charles Savage and he gathered himself. 'Calmly, now. Have I not explained ten times already? Your Hayden's aboard Flint's best ship, and the *Chance* is the hardiest vessel in the Indian

Ocean.' He met her eye but looked away too quickly. 'Look you, now, he's probably safe in Calcutta, having turned from Madras when he spied the storm. He's sure to be dining on roast beef at this very moment, snapping his fingers at the world and thinking of his wife-to-be!'

'Do you think that's true?' She smiled bravely, wanting to believe.

'Most certainly.'

There was a long pause, then she said, 'Father, if there is to be a war, shall we all be killed?'

The question seemed to amuse him. 'No. We shall not all be killed.'

'But there were rumours . . .'

'I think not.'

She thought about that. 'Will there be a surrender?'

'My dear, when Stratford Flint delivers what he has brought from Ceylon to the nawab, a written firman will come from Anwar-ud-Din ordering the French to leave us alone.'

'The French will do as the nawab says?'

'Surely. They must.'

'What if they do not?'

'Then a huge army will come from the interior and send them away.'

Arkali felt comfort at her father's words, but she knew that deep inside she did not believe him.

Her lip trembled as she heard the string quartet play forlornly, the scraping of their instruments almost drowned by the sound of wind and thunder. Hundreds of bottles of expensive wine had been downed by the guests, but many more remained undrunk. She realized that the Governor of Madras was readying himself to leave.

'Mr Morse, surely you're not going?'

The Governor looked briefly to Charles Savage, then back again quickly, producing a tight smile. 'I'm afraid I must. I have urgent business to attend to. My dear Miss Savage . . .'

'But to leave so suddenly? And in this weather?'

'The weather is the least of my concerns. A message has come for me, I'm afraid.'

Her father stepped forward. 'Arkali . . .'

'I'm quite all right, Father. But please don't stand down the servants, or the minister, in case Hayden should yet arrive.'

He forced a smile, knowing – as she did – that a flood of departing guests would follow now the Governor had left. Some news was passing round the room, alerting each of the guests in turn. Drunk or sober they began making for the doors.

'What's happening? Mr O'Farrell, please don't go!'

The merchant she had grasped looked to his wife and back. 'You must excuse us. All the properties are exposed! Not one of these houses is tenable in a siege! No one knows how long there will be to carry our goods inside Fort St George.'

'A siege?'

'There, my dear!' Her father came to her, wasted time comforting her, protectively propping up the illusion still, though he knew there was no longer any basis for it. He had known war would ruin him, and war had come.

Suddenly, a loud report came to them flatly on the wind: a big cannon had been fired. Arkali jumped for fear. A surge for the door followed.

'There, now. It's only the signal gun. A blank charge. No cannon ball.' He lowered his eyes. He was doing it again. Protecting her from the truth. Lying to her. He had to break the habit, but she was so vulnerable, so terrified. How could he tell her what he knew? In the end he said only, 'A large French fleet has arrived.'

'Fleet?' she echoed, her voice barely controlled.

'Yes. With some thousands of African troops.'

She was stunned. After a while she said, 'Will they want to billet their officers here?'

'Yes, I suppose they will.'

'Do you think Governor Morse will surrender?'

This time he did not answer her.

26

'You must believe so,' she said, nervous as a doe. 'Otherwise why should you have buried your silver under the floorboards of the house last night? You would have had it transported inside Fort St George.'

'You're most perceptive, my dear.'

She wrung her hands and faced him. 'Papa, I want to know. Will they – will they treat us decently?'

'I pray, don't consider such things. Though we are at war, the French are a civilized people, and Monsieur Dupleix, the Governor of Pondicherry, is personally known to me. And I . . .'

'Stop it! Stop it now!' she shouted. 'You can't continue to protect me from the truth. Tell me what you know. Tell me now!'

'I know we shall be treated well.'

She was silent for a space, then she asked, 'So they are Governor Dupleix's ships in the Roads? And those troops are his?'

'No.'

'Then whose?'

'They are Coffrees, from the French colonies in Africa. The ships are Admiral La Bourdonnais's.'

'Is he an honourable man?'

His gaze was once more drawn to her eyes. He steeled himself to answer her truthfully. 'La Bourdonnais has always been a privateer. Though he now sails under the French king's warrant he is interested only in plunder.'

She shuddered. 'Then his men will take what they want from us? Even though we're gentlefolk?'

He spoke deliberately to her, all pretence gone from him now. 'Arkali, I must confess a terrible truth. The French have come at the worst possible moment. You must know they have been trading hard out of Pondicherry in the last few years. Business has been bad. I am close to debt.' He stared as if stricken. 'If I am honest, I have to say that I don't know what's to become of us, or how the French will treat us, but I love you and I will always try to protect you.'

She stared back at him as if seeing him anew. 'But the

money? There's still the silver! I saw you and your servants bury a ton of bullion under the house last night. A great fortune!'

He took her hands in his. They were trembling, and his own palms were damp. He shook his head. 'Why did I ever trust Stratford Flint in this madness? But how could I have done otherwise? The money you saw buried was borrowed by Flint. It's neither mine nor his. It's a loan he raised for the endeavour on which we depended. The money, every last rupee, has been got at a ruinous rate of interest that compounds the debt every day the silver remains in our possession. Without Flint's ruby there can be no peace. Without peace I cannot use Flint's ships, or anyone's, to trade myself into profit. Even if I could . . .' He shook his head again, searching for words, then pointed out to sea. 'Arkali, the French have taken the *Chance*. Don't you see what that means? Flint's mission has failed. We're all of us ruined.'

'Oh, God preserve us . . .'

Her whispered prayer was faint, but it bit through his heart. When she looked up her eyes were red. 'And Hayden? My wedding?'

Ominously, as if timed to the chimes of the clock, the distant boom of thirty-six-pounder cannon echoed like thunder off the walls of Fort St George. The bombardment had begun.

THREE

Hayden Flint ducked out through the low door of the hut and cast a dark glance over the fishing village of Mavalipuram. He was dressed only in one of his diminutive host's longis. The faded black garment was made to reach from the navel to just below the knee, but instead of wrapping twice around his waist it was hung loosely over his hips, just sufficient to preserve a giant's decency. He knelt and looked at his reflection in the big water gourd. He was unshaved and his hair was hanging free.

By now the village was beginning to stir. Old men were rolling from their open-air sleeping places, young men scratching and yawning, women beginning to ghost gracefully towards the river with big earthen pots on their heads. A sharp movement caught his eye. Beyond the last hut, leaves of a big peepul tree shimmered. A man, all rib and sinew, his lithe black body painted with ochre, his hair long and in matted locks, stretched like a cat, then let himself down from one of its spreading boughs by a rope. The marks of Shiva were painted on his brow; he carried a begging bowl and a wooden trident.

Just their filthy saddhu godman with his horn of plenty and his magic wand, Hayden Flint thought. They're lunatic beggars, mendicants, rude and irritating surely, but also harmless. Just a holy madman the villagers believe is touched by God. At least he's stopped singing his dirges. They have a strange hold over the people as soon as they start to dance and yabber their cursing songs.

Hayden Flint saw the saddhu approach, seemingly unaware of his presence, but the man stopped suddenly, a couple of yards away. He turned slowly and, calmly extracting his penis from his loincloth, began to urinate in the dust.

'Good God, man! Have you no shame? I've no money for you! Get away from me!'

The saddhu ignored him, finished urinating, shook himself, readjusted his loincloth. Then he squatted and began to play with the dampened earth, sprinkling ash from a pouch, until he had kneaded the mud into a thin paste which he took up in his fingers and tried to apply to Hayden Flint's forehead.

He recoiled in disgust, but the godman moved with surprising speed and dabbed a smear accurately between his eyes.

'Get away, I said!' He lashed out with his foot and caught the saddhu's leg, tripping him as he danced back. 'Go on! Get about your begging, you heathen animal!'

He rubbed furiously at the mark. Though the pain in his chest had lessened to a dull ache now, the bruises were still livid on his ribs where Aravinth, the village headman, had used ancient skills on him. He had flogged the seawater from his lungs and hammered his chest to make his heart beat again. Any exertion now, no matter how slight, was painful. He leaned forward over the big gourd, poured a dipper of cold water over his head, gasping. Then he dropped the dipper, and it fell with a splash.

A cockerel crowed out, and Hayden Flint realized the villagers had begun to melt away. Automatically, his attention focused on the Moghul's hut, and he saw Muhammad Ali himself standing there, his talwar bound jauntily into his waist sash. He had seen everything, and he strode out, smiling.

So much fear has been loosed here by our coming, Hayden Flint thought as he watched. Perhaps the ruby inside me is truly cursed!

He cautioned himself. Take care. Rational beliefs are fragile in this land. Superstitious fear bubbled in him at that thought, a darkness just below the surface of his mind, a hell of fears separated from his waking thoughts by a very thin membrane. He felt the terror of them. Without his beliefs – in the order and lawfulness and logic of the world – what could there be but an unknowable chaos, an unpredictable and terrible Creation in which nothing could ever make sense, except magic?

But it was only the magic of European thought that had the power to destroy demons. Two hundred years ago in the enlightened Jerusalem of England men had begun to cast off the yoke of fear. Painfully the darkness had been pushed back and the fear banished, freeing, enlightening, and bringing reasoning sanity. He shook his head involuntarily. How could he, a man of that tradition, surrender these hard-won certainties of mind? How could he take in exchange the limitless voids of Eastern thought? How could he believe again in magic?

Hayden Flint regarded the village darkly, his back straightening. That the saving of our lives should have placed so heavy a burden upon these mild people is an injustice, he thought, clinging to that certain and guilty truth. To have brought any Moghul down upon them without warning would have raised panic, but I brought them Muhammad Ali, the man who owns them and everything around them – everything except the sea and the sky, which is the gods' prerogative.

Only the saddhu seems to harbour no terror of Muhammad Ali, and that's because he's a madman. Look at him, now. His insolence . . .

Oh, God! No!

Without any warning Hayden Flint had seen the first light of the sun flash off Muhammad Ali's sword. Strangely it seemed to hang there in the dawn sky, curving, recurving, crossing the silver of the old moon so that for an instant Venus studded the pommel like a diamond. Then the talwar rose and stood poised to slash down over the saddhu and Hayden Flint could not shout or stand or do anything except watch as the matted head dropped and rolled in the dirt, as the headless body staggered forward a pace and crumpled down.

The prince lifted the talwar again, examined its length, then put a critical finger to the undulled edge at the place where it had bitten through the bones of the godman's neck, and wiped off the blade. Casually he sheathed it and stepped out the twenty paces to where Hayden Flint stood.

'So,' he said, his eyes half-lidded. 'Now there is one less *heathen animal* to bother the world, eh, foreigner?'

Hayden Flint could say nothing. His eyes searched to make contact with the prince's humanity and all the while his mind hammered at him, willing him to believe it had been some kind of accident, or an act of self-defence, or that it was done for some reason. Any reason. There had to be a reason to kill a man.

The eyes Hayden Flint searched were not shark's eyes. They were liquid and alive and human, and they were very amused, and Hayden Flint saw in them the challenge he dreaded. His own whisper was a croak, intense and full of revulsion. 'Why?'

'Because he disobeyed me. I told him he must keep away from us. From me, from my wife, and from you, foreigner. Especially from you.'

Hayden Flint shook his head. 'But there was no need to kill him!'

Muhammad Ali's smiled dropped away. 'This is my country, foreigner. Mine under the laws of the One God. Everything in it is mine – everything and everyone – and those who live do so under my sufferance alone. Remember that.'

He smiled and turned and began to walk away.

Hayden Flint tried to control himself, stop himself shaking, stop himself looking at the hideous staring face of the godman. Then the anger tore out of his chest. It was the same blinding anger he had felt just before lashing out at his father. Magically his fear lifted, and he knew that for a precious moment he was free. For that instant he wanted only to come at Muhammad Ali, and tear him down.

'You bloody murderer!'

He had shouted it at the prince's back, yelled it at the top of his voice, but the prince was already twenty paces away, and the tension had made Hayden Flint's voice hoarse, and the insult had been shouted in English, and perhaps also the prince had affected not to hear him, so that he did not even pause his step.

In the silence, the rage began to crowd him again, and Hayden Flint began to walk, out of the village, towards the grove of ruined temples, to put distance between himself and Muhammad Ali's killing sword. He felt himself shaking with white-faced shock and he despised the ignorance and darkness seething in this decaying Muslim empire. He did not stop until he was safe among the huge timeless stones of Mavalipuram.

After an hour or so, she saw him get up from the sand and turn his back on the sun, following the beach, apparently lost in thought as the sun rose higher. Then he turned inland, as if his mind was made up.

From behind her screen, Yasmin Begum, wife of the second son of the Nawab of Arcot, regarded the feringhee with undiluted interest. What a bigger world this is than ever I thought, she decided. Not only their skin is different, they think differently, too. I thought he was going to attack Muhammad for killing the saddhu. It is well he did not, for then my husband would have surely ordered the death of every witness.

Aravinth's people were out in the fields. They laboured like dark skeletons in ground that had been cleared from the jangal and irrigated with sweet water raised from the Palar River by a great spidery treadwheel. As the Englishman approached the headman's hut he turned the heads of half a dozen women, who stared just as openly as their naked children.

Aravinth, the headman, came out, his face taking on its customary look of deference. He put his hands together.

'*Varuka.*'

'*Varuka,*' the Englishman replied.

She knew he did not understand the Tamil language, but

greetings were universal. Like so many other things. The voyage to the Isle of Lanka had taught her much about Englishmen, and this one in particular. As a youth his Calcutta tutors had given him Bengali, and some of the Indo-Persian spoken at the Moghul courts. They had not spoken to one another directly, but he seemed to be a sensitive man. He has poetry in his soul, she thought, with none of the violence and lust for silver of his father. Yet how he flared when his sense of honour was defiled!

She watched him bow his head in greeting to the headman and put his hands together, offering respect to the one who had saved their lives. Then he went to his clothes where they had been left, washed, dried and neatly folded, on the compacted earth beside his sleeping place. His father's guns had been returned to him, and he picked them up, weighing them with a look of purest intent towards the hut in which Muhammad lay. She passed the tip of her tongue over her lips thoughtfully. He has no powder, so his pistols are useless. Soon I must find a way to speak with him, to stop him from clashing with Muhammad, or else he will surely die.

It was almost noon and Yasmin felt the heat oppress her. The ground trembled, and she knew immediately what it must be. Horses. The sound grew as she scanned the grove of plantains screening the road. Then fifty horsemen were thundering into the village.

Their mounts were lathered and exhausted. Four riderless horses accompanied the party, and a fifth carried Aravinth's son who had been obliged to take a message to Arcot. He was lashed across the saddle; his body had been flayed and was caked with dried blood.

Aravinth's people, men, women and children alike, had stopped their work at the first sound of hooves and prostrated themselves on the ground. No one, except the Englishman, dared to move or look at the bloodied body.

'You! Come here!'

The lead rider was Abdul Masjid, one-eyed, a livid scar slashing his empty eye socket and trailing deeply across his cheek. He was mailed and fearsomely armed with circular dal shield, talwar and lance. A long-barrelled jezail musket was holstered in his saddle. He was an Afghan, one of the nawab's personal bodyguard, big-boned, muscular and deadly. When no one moved to his command, he dismounted and strode towards the cringing headman. He took off his pointed steel helmet, revealing a shock of black hair, greying slightly, as was his beard. He folded the helmet's chain neck-guard inside and looked sharply around.

'Eh, you? What is this place called? Who is in charge?' he demanded, nudging the trembling villager with a be-spurred boot. He glanced about, grinning. 'Ignorant peasants, there is not a Believer among them. What use are they to anyone?' He raised his voice. 'I said: where are we, and who's the patel? Interpreter, come here. Find out where we are, and how far we are from this Mavalipuram.'

Another of the riders dismounted and strode forward, his steel gear catching the light like fish-scales. He was darker than the other, and his eyes were bloodshot from exhaustion. As he came up beside his leader, he caught a movement in the doorway of one of the huts, and stopped abruptly.

She watched the tall, unsmiling white man dressed in his brocade coat and wearing his pistols emerge from the shadows. He came forward, cocksure and insolent, without obeisance and assuming superiority. He was about to intervene when Muhammad's rose-turbaned figure appeared.

Both horsemen went down on one knee before him, the one-eyed leader, slow and dignified. He said with great formality, 'Allah be praised that I have found you, Highness.'

The prince's reply was equally shallow. 'Allah be praised it is you who has found me, Abdul Masjid.'

Yasmin saw that Muhammad Ali's relief was far from sincere. No, she thought, as her husband motioned the men to rise, he'd rather anyone else had found us. Abdul Masjid

35

is my father-in-law's man, a mercenary, and, by the Prophet, the most terrifying son of a whore in the whole Carnatic.

'What is this godforsaken place?' Muhammad asked. 'How far are we from Arcot?'

'The road from Conjeeveram was difficult, Highness, while that from Chingleput was worse. That pathetic lump of dog filth you sent to guide us here could not ride. First he slowed us, then he put us on the wrong side of the river, so I had to teach him a lesson.' A passing afterthought overtook the Afghan's features. 'You didn't want him alive, did you?'

Yasmin considered the real reason why Abdul Masjid had flayed the villager to death. Undoubtedly to enhance his reputation among his cadre, probably for his own gratification, but certainly to maintain secrecy. She thought of the enchanted ruby, and a dreadful certainty flashed through her.

'Yes, I rode without stopping, Highness. Neither bread nor prayer delayed me, because I knew I had to find you. And now I have.'

'You made excellent time, but I ask again, where are we?'

'Ashraf!'

Another horseman dismounted and produced a map scroll from his saddle.

'It's no more than a hundred and fifty kos from here to Arcot, Highness.'

'You brought a native speaker with you?'

'Of course, Highness. Interpreter!'

Another trooper stepped forward. Muhammad said, 'Tell these people to fetch water and fodder. I want them ready to ride again inside the hour.' He eyed the Englishman suspiciously. In a lowered voice he asked the Afghan, 'I did not summon *you* from Arcot. Did my father send you?'

'No, Highness. That was my idea, and my idea alone. You see my men have orders to be particularly vigilant in times of political ferment. The piece of filth you sent as messenger was intercepted long before he reached the gates of Arcot. That's how we got here so quickly.'

Yasmin guessed at her husband's fears, but he only asked, 'You kept your destination secret from my father, and from my brother, Mahfuz?'

'Of course.'

'And no one questioned that a detachment of fifty men was leaving the capital without explanation?'

'I imagine it was questioned eventually, Highness, but I was long gone from Arcot before anyone thought to question me.'

The Afghan showed his even teeth, and a blade shafted Yasmin Begum's heart. She knew instantly the meaning of the smile. The autonomy that men like Abdul Masjid enjoyed was far-ranging. As warriors and intriguers, these Afghan mercenaries had no equal. They had risen to key positions in all the provincial armies of the Empire. They were reckless opportunists, totally ruthless.

'Of course, our departure was expected,' the Afghan continued. 'For a week now we've been awaiting the call to ride as your escort from the Angrezi fort, so we were in readiness.'

'I see.'

'It was common knowledge we would be summoned to meet you there as you stepped ashore – the son of the Lord of the Carnatic needs an appropriate bodyguard, eh? Especially when he's bringing back such a magnificent ruby as the Eye of Naga.'

Yasmin's blood froze in her veins as the huge horseman watched her husband's reaction closely. Allah protect him, she thought. He's truly in the tiger's mouth. How much does Abdul Masjid know? Did Mahfuz buy him? Muhammad cannot afford to let him know anything about the Eye, and he cannot afford to deny anything to his face.

'You *do* have the Eye, do you not, Highness?'

'There was a tufan. It turned us over, wrecked us. We were almost drowned. We lost a good deal.'

'So the messenger told me, Highness.' The Afghan looked back penetratingly, his voice honeyed now. 'You must have been worried, stranded here without any protection, and with such a prize in your keeping. But no need to worry now. No one else knows where the Eye is. No one else knows you are here, Highness. No one else in the world but I, Abdul Masjid.'

The Afghan's laugh was that of Satan.

'God is good,' Muhammad said quickly. The razor edge in the Afghan's voice had grown keener, and she saw the patch of sweat darkening the back of Muhammad's kurta. His breath caught drily in his throat as he made a fatal error of judgment.

'You did very well to get here before anyone else. I hoped you would. And you know it's my policy to reward loyalty. When we arrive at Arcot you must remind me to make you a present. An expensive present.'

The Afghan's eyes remained dead. He said nothing. His hand pushed down on the tasselled pommel of his talwar, so that the great curved sword thrust out behind him like a monkey tail.

Fool! Yasmin thought. Never appease a man like that!

Muhammad tried to summon the courage to look the mercenary in the eye, but his gaze slid along the row of procumbent villagers, and he cracked a sickly smile.

She stood up and approached slowly, almost casually. The Afghan became suddenly as wary as a wild dog, then he acknowledged her with cold politeness.

'Of course, you recognize my wife, Yasmin Begum?'

The unexpected interruption had momentarily thrown the big man. 'Salaam, Begum,' he said sharply, touching the fingers of his right hand to his forehead. Greetings, lady. 'You are well I hope. But your husband and I were discus – '

'I'm very well, thank you, Bodyguard Leader,' she replied imperiously. 'I trust you'll be ready to leave the moment my husband orders it.'

The Afghan stepped back a pace. 'His Highness knows he has only to speak and I will obey.'

'I'm glad to hear that, Bodyguard Leader, because my husband tells me you will have extra responsibilities on this escort duty.'

'Extra responsibilities? I don't understand, Begum.'

'Do you see the man with the two guns?' she said, pointing him out deliberately.

He glanced slowly to his right. 'The feringhee?'

'Yes.'

'What of him?'

'As I'm sure my husband has said, he's a very powerful man. The owner of a particularly large ruby. It's his property until he reaches Arcot, where he intends to present it to my father-in-law. I'm sure he will hold you responsible if it does not arrive.'

The ambiguity of her phrasing made him pause. Who will hold me responsible? he wondered with irritation. Anwar-ud-Din? I do not fear him! Or does her 'he' mean the foreigner? Who is he? And what's so 'powerful' about him?

He regarded the pistols with searching interest. 'The feringhee will have to be most careful with his jewel, Begum,' he said, his guile recovering. 'I have heard there are many dacoit bands robbing and plundering in these parts.'

You must be totally convincing, she thought. Your life and Muhammad's life and the life of the Englishman all depend on what you say next.

'I will say this, Bodyguard Leader, I pity the stupid dacoit who tries to rob this feringhee. For he has sworn to blow the brains from the head of anyone who attempts to touch his property.'

The Afghan stirred. 'One man could not resist an armed dacoit band for very long. And what feringhee knows the first thing about real swordsmanship?'

'This man is completely fearless. His guns are most accurate. They can cut down a man at thirty paces, before any swordsman draws near to him. I, personally, have seen him use his guns in anger. His tactic is to shoot the leader first. He says that followers always run about like headless chickens once their leader is dead.'

The Afghan's eyes narrowed. She looked back at him

ingenuously. 'Mr Flint is the finest shootist the English Company possesses. Do you know who is his father?'

'Who?' the Afghan asked, clearly disliking the Englishman's presence more than ever.

'The great Stratford Flint!'

'Lady, I have never heard that name.'

'You must have. Do you not know the Englishman who sank six of Tulaji Angria's pirate ships off Gheria five years ago?'

'I did hear something of that.' Abdul Masjid straightened suddenly. 'I understand you were shipwrecked here, Begum. The messenger said you were cast ashore, almost drowned.'

Yasmin began to lead him towards the veranda outside their hut, talking as she did so. 'A slight exaggeration, Bodyguard Leader. You know what these peasants are, they don't understand anything. There was no shipwreck. We came ashore in a little boat.' She stopped, and indicated a seat. 'You must be very tired after such a ride in your heavy gear. Please sit down. A rest of half an hour will allow you to recover your strength.'

He resisted her prompting. 'So, you were not cast ashore?'

The jangling of his panoply made her fear surge again as she lied. 'It was a difficult passage through the waves and high wind. Much of the boat's contents was swept away. One of the oarsmen was drowned, the rest Mr Flint sent north, on foot, to take the news of our safe landing to Madras. It is written that Allah looks after His own. Please sit down.'

'Just as you wish, Begum,' he said, seeming crestfallen that the secret of their whereabouts was known at Madras. He sat down slowly. 'As I said, I'm your husband's to command.'

'I'm sure my husband would like you to quench your thirst before anything else.'

'Yes, yes, of course,' Muhammad said. 'Drink. Bring water here.'

'I think Abdul Masjid has been at Arcot a long time now?'

'Many years, Begum. I first came to Hindostan with the armies of Nadir Shah, at the sack of Delhi, when we broke the Moghul's army by panicking his war elephants.'

'It is said Afghans are at their best when times are at their worst,' she said.

Abdul Masjid swelled up at the compliment, not detecting its double edge. 'Oh, we knew just what to do, Begum. We strapped platforms between pairs of camels, and loaded them with blazing naphtha to make them run berserk. And after, we showed the Unbelievers how a real ruler tolerates none of their cow-worshipping heresy.' He laughed, enjoying the fondness of the memory. 'Whenever we caught Hindu priests we used to slit open a cow, make them eat the entrails, then sew them up in the belly and bury them. It's amazing how quickly the rest forgot their scruples. We killed them all for being cowards. Oh, yes, we ransacked Delhi very thoroughly. One rich Hindu I recall murdered all his womenfolk rather than let them fall to our soldiers, but when he found his house had been missed, he ran outside and killed himself! We laughed like drains when we saw that.'

Abdul Masjid's grin stretched the skin knitting the wound on his cheek. 'Nadir Shah was a good man to work for. Plenty of plunder and plenty of excitement, eh? In one siege we killed forty thousand. Nadir ordered ten thousand of those who survived to be blinded when they surrendered. He told me to bring the eyes to his tent in silver dishes, and the Padishah sat up all night counting them out with the tip of his dagger. He told me that if he found one eye missing I would make it up with one of my own.'

'Is that how you lost your eye?'

He laughed again. 'No, Highness! I had made certain there were many, many more than the number he had specified. Ah, but Nadir Shah was the man! A great leader. You always knew where you were with him. And he, unlike some of today's people, knew which hand to wipe his backside with.'

Yasmin moved away. The Afghan had shed his weapons in order to sit down. Now he unslung the dal shield from his back, and took off his talwar. He accepted a dipper of water, wiped his mouth, then stretched himself stiffly. Yasmin tried to see in his movements if he had made up his mind, if the intended treachery was abandoned.

'That's good. Yes. It was a hard ride. Thirsty work, Highness.'

Muhammad sat down too. 'So,' he said, 'do you really think there's the possibility of an ambush on the road to Arcot?'

'As I've said, dacoits may still choose to attack us, Highness. As for anyone else, only your brother Mahfuz has the motive and the resources to mount an attack anywhere along the Conjeeveram road, but he's hawking with the Governor of Ambur somewhere out beyond Vellore. He's at least two hundred kos from here.'

'Excellent . . .'

Yasmin watched them talk from a respectful distance. By all the angels of Paradise, she thought, he's toying with us.

As the Afghan reached for another dipper of water, she took her chance to move towards the Englishman. He had walked away from the dead body of the messenger, apparently filled with disgust and anger, and stood a little way from his hut. He did not look up as Yasmin approached.

'I see you are saddened by what my husband's bodyguard has done to the villager,' she said in a low voice, holding the silk veil that covered her hair across her nose and mouth.

Hayden Flint could not find it in him to answer her, though he understood her words well enough.

'I must ask you, Mr Flint, what are the chances of taking revenge on the bodyguard? While he sits distracted by my husband's talk?'

His mind reeled. 'What did you say?'

'I asked, what chance is there of killing the bodyguard?'

He laughed his outrage. 'Are you insane?'

She looked back at him imperiously. 'The man is an

Afghan adventurer. A murderer and a thief. He knows about your ruby. He is the only one who knows we are here. And I truly believe that unless you kill him he will murder us all.'

'Lady, you're insane. There are half a hundred like him watering their horses here. They're all around us!'

'The others will take orders from my husband once the Afghan is dead.' She struggled to persuade him. 'We would all be dead now were it not for the lies I told him about you.'

Hayden Flint recoiled. 'What lies?'

'Please keep your voice down. I only said that you were an expert gunman who would blow his eyes out if he does not behave himself.'

'Sweet Jesus! You said *that*? To him? To Goliath?'

'His name is Abdul Masjid, and I had to. I know you are a brave and capable man.' Her eyes travelled momentarily down the length of his chest and returned to his face. 'And I think you are a man of honour.'

His voice fell to a growl. 'Lady, you're mistaken. I'm no expert with a gun. These pistols are not even loaded. A professional soldier would cut me to pieces if I – '

'But that is of no consequence since the Afghan *believes* you are an expert. He *believes* the guns are loaded. Surely that is all that matters.'

'And when he discovers I'm not, and my guns are not? What then? Lady, there's got to be a better way . . .'

Her eyes flashed angrily. 'I thought you were an honourable man. I was wrong. You are not. You are what your father called you – a boy! If you will not help me, then I will have to do it alone!'

She turned on her heel, walked away from him, and he watched her go. He saw her cross the open ground slowly, taking small, deliberate steps, until she was close to the hut where her husband and Abdul Masjid still talked. She moved round casually until she was out of the Aghan's field of vision, then began modestly to readjust the silk scarf that covered her head.

Hayden Flint saw the Afghan turn, then look quickly

away again out of decency. She was unwinding the veil as if to retie it more securely, but as Abdul Masjid turned his back on her, the veil came off and her hands worked swiftly to twist its length into a cord.

He watched, paralysed in the knowledge of what was about to happen. She can't be, he thought. She can't be! It's madness! But she had promised proof of her words. Soundlessly he willed her to stop, before it was too late, but her course was set. She looped the twined scarf over Abdul Masjid's head, then, bracing her foot between his shoulder blades, crossed her hands and dragged it tight against his neck, with all her strength.

Muhammad Ali froze, immediately, whether from fear or uncertainty it was impossible to tell. Hayden Flint was running towards her. He saw the Afghan's powerful arms go up, clawing the air impotently. Then the bodyguard overbalanced and crashed backwards off the beach on to his back. The force of his struggles threw Yasmin clear, but she held tight to the scarf which remained hooked under his chin.

His eyes bulged and his teeth champed in a furious grin. As he tore at the strangling scarf his face purpled, the vein in his forehead standing out as the blood pressure in his head threatened to burst it. Yasmin gasped. One huge fist lashed out at her, sending the steel helmet flying from the veranda, and a flailing foot demolished the flimsy woven palm wall beside him, then the Afghan's hand made contact with the scabbard of his talwar and he fought to unsheathe it.

Hayden Flint saw the terrible danger the woman had put herself in. His only thought was the sword in Muhammad Ali's sash. The prince remained immobile, his face stripped of expression. Flint grabbed the silver and ivory hilt and it slid free, slicing the bright steel up into his hand, a half-inch deep through the soft side of his palm.

There was no pain and no blood, just the shocking feel of parted flesh, and he almost dropped the sword, but caught it and stepped forward over Abul Masjid just as the curved

44

tip of the man's blade stabbed like a scorpion's sting into the earth beside Yasmin.

The Afghan ripped his sword free and it flashed back again, making Hayden side-step. He could do nothing to prevent a second swing. This time the blade plunged into the ground between her knees, pinning her salwa leggings.

He knew he had to make his own stroke count, but he was off balance, and he brought the sword down on the Afghan's chest, ringing the blade uselessly off the mail coat. The bodyguard twisted now and raised his sword-arm, so Hayden made a desperate second swing, wild and wide, that sent the Afghan's talwar spinning away.

Horribly, Abdul Masjid's fist still gripped the hilt. The empty wrist spewed blood in pulsing gouts as it waved, spattering everything around it.

'Finish him!' Yasmin's plea was desperate. 'Kill him, or his men will not respect you!'

Aghast at the duty, Hayden Flint placed the tip of his sword against the Afghan's exposed neck, and pushed. The blade slid deeper, until it would go no further. Blood lashed him. The man's body went rigid as if in a fit, finally slumping.

He heard the yelping of the bodyguards who had surrounded them. They had made no resort to save their leader, controlled by the oldest of their number, a grizzle-haired scout who had argued and held them back, until the matter could be decided.

He stared at them now, the sword hilt still clenched in his fist, its point still embedded in the throat of Abdul Masjid, and they stared back at him as if they had witnessed the killing of a man-eating tiger. He saw blood-lust in their faces: excitement, fear, a sly delight – but also respect. As for himself there was revulsion at the killing, regret for the necessity of it, and also shame that he had done it. There was another shame too – that dwarfing all these feelings was a vast and exultant sense of triumph.

FOUR

Stratford Flint threw open the double doors of East India Company House, and paused as the mob gathered at his back.

By the loaves and fishes, but we'll be lucky to carry this piece of treason off! he thought, thanking the devil for the crowd.

Those who followed him were mostly independent merchants and their wives, men and women resident at Madras, with families living on the lease. Some, like the McBride brothers, had prospered in the East and made themselves rich, others were less successful, but, like Stratford Flint, all stood to lose everything, and none felt any great love for the Governor, or the Company.

By God, Stratford, he thought grimly, they're all with ye and there's but one sergeant to keep them out. 'Tis a pity the filth've ceased their bombardment fer ye'll need all yer best thunders of retterick t'bend the Council t'yer will and prevent their cowardly surrender.

The crowd streamed along the corridor behind him, and through the ante-room, trapping the sergeant at bay against the great teak doors of the Council Chamber. The soldier raised his musket but when he saw the mob coming on regardless he turned and burst through the doors, seeking the protection of the men it had been his duty to guard.

Stratford stood on the threshold, eyeing the seven men who sat each side of the long mahogany table before him. They were the Council of the Presidency of Madras, men in whom the Honourable Company had vested all power concerning its affairs in the Carnatic. They were the men who could slam the gates of Madras shut against the

French, or lose the place for ever. At the table's head, occupying the tall-backed President's chair and writing with a goose-quill, was Nicholas Morse. He was dressed in a severe black coat and a new-powdered wig.

At once Stratford knew what he was contemplating. In his nostrils was a reek he had met with too many times before – it was the sick smell of fear. They all turned at Stratford's intrusion, startled rigid by the doors flying open and by the hubbub of voices flooding in from the ante-room.

'Damn me, sir, where's your manners? Can't you see we're in session?' He pulled on a pair of lozenge-lens spectacles, then he saw Flint, and started from his chair involuntarily. 'By God in heaven . . .'

Stratford advanced straight into the attack. 'Ah, don't waste yer prayers on my account, Morse! Or are ye thinking I've come to oust ye?'

Instantly there was uproar from the table, followed by a stream of oaths and recriminations.

Stratford's muscular bulk was the last thing any of them had expected. He knew they must have seen the *Chance* among the French fleet. They had evidently assumed her taken as prize, and with her their last chance to out-manoeuvre the French gone.

'Damn you, Flint, where's that ruby?' Morse's deputy, Screwton, demanded.

'Ah, I've not come to banter with ye, ye lickspittle, but to report t'yer master what misfortune overtook his money, and show him what can be done to save Madras, now that his penny-pinching's brought the fort to a state whereby it cannot be properly defended!'

More indignation boiled up at the insult. 'Answer us! Where's the ruby?' Morse shouted above it.

'Lost in the sea! I warned ye, Morse! I told ye what would come of neglecting the garrison. I told ye the filth'd come after yer hide one day, but ye wouldn't listen! Now I come here under a French truce flag – '

Morse recovered himself and plunged in. 'A truce flag?

47

Devil take me, that's a French wig he wears! As God's my witness he's in a treacherous deal with them! It's plain – he's sold us to the enemy with our own money!'

'But he hates the French! That's well known.'

'He loves money more than he hates them!'

The turmoil from the table rose again and the mob outside stirred in an ugly mood. Stratford waved the Governor down contemptuously, moving for control. 'Ah, sit ye down, Morse. And I'll thank ye t'keep yer slanders t'yerself. Ye knew the ruby was a desperation measure and no certainty. D'ye think I'd surrender me own livelihood up to the filth willingly?'

'You're a villain, sir! And one that has stolen ten lakh rupees of the Company's silver. What have you to say to that?'

'Just this: ye sanctioned the transfer and I've yer signature, and yer worm's here, to prove it.' He swept out a paper and brandished it in his fist. 'Aye, and the Hon'ble Company's stamp is on me receipt, so ye knew the gamble ye were taking!'

'You're a low corsair, sir! You've sold us out just as sure as your black heart cannot be trusted!'

Stratford's anger simmered. 'Have a care, Morse! Don't ye understand? The plan we agreed is in shatters. It's no fault of mine that the French mean to have ye out of Hindostan. If ye'd moved when I said instead of horse-bargaining with me fer a whole week ye'd not be squabbling among yerselves like washerwomen now, fer I'd not've got caught by no heavy weather, nor would I have had to raise a white rag to La Bourdonnais.'

There was more dissent until Stratford banged the table with the flat of his hand. 'I came here to tell ye what's to be done now. And perhaps ye'll all listen hard, fer I know yer Governor's not got the wit to see the way by hisself. He'd give all Madras away fer twopence three farthings and a safe passage out.'

Morse stabbed the air furiously. 'Villain! You insult the Council, you rob the Company and then dare to offer us advice! You'll swing for piracy, Flint! I'll have you strung up by tonight, by the Lord God above I will! Sergeant, come here and arrest this criminal!'

Stratford turned to the rest, his eyes slits. 'Ye should all be aware that the future of the world depends on the outcome of this pathetic burlesque of government.' He steeled himself and addressed Morse directly. 'And ye may stretch me by the neck, but first, if ye've sense, ye'll listen to what I have t'say.'

'Sir, you have no business – '

'No *business*?' Stratford seized on the word, turning to the crowd triumphantly. 'No business, he says, when two-thirds of me livelihood's in this Presidency? And, like me, all ye good folk have every last pin of property to lose. Now, are ye telling me ye'd see yer prospects squandered by a weak-minded civil servant who's anxious only to cover his own blow-hole with the Court of Directors? It's Morse who'd give up Madras, not me! He's the one who'd sell ye to the filth! Is he yer man in a crisis? I say no! I say we get rid of him, and then make a fight of it!'

Angry shouts for Morse's resignation burst from the mob. A chant of 'Fight! Fight!' struck up.

Stratford planted his feet wide. He looked down the length of the polished table defiantly and tucked his thumbs into his belt. He knew the time had come to fire his broadside. 'What if I tell ye I've stepped off the French Admiral's flagship? That I've supped prettily with La Bourdonnais last night? That we had an understanding of one another, he and I, and that this cease-fire is on my account?'

A hush fell, but noise began to swell again as the sound of soldiers running to the summons rose through the unglazed window. The crowd began to inch closer.

Governor Morse's anguish was plain. His voice rose to quell the tide of disquiet. 'Why, then, gentlemen, since you appear to feel this Frenchman's emissary has something to offer us, I'll give him two minutes. Then, by God, I intend to call on the guard to fix their bayonets and send the lot of you to the devil!'

'No, sir!' Stratford stared hard at the Governor, despising his gutlessness. 'Ye can be sure I'm no emissary of the filth, but we've vital business to transact here,' he told the crowd. 'Business that concerns ye all, and too important t'be ruled by a bloody Governor's watch. I told ye that last night I dined with the French Admiral in the stateroom of his flagship, and so I did. That's the truth and so is this: La Bourdonnais means to murder ye all if ye surrender.'

There was a vast silence as he paused, then the sound of more soldiers arriving in the ante-room. They were mollified by the quiet, and craned their heads to listen also.

'Aye,' Stratford told them all, knowing he had won. 'I talked with La Bourdonnais a'right. But only so's I might know his mind. And what I found was plain enough. He's mortally afeared that Curtis Barnett's ships will fall upon him while he's helpless at anchor. He's exchanged shots once already, that means Barnett's no longer off Mergui as yer Council thought, but hereabouts. And if I know the Commodore he'll be waiting his moment. Don't ye see? If Madras can outlast the French fer a week they'll be driven off!'

There was a shuffling and murmuring at that, and Stratford knew that he had grasped out for support but found only air. When Morse spoke up it was with a lawyer's sweetest venom. 'Mr Flint, I take it you are unaware that Commodore Barnett is dead?'

Stratford felt the colour drain from his face. 'Dead?'

'Yes, sir. Dead. Of a blood fever. We've known it here since a day after your departure to Trincomalee.'

Another confirmed it. 'It's true, Flint. Commodore Barnett's squadron is commanded by Captain Peyton now. We have it that they clashed with the French but that Peyton was bested and has retired to Calcutta.'

It can't be, Stratford thought, stunned by the news. The Royal Navy sent off by the rabble now anchored in the Roads? When they have the *Medway* and four frigates? That's not possible. God's blood, if Barnett's dead that's bad, but if Peyton's really sailed north to Calcutta that's a disaster, because it means he's a fool, or a coward, or both.

Stratford's mind began hunting desperately for an answer. Something, anything, to regain the initiative.

'I take it you have nothing more to say, Mr Flint?' Morse enquired crisply, a tight smile playing round his mouth.

'But that's ridiculous! Ridiculous! Peyton'd not do that. He'd know he'd be shot for dereliction as soon as he dropped anchor in the Hooghly River.'

'This is his communiqué,' Screwton, the deputy, said, holding up the letter. 'In Captain Peyton's own hand. I believe it expresses his intentions with perfect clarity.'

The Council stared at Stratford as he read it. At his back, the crowd that seconds ago might have been persuaded to turn the table over and oust Morse bodily stood shocked and aghast. It was disaster. Then Stratford's great laugh rang out confidently.

'Ah, but ye're a pack of fools! It's a feint! D'ye expect Peyton to write ye a letter and put it in a brig? Chapter and verse on his plan of surprise? When the filth're roaming about? D'ye not see through that? What if it were intercepted?'

Morse snatched up the letter and shook it in the air. 'But it was not intercepted! It's here in black and white! The squadron's gone to Calcutta!'

'Ah, Peyton don't trust yer courage any more than what we do. That letter was meant for the filth. Any half-clever man'd see its real message.'

Knowing he must rout out the doubts from them all with his fieriest words, Stratford raised his voice. 'Listen! Last night I played the broken-spirited man for yon French Admiral. I planted some deceits in his mind so that this morning he prettily toured me round his armament, believing I'd come and infect St George with despair and that way I'd win him a fast victory. But I'll tell ye this in honesty, me brave people: the filth've not the guns to reduce St George inside a week if we hold firm. We must get to the walls, and show them they'll not have Madras in a month, or in a year!

'We've two hundred guns and the powder to supply

them. We've three hundred militiamen, armed and trained. And a hundred gunners. And we've a fort round us built to keep any man at bay for a week! It's a quick submission that La Bourdonnais wants more than anything, for I assure ye all, he believes the navy's waiting to pounce on him! He'll surely put us all to the sword unless we keep him out! Now where's the coward who'll say we should sue fer terms, eh?'

'It was never our intention to surrender Fort St George to the French – ' Morse began, but Stratford cut him off.

'Good. Then that's settled. If we're to fight we'll need to enlist men as temporary militiamen. You! What's yer name?'

A bluff young man in his early twenties, one of the Company's clerks, put his hand to his chest. 'Me, sir?'

'Aye, you, sir!'

'Robert Clive.'

'Get yerself to the west-facing wall. Ye're to oversee the batteries there and to make everything ready. You, and you. Go with him. Ye're under his command as of this moment. Go!'

'Yes, sir!'

Stratford hauled the sergeant out of the press of men. 'Get yerself busy marshalling them three companies of Portagoosees who're to man the walls. Ye'r under the command of Mr Sowerby. So do as he tells ye!'

As the soldiers left, Stratford ordered each of the merchants and Company servants he knew by name into makeshift gunroom crews with orders to ready themselves and make reports. Others he appointed to the ramparts, sending still more to the stores to break out weapons, shot and powder, and the women to fetch and carry and make accommodation as secure as possible against the mortar fire that must soon resume, and all the while as the whirlwind gathered force, Governor Morse sat rigid in his seat, seeing he had lost the initiative utterly.

Within the hour Robert Clive came to report that of the three companies of infantry only two hundred men were fit for duty. 'You know that Morse has saved money by employing Portuguese sentinels, vagabond deserters from the military in Goa? They're the worst men in the world to rely on, sir. We've a further thirty-four in the hospital, and thirty more at least who're but young boys or old men.'

'Get them up, every one who can stand or hold a musket. Pull in the Indian customs officials, and those who maintain order in the native town. They'll drill with the first company of Regulars. How are ye faring, lad?'

'Well, sir! Hard work does the soul good.' Clive scowled. 'Hard work keeps the black thoughts off a man's mind.' He walked off briskly, trailing his retinue.

Stratford smiled, pleased with his choice of gun commander. Ah, but ye're fortunate, lad, he thought. Given two or three years' more of peace and the Company'd've squashed the juice from ye like a bed-bug, and ye'd be nowt but a stare-eyed slave. That, or dead.

He felt an arresting hand on his shoulder. It was Charles Savage.

'You lied to them, Stratford! I could see it in your eyes. My God, but you must hate the French more than I thought possible. Don't you know what those mortars will do to us? Hundreds of innocents will be killed.'

'Ah, we're all soldiers now. We've no choice but to fight. Have ye brought the bullion within the walls?'

'You'd ruin the whole of Madras just to save it from becoming French?'

Stratford faced him. 'Would ye not do the same if ye had the guts? Now, have ye brought the silver into the fort, man?'

'You have no conscience! Will you murder us all and sell out your own son? My God, you're a heartless bastard!'

Savage's daughter stood in shock, trembling at her father's side, her eyes accusing him. 'Where is he, Mr Flint? Where's my Hayden? How may I marry your son when he's stranded aboard a French ship, and we're to fight them?'

Stratford felt a pang of guilt, but angrily burned it up as he shrugged Savage's hand from his arm. 'Ye may marry

Hayden any way ye can contrive once ye've found him, missee, and to the devil with the both of ye!'

Her hysteria burgeoned. 'How can you say that about your son – '

'I've no son, by God!'

Savage grabbed his coat-facing and spun him as he began to turn away. 'What do you mean by that?'

'I mean he's gone to hell!' Stratford shoved Savage easily away and swept off his wig to show them the scalp wound. 'He did that to me, and that's a death warrant for any man! He left the ship in a boat. Left his vessel a thief, he did, with the saving of us all in his pocket. He took the Eye and the Moghuls with him over the side. Aye, and at the height of the wind too.'

'Oh, no!' Arkali's protest pierced the air.

Savage's face was contorted. 'You say they're all *lost?*'

'I neither knows nor cares. If he be dead, then the Lord God'll spit him out to burn in hell for his treachery, and if he be alive he's disowned. And ye can be sure I'll find him one day and pay him right smart fer his sins!'

The air in the women's cellar was as hot as an oven and Arkali was exhausted beyond the point of sleep. She felt a trickle of sweat run down between her breasts, and tried again to be grateful for the mercies of the moment. Soon the dread would start again, but not yet. Not just yet.

Suddenly a shaft of light slanted down on her, low and acute, a beam trapped for a moment between the battlements of the fort and the frame of the iron-barred cellar window. It picked out in scintillating motes airborne dust that had been shaken out by the bombardment.

The dust was beautiful, hanging in the air like purest gold. Yes, gold, she mused, gold in the air and gold in the bare white walls. Hang on to that thought and don't think of the dread that's building. See the gold illuminating the small, self-absorbed face of the baby in your arms, and think of this mite's greater misfortune.

She cradled the infant awkwardly in the crook of her arm,

feeling close to tears. At first she had not thought it seemly to accept servants' chores, nor even appropriate to be asked to sleep here right among the others, but after the servants had gone away she detected the hostility of some of the women, and knew her exalted position counted for nothing now.

'Ye'll muck in with us, won't ye, missee?' the bigger of the two McBride women had asked.

'Good. We'll appreciate that,' her sister said, and the matter was settled.

But even these hard trollops had flinched when some of the whistling shots had fallen in the street above last night.

'They got exploding grenades, them Frenchies,' the oldest McBride urchin said. 'And my da says their shot has the weight to come right down through a building – roof, three floors and all – and kill ye here where ye lie.'

'Hush yer mouth, Jossie!' Ellen McBride's thrown shoe had slammed into the boy's ear, but after that sleep had been impossible for Arkali.

As the night wore on, the firing had fallen into a rhythmic pattern, like the changes rung on church bells, but lethal and terrible: first a dozen shots from the north-west, then the mortars beyond the lagoon with their exploding bombs, then heavy ship cannon from the south-west battering at the walls.

Round and round us, she thought, on and on and on, night and day, without pause, robbing me of sleep, robbing me of the power to think until I'm driven almost insane by the terror of it. And then at night being locked in here with those who cannot endure, those like Flora Harlowe who go screaming mad. It takes a certain kind of anger or faith or some trick of the mind to believe that the random death falling from the heavens cannot in truth touch you, or that if it does it won't matter, but I've found some kind of faith.

Oh, Hayden, my love. I know you are alive, I *know* you are. And I know I am meant to marry you one day, and so I know the bombs can't harm me.

Concussions shook the building above as Arkail steered

55

another spoonful of sodden rusk into the baby's tiny bud-like mouth, carefully wiping the pap from his chin. He exuded a nauseating sour milk smell. She saw the pale blue eyes widen as he noticed the spoon, the red ridges of his gums, the tiny hands and fingers that tried to grip her giant finger. He was hot. His face reddened like a beetroot and he bubbled with mucus, and she wondered what to do.

He was the son of poor Mrs Mundy, who had died in the first hour of the bombardment. She looked at him pityingly: a tragic child. He was not yet weaned, already orphaned. Suddenly she hated the responsibility of feeding him.

She wiped back a thread of hair and resettled the infant, scraping the remaining morsels from the grey pewter bowl. She was desperately tired and suffocating in the sour air. It's exhaustion, she told herself. With my eyes open I can hardly remember Hayden's face, with them closed I can see nothing but his beloved features. Oh, my dearest, where are you now?

The baby vomited abruptly over her hand and filthied her dress. She looked up helplessly to the woman who had given the Mundy infant temporarily into her care, a huge woman, wife of one of the Armenian merchants, who fed her own baby from massive breasts. The two-year-old sucked on the big dark nipple lustily, eyes half-lidded, as the elder child cuddled her mother's side. The woman smiled impassively, her bovine contentment unshaken even here. Arkali looked away, despairing that marriage must inevitably one day make a cow of her too. Hayden's seed will do that to me. After the pain of sex my body will be transformed into a bestial thing with bloated belly and udders and I'll be a holy cow surrounded by rude infants, squealing and mewling and demanding and filthying and . . .

Another shuddering concussion woke her and jangled her nerves, then she realized it was the bolt being shot home on the door. Father, you promised you'd come to visit me here before sundown, she thought. You haven't come to me all afternoon, and now the guard have seen us locked in tight, ready for the hours of darkness. Oh, dear God in heaven, I pray the French troops don't breach the wall tonight –

'Shut yer mouth, ye whining little bastard! One more word and I'll hang one on yer ear, and that's me telling ye!'

The tousled brood of McBride children clung to their mothers and aunts in the furthest corner of the cellar as the eldest boy, ten years old, still brass-faced his mother defiantly, fists clenched. Because his father and uncle were absent he had chanced himself constantly, needling and wheedling to be let out to hold a gun, until his mother's raucous outburst had exploded.

Arkali bit her lip, wishing Molly or Ellen would give the unpleasant urchin his way. They were hard-bitten women. Sisters. Not at all ladies though they tried ludicrously to affect refinement in their dress and their manners because their husbands had trade money. No, they were obviously wharfside rudas doxies, women little better than common prostitutes who swilled around ports everywhere like human scum. These two had had the good fortune, if that was what it was, to marry Arthur and Willie McBride. And the match was appropriate. Two harpies hard as rock-salt for two tough brothers who had prowled the Indian Ocean in a heavily armed pirate grab for a decade before turning trader and prospering beyond the dreams of avarice. They were the kind of men Stratford Flint had mastered all his life. The sort who at the first rumble of war fell to becoming sergeants and corporals just as naturally as breathing. And their wives were adept at nothing so much as dropping brats once a year.

The dread crowded her. Howling laughter came from a distance. Undefined, feral shouting, men roaring and braying and the sounds of destruction. Brawling and looting and sin. The baby convulsed and ruckled another milky mess on to her dress.

'Yer've t'wind 'em when yer've fed 'em. Don't ye know that much, missee?'

57

'Won't you have him now?' Arkali said, dabbing at the front of her pale blue satin sack gown.

'Now din't I tell yer t' wear nowt but yer underbodice?'

The McBride brood smirked and shrieked around her. 'Just an underbodice? Like the Mussulmen women?' The thought appalled her.

Night came quickly in Madras. Close and hot and tropical. The purple sky, lit now by French ranging flares seen through the cellar's half-moon window, was windless and infinite. Here, in their shelter, bull's-eye lanterns were glowing, casting monster shapes on the whitewashed walls and pillars. A sickle hung on the wall above the Catholic Armenian woman, paradoxical as a Mussulman's crucifix.

The hysterical laughter of drunken men came from far across the parade square. It made Arkali feel half-naked. The yelling came again, much closer now, braying and yawping. Foul drunken men with burred voices. Rough men, these soldiers, without the acquisitive wit of the merchants, or the starchy discipline of Company servants. Her father had said they were deserters, these Company Topasses: Goanese, with angular European faces and long moustaches, lazy, and fractious because they had run from their own officers once before and knew all the tricks. They were cruel to the native prostitutes, they drank and fought cocks or pitted snake against mongoose for wagers and the joy of it, and now they had loaded muskets in their hands.

She panted in the breathless heat. Those men were moving overhead now. Laughing crazily, raw as hyenas. Footfalls on the boards six feet above. The McBrides drew their children towards them. Arkali heard breaking glass, a bottle rolling on the floor, the furniture of the office above being kicked over, and then the Armenian woman got up and crept past the pillars. She was holding a Malay parang, raised like a West Indian machete. It was sharp and heavy and could cut to the bone.

Ellen McBride hissed at her children. 'Keep still!'

'But the door's barred,' Arkali said. 'They can't get in without – '

'Quiet!'

The hush was broken by the sounds of more feet, and shouts in the echoing corridor, incoherent voices mouthing obscenities in dog-Portuguese, men thieving, looking for more wine. A flurry of kicks and blows rained on the thick wooden door. The blows became hacking, as with a bayonet. The stout door was the only way in or out.

An adolescent girl began to sob as the fear transmitted itself from the women. The McBride lad's face was a white oval now, his boy's hubris evaporated.

The crying gave them away.

'*Ola? Eh! Mulheres!*' Women!

'Quiet! Hush them up!' Molly hissed, moving forward.

'No!' Arkali shouted, getting to her feet. 'We must call for help. Call for an officer at the window! We – '

Molly caught her shoulders and slapped her, then hugged her close to speak in her ear. 'No one'll hear us, missee! Don't y'see? A Frenchie shot's busted open the wine stores and the scum's got themselves rotten on stingo and rumbo. The sound of women crying'll only serve to put them in a blistering passion!'

'But we must summon help!'

'I tell you, I know all about it, missee!'

'*Eh, senhora! Dona de casa!* You want jig-a-jig, eh?'

The man's voice was behind her, raucous and loud and clear. It filled the room with cackling laughter. A huge face was at the cellar window, hideously lit by the lanterns. Behind him another soldier, a bottle in his hand, knelt on the ground to unbutton his wine-stained breeches.

Terror and revulsion gripped her, then she saw Ellen McBride climb up on to the cotton bales and tea chests and with a boat hook jab viciously through the bars into the soldier's groin. He yelled in surprise and rolled in the dirt, avoiding the thrust.

'*Cachorra!*' Bitch!

A bottle thrown by the first soldier shattered against the bars, showering them with green glass and cheap brandy. Akali turned away, shielding herself, wanting to scream, to fill the silence with her own voice, but she could not. The younger children began to cry after the sudden violence, they would not be soothed now. One of the women started to whimper.

'For Christ's sake will you quieten them!' Ellen McBride hissed again.

Arkali clutched a wailing four-year-old to her and held her tight. When she looked again at the window the soldiers were gone. The incessant boom of distant guns peppered the night, throwing the battlements into sudden silhouette. The iron railings and stone gatepost ten yards away were broken down. Suddenly, as she watched, the wall of the building opposite collapsed into ruin on top of them, pushing a slender tree into the street.

A terrific bang on the other side of the cellar door turned her head and she saw the Armenian woman flinch away. The heavy dewlap of flesh that swung under the woman's raised arm shivered. She was praying aloud now and Arkali saw the fear on her face. The bang had been a musket shot and the door was being kicked in, the heavy iron bolts tearing out from the old wood. Arkali ran forward to help. A sickle had appeared miraculously in her hand, but Ellen McBride seized it from her and Molly picked her up and threw her bodily behind the nearest tea chest.

'Get down there!'

'But I – '

'By God, you'll keep your head down! You'll only incite them once they catch sight of that white neck!'

She sank down behind the great lead-lined box, her heart racing. Another flurry of kicks and the door began to disintegrate. She saw the Armenian woman jump forward, heard the sound of her struggle, of the parang ringing on to the stone floor. Then a big red-coated soldier pushed the woman back into the cellar, his hand round her throat, jolting her with tremendous force. He shoved her back against the wall like a rag doll and advanced powerfully into the sleeping space, a mad light in his eyes.

Others followed behind, ratlike. Three at first, then

another, and another. They looked round, crouching with suspicion, then they began to straighten confidently as they saw there was no guard. Children's cries rose up as the big man unslotted the bayonet from his musket and discarded the gun.

'You want jig-a-jig?' he said, fixing Ellen McBride with an evil grin.

'Get out of here, you bloody mongrel!' she shouted defiantly, raising the sickle.

He poked the bayonet half-heartedly at her, turning to laugh and to invite his comrades to laugh with him. Ellen McBride slashed the rice sickle at his eyes and he dodged his head back, laughing louder now, but the second swipe was too fast for him and she caught his cheek with the point.

He grimaced with pain, grabbed her wrist and pulled her to the floor, slitting her shift with his bayonet so that her breasts and belly spilled into view. Molly jumped out at him, screaming now. Arkali got to her feet, but the other men came forward and wrestled her away.

One of the soldiers threw Molly to the ground with immense strength, concussing her. Ellen flew at him, madly tearing at his eyes and flailing her knee at his crotch. The big man threw down his bayonet and took the sickle from her as if she was a child. He was breathing hard now. Blood was smeared on his face from the cut. He wiped at it, ordered the two youngest men to guard the door, then Arkali saw him grab Ellen by the hair and hook the sickle round her throat. He shook her back and forth until she spun away, her hand going up to the raw wound that had opened up on her neck. Then she collapsed, gasping for air.

Arkali felt herself dragged out; she saw herself pummelling him with her fists, but he was huge and hard as iron and he grabbed her and subdued her – with ease. Struggle seemed futile. One wrench of his hand tore away the front of her underbodice. He gripped her painfully, drinking in her nakedness through blazing eyes, and told her in Satan's voice, 'Now, I cut out your throat, *cachorra*. But first you get down on your knees and beg me to fuck you.'

'A pox on the filth, and a pox on the mangy sons of whores appointed to take this presidency off of us, and on La Bourdonnais and Dupleix in particular!'

Stratford Flint emerged from the smoke as it cleared from the battlements. He slapped the dust from his coat and breeches and fixed an eye on the flashes of the French batteries. A wisp of smoke curled up and away in the hot unstirring air amid a dark palm grove half a mile from the walls. A grenade from one of the coehorn mortars had looped high and plunged down to burst, demolishing the steps behind him and scattering his entourage.

A face appeared grinning in the blackness. 'I hope that bang didn't inconvenience you, Captain Flint!'

It was the young Company clerk he had put in charge of the guns of the west wall reaching down to offer a hand. He sweated now in a patched red jacket borrowed from the quartermaster's store. He was powder-smudged but grinning and unperturbed by the near miss.

Stratford glowered up at him, but allowed himself to be helped to the gun platform. As the gun crew stood by, shouldering their ramrods, Stratford regarded the clerk as closely as he could in the semi-darkness. The man was twenty-one or -two, an awkward mover, thickset, with a fleshy face dyed tawny by the climate and most probably an excess of cheap wine, and made darker now by the powder filth. His nose was blunt and his eyes were set shallow under heavy brows. As he walked round the gun, Stratford saw that the natural fall of his mouth was upturned at the corners into a false grin. I'll bet that twist to yer mouth makes ye seem by turns moody and insolent to yer superiors, and ye seem to have a grievance on yer mind. All in all, ye've a face like a bread pudding, Stratford thought with faint amusement, but that's how God made ye, lad, and ye've to live with that.

'Devil break me legs if I'm inconvenienced by French shot. And it's *Mister* Flint, if ye please. Captains are them as works fer me.' He relit his cheroot from the gunners' match.

The lad said pleasantly, 'A mite cooler now the sun's set, what, sir?'

'Quite so.' The day had been blistering, the French fleet standing with bare spars on a glassy ocean, their guns firing slower now. 'Aye, they're pacing themselves. Running out of iron shot, I'll wager. They know they're in fer a long haul now.'

He looked about him as the others emerged from the stair, coughing and dusting themselves, and drew in a mouthful of tobacco smoke, pleased with the young clerk's sangfroid and the ingenious way he had lashed up his cannons with ropes and planks to keep them aimed and firing, and to maintain the French siege at a respectful distance. It was true that the only real export the Company made to the East was raw courage, and that would serve as currency anywhere.

'Ye did well here, lad.'

'Thank you, sir, but if it's not "Captain" it's not "lad" neither, if you please. Lads is the rest of them.'

Stratford stared hard at him, taken aback, then grunted. 'That's fair, then, by God. Since ye've worked fer yer title, ye'll be Mr Clive. Now, were I not good enough to give ye the command of this station?'

'You were, sir.'

'I like the way ye work, Robert Clive.' Stratford drew a sabre and a pistol. They were Royal Navy issue, good and well made. Clive took them gratefully.

'Sir? If you'll sanction it, I'll chock the barrels with whatever I can filch, then go down into the Company offices to find what I can.'

'Sanction it? Don't ask fer my say-so. Ye're in charge here. Do what ye think's right.'

'Yes, sir! I surely will!'

Before he turned away, Clive set a torch burning to light his way. He crossed the parade square with the flaming firebrand in his fist. His thoughts were of the worrying vulnerability of the north wall where the native town could give ample and easy cover to a French assault. Then, almost too late, he saw the figure running from the shadows of an alley.

He thrust the torch above his head, trying to make the shape out plainer.

'*Khare raho*! Stand, damn you!' He laid his free hand on the hilt of the navy sabre but he did not draw it; he lunged instead and the fugitive ran full pelt into his thigh.

'*Tum kidhar jate ho?*' he demanded, grabbing the scruff of his neck. Where do you think you're going? Then he saw it was one of the McBride boys, the eldest. He was breathless and in shock.

'It's the sojers!'

'Soldiers? Where?'

'They're all jug-bitten, sir. Stone-mad they are, and amurdering!'

Clive shook the boy by the ear. 'French troops have got in? Is that what you're trying to say?'

'No, sir! Them Comp'ny Portagoosees – they're after killing my mammy! Killing her and the gels, sir!'

He stared at the child, dumbfounded. 'Where?'

'In the cellar! In the cellar!'

'Are you sure? Show me.'

He ran after the boy, trying to make sense of the garbled message, then, as he turned the corner, he stumbled over two men slumped in the road. He tried to pull one to his feet but the soldier was limp and insensible. The insignia on the man's jacket told him that these were the men who had been sent to guard the north wall. He picked up an empty brandy bottle, stared at it. Both men were stinking drunk!

'Damn them!'

Then the McBride boy was tugging at him, urging him on. As he rounded the next building he saw the cellar window and heard the screams.

'Fetch help!'

'But I want – '

'I said, fetch help, damn you!'

Horror consumed him as he realized what was happening. Drunken mutineers forcing themselves on the women, he thought, and Arkali Savage is down there! By God, if they've harmed one hair of her head they'll pay for their actions ten thousandfold!

He gave the flaming torch to the boy and pulled out his sword and pistol. The terrified screams spurred him like knives. He left the lad with another order to fetch more help before fighting his way into the dark building over a mass of tangled chairs and tables, and diving down the stone steps and into the basement passage.

Once off the stair his eyes were grateful for the dim orange light issuing from the cellar. It seemed to him that he had stumbled into one of the caverns of hell. Two laughing devils were viciously slashing at women and girls with hand held bayonets, ordering them to strip, taunting them with freedom but keeping them back from the shattered door. Younger children obeyed pathetically, cowering in the corners as their elder sisters ran back and forth screaming.

He came on, suddenly filled with savage rage, and drew back his sword instinctively. The blade soughed through the air, hacked at the throat of the nearest man, and the draw-cut went deep, severing the strings of his neck. The mutineer went down welling blood as the second man stared up at him, astonished, before recovering himself and turning to the attack. Without thinking, Clive straightened his arm and plunged the sabre through the mutineer's shirt and a foot deep into his navel, withdrawing the weapon sharply before the abdominal muscles could spasm closed on the blade and hold it. The man staggered down and lay helpless, absorbed in his own agony.

He had not used his pistol, and neither man had made a shout of warning. It seemed that the chaos of screaming had preserved an element of surprise.

He stepped past, horrified, crossed the entrance and flattened himself against the wall, his pistol in his left hand. He was alive to the danger and the need to tread carefully. There were shouts. How many men were inside? How were they armed? As his head came round the corner he saw three more mutineers sprawling on their female victims, ripping at their clothes and bodies, punching and shouting to subdue them. Then he saw Arkali Savage, and the hot dry air turned to ashes in his mouth.

Her struggles were futile. They had stripped her naked and the biggest of them had forced her bare back against a pillar. Her arms were dragged tight around by a second mutineer, a small, verminous man, who gripped her wrists. Her pale, slim body scratched, and smeared with blood, bucked as the big half-naked soldier tried to part her legs and thrust himself between her thighs.

For a long second Clive gaped at the scene, shocked to a standstill at its bestiality. Men were sprawling on their half-clothed victims, on the ground, on charpoys against the walls. The McBride sisters, covered in blood, were strewn like discarded dolls across the floor. Molly lay dead; beside her Ellen stared sightlessly, her throat slashed open.

He tore his attention back to the big man who was clearly the mutineers' leader. He was barrel-chested and his filthy shirt hung off him, ripped wide from neck to hem and soaked with blood. His face was booze-red and bleeding from a wound on his cheek, his eyes were fiery and sly, and as he pushed his breeches down, the dark stalk of his penis rose up grotesquely.

'No, please!' Arkali pleaded hysterically, her fingers spikes. 'No! I'm a virgin. Please. I'm a virgin!'

Clive bellowed incoherently. He burst forward and chopped his sword into the head of the man holding Arkali's wrists. The skull clove like a turnip and he fell to the floor.

The big man reeled off Arkali wordlessly, his dull eyes fixed on the blue steel of the navy sabre, his huge erection suddenly a laughable emcumbrance. '*Afsar!*' he shouted. Officer!

The other mutineers had already seen what was happening and come to their senses. Now the women struggled out from under them and fled for their children and the unguarded door as their assailants jumped to their feet.

Arkali stared, felt the red-coated officer grip her arm. She

66

flinched, unable to believe he was really there. This was a nightmare that was never going to end. She saw the four drunken soldiers begin frantically searching for weapons and the officer put out a protective arm to ward her away.

He shouted an order in their language, but they crouched like cornered animals, their eyes white on the barrel of his pistol. They were backed against the wall but spreading out dangerously, more confident now, and eager to take on the young officer who pointed his gun at each one in turn to cover their slow withdrawal. Then she heard more footsteps overhead.

The panic rose in her and she tried to warn him, but as she turned she saw a Portuguese sergeant armed with a pistol, and the McBride men, also armed, and the horror-struck little boy with them – and her father, at last, her father! He swept her up, swathed her in a blanket and held her tight and she saw that Stratford Flint filled the doorway and that he held a knife loosely in his hand.

As soon as they saw him the four mutineers fell back, wild-eyed like pigs on an abattoir ramp, as if they knew what would happen next.

'Give her yer pistol,' Stratford told Charles Savage in a strange, low voice. 'Let her have her justice on them.'

'No! Not Arkali!'

'It'll help heal her wounds, by God!'

'No!'

Stratford stared back at him, his eyes diamonds, then he nodded. 'It's your decision. Then ye'll clear the cellar and leave us to do the rest in our own way.'

Charles Savage drew back, deeply horrified by the carnage and by the significance of Stratford's words. The wailing was muffled as he helped Arkali to stand, and she was steered from the cellar, stepping stiff and cold and shaking over the blood-spattered dead. At the door he lifted her and carried her up the stairs, still numb, and thanked God she was alive. Below, only the young officer who had saved her, the two McBride men and Stratford Flint remained in the cellar with the four mutineers.

Four on four, as Stratford's barbaric code of honour demanded.

Before they reached the top of the stairs the screams started all over again. The first of the castrations had begun.

FIVE

The ride to Arcot was like a dream.

Hayden Flint and Muhammad Ali were mounted on the two biggest Marwari horses, chestnut mares of fifteen hands, splendidly groomed and impressively caparisoned in silk and gleaming brass. Yasmin Begum went ten paces behind her husband in a richly carved rosewood palanquin, carried across the shoulders of six slaves.

He had still been in shocked condition when the column left the village, his wounded hand bound up in a purdah veil, his clothes spattered with dried blood and the rage of the death struggle still ringing in his head. He could not think straight, events were impossibly mixed up. There was Yasmin Begum getting to her feet over the body; the Afghan's flesh rippling and twitching, though he had been dead more than a minute, and the startling groan he made as they turned his body over to drag him away.

After the killing Yasmin Begum had looked to him in triumph, the blood-lust still firing her eyes. Then she had thanked him. And Muhammad Ali praised him grudgingly, and the guard watched him with their strange silence, expectant as dogs at a dinner board. But he was in no condition to pay any attention to them. The fact was that he had killed a man, and even though it had been necessary he felt revolted at what he had done.

Trancelike, with the ache pulsing in his wounded hand, he had ridden away from the nightmares of Mavalipuram and slowly awakened to himself to find the bountiful land unfolding around him like a lotus blossom. The verdant green of rice fields along the River Palar were broken by dark wallows in which water buffalo waited out the afternoon. It was a landscape dominated by the wide, shallow river, waters glistering under the sun, and the fecund plain punctuated by distant women, bright in coloured saris, labouring in the fields. He passed mud levees, clusters of thatched huts and the huge yellowing leaves of plantains whose fruits hung in vast pendulous green fists, unripe as yet.

All day the heat increased and the sky grew vaporous and heavy, turning to the milky white of a blind man's eye, then the sun sank into the mountains, red and blear, and Hayden Flint knew that the season was pregnant with the onset of the monsoon.

He looked behind him, disappointed at their progress, irritated by the cumbersome and lumbering palanquin. It seemed to him the woman was imprisoned within its confines: a screened and curtained travelling litter made without wheels and hung instead from a freshly cut pole of green bamboo. The riders had sent to Arcot for the conveyance and it had arrived broken down into components and lashed across baggage horses especially for the begum. He had seen its like often in the dhoolies of Calcutta and Madras. The richer English traders went about in them, mainly to keep up appearances for the benefit of Bengali merchants and money-brokers to whom appearances were all. But his father had never used one, saying that the only time he would suffer to be borne aloft by six men was on the last voyage of all, when he lay in his burying box and could not properly decline the trip.

You are in Hindostan now, Hayden Flint told himself. According to custom, it's the only mode of travel, except the howdah of an elephant, that a Moghul noblewoman can respectably use. If only they'd relieve the poor wretches carring the weight of it more than once an hour. Can't they see the obvious way to speed our journey? The bodyguard could take turns. Rotate the work with fresh men to act as bearers. Perhaps I'll suggest it? He glanced at the prince.

Muhammad Ali rode his Marwari silently, his pugnacious air enhanced by his quiet mastery of the beast. The breed was incredibly tough. These horses were from the lands of the Rajputs, Hindu princes ruling the deserts to the west of Delhi. They were horses with distinctive ears that pricked inwards, almost touching; they had a reputation for endurance but owed their irritable temperament to their Arab blood.

'A fine horse,' he said to the prince, ruffling his horse's mane. 'I was told that this breed has come about by chance from stallions cast ashore in a shipwreck. Stallions which were then crossed with local mares.'

But the prince only looked at him with fury in his eyes and then away and Hayden Flint realized he had said something with a second meaning for Muhammad Ali Khan, something he had managed to interpret as an insult.

Well, damn you! Damn your thinking in riddles and talking in riddles, he thought, suddenly riled by the prince's irascibility. Yes, and damn your suspicious jealousy over your wife too. You watch her like a falcon and treat me like an interloper, and, by God, maybe you should because she's worth ten of you in every department and I'd take her away from you just to save her the trouble of your morbid company!

The burst of angry thinking did him good. After that his strength of mind began to return and he persuaded himself that he would soon be in Arcot and the matter of the ruby would be settled.

Where are you, Arkali? he wondered faintly. What are you doing at this moment? Are you thinking of me? I hope so. And, if you can hear my prayer, believe that I'll soon be back among sane people and I'll cherish you and we'll marry as we should have done. Perhaps then everything will be as it should, and I'll be as I was again.

Before darkness fell they rode through Chingleput where the entire population came out from their meal and threw themselves down on to the ground until the column had passed. A little beyond the hamlet they took refreshment in a roadside clearing while the night camp was erected. Yasmin Begum came out of the palanquin, remaining behind her purdah veil. She approached the fire dressed in a garment he had not seen before, still all-concealing, but made from a lighter, more yielding material that fell in shapely folds. In her hand was an exquisitely inlaid writing box, one of the womanly belongings that had been brought along with the palanquin.

She took out a bound book, opened it and began to write. The movements of her wrist were graceful as she penned the lines in Urdu script, right to left, with a swan quill. He watched her for several minutes, then she saw him and put her book aside. She followed his eye to where the body-guard were making camp. The men were arguing and disputing among themselves with kicks and slaps and a waving knife or two. She registered his unease.

'If they are disturbing you, you should not hesitate to chastise them, Mr Flint. You must not stand for in-discipline.'

He thought about that, unsure what to make of it. 'They don't bother me, Begum,' he lied.

'Good. Then you need say nothing.'

A moment passed and then she said, 'For the present, we are quite safe. They will not try to harm you.'

The lilt in her voice was one of amusement now, and prickled, he said, 'Surely it was *you* who tried to kill Abdul Masjid. They saw you attack him first.'

'Oh, but I am a mere woman.' She paused long enough for one of the guards to pass by, and perhaps also to ensure he had appreciated her irony, then she switched to English. 'You do not understand. These men are mercenaries. Low professionals, like – what can I say? – like seventh-rank prostitutes. They ride on behalf of whichever prince pays them most and they obey the commands of whomsoever they most fear. Because they owe no real allegiance to anyone, their loyalty is as the loyalty of whores.'

'I still don't understand . . .'

She laughed. 'In their eyes, Mr Flint, you were clever enough to send a woman to distract Abdul Masjid. It was you who delivered the death blow, and with the prince's own sword. Do not think the meaning of that symbol was lost on them. It was not. As far as they are concerned, you deposed their last leader quite legitimately and in a most artful manner.'

He scratched his head, dumbstruck by her explanation. 'But he was their officer!'

She shrugged. 'Of course. They were all afraid of him. Then you deposed him. Accordingly, what was his is now yours. Until someone deposes you, it is you they will follow.'

He cast a glance over his shoulder at the turbaned warriors behind him. They unstrapped their jangling saddles and unrolled tentage in preparation for the night, yet none of them approached him. He wondered if Yasmin Begum was hinting that he should give them orders, and if he did would they obey? Then he remembered how she had spoken delicately of 'deposing', and he wondered if any of them was yet ambitious for promotion.

'Don't forget, you are the English Company's finest shootist,' she said, the amused lilt returning. 'You can kill any man at thirty paces. By now, it is probably fifty. But now you must please excuse me. It is time for prayer.'

That night he lay beside a bright fire, the din of frogs filling the dark that surrounded it. At first he was sleepless, for now he had the ruby in his coat pocket again and he was not inclined to swallow it a second time. He got up twice in the night, the first time to goad the dying embers of the fire into flame and later to investigate the heap that was Abdul Masjid's tackle – the belongings he had inherited. At last, he found what he was looking for: the powder flask with which to make good the extravagant threat of his pistols. He filled them up and put them beside him before he retired to sleep dreamlessly.

The next morning he woke to the sound of Muslim prayers. The day was as close and humid as the first; away from cooling sea breezes the sky baked the land remorselessly and the mosquito bites he had collected on his hands and neck itched in the heat.

Halfway through the morning they left the river near an ancient tank, an artificial pond, large and rectangular and surrounded by stone steps, and followed the pilgrims' road north and west to Conjeeveram, the City of Gold. As they came to a lengthy rise, Hayden Flint turned to the grizzled chief scout, Mohan Das, and motioned sharply for him to approach. The man responded readily, so Hayden explained his idea that some of the riders, the dozen assigned to bring up the rear, might lend a hand with the palanquin.

The scout's old weathered face creased further. He was probably nearing forty, venerable for his profession, his black pagri turban was loose and he wore an absurd goat beard reddened with henna; he spat a quid of blood-red betel and showed teeth stained crimson by the stimulant he chewed.

'Not clever, sahib,' he said in colloquial Hindostani.

'Why not?'

The scout inclined his head quizzically. 'Why not, sahib?'

'Yes. Why not?'

'Because they are horse-soldiers, sahib. Sowars.'

'Yes, I know they are sowars. So?'

The scout seemed at last to understand. 'They are Kshatriya.'

'And do not Kshatriya have arms and legs like other men?'

Mohan Das grinned crimson once more. 'Of course you are correct, sahib, but they have dignity also. They cannot be palanquin bearers. That is not for them.'

Hayden Flint nodded. So, some of the guard were Muslim and others Hindu. 'I see. Thank you.'

He let Mohan Das resume his place in the column, knowing that in Hindostan no scheme could be made to work, no matter how important, if it overlooked the fact of caste.

By midday they had skirted Conjeeveram. They stopped for rest and more prayer. This was the Benares of the South, the scout told him, one of the seven most holy cities of the

Hindu, with its ancient temples and gopurams and sacred mango tree. Hayden Flint felt the magnetism of the place; an eerie whirlpool of religious devotion seemed to surround its thousand-pillared halls and stagnant tanks. A devotion rooted in tens of centuries.

Hundreds of pilgrims all painted with the mark of Vishnu, a white V-shape slashed with a vertical red stripe, were flocking in to choke the city and Muhammad Ali chose a detour to avoid their ox-carts and their tiresome and inevitable obeisances. He made camp two miles beyond the town as the sun began to set. The prince had been in the saddle all day; he posted three men as guards, then, once he had inspected the site, he stomped away deep into the coconut grove to relieve himself.

The fire flared comfortingly as Hayden Flint took his seat on a hollow log. Once more he took the opportunity of the prince's absence to exchange a few words with the Lady Yasmin. Since the events of Mavalipuram he had felt a bond of trust that made words easier, and he had thought long and hard over what were his best interests. On the one hand, she could be his guide and best ally in this strange land; on the other, he could not read her mind at all, and he dared not risk infuriating her husband.

'This is the best part of the day, I always think,' he said as pleasantly as he could.

'Oh, yes, Mr Flint. Now is called the Hour of Cow Dust, when the herdsmen drive their cattle along the dry roads. Dawn and dusk are indeed the best times in Hindostan, when the sun is not so fierce.'

'And which do you prefer?' he asked her. 'The rising? Or the setting?'

She turned her head, looking at him with clear piercing eyes. 'I enjoy the dawn for the promise it makes of the day. But I prefer dusk, for then the evening lies ahead and in my world the evenings are filled with music and laughter and good food and the stars of heaven.'

He nodded agreeably, stretching the weariness from his bones. 'Your world sounds enchanting, Begum.'

'So it is, Mr Flint. It is a woman's world. The world of the zenana, the harem. And it contains everything a woman could need or want.'

He listened to her words which were softly spoken yet definite and deliberate as was everything she said, but he noticed that the lilt had gone from them.

'You pronounce English most excellently, Begum.'

'And you speak our courtly tongue, which is very rare for a feringhee.'

He accepted the compliment as graciously as he could. 'Thank you, but I must confess I hardly think of myself as a foreigner at all.'

'The English are a restless people, are they not? A nation of traders and sea-nomads? Like the Portuguese, to whom we long ago taught respect, and the French and the Dutch who have yet to learn how to behave.' She stirred. 'Will the English go away for ever, now that the French have made war on them?'

'I don't know.'

'Ah, yes. But I forget. You don't know the English. You have never been to England. And you don't know about Hindostan either. So, tell me, what *do* you know, Mr Flint?'

He sighed. 'I've lived in Hindostan and other places, here and there, for more than twenty years. My father maintains houses in both Madras and Calcutta, and I've sailed all of your coasts on my father's ships. That has been my life since I was five years old. The fact is, I know a little something about a great many places, but perhaps not enough about any one of them, except Calcutta.'

'Ah, yes. Calcutta.' Her voice became distant. 'You told my husband you were taught there. But you cannot take Fort William to be Bengal, nor the lease of Calcutta to be Hindostan.'

'You think not?'

'I think not.' There was no guile in her voice. 'If you lived in such places for a thousand years you would never become anything other than a feringhee. Nor do I think you are the kind of foreigner who can ever really learn about Hindostan.'

He was disappointed by the remark. It seemed to him that another might think her haughty tone slighting, but he knew she was only speaking the truth she saw, and that, at least, was something he could respect. He nodded cautiously. She relaxed. Her long, slim fingers laced and clasped her knee. He saw that the nails of her fingers and toes were painted scarlet and the perfume she gave to the air was as delicate as lilies. Her golden bangles tinkled as she arched her back languorously.

'You are anxious to reach Arcot,' she said.

'Yes.'

'Then, if I may be permitted to counsel you in two ways: first, try to believe in magic, and second, learn patience. Patience is the chief virtue of this land – perhaps its only virtue. But if so, it is a virtue that can conquer all. And never forget that Hindostan is a universe of itself and unto itself. Nothing changes here. Magic still exists here. Here time is not measured in days or years or generations, but in the turnings of the cosmic wheel.' She paused as if deliberating what more she should reveal to him, then continued. 'There are countless examples of patience in this land, Mr Flint. I myself have seen at Chillapuram a chain stretched between two stone pillars set twenty-seven paces apart. That chain was cut from a single stone. You can hardly imagine the skill of the craftsman who made it, nor, I think, could you place a proper value on his patience.'

She stood up, the fire chasing the shadows from her eyes. In a darker tone she said, 'I will tell you also that not far from here there is a temple with a sacred tank into which the sacred River Ganges flows every year.'

He looked up at her quizzically. 'But the Ganges is a thousand miles away. How can it flow here?'

'Each year thousands of pilgrims come here to bathe in the tank, and as they gather and immerse themselves in the holy water they marvel at the surface rising higher from step to step. It is truly a miracle!'

77

'No, lady,' he said, grinning. 'That's only what we call Archimedes' Principle. Of course the water level rises when they crowd into it. It's the same when you load a ship and it sinks deeper into the – '

'Listen to me!' she cut in, still passionately serious. 'Listen to me with your mind and not just with your ears. You must believe that *magic* exists here! For your own good, Mr Flint, believe that.'

'Your pardon, lady, I was simply saying that according to science – '

Her eyes flashed at him impatiently. 'If you will not believe, then consider what has brought you here. The magic of a stone! If it were not for that, Anwar-ud-Din would have no use for the large spinel you call a ruby, and you would not be here!'

'That is the truth at least,' he muttered, not wanting her to converse with him so intensely for fear that Muhammad Ali would overhear.

'Mr Flint, in Hindostan there is a belief in the four pursuits. We believe that a man should look for wealth and for pleasure, but also he should seek to uphold order under the law, and it is also his duty to search for spiritual purity.' She straightened and he saw the passion animate her. She was frustrated by his ignorance and his cool politeness, and that made her angry. 'Know that you cannot pursue these aims in isolation. You must pursue them all. If you choose one, or two, or even three, you will not attain any of them. Pursue all four simultaneously and equally, and you will gain all.'

He smiled. 'Your philosophy is both ancient and honourable, Begum.'

Silently he thought of his father's self-satisfied summary of the Moghul fourfold code. 'Listen, lad, it's gold, gonads, government and God, fer them, in no pertiklar order, and ye can add guns to that if ye please. They've a great surfeit of all four amounting to a crushing burden, but thank the Lord a shortage of the additional factor. Theirs is an heretical form of Islam, soured and corrupted by two hundred years of Hindu mumbo-jumbo and ye should have no truck with it . . .'

Yasmin Begum's eyes dwelt on his own, urging him. 'There are things in Hindostan than you could never explain in your science. Know that. In Arcot you must think like we think, for if you think like a feringhee you will never succeed.'

'Allow me to thank you for your advice, Begum.'

'We will reach Arcot tomorrow.'

He looked at her, uncertain what precisely she had been telling him, then Muhammad Ali appeared and they fell into silence. Tomorrow, he thought, clinging to the real world where there was no magic and no foolish self-deceptions, but only rational explanations, tomorrow, I will deliver the ruby to Anwar-ud-Din. And tomorrow I will claim his help in driving the French from the gates of Madras.

Directly they entered Arcot, Muhammad Ali's thoughts left the ruby and turned instead to his two half-brothers. The Holy Koran is faultless, and the words of the Prophet – peace be upon Him – are wise beyond description, he thought. That a man should exceed the four wives stipulated in the scriptures is folly, even if that man is as rich and powerful as Anwar-ud-Din. The more wives a nawab has in his harem the worse it is for him in his declining days, for then the number of his offspring is great, and the turbulance of their disputes grows great also.

He looked steadily through the sun-blasted arch of the gate, and along the thronging street beyond, feeling that he had been away from the dispute too long. He ached to be back among those against whom he had sparred and struggled since childhood, and with those like Nadira Begum, his mother, who had nurtured and guided him. She knew that the turbulence was in his blood, that he needed to express it. She always understood that. She's still the most powerful woman in the women's quarter of the palace, he thought, virtual ruler of the zenana, and only with her help can I become nawab.

His mind explored the coming battle meticulously. Of the dozens of male offspring sired by Anwar-ud-Din, only a handful were dynastically significant. These were the sons of his father's wives, for the spawn of courtesans and consorts could have no legal claim to power, and of this handful only two were old enough to be a serious threat: the elder, Mahfuz Khan, and the younger, Abdul Wahab Khan. So far, he reflected, Abdul Wahab has shown little aptitude for politics, and even if he had he would be an ally against Mahfuz since Mahfuz is the man our father has named as his deputy and the son he wants as his successor, and against the favourite there must always be an alliance. But now that will never be. . .

He glanced to his right and saw the feringhee looking up from the street at the walls of the fortress citadel of Arcot. Its thick red sandstone walls rose up above the rocky slope at their foot. It was big enough to act as a refuge for most of the important townspeople when an invading army marched in, or when the filthy Maratha bandits appeared in force. It was strong enough to withstand a lengthy siege by any but the biggest armies. The population of the sprawling town of Arcot was perhaps one lakh in number – one hundred thousand – mostly Hindu peasants, the majority of them uninterested in the power struggles that went on continuously at the court. They knew that what happened in the nawab's white marble palace which stood symbolic-ally aloof, set apart from both the town and the fortress, was never any of their concern.

But soon it will be, he thought. There will be a revolution in the coming months that will affect everyone. If my father is astute, then no son will win and perhaps three sons will die. But if he makes a mistake, then one son will win and two will die. Then Arcot will have a new nawab. He smiled, delighting in the prospect now that Abdul Masjid was no longer an obstacle. How much did it matter to the great mass of people here which son would sit upon the masnad of power? he asked himself. To see them you would think it did not matter at all. In truth, it will matter more than anything else in the world.

He breathed deeply as he entered the gates of the ancient capital. It had taken a thousand years of history to confect this place. This was the *ganj*, the bazaar of the Old Town, rich with all the familiar essences of Hindostan; the smells of continuous habitation were grained like pungent wood oils into those old streets where the ways were crooked and narrow and hemmed in by tumbled hovels, where garbage choked the alleys, picked over by goats, and cattle, and scratching fowls, and children with streaming noses. One lakh of people and a millennium and more of their living. Their smells saturated the decaying fabric of the town: dust and dung and fust and bruised spice and dried fish and milk and rosewater and sandalwood and resin and incense smoke and currying and filth and rotting fruit and animals, and here and there a whiff of black stagnation and the sun in the sky fermenting everything.

The feringhee was looking about himself, sweating and uncertain, genuinely shocked by the way the guard kicked down the scum that raised inquisitive eyes to his stirrups. Oh, no, this is not Madras, the wide streets and white houses of John Company. No orderly life of marching lines and black ships here, no clean-swept straightness such as is found in the English fort. This is Hindostan, past, present and for ever! My land! And nothing, Mr Feringhee, nothing you can do will ever change it!

The crowds swarmed like locusts, a hundred thousand people, but whoever they were, everyone averted their gaze and parted for his horsemen. The shouts of his guard rang out, the men who ran ahead with their iron-shod lathis, switching at those who were slow to make way, and constantly the road opened before them,

Muhammad Ali shut his eyes, feeling the familiar scents thrill over him. The ganj was a hive: a swarm of *mofussil ryots* – country peasants – toiling their masters' produce to market; women in saris, labouring with baskets on their heads, or bargaining, or resting or gossiping. The young and the old, the poor and the prosperous, the strong and the weak.

Above the jangling bells of the horses, he heard the distant sound of the Islamic call to prayer floated out over the city from the minarets.

'*Allah-u-Akhbar!*' God is Great!

Above them now, carved wooden shutters, intricately ornate, hung loose on rusty hinges. Painted harlots and willowy, solemn-faced catamites enticed passers-by from these first-floor windows, glittering with fake gold and reeking of patchouli. A little further and there were holy trees, niches carved in them, daubed idols, and women on their knees doing *puja* for a barren daughter or a sick father in the meagre shade. The inevitable cattle with garlands of flowers and designs painted on their heads. Across the road a ruined garden; huge grey-hooded crows and carrion birds on the limed temple spires and sparrows twittering in the eaves. A monkey on a balcony. Bania women squatting behind cloths laid on the ground, laying out whatever they could sell: bunches of wilted spinach or chapattis or a few handfuls of winnowed dal lentils. Here were men wearing dhotis wrapped round their loins, men in turbans stained festive Holi colours, leaning on staffs, carrying gunny sacks: milk-sellers and tinkers, merchants and musicians, barbers and copper-beaters, craftsmen of all kinds, and thieves – young men hungry-eyed for the opportunities of the street.

They rode on towards the walled citadel, past the bigger houses of the merchant castes. The scum here think themselves superior and sophisticated and show far too little respect, Muhammed thought. They grow inappropriately rich by selling to the Europeans. But that will stop. My father is despicably lenient. I will have no Hindu in the palace when I become nawab. After all, doesn't their own holy book, the Gita, say as much? '*Better is one's own law though imperfectly carried out than the law of another carried out perfectly. One does not incur sin when one does the duty ordained by one's own nature.*'

He closed his eyes again but could not close his ears. There was the constant shouting. Vendors calling.

'Haircut!' 'Sweet papaya ripe!' '*Chai!*' Babies and bells and the yelping of a skeleton dog. The rumble of cart wheels. The swish of the lathis. Music blaring in the distance. A crowd down a side street cheering a hermaphrodite dancer, clapping the twirling erotic movements, others gawping at the buzzing reed pipe of the snake man.

He knew where he was, exactly to the pace. Here would be the fat-bellied man, and there the old Gujarati with the jutting beard who sat with hundreds of piles of coins built around him and the counting frames clacking in his sons' hands. The call of the muezzin grew louder and soon they were passing by the mosque and the cluster of temples where filthy saddhus lounged in vermilion and saffron, and innumerable beggars.

Here the beggars gathered like lice under the dusty awnings. Did not the Holy Koran make almsgiving the fifth pillar of Islam? And how the Hindu beggars knew it; for them there was refuge only among their gods of horror. There, crammed into the dark channels between high walls of old brick and the plaster monstrosities of the gopurams, were real living monsters! Not just Untouchable girls who borrowed starved infants to beg with, not just the hundreds of destitute mendicants crowding the steps of the temples and the mosques, but terrible human monsters. These were the lazar-house creatures, the human freaks who showed off their fantastic deformities for small coin. Here the man with gigantic testicles, like a huge brown pumpkin, that he pushed in a wheelbarrow before him, one leg normal, the other an elephant's; here the spider-boy in his home crevice, with legs and arms twisted up his back as boneless as serpents, making his queer, leering smile at the world as he had for years. There the lepers with their worn-down features and hands like newborn pigs, jangling their bowls. And among them, going in rags, women of the caste of Untouchables, who would strangle their daughters and fit their sons for a life of begging by inflicting novel wounds that never healed but jagged sharply at the heart of a passer-by. Soft young bones broken and set at pathetic

83

angles were common. Blinding was good for pity, so were the sores of loathsome diseases, and the application of hot irons to distort the features of the face. There was not a ruse to which some ambitious mothers would not stoop to equip their offspring for the ferocious competition of beggarly life. Thank the Prophet that Allah made me bodily whole and that I have a mother who makes me the centre of her universe, he thought, idolizing her. Nadira Begum is the only one in all the world whom I can trust absolutely. She alone is perfect.

His thoughts turned bleakly to Anwar-ud-Din. My father knows how much I want to be nawab after him, he mused bitterly, yet Mahfuz receives his beneficence because he is first-born and has the same-shaped face as his father. He should know I will never be satisfied with the little parcels of land that are occasionally tossed at me. One day soon he will learn that I am not a dog waiting below a window for chicken bones!

On my father's birthday Mahfuz was made his deputy. But me? What of me? He gave me the governorship of Trichinopoly! Ha! The second city of the Carnatic, he calls it. Trichinopoly! I'm killadar of a fortress built on a bare rock in the remotest southern tip of the country, a miserable city surrounded by enemies, with a small and insecure income and a reputation for being hard to govern. Trichinopoly! The place is a joke! An insult! But I shall redress that insult soon. With God's help I will create the ideal Islamic state on earth.

They had come to the gates of the palace. At the sight of it he felt an eagerness in the horse and his own mood lifting. The surrounding wall was serrated with tablet-like battlements of red sandstone, and the gatehouse was tall and elegant, incised with hexagonal Islamic patterns and surmounted by two domes. The gates themselves were missing, taken off after a previous siege, but the way within led up a steep elephant ramp made of stones scored across in chevrons to conduct away the vast quantities of strong stinking urine the royal beasts seemed to need to discharge as soon as they started up the incline.

The horses' hooves found purchase difficult. The ramp was deceptive and deadly, a shadowed slaughtering ground. Anyone trying to enter the palace uninvited would be trapped here as the ramp became a gauntlet overlooked by a second battlement on which musketeers could be stationed. Soldiers patrolled the walls with long-barrelled jezail in hand, or with sword and buckler. Others manned the gates at every checkpoint. A terrifying thought struck him. By Allah, what if there has been a coup while I've been away? What if Mahfuz has already made his move? Haven't the past weeks been the most opportune time? By all that's holy, my mother might be dead – or worse, his prisoner. What could I do?

The panic rose in him. He searched rapidly for a sign that something was amiss, any clue that there might have been an emergency in his absence, but in every way the Palace of Arcot seemed to be normal and as he had left it. The complex of white marble columns and fretted panels and courtyards and halls and domed pavilions were in quiet occupation. Men he recognized as loyal to his father were still to be seen.

At the top of the ramp, outside the entrance to the nawab's official suite, Mahfuz stepped out from the shadows to meet him. He dismounted and they embraced.

'Greetings, Muhammad Ali, my brother.'

Behind Mahfuz the palace guard stared sightlessly into space, their lances glinting in the sun. Mahfuz's face was sombre, his eyes liquid. The moustache he wore curled over his cheeks and his sideburns were long and wispy, extending to the angle of his jaw. He wore a dark green turban, hackled with an emerald-studded peacock feather, and a fine muslin jama, long-sleeved, turmeric-yellow and printed with leaf devices. It was round-necked, fastening across the chest from collarbone to armpit to a high waist, where a dark green cummerbund sash cut it and from which it fell away in a full skirt to the ankle.

Muhammad Ali stiffened under the embrace. His eyes slid down the rope of the big pearls Mahfuz wore round his neck to the fabulously bejewelled punch-dagger in his kamar sash. Mahfuz was dressed in the same clothes his father had worn the day he had been promoted to general in the Nizam's army. He was the image of Anwar-ud-Din's favourite portrait, and he had dressed this way deliberately today. With the realization, Muhammad Ali felt the tension between them increase almost beyond endurance. Mahfuz avoided noticing the foreigner.

'Greetings, Mahfuz. You are well?'

'Excellent. And you?'

'Very well, thank you. My father is expecting me?'

'Naturally. We knew you were coming since you struck camp just outside Chingleput. You will take refreshment?'

Muhammad Ali dismissed the riders and at a sign from him the palanquin was taken on round the path towards the back of the palace and the women's quarters. The guards' lances parted and they entered the cool shadow of the courtyard, the hooves of the horses clip-clopping. His own led; the foreigner's, still carrying him, came behind. He ducked his head under the dome-shaped arch, then dismounted.

'Make the search thorough,' Mahfuz told the guards.

The search revealed the foreigner's stolen pistols.

Mahfuz's wariness burgeoned. 'Tell him he can't bring them any further. He must relinquish them.'

Muhammad Ali made no translation, knowing it was unnecessary. The foreigner spoke up, hard-faced now. 'These guns are my property and it is our custom to go armed.'

The words were in court speech, and Mahfuz was surprised at them. 'You cannot bring them any further,' he said bluntly.

'It is also our custom to accept hospitality in the manner in which it is offered. Therefore, if I am to be a guest in your father's house, I can be trusted.'

'I'm sorry. I must insist you relinquish the guns.'

'Then you are insisting that I trust you when you refuse to trust me.'

'In my father's house, yes.'

'It is a point of honour to wear my guns.'

'The guards have orders to disarm everyone.'

'Then I shall disarm myself.'

The foreigner shook his head, took out one pistol and pointed it into the air. He discharged it, then did the same with the second.

The horses in the courtyard were startled. A cloud of doves rose up from the rooftops as the echoes of the rude weapons died away. Then, at Mahfuz Khan's orders, the guards seized the foreigner and wrestled him to the ground.

It was interesting to watch from here, the man at the marble-grilled window reflected. The view from the high casement had been particularly clear, and the feringhee prophesied by Umar's *gup* was indeed as arrogant and awkward as could be imagined.

'Oh, Mahfuz, my first-born son,' he said. 'You will have to learn to understand and deal cleverly with the European mind before I can allow you to have the Carnatic.'

He had spoken his thoughts aloud, yet softly and to himself. The sumptuous hall behind him contained a dozen ministers; all of them were within earshot and all of them had heard his words, but not one would dare admit it for he was Anwar-ud-Din Muhammad, one-time General of the Nizam of the Deccan, and a Commander of Twenty Thousand Horse in the army of the Great Moghul, now the Nawab of the Carnatic, the virtually independent ruler of the country, and his word was life and death.

He summoned Umar, his chaprasi, or personal messenger. 'My son and his guest will wait. Tell him they have ample time to wash and dress and partake of food before I shall require them. But have my daughter-in-law brought here at once. That is all.'

The chaprasi, a tall solemn-faced man, bowed and backed away three paces before straightening and turning.

As his will was done, Anwar-ud-Din smoothed the tip of his greying beard. He was fifty, a dainty man, slim and elfin, with sharp features and deep, soulful eyes. His skin was tea-dark, his turban jonquil-yellow. Everything about him was neat and quick. Intelligence shone from him. He wore, as did all the men present, the jama, a long-skirted tunic gathered at the waist by a kamar sash, the same that Mahfuz wore. It fastened across the chest, to the right for Muslims, to the left for Hindus. All the men carried dress daggers in their sashes, most heavily jewelled, and a long talwar on their left side, but whereas their hilts were unbalanced by gold and gem stones, Anwar-ud-Din's own was made for killing.

He watched the gangling chaprasi glide along the axis of the hall, his flowing white uniform flashing light and shadow as he passed the columns. The Diwan-i-Khas, Hall of Private Audience, was long and airy and built on two levels. It was flanked along one entire side by huge slabs of pierced red sandstone and white marble which acted as windows. Each was cut in its own unique mazelike pattern of holes, hexagons, stars and triangles, all fretted delicately until the stone was like lace. They filtered the harsh light outside into a milky translucence. Along the opposite side, the lofty vaulted ceiling was supported by scalloped arches standing on slender stone pillars which opened out on to a small inner courtyard and allowed the free passage of cooling breezes across the hall. Umar disappeared as he descended a flight of steps that split the hall, and re-appeared as he walked towards the main door at the far end. It was guarded by two men and led into the Diwan-i-Am, or Hall of Public Audience.

Anwar-un-Din thanked Allah for the chaprasi who was more than a chaprasi, more even than a minister at times. Umar was a consummate servant, one of those rare men who possessed a gift from God. He was a grand master of an ancient science, a master of *gup*, and therefore utterly priceless.

Gup was precious. Crucial. Essential. The whole empire ran on *gup*. Across all Hindostan, it was mixed with mothers' milk, yet it could feed the maw of government. It had the power to nourish, to placate or terrify high officials and the common people alike. *Gup* could entertain and inform and educate. *Gup* was the fastest way to communicate; it moved subtly, yet with the speed of the wind, and was always passed on the very best authority. No imperial firman or decree could match the respect it commanded. It could proclaim or prophesy or vilify magnificently, and destroy the reputation of years in a single day.

Gup raced in the pulse of the people. It was a currency more powerful than money. It reached everyone and, like money, passed through the hands of everyone. Like money it could be copper or silver or gold. It could be worn down or dirtied or bent or twisted or adulterated or traded – but never hoarded, for *gup* was alive, and it lived only so long as it was transacted. Those like Umar who knew how to orchestrate and to broadcast and to interpret *gup* were jewels, for *gup* was indispensable to a ruler. *Gup* was propaganda, rumour, gossip, hearsay, information, and the nugget at its heart could be truth, or it could be the kind of lie that revealed the desire of the people.

Umar had reaped the awesome *gup* about the ruby and the joyful *gup* that Abdul Masjid was dead. At first hearing, Anwar-ud-Din had been distraught that the secret was abroad, but then Umar had lifted a bony hand and there was shrewdness embedded in that cadaverous face.

He said that the knowledge had been taken by a fortune-teller from a scout who had sold it on to a pilgrim who knew a Brahmin who owed a favour to a friend who had ridden hard from Chingleput to see his brother who was a palace guard who had divulged it to a lady's maid to whom Umar often listened.

Anwar-ud-Din sat patiently while the chaprasi un-ravelled what he had heard, and finally he discovered that the nuggets were nuggets of truth: Abdul Masjid was indeed dead. The ruby was indeed coming, and moreover, it was in the hands of a feringhee, the same man who had killed the bodyguard leader. There had been a shipwreck of some kind, but the details of that were unclear.

'Our ship of state founders also,' he whispered to Umar, fearing the downfall of his plans. 'Don't you see? If the knowledge of the ruby is out, we are all of us lost!'

But Umar dared to give him a different opinion. He alone had that privilege, to speak his true heart and mind to the Master of the Carnatic without fear of reprisal. To the learned and disinterested Umar the deceits of Arcot were merely an academic mind-game, and his own purpose the accurate fathoming of them for his uniquely wise master. He squeezed his hands, the bulbous joints of his fingers cracking. 'Forgive me, lord, but you are wrong. There is another way . . .'

Anwar-ud-Din listened, then stood up and paced the hall and, finally convinced, he had sanctioned Umar to operate upon the rumour delicately and pass it back down among the people. In half a morning the ganj had been buzzing with it: an embroidered story of murder and shipwreck and war, and magic – especially magic. How quickly the travelling ballad singers would seize such ideas! Yes, the nautch girls would surely step out the story in a hundred places in the Carnatic tonight. And the people who watched would love to add their own personal embellishments to what was in fact a perfectly simple tale!

Without doubt, what was known today in the ganj at Arcot would be known tomorrow in the ganj at Hyderabad. The question of the Nizam's succession would suddenly be on everyone's lips, and the name of Anwar-ud-Din would be linked to it. The Nizam, Asaf Jah, was growing infirm and soon he must die, for how much longer could an old man such as he live? There would then be a power vacuum in the Deccan. There would have to be, because Asaf Jah had held on to power by force of arms and then by craft and then by magic.

For too many years Asaf Jah had depended on the Talwar-i-Jang, the War Sword of Islam, second only in holiness for the Moghuls to the Prophet's own sword in Stamboul. And with it he had kept the Hindu of the Deccan in awe because of the diamond in its hilt, the magnificent

Koh-i-Noor, which was accursed, so that any man possessing it should die. Therefore, how could Asaf Jah rule, they reasoned, unless it was the will of Allah, and unless all the gods of the Hindu pantheon agreed?

It was perfect for Asaf Jah! The people believed in the legitimacy of this man whom the diamond's curse would not touch. The rajas of neighbouring states paid tribute and would not clash with him; potential usurpers had long been intimidated by the Koh-i-Noor's baleful stare. It was an incredible stroke of political consolidation, but perhaps not quite perfect, because even Asaf Jah could not live for ever.

No, not for ever . . .

Anwar-ud-Din stirred, knowing that, irrevocably, he had made his move. The question was already being asked in high circles: 'Who has the power to hold the Talwar when Asaf Jah dies?' And because no one could yet answer, fear was starting to grow. A power vacuum would mean strife and anarchy and terror, and eventually the land would be laid waste and no one would be able to halt the devastation, unless – there was another against whom the diamond's curse was powerless. Without that man the dominion of Nizam-ul-Mulk would decline into violence on a scale that had never been seen in the history of the world, and both Hindu and Muslim alike would wash themselves to the shores of hell on a tide of blood . . .

But now the ruby was here, in the feringhee's pocket, and soon the feringhee would bring it out and offer it, and he would have to buy it, whatever the price.

Yasmin had allowed her two ayahs to take off her clothes in readiness to bathe. The main tank of the zenana was long and shallowly stepped and pleasantly set with abstract mosaics of colour. It was cloistered and open to the sky two storeys above. It was also empty of other bathers, which was unexpected. Yasmin was popular with her 'sisters' and they had welcomed her back, wanting so much to ask her about the world she had seen, but none had followed her to the pool. It's Nadira Begum's doing, she thought. Cow shit could not purify that woman.

Nadira Begum, number one wife of Anwar-ud-Din, mother of Muhammad, and therefore her mother-in-law, was the principal power in the zenana, the one to whom all the women owed deference, even if they did not afford her respect. Her nearest rival was the equally proud, equally unforgiving, Shahbaz, mother of Anwar-ud-Din's first-born, but only his second wife. There had been barely days between the births of Mahfuz and Muhammad Ali; even so, Anwar-ud-Din had never been moved by Nadira's persistent claim that though her own son was second-born, he was nevertheless first-sired.

Yasmin cautioned herself that the politics of the zenana could not be ignored and reminded herself that much of consequence might have passed in her absence.

What was it like, sahiba?' Gilahri, the younger ayah, asked her breathlessly. She was fourteen and wide-eyed.

Yasmin waded into the tank until she stood thigh-deep, her dark skin desiring the touch of water after the stale airlessness of the palanquin. Against the turquoise and lapis lazuli her body was like burnished bronze. Her long hair was tied up and pinned and she had shed most of her jewellery. She wore only a golden bracelet and a silver anklet worn after the Hindu fashion – silver as a mark of respect to the goddess Lakshmi, who did not approve of gold worn below the waist.

'What was *what* like, little squirrel?'

Gilahri's excitement overflowed. 'The sea. The sea!'

'Like this tank,' she said, smiling back. 'Like this tank, but deep as the deepest valley and as blue as a sapphire and stretching as far as your eyes can see.'

'Oh, sahiba! How can that be? Weren't you terribly afraid?'

'I was at first.'

'They say you were wrecked in a tufan,' the elder ayah asked her, her eyes full of concern. 'Now you tell me: is that true?'

'Oh, you shouldn't listen to silly *gup*, Hamida. You'll only upset yourself.'

Hamida was ten years older than her and her oldest friend and companion; she had accompanied her to this southern land when Yasmin had been sent to Hyderabad to marry. That was ten years ago, when Yasmin was twelve. Hamida was plump and plain, and the only time her pleasantly radiant nature showed any sign of anxiety was when she thought her Yasmin was not taking proper care of herself.

'I was very worried for you.'

'And I missed you, too.' She smiled again, broadly.

'Now, now, Yasmin Begum, you know that is not what I said.'

Yasmin bent her knees and immersed herself, delighting in the cool wash of water over her back and belly and breasts. 'So you didn't miss me, hey?' she said, mock severity on her face.

'Of course, I missed you, rose petal. But I was very worried all the same.'

'You're so beautiful, sahiba,' Gilahri said as her mistress stood up. 'So graceful. You rise from the waters like a goddess.'

Yasmin tweaked her nose playfully. 'You're so kind.'

'Oh, but I wish I had breasts like yours. Look at mine, they're so small and insignificant.'

'They will grow. In time.'

'In time for what, sahiba?'

'In time for you to marry.'

'Oh, I hope so!' She twisted about and put out her hand to stroke Yasmin's belly below her navel. Water coursed into the dark luxuriance of sable.

'Sahiba?'

'Yes?'

'Sahiba, why don't you shave down there, like the others?'

Yasmin answered her patiently. 'Because, Gilahri, I don't like the itching when the hair starts to grow again.'

'Ugh! Does it itch?' She frowned. 'Doesn't Muhammad Sahib object?'

'Why should he? This is how Allah intended a woman to be, not smooth and bare!'

'But doesn't Muhammad Sahib get the hairs in his – '

'Gilahri! You ask too many questions, you horrid girl! Now away with you and bring my best jama. I want to put on something clean and light tonight.'

She shooed her and splashed water and the ayah's screams went echoing up as she fled from the tank. Then Yasmin laughed and turned to Hamida, half serious now. 'It's good to be back. How was she?'

Hamida understood. She made a face, meaning that Nadira Begum had been no more unpleasant than usual. As a wife and a mother of one of the three sons, she held great formal power in the zenana and could have made it vastly uncomfortable for Yasmin's ayahs in her absence, especially Gilahri.

'You're sure?'

Hamida was brisk. 'Oh, don't trouble yourself about us. We know how to stand up to that old snake.'

'Yes. Please scrub my back for me.'

As she scrubbed, Hamida spoke softly, her mouth close to Yasmin's ear. 'You should know what's been happening while you've been away.'

'A good deal, I imagine.'

'Yes. Too much. But that can wait. What can't is that Mahfuz expects reprisals.'

'You mean in revenge for sending Abdul Masjid to find us?'

'That was Shahbaz's doing. I don't like it, Yasmin. There's something happening. That monstrous witch would do anything to get at Muhammad, maybe they will try to get at him through you. Yesterday, Gulbadan was listening at the curtain, and she heard – ' There was a familiar jangling of heavy gold anklets, and suddenly Hamida's face changed. Yasmin turned and saw that Nadira Begum had appeared and behind her, silent as ever,

94

the enormous fleshy blackness of the chief eunuch, Maqbool.

The metallic jangling that heralded Nadira's approach terrified most of the women, though she was slight of build and dainty. Her eyes were very dark, the lashes heavily emphasized with black kohl, and her lips were painted blood-red, but the whole of the rest of her face was astonishing to see for it was frosted with gold leaf. When she smiled, which was seldom, her teeth were seen to be lined with black, and she almost always kept her waist-length greying hair braided and hidden inside her veil. She went barefoot in the zenana and the nails of her fingers and toes were painted red, as were her palms and soles. Today she wore a fine gold muslin scarf over her head, held in place by a fillet of diamonds and pearls; more pearls hung round her neck, seven or eight strings of them, and heavy gold bracelets and anklets completed the effect. They jangled now as she approached.

'Yasmin, child. How are you? I believe you had an arduous journey?'

'Yes, honoured Mother-in-law. It was a little tiring.'

'Well, you shall tell me all about it.'

'Of course. I've almost finished bathing.'

The older woman inclined her head, sensitive to any hint of insubordination. 'Your bathing will have to wait. Come out.'

'I beg your pardon, lady?'

'I said you're to come out of there now.'

'Then I'll dry myself.' Yasmin's voice remained honey-smooth. She lifted her arms and allowed Hamida to wind a square of diaphanous muslin round her body like a sheath.

'You'd better hurry, child.'

'Yes, Nadira.' She stayed knee-deep in the water as Hamida dabbed at her skin.

Nadira Begum's chin lifted. 'My dear, for me you could stay in the water all day and all night. It is the nawab who has summoned you. You are to attend him immediately.'

Yasmin stepped out of the water, dried herself and

95

dressed hurriedly, aware of Maqbool's presence and his enigmatic stare, but untroubled by it. She left Nadira and followed the eunuch.

As they walked she wondered what his look could mean. What thoughts went through a eunuch's mind when he saw the ladies in his charge undress and frolic naked in the tanks? She felt a sudden great compassion. Of course, he had nothing in his dhoti. Everything had been cut away, so there was nothing to grow stiff, nothing to deliver the man's seed, nor even the delightful, delicate organs to produce it.

Was that why Maqbool and so many of the other eunuchs were so huge? The majority of this elite corps of protector-jailers were great bald-headed sexless creatures, and none more so than their chief. Massive thighs, massive upper arms, pudgy hands and feet, their heads and necks and chins were clothed with flesh. Maqbool's breasts were vast, hanging down over his big belly like the goatskin sacks of a *bhisti*, a water-carrier, his nipples flattened into ovals.

'What does he want, Maqbool?'

'I don't know that, sahiba.'

'Is he alone?'

'He is. Except for his hookah-wallah.'

If he's smoking, then he's thinking, she thought. 'Has he been smoking long?'

'Yes. And he has ordered glasses of Yemeni coffee for two.'

She smiled at Maqbool, liking him. Those breasts curved round under his arms and hung in folds. His moustache was just an eyebrow wisp, his voice rare and high. But what of his desire? Did he, deep inside, have the fire of a man? What a terrible thought: to have the fire, but never to have the means to quench it. A terrible thought! Far better to believe that Maqbool was no more than a thirty-year-old boy!

But that look he had given her as she dressed in fine white shabnam muslin, that was not the look of a boy for whom everything is to come. It had been the special look of a eunuch, the lingering, sad, locked-away look of a never-ever-man who understands what he has lost and can never ever have.

She made a conscious effort to cheer her thoughts, smiling inwardly at the absurdly exaggerated curled-up toes of Maqbool's ghatela slippers. She listened to the way his legs rubbed together as he swayed into his steps. Undeniably there was a grace about Maqbool that was like the grace of an elephant, and though his sword was constantly in his hand, he had always seemed to her a gentle person. A devil in her couldn't help imagining him squatting like a woman to relieve himself. What must it be like? How did he function? Was there at least a stump remaining?

Maqbool took the ring of keys from his belt and unlocked a huge iron-studded door. As he swung it open, Yasmin waited, reluctantly disciplining her mind to dwell instead on the coming interview.

'Ah, Yasmin! Come. Come.'

She emerged from the doorway from the women's quarters and approached the cushioned masnad.

'Revered Father.'

'Come. Sit here by me.'

The deep pile of the silk carpet was smooth under her bare feet. She knelt comfortably and clasped her hands in front of her attentively.

'Please excuse my lateness and appearance, revered Father, but I was bathing when your order came to me.' Anwar-ud-Din looked at her appreciatively for a moment. He took one more suck on the mouthpiece of his hookah and then dismissed the hookah-wallah so that they were alone.

'You may, if it pleases you, remove your veil, my daughter.'

'Thank you, revered Father.'

She complied with the order silently. Although it was usual for her to show her face to male members of the royal family, and occasionally to their chosen guests, she felt particularly naked under the nawab's eye. She knew he wanted to see her face now in order to gauge the truth of what she told him.

'The journey on which I sent you did not go as smoothly as I had wished,' he said.

'No, revered Father, it did not.'

'My prayers to Allah were constant. Tell me what happened.'

She told him about the voyage to Ceylon in detail, leaving out nothing of importance, and finished unhesitatingly on a warning. 'Twice your son came perilously close to death, revered Father. First a tufan nearly drowned him in the sea, and then there was almost an attempt on his life by Abdul Masjid. It is Muhammad's belief that his brother, your son Mahfuz, ordered his slaying.'

'*Insh'allah*,' Anwar-ud-Din said neutrally, watching her closely. 'The Hand of God. Is that not so?'

She met his eye fearlessly, but still respectfully. 'I think that the storm was the Hand of God, for what else can a sea-storm be? I believe it was *written* that French ships would come and that we would be forced from the English ship. It was also kismet that we would reach land. However, revered Father, I do not believe Abdul Masjid was motivated by God. It was only kismet that he died.'

Anwar-ud-Din stroked his beard thoughtfully. 'But you said it was the feringhee, Hayden Flint, who killed him?'

'He and I both.'

'And do you believe as Muhammad believes? That Mahfuz paid Abdul Masjid to kill him?'

'No, revered Father. I believe Shahbaz Begum may have alerted him to the existence of the ruby, but I think the rest was Abdul Masjid's own greed. He wanted to take the ruby for himself, for its monetary value alone.'

He grunted. 'Then he deserved to die. Both you and the feringhee are hereby absolved of his blood.'

'Thank you, revered Father.'

It was a formality, but Anwar-ud-Din, she knew, liked to be scrupulously precise when it concerned his duty as law keeper. That's what makes him so able an administrator, she thought. Attention to details. That's why, if it is kismet, he will make an able successor to the Nizam.

'Now,' he said, deliberately testing her. 'Tell me about the ruby and about the feringhee. And tell me what you think Muhammad has in mind.'

As a subject, Yasmin owed loyalty to the state, which meant to the nawab personally. As a wife she owed loyalty to her husband. For Yasmin there could never be any question of which loyalty was the higher one. She took a deep breath.

'Of those three questions, revered Father, the last is the most urgent. Ever since you appointed Mahfuz as your successor Muhammad's aim has been to kill him. I believe he will soon make a serious assassination attempt, and if he does he will have to include Mahfuz's mother and also . . .'

'And also?'

'And also yourself, revered Father.'

Anwar-ud-Din continued to stroke his beard, his eyes liquid. He had chosen Yasmin as Muhammad's wife, and he had chosen well. Muhammad had been a volatile youth, petulant and unstable and dangerously obsessed with the pursuit of power. He needed to be circumvented by a series of strategies, and one of them was the little dark-eyed girl his father had brought down from Agra.

'How soon is soon?'

'Perhaps one week. I believe he desires revenge as soon as possible. If you allow him to remain in the palace longer than a week he will have all the time he requires.'

'How will he strike?'

She stated her predictions as dispassionately as possible, but he saw she was full of disgust at the duty he had given her.

'And the ruby?' he asked suddenly.

She fidgeted uncomfortably. 'That is more difficult. I assume, from the way the people reacted when our column passed through the town, that the secret is a secret no longer.'

He made an affirmative gesture, delighted by her sharpness. She had a way of offering more than was asked of her, and making the unwary give more than they wanted to give, but this time he indulged her. 'Yes. You're quite right. Umar has released the story. You can assume that everyone in Hindostan knows about the ruby and its power to destroy the curse of the Koh-i-Noor.'

'In that case you have announced your candidature. There will be a stir in Hyderabad and unless you desire to incur the wrath of Asaf Jah you should keep your head low. It is said that the Nizam has a short way with threats to his authority. I should wait and let the immediate consequences blow over. The seed has been planted and it may be watered to spring up at any time in the future. If I were you I would not involve myself in a power struggle with Asaf Jah's probable successors yet. I would wait until after he's dead.'

He stared at her head, confounded as always by the presumption in her voice, but liking – as always – the candidness and the perception of her answers.

'You would?'

'Yes, revered Father. I would. That is, if I were you. Please excuse me.' She blushed and he let it pass.

'The feringhee,' he said, knowing he must summon the man soon. 'Tell me about him.'

As she spoke, he listened to her and watched her closely and he saw that she was telling him many things that were mere facts and that her true heart was shrouded from him. Therefore he only half listened and soon, sighingly, began instead to contemplate his son. Muhammad was a dangerous fool. His hero was Aurangzeb, the last great Moghul emperor to occupy the Imperial masnad at Delhi. Like Aurangzeb, Muhammad would turn away from the wise accommodations that the Great Akhbar had reached with the Hindus. Like Aurangzeb, Muhammad would reimpose the poll tax on non-Believers, he would expel the Europeans whose ports and factories made so much revenue, and he would mount jihad across the whole of the South. If Muhammad ever became nawab there would be a Holy War that would start with an orgy of temple-smashing and culminate in the destruction of the Carnatic as a *de facto* independent realm.

He brought his mind back to Yasmin as she tried her best to describe to a lord who was not listening the motives of the foreigner, Hayden Flint. Can it really be worth destroying this fine, intelligent, wonderful young woman just to cage Muhammad? he asked himself regretfully. What a pity she has turned out this way. If I had known that twelve years ago I would have left her in Agra, or married her myself.

As he listened without seeming to listen, his mind ranged over his problems. What to do about the damned foreigners and their irritating brawling? Didn't they know that his army, once raised, could crush them all out of existence as easily as an elephant could crush a pair of quarrelling rats?

And what to tell the foreigner about Madras? Should he be allowed to know that it had fallen to the French and that the English were no longer a presence in the Carnatic? Sooner or later Hayden Flint would have to know the truth.

So why not sooner?

It would certainly make it easier to obtain the astonishing magic ruby, and it might solve everything.

SIX

It was early and the long shadow of the Company's looted offices was thrown across the devastated fort. What the French had done, first with their bombardment and then with their occupation, was ruinous.

Stratford surveyed the damage – railings were torn down, windows gaped, fissures and holes brutalised the frontages of the grand houses and godowns. The random rain of destruction was revealed in slanting daylight that picked out the craters and heaps of rubble on the parade ground. Here a comically tilted weather cock, there a familiar tree split entirely in two, one half drooping and browning in the street, its twin still thrusting up from the wounded trunk, unbalanced, like one arm of wishbone. And in Sudder Street – a stench powerful beyond belief! – where the nightsoil wagon had been overturned, and its big barrels splattered across a lawn, the contents crusted and flyblown.

A little way from Charles Savage's office, under the shattered window of the cathedral, the street was covered in diamonds and rubies of stained glass, emeralds, sapphires and amber. Miraculously intact, the beatific face of St Anthony dangled, its halo surrounded by a ragged grey snake of lead piping, beneath the gothic frame.

Amid the counterfeit gems placid white cattle switched at early flies, and down the street goats rummaged through the contents of buildings that had been thrown out into the street: ledger sheets and thousands of bills, the documents of previous trade, their copperplate entries dispersed by the breeze and curling under the merciless sun; clothes and furniture and china and a little girl's dolly.

Stratford Flint's coat was new, his wig fresh-powdered,

his cocked hat his Sunday best – the one trimmed with ostrich feather – and the buckles on his shoes shone silver.

Ah, but ye look as fine as old Eli did when he set ye on the road to fortune, he thought fondly, remembering his self-made Bostonian benefactor who had sent him out of England in his youth and showed him the way to riches. By God, the riches may be temporarily in abeyance, but I've still got me belief and the same brain in me head as I've always had. Ah, yes!

He rubbed his hands together vigorously, the incredible news that had reached him last night still ringing in his head. Nothing could blight the day now. Nothing. But his instinct told him to lock the knowledge away for now, tight in the back of his mind, and make no sign to anyone of what he had been told.

The flag of King Louis stirred on the high pole as he passed beneath it. He spat in the dust and deliberately took the spring out of his step in preparation for dwelling on grimmer matters. He looked up and saw that the hands of the Company's great clock were six hours adrift – forked skywards where a French shot had stopped them at five minutes to one, the infamous moment of Governor Morse's surrender.

That disgrace had been three nights ago, and the victorious French had marched in the following morning, drums rolling, cornets blaring and their colours up on high. Two thousand Negro troops, cross-belted and proud as Romans, and the Council and its President shown the worst kind of ignominy in front of them. Morse and Screwton were detained under guard now, and serve the worms right.

Flint climbed the steps up to the fort's seaward wall broodingly, a deck telescope in his hand. His own parole was still good, giving him the freedom of the fort, and lunch with the Admiral was in prospect. The sentries left him alone as he made his way along the battlements to the place where four days ago he had shown his gunners how to prepare a weapon the French ships dared not use.

'Them vessels is all wood and tar, d'ye see?' he'd told

them. 'We'll give them a dose of Cayenne pepper t'keep them guns floating at a respectful distance.'

He'd watched the furnaces and charcoal grates heating cannonballs until they glowed bright yellow, showed the writers and clerks how to load shot into wheelbarrows lined with sand to transport them to the guns, how to use one dry and one wet wad between the shot and the powder, and he'd warned them, upon their lives, not to point their steaming muzzles at one particular fine ship anchored among the French fleet.

His belly heaved as he remembered his immense debt. A pox on despondency! he thought, his exuberance conquering all. Bugger Dupleix and La Bourdonnais, and bugger Omi Chand in Bengal who lent me the money, too. I can start a new career at any time! There's always Tulaji Angria. He's a pirate and a dangerous man, but he owes me a favour after I destroyed six of his pirate grabs but let him take his leave of me in the seventh. I could join forces with Arthur and Willie McBride and we'd be privateers and split fifty-fifty with Angria . . . ah, but I'm too old t'be hunting down French shipping in a grab, and it'd be too much like surrender.

He sighed, seeing his beautiful ship in French hands, but nothing, not even that sight, could take the shine off the day now.

The news he had received last night had jolted him. A mussoolah man off one of the catamarans, a man with kin south along the coast, had brought a garbled story to Robert Clive, and Clive had conducted the man straight to him, his face full of pity and regret. There was no way to disbelieve him because of the ring. A gold ring with the initials H. F. and the Flint pennant device of stars and waves. He swore that the ring had been pulled off the finger of a white man – a white man dead from drowning.

The news had devastated Flint and he felt like vomiting. For the first time he was forced to believe in his son's death. He wanted to send Clive away, unwilling for him to witness his loss of dignity, but he went instead to his desk to settle a tidy sum on the mussoolah man. Then something made him look again at the wide-eyed man who took the big bag of silver rupees, and he called in Shivaji to question him thoroughly in his own dialect.

'What village is it?'

'A holy place far away to the south – I don't know the place he mentions.'

'Did he come from the village himself?'

'No.'

'Then how did he get the ring?'

'From a brother's wife's cousin's friend who had a relative who saw it.'

'And was the dead white man alone?'

'Oh, no, sir!'

'Then who else was there?'

'There was the ghost of a dead maharaja that rose up out of the ocean, and a dragon with fifty heads and teeth that dripped blood appeared, clothed all in fish-scales of iron – '

Shivaji raised his hand and slapped the side of the man's head with undue venom. 'Tell the truth, you lying peasant!'

The mussoolah man put his hands together and cringed. 'I swear, lord!'

'What's that he says?'

'He says he swears, but he's lying, *na-khuda*. I know these people and their *gup*. Some nonsense about hundred-headed monsters from the deep.'

'Let him say his say, Shivaji.'

Eventually, they pared the story down. 'He says there was the ghost of a raja and his rani and two white men who were royal servants, but the one with hair of brass died and the other did not. And something about fifty armoured horsemen.'

'The feringhee who died,' Flint asked, 'did he have hair of iron? Or hair of copper? Or hair of brass?'

'Hair of brass, lord.'

'And the servant who did not die? What of his hair?'

'He says that was most strange of all, *na-khuda*. That one had human hair.'

Flint snapped his fingers. Though the story had been relayed and exaggerated in the Indian way, through many credulous and creative minds, the germ was of a black-haired man surviving a storm beaching. Black-haired like Hayden, because the lad Dan'l Quinn's hair was blond as straw, and the detail of his drowning was passed in the tale for certain.

'Not a word of this to anyone,' he warned Clive. 'Not a peep. Ye'll promise me!'

'Aye, I'll promise, Mr Flint. I'll not breathe a word to anyone, but . . . what about Miss Savage?'

'Especially her. On yer life, now?'

'On my life.'

'That's good,' he said. 'Hayden alive, damn his thieving eyes! And Muhammad Ali too. Ah, Hayden, you're the best possible news to my ears, though gunpowder in another way: what's the hope fer the ruby now? And the hope it'll get to the nawab? We'll have to be careful over that. And very, very quiet.'

Recalling his mind to the present, he pulled out the brass telescope tubes. Now what about ye, me beauty? he thought, squinting at the *Chance*. The morning was cool, the sun being newly up, a good time for thinking and working up a plan. He lifted the glass to his eye. His ship rode unhappily under her loathsome French ensign – a powder-blue field with lilies – and with a French prize crew aboard her. Her image in the telescope, blued and fore-shortened by distance, still invited his inspection, but she was no longer his pride, the ship he had struggled all his life to possess. He suddenly feared she was gone from him, and all he had amassed with her had gone too.

Stamp on that, trader! he warned himself. How can ye think evil thoughts on a day like today? There's no place fer pessimism in yer philosophy. Never has been! And ye'll not allow thinking like that.

Ah, but Free Trade, he thought, still loving the lifelong dream with a fierceness that hurt. That's the thing to dwell on. That's the big goal, and always has been. With the seas open to anyone to trade east of the Cape there'll be real commerce, real competition, real advancement. And with it real wealth!

Money's everything, he had told Hayden many times. Aye, everything. It's power and it's freedom and it's contentment, and it's anything ye want it to be. There's nothing ye cannot do when ye have money. Nothing. And there's too much ye cannot do when ye're without it. And the myth that money's evil is spun by pious fools who've never seen the horrors of poverty. And the rumour that money makes a man unhappy is spread by the rich who fear that other people want to take it from them. And the word that money's an impossible dream is spoken by those who're resigned and chained to beggardom. Ah, but there's no need to fear wealth, or hate wealth, or slander wealth, when wealth is absolutely increased by organized manufacture and overseas trade. By God, the wealth of nations would see a glorious increase if I had my way! Boatloads of money, aye, loads and loads of it, like the elephant-loads of gems and gold that the Moghuls have. That's what we want, and a black curse on all ye that says otherwise!

That's what Free Trade'll do. If we had that there'd be purest silver flowing down the Hudson River and the Delaware and the Susquehanna as well as down the crooked spine of Old Father Thames, and every man in England and New England and all the rest of the Colonies would have ten shirts unto his back and every woman her home and hearth and every child his belly full and shoes fer the winter. If we had Free Trade there'd be a hundred trading houses plying to the East. All independent. All competing fer the home market. And America freed from the Company's arbitrary rules and her goods freed from the Company's taxes. Within ten years all London and all Liverpool too would be sending ships to Canton and Bencoolen and Calcutta! And I'd be the king of tea in Boston and New York and the entire globe would be tied together with trade: English hulls filled with English manufactures and English cloth, with China tea and Virginia tobacco and Jamaica sugar and

Newfoundland fish; rice and cotton out of Charleston, hardwood from Honduras, furs from Hudson's Bay – but most of all, the wealth of Hindostan: bullion and specie. Think of it! A hundred English and colonial houses vying with each other, and Flint-Savage & Co. ahead of the lot, by God! Ah, what a world that would be – *will be*, one day!

He packed up his telescope and strode on a little further, sighing, patting his vest pocket for his stogie and tinderbox, then realizing he was bereft. Poor Arkali, he thought suddenly, remembering the night of the mutiny. Yer father says ye cry yerself t'sleep and have hollow eyes since yer experience. Clive says ye're distraught. Well, didn't I say yer da should've let ye get it out of yer soul with a gun. Ye had every right to revenge yerself, and to put a bullet in that scum's heart. I'm sorry fer ye now, lass, and I'm sorry fer the way I treated ye. I never wanted it to come out like this, fer me or fer yerself. But that's life and there's bugger-all justice to it, and though some men, good men, try to make it so. I'll bring ye better tidings by and by, so I shall, ye may depend on it.

He doused the warm feelings that were starting to kindle in him again. Faith! And where in God's name's the Royal Navy? Can it be that Barnett really is et by the sharks, and that Captain Peyton really is the snivelling coward that his letter to the Council makes him out to seem? What if the squadron has really fled away to the safety of the Hooghly River and Calcutta? He slammed his hand onto the stone abutment, wishing he had a new-rolled cheroot with him to suck on. Ah, ye know the truth of it. Don't deceive yerself!

So, what price freedom now?

He stopped and ran out the telescope once more, his seasoned eye taking a careful turn round the deck of the *Chance*, then by habit he took in imagination his customary morning constitutional along the weather side of the poop. The sun lit the waters through her masts and spars like beaten gold. By God, her lines are fine! Finest ship east of the Cape, and almost the biggest, and she's mine, by God! Mine! Aye, even now!

The smallest breeze stirred the dust at his feet and ruffled his ostrich trim. Instantly he spat on his hand and rubbed it on his breeches, then felt for the light air and its direction.

A smile split his face. All along the southern horizon a grey line of haze misted the junction of sea and sky.

He shortened his telescope and slid the brass lens cap shut, seething with the desire to get aboard his ship. He had seen what he had come to see and the knowledge fired him up like red-hot shot. First take stock, trader, he told himself sternly. Take a grip and see where ye're at, all the debits accounted one item at a time, and search out any credit ye can, and then ye shall have breakfast with the Admiral as his invitation requires and balance everything up on the bottom line.

You're a bloody fool, so help me, Robert Clive, he told himself, putting the flask out of Arkali's sight. You never think straight in the presence of ladies, and that's why they consider you uncouth and ungentle. And so you are because you don't know how to act properly.

He had visited her each morning so far, but she had hardly spoken a word to him. Today he had brought a silver flask with some brandy in it for her, thinking it might ease her, but the stink of the liquor only awakened raw memories of that terrible night and tears started to swim in her eyes.

'No, please don't. I only brought it to give you comfort. Really.' He offered her his handkerchief awkwardly.

'Please go away, Mr Clive.'

'Now there's no pleasure in sitting alone, is there?' he said as gently as he could. He thought he understood her melancholy

'I tell you I would prefer it.'

'Don't say that, Miss Savage. Your father allowed me to call upon you in the belief I might cheer you somewhat. Don't let's disappoint him, eh?'

She let his handkerchief fall into her lap.

'Perhaps I can persuade you to take a little tea with me?'

She shook her head. Her coppery ringlets rippled in the sun. She was very beautiful, but her face was pale and forlorn, and her eyes almost sightless as they stared into space.

Perhaps I embarrass her, he thought. After all, I did come upon her naked and otherwise helpless in the most bestial of circumstances, but by God, the least she could do is show me a measure of thanks for preventing a wholly worse outcome. Why, if it wasn't for me . . .

'I want to die.'

He stared at her, unable to believe she had spoken those softly numbing words.

'What did you say?' he asked stupidly.

'I said, I want to die. Now that Hayden's dead there's no longer – '

'Oh, no, Miss Savage! That's a terrible thing to say! Put that out of your head. Please, I beg you.'

Her body convulsed, her face puckered and she began to cry. He hesitated, horrified, then took her shoulders and clasped her to him, patting her back. She was like papier-mâché in his arms, fragile and insubstantial. Her vulnerability brought out a ferocious instinct in him to protect her, a desire to infuse her with some of his own sanguine spirit, and he knew he would have to break his word to Stratford Flint if he was to succeed.

Damn it to hell, he thought, my twenty-first birthday, the day I come of age! The only time I have to be alone with her, and she's for killing herself over Hayden Flint. I'll have to tell her he's alive. I'll have to.

But if you tell her that, a devil inside him said, she'll not look at you any more. And you can't break your promise to Stratford Flint.

He swallowed. But when I look at her, and I feel those sobs racking her whole body and I know she's so distraught she's lost her will to live – I have to tell her.

'Arkali,' he said, holding her at arm's length and insisting she look at him. 'I came here to tell you something wonderful . . .'

As he spoke, her eyes began to flick back and forth between his own, then she took the flask from his hand and drank from it until she choked on its fire. Clive watched her with astonishment.

'Where is he?' she asked, finally.

'I don't know. All we know is that he was reported somewhere to the south of Madras.'

'But we must find out where! We must try to find him.'

'Arkali, by the terms of our parole we can't leave the fort, much less the lease. And it's only a rumour.'

'No, it's true. I know it's true!' She suddenly hugged him and kissed him on the mouth. 'Oh, Mr Clive, you are my saviour. Truly you are! I must find Mr Flint and speak to him.'

'No, you can't do that!' But before he could stop her she had whirled from the room, leaving him to look at the flask in his hand and shake his head, knowing that he had betrayed Stratford Flint's secret.

Arkali ran down Church Street, towards the counting house, her heart thumping and her breath tight in her laced bodice.

Where's my father? He must be in the fort somewhere. He must be told right away. Right away! She went into the shot-pocked building, crossed the black and white marble-tiled floor and ran towards the great staircase that swept up to the offices on the first floor. The big corridor was eerie without servants or staff, and echoed to her movements. Debris blasted from the ceilings and walls lay scattered, shafted by sunlight from windows that had lost their shutters. Suddenly she ran foursquare into Stratford Flint.

'What's this, missee?' he said, gripping her upper arms.

'Mr Flint! Is my father here?'

'Ye're in a great hurry when there's nowhere t'go, lass.'

'I'm looking for my father. I want to tell him about Hayden. Robert Clive told me – '

'Ah, he did, did he?'

His sudden sternness made her doubt herself. 'Oh, tell me it's true, Mr Flint. Please.'

'It's only a report.'

'We must find him.'

'Now hold on, lass.' Flint gripped her harder, forcing her to stand still. 'Tell me exactly what's been said.'

She told him, words tumbling from her.

'Listen to me, ye can't go nowhere. This fort's under French control and them sentries'll shoot holes in yer hide if they catch ye outside the walls.'

'But – '

'There's no buts.'

A flash of sudden temper lit her and she pulled herself free from him. 'Let me go. Where's my father? You disowned Hayden. Yes, you devil! You don't want to aid him. Or help me to find him. Isn't that so? Where's my father?'

Her scream hurt his ears. He slapped her face lightly and she stopped.

'I'm sorry, lass, but ye'll have t'cease that or I can't think. Now . . .'

'Where's my father?' she whispered angrily, her hand pressed against her face.

'Yer father ain't here. He's talking with whatever Council members he can find, trying to get up some foolish petition to La Bourdonnais to have all English personnel, Company and independent alike, shipped out to Calcutta.'

'Calutta? But what about Hayden? What's *happened* to him, Mr Flint?'

Her voice rose again and he strove to calm her. 'Now listen to me! I'll tell ye where Hayden most likely went ashore and where he's trying to get to, but only if ye'll promise not to tell another living soul about it, and that ye will do nothing to interfere.'

'Tell me why I should?'

'Becos if the French find out what he's up to, he's as good as dead. And ye wouldn't want that, would ye?'

Her eyes hunted about. 'But why should that be?'

He tried to present a kindly face to her. 'Well, becos Hayden has the means to bring a Moghul army here and that would cause the French to leave – which is something they do not desire to do.'

'Don't patronize me, Mr Flint. Where is he?'

'A'right, a'right. Your word, now?'

'You have it. Now tell me.'

Flint had already weighed and rejected the possibility of telling her the truth. He was angry at Clive's betrayal, but blamed himself mostly for having trusted a lad who was so obviously in love.

Ain't surprising, when you look at her, and the lad knows he's her saviour. He's heartsick, and in that pitiful state a man'll say anything, do anything and spend anything – which I should know from two dozen years back when I was in just the same straits. But maybe there's still a way to recover becos she's just as lovestruck over Hayden . . .

'By the wind and tide,' he told her, 'I'll make my estimate that Hayden landed somewhere around sixty land miles south of here. That's a piece closer to Pondicherry than to Madras.'

'He's trying to make his way here? Is that what you're saying?'

'No, lass. He'd have heard the bombardment from ten miles away. Sooner, if he met with any of the refugees who fled away from here.' He paused, knowing he could not trust her with the truth, then he went on in a glossy voice. 'No, it's my guess he headed south. Twenty miles south of Pondicherry is another English Company fort at St David's beside Cuddalore. It's a walnut of a place, very small but built as strong as any of Sebastien de Vauban's fortresses, and the filth – that is, the French – won't have the inclination to besiege it until they've made Madras properly secure. Aye, Fort St David's where he'll be making fer, ye may depend on that.'

'You must help me to go to him.'

He stared at her and laughed dismissively. 'No, lass. That's not possible. The best course is fer ye to await events patiently. Do as yer father tells ye.'

Her face was set now. Suddenly she seemed very sober, and Flint could see her father in her.

'I've done with waiting patiently and doing as I'm told. I want to see Hayden again, And you, Mr Flint, will help me.'

He cocked an eyebrow. 'Oh, indeed?'

'You've no money,' she said. 'I know that. And I know exactly how much you're in debt. My father told me. But I know where you can find a fortune in silver. Fifteen lakhs of it.'

Flint felt the bottom drop out of his plans. It was the fifteen lakhs he had lodged with Savage, the silver Savage had sworn was lost to French hands when they scrambled into Fort St George just before the bombardment.

'Yer father told me what happened to that,' he said guardedly.

'Yes, he did. But he lied.'

'And I say ye're lying now, missee.'

'No! He's buried it. And I know where. I saw him.' She tossed her head. 'Now you'll help me. You will!'

An hour later Stratford Flint stood at the Arcot Road Gate in his best suit of clothes. Charles Savage met him, looking solemn and imposing with his stick and cocked hat and his silver-striped waistcoat buttoned all the way up to his collar against a wind that was getting up. The French sentries saluted on sight, and saluted again when they were shown La Bourdonnais's seal, and the watch officer was called. He looked at them suspiciously but allowed them both to pass as if they were natives and not English traders under a dubious parole bound for the new Governor's residence.

Once outside they took a gig with a dusty-flanked, scrawny horse for an impossible five rupees. The driver salaamed obsequiously as he took the silver in his hand.

'Robbery!' Savage said.

'Aye, but the populace has yet to trickle back to town and competition's thinner than this nag. We cannot walk fer protocol's sake, and ye know I'll not be lifted up by any damned bearer.'

Savage brandished his stick. 'Bloody usurers! Don't they know the Koran expressly forbids that?'

'Aye, they know, but they don't care any more about that than ye do about the commandments Moses brought down off the mountain.'

Savage shot him a deadly glance, then flicked a hand up Flint's coat. 'Why are you taking us out, Flint? And why the need for this natty apparel? If it's for the benefit of La Bourdonnais you can be sure it's wasted. He's the biggest pirate to come out of France. King Louis gave him his naval command in order to control him, and he was made Governor of the Mascarene Islands and Bourbon and Ile de France in the same way that Henry Morgan was made Lieutenant-Governor of Jamaica.'

'Ye're fergetting I supped with him once already, Charles.'

'And found him a kindred spirit, I'll be bound.'

Flint kept his voice level. 'Ah, stow them airs, Charlie. I don't recall ye refusing to handle the cargoes I brought ye in the early days, or enquiring too close where they come from. Ye don't smell so clean yerself – to them as really knows ye.'

The ride out from the fort took half an hour, down along Pedda Naik's Petta and along the dusty St Thome Road. Savage was sour and silent, turning his eyes away from the dust-laden wind, hurt by events and his losses. But he was playing the wounded party deliberately.

'Ye're still worried about Arkali?' Flint asked lightly.

'She's still in decline, sir.'

'Ah, but ye dote on that lass to the point of slavery.' And I'll bet yer wife did the same back in England, he thought, which is probably how she grew up t'be so snooty and so bloody impudent!

He hid his anger about the silver wonderfully, but he could feel it boiling inside him. Soothing chatter was wanted now.

'Surpassing pleasant day, though. Windy, mind.'

'Please don't attempt to small-talk me, Flint,' Savage

grunted. 'You still haven't told me what's in your mind for La Bourdonnais.'

'Ah, just a nice hot curry breakfast.'

Savage shifted his weight. The gig lurched over potholes, swaying as the traders' mansions came into view. The wind raked the palms, the rushing sound of waterfalls in their high heads.

'Just that, a curry breakfast?'

'Ah, yes, and why not? Ideal! Hot spice to give a man a good sweat early in the day. Cools the blood, so it does, and ye'll need it cooling before the day's out.'

Savage looked askance distastefully, and Flint saw that his suspicions were mounting. 'Aye,' he went on heartily. 'Then a glass of port or two to buoy us up fer the discussion, eh? And perhaps some business, eh?' He nudged Savage purposefully. 'Ha! Invited to breakfast in yer own house, what? But ye have to hand it to La Bourdonnais! He has style and some piratical humour, don't he just?'

They got out of the carriage and climbed the steps to the main entrance. La Bourdonnais did not show them the courtesy of meeting them in person, nor did he send a senior officer. They were attended only by servants. Savage scowled at the liveried men as he surrendered his hat, stabbed by the humiliation of being received as a visitor in his own house, but Flint saw that he was also wound up tight about the silver that lay under the adjoining room. It must be that, he thought. Or else I'm reading him wrong and Arkali was lying to me. Could she have been lying?

He fixed Savage with a dour eye. 'Ye did tell me that fifteen lakh I left with ye was definitely gone into the hands of La Bourdonnais and his officers?'

'Surely!' Savage lied baldly and without hesitation. 'I gave you no assurances, Flint. You know that. The French came upon us so suddenly here that there was no time to move a weight of bullion into Fort St George, and even if there had been, the silver would still have been taken when the French came into the fort.'

'I notice ye had time to take yer hall carpets and yer

Chinese crocks and yer long-case clock away,' he said, looking around him. The banging of loose window shutters filled the house with echoes of the bombardment, making the house seem even sadder and more abandoned.

Savage blustered. 'That was – that was my servants. They loaded a bullock cart after we'd gone and saved a few things. By God, Flint, what are you saying? D'you think I'd have left a fortune in silver for the French if I could have brought it away? I'll not have you blame me for that silver, Flint. If you hadn't let the French catch you – well, enough said on that, I think.'

Flint's forehead rucked and his mouth assumed a flat smile. 'A'right, then, that's the entire principal of the loan to repay, and with interest charged at fourteen an' a half per cent per annum, that's' – he figured the numbers rapidly in his head – 'that's damned near a thousand rupees a day, each and every day, including Sundays. There's nothing else for it, we'll have to go to Calcutta.'

'You want to go to Calcutta?' Savage was on guard again, but Flint played him like a fish.

'I've a feeling yon Admiral will give us leave to sail.'

'What?'

'In faith,' Flint said expansively, 'he does owe me a favour.'

'You? What on earth for?'

'Fer doing me best t'persuade the Madras Council to surrender. Have ye forgot?'

'But you didn't – '

'Steady now. He don't know that. And I maintain hopes of getting the *Chance* back.'

As they waited, Savage made a nervous aside. 'Look, Flint, even if you sailed for Calcutta tomorrow, you'd owe another ten thousand rupees by the time you got there. And before the *Kismet* and the *Karma* tied up, you'd owe another twenty thousand. That's if they come in on time! There's not a round voyage in the Bay of Bengal that's less than thirty days, and though you've two ships, what cargo can yield between fifteen and twenty thousand rupees? You'll never keep your wretched ships out of Omi Chand's usurer's hands, and that's on consideration of the interest alone. Think again. Sail for Canton or Bencoolen and get yourself another line of work.'

The agreement with Omi Chand and his bankers was for a minimum loan of two months with extensions of a month at a time, available by prior arrangement. Interest was two months down, which was already paid, and at each month's end on the nail for every month extended. To an Englishman, it was nothing but Oriental usury. Nothing in Europe approached it, except perhaps in Sicily, but it was the way the whole of the East worked from Stamboul to the Japanese archipelago.

'Let's see – I've been away from Calcutta seven weeks now,' he said, wanting to give Savage every last opportunity to repent. 'If I left tomorrow, by the time I got back that'd be nine weeks, give or take a day or two. Omi Chand'd be screaming fer his interest, and I'd owe him thirty thousand rupees, even if he was prepared to negotiate a further extension. Added to that, if he's learned of Madras's fall, or has got suspicious that the capital sum is lost, then he'll foreclose. When he finds half his security – that's our Madras holdings and the *Chance* – have already been confiscated by La Bourdonnais, he'll be an angry man. When he's certain I'm penniless, he'll have me killed if he can. And he can.'

That was putting the worst of it right in front of Savage's face. But instead of the penitent admission he had half expected, Savage adopted an air of moral superiority designed to magnify the tragic state of mind his daughter's ordeal and their joint misfortunes had created.

'You may as well give it up, Stratford. You've ruined us both, and all our futures. Bale out while you can.'

Flint's disappointment turned to anger. God, look at ye, he thought, covering yer sanctimonious blow-hole fer all ye're worth, ye sickening humbug – when ye know full and well that me fifteen lakhs of silver is salted away under these very floorboards!

'At least yer bloody daughter's alive,' he said harshly, then, suddenly conciliatory again, 'Like ye say, Hayden's most probably dead.' Savage did not look up, just remained slumped inside himself, and Flint's half-smile came back. 'But whatever and whatever, there's still business to be considered, eh?'

'Why, you thick-skinned devil! Have you no compassion?'

He looked at Savage, the anger undisguised now in his eyes, and Savage shifted, unsettled by Flint's demeanour. 'Ah, don't tell me ye've got a monopoly on the moral right, Charlie. Ye may show the world yer nice manners and piety when I show it only fists and a hard face, and most of the time the world believes ye a good man and me an evil one on the strength of that. But I know ye: we're alike in too many ways, except that ye hide yerself with hypocrisy and I do not.'

La Bourdonnais's clerk appeared and ushered them forward. They obliged and were admitted to the Admiral's dining room.

The Frenchman was as Flint remembered him. Just as impressive but now, since his victory, even more majestic. He was of middle height, the same age as Flint, his coat sea blue like his eyes, and of the best; his wig was centre-parted and coiled into tight ringlets – for vanity's sake the hair of a much younger person. Flint wondered what Paris pauper-girl had had her scalp shaved to make it. The Admiral's face was clean-shaven, dark through sailing, with a powerful nose and lines grooving his sculpted cheeks. The thrust-out lips were of the Gallic type and the inquisitorial eyes were set criminally close, features that raised the hairs on Flint's back. When the Admiral spoke it was with a nasal resonance.

That really is a prize French beak ye've got there, Flint thought genially, I'd be doing ye a favour to break it a little fer ye.

La Bourdonnais performed a perfunctory nod of the head as he was introduced, and smiled as he was told that Savage was the previous owner of the house. It was clear that the discussion was going to be in French and heavy-going.

The meal was a battle of face. Beneath silver candlesticks, several dishes of pickled chilli pods and mouth-puckering acid-lime chutney swam in poker-hot sauce. In the middle, an ornate decanter of water stood, with three highly polished crystal glasses, glinting like ice.

They started with huge, fragile popadums – plate-sized gram-crisps flavoured with cumin seed, followed by a tureen of the most intense eye-watering curried lamb ever to come out of Bangalore. The game, Flint knew, was to keep face and hold to the conversation despite a mouthful of white-hot shot, never to decline another spoonful when the stakes were raised around the table, and never to so much as look at the water.

'No, no, t'was but a small thing I did for ye, M'sieur Admiral,' Flint said modestly, his eyes giving nothing away, his lips and tongue raging with hell's own fire. 'Though I'll admit this: it did take me the best part of a week to convince our bold ex-Governor he couldn't stand against ye long. Ah, but he's a warrior and a half, is that Nic'las Morse. Be careful ye keep him closely under lock and key, sir, and, mark ye, don't listen to a word the lying schemer tells ye, or he'll have ye in knots. And now, might I be having my ship back, d'ye think?'

La Bourdonnais lost his humour at that. '*Impossible!*' He banged the table, sending rings shivering across the surface of the water jug. Then he shovelled up another spoonful of brown fire and consumed it, saying that the ship was a prize of war, and her profits already as good as divided among her captor's crew. She would be resold into the country trade at Ile de France, to a new French owner: the French would henceforth have need of good hulls, for the intention of Governor Dupleix was to double trade and double it again in the Carnatic. Might Mr Flint consider accepting a small sloop, the *Confiance*?

Flint smiled and gritted his teeth. 'Are not the French a justly famous people when it comes t'generosity?' he said.

'Ordinarily I would be most honoured to accept yer exceedingly kind offer, and remove to Calcutta the troublesome English who're languishing to no good end in Fort St George – or should I p'rhaps call it Fort St Louis now? – and also to bring the news to Calcutta, even though it might make the morale there suffer. Were it not fer other considerations . . .'

'Other considerations?' A trickle of spice-induced sweat emerged from under La Bourdonnais's wig. He dashed it away before it could drip on to the tablecloth. Now that credentials had been established, the real business could be commenced.

Flint put his hands together. 'It has been my good fortune, m'sieur, to have met with Governor Dupleix on several occasions. Ye may rely on me when I say I know what he wants with Madras.'

La Bourdonnais looked away, unconcerned, to the silent Savage. 'Water, wine or brandy, Monsieur Savage?'

'Why, thank you. A carafe of port wine would be my choice, sir. No doubt you found my cellars tolerably well stocked, though they are perhaps not purposely inclined towards the French palate.'

The barb went unremarked. 'Monsieur Flint?'

'Ah, a drop o' Charles's best brandy, if ye please, Admiral. And I'll trouble yer servant fer a light fer the stub on this gasper as soon as he likes. I'd offer ye one, but me supplies are temporarily held up, as ye know.'

'*Cognac et porto et Volnay.*' The table servants moved to obey. 'So! You presume to know what the Governor of Pondicherry wants? Perhaps you do. What is that to me? I am Governor here. It is my ships and my guns and my troops that have taken Madras.'

'Aye, but Joseph Dupleix is in charge. He called ye in, and it's he who has the Compagnie's mandate on the Indian mainland. And most important of all, he outranks ye.'

'I am *de facto* ruler here.'

Flint's flat smile reappeared. 'Dupleix wants to level Madras, ye know that, don't ye?'

'What do you mean – level?'

'Just that. He wants to flatten it until there's not one stone standing upon another.'

'That, m'sieur, is absurd!'

'Not at all. See, from his viewpoint Madras is nowt but competition. What happens when the Royal Navy comes back – as it surely will sooner or later? Or if Madras should be put back in the hands of the English by the nawab Anwar-ud-Din?'

'Most unlikely.'

'Not so, as I'll explain. And there's yer own fleet.' He indicated the purple and yellow iris flowers that swayed on their long stems in Savage's garden. 'Wind's getting up. The change of the southerly monsoon's here, and that means a gale of wind on the coast. There's no protected anchorages and ye may only escape it by standing out to sea.'

The underwriters of Lombard Street were wise to that. No Lloyd's insurance policy would cover ships on the Coromandel Coast from Cape Cormorin to Point Palmiras between the 16th of October and the 15th of December.

'Monsieur Flint, I am well aware of the constraints of the climate. And I have not been deceived by the part you claim to have played in the surrender of Madras. You are here because I have respect for you, please don't treat me like a fool.'

Flint leaned forward, his half-smile broadening. 'A'right. Let's get down to it. It's clear to me that yerself and Dupleix are vying with each another over who's got ultimate authority here. Dupleix is Governor of Pondicherry and therefore, in theory, once ye landed troops they became his to command and Madras his to dispose of. And don't ye deny it. He don't want ye to ransom Madras back to the English, he wants to knock it down flat, or at the least to keep it French, becos that's where his power lies – in keeping Pondicherry free of competition. Ain't that right?'

La Bourdonnais's eyes flickered to Savage who had sat up at the mention of ransom.

A slatted shutter banged against the paneless window. 'The south-west monsoons,' Flint said. 'Another storm could arrive at any time. Then where would ye be, with the *Achille* broken-backed on the beach? Ye know there're bad shoals all the way from Tranquebar to the Ganges, and there's no passage between Ceylon and the mainland fer a ship as deep-draughted as yours. That's why Barnett's squadron never came back fer ye. He knows the weather'll put paid t'ye without the expense of a single shot. Come on, why not settle now and get yerself and all yer ships away? That's yer instinct, if ye'll be honest.'

La Bourdonnais remained fox-wily. He looked down his nose. 'And why can't I leave Madras with all the booty I want already? Why should I have to negotiate some lesser ransom?' He raised his hands to the decor in demonstration of his point. 'Madras and everything in it is mine already, no?'

'No.' The trap snapped crisply shut as Flint sat back. 'Becos I can hand ye an additional ten lakhs of rupees – that's ten lakhs in hidden silver that ye'll never get without me – if ye'll agree to be gone from here before the month's end.'

Savage's mouth opened, then closed again.

Flint's eyes never moved from the Admiral's. He was at his hardest now that he saw the greed lighting La Bourdonnais's features. 'There's but two cast-iron conditions I'll put down, M'sieur Admiral, both what ye might call personal points of pride that I believe are wanting of redress. The first is that ye hand me back me ship on the day ye leave, and the second that ye have the decency to get out of Mr Savage's house immediately!'

SEVEN

The sun was waning over Arcot's Moghul pavilions, a pale disc lost in a featureless high overcast. Nadira Begum sat with her ayahs on a carved marble bench amid silk cushions and crimon- and gold-embroidered spreads; Muhammad lounged beside her, distraught.

'That is how it is with women, my son,' Nadira Begum said, infinitely sad for him. Privately she thought: It is a hard way for women, but it's harder for men. Restless, worldly, ambitious men, never growing up, always ungrateful, never stopping to enumerate the manifold blessings of Allah – never stopping until those blessings are gone like roses that bud and bloom and then wither in the gardens of the Great Moghul.

The gardens laid out below them were extensive, geometrically exact, four formal areas divided by long tulip beds and water channels that drank in the opal light of the sky. In this pavilion it was cool and shaded. Beyond the walls rose tall trees, cypress, plane and supari, and the ever visible towers of the mosque. Only Muhammad Ali and his mother and her two well-disciplined ayahs were here.

'My son, what troubles you? Come to me and rest your head on my lap.'

He looked up at her. 'It's Yasmin, Mother. I need you to advise me.'

She took his head and at once felt the unyielding tension in his neck and shoulders, and she began to salve him in the way she had always salved him. 'How many times have I told you that your marriage was a political marriage, Muhammad? A marriage decreed by your father, and his idea alone. I never agreed to it. He knows you are more able than Mahfuz in every way. You're a better horseman. A better warrior. A better Muslim. A better leader. And that's why Mahfuz has only jealousy for you in his heart. Your father named Mahfuz his successor not because he is first-born, but because he fears you.'

His face contorted and she gentled him.

Yes, she thought, your marriage to Yasmin was more than a political marriage, but didn't I tell you what to do two years ago? Then you had your chance to turn her to your own will. A wife should be loyal, obedient and subordinate to her husband, and you could have made her so – but you had to fall in love with her! That was a great mistake, my son. You should have made *her* fall in love with *you*! Why didn't you woo her? Why didn't you stalk her stealthily as you stalk the deer of the field? And then, when she was truly yours, you could have turned her against her father-in-law. O, my son, though you did not know it you held a jewel in your hands then. A jewel, a priceless jewel. It was within your power to make her yours for ever, yet you squandered her.

'Do you really think my father fears me?'

She answered him at once, her voice like silken steel. 'Why do you suppose Anwar sent you for the ruby, and not Mahfuz? He told you that you were the only one of the Blood he could trust to undertake so delicate a piece of diplomacy. And you believed him, my son. You believed him!' She whinnied. 'My son, that was false pride. You are many things, but you are not a diplomat. No, Anwar sent you to get you out of Arcot.'

He looked at her dully, unwilling to hear, but she persisted.

'And why do you suppose Yasmin was sent with you on the sea voyage?'

'Because she knows their feringhee languages.'

'O, my son, how this woman has the power to deceive you.'

Muhammad twisted on the cushions. The comforting softness of his mother's lap was an unction, but inside he

seared red-hot with remorseless passions that allowed him
no peace. Now it was as if his mother's words had unlocked
the dungeon of his mind, and the horrors he had kept pent
up came flooding out uncontrollably. He did not care that
each image of Yasmin he heaped on the fire inside him
threw the flames higher: the glossy raven of her hair half
concealed under a crimson veil of Benares silk; crimson, the
marriage colour. The colour of passion. Oh, the faultless
cream of her skin, her fine features, carved by God, her lips,
her big, clear eyes . . . and the foreigner looking at her,
drinking her in.

Nadira Begum shifted her weight regally. 'You have two
most beautiful local courtesans, and I have taken the
opportunity of purchasing the contract of Khair-un-Nissa.'

She was the most seductive courtesan in Hyderabad,
whose knowledge was broad and very special. She was the
woman to disengage Muhammad's affections from Yasmin
– if anyone could.

He dismissed the gift. 'There are many beautiful women,
but such beauty as Yasmin has is hers alone. It shows every
time she moves. What strength is that! Deliberate grace.
Mocking poise. A quiet, insolent composure. How the sight
of her maddens me! I want to possess her, but always she
retreats from me. She doesn't want me. She never has.'

One day I'll close her eyes for ever, he promised himself.
Those eyes. Always so cool and guarded towards me. She
doesn't want me. And it tortures me because I need to be
wanted by her.

His mother touched his temple and he whimpered.

Hasn't Muhammad always had everything he wanted?
she thought. I always took care of him. From a child, he has
always had the best. But I could not prevent him wanting
Yasmin, or that vile marriage.

'Tell me,' she asked him softly, probing his hurt, 'how
did she trouble you?'

He stared into the seamless white of the sky and imagined
the perfect skin that stretched from horizon to horizon slit
by a thousand small wounds, each a bleeding cut. He

pictured a rain of blood, each drop scarring his soul, mocking his impotence.

'On the English ship,' he began, unsure how to tell it. 'Whenever the feringhee and I were together, she would not retire as she should. And when I ordered it she would watch us from a distance. Even when my eyes challenged her she turned her head away, like this – haughtily.'

'Yes, I can see that disobedience is in her, my son. She is wilful and wicked.'

The fire in his blood consumed him. 'I saw it. I saw her doing it. She was comparing us. As men. As lovers.'

'As lovers?'

The sky's wounds dripped blood and the drops were tulip heads. They shimmered red in the garden around him.

'You really believe she has lain with him?'

He did not answer her question. It seemed too immense to be answered.

'Muhammad? Tell me. Do you believe it?'

He continued to look out at infinity, but then his stare decayed. 'No.'

'A pity.'

Nadira Begum's words were soft and he hardly heard them, but they jolted him.

'What?'

'I said it is a pity.'

His eyes were orbs as he looked at her. 'Why? Why say that?'

'Because, Muhammad, if you had said yes you would have had a way to escape her.'

'What are you saying?'

'Don't you see? You must denounce her. Destroy her before she destroys you!'

'Destroy her? I cannot!'

'You must!'

He tried to rise, but she took his chin in her hands and twisted it so that he was forced to look up at her. 'My son, she tortures you. If you could prove she has lain with the feringhee you could destroy her. Legally. Without redress. And no one could prevent it, not even Anwar. Promise me you will do that! Promise me!'

He closed his eyes, the sweat beading him. 'But I know they are not lovers,' he said. 'Though I know she desires it, still . . . still they are not.'

She released him and he sprang up, making the ayahs flinch.

'You said you knew her thoughts!' Nadira raised her voice at him. 'Her eyes spoke, did they not? Did they not?'

'Yes!'

'Ah! And she is eager to learn feringhee ways? Did she speak with him in his language? She might have said anything. They could have shared intimacies in your very hearing. Don't you see how she enjoys taunting you?'

He turned, staring at the rows of dancing tulip heads. 'No!'

'Yes! It gives her pleasure!'

'No!'

'You know it does! In your heart you know I am telling you the truth!'

He ran from the pavilion, vaulting down the steps wildly, his rage jerking him like a puppet. Then his sword was in his hand and he was in among the mass of flowers, kicking and whirling and slashing until the space around him was a ruin of stamped soil and fallen petals.

Hayden Flint closed his eyes and lay back. He had been given a suite of rooms in the part of the palace they called the mardana, a place removed from gossiping women, remote from noisy babies and children and safe from the spying and scheming of eunuchs. His rooms were light and airy and overlooked a paved courtyard. It was a suite befitting a guest of ambassadorial rank, with attendants to wash and anoint his feet, and flowing water so he could bathe and perform the ablutions of the Faithful. They had taken away his clothes and the dhobis had washed them and brought them back to him air-dried. Silk stockings and shirt and breeches all shining white, his coat brushed free from dust once more and his shoes polished. In the meanwhile he wore a jama and relaxed on the couch, meditating on the task confronting him, but he held the ruby in his hand, fearing to let it out of his grip.

That's irrational, he told himself. If anyone was going to steal it, they'd have stolen it before now. Perhaps that is an indication that in Anwar-ud-Din's court the honour of Anwar-ud-Din stands paramount, and that's important because if Anwar-ud-Din is without honour then I am lost.

He put the ruby down for a minute or two, but then picked it up again quickly, feeling much better with it in the palm of his hand. The touch of it comforted him; the thought of what it represented filled him with despair. This was the first time any European had sought to meddle in the politics of Hindostan. The Portuguese, the English, the Dutch, and now latterly the French, all of these trading interests had scrupulously avoided entanglement. They had attached themselves like barnacles to the hull of the subcontinent and stayed there within their forts and leases, playing to cautious rules. It seemed a sound policy, for Moghul politics was an octopus, many-tentacled and menacing, reaching out to drag the interloper into its coils, there to drown and devour him.

His father had always despised the policy. He had worked assiduously to break those rules. He wanted the English Company to confront the bloated and decaying Moghul power on its own terms, to contest its abitrary constraints, and to demand the trade rights a commercial power might properly expect.

Hayden Flint made an effort to fix his duty clearly in his mind. He squeezed the ruby hard, knowing that the moment of decision was approaching. Before dusk I shall have to formally hand the stone to Anwar-ud-Din, he told himself. In return, I shall request a firman, a decree addressed to Governor Dupleix in person, ordering the French to dissolve their blockade of Madras. That's what's been agreed, but –

He heard servants moving about in the adjoining room, and listened tensely, expecting his forebodings to materialize, but the servants vanished again, and after they had gone he got up and discovered they had returned his guns. There was no explanation. He examined them suspiciously. They had been thoroughly cleaned but not reloaded. Perhaps I can rely on Anwar-ud-Din's honour after all, he thought. I wonder what sort of man he is?

He considered that while he dressed and ate a light meal of spiced lamb and rice selected from a huge table of delicacies; afterwards, a self-effacing munshi, a tutor of etiquette, came to him with sugary words and excruciating deference to ask if he lacked anything.

'The Excellency did not find his unworthy meal too disgusting?'

'Indeed not. The food was very palatable.'

'The climate here suits the Excellency?'

'It is quite satisfactory, thank you.'

'Then the Excellency is not too uncomfortable?'

'I am most comfortable, thank you. I assume the hour has been fixed for me to speak with the nawab?'

The secretary looked at him in disbelief and spoke as if he had not heard the question, explaining that he had come to school the Excellency in the correct forms of Anwar-ud-Din's court. So Hayden Flint sat down and listened for an hour and accepted the munshi's euphemisms and round-about talk as gracefully as he could before asking again when he would meet the nawab.

'Surely the Excellency understands that such a thing is unknowable.'

His irritation increased, but he smiled. 'It seems to me a very simple question.'

'It may be God's will that one day the Excellency may have the good fortune to find himself summoned to the Hall of Private Audience.'

'One *day*?'

'*If* God will it.'

He stood up then, nettled by the man's cringing. 'I want

you to carry a message to the Hall of Private Audience. Tell the nawab I thank him for his kindness, but that I should like to transact our business as soon as possible.'

The munshi stared at him again, aghast, but Hayden Flint folded his arms and waited until the man disappeared. He returned later and brought with him a magnificent box of wrought silver, as big as a bible, saying that any gift the Excellency wished to offer the nawab – May He Live For Ever – might be presented with exquisite effect when set against the delicate green silk of the box's interior.

'A gift?' he asked, now completely exasperated by the fawning.

'Of course the Excellency knows it is customary to make a spontaneous gift to a great potentate such as Anwar-ud-Din, May He Live For Ever.'

'Oh, indeed?'

'Yes, yes, Excellency. A spontaneous gift is absolutely mandatory.'

'But I have nothing worthy of a great panjandrum.'

The munshi simpered. 'Oh, yes. Of course. Nothing could be a worthy gift to such as Anwar-ud-Din – May He Live For Ever, or for Mahfuz Khan – May Fame Attend His Footsteps, or yet for Muhammad Ali Khan – He of the Righteous Sword. But however insignificant the gift, the Excellency knows he must try to think of something.'

Now, two days later, he realized that what Yasmin Begum had told him about the virtue of patience in Hindostan was true: without measureless patience there could not even be a beginning. He resettled the silver box under his arm, praying that the waiting was over.

The munshi led him from his rooms, chattering continuously, to the spacious outer hall where the procession was assembled. The nominal reason for the audience, he was told, was the presentation of a new balaband for the nawab's turban.

A turban, the munshi explained, might seem to be nothing but a great length of dyed fabric twisted about a man's head, but it was much more. It had originated as a nomad's chief comfort, a shield against the sun, a pillow at night, a strangling weapon or head armour in times of conflict, a sling for a broken arm – on long desert rides a man could attach his water vessel to one end and use it to bring water up from deep wells, or employ it to keep dust from his eyes in a storm.

But at court a man's turban carried great significance. They were decorated with aigrettes and balabands and the tiara-like sarpej, showing the wearer's family and that family's prestige. It was possible for a knowledgeable man to read a turban as a scholar reads the Holy Koran.

Hayden Flint looked about him as he listened. Around him were fifty soldiers and perhaps a dozen distinguished-looking men, each in his own distinctive turban, and wearing a sword. They were grouped in conspiratorial huddles, enjoying the wafts of air as slaves played peacock-feather fans over them. These, he decided, were Anwar-ud-Din's sirdars and thakurs – the noblemen who formed his government. Then, one by one, the nawab's three sons appeared with their attendants. They came to speak with him, and the subject settled immediately and unshakeably on the weather. All other topics, it seemed, were odious to one party or the other.

Above the door was a great plaque with an embossed motto in golden Urdu script. He scanned the Persian-like words, reading their flowing, hooked forms right to left: 'A prince without justice is a river without water, or a lake in the rains without lotus flowers.'

It was a Hindu proverb, he knew. And beautiful. But strange that it was not a quotation from the Koran, as he had expected. Perhaps it's a good omen, he thought. I'll have to keep watch over what I say and do, especially after what the munshi was at such great pains to drum into me about proper etiquette. They certainly set enormous store by ritual and ceremonial.

The procession started to move forward. The gathering was formal and attended by great pomp, with ministers and lackeys, a column of mail-garbed soldiers and the beating of a pair of kettledrums, slung across a white stallion. The file was headed by the horseman and behind him the chobdar, a bearer who strode forward carrying the *alam*, or nawab's standard, a great showy thing of gold, shaped not unlike a Grecian lyre but mounted on a six-foot pole.

With Mahfuz and Muhammad Ali and the youngest brother, Abdul Wahab, going before him, the wazir, or chief minister, and his retinue immediately behind, Hayden Flint was at last conducted into the Hall of Private Audience across a gleaming marble floor as white as milk. He saw the sweepers grovel abjectly. They were flanking both sides of the procession, down on their knees, heads tucked in as if making themselves as small as possible.

Poor pathetic slaves, he thought, climbing the steps. Imagine the arid, barbarous power that so diminishes a man's life and soul; from birth their one duty is to switch away the fine specks of dust brought in here by the wind, no more and no less.

Ahead, the stallion began to mount the wide stair. Its tail went up and it dropped several moist balls of dung on to the steps. They bounced and rolled and reeked and the procession ignored them, but as the last minister passed there was no rush from the sweepers, for the gathering up of horse dung was the task of an even lower sub-caste, which, Hayden Flint supposed, was the rock upon which the self-esteem of these higher sweepers must perch.

How alien to them would be the idea of a station in life that was not fixed for ever, he reflected, filled with the power of the thought. Yes, the daring idea that a man could have pride in his occupation, yet at the same time aspire to rise through his own efforts to a higher one! How that would change everything, if it ever got a hold here! But it never will. It must seem as self-evidently foolish a notion to them as a man attempting to lift himself into the air by pulling up on the curly tips of his own slippers.

They crossed a hideously gaudy carpet and passed by a pair of over-ornate fountains, whose insistent sound made him feel like urinating. Each of Anwar-ud-Din's tributary sirdars slipped a golden coin into the water, their *nazar* – token gifts of submission.

So this is the durbar, he thought – the word signified a meeting – and that must be Anwar-ud-Din himself. My God, look at that throne! There's no doubt who's in charge here.

A sudden piercing cry filled the hall. He turned his head sharply, but it was only the jarring scream of a peacock strutting and displaying on the balcony. The procession fanned out and stood in a rank before the masnad. Hayden Flint waited, as the munshi had told him he must, and he felt the levity drain away from him.

The fear in the gathering was tangible now, visible even on the face of the wazir. The atmosphere grew silent and tense until the nawab ordered his three sons forward on to the choicest carpet. They, in turn, indicated that Hayden Flint should follow. Cushions were scattered around him and he was invited to take coffee and to smoke with them as an honoured guest. Good God, my shoes, he thought suddenly. Slowly, respectfully, he prised them off.

He felt foolish reclining on the carpet, propped on one elbow, but knew he must submit to the ritual, no matter how much he feared a loss of dignity. He took the long, flexible hose of the hookah and drew in a mouthful of water-cooled smoke, letting the pungent tobacco taste linger on his tongue. Like the others, he expelled the smoke slowly from his nostrils, but did not inhale, fearing there was hashish in the blend.

Relax yourself, yes, he thought, but you can't afford anything but the sharpest thinking here and now. Hashish is seductive. It affects the higher mind, and diminishes its capacity for analytical thought – worse, it makes a man feel falsely intelligent: he imagines great consequences from very ordinary ideas so that he feels he holds the secret of the universe in his palm, when there is naught there but a grain of sand.

The munshi had told him to listen, and to make uncontroversial remarks when spoken to. It was the nawab's prerogative to broach any subject. Privately, he had thought it a good idea to keep silent and watch the father and his two eldest sons carefully.

For half an hour he took no part in the conversation, but stole glances at Anwar-ud-Din, feeling his powerful presence and appreciating his obvious intelligence. He tried to remember the history of the man and thanked God he had at least half listened when his father walked him round and round the *Chance*'s quarterdeck and told him about the deadly politics that had put Anwar-ud-Din on the masnad of Arcot.

Anwar-ud-Din, the supremely powerful man sitting ten feet away from him, was the general who had been sent by the Nizam to impose his will on the Carnatic, and so end the bloody strife that had followed the Maratha invasion under Raghoji Bhonsla. The previous nawab, Dost Ali, and his army had been destroyed at Ambur, thirty miles further inland. He recalled dimly that Dost Ali's first son had been killed in battle by the Marathas who had gone on to overrun and plunder the entire country, even to the limit of standing before the gates of Madras and Pondicherry and impudently extracting a ransom before they would withdraw.

Something of his father's concern with those lawless days filtered back from the depths of Hayden Flint's memory, something about Maratha threats to burn down Charles Savage's mansion and the Governor's house, and of bribes and dirty money; certainly the affairs of Hindostan were rarely what they seemed – and never simple. What was it Stratford Flint had said?

'Make no mistake, son, the Nizam's devious statecraft is unparalleled in all Hindostan. It's my belief he deliberately allowed the Marathas to sweep into the Carnatic becos he hated the old nawab, and when the man's only surviving son, Safdar Ali, tried to take over at Arcot, the Nizam withheld his consent. Of course, without the legitimacy conferred by Nizam-ul-Mulk's word, Safdar Ali's claim was flattened and the whole succession was thrown open again. Ye know what dirty, bloody family feuds can grow up over money, son. By God, ye can

imagine what it got like in Arcot where there's an entire country and its great wealth to squabble over!

'*Safdar Ali's boy was only four years old at that time, so he posed no threat to his father, but he had two God-cursed aunts, and them and their greedy husbands both pounced on the prize.*'

The memory flooded back bright and clear. Those husbands had been Murtaza Ali Khan and Chanda Sahib, the former Killadar, or Governor, of Vellore and the latter of Trichinopoly. Within the year Murtaza had murdered Safdar Ali and proclaimed himself nawab, but the nobles at Arcot had set Safdar Ali's son, now just turned five years of age, on the masnad and Murtaza had had to flee back to the safety of Vellore, disguised as a woman.

This had been the crucial point at which the Nizam had intervened. He sent Anwar-ud-Din to act as Regent until Safdar Ali's son reached manhood. But the boy was murdered only days afterwards, and the blame pinned on Murtaza Ali Khan. Murtaza was still at Vellore, and Chanda Sahib had been taken off by the Marathas, never to be seen again. Thus both of Anwar-ud-Din's rivals had been swept away.

A bloody people with an equally bloody history, he thought. Watch them, and watch yourself. And no more slip-ups, God willing.

The durbar proceeded at a leisurely pace. At first the talk seemed to Hayden Flint to be good-natured, though strangely pointed. He struggled with the complicated court language and saw that there was more to the discussion than the teasing couterpoint of small philosophical disputes and abstruse arguments. After a while he heard a passing reference to himself, and knew he would soon be included in the conversation.

They began to argue about the colour of the Emperor's moustache.

'But what is, is,' Mahfuz told his father definitely.

'No, my son.'

'How so, revered Father? How so can black be white?'

'Because my word makes it so.'

'By what reason?'

'Because I am a Great Man, and a Great Man may not be contradicted, except by a Greater Man, is that not so, Mr Flint?'

He hesitated, remembering again Yasmin's advice and trying not to be lulled by the obliqueness of the talk.

'I cannot disagree with you, my lord,' he said.

Anwar-ud-Din nodded once, emphatically. 'You see, I may not be contradicted. A guest has said so.' The nawab clapped his hands. 'Therefore, what I command *is*. If I so choose, I can command that peacock to become a cheetah, and henceforth all subjects who see it will say it is a cheetah, for that is the command of their lord.'

'Only until an Even Greater Man commands that it shall be a peacock once more,' Mahfuz said sullenly.

Anwar-ud-Din stroked his beard. 'What Even Greater Man is that? Who may command that title here?'

'Only the Nizam-ul-Mulk, Father.' The title meant Grandee of the Empire.

'Or a too-favoured son,' Muhammad Ali muttered quietly.

For the first time Hayden Flint felt the overt bite of the brothers' animosity. It absorbed him. It was as he had thought: for all their airy circumlocutions this exchange still remains a test. The father is watching, feeling out his sons, and they him.

Mahfuz took the wise course, subtly parrying and deflecting the probe. 'Or by the Emperor. Yes, let us not forget the King of Delhi. Or by the Lord Muhammad, peace be upon Him.'

'Peace be upon Him,' they muttered automatically, but the eyes of the waiting ministers and nobles flashed to Muhammad Ali and saw that he remained impassive to the use of his name and the insinuation attached to it.

Hayden Flint watched, understanding enough to see the spider's web of hatreds waiting to catch the unwary. Something's happening, he realized. Something tremendously dangerous is moving just beneath the surface. Be careful! Remember what Yasmin told you: beware the princely houses for they are always in ferment. No nawab can afford to trust his own sons. And, in turn, no nawab's son trusts his brothers.

He sensed that the wordplay was coming to an end. Finally Anwar-ud-Din's gaze slid away from his son and his dark eyes began to examine Hayden Flint critically. 'So, Englishman. You are a prince in your own country?'

'No, my lord.'

'No? Then you must do as a prince commands.' He paused delicately, drawing in a great sigh, and Hayden Flint saw that here was a man capable of refined cruelty. Did he really smother Safdar Ali's five-year-old son, he wondered, as my father claimed, and make Murtaza Ali the scapegoat?

'Tell me about England. It is a fair country, is it not? Do you have many elephants? Are there great tigers in your jungles?'

'I fear that England is very poor in both elephants and tigers, my lord. England is a small, cold country, like Kashmir in wintertime, though without the great mountains.'

'And your villages? They are prosperous?'

He considered. 'There is one great city. Greater than all other cities in the world. It is full of poets and architects and men of science and fine virtue.'

'Lon-don, is it not? Which was all burned down because the houses are made of wood. And George King is the nawab, is he not? And in Lon-don there is also a famous bridge that has fallen down.'

'Quite so.'

'You see!' Anwar-ud-Din stretched and leaned forward, proud of his superior knowledge. 'And how great is the royal palace there?'

'That I don't know, my lord.'

'How can this be?' Mahfuz asked hotly. 'Why don't you give my father an answer?'

'Because I cannot, my lord.' He permitted himself a smile. 'You see, I have never been to England.'

There was a flurry of doubting comment, turning to frank disbelief.

'But are you not English?' Anwar-ud-Din asked.

'As I have already explained to your second son – He of the Righteous Sword, my lord, I was born in North America. In the – country – of Connecticut.'

Anwar-ud-Din absorbed the fact thoughtfully. 'Then what is your title?'

He spoke softly. 'I have no title, my lord.'

'He is a merchant's son,' Muhammad explained, pleased to diminish the foreigner in his father's eyes. 'His father is just a sea-pirate who calls himself a trader.'

Again a flurry, this time of indignation.

'Does my son speak truly?'

'He speaks half truly, my lord. My father does call himself a trader, for that is what he is. But he has never been a pirate.'

The nawab twined his pearl rope round his knuckle, and all who watched watched his face carefully, knowing what was coming. 'So. Muhammad Ali is a liar?'

Hayden Flint's eyelids closed and opened slowly; an icy calm lay on his smile now. 'I would simply assert that Muhammad Ali is mistaken if he believes my father indulges in piracy.'

'But is that not, therefore, only the assertion of a merchant's son?'

'It is without doubt the assertion of a merchant's son.'

'I think,' Mahfuz said, leaning back, 'that for a merchant's son he is not without honour. See, he has brought you a gift.'

The aigrette of Anwar-ud-Din's turban bobbed and he stroked his beard. Then his chin jutted at the box Hayden Flint had laid before him. 'You have brought a gift for me?'

'Yes, lord.'

'Let me see.'

Flint offered the silver box and Anwar-ud-Din took it. He placed it carefully before him and opened it so that the green silk lining illuminated his face from below. Then he looked up with an expression of profound surprise. His pronunciation was crisp as he hooked out one of the two pistols by the trigger-guard and let it dangle.

'What is this?'

'The fine gift of an – English – merchant,' Hayden Flint said uneasily. 'I can assure you that they are of the finest quality; they were made in London and are both powerful and accurate. You know, of course, that English gunsmiths are the most skilled in the world, and it was guns like these that carved out the Yankee colonies in North America. The colony from which I myself – '

'Enough!' Anwar-ud-Din waved him dismissively to silence. 'I am not a fool, Englishman. I have eyes and ears and a nose to help me make up my mind about Europeans and their wares.'

There was open laughter at the remark and Hayden Flint burned with embarrassment, realizing that he had foolishly allowed his mouth to run away with him.

The nawab took out the other pistol and looked at them both together, unimpressed. Then he cast them down heavily.

Hayden Flint's belly dissolved. Sweet Jesus, he thought, I've made the biggest mistake I could possibly have made. The munshi meant me to put the ruby in the box! That's the 'gift' Anwar-ud-Din expects. Of course! Now it all makes sense. It's beneath a prince to negotiate a deal. That's merchant's work. That's what the talk about traders was all about. You fool! They were hinting it was time to bring the ruby out, that I should offer it as a gift to the nawab. God damn their idiotic ways! Why can't they speak plainly and deal plainly? I've insulted him. And what in God's name am I to do now?

Anwar-ud-Din sighed and shoved the pistols forward. 'There. Take your pistols. And do not tell me that your country is pre-eminent in making weapons of war. We were fighting with gunpowder in Hindostan when your own people were hunting tigers with bows and arrows.'

'If I have offended you, my lord – '

Anwar-ud-Din's eyes dwelt on him. 'You have not offended me. You are a feringhee and your lack of proper manners is to be expected, as with very young children.'

'Your pardon, lord.' Flint's hand strayed to the pocket where the ruby lay. 'I apologize.'

'Yes. Perhaps I will give you pardon.' The nawab's voice became infinitely patient, as if repenting his outburst. 'Come and sit here,' he said, 'son of a trader, and watch. You will see how Indian merchants are superior to you in every way.' He snapped his fingers and the ranks of nobles parted. A man in plain clothing came grovelling forward with another box in his hands. He was halted by the nawab's secretary, the chaprasi whom the munshi had said was called Umar.

As the formalities of presentation were undergone, Anwar-un-Din whispered, 'This man knows he has just one precious chance to sell me a balaband. Both he and I know it is worth precisely thirty mohurs. Therefore observe and learn.'

The box was opened with a flourish, and the seller brought out a foot-length of gold-embroidered silk with golden drop-work sewn with small rubies and emeralds and edged in pendant pearls. 'See, lord, what a poor thing I bring to your court . . .'

He described it in an awed voice, holding the balaband with trembling hands. The pearls rippled and the stones glinted but the words of his description made small of the item. They were hastily curtailed as Anwar-ud-Din yawned into the back of his hand.

The chaprasi said, 'On behalf of my exalted master I will give you five mohurs, weasel.'

'A thousand thankyous, lord. I am truly honoured that so mighty a commander of warriors deigns to make so staggeringly huge an offer to so poor a seller of trinkets such as I. Your master's generosity is a worldwide legend.'

'True, true. Very true.'

'But this balaband is not worth even five mohurs. I know this because when the agent of the lord of a Far Country sought to buy it for five mohurs only yesterday I was forced to advise that were his master to buy it for twice that sum, then his own people would say he wears cheap jewellery, and if for twice that again they would say he cannot afford the best. But . . .'

'But?'

'But had his master instructed him to offer a hundred mohurs his subjects would say he is truly a Great Lord. Of course, I had to say: please don't insult your master by offering so small a sum.'

Umar leaned in on the seller aggressively. 'And was the lord of this Far Country greater than my master?'

'No, lord, that cannot be! This nawab was as dirt beneath your master's feet!'

'Then I shall offer you a thousand mohurs on my master's behalf.'

The seller's eyes glazed. 'The generosity of Anwar-ud-Din's noble servant is utterly beyond contemplation. In conscience, I cannot accept so vast a sum.'

'In that case, motherless weasel, I shall allow you to sell me the balaband for three times its value. Fifteen mohurs. And you shall have something also as a mark of my master's charity.'

'Your master's charity is at least as great as his generosity, lord.'

'Both are infinite, and so cannot be compared.'

'It is as you say, lord.'

Anwar-ud-Din clapped his hands and the seller crawled away from the masnad abjectly, fifteen mohurs of generosity in his right hand and fifteen of charity in his left.

Hayden Flint watched, disturbed by the ritual humiliation. He remembered Mavalipuram and the caste rigidity that permeated every level of society. Then, as the balaband seller retreated, something in the back of his mind made him decide on a tremendous gamble. He took the ruby from his pocket and placed it on the carpet before Anwar-ud-Din.

All eyes went immediately to the huge jewel. A gasp went

up, more at the outrageous breach of protocol than at the stone itself. Flint's heart hammered. The moment was upon him at last whereby Madras would stand or fall. His face unmoving, his eyes on the nawab's, he said, 'I am a trader's son, my lord, but I am not here to trade. Nor did I come here to enter into negotiations. I came merely to deliver this ruby into your hands. The stone is yours now. Please take it. Then, I believe, unless your court is a lake in the rains without lotus flowers, you will do what your conscience dictates.'

The women stripped Muhammad Ali of his jama so that he stood naked before them. They led him to the steps of the Pool of Great Wonder, and as his garment fell away he looked over the glassy surface of the water. At its deepest it was navel-deep, nine paces square and cut into solid rock that had been lipped with white marble and inlaid with jasper, jet and carnelian. A small star-shaped notch was cut in the far end over which water brimmed to feed an ever-running channel. There were many legends about its curative powers, many more to explain the unique ice-cold spring which fed it from below. But it was truly a mystery how such a pool could be. Truly a great wonder.

Without pausing he walked to the top step, descended it, descended the next, and the next, and once again, until the icy water reached his upper thighs, and then he turned and smoothly, as if lowering himself on to his favourite couch, he sat down.

He closed his eyes, anticipating the agony as he lay back and let the water of the pool swirl up around him. His shoulders and arms tensed on the stone lip and his head hung forward like the image hanging from the crosses of the infidels, like a man baring his neck for the executioner's sword.

How important it was for a prince daily to demonstrate unflinching control before others. That's why he came here. He knew that when the women retired they would whisper of his marvellous capacity to disregard physical pain, and so his reputation would grow and he would be revered. This he knew, and the knowledge made him strong, for he had learned to survive that exquisite space of time that lies between the infliction of hurt and the arrival of pain. Muhammad Ali Khan was of the warriors' line, and this was the interval given by Allah for the warrior to adjust his mind. Here, stone-cold spring water issued from a natural vent in the floor of the pool; from deep below the earth it welled up and bubbled. As he sat there it jetted into the cleft of his buttocks, played directly onto his testicles.

Aaaaagh . . .

He suppressed the gasp and remained still even though the icy current daggered him. He stared stoically at the fluted mosaics of the walls and the vaulted ceiling, containing within his chest a bellow of pain. Then he clamped his teeth together, feeling the flush of cold-pain to their roots and knotting in his temples and lower belly, and with a supreme effort of mind he forced himself to keep breathing without interruption. It was a simple release, a self-inflicted torture, but also a meditation, and one that he had lately come to crave. It was as if the all-pervading physical discomfort drove his most difficult inner problems to a deeper chamber of his mind, a place where they could be solved.

He knew that soon he would get out of the pool and feel his flesh burn with immoderate heat. The sensation of extremes is paramount, he thought. And how true the ancient wisdom that if a man would achieve an objective, any objective, first he must attempt its opposite. Oh, yes. Tear down the temple before you would build the mosque, fight in order to make peace, humble yourself to achieve great heights. And freeze the body with pain to experience the true pleasures of the heat of fire. But the fire will come later, after the cold has served to focus the mind, hard like a jewel.

Isn't that what the feringhee said before that astonishing interview with my father? A land like Kashmir, in the wintertime, without mountains. Heat enervates, but cold –

ah, cold invigorates. Isn't that the reason they are able to strive ceaselessly, and over so unworthy a thing as trade? Because they are from a cold land where summer never comes, and in their perpetual winter they learn discipline, and their minds become like crystal.

But why do they regard only profit? Profit through rapacious trade? Why do they not see there is no honour in that? Why? Because their souls are dead. They are not warriors, but unclean bania. Filthy, mannerless merchants who don't even know how to wipe their own bottoms properly.

Muhammad felt his muscles begin to spasm. The shivering was coming upon him and he forced himself into relaxation in the rigorous way he had been taught by the sufi ascetics.

I too have seen ice, he told himself, gripping the thought in his mind so that it distracted the pain. Remember it! See it! Fill your mind with it . . . Ah . . . Yes, it was at Delhi when I was a young child, with my father, who was accompanying the Nizam on a state visit to the court of Muhammad Shah, the Padishah. I thought those floating diamonds which the nobles made much of were things of great value. I secretly took one of them from the great ewer set before the Emperor's masnad and tried to hide it in my hand. But the harder I gripped it the more the ice stung. The ice was hard and transparent like diamond, but more precious than diamond. And yet in my hand it magically dissolved into water. It melted away as I watched, but I can feel the panic still, after all these years. Water dripped from my fist, and when it was gone I was terrified that the Padishah would notice I had stolen it and demand it back. How many years passed before I learned that the Padishah's ice was wrapped and boxed and brought swiftly to Delhi from the lands beyond the great Ganga, from the Himalayas. They told me it melted away under the sun so quickly that though a camel-load might start the journey, only a piece the size of a melon would arrive. Ice, more precious than diamonds, but still used by the Emperor in high summer to cool his drinks and to soothe his headaches . . .

Aaahhh . . .

The pain climaxed and his teeth began to chatter.

By the Prophet, he thought, biting his jaws together hard three times then relaxing them, I cannot do as my mother wishes. I cannot. The very thought of the feringhee and Yasmin sends me into a boiling rage. How can I plot to destroy her when I know I cannot live without her? I want her – all of her. Body, mind and soul.

This pool is unbearable today! It's far colder than yesterday. But that's good because such cold contains a lesson. It's the key to the Europeans. They are northern peoples, tempered by cold. That's why they are as they are. That's why Hindostan has nine times been invaded successfully from the north, never from the south. That's why the Nizam chooses Afghans and Pathans as his generals. They are fierce and they know nothing of mercy, because their minds have been focused by mountain cold, focused to a star-point, a bright, cold, blue-white star-point like the holy stone in the Nizam's sword . . .

Aahh . . .

A sudden tremor struck Muhammad but he maintained muscular control over his tensing stomach until the cramp subsided. He closed his eyes, feeling the cold right to the marrow of his bones.

Yes, I must learn to think how the cold-weather feringhee thinks. That is important now. Events have turned out astonishingly well for me. With a little careful planning I'll be able to apply my newfound leverage now that the ruby is here in Arcot. Will my father actually march on Madras? I hope so, because even an Untouchable may profit from the fight between a dog and a pig. In the world through which a prince must move the penalty for not staying one jump ahead is death, but I will be Nawab of the Carnatic, and it will be Mahfuz's head that rolls in the dung.

Aahh . . .

To beat back the pain he fixed his mind on the Emperor

Aurangzeb, knowing that he had more than a little of the great man's blood in his veins. A great man. The greatest. Aurangzeb had not scrupled to behead two of his brothers, nor to imprison his father. He had known how to deal with feringhee pirates who plundered the Haj ships transporting pilgrims to Mecca – he had forced the Dutch and French and English Companies to send ships to police the convoys, and had demanded compensation for every Moghul ship taken. Soon the Europeans will have to deal with such a leader again, he thought, and even the Hindus will recognize me as the living incarnation of Aurangzeb. Soon. Very soon now.

Muhammad was suddenly roused by movement in the water. He felt the lap of ripples wash his chest, but did not open his eyes. Always Fazhul sent the slave-girl to him. It was the same each afternoon, the same slave, an exceptionally passionate young girl, skilled and ritually cleansed for his enjoyment, and specially selected too. Chosen for her Rajput blood, her hot, strong sexual appetite and her manners, which were those of a tigress.

But this time he kept his eyes closed, looking at her instead with only the third eye of his mind, imagining her opposite him in the pool, sliding breast-deep across the water, her young and slender body hidden, her hair long and thick and black, the part framing her face still dry. She would smile, despite the pain of the cold, despite the fine hairs erecting in her dark skin. It would be a pure white smile just as he demanded. She must be as brave as he was in the cold or he would send her away for ever. She knew that.

He would smile back then, and watch her come to him. He would make her wait until she could not control her shivering, then he would take her and lift her up into the warm air and lay her on the marble lip of the pool, or carry her dripping to the couch, and there he would run his fingers over her body, which would grow warm, and he would feel her, but the pads of his fingers would be white and wrinkled and numbed with immersion, and her touch would be otherworldly, and all the time he would know she was praying that this time his seed would flow and be barbed so that it would catch in her belly and put her with child, because then she would be honoured and her position in the zenana would be enormously enhanced. When he felt the power rise in him she would straddle him and massage him so expertly, with such longing. Then they would couple and he would slip inside her and she would be like a raging furnace after the icy water. And so they would continue until he was sure that he had her entirely in his power, that she was holding nothing back, and only then would he dominate her and glimpse Paradise.

He opened his eyes, startled that he could feel no movement in the water. The Rajasthani slave-girl was not there, but another stood above the pool, reflected quiveringly in it.

This was not a girl, but a woman, older, and swathed in astonishing veils of ghostly muslin, pale turquoise and as insubstantial as moonlight on spring dew. She had rippled the water with her hand and drips fell from the red daggers of her fingers like diamonds. He started at her as if she was a vision and the shivering began to take him.

'Lady. . .'

He saw that she had undergone the sixteen rituals of adornment: her hands and feet were tattooed with crimson henna, he could smell the scent of her, musk and melon and sandalwood; her hair flowed blue-black from a knife-sharp parting below which a sindoor mark had been made. Her plucked brows were sabres, her sensuous lips bows. Her eyes were elongated with kohl. She wore silver at every joint, anklets, armbands, bracelets, rings on her long fingers and toes, and a huge sapphire in her navel.

'Lady,' he said, and began to rise from the water. 'Who are you?'

'My name is Khair-un-Nissa. I have come for your pleasure, lord.'

Her voice was like a fountain. She came towards him, stepping into the bright sunlight that dazzled the pleasure dome at the end of the chamber; her two attendants followed gracefully. The air here was cooled by the water, and the perfume of the gardens made it as sweet as wine. He stood before her, dripping cold water on to the marble and then on to the carpets, and the down-filled cushions, his shivering uncontrolled. He knew without shame that his lingam was shrivelled small as a walnut. Her young attendants towelled him, dried his skin and hair, whispering promises, rubbing piquant oils into his muscles, oils that gave a deep fire to him.

The courtesan was clearly one of the finest money could buy, fully skilled in the erotic arts. In appearance she was a houri come down to earth from Paradise, but women were often the most lethal weapon of the powerful. It was the simplest thing in the world to poison a man with a loving cup, for a courtesan's attendant to open a vital vein or reach down with a razor when he was striving for the Moment and sever him. He pictured himself raving in anguish down the corridors of the palace, naked, his lifeblood gushing away, his manhood irretrievable in some specialist assassin's crack.

The horrible vision melted as she began to reveal herself. Her attendants removed her clothing delicately and he touched her and together they sank into the silken nest. Then the attendants were naked also. They turned their hands on their mistress, touching her, drawing their nails along the insides of her outstretched arms, her superb breasts and flat, muscular belly, so that her nipples budded and her eyes rolled up into their lids. They kissed and caressed her and fanned her long hair out over the pillows to invite him smilingly, and the music of tabla and sitar drifted from a far pavilion beyond the marble moucharabya screens, borne to them on the hot wind.

He began to grow unbearably large as he watched them draw her legs apart to reveal the shaved mound of her yoni, the pucker of scented flesh that glistened now and held his desire. One of the girls marvelled at him, took him, her mouth succulent. The geometry of the screens fractured the sunlight and patterned the contours of their bodies with stars and polygons as they mingled, then the courtesan began to coo and moan softly and he knew he could do nothing but couple with her, not even if she held a razor of glass in each fist.

Outwardly, Khair-un-Nissa was a pliant, lusting vessel of desire. Each supple limb articulated at the perfect angle of temptation to invite him, each sighing, writhing movement hypnotic in its power to hold him. But inwardly she was dancing. The moves she made were learned skills, every technique a natural talent that had been refined and brought to sensual perfection by years of study and practice under one great teacher and a great many singular clients. She knew she could perform this act exquisitely, confident that her face and body were under total command, and sure, too, that her own private thoughts were invisible to the man who rode in her.

She felt him come to her, lay his hands on her, and her intuitive response was precisely the response he most needed. She felt his bull-like weight, measured his desire, opened her lips with her fingers, guided him. He was gripped by her passion; her head tossed and her breathing modulated. She gasped, this time without deliberation. Horribly, the cold of the pool was still in his flesh, his hair was lank, he felt like a man in death, a drowned man, but warrior strength was still in his thighs and biceps and they forced her down. It'll pass, she thought. The girls will anoint his back and buttocks and massage the life back into him. She gave the subtle sign and they began to manipulate him as he arched like a bent bow to position himself. Then she drew herself further apart to accept him and he entered her, grunting deeply with each heave of his muscular back.

Her cries whimpered higher as she matched her rhythm to his. He groaned as he rode her, but then, incredibly, his lingam's strength began to fade. She redoubled her movements, monitoring her inner feelings with concern, drawing every last skill from her repertoire, making herself moister by a conscious effort, as the yogis had taught her.

So that was it . . .

She had felt it, suspected it when Nadira Begum talked to her. *His very special needs.* That's what the old bitch said. What special needs? she'd wondered, knowing that whatever it was she could accommodate him. The ones with special needs were usually the easiest to satisfy, and by far the most grateful. He seems violent, but it's an odd kind of violence. A kind of frustration. What is it he's searching for? It's so hard to understand men, even after so long studying them. They're so completely different to women.

She knew instinctively that she must concentrate her body's being in her most highly trained muscles, in the depths of her yoni. He began to stiffen again, his flesh burning now, his hairy chest, matted with sweat, sliding against the erect flesh of her nipples. She smiled inwardly, blessing her mother for putting her into this most favoured of professions.

'But Mother, I don't think I'll ever understand the minds of men,' she'd said on a visit home one year into her training.

'Do you understand the minds of horses?' her mother asked shrewdly.

'No.'

'Then what is the problem?'

It was true. Looked at like that, there was no difficulty. Men were so easy to ride and control, much easier than horses, and much more rewarding. The life of a courtesan was a most remarkable life. She felt proud, for what other incarnation could have brought her into such intimate contact with so many rich and powerful men?

It was a pity she had had to leave Hyderabad. The zenana there had turned against her, had seen her through jealous eyes and wanted to banish her. That was why she had come here, before they could move against her. Arcot was a suitable temporary alternative, and Nadira Begum had convinced her that events were stirring here. Momentous events . . .

He continued to labour for his pleasure, seeking her depths, but his breath was husky in her ear, his heart pounding. What was he searching for?

151

As if striving for the ungraspable he became furious and she responded again. Her professional mind was helping him with all her ingenuity, but her private mind was wandering. Why was she here? What possibilities were there for her with Muhammad Ali Khan?

Why was the thought of Trichinopoly, Muhammad's southern jagir, or fief, so insistent in her mind? What use was Trichinopoly to her, or to him? An impregnable rock fortress rising out of the flat shallows of the River Cauvery –perhaps it was worth something as a place of last resort, a place to retreat to in time of war, but it was not a capital to rule over in splendour. In the far south of the Carnatic, Trichinopoly was even more predominantly Hindu than the rest of the country, a backwater of political power, a place granted to second sons as a sop to limit their ambition.

He faltered. Yes, definitely waning before the summit. He's not going to make it! Alarm thrilled through her. What's the matter? Surely it can't be me? Then her darkest worry. Please don't let it be me. Not yet. I've got years yet, I'm at my peak. Yes, it must be him. Only him.

The part of her mind that never ceased to think shut out her fears. It roamed over the opportunities she had discovered at Arcot as she coaxed him onward and feigned ecstasy for him.

'Oh, oh, oh, oh . . .' she moaned, urging him to spend his seed, raking his back with her fingernails, tightening her inner muscles again to maximize his pleasure on each thrust.

He pushed into her again and slid on her oiled body. She bit her lips together as if waves of pleasure were sweeping through her, driving her mind into oblivion. He thrust into her one last time, breathless, sweat pouring from him, and withdrew suddenly. His lingam was flaccid now, though he had not unburdened himself.

Khair-un-Nissa lay there shuddering beside him, gasping for breath, lavishing praise on his manly strength, on the size of his shaft and on his unmatched capacity to satisfy a woman. The attendants stared at their mistress, awed.

But beneath her seamless professionalism Khair-un-Nissa wondered at him. It was worrying. The first time she had failed to bring a man, any man, to the Moment of Unbeing.

Perhaps that's why he's so ferocious in his ambitions, she thought peevishly. Then, more practically: I must consult Jemdani, my student of the *Aupamishadika*, my herbalist and apothecary. Her magics contain a cure for every ill. She will prescribe the powder of the blue lotus mixed with ghee and honey, or perhaps milk that has had the testicle of a ram or goat boiled in it. Once he has drunk of that he will surely gain in potency. It will help draw that rage out of him, then he will be brought wholly under my spell.

He sat up like a busy man of affairs, without looking at her or speaking, or giving any indication of his mood, but she saw that all the muscles of his limbs and back and neck were rigid with tension. He dressed, declining the aid of her attendants, quickly wound his turban, and all the while she eyed him languidly like a woman so thankfully exhausted by a man's prowess that she could not even raise a full smile or move to close her legs.

That's good, she thought, as he left. Better than if he had spurted like a bull. No one knows except the two of us, and since my own reputation is at stake, as well as his manly self-respect, I'm certainly not going to jeopardize everything by letting him know that I know that he failed.

The music from the pavilion died away and she began to repair her make-up and put up her hair. She wanted to wash herself, but it would have to wait. The cold water in the pool was disgusting. No good for washing a delicate skin. Still, the payment is compensation, and there may be opportunities, just as Nadira Begum promised.

So what of Muhammad Ali Khan – He of the Flaccid Sword? she wondered. Already the part of her mind that made political calculations was beginning to go over the situation, giving her hope.

Years ago, when Muhammad Sa'adat-Allah ruled at Arcot, Trichinopoly had been governed by a Hindu raja. When Sa'adat-Allah died and his son Dost Ali took over, the raja had disdained to render tribute and Dost Ali sent his son-in-law, Chanda Sahib, to enforce the proper collection of taxes. Chanda had deposed the raja and become killadar there, but then a glitter of possibilities had opened when the Marathas invaded the Carnatic. Raghoji Bhonsla's marauding horsemen killed Dost Ali at Ambur and went on to lay siege to Trichinopoly, where Chanda Sahib was holding out. After three months the Marathas had taken Chanda Sahib prisoner and carried him off to their stronghold of Satara.

So what if Muhammad kills his father and half-brothers immediately? she asked herself. He will still have to persuade the Nizam to support his claim to power, and that could be difficult. There are two possible obstacles. Of the old clan descended from Dost Ali Khan, Safdar Ali is dead at the hands of his brother-in-law, Murtaza Ali Khan. Safdar Ali's five-year-old son was conveniently smothered by Anwar-ud-Din years ago, or so Nadira Begum swears. But there is still Murtaza himself, discredited by Anwar-ud-Din after the child's death – that was clever of Anwar-ud-Din to blame the smothering on Murtaza, but the fact that he's still alive at Vellore is something Muhammad must not overlook.

The foremost threat to Muhammad is Dost Ali Khan's second son-in-law, Chanda Sahib, she thought. He is still languishing in a Maratha dungeon, and here Anwar-ud-Din has been outmanoeuvred. Nadira Begum says that when the Marathas first took Chanda they tried to hold him to ransom, then they realized they would get nothing for a pretender's worthless carcass – why should Anwar-ud-Din pay for the masnad of Arcot? To kill him, perhaps, but for Chanda Sahib to be locked up in Satara was just as good as his being dead, wasn't it? And it was then that the Maratha general, Morari Rao, made his turnabout. He stopped saying, 'Give me so many rupees or I will hold Chanda Sahib for ever,' and began to say instead, 'Give me so many rupees or I will release Chanda Sahib tomorrow.'

Sooner or later, Muhammad Ali, you'd be wise to buy

Chanda Sahib's release, Khair-un-Nissa told him silently. Yes, and then you should kill him, or my plans and yours and those of Nadira Begum will never come to fruition.

She rolled over and put her eye close to the moucharabya screen. Muhammad stalked across the main axis of the formal garden. He was making for the royal zenana and she could see he was in a turmoil of unfocused rage. The eunuchs and the crones who huddled by the door with *gup*-hungry eyes made way, and then he was gone, rage and all, to find his only wife.

Hayden Flint sat in the howdah beside Yasmin and Muhammad Ali, sickened by the ceaseless rolling gait of the elephant. It was somewhere between the motion of a horse and a ship and ten times as nauseating as either, and the knowledge that the battle for Madras would be fought today, and that he would be in the middle of it, did nothing to settle his mind.

He watched familiar landmarks come into view, the tension in him screwed tighter by the muggy monsoon air. Before them the dusty strip of the Madras road ran away towards the Triplicane River and the lagoon beyond as they passed into the lease. To their right the hill of St Thome stood above a sleepy town of palm thatch and mud walls. Beyond it the sea stretched, blue as sapphire, to the horizon. The sound of the wind was like softly tearing silk, tugging at the fringes of their huge *chitr* umbrellas and the plumes of the horses and the elephant canopies of Anwar-ud-Din's royal van. There were seventeen elephants at the head of the vast column. The entire population of the *hathikhana*, the elephant stable, had been turned out – all bar three pregnant cows and half a dozen young. Mahfuz travelled in second place, after his father's mount, then came Muhammad Ali's beast.

It's like an omen of doom, Hayden Flint thought. Dull light, attenuated by rolling masses of cloud, strange shadows flitting across the waving green rice fields, the breeze restless in the palm tops . . . Every time I experience it, I never fail to wonder at the change brought on land, sea and air by something so simple as a monsoon wind! Sweet Jesus, why did it have to come to this? A bloody battle and another thousand souls sent out of the world. And it's all at my behest.

Yasmin's perfume filled the air around him. She has immense courage, he reflected. Riding calmly to war beside her husband, as if it was a Sunday stroll through the countryside. And how lovely she looks, despite the robes that almost conceal her. Look at her! I'd swear she's enjoying this, by God! Oh, if she knew the dread I'm feeling that she'll never talk to me again.

The white iced cake of Savage's Triplicane mansion came into view beyond the stands of bamboo, unsettling him further. It was deserted and ransacked, its contents pulled out and scattered across the lawns, its shutters and cane tatties ripped down. A fire burned at the foot of the steps where an encampment had been improvised. I should have been married in that house, he realized with astonishment. Married to a woman – no, a girl – an English girl called Arkali Savage whose face and voice I can barely remember now. Did I really court her here and walk with her in the groves of wild date and peepul trees and tamarinds, and throw a coin into the lake with my promise and hers upon it? How long ago was that? It seems part of another age, a lifetime ago. He shivered. It *was* another lifetime. Truly, time does not flow straight in Hindostan. Nor does it flow smoothly.

'Our advance parties found them abandoned,' Muhammad said gleefully, following his gaze towards the big garden houses. 'See how the Frenchmen have run away.'

'They've merely retired on Madras,' Flint said, sickened by the destruction. But he was thinking, was I insane to insist that Anwar-ud-Din bring this terrifying army down on Madras? After all, no European force has ever tried to stand against a Moghul army. Once it's brought into action can it be stopped? Or will it break up into a hundred

156

marauding gangs and will the whole of the coast be gutted by them? What have I begun?

'We shall join battle very soon,' Muhammad said.

Flint nodded readily. 'Perhaps it's a pity Abdul Masjid is dead,' he said, his nerves showing. 'Today he would have been invaluable. However, one has to say that if Abdul Masjid was alive now, then none of us would be here.'

'If! Then!' Muhammad grunted irritably. 'What foolishness! There are no ifs or thens. You infidels live inside your own crazy, arrogant minds. That is why you have no understanding of the real world around you. Only the Prophet teaches the true reality – that in this world there is no "would-have-beens" or "could-have-dones", there is only what is and what is written. And that is the will of Allah.'

What if he's right? Hayden thought, seized by the bleakness of the idea. What if everything is written and we have no free will? Then what's the point of trying to do anything? Surely it's a madman's doctrine to think no consequences flow from your own actions?

Totally irresponsible. But perhaps comforting too, because, if I believed their creed, then the guilt of Daniel Quinn's death would not weigh heavy on my soul, nor would the burden of causing an army to come here be destroying me.

The army of the Carnatic had assembled in Arcot over a period of days. On the first day of march, five thousand horsemen, crazed on bhang and screaming war chants, appeared in response to Anwar-ud-Din's order. Shots rent the air and Hayden Flint looked down from the howdah and wondered how anyone or anything could resist the ferocity of the wild horde that swept around them like a whirlwind.

They had ridden from the palace four days ago. At Muhammad Ali's invitation he had joined the prince and his wife on the draped couches of this swaying howdah built high on the back of their great bull elephant. A gold-fringed canopy shaded them from the sun, undulating on its canes; their mount's flanks and head, decorated in heavily worked gold, shone brightly in the diffuse light. The liveried mahout sat on the huge beast's neck, controlling its movements with deft stabs of his knees and occasional jabs with his ankus, or spiked goad.

At first the stately dignity of the elephant's gait, its regal bulk and their height above the road made Flint feel like a prince, but he could not relax and enjoy the experience. He was drawn taut by Yasmin's presence beside him. Her subtle perfume came to him on the air. He could almost feel the soft shapes of her body beneath the muslin that enveloped her and hear the soft jangle of hidden jewellery. My God, she radiates femininity, he thought. Everything about her is so sensuous, so much a delight, so distracting – she is so much a woman. I would like to know her, but of course that is impossible.

On the second day, Muhammad Ali had casually produced a scroll bearing Anwar-ud-Din's seal. 'My father has honoured you with this.'

He opened it and tried to read its archaic formula. 'My thanks to your father, but what is it?'

Muhammad maintained his unsmiling composure. 'You are hereby appointed a Commander of Fifty Horse.'

He digested that, unsure what to say. 'Then I am greatly honoured.'

'It is of no consequence. A matter of protocol only to permit you to ride with us in the royal vanguard, and to allow you to wear your pistols. My father is meticulous in matters of law. Now, when we engage the French, you will be able to come with us into battle.'

'Then there is to be a battle?'

'That is the favour you demanded.'

Later, despite himself, he had begun to ask Yasmin questions about the way in which so vast a mass of men and beasts had been brought together.

'Our tradition is an ancient one, Mr Flint. When the court moves, all its treasures and chattels move with it. Naturally, that means the women also.'

He had stared wonderingly at the scene around him,

thinking that she must be right, that the French would surely be intimidated by so gigantic an undertaking and would have no stomach or strength to resist.

'Then everything is brought along with the nawab?' he asked. 'Faith! The Palace of Arcot must have been completely emptied!'

'Almost. No nawab willingly leaves his capital for even one day when it contains everything of value to him. Especially when he is marching his army away from it. Even Anwar-ud-Din cannot be in two places at once. Therefore there is no alternative but to take everything with him.'

He looked back down the road. The column stretched for more than a mile: a vast organism of horse-soldiers, infantry, slaves, servants and beasts of burden stretching into infinity, obscured by the dust of their own passing.

'See!' Muhammad Ali had told him with fierce pride, meticulously pointing out the order of precedence. 'This is the way the Emperor Aurangzeb marched on campaign. We are descended from heroes who lived and fought constantly on the move. It has always been Moghul tradition that the heirs of our emperors are born on a horse-blanket spread on the floor of a tent. And in Delhi, the great Aurangzeb spurned his luxurious palaces and lived simply, in a tent pitched on adjoining land. That is how it should be for us. How it will be on our march to Madras.'

He drew his sword and pointed forward. 'A day ahead of the column the route-masters and advance parties will ride to give warning of our coming and to prepare the way. Their ox-carts contain tentage and with them go the servants of the household. They will procure food and firewood and other supplies from the people and build the camp that we shall occupy tonight. And because my father must have every facility for attending to affairs of state in the evening, after he has eaten and been to prayer, there will be tent kitchens, a tent mosque, tent courts and tent audience halls. All his quarters will be duplicated exactly after the pattern of the Palace of Arcot. And each night there will be a new capital.'

'Such effort for just one night? Each and every night?'

Muhammad turned on him irritably. 'A nawab must travel in the manner of a nawab. With the dignity of a nawab. Is that not yet apparent to you? Did you have no conception of the magnitude of the favour you were asking of my father?'

The banging of kettledrums announced the nawab's approach. He turned away from the head of the column, where his standardbearers and weapon-carriers rode on white horses to proclaim him. Immediately behind their own beast the rest of the elephants plodded, their backs loaded with burdens, and behind them camels similarly weighed down. The armoured bodyguard followed on horseback, their lances glittering.

'This must be the contents of the *jawarkhana*?' he said to Yasmin.

'You are correct, Mr Flint. Those first six elephants carry the treasury, a wealth mostly of gold and jewels and various religious items, together with the favours that the nawab will bestow upon his most deserving warriors after the victory. Then there is also the contents of the *tokshakhana*, which is courtly clothing and apparel.'

'I can see what must be a hundred palanquins over there, again with a strong bodyguard. What are they?'

'Those are the ladies.'

'Yes, of course.'

'And do you see your own bodyguard?'

The question perplexed him.

'They have not deserted you, you know, though you have been less than attentive to their needs. Perhaps you had forgotten them.'

He understood. This was the cadre of horsemen who had been led by Abdul Masjid, the men whose allegiance he had won. Am I expected to lead them in battle? he thought suddenly. Oh, in God's name, so that's what the scroll was about. Anwar-ud-Din has officially recognized my right to command fifty sowars, and now the scroll has made it legal! No wonder Muhammad was gloating.

She saw his discomfort. 'Do not be alarmed. As my husband has said, this has been done purely for purposes of protocol. A good lord wisely attends to details and always ties up the loose ends of his affairs.'

He heard the humour in her voice. He said, 'At tonight's camp I must thank him for his gift.'

'The soldiers are now your right to command, but also your responsibility.'

He hesitated. 'How much will I have to – pay them?'

'Nothing.'

His surprise took what he was about to say from his mind: that he had no means of paying them. 'Nothing at all? Then how will they live? What reason will there be for them to fight?'

'Common soldiers are not used to payment in Hindostan,' she said, amused at his puzzlement. 'It is their duty to fight. War is made for a share of the plunder they will take.'

His stomach heaved at that. 'They mean to plunder Madras to pay for the expedition?'

But she did not answer him.

They rode all day, the main mass of irregular horsemen 10,000 strong falling in behind them with swords and lances and jezails. In their midst, long trains of oxen pulled huge and unwieldy cannons, the biggest, which they called 'The Lord Champion Conqueror of Armies', had an ornate bronze barrel twenty feet long. In the rear a mass of sipahis followed, loose-robed peasant infantry armed with whatever makeshift weapons they could bring to war – the lowliest and least regarded in the entire army.

'How long will it take to reach Madras?' he asked, thinking, It's incredible. Such pomp and ceremony and encumbrance when the only important task is to stand before the walls of Madras and humble the French into leaving. This whole maddening, magnificent circus has been assembled when it would have been much cheaper and more effective to have sent a simple delegation with a list of demands. Why this lumbering monster and all these diversions when speed is obviously essential?

'When, always when!' she sighed. 'You will achieve nothing without patience. Slow is of God, as our proverb runs, and hurry is of the devil.'

'Yes, lady,' he groaned. 'And in Hindostan only the ways of Hindostan can succeed.'

'One day you will understand. Meanwhile do not waste your time trying to foresee what will happen when we arrive at Madras, or striving to comprehend the mind of our lord. There may be a battle, or not, as God wills. You cannot influence that.'

Messengers and couriers had thundered past the column at intervals, communicating the nawab's orders to his commanders or bringing in news of detachments joining the column. As he watched throughout the oppressive heat of the second day, he saw the scribes taking down order after order from Anwar-ud-Din's lips. Always close by were the timekeeper with his hourglass and gong and the men who hurried in relays beside the van with poles and chain marking the distance travelled. Ministers attended the nawab incessantly, but there were also cage palanquins containing hunting cheetahs and the rest of his hunting establishment, the most trusted men carrying hooded hawks on their gloves. On several occasions already a royal party, the nawab and his sons only, had mounted horses and ridden off for an hour or two in pursuit of distant herds.

'I myself have taken part in the shikar,' Yasmin told him, referring to the classic form of hunt where noisy beaters surrounded an area and drove game towards the shooters.

'For deer? Or antelope?' he asked, surprised.

'Neither.'

'Birds, then?'

She laughed. 'No. Man-eaters.'

'Sweet Jesus! A woman hunting tigers?' he marvelled. 'Is that permitted?'

She stiffened proudly at that. 'Why not? I can shoot as well as any man.'

'Indeed?'

'Oh, yes. I have Rajput blood in my heart, and with that

162

go proud hereditary rights. Among the Rajputs it is expected that a woman fit herself for battle by practising the martial arts, the sword and the spear. Rajput women hunt just as men do. Don't you know that in the north the Uzbeks have women warriors? In Oudh there is a whole regiment of women.'

The Rajputs are Hindus, he thought, excited by the revelation. That means Muhammad Ali has married a wife of mixed blood. That's not what I would have guessed. I thought he hated Hindus. I wonder how much of her is Rajput, and whether she took Islam or was born a Muslim? I wonder why she married Muhammad. They seem so totally ill-matched. Even here, where all marriages are arranged, there has to be a crucial reason to outweigh such massive incompatibility.

Now he looked one last time at the white columns of Charles Savage's mansion, a faint nausea rising in him again. So it is to be a fight, he thought. And what of me? When the battle is done am I just to return to Madras as if nothing has happened? When the French are punished, shall I go back and submit to my father's domination once more? Is it my destiny to marry Arkali? Once I wanted to dedicate myself to teaching her of the world, guiding her and watching her learn, but the idea of her innocence that once delighted and enthralled me does so no longer. Perhaps that's a sign that my own innocence is gone.

Last night he had learned finally that there would be a battle. Mahfuz's horse squadrons had surrounded Madras. His men had seized the sweet water wells on Pedda Naik's Petta which supplied the fort, but two pieces of news from the scouting parties and spies who covered the countryside to the south arrived to enrage them as night fell. First, the French had sallied from the fort and impudently recaptured Pedda Naik's Petta long enough to fill a dozen water carts. Second, and more important, Dupleix had dispatched reinforcements from Pondicherry: 300 French and 700 sipahis – French-trained infantry, all uniformed and equipped with musket and bayonet. At the Council of War in Anwar-ud-Din's magnificently appointed tent, Mahfuz Khan had assembled his generals and they in turn had brought in every officer until the durbar was heaving with three or four hundred men.

'The nawab is outraged,' Mahfuz told them all, speaking for his father who watched, grave-faced. 'No one has ever dared question his authority before. He is the rightful overlord of the Carnatic, granted his position by the Nizam himself. These feringhee leaseholders are infidel traders, here by his permission alone. Yet the French dare to ignore lawful command, they have made war on our lands despite Anwar-ud-Din's explicit prohibition, and now they intend to face us with troops!'

There were indignant calls and fists shaken in the air, a great press of men excitedly shoving forward. Then the ministers pored over the maps, loudly denouncing the gall of the French Governor, as Mahfuz, heedless of spies, put his plan before them all.

'If my father agrees, we will occupy the high ground here, at St Thome, eight kos south of Madras. And as the French attempt to cross the Adiyar estuary, here, we shall sweep down and destroy them!'

'No quarter!' someone shouted.

'No quarter!'

The cry was taken up by several voices. 'No mercy for the feringhee!'

Anwar-un-Din had nodded, his foremost son's strategy pleasing him. But Hayden Flint was shocked pale by the decision as the celebration of hatred erupted around him. There was a cruel justice that haunted him, and he almost laughed. Now, irrevocably, there would be a battle, and that meant he would have to stand alongside Muhammad in his war howdah, and Yasmin would be there too. Muhammad would take deliberate delight in plunging the elephant into the thickest part of the battle and all around there would be a terrible carnage and he would have to witness the deaths by trampling of a thousand men, deaths he had summoned like an evil djinn from the ruby. It was as

Yasmin had said: there was magic in Hindostan. A dark, powerful magic.

As the cries died down around him, he began to understand their intention. It was to be a steel trap, set and sprung, into which Dupleix's infantry would blunder. If the French were to attempt a withdrawal, Mahfuz's cavalry would fall on them and massacre them, and if they were to attack they would be caught in the water and cut to pieces. It was surely an impossible option, he thought. What infantry commander could conceive of fording a knee-deep estuary and then facing a mounted army that outnumbered his own by more than ten to one?

At the climax of the council, Anwar-un-Din called for his astrologers to pronounce on the auspiciousness of the battle. They pushed out of the crowd before him, one simpering, one bragging and one wise, with charts and dividers and a huge brass astrolabe. They told the nawab in flowery phrases that his life was presently ruled by a most fortunate conjunction of planets, that the moon was reaching apogee – again a sign of great favour – and, most propitious of all, the astonishing red star Mira, 'the Wonderful', had appeared in the constellation which the feringhees called Cetus, the Whale. That star rose to maximum brightness only once in every 331 days. Unlike any other star, it disappeared from sight completely for six months, but now it was brighter than Al-kaffaljidhina, brighter also than Menkar, and even the famous Diphda. Mira was as bright as it had ever been! The omen therefore was that the foreigners would be made to leave by sea, in ships that were big as whales, but that first Anwar-ud-Din's ruby would blaze forth in victory.

There were shouts of rejoicing, then Anwar-un-Din summoned Hayden Flint foward and bade him sit in the middle of the carpet before him.

'And you? What is your opinion on the matter?'

He looked at the nawab, his mind simmering with sick disappointment as everyone strained to hear him. At last he cleared his throat. 'It would not be appropriate for me to comment, my lord. I am not experienced in your ways of war.'

'Nevertheless I want your opinion.'

'Yes, but I don't believe I know enough to – '

Anwar-ud-Din cut in on him peremptorily. 'Do not argue with me, insolent man! You are commanded to give me your opinion!'

The excited gathering clattered arms on shields and catcalled bloodthirstily, then fell silent again. His face burned under the nawab's stare. How could he say that now he only wanted to avoid bloodshed? That he desired Mahfuz should meet with the French and arrange a demonstration of force that would send them running all the way back to Pondicherry? That there was no need to wipe out a thousand and more human lives.

'My lord,' he said slowly, realizing now that Anwar-ud-Din was not asking for honesty at all but merely demanding his approval before them all. 'I think it is likely that your army will destroy the French reinforcements.' He paused as they shouted their delight and hammered their weapons. 'However, their garrison in Madras have field guns – '

'We also have field guns!'

It was said with such unexpected volume that he winced. He was aware that the generals and nobles who flanked him, and the sons of Anwar-ud-Din who stared at him from his left and right, were watching him closely even as they showed their enthusiasm to their master. It was as if his words could seal their confidence, or somehow break it. As the hubbub fell away, he knew he would have to say what he believed, whether it upset them or not.

'Yes, my lord, but the guns the French have are better than yours.'

There was silence, then Abdul Wahab, the nawab's youngest son, jumped up indignantly. 'You lie, feringhee. Your guns cannot be better!'

The nawab leaned forward on his knee, his eyes steely. 'Answer me this: what is the biggest gun the French army can deploy on land?'

'I do not know about the French army, my lord, but the biggest field gun the English use is a twenty-five-pounder.' He made an 'O' with his thumbs and index fingers to show the bore. 'That is, it fires shot weighing twenty-five pounds, my lord.'

'Do you know that at Agra there is a Moghul gun, the Malik-i-Maidan, which I have seen with my own eyes, that weighs fifty of your tons, which has a bore of twenty-two of your inches, and which fires a shot weighing fifteen hundred of your pounds?'

He shook his head amid the triumphant jeering, unable to believe there could be such an immense gun, and knowing that even if it was true, and even if it could be brought here, it could not add to the slaughter that must take place tomorrow.

'Now you understand why I commanded you never to boast about European weapons at my court.'

A roar of amusement surrounded him.

'Yes, my lord, but – ' he began, his words almost drowned.

Anwar-ud-Din glanced round his kneeling nobles, his face impassive. 'So? You have more to say?'

'My lord, you commanded me to tell you my true opinion.'

'Then say.'

He turned to look at Abdul Wahab. 'Sir, forgive me, but it is true to say that the French cannon are better. Though they are smaller, they've very well designed, and ideal for their purpose.' He wanted to say, Because of their size they go where they're wanted and they fire faster than you may realise. He wanted to shout out that no Moghul could have the least conception of the technical advances in strategy and tactics that had swept Europe since the days of breastplated pikemen. He wanted to make them understand that they would need every last squadron of screaming horsemen if they intended to move against the French. But his words died in his throat when the nawab pulled a pistol from behind his cushion and pointed it at him.

'Do you recognize this?' Anwar-ud-Din demanded. Again there was instant silence.

'Yes, lord,' he admitted, sudden terror seizing him. It was one of his own pistols.

'And this?' Another appeared.

'Yes.'

Those who could see him were whooping and laughing. Then the whole place errupted as he looked down involuntarily at his own belt and saw that his pistols were there intact.

They shrieked and howled as Anwar-ud-Din tossed both pistols down before him. 'Pick them up!'

He did so, turning them over in damp hands, inspecting their brasswork and their engraved locks and the well-turned wood of their grips. They were identical in every way to his own.

'My craftsmen made them for me in two days,' Anwar-un-Din said. He snapped his fingers, extracting another morsel from the humiliation. 'Are they not selfsame, and one with your own? Well, then! Do not boast to me of the ability of Europeans to make weapons.' He stood up then, addressing his Council of War in person. 'You see! They have no advantage and we have every advantage! Tomorrow we ride to victory!'

Hayden Flint's mind dwelt now on the rowdy scenes that had followed that speech, the way he had been swept from the tent amid a tide of men, their muskets firing spires of light into the sky, their drums hammering out as they streamed back to their campfires.

He sat stiffly in the war howdah as it carried him and Yasmin Begum and Muhammad Ali unstoppably towards the sea. Behind them, the column had already begun to form up into battle order. On the near side of the river, infantry were concealed behind the walls of the small town of St Thome, with the 'Lord Champion' and his brother artillery pieces covering the crossing. Their own body, cavalry ranged three lines deep, stood back from the river in close cover, a deadly ambush waiting to fall upon the enemy. There they waited out of sight, Hayden Flint sweating in the heat, anxiety rising in him as Muhammad issued commands to his squadrons, relishing the decision to give battle.

Soon the French column came into view, and still Anwar-ud-Din's army waited in concealment, the whole force now drawn up in lines, silent as death, the wind rippling their war gear and tearing at the green flags that flew at their spearheads. Mullahs weaved in and out of the horde, dispensing God's certainty to the sowars, many of whom took bhang, drugged curd, for courage and ferocity, or stared eerily into the palms of their hands as if reading holy scripture from the pages of the Koran.

The French halted, their leader walking out ahead on foot, his sabre drawn, sensing something was amiss. He scanned the far bank for a long moment and turned to walk back to his troops.

In Abdul Wahab's battalions, the wailing of Hindu *bairagis* and *ghosais* began. They were naked fanatics, worshippers of the God of Destruction, who lusted for blood or death, leaping forward to throw themselves on the French. Then the *dundhubis* started to beat out the rhythm of war, and Hayden Flint saw Anwar-ud-Din's elite suicide squadron of Rajputs move forward. They were a part of the nawab's third wife's dowry. They put on turmeric-coloured robes, the *maranacha poshak*, or 'Robes of the Dead', signifying that they were resigned to dying, were dead already, and therefore beyond death, beyond fear. The sight of them raised the hairs on Hayden Flint's spine, for he knew that since his rebirth at Mavalipuram he also was beyond death.

The French column began to move forward, and he saw the astonished delight on the face of Muhammad Ali.

'They've decided to cross!' he exulted. 'Look!'

A messenger rode up, standing in his saddle to reach the mahout who passed the scroll to Muhammad. He tore it open and read its contents with undisguised delight. 'My father's scouts report that another French force has come out from Madras,' he said. 'Good. They too will pay for their Governor's sins.'

'How many men?' Hayden Flint asked, white-faced.

'Hundreds! I hope there are thousands! The more the better, for they will all die!'

'Do they have field guns? Are there cannon with them?'

'Whatever they have, it will soon be ours.'

Hayden Flint was filled with desperate anger. 'But you don't understand – '

'Get out of my way!'

'Listen to me!'

Muhammad shrugged off his hand. 'Damn you to hell, defiler! Get out of my way, I told you. Sit back there with the woman. My soldiers must see their prince!'

Hayden Flint was shoved roughly to the back corner of the howdah, where Yasmin sat silent and immobile, three tall jezails standing up beside her, their slim wire-bound barrels as long as a man and wholly unsuited to firing from a moving elephant. She selected one and passed it to him, picked another and put the heavy triangular butt to her own shoulder.

'You'll draw their fire standing like that!' he shouted. 'Don't you see what a target you're making of yourselves?'

'His men must have a clear view of him!' she shouted back. 'Or their morale will fail!'

'By God, lady, this is lunacy! You must get down! And tell him, for he won't listen to me. If the French are bringing guns out they'll load grapeshot and that'll devastate his cavalry.'

'We are taught that cavalry always beats artillery. They will be overwhelmed before they can reload.'

'That's only your kind of artillery! These gun crews can fire four rounds every minute and each cannon is like a whole battalion of muskets when it's loaded with grape! Better, because it can turn to face any direction instantly. They'll cut your horse army to butcher's offal if they've brought light cannon from Madras!'

'The rearguard will watch Madras!' She stabbed her

finger furiously at the infantry on the other side of the river. 'These are our enemy. They have no cannon.'

The French were wading across the river now, their muskets quartered across their chests, bayonets fixed, their lines unwaveringly straight even as the line of Moghul artillery was ordered to fire. The cannonade blasted out raggedly, ten huge reports in half as many seconds, filling the air with white smoke and one great smoke ring that soared up in an arc above the water. Then the French and their sepoys emerged from the water, their officer striding out in front, their sergeants and corporals keeping the lines die-straight and marching on remorselessly. They had caused the Moghul artillery to fire prematurely, and had taken few casualties from guns which had been improperly shotted with iron ball.

Hayden Flint steeled himself as the elephant under him was goaded forward. In front of him Muhammad was shouting like a madman at his commanders, his sword unsheathed, urging them forward, and the howdah bounced wildly, almost shaking them out as the animal broke into a lumbering run. Its grey and pink mottled ears flapped, the straps and metalwork on its massive head and neck clattered. All around them a sea of horsemen broke forward and streamed past in a cloud of dust and tearing robes and turbans and swords, screaming.

The wave descended like surf on to the two ranks of French soldiers who lined the bank, shoulder to shoulder, and still they walked on at the same pace, as if unaware of the collision that must come. The combatants closed in that last terrifying moment, two hundred yards, a hundred and fifty, one hundred, until the charge had coalesced into one surging mob at full gallop. Then the French officer raised his sword above his head; the walking ranks of blue coats and infantry tricorns halted. The officer stepped back between the two battalions and levelled his pistol. The first rank knelt as one, leaning into their musket stocks. The second stood and leaned in between them, harrowed into the gaps so that their long bayonets were interlaced like the tines of a comb.

Hayden Flint watched with horror from the bucking howdah as the entire line of uniformed troops disappeared, engulfed in white smoke. The fusillade that crashed from the French muskets felled dozens of the leading horsemen, thinning their ranks and obstructing those behind so that the remainder were pulled up, the force of their charge shattered. Terrified horses danced and pirouetted in panic, some throwing their riders to the ground as the second shock-wave smashed into them, then the French line opened up again, throwing down dozens more of the hapless sowars.

Those that reached the unflinching line veered at the palisade of bayonets and made off. Some fled for the cover of St Thome, where narrow, dusty streets might provide sanctuary from the lethal musket enfilade. Others retreated after their broken squadrons. On the right, the other squadrons had met the same fate, leaving the gunners on the huge cannon without cover. The Lord Conqueror stood proud, surrounded by a mass of men fighting to reload his immense maw, but the infantry marched on in their indestructible formation, their discipline taming the wild horde and dominating them.

Now the French musketeers were reloading, lifting powder flasks and ramrods like clockwork, tamping and shotting their pieces and levelling them once more. The second wave of Mahfuz Khan's horsemen went in in assault formation, the elephants in their midst, and as they reached the scattered corpses and kicking wounded horses they too were shattered and repulsed. Hayden Flint felt the charge break around him as the volley blasted into them. Twenty horsemen went down. Muhammad was screaming at his men to drive on when the elephant was hit. Its trunk went up and it slewed to a halt, trumpeting in pain, a bright blossom of raw meat ragged below its eye, the mahout staring at the stump below his own knee.

The elephant slumped, and the canopy collapsed over them, blinding them.

'My God, he's rolling over! Jump!' Hayden Flint

shouted. The stink of powder was in his mouth, dust swirled all around. The jezail went off in his hand. He felt himself knocked backwards as the howdah lurched aside, but he fought for balance and recovered himself just long enough to throw himself at Yasmin and carry her clear of the crashing beast.

His head hit the ground with a stunning impact and the wind was knocked from him, but he scrambled up. Yasmin sprawled at his feet. Thank God she's clear, he thought, lifting her and whirling as he heard galloping horses bearing down on them.

The third and last cavalry wave engulfed them, hurling themselves on to the French in one final show of insane courage. He stared, all sense smashed from him, seeing the victory he had engineered dissolving into ruin.

Where's Muhammad? he wondered, his head ringing. Then he saw Yasmin trying to drag her husband's armoured body from the howdah. His helmet was gone and his face was streaming blood; he lay with his arm trapped at the shoulder by the howdah's metal rim.

He's dead, he thought. And Yasmin will die too unless I can reach her. The felled elephant writhed, two blunt legs beating the air as Yasmin pulled Muhammad's trapped arm free. The horsemen began to stream back past them in retreat. He ran in towards the struggling mountain of flesh, another volley blowing great raw holes in the elephant, but its bulk saved them. Yasmin heaved with every last ounce of her strength. He pulled his pistols and waved them at the smoke and dust beyond to cover her, then watched in horror as the regular shapes of the French bayonet line appeared out of the thinning murk, now no more than fifty paces away. At any moment they might break and charge, scenting the rich plunder to be had from the royal elephant.

'Yasmin!' he shouted. 'Leave him! Get back!'

But she continued to pull single-mindedly at the inert form of her husband. He turned and stuffed the pistols into his belt and as he came up beside her he too began to heave at Muhammad's mailed body, but the prince was a dead weight and all effort to move him faster was futile. He pulled the body back ten yards, twenty, twenty-five, then ran forward again, drenched in sweat, determined to protect her as long as he could. He fired once into the nebulous figures, and a second time, then, filled with impotent fury, he cursed the world and threw his guns into the swirling dust.

As if in response the air began to clear. He saw the infantry, and the blue of their uniforms. He saw their faces, their white cross-belts and the light striking off their buttons. Astonishingly, they had halted. They were reloading!

Then riders came wheeling out of the dust. They were surrounded by bodyguards who jumped down and lifted Muhammad across a horse. Another leapt to the ground, giving Yasmin his saddle. At her command a second horseman stayed his menacing sword and pulled the feringhee up behind him instead. Hooves thundered, and Hayden Flint found himself hugging a mailed back. He heard cannon, and knew that the Madras garrison had arrived, and as they galloped into clear air he saw thousands of men fleeing for their lives.

The army of the Carnatic had been utterly devastated.

BOOK TWO

EIGHT

Arkali met Clive in the bright moonlight two hours after sunset and one hour after the tolling of the curfew bell had ceased.

The place of the tryst was secluded and high up, the deserted flat roof of the Savage godown, overlooking the sea wall. Huge clouds rolled overhead, ponderous galleons under full sail, blotting out the stars. Rollers crashed on to the beach, filling the air with a thunderous roar and a fine salt spume that settled on the lips. The air was humid but a warm wind gusted from the south, fluttering the flag and carrying away the shouts of the sentries. Apart from those sounds, a dreadful hush had fallen over Fort St George since the battle, a morbid expectation, but of what she couldn't say. It seemed impossible that so few French infantrymen could have destroyed so vast a native cavalry horde, but they had. And in the doing, not only had they defied the Lord of the Carnatic, but they had broken his power, leaving the French in complete control at Madras and without the least fear of being forced away.

'And that's why we must get out of here,' she whispered, her eyes full of pleading. She knew that her suggestion to go overland to Fort St David had staggered him. 'Mr Clive, we cannot do anything here ourselves. That much is plain. And now the French have driven off the Moghul army, they think themselves invincible. They'll grant us no concessions now.'

'Is that what your father thinks?' Clive's appearance was a conspirator's, his tricorn hat pulled down, the collar of his uniform jacket pulled up about his ears. His white breeches and giltwork were hidden under a full-length boat-cloak, giving him the aspect of a highwayman.

'I don't know what my father thinks. It's not important!'

Clive studied her suspiciously. His gaze was so coldly penetrating that she pulled the edges of her dark shawl tighter about her.

'Where is your father now? I have not seen him in two days.'

'He's at his house.'

'Beyond the fort?'

'Yes! You know that the French Admiral's staff withdrew from it when the nawab's army appeared? It's now so broken down that the Admiral does not wish to return. He has therefore given in to Mr Flint's requests that we be allowed to reside in it once more, as is only right.'

Clive's suspicion deepened. 'Why would La Bourdonnais do that?'

'I should say it's apparent that he has some sense of honour, at least. Perhaps he agrees it's not decent that European women should be confined inside the fort after what happened. There's nowhere we can escape to – or so they believe. Don't you see? It's our chance!'

'Indeed?'

She sighed, knowing how badly she needed his help, exasperated at his stubborn refusal to see it her way. 'Mr Clive, how may I convince you? There was some . . . some dealing between my father and the Admiral. That is how they bargained the house back from him. It is plainer than plain that since the battle the French have relaxed their vigilance. We can easily escape to Fort St David.'

Clive chewed on his lip. 'St David's is better than a hundred miles south of here. It's twenty miles south of Pondicherry. A most arduous journey, and with a lady in our –'

'You're afraid!' She twisted her hands together, maddened by his pudding face, his peculiar obtuseness. 'And to think I thought you a paradigm of decisiveness and courage.'

'I can see Dupleix wanting to smash St David as soon as he might. And he will do just that if he has a ha'p'orth of strategic sense. If he does, he'll have erased the last English presence in the Carnatic – indeed the whole of southern Hindostan.'

'All the more reason for us to go to Fort St David to reinforce their garrison!'

'Just we two?'

She turned away, thinking about what she had been told by Stratford Flint, that the French Governor, Joseph Dupleix, had departed Pondicherry and was now on his way to Madras. If pleading wouldn't sway Clive, perhaps there was another way. 'Did you know that Dupleix intends to destroy Madras completely?'

Clive digested her words thoughtfully, as if comparing it with what he himself had heard, or perhaps gauging what he could tell her. 'I had it from Stratford Flint that La Bourdonnais wants to ransom St George.'

'Neither Mr Stratford Flint, nor anyone, has the resources to pay for that,' she said too quickly.

'That's not what he says.'

She stared at him accusingly. 'And what does he say, Mr Clive?'

'That he's prepared to turn over a store of hidden silver for La Bourdonnais's private pocket, if only he will take his ships and troops away from Madras.'

'That's not going to happen,' she said, thinking about the fifteen lakhs of silver. She was still shocked at her father's fury and the way he had railed at her madly after his meeting with La Bourdonnais. Perhaps, she thought, his feelings had exploded because of the provocation of watching a French admiral eating off his best Cantonware plates, sitting on his furniture and making the lovely white mansion of Triplicane his own, but there had been no need to shout at her the way he had. Now the mansion was a ruined husk. All he had worked for over the years. Gone.

'Whatever possessed you to tell Flint about the silver?' her father had snarled.

'I thought he should know,' she replied, then, stripping the bark deftly from his argument, 'You told me that silver was your own. But it was really his. It was, wasn't it?'

'You stupid girl!' he had raved. 'Do you know what you've done? Do you know? A lifetime's work. Destroyed! Flint was ruined anyway. But now you've broken both our chances!'

The beast inside Charles Savage had erupted, fierce and uncontrolled. He brought her to tears before he finished, shaking her and making to strike, but then just as quickly he squeezed her tight and begged her forgiveness. It had been eerie, a demonstration of the unreasoning power a woman could wield over a man.

She stared at Clive now, her hand straying to his cloak. 'Won't you help me, Mr Clive? Won't you?'

He looked down at her, in an agony of indecision, then slowly he said, 'Soon a French ship will take you to Calcutta. Then all will be well. You'll see.'

'But it could be weeks before the French allow a ship to sail north with us on board!' She turned, her mouth set. How could she tell him the real reason she wanted to get to Fort St David? How could she say it was to find Hayden, and that the finding of Hayden was the most important thing in the world? There was no reasoning to explain. No logic to lay out for him. It just was. If Robert Clive could not be won by sound arguments of strategy, how could a declaration of her intuition make any difference? She longed to tell him that she knew beyond any question that it was the right thing to do, but she could not find the words to tell him.

'I don't feel safe here,' she said. 'We must get out. Soon. Tomorrow night.'

'I've given my parole as a gentleman not to attempt to cross the Madras bounds.'

The excuse was lame and she saw that he knew it. A gentleman! she thought scornfully. He told me his father was an impoverished Shropshire lawyer, and he himself is a lowly Company clerk, for all that he struts about in a soldier's red coat. How can he say that he's a gentleman? You only have to look at him: he's no patrician, he's a brute.

She lifted one eyebrow, seeing what her reply must be.

'You gave your word as a gentleman to observe the curfew. So you're not supposed to be here. But still you came.'

'I could not refuse the request of a lady. I thought – '

'You thought what?'

'I don't know,' he said, embarrassed. 'That perhaps you had something to tell me. About us.'

It was as if he had slapped her face. 'You came because you thought I was suggesting an assignation? Is that it, Mr Clive?'

He pressed his lips together, deflated by her hauteur, and looked at her as if trying and failing to comprehend what that night of terror must have meant to her. 'Miss Savage, may I assure you that the French are not planning to murder us in our beds.' He smiled his crooked, patient smile, an unbeautiful smile. 'And I am here to protect you. I swear I will stand guard on you day and night until we go from this place if it will make you easier in your mind.'

'Escort me to Fort St David. That's all I want.'

'That's impossible.'

'You're a coward, Mr Clive. Just a rotten-hearted coward.'

He looked at her a long moment, stocky and lumpish, a look of appraisal in his eyes. 'You know, Miss Savage – Arkali, if I may be so bold – I think that you've changed quite a lot in one month.'

'I can't expect a man such as you to understand.' She hunted about for a way to put it, sighing with frustration. 'It's no use telling you about feelings or instincts, I suppose. Oh, I was born in Hindostan. Since I've been here as an adult I've realized that it's not like anywhere else in this world. Things don't happen here like they do anywhere else. And because I was born here I know there's something of its peculiar magic in me. Always. Don't you see? I just know we ought to make for Fort St David. Please help me, I beg you.'

Sea salt made the air piquant. The wind ruffled her hair, frosted by the moon. She wiped at her eyes. Her face was oval and upturned and very white. He regarded her fragility, knowing what it cost her to abandon her dignity this way. But now she was beginning to make honest sense. Why do women believe they have a monopoly on feelings and presentiments and emotions? he wondered. How can I tell her of my true feelings for her?

He knew he should have left her then. He knew he should have gone straight down through the building and taken himself stealthily away, but he could not bring himself to part from her until she concluded matters.

'Can it be,' he said slowly, 'that you think, just because a man rarely shows his emotion outwardly, that he must be as tough and as cold as a stone through and through? By God, it's easy to think that pretty people are sensitive; it would be plainly ridiculous to expect such as me to quiver like a butterfly in sympathy with every damned ripple in the emotions of those around me! But that doesn't mean I don't feel within.'

'Mr Clive, I'm sorry if I have offended you.'

'I did not tell you this,' he said, ignoring her coldness. 'But earlier this year I tried to end my own life.'

She stared back at him silently, and he looked down, shadowing his face with his hat-brim.

'I had done with this world, as far as I knew. I wanted to get out from it with dispatch. And so I thought to shoot myself through the head.'

'Mr Clive . . .'

'I put a loaded pistol to my temple and pulled the trigger.'

She stared up at his face, stricken by the unearthly tone of his voice.

'But nothing happened. Just that. The lock operated perfectly. The flint struck the frizzen, sparks flew into the pan, but there was no discharge.'

'What did you do?' Her voice was awed.

'I examined the pistol, and poked the touch-hole clear with a pin in case it was clogged, which it was not. Then I tried again.'

'And the gun failed to discharge again?'

He laughed shortly. 'As you see.'

She felt her heart beating. It was loud in her ears in the taut silence. 'I'm very sorry I called you a coward, Mr Clive.'

'That's not the best of it,' he went on, not listening to her. 'After that second try I remember I experienced more than a little irritation that the damned-fool gun wouldn't do its duty. I was about to examine it again when Edmund Maskelyne came into the room and asked me quite innocently what I was about.'

'What did you tell him?'

'Only this: to point the pistol out of the window and fire it. Which he did. Quite without difficulty.'

'No!'

'Oh, yes.' He shook himself from his reverie, coming back to the present like a sleep walker. He was eager to open himself to her now, feeling she would understand. 'So you see, I do have that same notion about Hindostan being a peculiar place for fate. The lords of this land call it kismet, and understand it implicitly. No one would believe such a tale if you told it in England, but here it makes perfect sense! Here everything has a meaning. I'm sure you understand what my escape from death really meant?'

She shivered and drew her shawl close, his deep intensity troubling her. 'What?'

'Isn't it obvious? If I had died, then you would have died too. Because I would not have lived to rescue you. You see that, don't you? It was meant to be. Our destinies are inextricably twined together.'

She gazed at him, fragile and dew-eyed in the moonlight. Suddenly her relief was tangible. 'Oh, then you will help me get to Fort St David?'

He pursed his lips suddenly. 'Arkali, how can you ask that?' he asked with impatience. 'After what I've told you? Doesn't it all fit with Hayden Flint's inexplicable madness? With the destruction of every last barrier that once stood between us? Every turn of events since then has brought us closer. Isn't it clear that we'll sail for Calcutta soon, that here's the opportunity for us to start a new life, you and I, together?'

'Mr Clive . . .' She was shaking her head. 'Mr Clive, no. You don't understand.'

'I understand everything. There's a flow in life, and you must feel it, and go along with it.'

'Mr Clive, I – '

'Hush!' He seized her and turned her away from the moonlight that flooded suddenly from a canyon between the clouds.

The steps were unmistakable in their approach. Boots on the stone stair flagging, coming up from below, a hand skimming the iron railing.

Clive put a finger to his mouth. Suddenly sobered, he tried to enfold her in his cloak, but she pulled away from him. The boots had almost reached the top when they stopped warily. Automatically, he felt for his sword hilt then realized that he had not carried any weapon for days as a condition of his parole. He felt Arkali's warmth, heard the rustle of her skirts and, as they waited in the silent shadows, smelt the clean sweetness only a woman gives to the air. By God, how magnificent she looks in a blaze of moonlight, he thought. I want her. I would do anything to help her, anything to make her adore me as I adore her, but what she's suggesting is crazy! Against the flow of everything.

There were more steps.

A sudden fear froze him. Christ Jesus, perhaps she's to be proved right! If that's a sentry I'll have no choice but to choke the devil, then we'll have to go to Fort St David, and tonight!

The stairwell echoed. 'Edmund?' she whispered into the darkness.

A shape resolved itself in the blackness. 'It's me.'

'Maskelyne?' Clive hissed, his relief that it was not a French soldier second only to his annoyance at the intrusion.

'Yes. By God, Clive, is that you?'

'It's all right,' said Arkali. 'I asked him to come here.'

Clive tried to shake the killing tension out of his muscles. He had been prepared to launch himself bare-handed on to an enemy and his heart was beating like a tabla drum. He watched her explain to Maskelyne, saw her move closer to him, and felt the jealousy begin to burn in him. Part of him was amazed at his own foolishness; this was Edmund Maskelyne, a soberminded fellow, his closest friend, a good, moral soul. But Maskelyne, with his black hair and boyish face, was also very attractive to women. He normally affected a Dutch bedcap and a clay pipe in the evenings, and would suck it with a judicial air, as if considering a friend's problems with a depth of understanding that outstripped his twenty-five years. Yes, Clive thought venomously, and all that huff and puff just serves to cover a massive streak of indecision in you.

She had taken Maskelyne's hand in hers. 'Will you help me, Edmund?'

'I'd like to help,' Maskelyne said uncertainly. 'I suppose Mr Clive has already told you what the Council will have in store for us at Calcutta? You see, we were both a little too eager to offer our views to the Company during the bombardment.' He smiled, abashed. 'When Stratford Flint was in command things seemed quite different. I'm afraid we were both rather too liberal with our opinions. If we're shipped off to Calcutta, we will be reprimanded and probably sent back to England at the first opportunity the Company can devise. They do not tolerate troublemakers.' He looked to Clive. 'But my dear fellow, what do you think?'

Clive shrugged. He had totally forgotten about the criticisms he had voiced, and his own defiance on the night of the mutiny. Then he heard himself say stiffly, 'I've already told Miss Savage that I'll render her all the assistance she requires. We've agreed that such a course is unavoidable.'

She moved to him and hugged him. Pangs of desire went through him. It was madness. Total madness. But he knew at once exactly why he had agreed, and the gratitude she showed delighted him and was already beginning to confirm him in the belief that what he had agreed to was not entirely insane.

The air was heavy and electric and full of monsoon. The wind had dropped and everything was still; distant blue flashes lit the south and east silently, and the stillness was the stillness that precedes a storm. Inside the Company building the atmosphere was tense. Shivaji, Stratford Flint's chaprasi, stood just inside the door with a pair of pistols stuffed into his belt, his hands resting on his hips close by the guns.

'Well, then? Which of ye is t'come along with me and taste a bit o' glory?'

There was no movement in the assembled group. No assent from them. The writers and junior factors reluctantly made space in their dormitory and Stratford Flint found himself staring at thirty faces banded by moonlight and rattan cane blinds.

'What exactly is it you want, sir?' The questioner was a tall, blond-haired man, of six years' seniority, Prawley by name, one of the whist-playing crew who wore his breeches tight and thought himself sufficiently close to private trade status to have adopted senior factor affectations. The rest were disposed to listen to him. Their mistrust was strong, but Flint knew he needed them. Half a dozen. Better a dozen. Willing to haul for him and to fight. If the plan was to succeed he would need to talk them round for sure.

'Just a bit o' glory. I want ye to come with me over the walls and get away from here tomorrow night.'

'Break our parole? Our word of honour to our captors?'

Flint hated the Company for the way it trod the enterprise out of young lads.

'By God,' he hissed, his voice curdling with disgust. 'Hell's fire burn the Hon'ble Comp'ny and all its minions! What kind of deaf, dumb and blind juggernaut takes raw, spirited lads like yerselves and deliberately crushes the life out of them?'

Those nearest him recoiled in the darkness, but they couldn't tear their eyes away from him as he cursed their reluctance.

'No, it wants to creep forward at an inch a year, never risking, never venturing, which is what they call "good business" and "sure and steady progress". Eh? Eh? Am I right?'

He stared around at them again, raising his voice now as if he was careless of the curfew. 'Well, let me tell ye where ye're at, me boys! The Comp'ny burns out young men's souls when there ain't no earthly need. And their yeller gutlessness seeps out like a blinding fever to jaundice their vision. The French've been gaining on us fer years, and the Company's blind to that. Then a war comes and they're unprepared and they lose all they've built up – and again they're blind to that. And when war passes into peace, as it surely will, all trade'll be knocked back a decade and they're blind to that too. Ah, why must it be, when there's an obvious and better way?'

An obvious and better way? He could almost hear the question echoing in their heads.

'Yes, a boat to Calcutta,' Prawley said.

'Yer not going to sit here and wait on no boat t'take ye to Calcutta,' Flint said, grinning ghastly in the half-light. 'There ain't going t'be no boat, by God. And that's a fact!'

'La Bourdonnais's promised us a sloop,' one of Prawley's friends said definitively. 'The Council told us so.'

'I said there ain't going to be no boat! And Charles Savage, he says so too. Governor Dupleix left Pondicherry two days ago to come here.' He stared at the factors and writers evilly, thinking of the money he and Cornelius Morgan and the McBrides had just finished unearthing at the Triplicane mansion. The only problem was how to get so great a weight of specie away from Madras and La Bourdonnais. 'Make no mistake, when Dupleix gets here he'll have every last one of ye strung up fer yer dis-obedience.'

'We've heard your scare stories before, Flint! We know about you!'

'Ye don't know nothing,' he told Prawley. 'Ye don't know that the nawab's army only came here because of my son. It was brought here by a bribe delivered to Arcot by Hayden. It would not have come without him. All that was his doing and mine.'

'What does it matter? Look at the result! An army utterly defeated at the hands of a force less than one tenth their size! And with them our last hope is gone.'

Flint stared back, angered by their defeatism and apathy. This stinking season melted men's will, slowly boiled the virtue out of their bones. He knew he had to whip them out of their listlessness. 'That the native army failed to relieve us was becos Anwar-ud-Din and his sons've got the military skills of bloody cockroaches. But they came here, and ye're all witnesses t'that fact. I don't owe the Company a Wood's ha'penny. I promised them an army and an army they got, by God!'

One of the writers spat, muttering, 'That cowardly rabble can hardly be called an army.'

Flint cuffed him smartly. 'Button yer mouth, lad. I'll not have one of ye young lickspittles calling coward on anyone else when ye have no balls yerselves.'

'What do you want us to think?' the youngster blurted. 'Coming here with your man with illegal guns in his belt and all. You'll get us killed, so you will.'

Flint shook his head as if astounded, as if holding in a great urge to violence. 'I'm telling ye, Dupleix is going to flatten Madras and ye listen and want t'do nowt but complain about events that're dead and gone! What kind of Englishmen are ye? Not like the lads of my day when we'd crack the whole world open like an egg soon as spit fer t'get at the gold inside.' Flint smacked his hand on the arm of a chair. 'Listen! I'm warning ye: Dupleix has told La Bourdonnais what he intends, and now La Bourdonnais has told me. The Governor don't want Englishmen on this coast, and he means to get rid of ye as cheaply as he might.'

'That's all very well, sir, but we are all accountable to the Company here.' Another of the factors had spoken up, his voice drawling and unperturbed, his accent that of the minor nobility. 'We answer to the Council and to no one else.'

'That's not the opinion I heard from ye a week back, Sykes!'

'As you yourself pointed out, Mr Flint, we must look to our futures now,' Sykes said, sighing heavily. His face was wet with sweat in the still, close air. 'The Company brought us here. And it's the Company that keeps us. We came East to this damnable clime for no other reason than to make our fortunes, and I may say that those of us five-sevenths through our time are looking to our futures more than you are prepared to give us credit. We're owed a lot, and due to realize it soon – if we can reach Calcutta.'

'Yes,' another behind Sykes said. 'You may be able to whip up the independents to your whims, Mr Flint, and malcontents such as Robert Clive may be inclined to follow you. But we have to consider the Company and its rules. The Council has said we must have no more to do with you.'

Flint's lip curled. 'Ah, the Council's powerless. The Governor's deputy's gasping on his deathbed even as we talk! Strung out on his charpoy, with his liver black as coal. He'll never gain Calcutta, sloop or no sloop.'

They began to look from one to another.

'When ye think of yer futures, consider this: there was never a man who fought his way to the top of life's ladder with his soul intact. I'll tell ye now, ye'll go nowhere but to mediocrity by standing in line to kiss fat men's backsides!'

They lounged in the sweaty heat, enervated and wilting, their cotton shirts open to the waist and sodden at the armpits. Their faces displayed dull-eyed ennui. The eldest factor stood up languidly. 'Why should we trust what you tell us, Flint? You hoodwinked the Council into making a defence against the French and look where it's gotten us. Nowhere!'

Flint's contempt was livid. 'Ah, but ye're a real Comp'ny man ain't ye, Prawley?'

'I don't mind admitting that, Mr Flint.'

'Well, listen tight, and ye may learn something. I've put up a ransom of ten lakhs on St George and La Bourdonnais has accepted it!'

There was disbelief. 'What?' Prawley said. 'You're saying he's just going to sail his squadron away? Just like that?'

'Fer ten lakhs of silver, aye.'

'I don't believe it!'

'Then look out the windahs!'

They began to drift to the windows that looked out on the sea, pulling apart the rattan canes, putting their faces to the glassless spaces between the glazing bars, none of them with the least idea of what they were meant to be looking for. The blackness outside swelled vast and starless, lit only by a constellation of stationary ships' lights.

'The French ships are there as ever they have been! What's different?'

Flint's laugh was derisive. 'Yes, they're there, aright. But what else is out there? D'ye see it? A sea as flat as a looking glass! Not a breath of wind! See, Prawley, La Bourdonnais ain't got no choice. He can feel it in his pores how the weather's turned. He's been here long enough to know the signs of the weather. He knows it's the season of hurricanes that can smash his robbing navy to splinters. And he knows what this calm signifies. He'll take himself away if he has to warp every vessel off the coast himself.'

They thought about that, imagining French crews towing their ships out across the stillness, matelots pulling laboriously on their oars. Suddenly they felt the humid mugginess close in around them, heavy and dead. Sweat slicked their bodies; it could not evaporate into the moisture-laden air. Breath came shallowly. Everything was sticky; there was no respite from it when the breeze died, as it had. The clouds had closed suffocatingly over the world like a hot, damp blanket, containing them. The calm before a storm. They hung at the windows, wretched as scarecrows, prisoners of the climate.

Then they felt it.

Movement on their damp faces. Like the lightest caress of a mother's hand, on their brows and on their cheeks. A stirring in the air.

'It's a breeze!'

'By God, he's right!'

'I can feel it.'

'Jesus, I can feel it, too!'

Sykes turned back from the window. 'Mr Flint, if the French Admiral must leave, why did you promise him a ransom?'

'Ye must offer a man something if ye want him to tell ye his secrets. See, it takes half a week to ready a fleet. I had to know the date he planned to sail, so that everything could be made ready.'

'Made ready for what?'

Flint made a gesture of frustration. 'I see I'm singing psalms at me own taffrail, trying to talk to the likes of ye. Perhaps ye've more respect fer hard metal.' He patiently tried again, as if laying it out for three dozen obtuse children. 'Take it from me, La Bourdonnais'll set sail the day after tomorrow. There won't be no ship fer ye. So ye've but two choices: ye can stay here with this yes-maggot, Prawley, and be treated t'some more French hospitality when Monsieur Dupleix arrives. Or ye can come with me tonight and get the pay ye so richly deserve.' He dug a handful of heavy silver coins from his pocket and scattered them so that they rang and shimmered on the wear-polished teak floor. Some of the writers scrambled for the coins and began to test them with their teeth.

'Shivaji!'

The servant came up. 'Sah?'

'Tell them how much more of this ye've seen.'

'Plenty more, sahib. *Pandrah lakh.*' Fifteen lakhs.

They gasped. A writer's official salary was less than ten pounds a year – a hundred and fifty rupees. The sum Flint's servant had quoted was as much as each of them would earn in ten thousand years!

'Becos I need ye to come along, I'll give ye a hundred rupees apiece. And the promise that any that sails with me will be seen as heroes at Calcutta.'

'You're going to sail to Calcutta?' one of them asked.

'Aye. I just said so, din't I?'
'But how?'
'In the *Chance*.'

The two groups met on the foreshore the following night an hour after moonset. The breeze was getting up nicely, and the cloud was moving and parting in huge canyons in which the stars hid like diamonds. Cully with his lads for one boat, Flint with his for the other. It had taken them two hours to retrieve the last of the silver from Savage's Triplicane mansion and get it to the rendezvous. Now they had met up on the dark strand north of Madras.

They heaved the two 21-foot cutters through the surf and began to stroke out to the anchorage. The oars were muffled with rags. Flint took the tiller in his hands and passed an eye over what was in front of him. A dozen writers and ten others were crammed into a hull that lay low in the water. The silver was in strongboxes in the bottom, all roped to a 30-fathom line with a cork float on the end in case of an upset. Sitting astride it there was Cornelius Morgan and the McBrides, and, in the other boat, two or three other independents who knew what they were about. Charles Savage was not present. He knew nothing about the undertaking nor about his daughter's intention to go over the walls with Robert Clive and Edmund Maskelyne.

Flint grinned in the darkness, his mind relishing the coming confrontation. Ahead of him the familiar stars of the Scorpion's tail hooked down between two clouds towards the south-eastern horizon. A faint phosphorescence shimmered where the sweeps stirred it up out of the Indian sea. The sound of those muffled oars dipping repeatedly in the star-silvered water lulled him. Unexpectedly he thought of his Annie. The look on her face when she had presented him with a son half a lifetime ago. He felt a twinge of guilt over Hayden before his resolve hardened once more.

See what a wound I've took there? he thought bitterly of his dead wife. Ah, why did ye have t'leave me, Annie? Why does me heart open and bleed at intervals fer the love of ye still? Don't ye see how the thought of ye impedes me when I need t'be ruthless?

His grip hardened on the tiller. It's plain to any fool that romantic love's the game of imbeciles and fops. Ain't that so? There's no winners all round and no lasting advantage to it. Ain't that just so? What a force of effort spent on dandying and prettification! Aye, and in the end it's a game where young women're the only prize – young gels as don't know anything and can't defend themselves against the advances of such as Frenchmen. Not like trade, where a man gains wealth, and ye may see something fer yer trouble at the end of it. The Moghuls are in accord with our own aristocrats in this: marriages should be arranged fer mutual profit.

'Rest on yer oars, lads.'

The regular dipping of the sweeps halted and the forward way of the boat began to drop off. They looked to him as the boat lifted and sank on the swell.

'Why are we stopping, Mr Flint?' Sykes asked.

'Becos I've something to say to ye all. Some of ye think we're going fer the *Achille*, but if ye think that ye're wrong. We're heading straight fer the *Chance*.'

'But, sir, what about the Admiral's ransom?' one of the writers asked.

Flint chewed on the end of his unlit cheroot stub. 'What about it?'

'Do you mean that we hand it over to him aboard the *Chance*, sir?'

'We do not.'

A pause.

'But I thought that was the plan. To buy our freedom with that silver.'

'A waste of good specie, don't ye think, lad?'

'But surely he won't even let us get aboard the *Chance* unless you pay!'

'Then ye'll have t'persuade him another way, won't ye?

'Now just a minute! That wasn't what we agreed,' Prawley said.

'There's a price to everything, mister. Ye should know that.'

'You want us to storm the ship, from these boats?'

'What if they see us coming?' another of the writers asked, plainly terrified.

Flint stared at them. 'They'll not see us. It's like this: La Bourdonnais's ships have been readying all day. They'll sail at first light. We must get aboard the *Chance* only when she's fully made ready. Then it's a quick cutting of her cables fore and aft, out with me lascars from below decks and away before they have time to run out their guns or haul anchor to pursue us.'

'But how do we get aboard?'

'Did ye never hear of a cutting out?'

'A cutting out?'

'We'll row up quiet and surprise the watch. Swarm up her sides from bow and stern quarters. Then over the side with the filth what's aboard.'

'But what if they see us coming?'

'Don't ye worry. There's lads here has done cutting out dozens of times. No shooting, just slitting of gizzards. That's why we ain't brought nothing but knives and hangers.'

He pulled out two cotton bundles, one a foot long and the other three foot. Inside the bigger bundle was a half-dozen cutlasses; the smaller contained a couple of dozen dinner knives that had been ground to sharp points.

Prawley groaned. 'Flint, you're insane.'

'Ah, we'll be all right. Even a yeller-gutted bastard like yerself'll be all right.'

'I'll not do it!'

'What'll ye do instead? Swim home?'

Prawley looked down and saw the pistol in Flint's lap and thought again.

'Now row on, me boys. And keep it quiet becos we're coming inside earshot of the French.'

NINE

Dream terror beat through Hayden Flint as he sprang awake. Everything around him was blindingly bright, and for a moment he wondered where he was, and whether he could now muster the strength to pull out the lance shaft that impaled his chest. He knew that if he failed his lungs could not function and he would die; but if he succeeded there would be a great hole in him and he would bleed to death.

Sweat drenched his chest. He searched his mind, unable to breathe, then he realized that another vile dream had visited him and he collapsed back into the silken covers of the couch, thankful beyond reason.

The real Battle of St Thome was now many months in the past, but still it haunted him. It had been his battle, the battle he had bought and paid for, the one that had ended in a total rout. So many men killed, an unknown number – hundreds, perhaps thousands – bleeding and dying on the ground, and many more wounded crawling back in screaming pain, limbless or seared open by flying steel. For them there had been no waking from dream, no return to wholeness.

He breathed rapidly, gasping like a man drowning in his own blood. As he closed his eyes the terrible glory of the death charge lived in his mind again: the magnificent panoply of war shattered, so many horses and elephants and men blasted into carrion by the French guns, agony upon agony, and the insane, panic-stricken retreat raked by volley after volley of musket-fire from those dead-straight lines. It had been his fault. He had wanted it, had demanded it vehemently. All of it. And it had been given –

against Anwar-ud-Din's better judgment. God forgive them both.

'What is it, Mr Flint?'

He opened his eyes into the glare of afternoon and a pain seared his head. A huge iron sickle cut across the sky. A figure stood over him, her voice concerned for him. He remembered now. It was a festival day. He had been the honoured guest of Prince Muzaffar Jang, sitting with him and two of the Nizam's generals atop a strange tower, a ziggurat tower of many steps, remote from the main palace, in the midst of the astronomical gardens. Below were stone wedges and marble hemispheres and geometrical blocks set with graduated lines, many kinds of sun dials and moon dials and *gnomons* and *yantras*. Above, was a great star-sighting quadrant standing in the centre of the tower platform, its crescent free-swinging on an iron axis like an enormous weathervane or a gigantic version of one of his father's jealously owned navigational instruments. It dominated the sky.

This was the place the court astrologers came to at night to take their readings from polished scales of deeply incised Arabic numerals, to plot the progress of Mars and Jupiter across the zodiac and read what was written for the future. But the walled platform of the tower was laid with rich silk carpets and scattered with cushions and hung with delicate curtains; it had been transformed into a pleasure pavilion.

There were hookahs and wine and spiced delicacies and turbaned hench-boys waving peacock-feather fans over them for cool. And the bare-breasted courtesans of Hyderabad, their nipples rouged or traced with gold leaf, gems glinting in their noses and navels, gold chains looping from pierce-holes made in their flesh, tresses of the most astonishingly long black hair, talking as they played and sang and danced and smoked and applied make-up to one another's faces. It was a gentle noonday relaxation without politics but with snacks and a calabash of arrack punch instead, and they had come out here where the hot, dry breeze blew through fine muslin screens dampened with rosewater to cool them.

He had endured the entertainment patiently, hoping that Muzaffar Jang might be able to circumvent this endless waiting and arrange for him at last to present his petition to the Nizam. He had come armed with a letter.

'Drink, Mr Flint. Drink and enjoy. Drink and enjoy and relax. Here we have everything for you. So drink and be content.'

The favourite grandson of the great Asaf Jah was a forty-year-old, overweight boor, his smile insincere, his eyes swivelling in dark pits as he spoke, and he sweated perfume. Nevertheless, his luxuriance was skin-deep. He asked some penetrating questions about the Carnatic, and the details of the battle, before allowing his giggling girls to feed him sweet jellies and consume him with their laughter.

'May I at least ask you to pass on this letter to Asaf Jah – O Tremble at His Name – at your first convenience?' Hayden Flint asked finally, smothering his frustration with Moghul indirectness as best he could. 'Surely he cannot be so taken up with affairs that he has not the time to read what is a very short letter.'

Muzaffar's eyes slid behind their puce lids as his toadlike grin spread. He waved a careless gesture at the universe. 'What is time, but the revolving of the heavenly bodies in their courses? We shall have to see how the moon sets, Mr Flint. And see also how it rises. For sometimes today's moon is grown more plentiful by degrees than yesterday's, and sometimes it is grown slimmer.'

'I hope that tomorrow's moon is full, Highness. I have expected it overlong.'

The grin broadened and the words came again, caressingly, from his throat. 'You may hope. But do not be surprised if tomorrow's full moon is darkened again by eclipse.'

'That will not surprise me, Highness. Indeed, I have schooled my mind to expect delays to the end of time.'

'That is strange, for is not time endless?'

Hayden sighed. 'Highness, in the English world we have another view of time. It has been brought down from the heavens at the observatory of Greenwich, near London. Our time has been captured and contained inside mechanical contrivances. Thus tamed and regulated, time has become our servant; we find that our affairs proceed more evenly and with greater dispatch. In short, Highness, the English have procedure, method, organization. That is what makes us what we are.'

Muzaffar swallowed the criticism whole. 'And in the country of Paris too, we have heard, there is also an observatory where time is unnaturally regimented. It is, we have been advised, the location of the principal meridian of longitude of the earth.' He rolled his eyes up reciting the technical terms. Then he snapped his fingers and a woman – the most wanton of the courtesans – instantly produced an expensive silver pocketwatch. Muzaffar took it and flipped the cover open with his thumb to reveal a gorgeously worked rococo dial. 'You see! *Ajaib!* We already possess such a contrivance! Tak-tak, tak-tak ... Do you hear it? It is a useless thing, of course, of no purpose or consequence to me, but it is pretty, is it not?'

Hayden Flint took the watch and examined it, and slowly a brooding sense of unease crept over him: the maker's name painted on the face was 'Foubert', the place of the workshop, Paris.

Muzaffar Jang had made his point. Soothingly he said, 'Perhaps we will soon be able to do something to advance your interests. We have some small influence with our exalted grandfather at whose name all should tremble. Now please allow this beautiful creature, who is truly Excellent Among Women, to wait upon you. Drink and smoke as you please, for tomorrow, if the merciful Allah wills it, you may be gone from this timeless place, perhaps to return to your own country.'

Hayden Flint obeyed. Self-consciously at first, but as the dippers of punch thinned his blood he allowed the women to take off his coat and hat and then his shoes and necktie. He propped himself on his elbow with the tortoiseshell mouthpiece of a hookah between his teeth and sucked in the cooled but pungent smoke of strong Turkey tobacco.

'Tell me about yourself, Mr Flint. Tell me. Tell me all.'

He saw the toad grin broaden. Things had begun to swim in the heat. The emerald in the nose of the most beautiful courtesan glinted, green as a serpent's eye. 'Highness, there is little to tell . . . about a humble man . . . but I will tell you . . . whatever you wish.'

'Come, Excellent Among Women. Put your hands on the Englishman's brow. I want to know how he came here. Before that, how he came to Arcot. And why does he accompany this extraordinary embassy now?' Among the caresses a jowled face loomed. 'I have heard about a gem you brought to Anwar-ud-Din. It is said to be a very special ruby, Mr Flint. Yes, tell me about that ruby . . .'

The pleasure pavilion atop the ziggurat was deserted now. The shadow of its lobster-tail dome had moved with the sun. The others had gone from the astronomical garden to some other part of this huge and fantastically impressive palace complex – whether by design or not he could not tell – leaving him alone, asleep and exposed. He had lain directly in the sun's powerful noonday rays for more than an hour.

'Yasmin Begum? Can it be you?'

His mouth was dry as dust. He tried to get to his feet, ashamed at his sore, sweat-slicked face and dishevelled hair, and succeeded only in falling back. His heart still thumped. 'Excuse me. I fell asleep. I had a dream.'

She was a black shape eclipsing the sun. She wore long skirts of many diaphanous layers that fell from her waist to her ankles. Her midriff was bare; a close-fitting choli bodice covered her breasts, fastening at the front. An orhni mantled her head and shoulders with delicate gold border-work on a gauzy material. It was pulled across her lower face. She said, 'I was walking among the yantras below and I heard your cry. I thought you had found a scorpion, or perhaps one had found you. What was your dream? Tell it to me and I shall tell you its meaning.'

'I . . . it was nothing. I'm all right, thank you.'

'Do you not realize that it is dangerous to go to sleep in the sun? That it brings on madness?'

'I did not mean to do so.'

Around him was a wreck of pummelled cushions, spilled wine goblets, plates of half-eaten sweetmeats, a dormant hookah; rice from a pillau dish was scattered across the carpets and dhurries. He looked away.

The kanat screens hanging around them were as dry and white as desert bones. They obscured the view over the arid plateau, but also protected the pleasure pavilion from vulgar gaze. From this vantage point they could see anyone coming up the steps, but no one could see them.

She approached him. 'Your face is very red. Let me see it.' She knelt and took a bottle of amber oil from between the cushions, then she poured some into her palm and delicately applied it to his cheeks and forehead. 'This jadu is a special oil the courtesans use. It will kiss your skin and prevent it from peeling away.'

Instantly the burn left his face and the touch of her fingers lingered as he looked at her. 'That's most kind of you, lady,' he sighed, surrendering to the delight. 'Most kind.'

'You did not go with the others,' she said matter-of-factly.

It was not a question, but still he felt he had to reply. 'Go with them? No. I fell asleep and . . . I think it must have been the punch.'

'Muzaffar Jang's . . . hospitality . . . is not what it seems.'

'That's very true, lady.' He smiled, calmed by her. 'I underestimated how much arrack was in the mixture. I assumed it was mostly fruit juice and I was very thirsty, and what with the heat I suppose that I . . .' He moistened his lips and looked up. 'I drank too much.'

'Perhaps.'

· 'I thought the Koran forbade strong drink,' he said sheepishly. 'And the way the prince's ladies were dressed . . .'

She adjusted her veil, which was thin and almost transparent. 'The Koran gives guidance on many matters, but in this world each person takes of it only what his or her strength or vanity allows.' She ran more oil into her fingers and rippled them sensuously against her thumb. 'I think that the courts of the Moghuls are intended as a paradise. It is as if we are already dead and judged. In such a place earthly sins have no meaning.'

He looked at her for a long moment and when he spoke his voice was stronger. 'However, we are not dead. And it has surprised me, lady, in our time here, that there is no prohibition on the drinking of alcohol or bhang at the Nizam's court. Nor on the smoking of tobacco – or even hashish.' Bhang, the preparation of milk, curd and hashish, was frothed with fruit juice and enjoyed by the nobility.

'It is true that the Nizam is a Muslim, and an upholder of the Faith, therefore his court observes the daytime fast during the month of Ramzan.' She gestured with her hands like the seesawing pans of a weighing scale. 'But he is also a mindful ruler, who enjoys the festival of Holi at the equinox, which is a Hindu observance.'

'He sees no inconsistency in that?'

'In Hindostan, or Bharat, as the Hindu themselves call it, you will find many strange blends that arise from the meeting of cultures. On the shores of Bharat all men have come together. After one hundred years the English drink China tea and Yemen coffee here, do they not? In the Madras lease they eat curry, do they not?'

'Indeed.'

'Do not forget that Islam has been in the Deccan – the southern lands – for almost five hundred years. And here, therefore, the Deccan has been in Islam for just as long.'

Yes, he thought. She's right about that. That's why it's so hard to make sense of these people. They're a curious mix. They're not pure Muslims, nor are they Hindu. In some matters they think one way, in some another. And they're not remotely like us. Our church and our laws, our king and our God, our traditions and ideals, they're completely different.

'But all people are the same, underneath,' she said sensing his thoughts. 'Is that not so?'

'I don't know.' He regarded her thoughtfully. 'If you mean that we all suffer pain, I would agree. If you mean that we all experience joy, or grief, or ecstasy, or sadness, or delight, or torment, or inner peace, again I would agree. If you mean that we all pursue those things or hide from them, I would agree once more. But if you mean that we think the same, your people and mine, then I would say that we almost certainly do not.'

'So! You are a reader of minds?'

'I simply observe it as a fact of behaviour.'

'Do not forget that you too have behaviour.' She inclined her head. 'By the gestures of your hands I see you are a man remote from your own feelings. Am I correct? Do all English have this problem?'

He smiled shallowly. 'I'll say only this: that is a question you would not ask if you were English.'

There's more to it than that, he thought, prickled by her criticism. We're from a culture that's a young oak – strong and upthrusting and growing in power and wealth, whereas this civilization's a gnarled fig tree, a power in decline just as much as ancient Rome was in the days of its destruction. I've only understood that since the battle. And since I've been here in Hyderabad I've begun to see that its heart is decaying wood; only the outward show continues. They're at the end of their glory, a fruit ripe and fated to rot – or be picked and gobbled up. My father always believed that, but I could never before understand what he meant. I could not see how a tree so manifestly strong and powerful and so plentifully hung with golden pagoda fruit as the Moghul's tree could be so rotted away at the core. He said it was, and he was right. Now, I see that.

Stratford Flint had warned the Company many times that the Moghuls were sinking into decadence. He had called it a natural process that afflicts all empires. 'Ye should learn that in a mortal creature the vigour always fails eventually, no matter what or who it be. It will in me one day! Aye, and in yerself! Which is why ye must strive while ye yet can! And empires are like the men what builds them, they grows old and decayed and too weak to defend theirsels. So ye must ekspect the filth to yearly find this land an increasing attraction.'

As Hayden Flint remembered his father's monologues on Hindostan great articulated wasps banded in black and lime green visited the browning cores of apples in the bowl beside him, their comma abdomens breathing on needle-slender waists – golden eyes jewelled as they ate. They buzzed away in relays to their brood hive built in a cracked Moghul arch.

According to Stratford the fissures had begun to yawn open forty years ago, when the Emperor Aurangzeb died; but long before that the Moghuls' much-vaunted empire had been dying – from the inside out.

Anyone can see it now, he thought, looking out over the basking glory of the Nizam's palace. Despite all this, their imperial domain is shrunken and enfeebled, the six subahs of the Deccan have split away, and the viceroyalties of Oudh, Bengal, Bihar and Orissa are all but independent. Malwa, Bundelkhand and Gujarat have been overrun by the Marathas, and the Rajput states are out of Delhi's control. New incursions from Persia and Afghanistan are sweeping down from the north. It's only a matter of time before the whole of Hindostan falls into chaos. I'm learning so much here, so much that I'm beginning to make sense of my father's ideas, and of Anwar-ud-Din's policies too.

After the débâcle at the mount of St Thome, it had been strangely clear to him how to carry events forward on his own initiative. He had known that he must resort to a higher authority than the Nawab of the Carnatic for help in making Dupleix relinquish Madras. In Arcot, he asked the nawab for permission to take his request for assistance to the Nizam of Hyderabad, the bearer of the Talwar himself.

At first, Anwar-ud-Din had refused, not wanting to give Asaf Jah any reason to send troops into the Carnatic. But then he chose to send an ambassador to Hyderabad, knowing it was imperative that the French be disciplined as soon as possible. Now, that could only be done by Asaf Jah's army.

As soon as an official pretext could be found, Anwar-ud-Din had sent Muhammad Ali, Nadira Begum and Yasmin with their full establishment of women, servants and guards on an embassy to Hyderabad. The official reason was the failing health of Muhammad Shah, the Emperor at Delhi: Muhammad Ali was to consult with the Nizam's court on what arrangements should be made in anticipation of the Emperor's death. Only on the eve of departure, after very careful thought, and for reasons Hayden Flint could not yet discern, had Anwar-ud-Din decided to allow him to go too.

They had been in Hyderabad for many months. The elaborate negotiations had dragged on and on, and now Muzaffar Jang had told him casually that the twenty-nine-year rule of the Light of the World, His Imperial Majesty Muhammad Shah, was ended, that the filthy, debauched, opium-sodden lecher had died some weeks ago – and about time.

That's rich, coming from you, he thought at first, then he saw that Muzaffar Jang was much sharper in his mind than he wanted people to believe, and that perhaps he was signalling that the time had come for events to move forward, that the diplomatic paralysis was, at last, coming to an end. Perhaps.

He thought of the Paris-made pocketwatch again and queasy misgivings bubbled in him. Muzaffar Jang is taking presents from the French. And there was still the bloody ruby – what had happened to that? Wasn't its usefulness spent? Since the battle there had been no value in thinking of it . . .

He put his hand to his temple; the brightness and his overindulgence had completely robbed him of strength and his head raged. 'Oooohhh.'

'The Koran says that in strong drink and gambling there is both usefulness and sin,' Yasmin told him pitilessly. 'But that the sin of them is greater than their use.'

'Your book is very wise, lady.'

'Take heed then, especially concerning gambling.' her eyes flicked carefully right and left, then she continued, an edge of warning in her voice. 'I will tell you this: the Nizam's court is a morass of intrigue that makes Arcot seem as pure as the waters of the holy river Ganga. Muzaffar Jang and Nasir Jang are the two main players manoeuvring for position in Hyderabad. The stakes are very high and growing higher by the day, so take care how you tread, Mr Flint, and above all, don't be seen to back the wrong side.' She urged him to lie back more comfortably and produced a second oil to put on his face. 'You said you were dreaming. The dream made you shout. What was its substance?'

The dream . . .

After the battle the ragged remnants of Anwar-ud-Din's army had gathered then dragged their heels back to Arcot. Anwar-ud-Din himself was pale-faced and silent in his war-tattered howdah, shocked and humbled by the un-expectedness of the defeat. He understood only partially the immense implications of the outcome. It had been a total humiliation for the nawab, his authority defied and his army smashed into retreat, and by a force perhaps one fifth, perhaps even one tenth, the size of his own.

But it was much more than a humiliation. It was a precedent. For the first time, a line of lowly feringhee foot-soldiers and their trained sepoys and four light field cannon had withstood the massed cavalry assault of a Moghul horde. The charge had broken and fled, and with it had fled also the ultimate sanction of overwhelming force that lay with the Moghul overlord.

'I said, it was a dream that made you shout.'

Again the question that was not a question. Again it laid his guard low.

'I thought myself back in the nawab's vanguard,' he said distantly. 'In the charge. It was a terrible dream.'

'You have very little taste for war, Mr Flint.'

He looked at her hollowly. 'The truth is, I don't have the stomach for it.'

She took his admission without comment. Another long moment passed, then she said slowly, as if reciting a verse stored for years in her mind, 'Warfare is ordained for you, though it be hateful unto you; but it may happen that you hate a thing which is good for you . . .'

He gazed at her, mystified by the Koranic paradox.

'. . . and it may happen that you love a thing that is bad for you.' She looked back now, into the depths of his eyes, and he saw her compassion, and he could not stop himself from reaching up to her to touch her veil, then she looked away again and his hand fell away also. 'Allah knoweth, but you knoweth not,' she said.

She did not rise as he expected, but stayed and worked more oil into the skin of his face, and he closed his eyes and considered her words. The danger of his situation fogged his mind: it's beyond the strict laws of the court to be alone with a lady of rank, or even to be in her presence without the express permission of her husband. Even on a festival day such as today, and with the dispensations granted to me by Anwar-ud-Din, even in a place such as this astronomical garden where both men and women may enter – if Muhammad Ali were to come here and discover us, he would be within his rights to have us both punished. It's true that their punishments are excessively severe. I wonder what the punishment for adultery is? Has she thought about that? My God, we've been here months, and each time we meet she talks to me using less and less formality, we converse with greater and greater enthusiasm, covering all kinds of subjects; where else can it be leading?

Why did she happen to come by this particular place when I was alone here? Perhaps she's right that in this world we choose to obey whichever laws we please. And perhaps I am beginning to love a thing that is bad for me. She's so beautiful that I could . . .

He reined in his thoughts sharply, but he could feel her supple fingers on his cheeks and neck, he could feel her eyes on him, smell the sweetness of mint on her breath, and the longing in her. No! No! That way lies only destruction!

Think about why you're here. Think about the battle. Think about hell-damned Moghul politics. Think about anything except Yasmin.

He sat up suddenly, the excitement of his body an ache pulsing in him. He began to gather up his shoes and hat and don them hastily. 'Thank you, lady. I should like to go down now. Alone, if you don't mind. Thank you again for your attention. Thank you.'

He got to his feet and descended the steps as fast as the dizziness in his head would allow him, and she looked after him as he staggered, wondering if he could really be so susceptible to the punch he had drunk. If he had slept so heavily and awakened so unhappily and so confused after just a little arrack, then the legendary capacity of feringhees for handling strong drink was greatly exaggerated.

She smiled at the embarrassment he had shown at her touch, and the astonishing way the shape of his member had begun to show inside his tight white breeches. His member had betrayed him, showed what his thoughts really were. For a moment his eyes had glazed under her tender ministrations and he had seemed about to make a grab for her. But he had not.

What would I have done if he had? she wondered. But she already knew the answer to that.

It was strange how men behaved when the moon was in a certain heavenly house, especially since he had been enjoying the company of Muzaffar Jang's courtesans before he fell asleep. Doubtless the rest of the men in the drinking party had retired with the choicest women to private apartments to slake other thirsts; why then had he not followed?

A sudden suspicion overcame her. Which courtesans, I wonder? Oh, you'll have to be more careful than I thought, Mr Hayden Flint, she told him mentally as he reached the foot of the ziggurat. If you can be drugged for your secrets – and perhaps you were – you can just as easily be poisoned.

She capped the bottles of oil, wiped her hands and started to descend the steps. Carrion birds wheeled and winged on the hot air over the plain.

So, she thought, hurrying from the Star Garden, Muhammad Shah, the Emperor, is dead. That's what Muzaffar Jang's women are saying, but Muzaffar is a grasping, ambitious, treacherous schemer even by the standards of Hyderabad and everything he originates has to be examined and compared with other reports. The stories of what that gross and filthy-minded nawab did with the courtesans who consented to go with him had been the staple *gup* of Hyderabad for almost a year. They were paid massive sums, and always obeyed the courtesan's code of elaborating and half divulging *gup* so that even one such as Umar could not begin to unravel fact from fantasy.

The calling of birds had ceased in the noonday blaze. Yasmin approached the huge guards who stood at the studded door of the zenana and waited for them to allow her entry. It was a harem guard's duty to protect the privacy of the ladies of the court from prying men, and to prevent the disaffected from leaving. Some women were kept prisoners. She remembered her own confinement in a zenana, the first homesick months she had spent at Arcot. It had been horrible, especially those first nights. But then the other women gradually won my trust, she reflected, and I accepted my sequestered life patiently. It might have been worse. In the province of Oudh, the perimeter of the zenana is patrolled by a regiment of women, each carrying a musket. At least here, as at Arcot, the regiment consists of eunuchs, but since I am not of the Nizam's harem, but rather a member of the embassy of the Carnatic, I may come and go past them as I please.

She made her way through the labyrinthine interior of the zenana to the spacious quarters where the women of the Carnatic embassy were lodged. Besides herself, there were twenty women accommodated there, Nadira Begum and the courtesan, Khair-un-Nissa, among them. As she came to her landing she met her older ayah, Hamida.

'Is Khair-un-Nissa within?'

'No, sahiba.' Hamida grimaced. 'The tigress hasn't been here for hours. She's out sharpening her claws somewhere, but I don't think she went at Muhammad's pleasure.'

'Oh?'

'She and Nadira Begum spent some time talking this morning. They're planning something together. I can sense it.'

Yasmin considered the conclusions she and Hamida had already reached concerning the courtesan. Khair-un-Nissa was Nadira's purchase, but it was doubtful that she had been perfectly frank with her contract-holder. Of course, before settling the figure, Nadira would have demanded to be kept fully and exclusively informed in all matters relating to Muhammad, and naturally Khair-un-Nissa would have agreed to her conditions, but the courtesan was not the type to divulge everything.

'She's devious,' Yasmin said. 'She's spent too long at Hyderabad for her own good. My guess is that she came to Arcot because of some embarrassment. The rumour is that her shampooer is a poisoner.'

'That witch, Jemdani, her so-called herbalist!' Hamida's eyes flashed. 'Some say they have seen Jemdani practise *kimiya* – alchemy. Those whom Khair-un-Nissa protects say Jemdani was employed because she is expert in the skills of the *apadravya*.'

'Indeed?'

Hamida shrugged. It was a delicate matter. *Apadravyas* were worn on the man's lingam for support. 'So I was told, sahiba. But I don't believe that's the real reason.'

'No. Muhammad has no problem with size or stiffness, and he never wanted for vigour with me. I wonder if he . . .' She shook her head. 'But that's not what I wanted to know. Tell me, does Khair-un-Nissa ever wear a poison ring?'

Hamida pursed her lips. 'It is quite possible, but so difficult to tell. Jemdani could obtain one easily, and it wouldn't surprise me if the tigress goes habitually about the palace with deadly powders hidden in all her jewellery. She is a walking arsenal of deceits!'

'Do you have any idea where she went this afternoon?'

'No, sahiba. But I know that she went out by the gate of the star gardens before noon. Do you know if there were any pleasure picnics planned by the men there at that hour?'

Yasmin bit her lip. 'Tell me, have you heard any more about Asaf Jah?'

Hamida swallowed and their eyes met. 'The *gup* is variously that he spends his waning days in prayer, or that he is insane and chained in a dungeon beneath the palace, or that Nasir Jang has put out his eyes and has him tortured daily to try to make him confer Hyderabad on him, or again that it was Muzaffar Jang who did the blinding.' She shrugged with dissatisfaction.

'Yes, I agree. The rumours are without focus. Stay vigilant, Hamida. I want to know what Khair-un-Nissa is up to. But also be careful!'

Yasmin kissed the ayah's cheek and dismissed her.

So, she thought as she made her way towards Muhammad's quarters, Khair-un-Nissa was not with my husband as I thought. She could have been with Mr Flint, after all –possibly. And she could have drugged him – again, only possibly.

I must talk urgently with Muhammad. He must surely now believe Nadira Begum when she tells him that I am spying on him on his father's orders, but perhaps even she underestimates the degree of confidence that exists between Anwar-ud-Din and myself. Does she realize, for example, that I know Muhammad is really here to dispose of the ruby? Does she know that truth herself? She must do. I know that Anwar-ud-Din has charged Muhammad with the task of choosing who shall receive the ruby. There are only two possibilities, but Muhammad must now be guided to the correct choice.

As she threaded her way through the crowded zenana Yasmin smiled at those she saw and they smiled back at her. During her stay at Hyderabad, she had talked with the Nizam's women and learned many invaluable facts. For one, it seemed that Asaf Jah had not appeared in public for almost ten months, creating all kinds of scares and rumours. For another, the Nizam's eldest son was

Ghazi-ud-Din, but he was not the heir. According to the most reliable sources, he had abandoned himself to a life of decadence and voluptuous living at the Delhi court. He had no desire, evidently, to take up the heavy responsibilities of the Talwar, nor any wish to bring the curse of the evil-eyed diamond down upon his own head.

Asaf Jah had apparently prevailed on the Emperor to issue a firman appointing Nasir Jang, his own much younger son, as heir, but that information was disputed by the women who had allied themselves with the noxious Muzaffar Jang. They thought Nasir was trying to usurp the Nizam's masnad.

It is a fascinating power struggle, she thought, and we are at the fulcrum of it, able to affect it to our advantage – if we are clever.

She considered. Muzaffar Jang himself was already Nawab of Adoni and Bijapur, two provinces of the Deccan; he was also the favourite grandson of Nizam-ul-Mulk, and the main contender in the battle for ultimate power in Hyderabad. His campaign had been gathering pace; already he had worked himself into a most advantageous position militarily, and now he had begun to claim that Asaf Jah had promised him nawabship of the Carnatic.

That changes everything, she thought. The critical move has been made and I must inform Muhammad and then cause him to move in the correct way. He is such a changed man since the battle that he can no longer be relied upon to do what he must, and that worries me.

She turned into a long, narrow corridor that was cool and thick-walled. The windowless gloom made her hurry. One last piece of *gup* occupied her mind as she walked. She had discovered that Khair-un-Nissa's contract had once been owned by Muzaffar. I wonder if he's using her to get at Mr Flint, she thought. And if so, why? What exactly does Muzaffar want from him?

In sight now was the door to Muhammad's quarters. At the portal she spoke to one of the eunuchs, who sent a gap-toothed ten-year-old boy with her message to her husband.

Moments later the boy reappeared and whispered to the eunuchs. They would not admit her, of course, to the sacrosanct male quarters, but one of them showed her to a waiting hall where Muhammad appeared within the hour.

Since the battle a great change had come over him. He was quiet and had seldom emerged from his room. She hadn't seen him for weeks.

He was stiff in his bearing, his arm still held strapped up across his chest, and he was grim-faced as he approached. She felt a pang of guilt at the thought of his decline. To have been defeated by a pack of feringhees and their trained sipahis was dishonourable; but to have been dragged from the field of battle by a woman with his sword-arm shattered was ignominious. She should have left him to die a warrior's death, but she had been unable to do that, and in rescuing him she had robbed him of his destiny.

That was a terrible crime, one for which Muhammad would never forgive her.

His dignity in shreds, he had been unable to hold his head up. Without full health and his daily cold baths he became lethargic and morose, and the heavy wines and rich foods of the Hyderabad court had burdened him with extra flesh. He stopped six paces from her now and she smelt the acid tang of his breath. He had been drinking.

'Well?'

'Thank you for coming at my asking, lord,' she said formally.

'Lower your veil when you speak to your husband!'

She bared her face obediently.

He looked at her with hate in his eyes. 'What is it you want of me?'

'Ask rather what I have to give you.'

'I know you have nothing to give me.' His voice was icily vacant of emotion but his words were still cutting. 'You never give me anything.'

She lowered her eyes. 'I have brought you an important piece of information.'

He sat down in the window seat, his back to her as if he could not bear to face her. 'As I said: nothing for me.'

'It is important. Very important, my lord.'

Suddenly he turned, his voice filled with a grinding rage. 'My name is Muhammad! Muhammad! Or have you forgotten?'

She waited as she always waited, silent, head erect, maddeningly superior, secretly laughing at him. He had been told she had been seen in the Star Garden, mounting the steps of the tower, and that some minutes later Hayden Flint had come down from there, dressing himself as he descended.

'Well? Speak!'

'It has come to me today that Muzaffar Jang has laid formal claim to the masnad of the Carnatic. If Asaf Jah can be persuaded to sanction it, it is possible Muzaffar will attempt to oust your father from Arcot.'

He stared at her, his eyes travelling her face. 'Anything else?'

'Is that not enough, my lor – Muhammad? I think it is significant enough to warrant immediate communication to your father. If you sent a horse messenger today – '

'I asked if there was anything else. Confine yourself to passing on what you have heard. Your opinions are of no interest to me. Now, do you have anything more to tell?'

'No.'

'Then get out of my sight.'

She put her hands together and backed away elegantly with bowed head, not even trying to show humility, and then she looked up. 'Perhaps . . . perhaps there is something else.'

'Well?'

'Some of the women believe that Muzaffar Jang has a secret plan to help him gain the Carnatic. It is a complex game and you and Mr Flint are both bound to be key players in it. If I am to make sense of what I hear, I must know about the Blood Stone.'

'I have it safe,' he murmured, torn inside by her mention of the feringhee's name.

'But I must ask: what do you intend to do with it?'

Muhammad looked accusingly at her. 'Why? I hate the ruby! It is a foreign thing. A dirty thing. It is truly cursed and truly it has brought disaster down upon our house! I shall shatter it into fragments and grind the fragments to powder and scatter the powder over the waves of the sea!'

'With respect, was not the ruby entrusted to you by your father? I wonder, what did he want you to do with it?'

He studied her in silence, enraged by the knowledge that she knew Anwar-ud-Din's intentions as well as he did, but that still she continued her conniving game. You owe your loyalty to my father, not to me, he thought. You never treated me as a wife should treat a husband. Never. He said, carefully, 'You may also wonder about this: my father has now given up his ambitions to gain the Nizam's throne.'

'Was that ever his intention?' she asked softly.

'It was.' There was triumph in his voice now. 'But after the defeat, the reputation of Anwar-ud-Din is as dirt. He and my brother are marshalling the pathetic remnants of their army, using them to assist the English at their last stronghold. They are grovelling at the feet of foreigners! And yet I am sent here to dispose of the filthy ruby in a way that might save my father's dishonoured neck from the Talwar's cut?' He raised his head dangerously and his gaze had the amber fire of a tiger's. 'But of course you know this already. For you are my father's eyes and ears, and you boast that you know his mind better than I do myself.'

The bitterness in his voice was intense. She looked away and kept her eyes averted. 'Both Nasir and Muzaffar want the ruby for its power to destroy the curse on the Talwar stone. Which of them shall have it? And what shall the price be?'

'I have yet to decide the answer to either question.'

'Give it to Muzaffar Jang,' she said levelly, 'and you arm him with the advantage he needs to take Hyderabad. If he can be Nizam he will no longer want to be Nawab of the Carnatic.'

'Enough! How dare you attempt to counsel me!'

She stared at her feet again. 'I apologize.'

'You cannot apologize!' he said, thrusting his face into hers. 'You have no sincerity! You have played with me all these years! You have betrayed me! Your heart is black! Why do you torment me?'

The strike was as fast as a cobra. He grabbed her jaw and forced his mouth on hers. She staggered under the sudden passion of the movement but tried not to turn her head aside in disgust. But her standing still, unresponsive as a wooden doll, only enraged him. Her teeth gritted as he grabbed at her throat with his left hand.

'If you will not love me then you shall fear me!'

His fingers dug into her neck, his thumb pressing hard on the vein. She pulled away, gasping. Without the use of his right hand he was powerless to drive home his attack unless he could throw her down and pin her. With an agile movement she put six paces between them.

'Why, Yasmin? Why do you hate me?'

'I do not hate you! But I can never love you. And I refuse to fear you.'

'You prefer the company of that filthy feringhee to mine! You are my wife!'

'Muhammad, I am myself!'

He sprang at her like a tiger and his left hand slammed into the side of her face, the power of it throwing her bodily to the ground.

'Then go to him! Go to him! And take him!'

Her feet gripped the warm, hard marble of the floor as she got up. The back of her hand was red with her own blood, but her dignity was whole. 'Remember you are your father's ambassador here!' she gasped back at him. 'Please try to conduct yourself accordingly.'

She turned and fled, and all the way along the gloomy corridor that led back to the zenana the terrible broken crying of Muhammad Ali Khan followed her.

Salim the falconer was a small gaunt man in his forties, very light-skinned and with glaucous green eyes. He was a

Circassian by blood, from a land beyond Persia, in the Far North. He had kept Asaf Jah's birds for twenty years.

Hayden Flint took the hawk from him and held it firmly on the rough leather of the glove, gripping the varvel jesses attached to its legs. He was impressed by the powerful grip which the bird's claws exerted and the weight which his hand was obliged to support. Salim grinned at him proudly, a man totally absorbed in his profession and anxious to explain its secrets.

'You like Ruqayya?' he asked.

'He's superb. And quite heavy.'

'Oh, no! He is a she, sahib!'

Hayden Flint raised his eyebrows, taken by the majesty of the bird and the perfection of her plumage. He looked to Yasmin; after more than a week the swelling on her face had gone, but there was still faint bruising on her neck and cheek.

He turned back to Salim. 'How old is she?'

'Two years and three months, sahib. There are many kinds of hunting bird in Hindostan. All are either long-winged birds that kill in the air, which are falcons, or short-winged birds that kill on the ground, which are hawks. My beautiful Ruqayya is a falcon – she kills in the air, sahib.'

His eyes strayed to Yasmin and back to the falconer. 'Can you tell by looking at her which way she kills?'

'Yes, sahib. You can tell because a falcon has a dark eye, whereas a hawk's eye is always yellow.' Salim spread the wing expertly and the bird screeched at him. 'See also the second wing feather is the longest. So this bird is most certainly a falcon.'

'The training of a hunting bird demands infinite patience,' Yasmin told him, adoring the bird. 'A falconer must choose the exact moment at which to take the young eyas from the nest, just as the brown feathers have replaced the down. Earlier, and the eyas will never learn to hunt properly; later and she will revert too easily to wild ways.'

He turned and looked into her eyes, seeing once more the burnished darkness and recognizing that in one of her

216

previous lives Yasmin Begum must surely have been a falcon.

Yasmin's silver anklets tinkled. 'The young bird must be taken straight to the loft and bells put on her jesses, but then she must be given her freedom. Do you see, Mr Flint? She must fly at hack with liberty so she gains strength of wing and confidence in herself. Only then can she be happy and fulfilled and do her duty to her master.'

He nodded, but it was more than understanding. He felt he had taken more from Yasmin's words than she had intended him to take. He had learned to read the parables of her thoughts, and the knowledge warmed him. When were you taken from the nest, my lady? he asked her silently. For as it is with falcons so it is with people. We learn and we grow and we become what we must, and then we stop learning, and from that day we are fixed for good – or for ill.

Salim showed them the hawk's feeding platform, still intense, zealous to convert him to the joys of hawk-rearing. 'The begum is very correct. If the falcon is given this vital freedom and is relied upon to return at sundown to her food she will not fail.'

The hack board had been scarred by generations of talons. Shreds of bloody lamb meat and smears of raw egg attracted a mass of flies.

'As the falcons grow older we give them small birds or rabbits so they may learn to recognize prey. Every day for a month, at dawn and dusk, the food must be presented here. Punctuality is of the essence, sahib, and the falcon must never be suffered to carry away the prey, only to pull at it on the board. It is during this time that she is caught and hooded and the training may begin. A falcon that has twice missed feeding has undoubtedly started killing for herself.'

The hawk seemed unsettled by the sight of the board and began to flap its great wings. He handed it back to Salim who took it to its post.

'You must be very skilled, Salim.'

'It is a long and difficult procedure, sahib, to bring a bird like Ruqayya through her education. But the fine, hot-tempered bird who shows fight and passion at first is the most easily tamed. All the while there must be no disturbance.'

Yasmin looked at the bird with delight. 'A single impatient action,' she said, her voice becoming husky, 'and the hasty falconer undoes the work of weeks. These birds love to be stroked with a feather and whispered to with the utmost tenderness.'

'Indeed?'

'Yes, Mr Hayden Flint. They are brought to obedience by love. And then they will kill on request for their master.'

Like a woman, he thought, but dared not say it.

She moved away, towards the battlemented walls that overlooked the great paved square below. As he walked to join her he wondered about her desire. Nothing else mattered. She had unsettled him that day in the Star Garden. His nerves jangled with each thought of her. And when next they met, days later, amid the roses and perfumed fountains of Asaf Jah's gardens, it had been electric.

He saw the marks on her neck, the bruises she would not speak about. His insistence had angered her. Her anger had outraged him.

'Lady, I'm asking you to tell me. How did it happen?'

'And I am telling you not to concern yourself.'

'I am already concerned.' He almost checked himself, but then went on recklessly. 'Because I suspect it was your husband – why turn away from me like that, Yasmin Begum?' She set her face. 'So, I'm right! It was Muhammad who did this. Of course. No one but a monster with a love of cruelty would want to. No one but a fool would dare claim the right!'

'It was my fault.'

'I'll thrash the devil out of him, so help me. I'll teach him to respect you!'

She sighed, standing still. 'I said the fault was mine.'

He faced her, his voice almost drowned by the rushing of the big central fountain. 'How could it be your fault? What right could he possibly have to do this to you?'

'Every right.' She daggered him with her eyes and walked on faster than before. 'Every right in the world.'

Then she feigned light-heartedness and laughed at his pompous indignation in order to distance him, and he had been deflated, but a little later he said to her, 'Lady, you do not fool me with these antics.'

She stopped again. 'You are a strange man, Mr Flint. A kind man in head and heart. A man of good thoughts and temperate emotions – *allah maloom*, God knows. You are impossibly direct, despite which I still appreciate your intended sympathy. But you madden me intensely! Now, please, the matter is closed!'

'Lady, I am concerned for you.' He placed himself in front of her. 'Unless you forbid it expressly I will avenge you this minute!'

'*Bismillah*! Then I forbid it expressly.'

'In that case I shall protest to Muhammad Ali Khan's ignorant face, in terms so direct he will have no option but to give me good reason to demand satisfaction!'

She huffed at him. 'Oh? You want to duel with him? But that is not of our tradition. If you threaten him he will simply have you killed. And in any case such a match is beyond your own English code.'

'How so?'

'If I understand it correctly, you cannot demand a duel with a man who has lost the use of his sword arm, since you would then be at an intolerable advantage.'

'Lady, that is not an insuperable obstacle. We may negotiate a solution to it. We may fight using pistols!'

'Oh, no, Mr Flint. Not when your fame among this Moghul durbar is as the foremost shootist of the English Company, and when my Muhammad must use his unclean left hand to save his life.'

He had no reply to that, and after a moment he said, 'Yes. You're quite right. Of course.'

She stared into his eyes, then laughed – a genuine laugh this time, wistful. 'It fascinates me: the way you seem to think and feel at the same time. Your thoughts appear always to be tempered with compassion, and your passion is always considered. It is not often so among our women, even less, I think, among our men – or any men. I believe you are an admirably made person.'

'Lady, please!'

'You see? No matter what the circumstance, your mind is always making and making. You are never overwhelmed. You have a very clever knack of balance. On the soul of my mother, you are difficult to deter. But your rational logic should tell you that you cannot make correct conclusions from false beliefs.' She broke off, considering, then she said, 'How, instead, if I tell you everything? Will you promise not to interfere?'

'If it is your wish.'

'It is my wish. But you should promise first.'

He hesitated, but then said, 'I promise.'

'You swear by your God?'

'I swear on my honour.'

He walked with her for longer than an hour. She talked freely, telling him how she had been charged by Anwar-ud-Din with the task of controlling her husband. How it was now up to her, and to him too – if he would consent to be her ally – to use Muhammad and the ruby to shape the future of the Deccan. She won him with her words; astounded him with her revelations. She also confirmed something else in his mind: he knew he would have to have her.

Now, as they stood at the battlement separated by a yard of air that seemed to him at once a thousand miles and nothing at all, the beat of distant drums came to them on the wind. The rhythm grew louder and he heard another sound mingled with it. A dreadful sound. Pitiful. Keening. It unnerved Ruqayya on her perch. Yasmin pulled the corner of her orhni mantle across her shoulder and leaned out to find where it was coming from. From these high walls they could see everything.

They watched a curious crowd gather below, awaiting a procession that seemed to be leading into the outer precincts of the palace complex. The wailing was that of a young woman. As she came into view, they saw that she was distraught with terror. She was led stumbling and crying on a chain by a darogha; a body of a dozen guards in dark green surcoats and black turbans followed. They were led by two young drummers, barefoot and bare to the waist, thrashing their long drums with curved sticks to give warning and a summons. An official came forward and the rhythm stopped suddenly, but the wailing continued.

Yasmin watched, horrified, as a proclamation was read out.

'What is it?' he asked, unable to catch the words himself.

'*Zina*,' she breathed, staring down at the milling crowd.

The word meant nothing to him. '*Zina*? What's that?'

'They have invoked the law of *zina* against her,' she repeated, her voice heartsick. 'It was his word against hers and she is but a woman so her testimony was deemed inferior.'

'Do you mean she's been found guilty of perjury?'

'No, Hayden Flint. Not perjury.'

The young woman's crying intensified. She stood facing the crowd insensibly, her head uncovered, shoulders sagging, arms hanging. The sound that came from her was a howling sob, the same note of supplication a young child makes after breaking its parent's temper. Then a sudden yelp, followed by louder cries, as if the parent had given another slap. But Hayden Flint saw that it was no slap that had made the cries change pitch.

Jagged lumps of rock, some the size of a china teacup, others smaller and fast and venomously thrown, thudded on the ground and struck off the walls. The official who had read the proclamation berated the crowd's ill-discipline.

He stared, in horrified fascination, until a large rock bounced off the girl's head and knocked her to the ground, then he flinched, as if feeling the numbing pain of it himself. As she began to crawl, the shouting crowd encroached on her in a crescent of hatred, rocks scoring hits on her legs and arms and body until they had driven her back against the walls, cornering her like a baited animal.

I must do something, he thought. He shouted at them to stop. '*Roko! Bas! Tumko usko marna nahin chahiye!*' He yelled until he was hoarse, but his shouts were not heard, or if they were they were ignored.

For minutes he remained paralysed as he watched her knocked down time and again. Blood poured from her head now, matting her hair, staining her clothing and spattering the dust. The screaming began again. She fought hysterically to escape through her assailants and was thrust back. She tried to dodge and fend off the rocks with her arms until she could no longer get up. A rock the size of a pineapple cracked her hip and she lay hunched on her side, cradling her head until the crowd came near enough to rain the biggest stones on her, illegally heavy stones, stones so massive they were hard to lift. The mob closed in; there was a flurry of violent movements and she was lost to sight.

When it was over Hayden Flint looked up at Yasmin Begum, shocked. 'It's barbaric!'

'It is the law. The punishment ordained for such cases.' Her voice was low, on the point of breaking.

'Then your law is barbaric! What in God's name can she have done to deserve that?'

She touched his hand, squeezed it gently, her face full of pity. There were tears in her eyes. 'Her crime was adultery, Hayden. The penalty for that is stoning to death.'

TEN

Arkali's hopes fluctuated as she walked with Francis Covington, the Governor of Fort St David. Behind them, afternoon light spilled over walls that were still manned by defenders, though the native population had fled long ago. She felt suddenly astonished at her own fortitude. This was a very long way from home.

Covington was an affable man in his mid-fifties, cadaverous of features but optimistic in outlook. His stubbled cheeks dropped over a weak jawline that swivelled this way and that over a rooster neck tied with a sweat-soaked stock of once white muslin. His battered hat was dusty and his coat cuffs fraying. Everything faded and rotted and wore thin so quickly here, but Covington himself was indomitable.

He lent her his arm and strolled with her towards the native town of Cuddalore. He had been explaining how important it was that the French be kept out of the whole settlement as well as Fort St David itself.

'It's the wells, you see, lassie. They cannot be allowed to fall into French hands. The underground watercourses communicate with those inside St David. Two or three carcasses thrown down there and we'd all be taken by the cholera inside a week.'

She sighed with frustration. The defence of St David was deadlocked, she knew. French guns had been firing for many days now, and several breaches had been blown in the walls of Cuddalore, but the stout walls of Fort St David were still almost unmarked, and the garrison of one hundred men were well disciplined and of high morale. It was possible, she had thought fervently, that Covington might see her point of view about Hayden, if she were to catch him at the right moment. How wrong she had been.

She had already discussed the situation at length with Covington, seeking a way. Without a fleet in the Bay of Bengal and the troops and big guns that could only be landed by another battle squadron, the French could not get into St David – and the English could not get out.

Robert Clive had been gloomy about their prospects. 'We've no choice,' he said. 'No choice but to sit tight here while the French wait outside Cuddalore and prevent trade.'

He said that Dupleix would be waiting for the Honourable Company to decide to pull out. Without Madras and without trade, Fort St David might seem to be too heavy a burden on the exchequer. Dupleix would probably be hoping the Company would decide to capitulate and evacuate to Calcutta, which is where they should have gone in the first place.

Robert's a stubborn man who wants everything his own way, she thought, disliking the dominating strength of Clive's personality. And in this case he's wrong. Governor Covington has said that an order to evacuate St David could only come from the Council of Members in London, and that was at least a year away. Meanwhile he says he'll never surrender to the French, nor will he withdraw. Hardship or no.

But there will be hardship – the problem of the wells in Cuddalore will see to that. Already food supplied for the two hundred souls in the Governor's care is running dangerously low. I wonder if I shall ever see Hayden again now? I wonder why he wasn't here when I was so sure he would be? I wonder if my other thoughts about him are equally in error?

'What's that you say, lassie?' Covington asked, squinting far away at the treeline.

'I was speaking about the reason I came here.'

'Well, you certainly did a brave thing bringing your young men here,' Covington told her again. He patted her

224

hand in a fatherly way. 'We had need of men, and what good soldiers your boys are proving to be.'

'They're not my boys, Governor Covington,' she said, irritated by his amiable way of not listening to anyone but himself. Despite the lapse of months her disappointment at not finding Hayden here had not diminished and she raised it with the Governor at every opportunity.

'Oh, yes, my dear. Especially young Clive. Do you know his grasp of military tactics is quite astonishing for one who has had no training and no exposure to the great manuals of war. Says he's never read Thucydides or Suetonius or Sallust. But he's quite remarkable with the men. I've recommended him for a commission.'

'Mr Clive wanted to run off to Calcutta like all the rest,' she said, piqued by the praise that was being showered on Clive. The man had not left her alone for a single day in the time they had been here, and his company was becoming irksome. 'Before I myself dissuaded him he was all for going to Calcutta in an old French sloop.'

'Oh, really?' Covington said it with that maddening faintness that told her he did not believe half of what she said.

'It's quite true, Mr Governor. Clive thought Admiral La Bourdonnais would be disposed to give them a ship to complete the journey. I didn't think so. If it hadn't been for me, they'd still be in Madras now, locked in irons like my own dear father.'

'Oh, yes. Charles Savage. Singular man. I've known him these twenty years. Twenty-five, if it comes to that. Faith, the finest whist player I ever saw!'

She stopped walking, cut in on him, knowing there had never been much goodwill between Covington and her father. 'Mr Covington, since there has been no sign of Stratford Flint, and your enquiries seem to be dragging on inordinately, perhaps you could arrange some kind of search party for his son.'

Covington stopped too, sighed, his eyes avoiding her. 'Cannot be done, lassie. No. Wouldn't be practical.'

'But why not?'

He shrugged. 'Not enough men to go swanning around the lease. And there's the French.' He waved a hand vaguely at the northern sky. 'They've still got us hemmed in to landward.'

'It wasn't the lease I wanted you to search. Mr Governor, we brought five men here who all got in. Surely three could get out again. You could allow that. Send one north to Bahur and one inland to Trivadi, both asking questions. The last could go all the way to Arcot itself.'

'No. Cannot be done.' ·

'Why do you keep saying that?'

Covington grew peppery. 'Well . . . in the first place, it's not in my power to issue passports to allow Englishmen to cross the lease boundary. That requires permission from the nawab.'

Her fists balled with frustration. 'But how can you get permission from Arcot if you can't leave the lease because you don't have permission which can only be obtained at Arcot? Oh! It doesn't make sense! It's a nonsense!'

'That's the rule.'

Her temper broke. 'But we're at war! You can't treat the normal rules as sacred under these circumstances. The French are breaking the nawab's rules by marching whole regiments over his soil! They've attacked and driven off Anwar-ud-Din's army! They're firing guns at us from our own lease. For pity's sake, wake up!'

'I'm afraid I can't help you, my dear, because in the second place –'

'You're just being deliberately obstructive!'

Covington's face clouded. 'Because, in the second place, it's too dangerous. I cannot order a man to walk to Arcot – it's a hundred miles away and across some terrible terrain.'

'It's no longer than the journey from Madras. The terrain is no different to that I crossed to come here, and I, a mere woman! Please, Mr Covington, I beg you. Order Mr Clive to go.'

'Really, my dear, I assure you. It cannot be done.'

She gave him a freezing stare. 'I feel sure you would comply if Stratford Flint was making the request.'

He shrugged, and she fell silent, thinking angrily of Hayden and why she had wanted to come to Fort St David in the first place. *I won't give up. I won't! Covington's words are full of guile, his friendliness hollow. The journey overland was arduous, yes, and full of natural hazards, certainly, but we completed it. I'm sure that Clive could make his way to Arcot. I don't like him here, his presence bothers me. If only Covington can be made to order it.*

There was the sudden crack of a small cannon. A signal from the Water Gate, and John Seddon, one of the Governor's young writers, a boy of fourteen, was running towards them. Covington's narrow face looked up at the interruption. 'What the devil –?'

'A sail! A sail, Mr Covington, sir!'

'Which way?'

'To the northward.'

He pursed his lips. 'By the Lord, she'd better not be French.'

'Is that likely?' Arkali asked.

'Well, lassie. Pondicherry's to the north.'

'And so's Madras,' Seddon said breathlessly. 'But then, so's Calcutta.'

'Aye, I'd've expected the French to come from the south. That's where La Bourdonnais went. When he returns, or when any new squadron enters the Bay of Bengal, it's bound to come from the south.'

Covington sent for his glass and within minutes his servant brought it. He peered at the vessel, then Arkali asked to be allowed to look through the telescope herself.

'You have no need to worry,' she told him with cold anger. 'She's an English country trader.'

'She looks like an Indiaman to me,' he said, unconvinced. 'Y'see, lassie, all ships in the Bay of Bengal live by trying to appear to be something they're not. Many Indiamen are built in Hindostan – at Surat and elsewhere. Country traders try to make their ships look like Indiamen to avoid pirates, and Indiamen are patterned after men-of-war for the same reason.' He stared again at the blue image in the glass. 'Even the Royal Navy's ships are often French-built, captured as prizes, y'see?'

Arkali's anger simmered. It was not anger at Covington and his patronizing attitude, but at what was to come. She knew that what she had to tell them should make everyone in Fort St David jump for joy – everyone but herself.

'I have learned enough about my father's trade to understand that,' she said cuttingly. 'But I know that vessel is the *Chance*. Stratford Flint's ship.'

'Lassie, you cannot possibly tell that from this distance. And a lady cannot be expected to –'

'Sir! Whilst at Madras I spent many hours watching that very ship through a telescope far better made than yours! I know what she is!'

'Lassie, please don't agitate yourself.'

'Then don't treat me as if I were a child, Mr Covington! And please have the goodness not to call me "lassie" again! You cannot imagine how irritating it is.'

An hour later, the ship had secured her moorings and the first boat was crashing over the surf, a huge, dominating figure in the prow.

'By God, Covington, ye're a stout feller,' Flint said, jumping down knee deep into the surging water and striding up to grip the Governor's hand. 'And I've come with powder and provisions to help yer fight, and grand news from Calcutta!'

Arkali pushed forward, seawater soaking her dress. 'You, sir, are an honest man!'

'Ah, now what's this? But ye're a goodly sight to greet a man, Arkali Savage. So ye came to St David after all, did ye?'

'Yes, sir, an honest man. As honest a man as any that are in the deck when the kings are out. That is to say, a knave, sir!'

'That's an accusation!'

'Yes. Because Hayden's not here!'

He stood back on his heels as the sea sucked the sand out from under him. 'Is he not?'

'No! He never was. And you knew it! You lied to me!'

'Steady now, lass.'

'You lied to me! To get your hands on that silver!' She slapped his face and pulled back to strike again, but he caught her arm.

'Don't ye want to hear about yer father?'

One of Flint's men took her around the waist at a nod from him.

'Put me down!'

'Aye, put her down.'

The lascar dumped her in the surf as it surged in. She got to her feet, drenched to the waist. Flint turned to her, smiling. 'Yer father's affairs are proceeding in Bengal, and I'm keeping the old firm alive while Charles is stranded in Madras. Ye should be thanking me.'

'You left him there deliberately! To the mercy of the French. You –'

'Ah, now! Ye cannot say that. He put his shirt on La Bourdonnais giving him an old sloop full of teredo worm and with a rag fer a sail, so's he could get hisself and all them weasels of the Madras Council up to Calcutta. That was his mistake, not mine.'

Clive came up beside her protectively, but she was too incensed to register him.

'You double-dealt my father!' she said. 'The reason La Bourdonnais changed his mind about that sloop is because you stole the *Chance*.'

'Stole it back, ye mean. And a good thing too, becos now ye may dine on succulent pork chops and old port tonight; not salted houndfish and hugmatee. If ye'll accept me invitation.'

'Dine with you, you shamming huckster? I'd rather eat ship's biscuits and drink seawater!'

'Ah, well, I'll tell me cooks to oblige ye in whatever ye require.'

Flint's men laughed as he strode away. He cast a glance back at her and saw the humiliation burning in her. By God, but she's growing up all right, he thought. Last time I saw her she was sick in the head, and the time afore that a hoity-toity thing – all giddy and thoughtless. A shame she's yet got a swinging arm on her as limp as seaweed, but she flew at me passing well, and that's summat! Then he wondered in passing whether it was time to tell her what had really happened to Hayden.

Flint went immediately with Covington to the Governor's residence, the St David's Council following like a gaggle of black-coated geese.

They retired to the dining room. Covington ordered good brandy uncorked, then laid out the situation as he saw it: that the French were obliged to attempt Cuddalore in great force at some point. Flint listened in silence and lit up another mellow cheroot, then it was his turn to speak.

'Right, now. Here's the size of it fer ye. There's a small squadron of Royal Navy ships heading towards the bay under Commodore Griffin. He ain't no lily-faced Edward Peyton, so I heard, but he ain't no Curtis Barnett neither. I don't b'lieve his force is big enough to retake Madras, but at least it gives some hope that the French might be kept out of St David indefinitely. If it arrives.'

He sucked on his teeth and went on. 'Now, if La Bourdonnais stays over by his base at Bourbon, and if Dupleix don't get reinforced, and if the Admiralty has sent the right orders, and if Griffin's a bolder man than some at Calcutta gives him credit fer being, then there might just be a chance of taking Pondicherry.'

They delighted at that, but he quelled them. 'That's a lot of ifs. But it's your task to keep St David alive.'

'Rest assured that's our avowed aim, Mr Flint,' Covington said, roused by what he had heard. 'We were not put here to give Company property away gratis to the French. No, sir!'

Later, Covington 'ahemmed' privately, and said something watery about sending a search party out for Hayden.

'My lad? My son, ye say?' Flint arched his eyebrows at the man. 'Why, I have none!'

The Governor stared back blankly. 'Mr Flint, I meant your son, Hayden. I'm told he's not perished as you might have thought, but is inland these several months, lodged with the Moors on some complicated mission of diplomacy designed to rescue us. Do you not know about that?'

'That man? Ah, we share a surname, that's all. I used to have a son, but he betrayed me wickedly, y'see, and he's none of mine now!'

'I'm most sad to hear it.' Covington's narrow face looked suddenly mournful. 'Seems I've had a garbled tale from somebody. So you've disowned the lad? It's a blood tie nevertheless. Can it not be repaired?'

'I'll thank ye t'mind yer own business, Mr Covington,' Flint said dangerously. 'If I set eyes on him again I'll likely cut his gizzard out fer his crimes against me.'

Aye, he's disowned, he thought as Covington tactfully steered his conversation into new waters, but it's true I've changed me mind a fraction on him. There's no doubt he brought that nabob's army down on Madras like he said he would. Now they say he went up to Hyderabad to talk with Asaf Jah hisself! He's surely sticking to his task . . .

Clive saw Commodore Griffin's squadron come down to the coast some days later, just as Stratford Flint had said it would. Five hundred sailors and a hundred and fifty marines were put ashore to reinforce St David and with them came Company commissions for himself and Edmund Maskelyne. Now he had the official sanction to command troops in the Company's pay, and the prospect delighted him.

By the night of the ball the Governor gave to celebrate the reinforcements, Clive had received his dress uniform. It was a handsomely cut thing of red and white and black and gold, though the jacket pulled a little tight under his arms. He noted Arkali on Maskelyne's arm as he arrived at the Governor's residence; her dress was said to be cut down from one of Mrs Hardy's, a Council member's wife and senior matron, and though that was the case, and her jewellery borrowed, Arkali remained unquestionably the most attractive-looking woman present. Her hair was elfed up in plumes of pearls and ribbons, and her pale blue taffeta gown enhanced her coppery hair.

Clive's stomach turned over at the sight of her on Edmund's arm. How dare Maskelyne agree to escort her after what I said to him? he thought as disappointment sickened him. I told him what I wanted, I told him. I'll beat the tar out of him.

A spacious balcony had been set with chairs, a long covered table was loaded with imaginative dishes of local origin, pillaus and kebabs, marinaded chicken legs and succulently dressed fruits. The drink was also of the best: wines of every description, sherbets and a huge silver punch bowl in the shape of a South Sea clam.

Clive eyed the host stiffly. There was Covington himself, with the Commodore and Mr Flint, all trailing dress swords and in their best coats with their collars turned up, manfully ignoring the heat. He saw the way Arkali looked pointedly away as Flint made a little bow to her and kissed her hand.

Clive could not take his eyes off her. With growing jealousy he watched officer after officer from Griffin's fleet present their compliments. She declined everyone's attentions, and stood with Maskelyne who seemed lost and forlorn beside her. Clive willed him to move away so that he could waylay him discreetly and take him into the garden, but Flint sailed in under full canvas and took them both to the punch bowl.

He summoned Clive with a finger. 'Have a bumper o' this, lad. You too, Maskelyne. Ah, but excuse me manners. A cup fer the lady first, isn't it?'

'I don't think so.'

'Nonsense, missee. Ye'll drop in a faint unless ye drink something, and this here's a delicious fruit beverage designed special fer the silly sex.'

'Sir, did I quite hear you correctly?' she asked frostily, holding her brimming glass of ruby liquid so that it dripped clear of her skirts. 'The *silly* sex?'

Flint nudged her escort and winked at his glass. 'Get it down ye, Maskelyne.'

'Sir.'

'What's yer opinion, Clive?'

He sipped and recognized the strength of spirits that underlay the fruity camouflage. 'It's . . . good . . . God!'

'Remember now, it's a recommendation to the ladies that we're after from ye! Did ye hear him say "good"? Ah, what a judge!'

Flint hooked Covington to his side. 'Ye see, like I told ye, Miss Savage and me is quite repaired now. The misunderstanding on the strand was just that. A misunderstanding. She begs yer forgiveness fer being so rude.'

Covington beamed and tossed his head as if disposing of a trifle. His narrow arch of front teeth were bucked, like a horse's. 'Oh, think nothing of it, lassie. We've all been under a good deal of strain here, and none more than yourself.'

Arkali's eyes flashed at Flint, then she forced a momentary smile for Covington, but Flint was not finished.

'Now, Mr Governor, sir. Are ye not the fountainhead of our law here? What say ye give us some of yer legislation this instant? A special ruling t'cover this state of emergency?'

Covington took the bumper of punch that was thrust at him. 'What, sir, did you have in mind?'

Flint made as if to think. 'A law that every lady we capture shall down at least one such glass as a condition of remaining! As a specific against the heat, ye might say.'

'Excellent! My, but this fruit punch is quite the best I've tasted.' He approved another draught of it. 'A capital notion. Yes, indeed.'

'Now, Miss Savage, ye'll not embarrass yer escort by defying the law and the Governor to his face, will ye?'

He fixed her with a beady eye and she drank a sip if only to show Covington that she wanted to undo the embarrassment she had caused him at the landing.

'Well?'

The solemnity of her face was unbroken. 'It's . . . a pleasant enough drink, I'd say, thank you, Mr Flint.'

'Drink up then, missee!'

As Flint badgered Arkali to finish her bumper, with Covington grinning on, Clive took Maskelyne aside. 'What's your game?' he whispered fiercely.

'Clive, I'm sorry. I'd no idea!'

'I told you.'

'She came and asked me. Just like that. What could I do?'

There was pleading in Maskelyne's eyes, but Clive trampled it underfoot. 'You'll retire hurt – one way or another. Through drink or through me. Go and take a bellyache to her, and then away with you. Understand me?'

'But I'll miss the ball.'

'You'll miss your guts more.'

Maskelyne's brow furrowed. 'I don't b'lieve I care for your tone.'

He felt Clive's will focus on him frighteningly. 'Do it, Edmund.'

Maskelyne sighed and folded his arms across his chest. 'If that's what you want. But you should know you're going a rash way, Robert.'

'I am resolved to put my proposal to her tonight.'

'But it's doomed.'

'Why?' Clive's eyes were full of false hopes. 'I'm equal to her, aren't I? A commissioned officer. See that braid? These buttons. I'm of recognized standing now, and I have prospects of enriching myself. Good prospects. My family's origins are better than hers, I'd say. Her father's a bankrupt, insolvent and discredited and a prisoner of the French.'

Maskelyne was shaking his head. 'It's not a question of quality, or rank. Or even of prospects.'

'Then what?'

'I know you, Robert. I know what sort of woman you need, and she's nothing like Arkali Savage. She's a thoroughbred; high-strung and flighty. You need someone like my sister Margaret back in England, a plain drayhorse by comparison, I grant you, but loyal and calm in her mind, the sort that follows through thick and thin, a girl who'll accommodate a compromise, who's good with money and content to have a solid man to father her children.'

'Damn your whining philosophies! I know my own desires, and what sort of woman'll benefit me best!'

'I'm trying to help.'

'You'll get no thanks from me for doing that!'

'She wants nothing of you, Robert.' Maskelyne pursed his lips, unfolded his arms. 'She thinks you a boor.'

Clive watched him walk away, his dandy little dress sword hanging at his side. If this moment was not already determined, he told the retreating back, infuriated, I'd run you through.

He strode back to Arkali and took the empty glass from her hand. She was momentarily so shocked that she allowed him to steer her away from Flint and Covington with a brusque, 'Your pardon, sirs.'

'What? Do you propose that we dance?' she asked dubiously, then when she got no direct answer, 'Where is Edmund gone to?'

They approached the big window doors. 'Please, Miss Savage – Arkali – step out with me into the garden. I have something exceeding important to tell you.'

As he steered her across the lawn a bulbul flitted from the branches of a tree, startling her. Oh, perhaps Clive has heard something about Hayden from one of Flint's crew, she thought. Something Flint would disdain to tell me. Her hopes rose as he faced her, a strange light in his eyes, waiting, as if calming himself. Then he handed her down on to the rustic bench beneath the tree and sat down beside her, his earnestness unnerving her.

'Do you know what sort of tree this is?' he asked at last.

She looked up and saw the tracery of branches against a starry sky. 'I confess I do not.'

'This is what the natives call the champaka – what we call the pagoda tree,' he said. 'Smell the sweetness it gives to the air. Here. For your hair.'

He reached up suddenly into the leathery branches with their dense foliage of pointed, glossy leaves that shimmered at his touch, and plucked one of the blossoms. It was creamy yellow and resembled a saffron flower.

She took it from him. The music from the house was distant. 'Why, thank you, Robert. That was a kind thought.'

'Have you heard the phrase, "to shake the pagoda tree"?' he asked as if it were a matter of life or death to him. 'It means to brave the hardships of this land and to seek its unimaginable wealth. To get rich. We have come here, all of us, to Hindostan to do that, have we not?'

'I believe a pagoda is a local gold coin?' she asked lightly. 'Of seven shillings' value?'

'Yes.'

'Then I suppose I see the pun.'

'Now I am commissioned, my prospects are excellent. Soon I shall be empowered to trade. And when this war is over I shall make a good deal of money in Calcutta.'

'You will shake a pagoda or two into your own pocket, I have no doubt.'

'But that's just it! These flowers are not only golden coins!' His sudden and intense agitation shocked her. 'They are tokens of that other commodity a man must have to make his contentment complete. The champaka is the pagoda tree to us, but to the Gentoo it is much more. It is a tree sacred to love. It is far too holy to be cut down – images of the Buddha are carved from its branches – and all because it is Kama Deva's flower, the Cupid of the Gentoo. Do you not smell in its perfume a sweet narcotic? Can you not imagine their god of love blessing you? In its sacred embrace, Arkali, I can tell you: I want you to marry me.'

She stared back at him, dumbfounded.

'Say "yes" to me, Arkali. Then I would be rich. Be my wife.'

She got to her feet, but he rose and caught her.

'You must see that I'm right. It's your destiny. As I've always told you. Don't you see?'

'Let me go! I'm promised.'

'Hayden Flint's dead!' he blurted out.

It was said more in exasperation than anger, but his face set hard and that checked her.

'What?'

He had spoken hotly, impetuously, and nothing now would undo what he had said. More words came tumbling out. 'He's dead. Of course he's dead. It goes against all reason for him not to be. He was with the army of Anwar-ud-Din. He rode with Muhammad Ali Khan in the battle at St Thomas's Mount. It was a massacre. A bloodbath. They rode straight into French artillery.'

She stood gaping at him as if he was a ghost. 'How do you know this? It's from Stratford Flint, isn't it? Another lie from his scheming brain?'

'No! It's not from Flint. It's from my own native spies among the men,' he said. 'I pay them to tell me things. The French slaughtered hundreds that day. It's inconceivable he survived.'

She shook her head in disbelief. How could anyone who knew how much Hayden meant to me have kept so vital a piece of information back? 'You knew all along! You've known for weeks!'

'No.'

'Yes! You knew even before we left Madras to come here. And yet you thought you would let me live in hope until the moment was right for you to make your own sordid suggestions. I see it all now. I see what you had in mind that night we met on the Company roofs in Madras!'

'Arkali, no. I swear. I learned just two days ago. Thousands of men ran from the battle in disorder, many returning to their villages in jagirs hereabouts. Please believe me, I've troubled hard to find out what I could about Hayden Flint – for your sake.'

'For your own sake! What if you'd heard to the contrary? Would you have told me then?'

He was affronted. 'I've told you exactly what I myself have heard. The word was of an Angrezi shot out of the howdah of Muhammad Ali's war elephant. Who else could it have been?'

'You say you knew all this two days ago?'

'I couldn't tell you before, what with the ball coming, and all. I wouldn't have told you tonight even, 'cept that . . .'

'Except that your pathetic proposal of marriage went so wrong.' She looked at him directly, her anger cold now, but her face still bloodless from the shock of his words.

'Arkali . . .'

She addressed him in flat tones of detachment. 'And when I would have nothing of it, you lost your temper and found spite enough to invent a vicious tale. Well, I don't believe you, Robert Clive. I think you are deliberately lying to me in a forlorn hope that I shall change my mind over you.'

'Why do you cling to him?' he demanded. 'I can't understand it! He was a thief and a ship-jumper, disowned by his own father. A notorious coward of no account. I saved you from a terrible fate. I have shown you that I am no coward and my prospects are increasing daily. Can't you forget him and marry me? You owe me some consideration.'

'I have considered long enough, Robert Clive. Yes, you saved my honour and perhaps also my life, and for that I have thanked you.' She took several paces from him. 'But I would not marry you if you were the last white man in Hindostan.'

She turned away, leaving him in hell. He watched her silhouette recross the lawn and ascend the three shallow steps to the house, trailing a long shadow. The suffocatingly sweet smell of flowers sickened him as he caged his head in his hands, and the rage inside began to burn white-hot.

The walls of Fort St David stood darkly haunted by the moonless night as thin mists rolled in across the maidan. That flat space surrounding the fortifications, on which no houses stood or trees grew, had been extended so that nothing except the shallow, dry-bedded nullah afforded cover for a besieging army.

Edmund Maskelyne nipped at his flask and felt the spirit warm his throat fiercely as it went down. Now he stood ready to inspect his men on sentry-go. Since the night of the Governor's ball, the French had been moving troops and guns down from Pondicherry and great vigilance had been necessary, especially on nights of the new moon such as tonight, when it was very dark. Never, he thought uneasily, had the atmosphere inside the fort been so tense.

On such a night it was possible for the imagination to run riot. The situation had worsened. A huge French army was gathering, unseen, just over the horizon. For all the officers there was the sense that titanic forces were moulding events beyond the control of mortal men, the fear that dealings in the Carnatic were moving unstoppably to a bloody and final crisis.

What's making my back prickle so? he wondered. He took out the flask once again and took another nip of brandy. Perhaps it's the sudden way the Major pulled the defences out of Cuddalore this afternoon. What can be in his mind? There's no doubt something important is about to happen. Perhaps Clive knows. But if he does, would he tell me?'

He straightened his hat and considered the sequence of events.

Some months ago, an experienced ex-King's soldier, Major Stringer Lawrence, had arrived, originally sent out to Madras by the Company directors in London. He had landed at St David, and within hours had announced himself, assumed command of the Company's forces and begun furiously to take the defences in hand, organizing the fort's rabble into a small army of seven companies with a draconian military code to punish indiscipline.

Then some weeks ago, Stratford Flint had disappeared again, taking the *Chance* away to Calcutta and leaving dire warnings that a big French squadron was imminent on the coast. Griffin had taken note and put to sea, unwilling to be surprised in the anchorage. The French ships had showed sail the next day but they had pushed on northwards to

Pondicherry or Madras, no doubt to land Dupleix his looked-for reinforcements.

Now, some days ago, news had arrived that yet another Royal Navy squadron was on its way from St Helen's, a fleet of six ships-of-the-line and five frigates, carrying 2,000 soldiers. It was thought to be commanded by no less a man than Admiral Edward Boscawen, Rear-Admiral of the Blue. I heard that Brave Boscawen had been laid low by a musket ball in the shoulder in an action off Cape Finisterre, Maskelyne reflected, but apparently not. If these new rumours are true, and Boscawen is coming here with so substantial a force, then the French would do well to be in possession of St David by the time he arrives.

Maskelyne felt a hot turbulence in his belly as he looked out over the maidan. Damn the differences I've had with Clive, he thought. I'm still rattled by that offhand remark he made half an hour ago, a petty argument over shoes, wasn't it? Why do I let the thought of him bother me? We've had nought but differences since the night of the ball. That was the turning point. That was the moment he ceased being the Robert Clive I used to know. The night I saw something terrible in his eyes.

He looked round sharply. But I'm sure it's not that that's prickling the hairs of my neck, it's something else. I feel as though someone's watching me – it's exactly as if a gun is following me.

His hand strayed again to the pocket that concealed the brandy flask, but this time he checked himself. He thought he heard a faint click, like the breaking of a twig out in the darkness beyond the wall. He controlled his urge to stop or turn around, and took himself along the wall steadily, checking to see that his sepoys were present and ported their arms correctly at his approach. If there was anything down there in that morass of black shadows, his sharp-eyed sepoys surely would have seen it. Major Lawrence had told them all to be especially attentive to orders tonight.

He admonished the third man for having the chin-strap of his cap set too loose. '*Chhati bahir nikalo*,' Maskelyne told him mildly. Keep your chest out. Out came the man's chest and Maskelyne moved on.

The new commander was a stickler for discipline, and it made sense to carry out his wishes to the letter. He knew how to get things done his way, and heaven help the man who obstructed him.

According to Clive, Major Stringer Lawrence was a King's Army veteran who had risen from the ranks to become an officer. At the age of thirty he had been commissioned into Major-General Clayton's regiment, the Fourteenth Foot. He had served in Flanders and Spain and risen to Captain; on the death of Major Knipe, the Company had appointed him to the post of Madras Garrison Commander at two hundred and fifty pounds per annum. Astonishing, Maskelyne thought, that the Company could have gained the services of so dedicated and able a soldier when its efforts in the past had bought it a lamentable line of drunkards and destitutes and the dishonourably discharged.

Clive's got a fellow thinker in Lawrence. He seems determined to give responsibility to anyone who both deserves and desires it, and Clive certainly does that. If only the Major had seen what I saw the night of the ball – perhaps then he might think twice . . . well, talk of the devil!

Maskelyne saw Clive coming in his direction along the battlements fifty yards away. He cast his mind back to the black passion that had engulfed Robert Clive that night; he had flung in from the garden and drunk down several glasses of Stratford Flint's pole-axe punch one after another before stalking away to a side room where he found suitable company for his devilment.

He had begun by taking on a tableful of notorious officers in a few dozen tricks of whist. They had seen him coming, a drunken booby, ripe for the fleecing. Then, after the last rubber, the time had come to settle.

'We'll double the silver on another rubber! Or aren't you sportsmen in the navy?'

The officers resented the remark, but one had tried to

cajole him. 'Come, come, it's a footling amount. Thirteen rupees. Pay up, Comp'ny boy, and let's have done!'

'The amount is not footling to me.'

'Pay up, I say. Squarely. What's a few rattling rupees to a man in a red jacket? We're all officers of one sort or another here.'

'You may be officers,' Clive said pugnaciously, 'but you're far from being gentlemen.'

There was a general loss of humour at that, but Clive spoke into the silence, deliberately raising the tension. He gunned a finger at the officer who was clearly the leader of the group.

'You, sir, I say you cheated me.'

The lieutenant from the *Eltham* took it up, cold as ice. 'You realize that if you do not withdraw that word, there is only one course open to me?'

Clive had lounged back until the challenge came. Then he was obdurate. 'Outside with me. Here and now.'

I had to step in, Maskelyne thought, reliving the moment. If I had not stepped in, I could never have forgiven myself. After all, he was three parts drunk. Even at that point there was something in his eyes that appalled me. A frightening void.

'Robert! For God's sake! Let me settle for you.'

'Keep out of this.'

How could I say it? Of course they had been cheating! It was understood. Their notoriety as dangerous devil-may-care sorts was widely put about, and it was a reputation they delighted in. Clive had taken them on knowing full well their mode of entertainment. He had intentionally upset them. Alone and in the midst of their territory he had as good as slapped their leader's face. And therefore they were obliged to rise to him. It was a matter of form – in a strange way of honour too. A challenge had been inevitable.

Even so, the way these things went was generally a matter of bluster and bravado, coming to nothing in the end. Bluff and bluff back again until they settled in some fudging way. But here Clive was calling the bluff. He was calling

Lieutenant Keene from the *Etham* out – immediately – and no two ways about it, sir!

They had left the Governor's house in orderly fashion and found a quiet spot. No seconds, and no way out. This was dirty play now. A squalid dispute. Hard as iron. A deadly clash of wills. The white-faced lieutenant, hooked like a trout on his inflexible pride and the honour of his service, handling pistols in a dark alley. Clive, strutting, bent on either self-destruction or murder to discharge the pain of passion inside him. Did it matter to him which it was to be? By his expression, not at all. Oh, they had mistakenly picked on a quiet maniac in this Comp'ny lad. What a mistake. I'd never seen eyes like that before. Empty, they were. Unholy.

Maskelyne wiped his forehead, remembering that sickening failure. No doubt it's the memory of it working my pores open, he thought, feeling salt in the corners of his eyes. But it shows you how quickly alcohol and bristling pride can make dead meat of a man. Two hours before and he's fluttering like a lady's fan over Arkali, and there was I enjoying the Governor's ball and the champagne. Then, within minutes, the evening was turned to dregs. It had come to a duel in a dark street.

He had gone down, knowing he must, for Clive's sake, still looking to conciliate. But there was to be none of that. A brisk business it had been. The plaintiff and the accused had marched apart, then Clive had turned at the appointed place and fired – a bright flash and a hellish bang. But the lieutenant remained upright, unhit. A miracle, really. The wind grazed his chalk-white cheek and suddenly he realized and rocked back on his heels: now the opportunity was his! Free and clear to do with as he liked. A flush rose through his face like red wine. He levelled his pistol with relish and directed it towards Clive's heart. They stood watching like a pack of lunatics, silenced by dread, willing something to happen. But Keene had neglected to fire.

It was an unheard-of breach of etiquette, a Royal Naval lieutenant walking back up to Clive slowly like the bully he was, a petty tyrant versed and schooled in the cruelties of the midshipman's berth.

Keene put the gun to Clive's head. To his left eye to be exact.

'You, sir, said that I cheated.'

Clive stared on in that inhuman way, one eye eclipsed by the blackness of the muzzle as Keene prepared to make him beg.

'Now, Comp'ny boy, you will retract your accusation.'

But Clive stood there still, as if calculating in the steaming heat, a loaded pistol just a light squeeze away from blowing his brains into the street.

'I will not retract.'

'Retract, I say!'

'And I say: fire and be damned. I say you cheated. I say so still. I will never pay you.'

Clive's will locked against the other's. The pistol quivered, steadied . . . then it was put up.

Perhaps Clive had read something in Keene's face, heard his heart thumping with relief and triumph, had decided to gamble again. Or maybe he had resolved to tempt death. Was that it? Whatever his purpose, he had accomplished it with the look from a single terrifying eye.

The lieutenant slumped. The navy fellows milled about anxiously, trying to cover the shame of their man. Then they found a formula: insulting Clive between them.

'He's mad! Stark staring!'

'Yes. Insane. Been out here too long.'

'Not worth being cashiered over!'

'Let's get ourselves away from here, gentlemen. After the gunfire it's no place for any of us.'

There was detectable fear in their voices. They slunk away, a little like curs whose barking into a cave had brought out an unexpectedly large bear – but more like ordinary men who had witnessed something incomprehensible yet powerful, something almost supernatural.

The next day had seen enquiries made Company-style: tentative at first, feeling out the truth of the matter, and threatening monstrous consequences, for the penalties on duelling were severe. Clive was called to account but refused to blame anyone. Finally he told both Covington and Lawrence flatly that his unnamed opponent had granted him life and he therefore owed the fellow his liberty. He would neither associate with him nor testify against him. At a word from Lawrence, Covington agreed to drop it, and Flint placated Commodore Griffin for them with a case of good brandy.

That nobleness of spirit in the enquiry had won Clive the admiration of all the Company's servants at St David, Maskelyne reflected. The men adored his courage, and the straight account of it was good enough currency to bring it to everyone's ears – a hard lily for even them to gild. But the admiration had not helped to heal his heart. There was a worm eating at the very soul of Robert Clive, souring him, embittering him. It took me long enough to realize what it was.

Maskelyne took a last nip of brandy. One for courage. No good saving a good label when it might go down a French throat tomorrow. When Clive was twenty yards away he made a gesture of recognition, his white glove like a dove startled from its roost.

My dear fellow, Maskelyne thought, returning the greeting with a twinge of guilt. I wish we could turn the clock back to the day before Arkali came to the Carnatic. I never imagined until the night of the ball what she had come to mean to you. How idiotic of you to have thought to propose to her. How thoughtless of her to have let you down in the way she did. How naive of me to have explained her true feelings towards you. And now you're in that black pit of the soul, with a broken heart beyond the reach of everyone, and you act as if your life means nothing much at all to you – you chance yourself with death and volunteer for all the most dangerous duties. No wonder the Major thinks so much of you.

Clive stopped in front of the rigid sentry and told the man to stand easy before he spoke to Maskelyne. Astonishingly, he was in a buoyant mood, completely turned about from the blackness that had been in him three hours ago.

'Ah, smell the air! Ain't it like wine? This is the night we've all been waiting for, what? And why not, eh?'

'You seem very certain of that,' Maskelyne said cautiously. 'You've come from the Major?'

'Directly. I just found out marvellous news. The scouts report the presence of French forces preparing to overwhelm both our fort and the native settlement. Eight hundred French and a thousand Indian troops are coming to us. Major Lawrence expects them here very soon. And why not?' He rubbed his gloves together in anticipation.

'It's good to know the French are according well with his schedule,' Maskelyne said flippantly. 'I wonder if they know what is required of them?'

'You should know that Stringer is very capable.'

'Stringer, indeed?' Maskelyne paused, then found himself willing to venture a little more with Clive alight like this. It was a fire very different to the blue flame of alcohol that burned inside some men. 'Well, if "Stringer" is so very capable, why in heaven's name did he choose to unman Cuddalore? Any fool could see we had a reasonable chance of holding the walls for some days at least. And if Boscawen could be here soon – '

'That's why I'm here now.'

Maskelyne was perplexed. 'Why?'

'Orders from Major Lawrence. You're to take your company back into Cuddalore and man the walls.'

'What?' Maskelyne's irritation surfaced. He sighed, white-gloved hands on hips. 'But that's precisely the place from which we withdrew this afternoon.'

'Not precisely. You were manning the southern wall. Now you're to dispose your pieces along the north-west ramparts.'

'Hell's teeth, Robert! It took us three hours to get those guns back inside the fort. I understand that the Major likes us to be kept at tasks for the sake of morale, but shifting stores and guns and men back and forth and back again like this doesn't make any sense!'

'Edmund, it makes perfect sense.'

'I don't see how.'

Clive eyed him with something like pity. 'You don't. And that's why you'll never be a major.'

Maskelyne sighed. 'Whereas you are doubtless capable of explaining it all to me.'

'Easy as light and dark, Edmund.' He waved his hand in the air, the dove winging to the horizon. 'Day and night. And why not? The French have spies watching us. Of course they do. Their army is not more than two hours' march away. Therefore they saw us withdraw from Cuddalore in this afternoon's brilliant sunshine. They saw us fall back on the fort and abandon the much longer perimeter of the native town – a reasonable, though, as you properly say, premature precaution. The French saw us abandon Cuddalore, Edmund. They'll believe the evidence of their own eyes.' A lop-sided smile broke over Clive's mouth. 'They won't as readily believe we've remanned it in pitch blackness.'

'You mean we're going to *ambush* them?' Maskelyne said, taken, despite himself, by the brilliance of the ruse.

'And why not? We'll re-man Cuddalore in absolute silence. In secret and under cover of night. Dupleix's man'll be here come midnight, and we'll shoot him to bits. Why, he's dead already. Then Asaf Jah'll see whose side to come down on.'

'I hope you're right.'

'Yes, I'm right. You'll do me a favour, Maskelyne?' He took off his right glove and lodged his hand inside his coat for an instant before pulling out a kid pouch. Maskelyne had seen it before: it was a runner's pouch, used to contain orders. But instead of orders there was a neat envelope within. It was addressed in thin-looped copperplate script: *Miss Arkali Savage*.

'Supposing I fall in the action and you survive, I expect you'll see yourself clear to passing on these sentiments for me.'

Maskelyne took the envelope reluctantly. In Clive's

mind, clear as sunshine, was the hope, the intention – the certainty! – that tonight would see him demonstrate his courage. And so brilliantly would he show it, and so incontrovertibly, that Arkali Savage would have no choice but to see him in an entirely different light. Beyond that it did not matter if he lived or died.

'What makes you think I'll survive and you won't?'

Clive's characteristic half-grin passed briefly over his face. 'Let us just say that this way fate has to kill two men to prevent me saying what I must say to Miss Savage.'

A faint stirring in his belly prompted Maskelyne to pull out his flask and sip. The fierceness made him shiver.

'What's the matter, Edmund? Somebody walk over your grave?'

Maskelyne passed the flask to Clive who likewise took a swallow.

'I wish you didn't put things quite the way you do, Clive.'

Maskelyne's company stole back into the native town dragging their field guns, the wheels bound with hessian to silence the iron tyres. The other companies did the same, the men picking their way nimbly through the darkness to their loopholes and hidden positions among the narrow byways and tumbledown hovels. Each man carried a good flintlock, a bayonet and thirty rounds of powder. Each found a comfortable hiding place a little way back from the walls in the jumble of mud-brick and chunam and rattan and bamboo and thatch of the shacks.

Clive's optimism burgeoned. He began to calculate again. By listening carefully to the Major's words, he had learned much and he had stored the information away carefully in his mind for later use. Commodore Griffin's arrival had allowed reinforcements from Bengal and Bombay to be landed, but the total at St David was still only 473 Europeans and 371 Topasses – the same kind of untrustworthy Portuguese scum who had failed Madras – and 1,000 native sepoys. On the other hand, Griffin's departure had allowed the French Admiral, Bouvet, to land his troops at Madras and march them to Pondicherry. According to the spies, these troops had marched out of Pondicherry again under a commander called Mainville. They had moved south and inland twenty miles and tracked along the bounds of the English lease until they had come to face the southern part of Cuddalore's defences. Cuddalore's ruinous walls were two miles long.

An even fight, thought Clive. Without a doubt there'll be a French attempt to escalade the southern side of town where the wall is at its lowest and can be most easily climbed. That's what I'd do, and that's why I asked for these positions for my company, why I asked Stringer to swap mine with Maskelyne's. That's where the hottest fighting'll be. That's where I'll cover myself in glory – or a bloody shroud. Either way it'll be an end to this hell.

He settled down in the quiet dark, absorbing the sweltering summer night, giving occasional whispered encouragement to his men. There they waited, united in spirit. At midnight there came the unmistakable sound of a column making its way along the Devicotta road. They appeared with a baggage train, six bodies of foot-soldiers and a head of six mounted officers. A detachment came forward. They disposed themselves round the Devicotta gate, confidently marched up to the walls and loudly erected a sixteen-foot bamboo scaling ladder to enable them to climb in and unbar the big wooden gates to their army. Then they lit firebrands.

Clive put his head down, and his men did likewise. He heard the boots of the French sergeant crunch on the parapet as he jumped over the battlement. A shower of sparks and shadows danced riotously in the orange light. The sound of the Frenchman's breathy voice as he counted his men in was loud in the silence.

The men in the unfamiliar uniforms were vigilant as stoats as they came up over the wall. They spread out a little way along the parapet looking for the steps that led down to the gates. They were men preparing to take over what they presumed to be a deserted town.

Clive saw the whites of the eyes of his own men. He met their gaze, infusing them with confidence, willing them to be still and quiet in these last critical moments.

The heavy bar planks were lifted down and the gates swung back and secured in their niches. Then orders came from the outside and the French column began to march in to corporals' shouted orders.

Oh, how the French come on when there was no resistance, he thought. Jaunty as cockerels! Officers with their noses in the air! A picture of most self-assured superiority.

When two or three hundred men had marched through the gates the head of the column reached the marketplace. A raucous English order was yelled out and men and guns appeared in the vacant window-holes overlooking the street. A tremendous roar blasted the night, flashing fire into the sky, and a wholly unexpected salvo of musketry and grape poured down into the French column, tire after tire of lead scything into the occupation force. The surprise was absolute. As their ranks dissolved, screams and yells escaped the churning stew of men, all control broke down and the French ran hither and thither in panic for the gate.

Clive could hold himself in check no longer. He stepped out from his barricaded doorway, his navy hanger in one hand and his pistol in the other. His men sprang out after him.

I'll show them what it means to be an officer, he told himself, his thoughts clear as ice crystals. I'll lead them and we'll see if they at least love me! The devil that she's not here to see me now.

He raised his sword. 'Arkali!' he shouted, his heart pumping, the battle shout raw in his throat.

Ahead of his men, he ran into the mêlée and threw himself bodily into the murderous fray.

ELEVEN

The Tower of Earthly Delights stood at the eastern
extremity of the Nizam's palace, a wondrous pleasure
pavilion of commanding height and breathtaking views, yet
with a seclusion precious in Hindostan. It was built on three
levels, like the tiers of a wedding cake, but open and made
entirely of sandstone, each platform surrounded by a low
stone fence of pierced slabs, each higher level smaller in
area and artfully balanced on four carved pillars, as slender
and efficient as thighbones. The whole structure was
capped by a Moghul dome sixty feet above the plain, a
spiked hemisphere surmounting a stone apron so perfectly
proportioned that it drew sighs from Yasmin's heart when
she saw it in silhouette against the sunset.

Hot wind rippled the dry muslin hangings. She heard the
muezzin's last call to prayer, the *adhan*, the echoes carrying
from the distant masjid, the sounds reflecting from huge
fortress walls and reverberating, layer upon layer, until it
was dreamlike. '*God is most great. I testify there is no god but
God. I testify that Muhammad is the Messenger of God. Come
to prayer. Come to salvation. God is most great. There is no god
but God . . .*'

She did not respond to the call.

They had climbed the tiers together, he following her up
the narrow stone staircases that rose higher through oblong
apertures in the levels, and from the topmost tower of the
pavilion they watched the clouds rolling towards them, vast
expanses of opaque blackness that filled the sky, making it
darker than the land.

He stared in wonder, awestruck. 'Look at the sky over

there, Yasmin! Isn't that the most wondrous sight?'

'Truly!'

'I wonder what it's like down on the coast.'

'Very bad, I think.'

'Yes. I think so, too. And here, soon, it will be the same.'

'We should go down while the air is still somewhat quiet.'

He seized her arm. 'No. Let us stay. Whatever the danger, I would stay – if you would.'

She hesitated. 'This tower is too delicately built.'

'It is old. Therefore it must have stood through many storms.' He looked at her penetratingly, regret in his eyes. 'But perhaps we should go down.'

She did not move. 'As a child I used to come to a place very like this to seek solitude.' Her voice was husky with piquant memories. 'When there is no one here, such as now, I can imagine I am back in the palaces of Delhi, or on the battlements of the Red Fort, overlooking the bend of the Yamuna River on which stands the Peerless Tomb of Agra.'

'You make it sound a great and mysterious place.'

'It is a monument to a great love, Hayden: the white marble mahal of Mumtaz, wife of Shah Jahan. There can be nothing in the world to compare with it.'

He watched her eyes, met them as she looked up.

'Only once in their lives do people fall in love,' she said. 'Then they must live with love's pain, die with love's pain.'

They were alone in a deserted landscape. Close and seized by the moment. Together. Wordless. They stood very close.

Fine airborne dust gritted the silk cushions and the carpets as they sank down. The return of light sheened brightly against a ghastly sky of impenetrable grey as silent forks of brilliance stabbed from the thunder-heads rising over distant mountains, astonishing and delighting him, but frightening her.

'Listen,' he whispered. 'Do you hear it?'

'*Garaj aur bijli.*' She put her hand to her mouth suddenly. 'What? You're not scared, are you?'

She hid her head in his shoulder. 'The Hindu say it is their gods warring in the sky. Bijli is the weapon of Indra, the thunderbolt; garaj is the bellowing of the dragon Vritra, the Enveloper, as he is defeated.'

'You don't believe that. And you were brave in the sea-storm. Why are you trembling now?'

'With his lightning he splits mountains to make the rivers, and clouds to give us back the sun and the dawn. It is dangerous! The common people say that Indra has great powers. Have you never seen a tree split and burned by his bolts? It is foolish to stay here in this high place, Hayden, insolent and tempting to their gods, and such disrespect will be punished.'

'You do not believe in Indra. You are a Muslim. If that lightning is made by Allah, what can it avail us to run from it? Let's glory in His work.'

Electrical storms are magnificent, he thought, filled with feelings of elation.

'I can prove to you there is nothing to fear. Trust me.'

As she looked up at him a huge flash lit up the east and again she stiffened. The words of the poet Dryden came to him – 'the electrick flash, that from the fond eye darts the melting question . . .'

See how she loves you!

'Quickly now, count the seconds! *Ek, do, teen, char, panch, chhe, sat, ath* – count with me, Yasmin – *nau, das, gyarah* – there now, you hear it!'

Why do you count, Hayden? Is it a talisman? An English charm to protect you?'

'No! To measure the distance. Every five seconds is a mile. The last strike was more than two miles away. It can't harm you.'

Another flash, huge and violet and lingering, and still there was no rain, but the dust swirled on the ground in wild eddies fifty feet below. 'From electric fluid, spirits may be kindled!' he said, full of wonder. 'A marvellous thing! Do you know that in Europe they have machines that can make lightning?'

She listened to him, pressing closer to his chest. 'Your jokes are very strange. I do not like them.'

There was gooseflesh on her arms, he felt it under the diaphanous muslin that covered her. He pressed the short, silky bodice that hugged her ribs, and looked at her.

'It's not a joke. It's the truth. I have heard of a machine that works by friction. It has a crank handle and anyone may turn it to make a crack and a small lightning bolt just this long.' He measured out an inch for her between his finger and thumb.

'That is not thunder and lightning.'

'The great natural philosophers of Europe say it is. I have read that in the Low Countries, in the city of Leyden, they have gone further still.'

She frowned at him. 'How so?'

'A glass bottle, or a jar, if you will, that contains the very shock of lightning when you touch it. The electric substance, which is actually a fluid, may be stored up.'

'The sages of Europe are great indeed if they can do this. But it will avail us nothing. Because we ate of the Tree of Knowledge in the Garden of Eden, we are all damned.'

'Why are you trembling?'

'Hold me, *baba*.'

Her voice was tiny, and he enfolded her with his arms when she flinched at the next cascading crack of thunder. He had never seen her like this, revealed in this unholy, unworldly illumination.

He looked into her eyes once more and saw her head tilt and her lips part, and he leaned forward and then he kissed her. Hungrily, meltingly, and in certainty that it was very wrong, but in certainty also that it was very right.

And the rain began. Big slow drops like the gods' tears falling in splashes on the dusty stone around them, soughing louder off the dome, until suddenly they became a drenching downpour, forcing a haze of spray that wetted the carpet with spangles, wetted the silken cushions, wetted their naked bodies as they moved as one, as he did what he had desired to do from the moment he had first seen her, as she received him as she had ached to receive him from that same moment.

The sun was closing the lotus flowers of Brahma when Muhammad Ali Khan stirred.

He knelt alone on a circle of maze-patterned rugs in the middle of the Water Garden of Quli Qutub Shah in the last dying hour of the day. His eyes were closed as he wrestled with the problem he was daring at last to face, as his mother had told him he must.

He occupied the centre of a square island of white marble built in the middle of a small tank. The island was fenced to knee-height in geometrically pierced slabs of sandstone the colour of sheep's liver. Four little bridges, only ten paces long, connected the island to the edges of the tank. The surface of the waters between reflected the waning blue of the sky, and on them three kinds of lotus flowers floated, their cups of rose-tipped flowers rising on slender stalks above huge leaves. Under those dark green pads, old golden carp – a gift long ago from China – breathed torpidly in the shadows, brooding.

Muhammad's breathing was slow. His semi-naked body was warming in the slanting rays of the late sun, his skin still glistened with the oils of the masseur who had recently completed another session of palpation on his arm. His shoulder was almost healed now, and meditation was focusing his mind once more on the difficult choice he had to make.

He roused himself with a deep inhalation of breath and stirred, breaking the reverie. A few experimental sword cuts and he smiled. There was no pain; the feel of grinding gristle in the joint of his shoulder was almost gone. And the pain in his belly, the heartache he had suffered for so long, that was almost gone too.

Yes, he thought. Now I can make the answer yes.

The day had been unusually languid and deliquescent, a day made for lions. And like a lion he had lain with Khair-un-Nissa and then with her maid, and afterwards he had drowsed and taken a little food. But a cool breeze rose before midday; the atmosphere had subtly changed. His mother had come to him, hissing her undeniable challenge, and her ultimatum.

'What are you going to do about her? If you don't move, I shall be forced to, my son. It's over. Something else is coming. There is no more time!'

Now that something was palpably in the air. There was a smell, a definite quickening of the pulse of the Nizam's palace. The signs were discreet, but definite: messengers trying not to appear urgent; a change of guards to older, more trusted men. And whisperings everywhere.

Last night there had been other portents: in the zenana gate an old woman seer wailing until she was quickly hushed by a chamberlain; four grey-headed crows disputing above the dome of the Mecca Masjid until one fell to the ground; one of the younger princes falling in a fit at prayers, four body-servants bearing him away . . .

He had ridden down to the Char Minar – the four minarets of Muhammad Quli Qutub. And so strong had been his feeling that something was turning that on his way back he had stared long at the sky, seeking for comets.

He stood up, crossed one of the little bridges and went to find his mother.

Nadira was on the screened balcony of a reception room next to the women's quarters of the ambassador's residence. She awaited his return impatiently. A complex network of niches and purdah screens decorated with a dozen or more tiger skins occupied one wall of the long, classically dimensioned room. The opposite wall was fashioned in curtains of white stone, elegantly curved, like nothing she had seen before. Early light flooded it with cool shadows. There was something undefined about the room that bothered her. It was not the Nizam's tiger trophies or their camphor smell, but another scent.

'My son, have you now thought upon it?' she asked him formally.

'Mother, I have.'

'And will you do as I suggest?'

'I will.'

'And you will take me completely into your confidence at last?'

'Yes.'

'With a clear conscience concerning your father, I hope?'

'Yes. You alone shall be my counsellor.'

Her eyes widened. 'Good. Very good. You will not regret that decision.'

She realized suddenly that there was the faintest smell of attar of roses on the air. That was what it was! A fabulously expensive perfume Yasmin sometimes used, a scent that lingered. She had been in the room. When? Overnight some time? Why?

'Yasmin is the heart of your problem.'

'Yes.'

'Then tell me what that wolf-bitch advised.'

'She said I should offer the feringhee's ruby to Muzaffar Jang.'

'On the grounds that he will relinquish his claim to the Carnatic if he succeeds Asaf Jah as Nizam?'

'That's what she said.'

'Oh, she was lying to you again!' She brushed at her lap as if disposing of his first problem with ease. 'Obviously she hoped to sway you against Muzaffar by making him her choice. She believed you would automatically go against her advice, and that you would therefore choose Nasir Jang. Don't you see?'

He looked back at her, bewildered by her intuition. 'How do you know that?'

'Because I know the devious way the she-wolf thinks, and because I know your father's mind. Now, what has the Englishman been doing?'

'Why do you speak of him?'

Patiently, she told him, 'Mr Flint's part in this matter is not insignificant.'

Muhammad's lip curled moodily. 'He is still attempting to persuade Muzaffar to petition the Nizam to move on behalf of the English Company. He has tried to make contact with Nasir Jang too, but so far he has had no response. Nor shall he. What business do princes of the blood have with mongrels?'

Nadira smiled. 'That, as you shall see, is the kernel of the matter. Your father's plan – '

'My father's plan is a counsel of desperation, believed in by fools,' he interrupted.

'No! It is far more than that. It is a beautifully crafted web spun to hold all his possibilities in place until he can move on them one by one.'

'I don't see – '

'In the first place, Anwar knows that you must try your best to secure confirmation of his position. You are forced to do so. We must assume that Asaf Jah has read the reports of indiscipline among the foreigners in the Carnatic. If he should interpret them amiss, and take it into his head to replace Anwar as nawab of the province, then you, Muhammad, will never succeed as you hope. You will become merely the second son of a displaced and disgraced general who once lost a battle against foreigners, and your claims to Arcot will be as worthless as goat droppings. Your father knows that. And he knows that you know that. So, you are forced – no matter what you think of him – to do your best on his behalf.'

Muhammad nodded slowly. 'That's why he entrusted the Eye of Naga to me: to present to Asaf Jah, and to no one else. And that's what I would have done were not Asaf Jah hidden away in the depths of his own palace. His vizier is a weak and frightened man, and everyone else in his government is in the pay of either Nasir or Muzaffar. I cannot get near Asaf Jah – any more than the Englishman can. My patience is at an end.'

Nadira waited for him to finish before resuming her instruction. 'Something more than patience is needed in this, my son. I know you are a proud man, but you must realize that Anwar is only seeking to neutralize you by sending you here on this ultimately futile embassy while his

258

army is in disarray. Your injury was heaven-sent: it permitted you to be conveniently packed away to Hyderabad while the real work is happening on the coast. While you are here, Mahfuz and Abdul Wahab are marshalling their father's forces, ready to pursue and punish the French throughout the Carnatic on behalf of the English. And all this without having to worry about what is happening at Arcot.'

Muhammad's jaw clenched. 'My father is siding with dogs!'

'Thirdly he has sent Yasmin Begum here to choose who shall have the Eye of Naga. She is in the one place where she can accomplish the dual ends of protecting herself from you while still remaining close enough to you to monitor and influence you.'

'I hold the ruby! I, Muhammad Ali Khan! It is locked in a box in my apartments and guarded day and night.'

'You hold it, yes. But Anwar knows he can depend on Yasmin to dispose of it correctly. She must also be under orders to manipulate the Englishman, for there is a more essential business here that has nothing to do with the Eye. She has been told to steer you to the correct choice, but she is also here on a much higher mission.'

He looked at her, astounded. 'What higher mission?'

'Do you not know that Yasmin is gathering intelligence on behalf of your father about French intentions?'

'She is a daughter of Shatan!'

'Praise be to Allah that your eyes have been opened to her at this last possible moment.'

He looked at her without understanding. 'Why do you say that?'

'Do you not feel the breezes that blow through the palace? They portend a great change. Hasn't that ever been the case in high politics? So much waiting, so much raising and dashing of hopes, and when the real crisis comes everyone but the most astute is found unprepared. You must make your choices now in these last hours.'

'Last hours before what?'

She gestured at the lightly swaying stalks of flowers growing outside the balcony. 'Don't you know what that breeze is? It is the breath of Heaven. Power is passing out of the hands of Asaf Jah. His spirit is preparing to leave his body and begin its journey to Paradise. His body is going to the grave, and his name into the histories.'

'What do you want me to do?' he said, unable to see the answer. 'Who should have the Eye? The Nizam's son or his grandson? The uncle or the nephew? Nasir or Muzaffar?'

'You must offer the ruby where it commands the highest price. Consider Muzaffar. For him it is vital. That is why he has been so much more open to you than Nasir who holds himself aloof. Unless Muzaffar gets the Eye he will lose the power struggle here, and Nasir will become Nizam. With the Eye in his control, Muzaffar may just succeed.'

He looked back at her, at a loss to understand how she could know so much.

Nadira smiled. You poor boy, she thought. How you let your prejudices cloud your judgment. How your mind seems blocked to higher understanding. If only you knew how much politics is conducted through the zenana. Few men feel the shocks reverberating through Hyderabad as clearly as we women.

'I chose well when I bought Khair-un-Nissa for you,' she told him. 'She spent her learning years here and she is a rich fount of information. She says that Yasmin really wants you to present Nasir with the ruby because he is the most likely of the two probable heirs to entertain the English cause on the coast. That is so because Muzaffar has been in secret communication with the French.'

'What importance can that have?'

'Just this: by supporting the English against those who destroyed your father's army, Nasir Jang will re-establish Moghul pride of arms. He will desire to help the English crush the arrogant French, and Anwar-ud-Din, whose army is already aiding the English in their struggle, will be too valuable an ally to replace as Nawab of the Carnatic.'

'I told you: my father is siding with dogs! Nasir Jang will

never do that. No bearer of the holy Talwar would descend to involving himself in the petty squabbles of feringhees. And nor should my father.'

'He has no choice. You must allow yourself to under-stand – to fully understand – that everything is changed. Less than a thousand French foot-soldiers broke your father's army of ten thousand horsemen. Since then, our spies tell us that thousands more French and English troops have been brought to the coast in their giant warships to continue their feud. Thousands of Hindu peasants have been seduced from their proper stations in the fields to be trained by both sides in the feringhee ways of fighting. How big an army would the next Nizam of Hyderabad need to throw the English and the French into the sea now?'

She saw that Muhammad was in turmoil. Every fibre of him was repelled by the idea of admitting the truth, but at last he nodded, knowing in his heart that his mother spoke wisely.

'Therefore,' she said softly, 'Nasir Jang needs an ally at Arcot. Moreover he needs one whom the English already know and trust as a friend. Besides that, of course, Nasir wants to be seen as the legitimate heir of Asaf Jah. If he succeeds he will naturally be inclined to endorse Anwar as Nawab of the Carnatic since Anwar was Asaf Jah's choice. Nasir could not very well depose your father, even if he wanted to.'

'Yes.'

'Now, my son, we must talk about Yasmin.'

'I understand.' He said it so tightly his mouth seemed full of bitter bile.

Nadira told him what he must do to solve the problem of his wife, then she sat back, her huge earrings sparkling with Golconda brilliants. The stirred air brought another whiff of attar of roses to her. It was a royal essence, discovered by the legendary Empress Nur Jahan herself. The foremost wife of Jehangir – Seizer of Worlds – had made known her pleasure to bathe daily in water scattered with the petals of a thousand roses; she had noticed the intoxicating oil that cast a rainbow on the waters and ordered it refined and bottled.

'*Ajaib*,' Nadira said, pleased with herself. 'I think statecraft is your father's greatest strength. His policy is artful and it is also sound.'

'So you think Yasmin is right? That I should offer the Eye to Nasir Jang after all?'

She put her hands flat on the table before her. 'On the contrary, I have a much better idea. Khair-un-Nissa says that though Muzaffar's aim is to become Nizam, he is nevertheless terrified of the Talwar. I think he will remember and reward the one who made the ruby his.'

He looked wonderingly at her. 'Why do you want Muzaffar to succeed?'

She said darkly, 'Because I think he is a dirtier fighter than Nasir. I believe that once he has gained the masnad of the Deccan he will set the French and the English at one another, and allow each to rip out the other's throat. Then he will turn on the victor while he is still reeling, and destroy him utterly.'

Muhammad could not contain his zeal. 'Then I will give the Eye to Muzaffar!'

'No, my son. You must not give it to him.' She smiled at him. 'You must sell it to him.'

'Yes!'

'Go now, and tell him this: that you come from your father who since his defeat is raving and insane. Say he is riding about the Carnatic kissing foreigners' bottoms with disgusting servility. Tell Muzaffar that it was you who chose to bring him the ruby. That you see him as the only leader who has the correct attitude towards the feringhee. Say: "Muzaffar Jang, I will give you the key to Hyderabad, if only you will give me my heart's desire. Make me Nawab of the Carnatic in my father's place! You will not regret it." '

'Oh, yes. Yes!'

'Soon we can be gone from here. Soon we can be in Arcot once more, and all your other scores can be settled.'

Muhammad got to his feet, fired with the idea of shedding the burden of the ruby and returning at last to

Arcot. But as he rose, Nadira caught a half-glimpse of something moving on the very fringe of her vision behind the dangerous stripes of a tiger skin.

Her heart missed a beat. Behind the purdah screens the dark shape froze. Muhammad noticed nothing. As his footfalls echoed away, she moved close to the screens, paused deliberately and rang the hand bell for her servants. Whoever was concealed in the niche was trapped; she could not rise and flee without giving away her identity. She had no choice but to sit and hope.

Nadira was careful to show by her actions that she suspected nothing. But she remained standing close to the eavesdropper as Jauhar, her ewer-bearer and chief eunuch here, came to her summons.

'Have Khair-un-Nissa attend me presently.'

'Your command, my lady, is my duty to perform.'

A tremendous feeling of power washed over Nadira, as it always did when she reached a fork in the road of her destiny. Moments later, the courtesan appeared.

'My lady.'

'Ah, Khair-un-Nissa. Come. Sit down here. Will you take coffee? Or perhaps the hookah?'

They exchanged pleasantries, Khair-un-Nissa refusing all that was offered with courteous finesse.

Nadira watched her, smiling. Together we are a force to be reckoned with, you and I, she thought. By going along with my plans, and allowing Muzaffar to have his will in that disgusting Turki way – which must have been a painful experience – you have gained, if not his trust, most certainly his gratitude. Your magical powders have loosened Mr Flint's tongue, and we have discovered what he really wants here. We have also found out just how much Muzaffar is depending on this so-called Eye of Naga. What we have yet to learn from him is where he stands with the French, and precisely what accommodation he intends to reach with them.

She whispered to her servant who moved away silently, then steered the courtesan to the far end of the room and said in a low voice, 'Can you find out what Muzaffar is planning?'

'In what respect, sahiba?'

'In respect of the French, of course.'

'He is guarded in this.'

'You said he showed you the little clock he was given by the French general.'

'Only because he was planning to score a point over our own feringhee.'

'Can we know anything of Muzaffar's mind on the French?'

'He will never willingly tell us.' Khair-un-Nissa's eyes turned to the pierced balcony screens, then flicked back. 'But then a direct approach would be artless.'

Nadira thought carefully. The faint scent of attar of roses came to her again, throwing her mind into sudden panic. Oh, *bismillah*!

'Yasmin.'

'That's right, my lady. Yasmin.' Khair-un-Nissa nodded, unaware of the eavesdropper and the double play in Nadira's mind. She looked quizzically at her contract-holder and asked, 'My lady? Are you all right?'

'Yes. Yes, quite all right.' She rang the hand bell to summon Jauhar.

Khair-un-Nissa continued. 'It has to be assumed that Yasmin Begum's lines of communication with the Carnatic are good, and that Muzaffar's messengers are probably being tracked, maybe even intercepted . . .'

Nadira stayed her with a raised hand. 'Are you sure you will not take coffee, my dear?'

'Thank you again, sahiba. But no.'

Where's Jauhar? Nadira thought, almost frantic. I can't very well confront Yasmin and berate her for eaves-dropping. She will easily be able to face me down after all I've revealed. It's too difficult to feed her false information now, and nothing I could say would recover what I've already said. What can I do?

Suddenly her mind became very still. There was only one solution now.

When Jauhar reappeared she told him to bring the room guard before her. He came, his eyes fearful and averted, his long jezail musket held tight across his chest.

'The tigers in this room bring many memories back to me.' She turned to Khair-un-Nissa and moved her towards the door. Well out of earshot. 'My dear, have you ever been on a shikar?' she asked.

'A tiger hunt? No, lady. Never.'

'Let me show you how it's done.' She tossed back her hair and spoke softly to the guard. 'You, soldier. I want you to fire your gun at that skin. Aim to hit the middle of the back. I will have you as a eunuch if you miss.'

Hayden Flint watched Muhammad Ali as he moved across the deserted rooftop, hating him. Long shadows fell across the great flat roof of the embassy now; in some places awnings had been pitched but the areas that had been in the sun had grown hot enough to bake bread. He could still feel the heat seeping up through the soles of his shoes from the stone slabs, and he wondered how Muhammad was able to stand such heat on his bare feet.

Flint had come here to meet Yasmin. They had arranged it two days ago, and since then he had been unable to stop himself wishing the slow moments away. He had waited and waited, since before the appointed hour, but she had not come, and now Muhammad had appeared in her place.

'*Salaam aleikum.*'

He did not expect a greeting from the prince, but returned the formula politely, on guard against Muhammad's double-tongued speech. '*Aleikum salaam*, Highness.'

'That is well,' Muhammad Ali said. 'I think you have learned much about us during your time here. Perhaps you would learn more.'

'Perhaps,' he returned. 'What was it my munshi taught me about your form of government? That the Great Moghul, who is a Muslim, rules all Hindostan from his Imperial cushion in Delhi: the Punjab and Rajputana,

Oudh and Bengal in the North, Orissa and the Circars in the East, and the Deccan here in the South. That land, and the tenure of land, has ever been the basis of your system. Is it really true that the emperor himself owns all of Hindostan personally?'

The other turned proudly, staring out at the mother-of-pearl waters of the Musi River. 'Oh, yes, Mr Flint, certainly. For that is what it means to be a Great Moghul. In Hindostan no one can buy or sell land. Only rights to it are granted, rights to use the land for peasant cultivation, for grazing, for woodcutting – and rights for foreigners to buy: merchants rights to carry out their low business across it.'

'And then the Great Moghul's underlings tax those foreign traders,' Hayden Flint said crisply, also looking away. 'Like sucking parasites and leeches who do nothing for themselves but draw a living off the blood and bone of those who work the fields, or those who make and move merchandise.'

Muhammad Ali's voice remained level. The remark was designed to stab, to curtail the conversation, to make him stomp away, but he did not rise to it. He only indicated the burnt land vaguely.

'The Emperor gave these provinces of his empire into the keeping of his viceroys. Each viceroy hands power down to his nawabs – his deputies. It is they who tax the land, and they are honourable men. My father, as you know, is a nawab. Is not he an honourable man, son of a tea pedlar?'

Alarm bells rang louder in Hayden Flint's head. What was Muhammad's intention? Why couldn't he pick up the duplicitous under-thread to his words? Did he know that Yasmin was due to come here? He must do, of course he must. I'm not scared of you, he thought. I've learned more about you than you could guess.

He brushed back his hair, again deliberately affronting Muhammad with his directness, his own ire rising. 'As I have said before, Your Highness, I think that to be the son of a merchant is a greater thing than to be the scion of a corrupt and failing dynasty. Trade is the most powerful

266

thing in the world. We pedlars know that. We mind our businesses and build up our wealth a penny at a time. But one day we shall buy and sell the likes of you, Muhammad Ali Khan. You may count on that.'

The prince heard him out without reaction. 'I see that to call you the son of a tea pedlar – which is avowedly what you are – prickles you. I wonder why? I wonder what, truly, is your idea of honour?'

'Who do you say is the most honourable?' asked Flint, locking swords with his adversary. 'Muzaffar Jang or Nasir Jang?'

'Both are equal in honour.'

'Well said! One treats with Frenchmen, whom you call dogs, and the other, soon, will treat with me. Equal indeed.'

Muhammad's eyes half-lidded. 'I say both are honourable men.'

'And which is to be Viceroy of the Deccan?'

'Either one would uphold the laws of our Muslim land if he were ruler here. But, as you know, Asaf Jah is Nizam-ul-Mulk.'

Hayden Flint faced the prince squarely now. 'If you had the wit of your father you'd choose to work with me, not against me. Who are you going to offer my ruby to, Muhammad Ali Khan?'

Muhammad stood motionless, then he raised his eyes and presented the palms of his hands in the way an Englishman might shrug. Somewhere in the palace a gun fired and the report sent multicoloured doves scattering from the arched gravestones of the battlements.

'*Inshallah*,' he said. 'Who may say?'

Hayden Flint turned angrily on his heel, but the Prince called him back. 'Why do you leave, Mr Flint? I have sent word to my wife to join us here. She will arrive presently. In the meanwhile, you will take coffee. Hatim!'

Sweet Jesus, he thought. He does know about us. 'No, thank you.'

'But I insist.'

He sat down and they waited for Hatim, the servant, to bring the thick, bitter cup that still sparked in the nerves an hour after the first taste.

'The will of God is a concept with which you have great difficulty, Mr Flint.'

'Our beliefs are quite different.'

'Islam is a faith that, to outsiders, can seem harsh. That's because the rules are built on rock. There are five pillars of wisdom that support us. First we say: "There is one God, Allah, and Muhammad is His prophet." Then there is a prayer, our humility offered five times a day to God. The third pillar is the pilgrimage to Mecca, the Haj. Perhaps now you can understand why we are so sure of ourselves.'

'You are not sure, Muhammad Ali Khan, you are lost. Lost and self-deluded. Like a child.'

Suddenly Yasmin appeared from behind the awnings, sheathed in diaphanous blue muslin. She looked to her husband. It was clear that she had been there some time. Muhammad Ali stared at her as he went on.

'Fasting is also for the faithful, Mr Flint. Abstinence. In Ramzan we suffer without food or drink from sun-up to sundown. We learn the pain of need and the self-discipline of commanding the complaints of our bodies to be silent. This is to honour the Night of Power when the Holy Koran came down to us. We indulge in no form of sex for the duration of the ninth month.'

He felt the brooding power of Muhammad's will, the turmoil inside him and the slashing cut of his words.

Then Yasmin spoke. 'But the fifth pillar of Islam is giving.'

Muhammad seemed to look through her. 'Yes. As she says, Mr Flint. The fifth pillar is giving – the giving of alms to beggars and scavengers.'

She watched as Muhammad turned back to him, but Hayden Flint said nothing in reply. The Englishman's cool blue eyes were unblinking; the dark, burnished eyes of her husband remained expressionless.

'I give you the services of my wife, Mr Flint. Let her

show you what she will. Ask of her whatever you wish to help you understand us better. You have my permission to walk alone with her.'

He turned and walked away, leaving the roof, leaving Yasmin clutching her veil to her cheek, leaving Hayden Flint watching.

After a moment she said, 'You did well not to allow my husband to intimidate you over matters of birth.'

He shook his head as if shedding a perplexing dream. 'How long were you listening?'

'You knew what he meant by "beggars and scavengers". You knew he was insulting your family.'

'I have nothing to feel shame about,' he said openly. 'My ancestors are as good as his – or yours.'

She looked at him another long moment. 'You say that too quickly, Mr Flint, too hot and too sharp. As if you do not truly believe it. My ancestors were Rajput princes. Royalty.'

He made no reply, feeling extraordinarily transparent to her, yet trusting her even so. Her great brown eyes looked at him, but they were depths that were calm and without threat.

'My own family history is a long and complicated tale,' he said at last. 'My father knows his blood back six generations for certain, to a Captain Tavistock, who fought against the Spanish Armada – an invading fleet of foreign ships – a hundred and sixty years ago.'

'Is that what drove your father to the sea? His blood?'

'I believe that was his ambition. The wish to better himself, to see America – and more than a little patronage from a rich man.'

Hayden Flint thought of himself then, and was suddenly overwhelmed by the immensity of odds against his existence. He was the product of such an unlikely combination of circumstances that it was impossible to understand the reason in it. 'Yes,' he mused, 'the patronage of a rich and kind man.'

'Your father is passionate. I think he married for love.'

269

'Of course there's no doubt. Yes, he loved my mother very much.'

'He is a great man. I often see him in you.'

'God forbid!'

'Oh, you should not hate him so much! Be dutiful as your Bible says.'

He pursed his lips and his brows knitted. 'My father believes in trade and ships and commerce and the amassing of a fortune. I don't want any part of those things.'

'That is not what you told my husband,' she said, her eyes sliding up to meet his. 'That trade is the greatest thing in the world? That one day you would buy and sell us? Or perhaps you were merely blustering.'

He sighed, torn by her probing, unsure now what he really did believe. 'I was speaking as a feringhee when I told Muhammad that. To you, I speak only as myself.'

Suddenly she stiffened, hearing the sound of weeping. A young girl was sobbing her name as she staggered across the rooftop towards them. He recognized the youngster as one of Yasmin's personal maids.

'Gilahri!' she said. The young ayah was in a delirium of distress, her face shocked, ravaged by crying and streams of black kohl that made her cheeks hideous. There was blood on her hands, masked at first by the red palm decoration she wore. As she clung to Yasmin, it stained the soft blue muslin.

'What is it?' Yasmin asked hugging her and wiping her face. 'Tell me, little squirrel. Whatever is the matter?'

'It's Hamida! Hamida!' she cried, barely able to speak. 'They've killed her!'

'Show me!'

The two women made for the stairs that led down to the zenana. Hayden Flint began to follow, but Yasmin put up her hand. 'Stay here, Hayden. In this you cannot help.' She rushed away, her slippered feet carrying her deep into the shadow world of the harem.

The sight that met her on the balcony outside her own quarters stabbed her to the heart. The inner court was shafted by light, the air mint-fragrant, cool as stone and laced with the sound of a fountain, but Hamida lay on her charpoy, her kurti red with blood across the right breast. Her eyes were closed and her face was a ghastly grey, and set as if made from wax. At her side Nadira sat regally, watching unmoved as Khair-un-Nissa's shampooer poured a little lemon water from a brass jug into a bowl. She lifted Hamida's head and tried to induce her to sip, while everyone else down to the lowest lady's maid crowded around in a semi-circle and watched. Yasmin burst through them and dashed the bowl to the floor, smashing it. 'Get away from her!'

The shampooer looked up, astonished. 'My lady?'

'Get away from her! All of you!'

They had never seen her show anger before, and they drew back as one. Only Nadira remained where she was. Yasmin whirled on her.

'You!'

'A most regrettable accident, my dear. One of the guards fired his gun, and the fire touched her. It was a terrible mistake.'

'No! This was your work, Nadira Begum. It carries the mark of your despicable scheming. Damn you to hell!'

'Yasmin Begum, you will pay for these slanders! I have two dozen witnesses. Everyone has heard your filthy mouth. When we return to Arcot they will all report how you have slandered a wife of Anwar-ud-Din. The nawab shall know how you have disobeyed and reviled your own mother-in-law, and the court shall order you striped with lashes!'

Yasmin looked round defiantly. These were the women of Nadira Begum's establishment. They would testify just as she told them. Despite the rage she felt, she knew she must do something to protect herself.

'Then let them report this also,' she said, picking up the long-necked brass jug. 'Let them report the depth of their own conviction. Which one of you will drink of this lemon water? Which one? And which among you will lie to

271

Anwar-ud-Din when he asks directly who was offered to drink?'

The women began to melt away into the darkened colonnades, their shame clear.

'Now leave my quarters!' she told Nadira. 'Leave! Or will you refuse to take your leave? Will you prove that you cannot rest until Hamida is dead?'

Nadira retreated and took her retinue away. Yasmin turned to Hamida, and knelt beside her where Gilahri shivered and sobbed. She took Hamida's hand. It was cold and pale. 'Hamida? Can you hear me?'

The ayah's breathing was shallow. She had lost a lot of blood, but she made a supreme effort and her eyes flickered open dully. 'Yasmin Begum,' she whispered. 'I am so sorry to be a burden.'

Hamida's eyes closed again. There was something she had to do. Something important that couldn't wait. Yasmin has been in an unfathomable mood for the last few days, she thought. Yesterday she chastised me for stealing a tiny dab of her perfume. She drifted, fighting the black sleep that would close her eyes for ever. She fought, but still she drifted . . .

She had prayed silently that Nadira Begum had not seen her, would not see her. It had been the barest chance that she went there at all. Just a fortunate piece of *gup* from one of the toothless hags who had lived in the zenana since the early days of twenty and more years ago, when Asaf Jah first came here to declare himself Nizam-ul-Mulk against the wishes of the late Emperor. The gossip was about the clever architects who had built this palace.

'Now it is just a room in an embassy, hung with Asaf Jah's prized tiger skins, but then it was the private audience chamber of Quamar-ud-Din. Ah, dear old Chin Quli Khan.' The crone laughed to herself at the memory of the glorious days when she had been a favourite courtesan of the Nizam-ul-Mulk's. 'He liked to read poetry to us in this room, and many we were. He had a great voice for Persian. There is an alabaster wall shaped in curves that throws the sound clear across the room and through the purdah screen. It magnifies a whisper so you can hear it wonderfully. But you have to sit in certain spots. They are marked by tiger skins.'

Hamida had gone to hear this marvel, had found the very places, a dozen of them, each a niche. Close by each niche, the rosewood screen was hung with a huge tiger skin. She sat down behind one and listened, then realized that unless someone spoke from the table near the balcony there would be no way to try the experiment. I shall stand a bulbul in a cage on the table, or one of Ghulchira's mynah birds, she thought. Or I'll fetch Gilahri and she will read to me. But then Nadira had come, and she wondered at the clarity with which she could hear the tinkle of the begum's jewellery, and the roughness in her breathing. And when Narida rang for Jauhar to admit her visitor, the sound was deafening.

It was one of those secrets worth knowing and keeping. Hamida sat very still. Then Muhammad came and the talking began, and what priceless talk it was! To know Nadira Begum's most private plans was purest gold. This will restore the balance in my mistress's favour, she thought. At last!

'Hamida . . .'

She heard her name and stirred, opening her eyes against the appalling tiredness. There was a vision of Yasmin before her, but the princess's face was misty as if in a dream. Was it then a dream? And why was Yasmin Begum crying tears?

Suddenly Hamida was drifting again, back behind the screen, to the fear she had felt. She had almost gasped as beyond the tiger skin Khair-un-Nissa appeared. The courtesan had paused on the steps of the room, rippling with deceits. Her carriage was as graceful as she was beautiful; her poise as exquisite as her heart was false. She touched her fingertips to her lips and brow. The despicable tigress, Hamida thought, and then she had listened again, praying that she would not be discovered.

Alhumd-ul-Illah God be praised that I have heard what I

have heard. I must tell Yasmin. I must warn her! . . . Then the gunfire had shattered the world . . .

Yasmin felt the hand she held change as the spirit went out of it. Gilahri stared at Hamida's immobile face expectantly, then looked up at Yasmin, swallowed and looked back. It seemed to Yasmin that the young one would keep vigil for Hamida's next breath all night unless she signalled an end. She put out her hands to Gilahri who refused for a moment but then flew to her mistress to have her grief cradled away.

'So, feringhee, tell us: how did you come by it?'

Nasir Jang watched him gravely as he set down his cup. He was a slim, neatly bearded man, son of the great Asaf Jah – in his forties, Hayden Flint judged. His bearing was regal, aristocratic and heavily mannered. He had officiated as deputy for the Nizam for many years, and had assumed the full mantle of responsibility during Asaf Jah's long illness – all responsibilities but one: until the Nizam died, he could not formally become bearer of the Talwar. Strangely, he wore a silver key round his neck, suspended on a silver chain.

Hayden Flint felt the sweat seethe at his temples. He could hear his father's tough voice telling him to get hold of himself. 'There's no such thing as an "equal" to a Moghul, son. They're conquerors. You know what that means? It means you're not one of them, so you're either their superior, or you're dirt beneath their feet. They'll take one look at you and make up their minds for ever. Never let them take you for dirt, son. Never.'

He regarded his adversary's coterie with equal care, observing that they would not look at the box in which the Eye of Naga lay. They knew what was inside and what was its import, these ministers and lackeys and nobles of the blood, but still none would admit so much before their master.

'They say the English like to talk in specific terms,' Nasir Jang said, as if encouraging a shy youth. 'Please, speak therefore in specifics. Tell us every detail.'

'My own father set sail for Hindostan from the Isle of Serendip with the Eye the principal item of his cargo. I myself brought it ashore when it was threatened by the French.'

'Threatened?' Nasir looked to his advisers as if he had uncovered a significant point. 'How may a stone be safe or unsafe? Perhaps you mean "ownership" – that its ownership was threatened by the French?'

'Quite so, Highness.'

'Yes, we can see that it would be unthinkable for the French to have taken it – would it not?' He looked up again at his grinning coterie and back. 'And you brought it to Anwar-ud-Din for what purpose?'

Hayden Flint feigned surprise. 'Can it be that you are as yet unaware of the singular nature of the Eye, Highness?'

Nasir Jang inclined his head and waved his hand dismissively. 'We have heard *gup* of a ruby supposed by some to possess certain powers.'

Hayden Flint pursed his lips, remembering the seller of balabands who had haggled with Anwar-ud-Din so artfully. He knew he must sell the Eye by not selling the Eye. But how? How to begin? Perhaps by selling the Eye's past. He swallowed and looked up, praying he was ready to reveal the myth he had so recently created.

'Such power it possesses, Highness, some may say is no great thing today, when so few believe in the power of magic, but once it was the terror of nations. It was discovered many years before the Buddha's birth in the hills of the Land of Mogok, a place in the distant east, somewhere beyond Ava and beyond Pegu. At that time it was a diamond, just as your Mountain of Light is now a diamond, pure white and brilliant, but it was charged with evil. He paused, looking round Nasir Jang's advisers challengingly. 'The king who first owned it wore it on a great pendant round his neck, but though this king was beneficent and good, the evil contained within the diamond was stronger than he. It drained his goodness and soon the king became barbarous and evil.' He kept his eyes on

275

Nasir's face and dropped his voice, desperately hoping that his inflection and gestures were convincing enough to hold the heir's interest. 'This king would cut off the heads of newborn babies with his sword – like so! – and eat their brains when they were still warm as an aphrodisiac. He would cause those who displeased him to be trampled by elephants. He would make his women lie with trained animals. And he indulged in other crimes too horrible for me to relate.'

Nasir Jang frowned. 'This aphrodisiac . . . And you say he had criminals trampled by elephants?'

'Yes, Highness. Oh, this king became a very demon.'

'Trampled by elephants?'

'Whenever possible. Remember that he was the very basest, most uncivilized king there ever was.'

'And what was the name of this king?'

'His name? King . . . Massachusetts, Highness.'

Nasir Jang considered, then grunted, signalling him to go on.

'As his evil deeds mounted, his country fell into despair, and it was noticed that the gem hanging about his neck began to cloud with blood, and the name of it was in the Mogok tongue, "Connecticut", which is to say, the Eye of Naga, or in our English manner of speech, "Snake's-eye".'

Nasir stirred. 'You are a foreigner, and perhaps that is why the moral of your tale is unclear to us. It seems to our mind that the crimes of this king have paid him hand-somely, for by his evil he has transmuted a diamond into a ruby which is worth much more. Can this be?'

'Ah, but this is a history, not a legend,' Hayden Flint said, smiling to cover his anxiety. 'A history of the olden days, when the forces of magic were much stronger in the world, and my history is not yet finished, Highness. Not by a long way. Because, you see, it happened that one day the King of Mogok was deposed by his people who could no longer endure his excesses. He was murdered in his own palace by priests. He died clutching the gem, thus, to his breast. And it is said that the priest who cut it out of the dead king's hand devised a plan to prevent such a monstrous power from ever again falling into the hands of a tyrant. He laid a spell on it that henceforth anyone who owned the jewel would die. And since no one would dare to claim it, it hung in the marketplace, a fabulous wealth, yet untouched on its chain of gold for seventy generations.'

He saw Nasir Jang's ministers look to one another at that, and realized his invention was growing beyond his control, and perhaps straying uncomfortably near to the history of the Koh-i-Noor itself. How close to the wind can I afford to sail? he wondered. Perhaps it's no bad thing that the point is driven home with force in terms they can understand directly. But I can't afford a mistake now.

'We see,' Nasir Jang said darkly, stroking his moustache, 'that it is your intention to insult us.'

Hayden Flint's heart fell to his boots. 'I beg your pardon, Highness?'

'You say that this king practised trampling by elephants upon his criminals. You say this is a mark of barbarity. Yet it is a punishment prescribed by our own laws. Therefore you are offering a deliberate insult to the Nizam's court, are you not?'

He damned himself for overelaborating when there was no need, then saw the way out. 'I apologize, Highness, for not making myself clear. It was not, in fact, criminals this king committed to trampling, merely those who displeased him in trivial ways – servants who perhaps stood too close to him, certain mild and obliging wazirs who failed to keep up with the caprices of his policy, members of his own family who annoyed him at the breaking of bread. But that is not the point, Highness – '

'Do you understand the nature of my power, Englishman?'

'Yes, Highness. I believe I do.'

'Then take care.' The prince motioned for the history of the Eye of Naga to continue.

'So, Highness, it came to pass that the new King of Mogok was a good man, and a son who was his heart's desire was born to him after many years, and this son was so precious to him that he kept him confined to the palace and would not allow him to go beyond its walls. But one night, when the boy was eighteen, he climbed the walls to satisfy his curiosity and went wandering in the guise of a beggar until he came to the marketplace.'

'And there he found the ruby!'

'Yes, Highness. And this innocent son of a virtuous king took the Eye home when he returned to the palace in secret with the coming of the first rays of dawn.' Hayden Flint shook his head regretfully. 'And there, in his bed, he dissolved in a pool of blood before the sun was fully up.'

There was a muttering among the ministers of Hyderabad, but then Nasir Jang leaned forward, hushing them. He asked, 'And then what happened?'

Hayden Flint shrugged, sadness still in his voice. 'So stricken with grief was the king that he searched far and wide until he found a certain sect of monks who might destroy the power of the accursed jewel. He gave the Eye into the keeping of these monks, they of the shaven heads and the robes of saffron yellow. Mendicants they were, men not of this world, men who relied upon the charity of others to fill their bellies each day, men who had renounced all property.

'These monks were charged with the task of creating an instrument of good from the jewel. It was to be a weapon against evil, a defence. But that, they said, was a difficult and lengthy task. Nevertheless, the ruby was taken to their heathen temple and built into the forehead of their idol, Naga, as a third eye – which is, you see, how the stone first took its name – for they said it had caused so much wickedness that it was henceforth only to look upon the devout and witness their devotions. And that when the name of God had been spoken before it ten thousand times ten thousand times, then . . .'

'Then?'

'Then it would be pure and so filled with power that it would be able to undo the curses that might be laid by any other evil gem that came into the Kingdom of Mogok, thus rendering it innocuous.'

'*Bas!*' Enough!

Nasir Jang clapped his hands in dismissal. His ministers rocked forward on their haunches and laid the weight of their bodies on their feet, standing like worshippers rising from prayer. Then they made formal obeisance and backed away to the far end of the audience chamber. Their master motioned for Hayden Flint to stay.

When they were alone, Nasir Jang put his finger to his lips and said, 'Do you really understand the nature of our power, Mr Flint? I wonder.' He flicked a hand towards his ministers. 'They are our brother's vassals, and dangerous men – but see how they obey us? Not one of them would cross the courtyard to save us if we did not have power over him. Not one of them would hesitate to kill us if he thought it would advance him to do so. And yet they follow us like sheep.'

Hayden Flint said nothing, and Nasir Jang sighed wearily. Then his voice hardened. 'Now, tell us: how did you really come by the Eye?'

'It was as I said, Highness. That is the story told to my father by a Dutchman, then my father told it to me.'

'Allow us to congratulate you. It was . . . amusing, and pleasantly told, and what more can we ask of a tale? However, all talk is mere words, and words are as wind over the desert. Do you not agree?'

'No, Highness. Words are tools. And words are weapons. They may shape the world as builders do, or as armies do, if you will let them.'

'In Hyderabad we are most sophisticated. We cannot afford the luxury of credulous belief, no matter what our yearnings for the glorious days of the past. Events are moving fast – we must soon address ourselves to matters of state.' He coughed delicately against his crooked, be-jewelled index finger. 'Was it not your intention to offer the Eye to our servant, Anwar-ud-Din, that he might over-throw our brother?'

'It was offered to Anwar-ud-Din only that he could offer it to you.'

'Through his son, no? We will tell you freely: we had expected his son Muhammad to approach us with this stone.'

'It is true that Muhammad Ali Khan was charged with the task of bringing the Eye to bear as a lever. He was to bargain it against the masnad of Arcot: Hyderabad for the price of his father's nawabship of Arcot.'

'Then why did you steal the Eye back?'

'Because it was never Muhammad Ali Khan's intention to offer it to you. I, alone, could ensure that – '

Nasir Jang snorted. 'So. Then it was you who sent me the silver key?'

He was utterly perplexed. 'Silver key, highness?'

'Then it was not you who sent it?' Now Nasir Jang sounded mystified. He lifted the silver key from his neck. 'This key.'

Hayden Flint stared. Damnation, he thought savagely, it's obviously the key to the box. How could I have been so stupid? The box is locked. I never considered the key, or where it was. Yasmin must have sent it to Nasir Jang anonymously. A creeping suspicion overcame him. But why didn't she mention it? Certainly there was little time. We met only fleetingly when she gave me the box, and implored me to seek an immediate audience with Nasir Jang. Even so, could she have forgotten something so important?

'Please, Mr Flint, do me the courtesy of not taking me for a fool in my own citadel!'

'My lord,' Hayden Flint said, meeting the other's eye with difficulty. 'I know you are no fool. The key was missing. I am pleased it has come to you, though by what agency I cannot say. What I do know is that you will soon rule a crore of subjects who believe what they believe about the Talwar. As for myself, I would prefer your rule in Hyderabad to any pretender's – for my own reasons. My intent in bringing this gift to you will soon be clear enough.'

He felt the tension of the moment crystallizing. Be careful! he thought. This man certainly believes in the Talwar as the symbol of power, but there's more in his mind than that. Look behind his eyes! Look deep, as your father looks deep, right into the soul of a man. Is Nasir Jang convinced of the Koh-i-Noor's curse like the rest of them? Is his coolness genuine? Is he really worried? Is he praying to Allah that the Eye is all I say it is? Or is he trying you? Testing your own belief in the power of magic? His eyes give him away – look at that almost imperceptible tremor in his hand! You must believe, Hayden Flint. Believe in the power of the Eye as you've never believed before. Show him you think that stone's worth half the world.

'What my father's subjects believe is of no concern to me.'

'On the contrary. You must have the Talwar to show them you are Nizam. No one in Hyderabad, or in all the world, can understand how the great Asah Jah – O Tremble at His Name – has avoided falling under the maleficent spell of the Mountain of Light. No one has explained it. Nor can you.'

Nasir Jang's words were razor-edged. 'You presume to speak to us that way? You, who says he has his own reasons to want our rule in the Deccan? Englishman, you have no idea how dangerous is the game you play.'

'Perhaps so. But it is the hard reality of the world that interests me. My father is a merchant; what he cannot count he may not deal with. These specifics are clear enough to me. And I dare say that you yourself will not move without knowing precisely how the stars travel in their courses.'

'Explain yourself.'

He drew breath, his heart beating like a tabla, and launched into the biggest gamble of his life. 'I think you will not move to announce the death of your father, Asaf Jah, who is most certainly dead, and has been these past four-and-twenty hours – you will not do that until you can be certain Prince Muzaffar Jang's faction has lost all hope of wresting the nizamship from you.' He returned Nasir's steely gaze steadily. 'If only there was a way to squash your father's daughter's son, eh, my lord?'

Not a glimmer of admission crossed Nasir Jang's immobile face. 'And if there was?'

'On behalf of the English Company, the President of Madras and his Council, and King George the Second, of Great Britain and all his domains.' Hayden Flint took the box in both hands. 'I offer this to you.'

Nasir Jang drew himself up, called his ministers, guards and servants back around him. The important among them resumed their cushions and turned politely to hear Nasir Jang's words.

'See! The mystery of the key is revealed. The English Company has a gift for us,' he said grandly. 'What do you think of that? Should I accept it?'

They looked at the box, saw how it glinted in the feringhee's outstretched hands. Then the wazir said 'Ah!' and one after another, in a way that laid bare their alliances, they added their own approving noises.

Nasir Jang hushed them. 'And what is the price of this gift?'

'It is freely given, Highness.'

'So.' Nasir Jang took the silver key from around his neck. 'This is the key to the Deccan.' His pun drew no smile from his ministers. 'We have lived long enough,' he said, 'to know that nothing is ever freely given to a prince.'

He received the box from Hayden Flint's hands and cracked the lid open. Then he slammed it shut and his eyes flashed to the Englishman's face, stark shock in them, swiftly overtaken by an icy rage.

A shocked cry went up. '*Naja! Sanp! Sanp!* A seven-stepper! Get back!'

The hookahs were overturned, the cushions scattered. Everyone recoiled as the banded krait slithered from the open box, everyone except Nasir Jang who was staring, rock-still, as if at an assassin.

Sweet Jesus, how did that happen? thought Hayden Flint frantically, staring at the krait as it tried to dart under a cushion. He knew the bite of the krait was lethal. It was by far the world's most dangerously venomous snake, the one known in the Carnatic as 'the seven-stepper', where it was believed that a man, once bitten, could take no more than seven steps before dropping lifeless.

A huge black servant ran across the hall with astonishing speed and stroked his sword up, lifting the royal cushion on its tip. The silk tore, cascading white feathers, and the snake struck at them as they fell, until the second stroke of the sword cut it neatly in two and its halves twisted in death.

Hayden Flint tried to recover himself, but soldiers rushed forward and seized him, and he was marched struggling from the hall.

The palace drowsed peacefully in the tropical darkness. No evening breeze blew in from the east tonight, and the paved rooftop decks still radiated the warmth of the sun. This was a lordly place in which they camped, a private domain of spread carpets, high above the sleeping world, amid the towers and domes of night and the very stars themselves. Tonight they would eat a meal of celebration, and then they would make love, also in celebration. For tonight the plans of the Englishman and the faithless wife were in ruin and victory over them was assured.

Khair-un-Nissa, in her most arousing attire, knelt in the sultry night. She massaged Muhammad's temples and listened as Govinda the musician tuned the long-handled sitar. It was many-stringed, with a huge gourdlike body. Govinda's tabla players squatted beside him with their drums, then the cascading music began, like icy streams at the headwaters of the great River Ganga, the notes thrilling and bending, carrying high into the air, an ancient *raga* telling of the days before the world when the gods loved one another in cosmic splendour.

With a snap of her fingers Khair-un-Nissa summoned her eunuch body-servant. The windbreak was parted instantly.

'Bring coffee.' The curl of her lip was commanding.

The eunuch was young, in his mid-teens, unhappy, scared of her now. He had thought himself better than others, better than her. So he had come from Arcot at her special suggestion to learn humility. Here he was easy to handle.

She listened to the bending notes of the *raga* for a while, her thoughts coiling and uncoiling, like hookah smoke, like a nest of serpents. How right I was to side with Nadira in this dispute, she thought. What a remarkable politician she is! And how clever of her to think of the krait. Muhammad is waking up; soon I will find out what happened. That wife of his has played into Nadira's hands all along, and now she has ensured her own death, leaving me to control the man who will be the next Nawab of the Carnatic.

'Tonight you shall sing of love,' Muhammad said drowsily, his hand stroking her thigh through the diaphanous material of her pyjamas. His eyes dwelt on the strand of tiny pearls that touched her cheek, linking her nose and earrings, then his gaze dropped to the fine-braided strings of large pearls that hung between her barely covered breasts.

'Drink. This is to be your night of pleasure, my lord. A night when all dreams shall be fulfilled. Now you are to be confirmed nawab, anything you desire shall be yours.' She poured more of the heady wine into a goblet of rare Venetian glass and offered it coyly, meeting his eyes. 'I live only to serve you.'

He took the wine and savoured it, enjoying the forbidden thrill of its alcoholic bouquet. 'After the victories of this day I now have time to appreciate your beauty properly, Khair-un-Nissa.'

'Thank you, lord. You do me a great honour and in return I shall give you pleasure like that given by the houris of Paradise.' The nymphs of Islam's heaven were voluptuously beautiful, black-eyed like gazelles, insatiable in their desire. Khair-un-Nissa felt suddenly light-headed. The huge brass fretwork lamp that hung overhead cast complex shadows across the flagging. All around, the deckroof of the palace, surrounded by its sculpted battle-ments and muticoloured awnings and windbreaks, basked in the light of ten thousand stars, and beyond, in the void, the windless sky shimmered in the heat. She thought she saw a brief streak of light flare in the darkness – a falling star, a spirit that had become detached from the firmament, one that only she had seen fall. She gathered between her fingertips a morsel of pillau from the great hammered gold dish that was laid out before them, and he opened his mouth.

'The most delicious food is that taken from the hand of a beautiful woman.'

'My lord, it is a poor offering for so great a prince as you will be.'

She had laid out a delicate repast for him on a jade platter: thin slices of fresh mango and papaya. She took them, hungry now, and fed them to him. There were chinga prawns in a red-hot sauce, saffron rice and spiced cubes of lamb cooked in mint and yoghurt. There were palm leaves containing tiny banana and coconut delicacies, lime and rosewater juleps, and long-spouted jugs of arrack and shiraz wines.

She fed him until he wanted no more, until his eyes wandered in dreamy forgetfulness along the milky path of the sky, absorbing the mystical reflection of the holy River Ganga.

'Tell me,' she said. 'What are you thinking?'

'I am thinking that this is a perfect night.'

'Yes. So perfect.'

I was clever to switch the boxes, he thought. A ruby for a snake. Now the Englishman is imprisoned and the ruby is with Muzaffar Jang. Tonight his men will break into Asaf Jah's apartments. They will slay the Nizam, or, if he is already dead, they will stamp out his memory, and after that Nasir Jang will die.

'What of Yasmin Begum?' whispered Khair-un-Nissa, hardly wanting to mention her, but desperate to know Muhammad Ali's mind.

She knew she had made a mistake, because his face changed and his muscles became rigid. 'Yasmin Begum will return with me to Arcot,' he said. 'She is a thief and an adulteress. At Arcot she will atone for her crimes, as the Book decrees.'

'As the Book decrees.'

Gilahri woke Yasmin at a godless hour.

The night seemed almost over. Perhaps dawn was about to break. The moon was sinking into the west like a great bloodied ruby. The flames of the lamps had become so etiolated that they could no longer bear the weight of the darkness. On the window ledges flowers had withered in their jars and the pollen of the lotuses had been turned to cold paste by the dew.

Asaf Jah was dead. Flint was imprisoned by Nasir Jang. They had been tricked by Nadira and Muhammad.

Gilahri shook her again, wordlessly. Since the death of Hamida two days ago she had not spoken a single word.

Footsteps ran through the courts and gardens. Shouts and the screams of women. Then shots, the bright flare of muskets casting shadows on the ceiling.

Yasmin ran to the window. '*Bismillah!* No!'

There were horsemen in the square below, their spiked helmets and fish-scale armour reminding her of Abdul Masjid. At the gatehouse a dozen men struggled to lift a great timber bar into place, but the horsemen were spurring towards them. Suddenly a rash of firing began in the outer courtyard, the sounds magnified inside the echoing hall of columns from which the flashes appeared. Men were running. Others were trying to turn a gigantic bronze cannon towards the gate. A figure fell from the walls, impacting with a sickening thump. Then fire-devils – tar-soaked collars impregnated with sulphur and worn on the shafts of arrows – were raining on to the gate, sticking there and dripping bright fire down the old dry wood.

Gilahri seized her hand, her eyes imploring.

'No! We shall stay here. This is the safest place. They will not harm us here.'

Privately, her reason said otherwise. Her greatest fear was being enacted. Muhammad and his power-thirsty mother had taken the Eye to Muzaffar Jang, prompting him into a bloody and unnecessary rebellion.

'The fools!' she shouted. 'The blind fools!'

There was the noise of men on the roof above, ropes were thrown down from the eaves, and the oiled bodies of special fighters, fierce men recruited from an ancient and secret society of the killing arts, slid down the ropes, long knives slung over their muscular backs, steel tiger's claws looped from thumb to little finger of the left hand, their stomachs bound tightly into strange white loincloths. Some of them wielded thin whip swords twelve paces long, flexible razors of steel that thrashed and flickered from their hands like lariats, rippling and looping in astonishing patterns about the swordsmen, cutting down the men of the guard.

Suddenly a rope snaked down outside her own latticed window. The assassin slithered down, agile as a spider, his lithe body almost naked, glistening in the light of flares. He stopped as he came level with them, the whites of his eyes bhang-reddened, his face that of a madman. Gilahri broke away and ran, panic sending her out across the landing and down to the entrance hall, weaving as she fled. Yasmin tried to follow her, past knots of frightened women and towards the place of escape.

'Gilahri! Stop! Come back.'

She turned a corner and halted, lost, turning to see in which direction Gilahri had gone. There on the stone floor was Jauhar the eunuch, his ribcage laid open by a sword slash, dark blood pooled all around him.

'Gilahri!'

She saw the girl standing in the threshold of an open door, transfixed by fear. Twenty yards away, a dozen rebel horsemen kicked their mounts up the marble steps outside, swinging heavy swords that were dull with blood. They were chasing the men of the palace guard, hacking them to pieces as they ran screaming for any cover they could find.

She dragged Gilahri back and slammed the door just

before the heavy body of a man crashed into it. She heard his terrified cries as he begged to be admitted, then the shudder as he was impaled on a lance.

Gilahri started to scream, her body paralysed by terror. Her clinging fingers were like wire, her limbs stiff as a corpse's. Yasmin pulled her into a dark room where a wellhead gaped fifty feet down into the bedrock of the palace, a circular hole full of black echoes, lipped with stone and surrounded by a hundred huge jars, filled with water. There they hid, Yasmin cradling her maid on the floor, in the dusty space between the stoneware jars.

'What if they come? What if they find us?'

'No man can lift these jars when they are full of water, little squirrel. Look how they have fat bellies and narrow feet. We could crawl into the gaps and hide and no soldier could follow in such a maze.'

When the firing and the shouting stopped, Gilahri asked her shakily, 'Who are those men? What do they want?'

'Assassins. Supporters of the pretender, Muzaffar Jang.'

'The great Nizam's grandson?'

'Yes.'

'What if he wins, Yasmin Begum? What if he kills the Nizam and his true heir, and takes control of the palace? What will happen to us then?'

'Hush, now, little squirrel. Try to sleep. I will wake you when the battle is over. When safety has returned. Then we shall go back to the others. Everything is well.'

But she knew that everything was not well; that whatever happened now there could be no escape. If that treacherous hyena, Muzaffar Jang, prevails, she thought, we shall remain at Hyderabad – as captives, awaiting death. And equally, if Nasir Jang has escaped the attempt on his life, then he will cherish no love for those who made the revolt possible.

I hope you are not dead, Hayden Flint. I hope that with all my heart.

The blood had been washed away and the corpses burned.

Hayden Flint stumbled on the steps, the chains loading him, weighing heavily on his wrists and neck. Last night he had listened to the violence of the coup through the bars of a dark and airless dungeon, trying desperately to fathom which way the fighting was turning. It was the night that Hyderabad and all the forces that would shape the future of Hindostan had awaited during these last failing years of Asaf Jah's glorious reign.

Hayden Flint spent the night cursing his luck, damning his stupidity, running through in his mind the possible ways the krait could have got into the box that Yasmin had sworn contained the Eye.

I pray God she has not deserted me, he thought, as he was led solemnly into the shade of the Hall of Audiences. I pray God that Nasir Jang has triumphed, or else hope is gone, we are all dead, and the English confounded here for ever.

The marble hall of the Nizam's palace was clean and cool in the morning light, the air perfumed once more, as he was escorted through it in shackles, his hat clapped on his head awry. Hundreds of armed guards stood motionless in alcoves along the entire length of the audience room. A breeze blew in through high-scalloped arches above them, carrying the harsh light of another blistering noonday within. When they reached the Nizam's rostrum, Hayden Flint counted seven noblemen. Two were important enough to warrant huge feathered fans playing over their heads, but it was the eighth man, a European in a tricorn hat, who made him exclaim in despair.

'By God! I should have guessed!'

As he and his guard approached, Nasir Jang shifted on his masnad, the silken throne-cushion signifying his over-lordship of the Deccan. His calculating eyes watched everything. The Englishman's eyes looked him over. He was swathed in a gold-threaded cotton achkan; a skirt of fine pleats fanned out around him from a high waist, almost hiding his pyjamaed legs.

Then he saw it. It was like no sword on earth. The scabbard was thickly jewelled and worked with gold, the hilt and handguard magnificently fashioned. It was a sight he knew he would never forget. And the hilt of the Talwar-i-Jang was set with a single glassy object that sparkled with what seemed like the white fire of hell. It was a huge diamond. The biggest in the world. The Mountain of Light.

To Nasir Jang's left on the rostrum, similarly robed and turbaned, lounged his wazir, or chief minister, and five of his white-clad generals seated cross-legged on cushions. All were similarly armed with ornate swords, all wore fearsome, triangular-bladed punch-daggers at their waists. They looked to one another, interested in the Englishman's open astonishment. Then the spell was broken as the Frenchman also smiled.

He was clean-shaven and patrician, his dress crisp and well-cut. He seemed at ease with those at his elbows, in control of the situation. He stood up.

'Allow me to introduce myself, monsieur. I am Charles Castelnau de Bussy, of the Compagnie Orientale des Indies, member of the Council of Pondicherry and ambassadorial representative of His Most Christian Majesty Louis Quinze to the court of His Imperial Highness Nizam-ul-Mulk.' He swept off his hat and bowed with overwhelming irony.

Nasir Jang's searching gaze broke away from de Bussy. He whispered something indistinct at Hayden Flint, who still stared at the diamond. Somewhere nearby a column of crystal water played from a fountain; its sound filled the moment with haunting music.

'*Kya hua?*' Well?

His chains were heavy. They clanked as he moved. Insect bites covered the tender parts of his body, itching madly. The filth of the cell stained his sweat-foul clothes. He fought to master himself. The Nizam wants me to bow to de Bussy, he thought. Bow to the filth. I'll not do it!

His parched throat was dusty-dry from his confinement and fear tautened his belly, but his voice came strong as he whispered, 'This floor sweeper's not fit to sit beside you, Highness. I refuse to acknowledge him.'

Nasir Jang's voice was suddenly raised angrily, '*Jo ham kahta hai wo karo!*' – Do as you are commanded!

The Nizam nodded sharply towards the sipahis who ringed the prisoner. One knocked off his hat. Another stepped forward, and he felt a sharp blow crash into the pit of his stomach. He went down on one knee and was held there. A drawn sword was put at his throat, and he began to tremble as the nick at his Adam's apple started to bleed on to his shirt.

Fear mingled with guilt in his belly. Terrible regret that he had failed in his mission, failed in his promises, failed his father. His head came up angrily, and his eyes went to the Frenchman who he knew had him precisely where he wanted him.

'Have you told him the true reason you're here?' he asked savagely. 'Have you told His Highness about your dealings with Muzaffar Jang? That together you planned to install him as Nizam, and then to put Chanda Sahib in charge of the Carnatic?'

De Bussy thrust out his lips thoughtfully, unruffled by the Englishman's words, prepared to give him nothing except enough rope on which to hang. 'The Nizam doubtless has his own very good reasons for tolerating a French embassy,' he parried. 'For our part, Monsieur Dupleix wants merely to see the Carnatic ruled by the rightful heir. Only then might we expect to get a proper normalization of trade.'

'French trade! French trade, because there'll be no one else here to compete with you. Isn't that right? Get rid of the English and you'll have the whole of Hindostan under your heel. Have you told the Nizam what Dupleix will do with him and his kind when you've succeeded in kicking every last Englishman into the sea?'

His eyes went to Nasir Jang, and he wondered how much the Nizam knew about the French plan and the man they sought to install at Arcot. Chanda Sahib had lusted for possession of the Carnatic since the chaos of the Maratha invasion eight years ago. Though born a Hindu, Chanda had married a lesser daughter of Dost Ali, the Nawab of the Carnatic before Anwar-ud-Din's arrival.

Chanda had commanded Dost Ali's army until the Marathas came and slew the nawab at the Battle of Ambur. Then the old man's only son, Safdar Ali, had been forced to contest the succession with his brother-in-law, and first cousin, Murtaza Ali.

Chanda had sided with Safdar Ali. He was rewarded with the governorship of the city of Trichinopoly, but the Marathas had besieged it, and taken him with the hope of getting ransom.

Yes, Flint recalled, watching his captor, while Chanda Sahib was locked away in Satara the Carnatic passed to Anwar-ud-Din, on the orders of Asaf Jah. As Nizam, he had asserted his absolute right to choose which of his vassals might rule the Carnatic, and Asaf Jah had no love for any independent-minded clan. It wasn't surprising that Anwar-ud-Din showed no inclination to ransom Chanda. So he stayed in his cell for seven years, until someone paid the Marathas what they wanted. Who paid that ransom? Who else but Dupleix.

He gathered all his strength, sure that he must mount an immediate offensive against de Bussy, or be swept into oblivion.

'Do you deny that you and Muzaffar Jang planned the rebellion together?' he demanded of de Bussy. 'But your coup failed! You miscalculated! You lost! And now look at you, trying desperately to recover your position with the man who did become Nizam!' He faced Nasir Jang in open appeal. 'Highness, the English Company has always maintained that you've every right to occupy the masnad of Hyderabad. The Carnatic is yours and should be yours. But by embracing Monsieur Dupleix and his minions you'll throw the will of the English against you. And that is not a policy I would recommend.'

Nasir Jang's eyes half-lidded momentarily, then he answered. 'This is our land, Englishman. Not yours. Not France's. It is the English who have made a mistake, for they have chosen to make Anwar-ud-Din their vassal, and to turn him against his rightful lord.'

'We have no vassals, and we seek none. Anwar-ud-Din was the choice of Asaf Jah. We recognize that the Carnatic is a province, not an independent realm. The English have no ambitions there. We desire only to go peaceably, and to trade as we have always traded, since the Company first came to Hindostan five generations ago.'

He saw Nasir Jang's languor leave him. 'Asaf Jah is dead. Who now shall say Chanda Sahib may not rule in the Carnatic?'

'I do not say that,' Hayden Flint said carefully. 'If it is your choice. I only say that it should not be a Frenchman who chooses.'

Nasir Jang sat up and stabbed a finger at him. 'Our father willed the Deccan to us! We decide how we decide! No Frenchman chooses! Nor shall any Englishman!'

Take great care, Hayden Flint told himself. One false step and they'll cut out your heart. He hesitated deliberately as Nasir Jang's anger echoed away, but the raw nerve the man had exposed astonished him, and he knew he must stake his life on it. Very clearly, in courtly Persian, he said, 'Asaf Jah had no right to will the Deccan to anyone. Only the Great Moghul in Delhi may do that.'

Instantly, Nasir Jang's wazir was on his feet. 'Hold your mouth, dirty feringhee! I say you are an assassin. You tried to murder our lord. It was you who wanted Muzaffar to rule here, but soon we shall find him, and his bare head shall be trampled in the earth! That is the reward of usurpers! That will be the reward of Muzaffar Jang!'

It was like the clearing fogs of early morning, the lifting of an obscuring cloud before a man given to vertigo by great heights. A great precipice had been revealed before him. He felt the warning prickle his back, and willed himself not to look at de Bussy.

So, Muzaffar was still alive! The Frenchman's grand strategy had suddenly become terrifyingly clear. Dupleix wanted not only to seize control of the Carnatic, but of all the Nizam's realm.

My God! I should have realized. Dupleix's vaunting ambition will not be satisfied until he has the whole of southern India in his fist. The Deccan stretches clear from coast to coast, from Bombay to Madras. With his nominee in Hyderabad he'll be able to control everything south of the Godvari River, and even threaten Bengal! If de Bussy succeeds in winning the Nizam over, all three English presidencies must eventually fall. And there'll be nothing we can do to stop it.

He tried to keep his face blank, paradoxically grateful that the razor-sharp talwar held against his throat had prevented him from showing any greater fear.

He looked Nasir Jang in the eye, the flashing of that astonishing jewel hidden in his blind spot. 'Highness, I repeat: we English are merchants. We have no interest in your dynastic disputes. We want only to trade peaceably, to pay our due taxes to the legitimate ruler, and in return to enjoy the protection of Moghul law. Remember, it was the French who cravenly attacked our lease at Madras. They are the aggressors. We asked Anwar-ud-Din to aid us not because we had any particular love for him, but because he legally sat on the mansad of the Carnatic – by that same legal authority by which you yourself now sit as master of the Deccan. To us, the rule of law is paramount. We have done nothing to contradict that.'

'You have tried to kill us!'

'Highness, as I have continued to say from my dungeon cell, that was a French conjuring trick. The box was locked. I did not know what was inside. If I had truly wanted to kill you, would I have chosen to use a snake?'

Nasir Jang considered, then asked, 'So, you say the English will recognize our authority?'

'That is beyond dispute. I want only to open your eyes to the ambitions of the French who surely seek to lie to you, and dominate you, and to eject us.'

Nasir Jang sat back. 'Is that why you came to Hyderabad? To warn us?'

'Yes. And to aid you. And most of all – '

'He's a spy!' de Bussy interrupted scornfully. 'He's nothing but an intelligence-gatherer sent here to discover how best to destroy you!'

'I came here above all to ask a favour of the Nizam-ul-Mulk.'

Nasir Jang remained grave-faced. 'What favour?'

'I came here to ask him to send his armies into the Carnatic. To oblige the French to vacate Madras. To restore it to us, as it was before the war in Europe spilled into your lands.'

De Bussy watched the Englishman with a growing feeling of insecurity. An hour ago, when Nasir Jang had ordered Hayden Flint to be brought before him, he had thought there would be a swift and final end to it. He had accused Flint of spying, believing he could persuade the nizam to execute him, but so far the Englishman had played his hand with great skill. Nasir Jang was, moreover, an honourable and chivalrous man, and that was dangerous because it made him less malleable. He was also the thread from which the entire future hung.

Dieu, de Bussy thought. The Englishman's too well aware of what we've been doing.

'You came to ask for an army?' Nasir Jang asked the prisoner, intrigued by the reply.

'That is so. To restore Madras that was so perfidiously taken from us by the French, without any cause.'

De Bussy said, 'Your ships provoked the attack. English ships preyed upon French trade. You had turned Madras into a veritable pirate base!'

Nasir Jang raised a hand for silence, and Hayden Flint continued.

'I made Arcot the object of my quest. I promised Anwar-ud-Din I would give him the Eye of Naga if he would relieve Madras. He promised me he would try.'

'You went with his army?' Nasir Jang asked quickly, his

eyes aglow with the reflections of the vast diamond at his waist.

'I did.'

'You were at the battle where Muhammad Ali Khan was wounded? Riding with him? A warrior? You saw the destruction of his father's army?'

'Yes.' Hayden Flint's head bowed slightly. 'I witnessed that. I saw how it was that the French gained the day. And I understood the secret of their victory.'

'Look at him!' de Bussy said. 'He's plainly lying! He's just a spy, sent by the English Major Lawrence.'

'Enough!' Nasir Jang looked at Hayden Flint for a long moment, then he said, 'Tell us why we should listen to you now. Tell us why we should prefer the English over the French. Tell us why we should not simply execute you as the monsieur wants.'

Ice water trickled down Hayden Flint's spine, but he balled his fist and urged Nasir Jang with all the feeling he could muster, playing his last and greatest card. 'Because, Highness, England's war fleet is the greatest in the world. Soon, an English squadron under Admiral Boscawen will appear on your coast. I don't know when it will arrive, but it will certainly come. And when it does a powerful army will land. A force that will destroy the French. And' – he looked regretfully at Nasir Jang, inwardly terrified at what he was about to say – 'and if you have lent your support to them it will be the worse for you.'

Nasir Jang remained silent. Then he put his hands together, a half-smile illuminating his face as de Bussy leaned forward and crisply delivered the crushing blow.

'Can it be you have not heard what has taken place on the coast these past three months?'

'M'sieur?'

'Then you don't know that some time ago four thousand English troops were landed on the coast? That since then, those four thousand troops have failed to capture eighteen hundred Frenchmen? That they have failed to reoccupy Madras? That they have failed to conquer Pondicherry, as

296

was their aim? You do not know that their commander, and your own spymaster, Major Lawrence, has been captured? Or that the only other senior English officer is now dead? Surely you cannot be ignorant of all these things?'

'Liar!'

Hayden Flint felt the blood drain from him; he began to speak, but Nasir Jang motioned him to silence as de Bussy went on. 'If you will permit me, there is more. Some days ago a typhoon hit the coast. It destroyed the English fleet, including Admiral Boscawen's flagship – the *Namur*, I believe. Since the remains of his squadron have now sailed away it is clear that the salvation which the Carnatic English have looked to their navy to provide has – for the foreseeable future – evaporated. Their position is now far worse than it was before the great Admiral Boscawen arrived. My superior, Monsieur le Gouverneur Dupleix, has ordered his troops to hasten to the bounds of Cuddalore, and to take the fort of St David with all speed. In view of these facts, let me ask you this question: why should the Nizam move to aid your powerful English Company now?'

Hayden Flint opened his eyes which he had shut at de Bussy's words as if against a blinding light. The news had crushed all his hopes, undermined whatever slim position he had thought to build his arguments towards. How hollow his recent bravado sounded now. He understood the great significance of what Yasmin had told him and knew that he must carry his information to Fort St David without delay.

'In that case, Highness, I beg leave to be allowed to depart Hyderabad and rejoin my compatriots in their final struggle,' he said steadily.

Nasir Jang inclined his head and looked sidelong at de Bussy before answering.

'Strike off his bonds,' he said simply.

'But, Highness, I must prot – !'

'Monsieur de Bussy, we have spoken. We are assured Mr Flint is a man of honour. The embassy of Anwar-ud-Din is at an end. Muhammad Ali Khan will leave today for Arcot with our decision: his father will, for the moment, retain the Carnatic, but our court shall deliberate upon the request of the claimant, Chanda Sahib.'

De Bussy baulked at the delay. 'Freedom for a man who sought to kill Your Highness?'

'We find that is not proven. He shall have our permission to leave Hyderabad immediately. He shall carry papers of safe passage, so that he may return to Fort St David and serve his master faithfully, even as he requests. Perhaps by that time your valiant French troops will have stormed and taken the place. Perhaps another great English fleet will have arrived to save it. Who but Allah knows? We hereby place his life in the hands of God: our permission is granted. *Insh'allah.*'

They released Hayden Flint from his chains, and he walked from the durbar hall unchallenged by the guards. They watched him: Nasir Jang, his ministers, the princes of the blood, the damnable Frenchman, and the evil eye of the accursed diamond.

He steadied his step as he left, knowing that he must leave the hall with dignity, praying that he still had time to reach the gate and catch Yasmin. If she had gone, he knew he would never see her again. Never, this side of Paradise. Do the Muslims sometimes go to our heaven or we to theirs? he wondered absurdly. Will there be a chance to meet the life everlasting? If not, I would rather go down to hellfire
. . .

As he descended the steps, it took all his composure to suppress the panic inside him. There was a mass of men moving down the elephant ramp, leaving the citadel: five, six white horses, two dozen pack camels. Following them were two hundred troops, a mounted bodyguard with green pennants trailing from their lance-tips, and foot-soldiers, in yellow turbans, white robes, and with small lenticular shields hanging at their sides. Then came the huge bulk of Makna, the tuskless male elephant, with Muhammad Ali Khan staring unseeingly ahead from the howdah. Behind, attended by saried women who walked alongside, were a half-dozen closed palanquins.

He gasped involuntarily as he looked at the swinging tassels of the suspended box that came second last in the procession, the crimson curtains of Yasmin's dhooli.

The certainty blew up like storm thunderheads, scattering his hopes and contingencies, his ifs and buts, like straws in a gale.

That was it. He had missed her. She had gone, she would be gone for ever. For ever.

He burst into a run, alerting the guards at the gate who clashed heavy swords across his path as he tried to pass. His fingers clawed at them, but they held him, and more came from the guardhouse to hold him down in a wrestler's grip.

There was no way to get out. No way to get to her. No way to stop her leaving. He shouted as the horrible thought slitted his guts.

Muhammad Ali craved revenge on his wife. Once out of Hyderabad and into the domain of the Carnatic he would have her at his mercy. She would be accused of *zina*. She was going to her destruction. They would stone her to death just as surely as they had stoned that poor creature whom they had watched broken in agony. And there was nothing he could do.

He gazed helplessly at the palanquin passing below, fifty feet away. He shouted, and his shout echoed round the canyon walls of the elephant ramp. Then he saw the curtain of the palanquin twitch back and a veiled figure lift her fingertips to forehead, lips and heart before the maids walking alongside closed it again.

TWELVE

The deadly barrel of a long-pattern musket jutted out from behind a rocky outcrop, wavering as it followed its target. The musket was aimed at a lone horseman who had steered his mount into the dry gully below. He came on at walking pace, leaning back in his saddle, picking his way down towards the Pondicherry–Bahur road. Robert Clive knew this place was a pinch-point, an ideal place for his ambush. Eventually some unsuspecting French officer would be tempted to take the short cut through the gully, and when he did he would die.

The last three months had not delivered them a victim such as this. Clive's half-dozen native troops crouched low, watching the feringhee, their dusty turbans blending with the outcrop. Not one of them chewed pan now; they had put their slim tobacco sticks out, and their murmuring had stopped. All eyes were on the steep twists of the gully. The party had left the English fort secretly before dawn on random days scattered over the past three months. They had caused the French and their allies great annoyance, but today's patrol had yielded nothing – until now.

The chirring of crickets tore the air softly.

Suddenly a whinny rang out. The horse in the gulley had missed its footing on the loose scree. It recovered, but pulled up. The rider stroked its neck and obligingly dismounted, slipping his right boot from the stirrup and swinging his leg up and over the front of the saddle. He took the reins and started to lead the beast down when the leather suddenly jerked out of his hand as the horse's head catapulted violently to one side. The intended victim recoiled. Then, a split-second later, he heard the musket report and froze.

Dislodged stones rolled down the gully and came to rest. The report echoed into nothingness. Eerily, the cricket noises had stopped.

The lone man scanned the outcrops, heart hammering. When he looked down, his horse was lying in a cloud of dust, kicking its life away in death throes as a pool of dark blood spread out from its head. Whoever had fired had put a neat hole in its brainpan.

'*Kaun hai?*' Who's there?' '*Kya mangte ho?*' What do you want?

An answering shout echoed back. '*Wahan kare raho!*' Stand still!

The crickets began to scream again. He heard footsteps scrambling towards him from behind and started to turn, but the order was shouted again and he obeyed until the feel of a hot steel barrel behind his ear made him flinch.

Dark hands came round him, pulled out his pistols, then he was whirled about to confront a rough-faced man in a sun-faded red coat.

'You!'

Robert Clive's jaw dropped. 'Good God! Hayden Flint?'

'Clive, by all that's holy, I've never been so happy to see a human face!' His own was lit by an expression of pure relief.

'What in the devil's name are you doing here?'

'I might ask you the same question! You've shot my mount to death.'

'You, sir, look too French!' The shock of their meeting had worn off, and he found an unexpected hardness in Clive's voice as he turned away. 'You weren't looked for here, Hayden Flint.'

'I have intelligence for Governor Covington. How else can I get to St David except by Villanour and Bahur?'

'This way is a main short cut to Pondicherry. They now have garrisons at Tiruvadi and Gingee.'

'Is that good enough reason to fire on me without a challenge?'

'As good a reason as you'll get from me, sir. Where were you going?'

'I've already told you – what do you mean?'

Clive's manner was unyielding. 'You maintain your destination isn't Pondicherry?'

'Of course it isn't Pondicherry! What do you take me for?'

'There's been hard times for Englishmen on this coast since you were last on it. And you were not looked for here.'

Hayden Flint knelt over the horse's head, angered by Clive's ridiculous suspicion. 'Look at the nag that brought me all this way! I mean to say, don't trouble yourself about my horse, sir! Don't offer your friend any apology!' He rubbed the sweat from his face, then tried to be a little more conciliatory. 'Well, it's a pity, but I guess there's nothing for it now but to leave her for the vultures.'

Clive shouted after him as he turned away. 'Yes, a pity! Our chances of making an ambush here again are ruined. Can't properly surprise a man when a stinking carcass is lying in the road – not with every damned carrion bird for fifty miles circling round as a warning. And we can't shift it away, or bury it in the rocky ground here.'

Hayden Flint checked his step. 'Well, sir, then you shouldn't have shot it dead here, should you?'

'You're very lucky I didn't shoot you – friend. I was trying to.'

He faced Clive, and saw black fire burning in his eyes. 'Well, this is a pretty welcome back to English territory, I'll say that!'

As they rode back through the dusk, Clive told Hayden Flint stiffly the bare essentials of what had happened at Madras, from the *Chance*'s capture, through the fort's occupation, to their own escape to St David. He mentioned that Arkali Savage was at Ford St David, but could not bring himself to say why – that she had risked the journey there from Madras, guided by himself, in order to seek news of her fiancé. Instead Clive told Flint about his father, how Stratford had embarked on a secret voyage, a mission that, if successful, might deliver them all.

'Not another damned ruse with rubies and diamonds?'

Hayden groaned, thinking that with Asaf Jah dead and the succession settled on Nasir Jang there was little use for a second curse-laying stone.

'I don't know what it is, except that he has a rendezvous with coast pirates. Men who owe him a favour.'

'Was he dull and guarded over it? Or did he seem to you full of confidence?'

Clive remained unsmiling, his voice flat and terse. 'He kept it close to him. I only learned this much because he had to give some word to Governor Covington to raise his expectations of a deliverance.'

'But this manner?'

'I should say he was very dour over it.'

'That's a good sign!'

They reached the fort just after dark. There did not appear to be a heavy French presence in the surrounding country, but even so Clive insisted on a careful approach to the pickets. The less the French knew of their comings and goings, he explained, the better.

Inside the fort the first man Hayden Flint met was Edmund Maskelyne, who embraced him and expressed genuine astonishment and pleasure at his return.

'But this is magnificent! A happy apparition! Wait till I tell the others! Half of us thought you must be dead. And I confess that I myself doubted all the rumours that it was you who had raised Anwar-ud-Din's army in that heroic effort to save St George. Was it you?'

'I played some part.' He felt a hollowness in the pit of his stomach. His voice dropped. 'Edmund, how is Arkali? I've asked Clive about her, but he seems unwilling to give me a straight answer.'

Maskelyne's eyes clouded momentarily, but then his smile reappeared. 'We've all had a hard time, but have no fear, Arkali's well, and lodged in Governor Covington's house. She has looked for your return every day without fail, and she for one never doubted that you would return to her. Staunch! Resolute, you see! And faithful! You're a lucky man to be the focus of so much love and loyalty, and from so delightful a person. If I was betrothed to someone like her I'm sure I'd be the happiest man on this earth! Shall I tell her you're here?'

The hollowness grew inside him. 'No. She'll learn that soon enough.'

'But . . .'

'Please, Edmund. Of course I'm pleased she's safe. I'll meet with her directly I've spoken with the Governor.'

'As you wish, Hayden . . .'

Flint became brisk again. 'As for Robert, I've never seen the like of it. The change that's come over him . . . Is that what war does to a man?'

Maskelyne pursed his lips as if picking over a delicate matter. 'I would say – just the very opposite.'

'What do you mean?'

'Not war.' Maskelyne's head tilted. 'Love.'

'Tell me as we walk to the Governor's house, Edmund. If you do, I'll tell you something.'

'I will, then. I must, I suppose, for your own good. But when you've heard me out I beg you to remember that I'm trying to help you. And that I still count myself Robert Clive's friend also.'

Still stunned by what Maskelyne had revealed, Hayden Flint was recognized by the sentry in the light of a coaching lamp. The sea air cleared his mind as he waited to be admitted to Governor Covington's apartments. Hard to think that Arkali was in this very building, so close yet so very far away. He forced his mind to think about what he could tell the Governor, and how best to put it.

Covington welcomed him immediately, and poured two bumpers of crusty port before dismissing the servants from earshot and sitting down.

'So here's to you, sir!' Covington said.

'I don't believe I bring any reason to toast.'

'Have a care, sir! A compliment is a difficult thing for most men to pass – especially to a younger. It's even more difficult for a man to receive properly. Accept it gracefully, if you can.'

'In that case, thank you, Governor.' He made a vague gesture of acceptance and sipped his wine. 'But I still don't see why I rate compliments from anybody, much less the President of Madras.'

The 'Presidency of Madras' covered all HEIC leases and factories on the Coromandel Coast, including Fort St David. Covington inclined his head. 'The title is somewhat absurd under present conditions, don't you think?'

'Who can say?' Hayden Flint gave an open-handed gesture, which Covington seized on.

'Oh, I see by your manners you've been among the Moors too long. You've been at Arcot all the while?'

'Yes. And latterly at Hyderabad.'

Covington's scarecrow frame jolted with delight. 'Hyderabad, eh?'

'And I believe I've brought back news of the greatest importance to the Company, though it will sour your wine when you hear it.'

'Oh, not this wine. No.'

'Will you not call Major Lawrence to hear what I have to say?'

'Not for the moment, I think.'

He told Covington about the death of Asaf Jah. How Nasir Jang had taken the lead in the power struggle, and had seized the succession at the palace.

'Sir, Nasir Jang maintains spies everywhere in the Carnatic. Many more than we might have hitherto imagined. There's not a thing happens in the whole of the Deccan that he does not come to hear about. And that is most certainly also true of Monsieur Dupleix.'

'Indeed?' Covington said, getting up and pacing distractedly. 'If only we could have known about Asaf Jah's death two months sooner. Then we might have been able to goad Monsieur Dupleix into a hasty decision. As it is, the outlook's not rosy. Not rosy at all.'

'Sir, I regret that circumstances at Hyderabad prevented me from – '

'Oh, no, no! I meant no criticism of yourself. Of course,

you've done superbly well. But that two months would have made all the difference, do y'see?'

'I came with all speed, sir.'

Covington cocked an eyebrow at him. 'And almost in a wooden box, so I hear, eh? Our Mr Clive is a dedicated officer. Brave as a tiger, and perhaps as ferocious at times. I must apologize for his zeal on this occasion. Of course, the Company will reimburse you for your horse. Remind me of that later. Now, I must write to Calcutta. The captain of the last vessel to come by has promised to brave the dangers and drop anchor on his return. She'll be sailing from Trincomalee on her way to the Hooghly. She's overdue two days. Let me draft the letter this instant. With you here there'll be no mistake.'

Covington sat down heavily at his writing desk. As he addressed the blank paper with a charged nib his shoulders sagged under his coat. 'Oh, but this is the most wretched duty. A cry for aid that cannot possibly be answered.'

'Do you think so, sir?'

'I might as well toss it on to the waves plugged up in a bottle. The Calcutta presidency cannot supply us with reinforcements, and according to Boscawen nothing is coming to us by way of the Cape. Bombay has even fewer defenders than Calcutta, and we have no idea if the French have dispatched another fleet.'

'We cannot give up hope, sir.'

Covington's narrow smile lit his face fleetingly. 'A man should never give up hope. But it could be we are facing our final snuffing out. One more attack from Dupleix's legions and we'll be obliged to strike our colours.'

As Covington applied ink to paper Hayden Flint thought over what Maskelyne had said concerning Arkali.

'Robert's becoming crazy over her. You'll know it sooner or later, so you may as well hear it from me now. He's conceived this mad notion that their destinies are somehow linked, that they're fated for one another. For a while he talked about her all the time, and now he won't talk about anything whatsoever! He's getting out of his right mind with it.'

'And she won't see him?'

'She doesn't care tuppence for him.'

'I see.'

'Hayden, she's almost as mad for you as he is for her. He irritates and repels her so she avoids him, and that deepens his resentment.' Maskelyne's face was full of human concern. He shook his head and threw up his hands. 'The passion of love leads to a dangerous madness. I can't say I understand it perfectly, being a man of even moods myself, but I've seen its effect in others, and it's more dangerous than the cholera. Arkali is sighing and swooning, and Robert is in hell with it.'

'He sees me as his rival?'

'Of course.'

'If only he knew!'

'You must take care! Robert has already proved himself a reckless duellist, and this spurning has done nothing to improve his humour.'

He laughed bitterly and told Maskelyne how much crueller the twist of it really was, confessing about Yasmin, their love and the final parting.

Maskelyne was shocked. 'As your friend I'm bound to tell you to put the Moghul woman out of your mind. It's obvious there can be no future to it.'

'I love her, Edmund.'

'Say that to Arkali and you'll break her heart in two.'

He hung his head. 'Yes, perhaps I will. But it is the truth.'

Back in the present, Hayden Flint looked up at Governor Covington's expectant expression.

'I'm sorry, sir? What did you say?'

'I said, your father's been here twice in your absence.' Covington paused. 'Do you know yet that he's disowned you?'

'Yes.'

'I think it's fair to say he bears you some kind of grudge.'

Covington's understatement triggered a show of bitter amusement. 'That really would not surprise me, Mr Governor.'

'It's no laughing matter. Or it won't be if the *Chance* should appear again.'

'I'm ready to face my father man to man at any time.'

'Then you're a braver man than I, Hayden Flint. He is a most formidable individual, your father. His grudge is over your "theft" of the ruby. He has been put in a difficult position. He says he will not forgive you.'

'Have I completely ruined him?'

Covington paused. 'You must never let him know it was I who told you, but it seems he may have mended most of his affairs in Calcutta. But it was done at a heavy price. He has twice returned here, bringing us support and news, doing what he can. No one can clearly judge what moves inside that head of his, but I may tell you this: he is still smouldering over the collapse of his Madras endeavours. He often repeats that the ruin of Charles Savage, and the consequent loss of the opportunity to merge their interests, has put his life's aim out of reach. They say he saved his own ships only by mortgaging himself enormously to a clique of Bengal moneylenders headed by a rapacious individual named Omi Chand.'

'Where is he now?'

'Your father departed here some days before the disaster.'

He nodded, knowing that Covington meant the typhoon that had driven the *Namur* ashore.

The Governor poured more port. 'When Stratford warned Admiral Boscawen to get off the coast before the monsoon season turned the Admiral would not listen. I was not surprised when Stratford suddenly upped anchor and made sail. Nor was I surprised when, two days later, the typhoon hit us.'

'Where is he now?'

Covington shrugged. 'That question everyone is free to guess at. Calcutta, I would have to suppose.'

Hayden digested that thoughtfully. Maskelyne had said it was Clive's opinion that this time Stratford Flint had not gone back to Calcutta at all. According to Robert Clive,

Stratford's departure had been prompted by a piece of intelligence bought from one of the Indian pirates with whom he had dealings.

He's looking to make a deal with one of Tulaji Angria's men, he thought. Robert said my father was expecting to learn something important. Something so huge it could set everything to rights. What can the devil be up to? And can I trust what Clive says? I wonder what it can be. Covington drained the decanter into both glasses. 'Read that over, if you would be so kind.'

He took Covington's still-wet draft and looked at it. The situation was set down accurately; the final paragraph begged Calcutta for aid.

'There's not much else can be said,' he murmured, looking up at Covington.

'That's my view also. And now business is concluded I'll not detain you longer.' Covington's narrow grin came again. 'There's one lodging in my residence who is longing to see you. I've not disturbed her as yet. Doubtless you'll be eager to do that now.'

The moment she heard the sally-gate being opened Arkali's heart began to pain her. The thought of Robert Clive back inside St David brought down a dull despair. For months now she had been avoiding him, feigning illness, dressing in a man's shirt and breeches, locking herself away in the Governor's house whenever he was in the fort. She had already given a thousand reasons why she could not walk or sit with him. But the man was an imbecile; impervious to hints and insults, carrying on about destiny and his supposed love for her.

She set off across the unlit parade ground, making for the private quarters which Governor Covington had provided at the back of his residence. The last Indiaman had taken away the remaining dozen ladies, but she had refused to go, and the Governor had finally obliged her.

She let herself in through the garden door and climbed the dark, narrow servants' stairs at the rear. If it had not been for dear, kind Edmund, she thought, I would have gone mad with Clive's unremitting attentions. Fort St David is too small a place; it's like being in a cage with a tiger. If only Hayden was here to protect me and love me and take me away from here! I'll never forgive Stratford Flint! Never!

She hurried to her bedroom, entered, slipped the bolts and lit a candle. It was a passable first-floor chamber, though very small – cool white walls and a high ceiling lost in the light of a single candle. A polished hardwood floor gleamed under Bengal rugs. The bed was high and comfortable, with a good horsehair mattress. Full-length louvred shutters opened on to a private balcony that overlooked the Governor's small walled garden. Below, banana plants thrust up their huge fronds against the bars of the balcony rails.

She unbuttoned the waistcoat she had made for herself, slipped off her shoes and undid the knee buttons on her breeches. There was sufficient water to permit her to wash once a day. It was a relief to roll down her hose and knead the soles of her feet.

She took an Indian Ocean sponge, soaked it, then put it to her face. The touch of it was delightful. She dabbed water on her neck, shoulders and chest and rubbed a tablet of hard soap across her skin, rinsing herself with the sponge. When she had finished, she used towels to dry herself and climbed into a long nightshirt. She would use up half an hour of her precious candle to write in her diary, then she would climb into the big bed and sleep.

The knock startled her. 'Who is it?'

'Do not be alarmed, Miss Savage. It's me, James Covington.'

'Mr Covington? I . . . I am in my nightgown and about to retire.'

'Then don your shawl, my dear. I have a surprise for you.'

'What kind of surprise?'

She threw the bedcover around herself and went to slide

back the door bolts. The door opened, she saw, took a step back . . . and felt herself falling.

Hayden Flint caught her as she collapsed. He carried her to the bed and laid her on it as Covington went to fetch salts.

He leaned over her and watched with concern as she came round. Her eyes opened, cleared, and registered him. She put her hand up to touch his face: his chin, his unshaven cheeks and his mouth. Her fingertips lingered and then she burst into tears and reached up with both her hands to grab his neck and pull herself to him, racked with sobs.

He put his hands on her wrists, tried gently to disengage her, but she would not release him. Her grip was like steel, so he put his arms round her to support her, and she hugged him for a long moment without a sound.

When she spoke, the words gushed out. 'Oh, Hayden! Hayden! Oh, Hayden! Is it really you? I knew you'd come back to me. I knew you would. Oh, Hayden. Tell me it's you. Tell me this is no dream.'

He could not find it in him to reply to her.

Covington stepped in with the salts and saw her clinging to her fiancé. He left tactfully, closing the door behind him.

She would not release him for many minutes. 'Hold me. Hold me, Hayden,' she murmured whenever he tried to pull away. His cheek was wet; he felt the salt of her tears sting his eye. Her breathing came in gasps.

'Arkali,' he said softly. 'Arkali, listen to me.'

'Oh, yes. I have so much to tell you. But we are together now and for always. There's all the time in the world. I love you, Hayden. Hold me tight. Promise me you'll never go away again.'

'I cannot do that.'

She had not heard him so he spoke again. 'Arkali, I said, I cannot make that promise.'

Her eyes questioned him. She was so vulnerable in that moment, her soul so bared and fully open to him that he could not go on. The truth was a dagger to be plunged into her heart. How could he possibly use it?

'Arkali, we must talk.'

She heard but refused to acknowledge the regret in his voice. 'Hold me, Hayden. Love me, now.'

He pulled back stiffly. 'Please listen to me. I'm most relieved to see you, Arkali, and so very glad you are well. I suffered greatly at the thought that you might have come to harm because of me. I never wanted to hurt you.'

'My darling, I am not hurt. Everything is made right again. We're just as we were before. A boat will come soon and we'll be married in Calcutta, and it will be as if this nightmare had never happened.'

'No. This is not a nightmare. This is real. We're not the same as we were. I have changed. And you also.' He released her hands. 'Sleep now, and when you wake we'll talk about the future.'

'Sleep? How can I sleep? Don't leave me, Hayden. I need you. You must never leave me ever again.'

She pressed herself to him, hung round his neck, and he felt her whole body trembling. She was pale and beautiful and her red hair cascaded round her face in coppery curls. Her small breasts shaped the thin cotton of her nightgown. The pupils of her eyes were huge as if thirstily drinking in what they saw.

Waves of conflicting emotions clashed within him. I must find some way of telling her, he thought desperately. I don't want to hurt her, but I must tell her. Every minute I allow her to carry on believing in me the wound cuts deeper, and the deception grows dirtier. She must be told I cannot marry her. And she must be told why.

Her voice was breathy, urgent and demanding all at once. 'Stay with me tonight. I could not bear it if you were to go out through that door. I will not sleep unless I lie in your arms. Love me. Oh, love me!'

She lay back on the bed, her eyes fixed on his. The moisture of her lips glistened in the candlelight, there was a red flush in the skin of her face and neck, mottling her chest. She had offered him all in that astonishing invitation. Then she bucked her hips and crossed her hands in front of

312

her, and in the most wanton way lifted the nightshirt up over her head.

The agony of his decision was intense; the moment burned white-hot. His body was screaming at him to do as she wanted, to give her the love she craved in one consummately passionate act, but he knew that if he kissed her the moment would be lost.

Instead, he threw off her arms and began a halting explanation that he would have given anything in the world not to make.

A maroon split the darkness, like a firework exploding at the top of its flight. It was the warning signal for a sighting at sea. Then three distant reports – cannon-fire made in reply.

Inside the house Hayden Flint came to the head of the stairs to see Covington fighting off his servants. His people were clearly agitated by the notion the vessel must be French, and the herald of a grand assault. He went down to the hallway to be met by Maskelyne, whose company of men were standing guard by the Water Gate and who had let off the maroon. He had brought a gaggle of people of no account with him.

'A ship, Mr Covington! A ship of five hundred tons burthen, or more! In the Roads and fixing to turn broadside-on, I think. She's fired on us.'

The faces of Maskelyne's companions were variously full of alarm and anticipation.

'What d'you say, sir? French?'

'Yes, sir. Though it's dark as a tar barrel out there, there's a rake to her masts that makes me think – '

'Och, she'd better be one of our Indiamen, or best of all a navy frigate.'

They hurried to the Water Gate, where Major Lawrence was waiting, vast in his red coat, jowly as a bulldog. He had been released by the French some weeks ago, in exchange for one of their officers.

'Our concern is mostly justified, Governor,' he roared.

'She's come under our guns this moment, happy as you please. You may see her lanterns burning brighter than brass buttons – all manner of lights shining out of her! Neither is she afeared of our ordnance, ergo she cannot be French, which most likely makes her Royal Navy, and therefore an even bigger danger to our continuing here.'

'Thank the living God for that, Major. This is surely the most timely of all our good Lord's interventions.'

Lawrence shook his head. 'She depended mightily on my forbearance, though. Soon as she saw the maroon she came back with three twelve-pounders full of wads – if the sound of navy guns is at all to be trusted. I might have had a booby on watch and blown her into the Kingdom to come.'

'Perish that thought.'

Hayden Flint considered. No officer late of any of the King's line regiments thought much of the navy in the best circumstances. Lawrence was probably no different, having seen Admiral Boscawen's notable failure at close hand.

'She's a frigate, then, sir?' he asked.

'Damme, who is this fellow?' Lawrence growled, casting about to see his men standing at a respectful distance. He posed on his stick, bearing his weight on it; a crusted cuff half-covered the back of a hand as big as a ham hock. His formidable chest was a ribcage of braid and buttons.

'This is Mr Stratford Flint's son, lately come from Hyderabad.'

'Is he?' Lawrence seemed dented by the answer. 'Well, tell him not to question me about boats. They're all oversize Dutchmen's clogs tied up with string to me, the entire lot of them. And populated by fools – look, there's the cudden yonder in the waist, waving a damned lantern to and fro like a madman. Is it a signal y'recognize? A distress, perhaps?'

'Not at all.' Covington peered into the moonless dark, seeing nothing on the tropical ocean but a tight constellation of bright yellow stars peppering a darker than dark shape.

Lethargic surf crested on to the beach. Everyone

regarded the ship with a hushed prayer in his heart. They heard the faint sounds of shouted orders on the breeze, the splash of a falling anchor. Then Hayden Flint broke the silence. 'Sweet Jesus,' he said, 'I believe I know who our visitor will be.'

'In answer t'yer question, Guv'nor,' Stratford Flint slapped a big satchel down on Covington's desk, 'that's what I've brung ye this time. And nowt else. Though as ye'll see, it's likely quite enough.'

There was a universal gasp.

Twenty men, officers, soldiers, officials of the Company, and all of Covington's Council, stood around Stratford Flint expectantly. Had he brought them powder? Was the *Chance*'s hold stuffed with provisions? Did he have soldiers from Calcutta to land? They had badgered him as he strode up to the Governor's House, but he had been tight-lipped.

'None of ye have come close to what I have fer ye. And I doubt ye will guess it.'

'We thought you'd deserted us for another place, Flint. There was talk of you going to Cochin, or was it of you throwing in with some piratical elements?' Covington turned to Lawrence. 'Didn't Boscawen say something about Marathas?'

Flint knew what Covington meant. The Marathas, who now annoyed a vast tract of land clear across the middle of the Moghul Empire, had in the early days of their plundering enlisted the help of certain country seafarers who had since found piracy to their taste.

'Ah, well, I do not deny it! Aider and abetter I was. But it was a working arrangement. Neat and tidy, tidy and neat, with nobody worth a damn the loser – I'd feed Angria's men biscuit nibbles: the sailing times of Comp'ny ships, bills of lading, whatever I'd decide on. Once his boys knew which ships were Comp'ny – which were the real wasps with stingers in their arses, and not just shit-flies painted up to look like – well, then he'd know what to avoid. He was better guided, getting rid of the likes of Dutchmen, and

315

ships belonging to the filth, and some of me lesser competition, see? Ah, that's how I grew so big so quick. I had a hackwisitive heart in them days, Lord save me. Aye, days when I weren't as mellow as what I am now. I allus knew what I wanted, by God!'

Lawrence eyed him steadily. 'It's common knowledge you have filthy dealings with pirates, Flint. Why do you choose to make your admissions now?'

'I like ye as a man, Stringer, so I'll let that comment pass. Ye may not have been here long enough t'know that some enquiries it ain't quite prudent t'make of me.'

'Why don't you say what you've come to say?'

'Why don't ye have a good look at the satchel what I brung ye?'

Covington examined the salt-crusted mail satchel balefully. Branded on the stiff leather in big serif letters was the legend: *H.C.S. Diomede*.

'I had hoped, as we all did, she might have made Calcutta after all, or been delayed at the Cape and missed the season. So we may take it she's gone down?'

'Aye, sunk in the sea by a storm, she was. Thirty leagues south of Goa.' Flint's cheroot burned bright red at the tip as he sucked on it. 'Ye might like t'see the papers she was carrying.'

'Letters? You mean there's correspondence? Intact?'

There was general muttering. Covington's eyes were alight. The *Diomede* had been sailing from London. The Honourable Company ship was long months overdue, but had she survived she would have been the only vessel to deliver word from the Directors since Boscawen's arrival.

'Ye cannot call them intact, exactly.'

Silence fell.

'How did you come by these, Flint?' Lawrence demanded. 'Papers don't just wash ashore dry.'

'I told ye before not to make enquiry into my affairs.'

The silence deepened. Lawrence sat back, a significant look on his face. 'Then we might suppose that you did obtain them from coastal pirates.'

316

'Ye may suppose what ye like. I'm a man who listens far and wide. I merely came by a Comp'ny satchel, and thought it was worth the purchasing – on behalf of the Comp'ny, that is, y'understand?'

At what a cost, he thought. A big favour repaid by Tulaji: his life when it was once mine to give. I could've let him die on the yardarm of the *Bellerophon* in '38, if I'd wanted. But what use is a dead man? That's what I asked meself. A vigorous man in business he is fer sure, that Tulaji Angria, and not self-effacin' when it comes t'setting a value on his own neck. So that debt was cancelled, plus several lakh of Chinese tael silver, a full fortieth part of his life's hoard, fer that little leather bag. But he knew what was its import. He knew the price I paid to him was nowt compared with its value to me.

'On behalf of the Company, you say?' Covington was warily suspicious. He reached out towards the satchel but Flint's hand banged down over it.

'Ah, no!'

'How much?'

'Ten lakh, and that's a bargain.'

'Ten lakh?' Lawrence exploded. 'You've a gall to try selling the Company back its own property! For heaven's sake, Flint! Ten lakh is monstrous!'

Flint grinned. 'How do ye know that when ye don't know what it is ye're buying?'

Covington wrung his hands. 'Well? Is it worth the money?' he asked flatly, ignoring Lawrence's protests.

'I guarantee ye this: the paper in this will save yer fort here. And a lot more.'

'Save St David?' Covington digested what he had been told, sucking on his lip. He walked up and down, then turned suddenly. 'Are you in earnest, Flint? Are you certain?'

'I said: this paper'll save Fort St David. And more.'

'What more?' Lawrence asked.

'It'll get ye Fort St George back too.'

'Impossible!'

317

'No, sir! Not impossible. Certain.'

Lawrence's jowls quivered. 'When Boscawen brought thirty vessels here! Thirteen ships of-the-line! Twelve companies of a hundred regulars each! Eight hundred marines! God damn it, Mr Flint, when four thousand men cannot do it, how shall you and a miserable letter from the Directors do so?'

'Ye can trust me word! I guarantee that paper'll frustrate the filth's ambitions to take St David. And ye'll get the return of Madras as a consequence.'

'We'll have a pledge to that effect.'

'Then ye'll authorize payment for eight lakh on a Comp'ny bill hekspeditiously redeemable in Calcutta?'

'Seven.'

'Seven and a half!'

'Done!'

Flint nodded with satisfaction. 'Then it's yours as soon as the ink's dry. And I'll forecast the purchase'll please ye mightily.'

The contract was drawn, worded and signed, and copies run down to the boats. Lawrence watched with increasing anger. He grabbed up his hat. 'I'll not stay and watch this sham to its conclusion.'

'Do you not want to know what's in the satchel, Major?' Covington asked.

'No, sir! I do not!'

Flint's eyes followed him. As Lawrence reached the door the sentries stamped, pulled back their bayoneted muskets and opened the double doors. The Major narrowly missed bumping into a tall figure who had been waiting in the ante-room.

Stratford Flint's jaw knotted, the ash fell from his cheroot, then he recovered. Wigs turned. All eyes went to the door to see what the trader had seen. Those who knew how things stood with him paled.

'Hello, Father.'

Flint's jocularity evaporated instantly. The easy humour of the last few minutes froze solid in the silence.

'So it's ye, is it?'

'As you see.'

'And did ye bring back me ruby that ye stole?'

'I stole nothing.'

'And me coat? And me best pair of pistols? And a ship's boat?'

'I don't owe any debt to you.'

'Ah, don't ye? Well, it's all set down in me accounts book. So what about Dan'l Quinn? Have ye lost him too?'

'Quinn's dead.'

'Aye, like ye should be.' He spat and turned back to Covington. 'Open yer satchel, Governor.'

The leather flap cracked back stiffly. Covington drew out the packet. Government papers. Vellums folded like legal instruments, stiff and waxy with bright red seals. The seals had been broken.

Covington opened the documents and read, and as he read, his face changed. He looked up at two dozen expectant faces.

'But this is momentous,' he said, awed by the paper he held. 'This confirms the Anglo–French war is at an end in Europe. All conflicts worldwide between contestant nations are to be ceased forthwith, and further, the ministers of King George have negotiated a peace treaty with the French Crown at Aix-la-Chapelle – ' his eyes widened ' – in which the return to France of Louisbourg fortress on the Isle of Cape Breton, Nova Scotia, is ordered, and so in consequence is the restitution of Madras to the English Company!'

There were gasps, then jubilation overwhelmed them.

'Dupleix has been sold out!' someone shouted.

'And by his own government!'

'The war is over! Huzzah!'

'To the walls! Let the French know they're confounded!'

Covington led his Council from the room, the vellum grasped in his hand. Soon only two men were left, father facing son across an empty chamber.

'Father, I – '

'Don't call me that, by God!'

Hayden Flint hung his head, trying to master the intense feeling within him. 'Sweet Jesus, give me a chance! That's all I want. All I've ever wanted from you. We should be thanking God that the war is over. Damn your pride! Can't you allow yourself to make peace with me now?'

His father was contained but fearsome. 'So. Ye think this can be the end of it? That ye may worm yer way back now? That it'll be business as usual, just like it was before, when I'm still fifty lakhs adrift?'

Hayden Flint shook his head. 'I don't want any part of your damned business. I just want your respect.'

'Respect? The only reason I've not leathered ye all over this floor is that ye somehow got that ruby to Anwar-ud-Din. But ye'll get no praise fer that. Ye botched it and botched it again! Yer cack-handed interference ruined all me stratagems, and ye never did it once how I meant it t'be done. Ye're nowt. And ye've got nowt. And if it's respect ye want from me – then, laddie, ye'll have t'do better'n that!'

He watched his father stand up. Watched him walk from the room. Saw the way he doffed ash as he passed out of sight without looking back. Hayden punched the table hard enough to make his knuckle bleed, hard enough to release the anger he had stored up.

The hard-man trader, he thought, full of rage. The tough, unforgiving man of commerce! Where's his heart? I'll cut him again to find it, by God!

He beat his fist again on the Governor's table, then held his head, his thoughts a furious jumble. What did I steal? When did I cheat him? What does he want, by God? He'll not be satisfied until I bring him the very Koh-i-Noor diamond itself!

Outside, Stratford Flint turned a corner and ran flat into Robert Clive. A cutlass was in his hand; his anger was boundless.

'Where is he, Stratford? I swear I'll kill him!'

'Hold there, don't ye know the war's finished?'

'It's no Frenchman I mean, but your son.'

320

Stratford seized Clive's wrist without any loss of amiability, and broke it back in the Chinese style, until Clive yelled.

'Well, let the steel drop, man. What are ye? A fool who'd prefer a broken joint to a polite conversation?'

Clive gasped, but the cutlass fell. He cradled his arm.

'I'll teach ye how t'do that, if ye like.' Stratford's voice was unruffled, slightly humorous, but he kept hold of Clive's lapel. 'Ah, don't scowl at me. Now what's the bother?'

'Sir, he has dishonoured her!'

'Who?'

'Miss Savage – '

'Ah, little Arkali. Aye, and ye have a light in yer eye fer her still, don't ye?' Clive grimaced, but Stratford shook him. 'Don't ye?'

'Yes.'

'Well and good. Yer path's likely as clear as it'll ever be.'

Clive stared back, astounded. 'You think that – '

'Well? Do ye want her or don't ye? It's all a case of valuation, lad. What's a gold dollar but a fillet of yeller metal with the King o' Spain's likeness 'cept some Spaniard thinks otherwise of its purchasing power, eh?' He put an arm round Clive's shoulders and began to walk him away from the Governor's residence. 'What say we has a drink, just ye and me, t' wet the peace?'

They went out through the Water Gate, Clive uncertain but unable to decide what else to do, and all the while, as Stratford led him away, the walls seemed manned by madmen, all shouting and whooping and firing off shots into the night.

Soon they reached the sand and the deeper shadow of the seaward walls that stretched out almost to the surf. In the boat there was a bottle of the best and Stratford told the guarding lascar to uncork it.

'I been saving this, in case I ever set eyes on ye again. Did I p'raps tell ye a tale I heard from a wily Turk about the mighty Sooltan who had a fop fer a son?'

321

'I don't recollect that, sir.'

'Then listen, and maybe learn.' Stratford looked up at the starry sky and paused long enough to hitch his coat and lodge his backside on the top strake of the boat. Then he began in a faraway voice. 'There's this father, see, a Sooltan of Turkeyland. That's a country that lives by trade, like we do. And he sends his beardless heir across the waves t'make his fortune against the smack of tide and wind and the enemies of his nation and all. But the boy only sails down the coast aways and lands and sends in secret to his mother who always doted on him. Then, see, he tells her his plight and he asks her fer gold fer t'fill up his holds, and she obliges him in that, and off he sails.

'So after a space he comes back to the main harbour with pennants broke out at his masthead and he applies t'see his father who as a Sooltan needed that kind o' formality. Well, the Sooltan has this great pit filled with crockerdiles and he receives his son by it. And the son brings by the gold and he says: "There, Father, what a fortune I have got through trade, just like what ye asked me." And the Sooltan takes a dollar of it and looks at it right queer and looks at his son likewise, then he throws it in among the crockerdiles. And the son just stares at it and says: "Why did ye do that?" And the father fetches him a clout on the ear and calls him liar and sends him off again t'trade fer another boatload of gold.'

He handed the brandy bottle to Clive, who quaffed and wiped his mouth. 'I don't see – '

'Let me finish. So. This time the lad goes out and starts to trade proper, like. He makes his way in the world. Fer a full year he overcomes sea monsters and the roused elements and all the deceits of men, and he wins his own profit, by sweat and ingenuity. And when he comes back safe to harbour he comes before his father who is down yonder at the pit. And again the lad shows a golden dollar to his father. And again the father throws it in among the crockerdiles. But this time, the lad vaults over the side of the pit and grabs the dollar from among the snapping jaws and brings it out. And this time the father lays his hands upon the son's shoulders and tells him he is a man.'

Stratford looked aside, and saw Clive nod his head. 'That's me favourite parable. One I told me son when he were a young'un, though I might have held me breath fer all the good it taught him. But ye see the meaning, don't ye, Mr Clive?'

'That I do, sir. I've always held that it's not what a man has, it's the way he gets it that makes him.'

Stratford handed the cutlass back to Clive. 'Then mind ye go carefully. And take no heed of anyone who says I want Hayden Flint dead.'

As Clive sullenly took the blade, Stratford swigged at the brandy again, then handed it back to a lascar. That's a pissy shallow reading of me parable, he thought. And I supposed young Clive knew a thing or two about Hindostan and the ways of fate. Hayden's changed. My lad's returned from his first journey. He's learned to recognize destiny, but he's yet to go on his second, where he'll discover how to mould it to his will. That's the work of a man of forty years and more, but who says it can't be done?

'So the war's over, is it?' Clive said desolately. 'That was it, though I'd counted on ten years. I suppose it's my destiny to be a damned clerk after all, for that's what they'll put me back to now.'

The words jolted Stratford. It was as if Clive had heard his thoughts.

'Courage!' he told him. 'Ye don't think Dupleix'll give up the war just because the King of France has ordered it, do ye? Ye don't suppose Madras'll be handed back by the filth just like that?'

Clive's face lit as he heard Stratford Flint's words. 'But the treaty is signed and sealed. The Company and the French Company – both our government and theirs – all have agreed. How can Dupleix maintain his plans now?'

Stratford laughed shortly. 'Think on that one, lad. Think on it hard in the coming months. Aye, and keep yer powder dry.'

BOOK THREE

THIRTEEN

It was the summer solstice and the wide boulevards of Pondicherry sweltered under a sun that rode well north of the zenith. For weeks now the heat had been growing in intensity, each day a little less endurable. Above street level inside the citadel of Fort Louis, the architecture was that of a French provincial city in midsummer, glaring white walls, louvre shutters and red pantile roofs, solid and in harmony with the infinite blue of the sky. But below, the streets were khaki, the colour of Indian dust, the pavements shaded by awnings, and in the shade squatted saried women with studs in their noses and men wearing dhoti and turban, and the heat was of a kind never felt in France.

Beyond the Governor-General's residence each window facing the minuscule breeze had been equipped to provide relief. The bhistis, or water servants, had hung frames with woven screens soaked from their mussaks so the air that entered the houses would be cooled. Overhead, the lofty ceilings were rigged with ingenious punkahs, broad fabric paddles pulled this way and that by string and pulley and the lethargic tug of the punkah-wallah, as if, unless the air was stirred, it must set like glass.

Joseph-François Dupleix, Governor-General of the East Indies, looked out over his fine buildings. They stood in regular blocks, on wide streets that met at right angles. Evidence, he mused, of French love of order, of our reason and logic. This is inherent in all things French, the quintessence of our civilization that sets us apart from others. These buildings are solid proof of the enlightened philosophies of the people who are destined to show all

Europe, the whole world, how the future must be made. France shall lead the sublime destiny of human kind.

A hundred yards away in the centre of the barracks parade ground, a lone soldier in full kit stood at attention, stiff as a nail, suffering for some infraction. He wavered momentarily, then collapsed. Two corporals, who had been set to watch him three hours ago, came out of the shade to stand over him.

Inside, the Council members were sweating in the mandatory heavy brocades and silks and powdered wigs: Duval d'Espremenil, Charles de Bussy, Philippe Mainville, and on the far side of the table, Louis d'Auteuil, old Danton and the youthful le Fevre. How Danton was droning on! *Quelle barbe!*

The untouchability of genius, thought Dupleix, feeling their eyes on him. I know how that feels. All my Council – indeed all who know me, with the possible exception of Charles de Bussy – regard me as a cultured man, well-read and intelligent, but I know they also consider me utterly untouchable.

Charles de Bussy watched his superior regarding the rest of his sweating, bewigged Council as a schoolmaster might a class of six adolescents, his bright eyes knowing all the answers when they did not.

Though nearing fifty Dupleix had maintained his health, and the rigours of the climate, combined with a careful diet, had preserved the youthful trimness of his figure. That was important, for respect's sake. 'The secret's quite simple,' he had once heard Dupleix tell Louis d'Auteuil. 'You see, I have no interest in growing fat and comfortable. All my life, Louis, I have dedicated myself to servicing the expansion of French interests in Hindostan. First at Chandernagore, where I built up a trade centre to rival Calcutta, and now here, in the Carnatic, where I have been given the opportunity to wipe out Madras. That is what I want from life. Not the pleasures of the gourmet, or the satisfactions of great personal wealth. I ask only that *Compagnie d'Indies Orientales* – and posterity – should remember me for bringing the prize of Hindostan and all her wealth under the control of France.'

De Bussy continued to examine the Governor critically: his dark hair was natural, his face ageless. He sat propped elegantly on the sill of a paneless window. Glowing white breeches, tight to the skin from waist to below the knee; white silk stockings; loose white silk shirt, open at the neck; sleeves ruffed at the wrists – an ensemble that gave him the cool, unsullied aspect of a Versailles fencing master.

'What does it matter, Philippe?' Dupleix asked the speaker when the man had finished his irrelevant monologue. The Governor's head inclined enquiringly. 'Well?'

Mainville raised his hands as if contending against unreason. 'But it's the end of hostilities, Monsieur Governor. By order of the King. The war is over.'

'I do not see your difficulty.'

'My difficulty? Monsieur Governor, I – ' Philippe Mainville struggled again to confront the issue, but Dupleix brushed his objection aside. He left the windowsill and began to walk the length of the table, the members watching him.

'It's quite simple. The dispatch says there has been a final settlement. By the treaty of Aix-la-Chapelle, His Majesty's Government has seen fit to squander our advantages in the Carnatic. What's so hard to understand about that?'

There was an uncomfortable silence, then Louis d'Auteuil spoke measuredly. 'We are ordered by the *Compagnie* to return Madras to the English. Are you saying you will not comply?'

Dupleix adopted a pious expression. 'By no means, Louis. We must comply. As you point out, it is the ruling of the *Compagnie* and of the government. It is their considered opinion that the vastly important fortress of Louisbourg on Cape Breton Island is more significant to France than Madras will ever be. The British have agreed to return Louisbourg to France, so – ' he shrugged, his sarcasm turning to matter-of-factness – 'we must return Madras to the English.'

They looked at his unconcern with open amazement.

'I cannot understand, Monsieur Governor,' Louis d'Auteuil said at last, his voice working under tight control, 'how can you remain so calm. Isn't a French Madras what we've always worked for? What you yourself dedicated your whole life to bring about? And now you smile at this instruction as if it was a commendation from His Majesty. I can't understand. Don't you feel anything?'

Dupleix's smile broadened. *Mais oui*, he thought with satisfaction, I feel it's time to pursue another policy, and the *Compagnie* feels that too. They have seen my methods working, and they like what they see. That is why they promoted me to Governor-General of the East Indies after Benoist's retirement. There can be no doubt that the Cardinals of France, perhaps even the King himself, have approved my plans for the future. I am within a few months, weeks perhaps, of achieving my ambition. The war has ended? So what? There has to be a treaty, they have to send me this letter. But I know how to read between the lines.

'Gentlemen, it's time to turn away from considering the English and matters on the coast. Our future lies inland, with the Nawab of the Carnatic, and ultimately with the Nizam-ul-Mulk.'

Over the next hour Dupleix discoursed on his plan of action. He brooked no interruption and after a while none was offered, for the ideas he expounded were complex and the patterns into which they were woven bore the intricacy of his particular genius. The plan harked back to the struggle for power that followed the death of Safdar Ali Khan. When Anwar-ud-Din had succeeded to the masnad of the Carnatic, only the supposed child murderer, Murtaza Ali, and the imprisoned ex-Killadar of Trichinopoly, Chanda Sahib, remained to dispute it. Because of his alleged crimes, Murtaza had ruled himself out of consideration, but Chanda Sahib's claim was in this respect untarnished. If he could be secretly brought out from the Maratha stronghold of Satara where he had been under arrest since the Maratha invasion, then he could be used.

'Used for what?' Danton asked.

Dupleix stared at him, amazed at the man's lack of understanding, then he said, 'To carry on the war by other means, of course.'

Danton shook his head, lost.

'I might explain,' de Bussy cut in, 'that Anwar-ud-Din was nominated by Asaf Jah, but since Nasir Jang has become Nizam, he will naturally want to give the Carnatic to his own man if he can.'

'And you want to persuade Nasir Jang to give the Carnatic to Chanda Sahib?' Danton asked.

'I do!' Dupleix laughed. 'But there's no possibility of that.'

'Then what?'

'A little meddling. It's obvious! If Nasir Jang won't appoint Chanda Sahib, then we shall have to create another Nizam who will.'

The entire Council, with the exception of de Bussy, were openly shocked.

'*Dieu!* Do you realize what you're suggesting?' D'Auteuil sat up. 'That's not meddling in Indian politics! That's shaping it in its entirety!'

Dupleix raised his index finger. '*Précisement!*'

Suddenly, everyone was talking.

'*Bof!*'

'It's impossible!'

'Think of the consequences!'

'Why not?' Dupleix shrugged. He rose and stepped to the window, his hands clasped at his back. 'Why not shape events the way we want them? Why not put Chanda Sahib on the masnad of Arcot? I have it that he is brave and warlike and ambitious, and what's more, inclined towards us. It is my opinion that he will make a very fine nawab.'

'Chanda Sahib?'

'Yes. Can't you see it? He'll be our friend for evermore. He'll strangle the British the moment we ask him, *et*

331

Madras est foutue! And then he'll give the trade of Madras to us.'

'There's just the little problem of Nasir Jang,' de Bussy said lightly.

'There is no problem.' Dupleix's eyes were alight now. 'You're forgetting the Battle of St Thome. Our troops have proved themselves beyond all doubt against Moghul horsemen. What was accomplished on the banks of the Adiyar River was glorious, but it was much more than that. It was a turning point in history. The corruptness of Moghul power has been exposed. They're in awe of our infantry now. They live in fear of us. Don't you see what that means?'

His question reverberated into the silence. He sighed and made a gesture as if he had been strewing pearls before swine. 'Oh, you blind men! But I suppose I cannot expect everyone to see things in the vivid colours that I do. Let me explain: the facts are clear enough.'

He began to tick them off on his fingers. 'We maintain Chanda Sahib's relatives – his son, Raza Sahib, and all his close family, are here in Pondicherry as our guests. Don't forget that he's a Navait, and many of that sect still hold jagirs all over the Carnatic, making them useful allies. Then there's Murtaza Ali at Vellore, and the Killadar of Wandiwash, and plenty of other nobles who were once happy to be Chanda Sahib's friends, and who only suffer Anwar-ud-Din because they have to. As soon as his army threatens to approach they hide themselves away inside their forts like so many snails, and wait for him to go away. They will certainly switch from cowering neutrality to open support for Chanda once he proves himself.'

'Oh, yes, if he proves himself,' d'Auteuil said. 'But how will he do that? He has no chance of overcoming Anwar-ud-Din's army, even in its present reduced condition.'

Dupleix was triumphant. 'We'll not only release Chanda Sahib, but arm him too.'

'With our own troops?'

'There may be no need. With the right persuasion, and two or three lakhs, we could approach Balaji Rao, who, don't forget, is both Chanda's jailer and chief of a large Maratha army. He could raise twenty, thirty thousand men!'

'The Marathas won't move on the Carnatic for three lakhs,' d'Auteuil said, 'or for three hundred.'

'No. But they will for religion.' Dupleix grinned. 'We'll speak grandly of the restoration of Trichinopoly to Hindu rule. Chanda will cede that gladly. What's Trichinopoly? I'll ask him – and the Raja of Tanjore claims it anyway, and so does Mysore. It'll probably fall to a Hindu ruler soon in any case. Let it go, I'll say, and with it you can purchase the rest of the Carnatic.'

'You really believe he'll be able to overthrow Anwar-ud-Din?' d'Espre-menil asked.

'Without doubt. And just to make sure, Raza Sahib can go to him with two thousand of our trained sipahis. Anwar-ud-Din's army will turn and run when they see French uniforms.'

The glare from the window hurt de Bussy's eyes as his glance followed the Governor-General. I can't prevent this, he thought unhappily, so I'll have to go along with it. 'What will you do about Nasir Jang?' he asked, politely omitting to mention the half-million-strong army of the Nizam.

'I don't know yet,' Dupleix said, his eyes gazing back. But the smile on his lips said otherwise, and de Bussy saw that his superior had lied: Dupleix knew exactly what he was going to do.

Although he had asked the question, de Bussy knew too. It was contrary to the wishes of the *Compagnie* and the King of France, and flew in the face of the Nizam's stated policy, but Dupleix would buy Chanda Sahib, the pretender to the nawabship of the Carnatic, out of captivity, and together they would plan a coup. Then he would bring in Muzaffar Jang, Nasir Jang's defeated nephew, the man who was driven from Hyderabad after Asaf Jah's death. Dupleix would make available French military advisers, a body of infantry and enough money to raise an army. It was just as the Englishman Flint had been unwise enough to explain to Nasir Jang.

At present Anwar-ud-Din's army was conveniently assembled at Ambur. What better time to fall upon it, and stamp it into the ground?

The settlement of Ambur straddled the pass through the Javadi Hills. It lay quiet within its ancient walls, spurned by the guardians of Moghul power. For Anwar-ud-Din's people the tents of their forefathers, pitched precariously on the slopes of the hard earth, and under the crescent of the five-day-old moon, provided sufficient comforts.

It was the hour after evening prayers, in the first hour of true darkness, and the whole encampment had come to throng the hillside around their nawab's tent.

The gorgeous shamianah of the Lord of Arcot was packed with hundreds of men. The lesser canopies of his nobles that surrounded it stood empty, islands in a sea of men, and beyond them again the many shelters of the soldiery were unattended right to the bounds.

Dusky light shone from a doorway where necks craned forward so that eyes could see. Under the greatest of the pierced lamps within the grand shamianah Anwar-ud-Din sat stiffly in his high place, his advisers on either hand, his three turbulent sons below him, and the qasis and mullahs of the Faith present to give their judgment in the grave matter now before them.

Muhammad Ali was silent now, temporarily mollified by the peace of the *salat*, but he had flared with affronted righteousness before prayers, when Anwar-ud-Din used the present of the English merchant, Stratford Flint, the wonderful brass machine, to determine *quibla*.

'It defiles us!' he had shouted, and many of the religious scholars had nodded. 'To use an infidel device to point the direction to Mecca is a sacrilege!'

'My son, it was a well-meant gift, sent in acknowledgment of the return of the English merchant's son.'

Muhammad spat at the mention of the name.

'It is this kumpas machine that guides the great black ships of the feringhee across the two oceans of the world. If such a machine points truly then who will say we may not use it for *quibla*?'

'I say that! It is an engine of Shatan!'

Muhammad's exasperation at being overruled was immense. His anger betrayed his inner feelings, betrayed his plan. 'I demand you convene a court! I have a quorum. That is my right!'

'For what purpose?' Anwar-ud-Din said, unruffled, though he knew that it was only a pretext. 'We may discuss *quibla* privately.'

'No, Father. This is a matter to lay before the whole camp. That – and another matter.'

Now the nawab adjusted the fall of his robe as he regarded Muhammad. Oh, you have quietude in your mind for the present, he told him silently, but your heart is full of cruelty and your whole being is a tangle of plots. You will not rest until you have forced your wife to embrace public disgrace and then death. You will not rest until you have unseated me and taken this realm into unholy war. Unfortunately, I can do little to stop you, should you succeed in getting the spiritual leaders on your side. Once they come together they outweigh my power.

His eyes moved methodically along the row of religious judges who had been convened to consider the question of *quibla* but had now, as tradition demanded, turned their attention to petitions. This time there was only one: the amazing case of Yasmin, the wife of Muhammad Ali Khan, Prince of the Carnatic.

He looked at her, standing in the smoky light, silent and chaste in her veil. No one but I can know her courage, or the true passions concealed by those downcast eyes. But what may be done? If it comes to pass that she dies, then surely that is what Allah wants. How may I meddle in her destiny? How can I, a mortal man, save her life when it is an issue so clearly in the hands of God? Every issue is in the hands of God. Not a leaf stirs, not a butterfly's wing trembles, but that He commands it.

He resettled himself. *Insh'allah.* She was born to live,

and she has lived. Let us be thankful for that, and beseech God in His Heaven, for it is certain that once she is found guilty under the *zina* law, no power in our world can prevent her death by stoning.

'Know, Yasmin Begum, that you have been accused by your husband, the Prince Muhammad Ali, of lewd behaviour, in that you showed yourself to a man though this was not approved by your husband. Know that you are further accused of passing time alone with this man, though he is an infidel, and fornicating with him, though you are a married woman. Know that it is your purpose here to weigh your guilt against your innocence, and that if the case is proved against you, it shall be our task to pronounce due punishment. Do you understand?'

Yasmin stood alone, swathed in a sari-like garment of sombre black. She was conscious of the curved dagger concealed at her waist, her one consolation in this hour of loneliness and hellish lies. She looked up as the words of the prosecutor filled the dead air of Anwar-ud-Din's tent. Muhammad's sensational denunciation after prayers had brought everyone who could justify their presence. The door was packed with men, straining their necks, packing against the guards, and as she listened to the charges laid against her she could sense a wall of hidden female eavesdroppers cupping their ears to hear the proceedings beyond the hangings.

'Do you understand?'

Her voice was a whisper behind her veil. '*Han.*' Yes.

She tried to control her fear, but memories of the obscene stoning at Hyderabad haunted her. She turned to other memories in order to escape the fear – wonderful memories, happy recollections of the love she had felt for Hayden Flint, and of the times they had spent together, but all these seemed to isolate her and underline the truth of her guilt.

'Prince Muhammad Ali Khan shall speak.'

She watched Muhammad deliver his diatribe, an impassioned catalogue of dates and places, her trysts and assignations in Hyderabad, all meticulously noted and recorded by his spies, and delivered in a wounded tone that also damned her. I hurt you, she thought. That's quite true. I hurt you and hurt you again, and I did not care. Some men are easy to hurt carelessly because they have delicate souls; some are easy to hurt out of spite because they are insensitive as oxen. I only hurt you, Mohammad, because pride was your weakness. I never hated you, I only ever pitied you. And that is what hurt you most.

She endured the lies of witnesses, and vowed silently that whatever else might be said, there would be no admission from her. No confession. No defence. She would say nothing, absolutely nothing, and thereby imply her contempt.

She looked to Anwar-ud-Din, who returned her gaze momentarily before turning away. If he refused to speak on her behalf there could be no hope, and no course left to take. Or, at least, no course with honour. The only possible defence was to plead a conflict of higher interests, of lord over husband, but she had decided against that.

'Will you say nothing in your defence?' Anwar-ud-Din enquired at last. He spoke as if addressing a child.

She held her peace disdainfully, as if the question had not been asked. Her fingers strayed to the hilt of the dagger that was hidden in her waistband.

'I command you to reply!'

'Then, lord, hear this: I have no plea. I admit nothing. I deny nothing. If you have the power and the desire to illuminate the understanding of this court – for God knows it wallows in darkness now – then you must speak. You are Anwar-ud-Din, Lord of the Carnatic, and all here present know that your word is law.'

The nawab shifted uneasily; he was unnerved. She had read him with confidence. He had applied as much pressure upon her as he dared. The imperious command to speak, what a sham! The truth was as fragile as eggshells. What if she broke through now? How then the mighty lord, beset by intrigues? If they knew what Anwar-ud-Din had ordered! If she were to say that he had commanded her

337

married to his son for the express purpose of controlling him, what outrage they would show. Such a scandalous admission would bring him down; Muhammad was rising to his zenith on a tide of religious zeal, carrying the army with him. She could see the working of his mind too: a revolt in the camp at Ambur; manipulated factions; a night of butchery. Then a triumphant return to Arcot for Muhammad Ali Khan, the new nawab, his father's head dripping red in a carpetbag at his saddle.

But Anwar-ud-Din knew his people, and he knew Yasmin Begum best of all. She would not reveal in public the onus he had placed upon her, the duty of spying on his most dangerous son. She would not speak of it even though it was the only possible way back to life.

The nawab's fingers teased his beard, then he addressed his son directly. 'It would be proper for you to produce the man who you say defiled your wife. His reputation is diminished by your claims, therefore it is only fitting he be allowed to speak in his own defence.'

'That is not a requirement,' Muhammad said. 'I have produced witnesses enough. That Hayden Flint has fled from justice is not our concern. And what reputation has an infidel feringhee that we must consider it? Are they not all liars and cheats and adulterers?' He paused to stare around at the bearded scholars. 'I believe these wise heads have heard more than enough. They know the truth. They know what must be done.'

Beyond the screens, the crowd stirred impatiently, but Yasmin remained impassive.

The common people had found her guilty already. Unanimously.

One by one the qasi signalled their decisions, each with a stroke of the hand. And Anwar-ud-Din stared back, not unmoved, but sighing. He accepted the loss of this woman, his favourite instrument of statecraft, with the same regret that he had last year accepted the loss of a favourite horse.

Two big eunuchs laid rough hands on her. She was no

338

longer a princess, not even a lady. Now she was no better than a whore, a woman who had betrayed her husband.

Terror clutched at her. She heard shouting as the verdict was given. The calls for punishment increased. She became keenly aware of the dusty, fusty smell of the tent, the suffocating stink of hot grease from the huge brass lanterns.

The swelling crowd outside was quickly becoming a mob. She felt its mood darkening. It would be a dangerous force when ignited by the fanatical demands that Muhammad would know how to whip up. I can see it, she thought, giving in to the terror despite herself. I can see their torches lighting me to hell. God save me! In moments it could be over! I could be gone from this world!

The eunuchs gripped her arms tightly and lifted her to lead her away. The overwhelming power of their hands sent another surge of fear through her. They pushed her forward so violently that she fell down on to the carpets and slid with outstretched hands, her veil torn from her head. The fall knocked the wind from her, and a wave of panic submerged her. She felt kicks and punches on her back and head before the eunuchs pressed through the mob and took hold of her again. Their size and strength made them irresistible.

At the entrance to the tent they thrust her out into the open air. The hillside was a constellation of burning brands, white corah cotton and dark faces dancing like devils in the night. She heard shouting, and now jezail shots. Muhammad's voice was exhorting them above the din, but it seemed in the darkness that the fiercest noise was coming from the far fringes of the gathering.

Heads began to turn. Thousands of men, the horse warriors of Anwar-ud-Din's levy army, were running down off the slopes, dispersing into the night, making for the valley where the horses were corralled. Suddenly a volley of shots exploded off the crags and a fan of fire stabbed out in the night like the tines of a hair comb; a lone trumpet sounded, terrifyingly close. Then the foreign soldiers crested the rise and moved out of the shadows into the moonlight, a sight to freeze the marrow in any man's bones.

As she watched, the front rank reloaded as the rear rank advanced through them to give cover. There were hundreds of them, white men and trained uniformed sipahis in their separate companies, drawn up in close order, spaced only an arm's length apart. A drumming started up, powerful and loud and confident, and as regular as the ticking of a European clock. The soldiers marched forward, the front rank charging their spiked muskets, holding them outstretched at belly height, white hose flashing in unison on their shins, their tricorns cutting dark silhouettes against the pearly sky, the glitter of gold tape and buttons on their Brandenburgs making them seem like demons made of metal, as they knelt to fire.

The effect of the rippling volley on Anwar-ud-Din's army was immediate. At Madras, Yasmin had seen these men ride their horses time and again on to the disciplined bayonets of French troops, driven on by raw courage and faith in the Prophet's mercy. But now it was different. Not a man among them had failed to hear the terrifying stories of the unbreakable line of blue-jacketed men who dealt bloody slaughter to any who dared approach them. This, she knew, would be their worst possible nightmare: that the awesome killing machine should pursue them into their encampment, in the heart of the Carnatic.

She too was outraged. Warring at night made no sense. Who would see the glory of battle? Who would bear witness to the heroism? It was the work of jackals to ambush their opponents at night. Jackals and filthy carrion-eaters.

She felt her Hindu warrior blood surge. Then the grip on her arms slackened as the line of French troops began to harrow the camp. The eunuchs beside her stared open-mouthed. Neither had experienced so much as a year of life beyond Arcot's zenana walls. In all directions the nawab's best warriors were throwing down their firebrands and cascading away from the camp in terror. They saw Anwar-ud-Din's generals issuing from the shamianah, astonished at the barbarity and callousness of the night attack, their calls to rally going unheeded. They saw the royal choukedars streaming out, never without their bright helmets and mail, their swords drawn. But the rest were fleeing, fearing they would be ordered to stand against the French. The crush of men threw down tents and trampled everything in their path except for the great shamianah of Anwar-ud-Din itself.

Yasmin found herself slammed to the ground, and almost in the same instant the French infantry ranks parted and a cannon opened fire. It was near, no more than a hundred paces, and its throaty roar deafened. She saw the broad swathe of death scythe towards her, smoke ballooning out to cover the destruction, and felt one of the eunuch's beside her collapse like a shot elephant.

She got to her feet, gasping with horror, and ran back towards the shamianah, where she was trapped against the side of the nawab's tent. To her right was the entrance: a dense mass of men fighting to escape; to her front the thousand bayonets of the French line; behind her a blank tent wall. She was pushed towards the taut plane of reinforced fabric that barred her way. Her fingernails tore across the smooth blackbuck-skin decorations, but she could find no purchase on the surface. She managed to turn again, and saw the European soldiers, their inexorable steps marching closer.

She dragged at the nearest guy rope, the harsh fibre drawing blood from her palms. Panic seized her again, but the pain helped her to fight it down. She tried to lift the edge of the tent off the ground, but it was pegged down by long iron spikes that had been hammered into the rocky earth, so close-spaced they would not permit even a boy to wriggle through.

'*Punah i khoda!*' she cried out. God save me!

There was a trumpet blast; the drumbeat checked. The French line halted in swirls of smoke. She saw the tail of the officer's horse flick, his sword glinting in the moonlight, then he screamed an order. Instantly the front rank raised their muskets to their cheeks and loosed off another terrible, flickering volley that stabbed tines of fire into the

341

night. She threw herself to the ground, and as she lay there cradling her head she felt a sudden pain. It was barely perceptible at first, but when she tried to turn over something sharp dug at her groin.

Behind her some of the choukedars of the Royal Guard had managed to steady themselves. Unused to fighting on foot, many of them had fled to their tents to gather up arms, then gone down to their horses. The bravest dozen had ridden back, wielding swords or lances, throwing their unsaddled mounts into the advancing French. With only a namdah saddle cloth under them and nothing but their horse's mane to hold on to, they were easy prey for French bayonets.

More sowars gathered and bore down on the French line, but three cannon were already trained on them. The first forlorn hope was smashed as it closed on the infantry, the second was cut to pieces by another volley of musket-fire.

One horseman miraculously survived, pressing himself hard down against the neck of his mount, his swordblade held out like a sickle as he skidded and wheeled into the line. She saw his insane intent was to take the *alam* of the enemy. The flag carried close to the mounted officer was pale, with gold designs like axe-heads or stylized flowers. From the way it was borne up, much honour seemed to be vested in it. As the rider reached the close-packed line of bayonets his horse baulked, a dozen spikes plucked him up and pitched him to the ground. Yasmin saw the cleverness of the foreign way of fighting. How great the control with which they move, she thought. So long as they take care always to have one rank with loaded muskets they are ready to repel any assault. So long as each man stays with and protects his brothers to left and right they can take ground and hold it. Their march cannot be stopped.

A great cry of dismay went up nearby. Along the valley, dimly perceived at first, but growing more visible as they advanced, was a great army – five, ten, fifteen thousand, in ghostly white pagri and jama, moving up to fill the space cut by the French line. Yasmin gasped. This could only be an army raised by Muzaffar Jang and Chanda Sahib. Following the French shock assault it began moving on the nawab's tent. A man stumbled into her, and she felt again the sharp pain in her thigh. Her hand went to the source of the pain. There was blood.

'*Barik Allah!*'

It was her own curved dagger that she had wound into her waistband. Muffled shouts and the shapes of bodies struggling against the tent walls came from inside. Faithful to the rule that no man may enter the lord's tent armed they had laid aside their weapons when they packed in to see her tried. Now they were imprisoned. Quickly she drew out the knife and hacked into the wall, cutting a long vertical slit. There was a sudden and unexpected brilliance, the slit ripped and half a dozen men burst through and scattered. She slashed two more panels, shouting a desperate warning, but many of those who stumbled out ran blindly into the deadly foreign war machine and were impaled. Then, as the rush began to move the other way, she found herself forced through the gash and into the tent.

There was chaos in the great assembly space. High overhead something was burning, filling the top of the tent with light and smoke. Below, the collapsible screens and draperies that divided the interior into many separate sections had been torn down or overturned. The women's section, which had been sealed off, communicating only with the screened zenana tents behind the shamianah, was now violated. The fifty or so women of the royal harem screamed as scores of men burst into their midst. She saw cheetahs snarling in their cages, their handlers nowhere to be seen. Then the brilliance overhead flared brighter and one of the three huge brass lanterns came crashing down. Flames started to flicker up the central pole.

On the far side of the tent, perhaps fifty paces away, hundreds of men fought to get out before the burning canopy parted and caved in on them. Nearby, royal furniture and hangings were passed over the heads of the frantic mob: the masnad, Anwar-ud-Din's fine chillum, a dozen of his biggest and most precious wine jars, gold incense holders, a huge silver-bound Koran, all being conveyed to safety. She saw Muhammad marshalling the loyal van of troops that would protect Anwar-ud-Din's person as they withdrew. Then, on an instant, the far wall of the tent was enveloped in a rush of flame as the impregnated fabric caught a draught. It was consumed with frightening speed as she watched. With helpless certainty she saw the supporting stays burn through, the blazing canopy collapse. She heard anguished screaming and for a moment she was covered in folds of heavy fabric, but there was no fire here, and she used her dagger to cut her way out to the open air.

She emerged into hell. A squadron of hostile sowars rode in like evil djinns, their lance-tips and talwars flashing as they circled the fringes of the blaze, hacking down the fugitives from the fire. Some kicked their horses into the flames to slash at the whirling, stamping men trapped and burning within.

As Yasmin dived down among a mass of tent shrouds she recognized the terrible bearlike figure of Shaikh Hasan, notorious jemadar of the French sipahis. Bellowing, he led his men on a final charge towards the royal van. Mahfuz Khan was swept down as he tried to protect his father; Anwar-ud-Din's brother was bayoneted. Desperately, from her hidden position, she looked for Mohammad, but the bodyguard seethed around in a tangle of limbs and weapons, until the huge Shaikh Hasan ploughed into their midst. His great battle sword rang on steel and bone, opening a path to Anwar-ud-Din himself.

'*Bismillah ir ruhman ir ruheem!*' she prayed. In the name of God, the most merciful and beneficial. 'Save my lord, Anwar-ud-Din!'

But the single combat was clearly hopeless: the once-talented swordsman was now too old and too slow to deflect, with his delicate fencing strokes, the clashing sweeps of the monstrous Shaikh Hasan. The bear clove Anwar-ud-Din's ornate sword aside, and with the next stroke axed the blade through his quarry's neck.

Yasmin stared in horror as the nawab's head was snatched up and held aloft, dripping red. The balaband of pearls had slipped down over his now sightless eyes, but the grey face, contorted in shock, was recognizable to his people.

'See! See!' the enemy shouted. 'Your despicable pretender is dead! Long live the true Nawab of the Carnatic, Chanda Sahib!'

All resistance dissolved as the forces of the new Lord of the Carnatic surged forward. In that moment the nature of the battle changed: its pace quickened and its mood polarized to extremes of joy and despair as it became a rout.

Suddenly, Yasmin realized that the wavecrest of battle had swept past her. Blasted out of her stupor, her first thought was to run forward, to raise her knife and throw herself at Shaikh Hasan in vengeance, but rising up before her, appearing from beneath a smouldering piece of tentage, was a nightmarish sight.

Muhammad, his sword in his hand, clothes smoking and glowing in scarlet rings where holes had been burned through to his skin, staggered towards her. He clutched his arm across his eyes like a blind man, tottering as if drunk, moaning and cursing, slashing at imagined attackers.

In that instant she felt the power she had over him. It would be so easy to steal up and plunge the knife into him, or slit his despicable throat. It was as if the ivory of the handle pulsed with an intent of its own; her palm itched to bury the blade in his heart.

As he passed, unaware of her, she ambushed him, leaping out from her cover and grabbing him by the neck to pull him down. His sword flew from his hand. At the same time she shouted his name, and pulled him to the ground.

'Muhammad, Muhammad! It is me! Me, do you hear?'

'Oh, torturers of hell,' he shouted, half mad at the pain. 'I hear her voice!'

'Come with me!'

'Am I dead then? I cannot see! My eyes are plucked out!'

She dragged his arm from his face, and saw the raw and

blackened flesh of his cheeks and forehead, as if he had caught a firebrand in the face.

He tried to crawl. 'Help me, Yasmin!'

She snarled at him. 'Carrion! I desire to kill you, as you desired to kill me!'

'Mercy!' He made to shield himself from the killing stroke.

'Do not cower, Muhammad Ali Khan! Not at this moment of your fondest desire!' She shouted at him, hating him. 'Your father is dead. So too is Mahfuz. You are granted fulfilment, Lord of the Carnatic!'

'Ugh!' His voice was cracked with loathing. 'You would not kill me?'

'I would happily kill the gutless maggot I have as husband, but I cannot kill the lord to whom my word is pledged. Come! You must flee to fight another day. This battle is lost and Anwar-ud-Din is murdered. You must live, so that one day you may avenge him!'

'Lead me, then! Lead me from here – ' His voice begged her, strengthened now by pathetic hope and a sickening show of gratitude. 'If you will save me, I shall reward you with anything you desire. *Allah hafiz!*'

'With God's aid, we may yet rally those you can trust. With His help you may yet reach the treasury of Arcot, and then you can flee south to Trichinopoly to raise another army.' She scrambled up, pulling him after her. 'Follow this way. Down the hill. To the horses, and freedom.'

FOURTEEN

The Untouchables were lifting slaughtered cows from Madras's main well, using a timber tripod and a block and tackle. These were the hollow-eyed men, non-men, doomed from birth by their own gods to a lifetime of filth and pollution and degradation. Their hair was cut to the bone and their nakedness covered by Company pyjamas, but Hayden Flint saw no sign that they wore their European clothes with the self-respect the Company had intended.

A languid sentry spat betel beside a row of reeking carrion. '*Hankar ek saf!*' Hoist away! '*Is taraf! Us taraf! Is taraf! Jaldi!*'

Sinews strained until the knotted rope that was looped round the thinnest part of the cow's hind leg jerked up hard to the block. The sagging carcass was blackened, the stench putrid. Water trickled from the decomposing snout back down the well, until they manhandled the bloated form to the dust.

Hayden Flint looked away, compressing his lips, trying not to breathe. A wave of faintness from the fever he had caught forced him to sit down on a low wall nearby, but the news he had overheard was urgent. After a brief respite he got to his feet again.

It was the burning height of the day. Waves of intolerable brightness flushed over the war-striped walls and spires of Fort St George. Madras had been brought low by the occupying French, and massive rebuilding was required. The ill-treated masonry appeared alien to his eye after so long at Hyderabad. Here the rational had once ruled with iron certainty, superstition had been banished, and with it the magic of the land. Now the English forms were broken,

347

their insides laid bare. The place was worse than if the Enlightenment had never been. Once banished, he heard Yasmin tell him, magic can never return.

At Triplicane, outside the bounds of the fort, he had seen Charles Savage's house, standing caged in a scaffold of bamboo. It had been reduced to little more than a shell after serving as a domicile for French officers. It was said that the floor of the merchant's main room had been pulled up and the bullion he had hidden there taken. Even so, Hayden Flint thought, the man cannot have been totally ruined for he has returned from Calcutta and now the rebuilding is almost complete. How long will it be before my father chooses to build a bigger mansion than his on the adjoining plot?

A gargoyle broken off from the ruined church grinned at him as he passed. In his fever it resembled the devil he saw in Clive. I have seen dozens of young Company writers die within their seven-year terms, he thought. My suspicion was always that in hard times the most odious fellows went unscathed, while the best of characters died young. Like poor Quinn – there was a blameless soul! Yet he was drowned, whereas I was not. So what are we to believe? Is life truly raw and random and impersonal? Is the Reverend Forde right in his sermons on free will? Are the mullahs correct when they speak of the will of Allah? Or is it that we are, in fact, ruled by a Chinaman's constellations, and subject to a universal law that those born under the sign of the rat or the snake are destined to outlive those born as rabbits or tigers? Then again, is there a deeper and more subtle way to it as my father holds, and as Yasmin always swore? It is too complicated for science! I cannot comprehend it!

Ah, but Yasmin . . .

It was never my forecast that she was fated to fail. Strength shone from her. If ever there was one well starred . . . I cannot make myself believe in her death, but even if she lives, her adventurous spirit must be trapped once more in the small world that was most hateful to her.

His thoughts turned away as the pain of the news he had overheard daggered him. He stumbled, reached out to steady himself, gripped by the urgency of passing on what Governor Sawyer, Morse's successor, had just learned. He had to find Clive and tell him immediately, before Sawyer discovered what he had overheard and commanded him to silence.

This mission is too dangerous, he thought. To seek out Robert Clive is the last thing I should do. The gulf that stands between us now is deadly. In Arkali's name Clive has threatened to kill me the next time we meet eye to eye. His grudge is implacable, and inexplicable – too relentless to be purely a matter of honour.

As he passed into the shadow of the Company office, a hard knot of reluctance grew in his belly at the thought of facing Clive. He reached the side door, shivering despite the heat, and opened it on a game of whist. The table was round, elbow-polished, scattered with silver rupees and playing cards. Four squat wine bottles had already been emptied. Maskelyne and two other players in red Company jackets studied their hands or fanned themselves languidly. Clive, once more a civilian after the cessation of war, was digesting a heavy lunch; he sat squarely with his back to the door. At the sound of it opening, he turned, registered the identity of the newcomer and returned his attention to the game.

'By God, Maskelyne, but the nightsoil's rank today. Wind must be blowing from the midden.'

Maskelyne put his head down, embarrassed, but unwilling to oppose Clive.

'Another trick,' one of the players said, picking up the cards he had trumped.

'Clive!' Hayden's voice was weary, the snub unnoticed. His face was cold and sweating. 'Clive, I need to speak with you.'

Clive rose, a truculent grin suddenly distorting his unbeautiful features. 'Ah, no wonder there's a stink in here. Look what's swilled in under the door.'

Maskelyne came forward and put a hand on his cuff in an attempt to placate him, but the gesture had the opposite effect and Clive's face coloured up in fury.

'Clive, for God's sake – ' Maskelyne's hand was knocked away. His wine glass pitched from the table, smashing on the floorboards.

'You have front coming here and asking to speak with me, sir!'

'I have news – '

'Well, then, tell me. And then get out.'

Hayden's control faltered. 'I warn you, sir, do not talk to me that way.'

Outraged amusement burst from Clive. 'You do what? You warn me?' He turned to his frozen-faced companions. 'He warns me. This mannerless prick wants the respect due a gentleman, when he is no gentleman at all. And he has the effrontery to warn me!'

'Clive. I came here to tell you – '

'You, sir, shall not talk to me. Here or anywhere else. You have insulted a lady, and you have yet to collect your punishment for that!'

'Listen to me!'

'No! You listen! You are a strutting peacock, and I'll have satisfaction from you! D'you hear me?'

Hayden Flint's own anger crescendoed, pushing up through his fever-weakened body. Who was this man to tell him how to conduct his affairs? How did he imagine he held such rank?

'What passed between myself and Arkali Savage was none of your concern, Mr Clive.'

'Did you think I'd stand idly by and watch you torture her? Did you? No, sir! I've decided that you shall pay. You shall account for yourself on the field!'

A silence opened between them.

Hayden Flint broke it. Clive's words acted on him as if a pail of water had been thrown in his face. 'Duelling is strictly forbidden. The crime of monomachy is punishable by – '

'There we have it! As I said: a coward. Despite all his big claims.' Clive's face loomed, rage-filled, maleficent. 'You're a cowardly prick, and I'll cut out your liver if you do not consent to give me satisfaction!'

'For God's sake, Robert, Hayden's right. You'll both be transported.' Maskelyne made to come between them, but Clive shoved him away easily.

'Is it a brawl here and now that you want?' Hayden Flint said, his heart pumping, his head lightening.

'Oh, no!' Clive's malice showed naked. 'You don't get away like that. I, at least, am a gentleman. We shall have pistols, sir! The bullet! That's what you will face. Twenty-six paces, and I'll blow your cowardly heart out of you and into the dust. See if I don't, by God!'

'Look here – '

'Will you or won't you?'

'You're drunk, sir!'

'Answer me, damn-you-to-hell!'

Hayden Flint was suddenly appalled. He felt a wave of weakness hit him as he faced the savagery of Clive's personality. There seemed no way to avoid it. He could not imagine how this grotesque pass had been reached. The wrong word now and both their lives and futures would be plunged into senseless jeopardy.

If only Clive had not downed two bottles of red wine, he thought despairingly. Sweet Jesus, look at his eyes! He hates me. I do believe he wants to kill me, as he says. I shouldn't have come here. If I'd not overheard the Governor's words this morning, or if the message had not arrived, I would not have known. But it did arrive, and I do know. These things have happened, and the chaos has come upon us. It's just kismet.

'You leave me no alternative,' he said tightly.

'There is only one: you may slide out of here on the flat of your belly!'

'Tomorrow, then. At first light, on Pedda Naik's Petta.'

'Excellent.' Clive's chin jutted. 'Edmund, you will be my second.'

'I'm sorry, Clive. I will not.'

'As you wish.' Clive's eyes never left Hayden Flint's face. 'Then you, John Anderson.'

'Yes, Clive. If you want me to. I'd be honoured.'

'In that case I'll second Hayden,' Maskelyne said suddenly, his voice firming.

Clive glanced at him. 'Deserting me, are you? When I'm upholding a lady's honour? You've got a sister, haven't you? What if it had been Margaret he'd used like that?'

'You're drunk, Robert.'

'Not so drunk that I don't know a coward when I see one. A coward who – '

'That's quite enough!' Maskelyne said.

' – a coward who has broken the spirit of a helpless girl. Broken it along with his empty promise and stamped it under the heel of his boot. Without a second thought. Without any feeling. You make me want to spew my guts, Hayden Flint. Why a lady should think anything of you eludes me. You're an unfeeling reptile who deserves death. And I mean to give it to you. D'you hear me?'

Hayden Flint listened to the tirade unflinchingly, but Clive's words speared him again and again because he knew they were true.

'I came here to tell you all . . .' he said, and stopped as the trembling took him.

Clive glared at him. 'The man's a lunatic,' he said, walking away contemptuously. 'Is that all you have to say? By God, the fellow's ripe for Bedlam!'

'Good God, Clive, can't you see he's unwell?' Maskelyne cut in. He steered Hayden to a chair and sat him down. 'Go on,' he urged. 'What is it?'

Hayden roused himself as the shivering left him. 'I came to tell you – to tell you all – the news that's reached the Governor. The nawab's camp has been sacked. His army is scattered. Anwar-ud-Din . . . is dead.'

There was a stunned pause, then Clive asked, 'Anwar-ud-Din? Are you certain of that?'

'That was the message conveyed to the Governor.'

Anderson said, 'But that's impossible!'

'How did it happen? A revolt?' Clive demanded.

'No . . . Chanda Sahib and . . . Muzaffar Jang.' He started to cough.

Maskelyne moved in time to catch him as he began to pass out. 'Give him a drink somebody. *Bhisti! Ek glass pani lao! Jaldi!*'

Hayden Flint drank gratefully, though the water was warm and tainted. 'It seems that Chanda Sahib's army fell on the nawab's camp at the Pass of Ambur, and routed him. Thirty thousand men. It was a total defeat.'

'And a total victory.' Clive's eyes were looking at his own private vision. 'And did the messenger say that Dupleix sent French troops, or French-trained sepoys, in support?'

'Yes, he did.'

'I knew it. By God, then that is a disaster!' Clive's expression was unreadable. 'Don't you see? If Dupleix has unseated Anwar-ud-Din, then he's gone too far. There'll be all hell to pay. It's a disaster.'

'For us?' Anderson asked, perplexed by Clive's reaction. 'Do you mean a disaster for us?'

'Not for me, my boys! Not a bit of it. I'm headed for an end to the tally books. I'm headed for glory.'

A commotion behind them signalled the arrival of half a dozen other writers, and soon the news was being shouted all over the building.

'It's said that Anwar-ud-Din was beheaded by Shaikh Hasan, the jamadar of the French sepoys.'

Clive wiped at his mouth. The news affected him, sobered him almost immediately. He closed the furnace door on his rage in a way that Hayden Flint marvelled at. His grasp of political consequences was second to none, and everyone in the room naturally looked to him.

'What else? What about Mahfuz Khan?'

Hayden Flint shook his head. 'It's said that Mahfuz Khan is also dead.'

'By God! And Muhammad Ali?'

'I have no certain news of that.' Hayden felt the fear

crowding him, and he prayed inwardly for Yasmin. ' "Great bloodshed among the royal party" – that's what the messenger said. The pretender's orders were explicit. Anyone at all, male or female, connected with Anwar-ud-Din's family was to be – '

'Yes, made meat by their swords, no doubt,' Clive finished for him. 'By God, you can be sure the Moghul are at their worst in a dynastic fight.'

'What does it mean?' Maskelyne asked.

Clive strode up the room and back. 'It's obvious. Dupleix will not rest until he has made a French empire in India. We already know that. But how can he do it when we're here? Certainly the French government and their *Compagnie* have put a stop to his war and given us back Madras, but remember this: there can be no prohibition on native princes prosecuting war upon one another. And, we may assume, no prohibition on French troops training, or even accompanying, native armies.'

They looked from one to another, then one of the younger writers asked, 'I don't see why we can assume that.'

Hayden Flint told him wearily: 'Because, Mr Glass, there has never been any need to make such a prohibition. Think! Until the French took their troops across the Adiyar River and smashed a mounted army that outnumbered them ten to one, everyone imagined the military power lay entirely with the Moghul princes. Why would the *Compagnie* prohibit something so improbable as using European troops as auxiliaries in a Moghul feud?'

Young Glass nodded in understanding.

Another of them asked, 'But you're saying this is a French scheme?'

'I'm saying that behind the fiction of French "tactical advisers" helping Moghul armies to combat one another there is an ulterior reality.' They gawked at him in silence, disturbed at the fearsome consequences of his warning. 'That ulterior reality, gentlemen, is this: it is not the five hundred Frenchmen aiding an army of ten thousand, it is the army of ten thousand legitimizing the actions of the five hundred. Dupleix's war is continuing. It is only ourselves who have stopped fighting.'

Another writer, Trenwith, shrugged. 'But doesn't it go against the principle of non-interference in Hindostan's political affairs?'

Clive cocked his head indulgently. 'We have always had more love for that idea than the French, Mr Trenwith. All Frenchmen have a passion for interfering with the internal politics of any people whom they consider to be barbarous or half-civilized. They are an expedient people, and none more so than Joseph Dupleix. If there's profit, or any advantage, to be had he'll not hesitate to interfere. And if Dupleix has interfered – as we now know he has – we can be certain he's done it, in the main, to further his cause against us.'

Hayden saw how Clive's realism stood out solid against their naivety like a mooring post in a fast-flowing tide. Most of John Company's writers rate him their leader, he thought. Look how they admire him. You can see it! He has a firm grasp of what motivates ordinary men, and he's invariably right in his assessments of them. Sweet Jesus, he has a strength of belief in himself that I'll never have. He has it right down to his boots. And a temper to match it. How could I have agreed to fight him tomorrow?

The morning was luminous, the sky a still, tropical purple. Dew lay on the earth where the stars had wept. Faint traceries of mist hung over the western watercourses. Edmund Maskelyne looked to his friend and companion with mounting agitation as they passed the sleepy guard, then walked out to Pedda Naik's Fetta. He tried to disguise it as hopeful sanguinity whenever Hayden Flint turned to him, but as they crossed the Garden Bridge, the tension grew too much for him.

'Hayden, for heaven's sake, won't you let me dissuade you from this folly?'

The other was pale-faced and drawn. He was weak, but

the fever had gone. He said quietly, 'I simply want to be at peace with myself.'

Maskelyne made a face as despair flushed through him. 'Well, nothing short of an ambush will prevail against Clive. You know that, don't you?'

'I have it that he's a poor shot. He missed his own head twice.'

'He killed your horse, right enough, Hayden.' His placidity had roused Maskelyne. 'And he'll kill you too! He's in love with Arkali, and he knows she'll never accept him while you're alive.'

'I suppose he wants to change her mind by becoming my murderer? Is that his logic? Edmund, Clive is many things, but he is no fool.'

'You don't understand. Robert may be an analytical thinker of the first class when it comes to war, but in love he is asinine. I don't believe he's thinking at all in this matter. He's reacting from the heart, and you know how dangerous that can be in someone of his nature. He's more than just your enemy.'

Hayden Flint felt the cold penetrating his bones. He turned to his second, wanting to make his position completely clear. 'I rejected Arkali because I was in love with another. That other may now be dead. Don't tell me I don't understand Clive's passion, or his despair. I have known both.'

'Then you'll see why he insults you. Please let me arbitrate between you. I'm sure I can disentangle this idiocy before one of you is killed and the other sent for trial.' Maskelyne's boyish face hardened. 'You're not English-born, Hayden. You know that technically the Company is not permitted to carry out executions. They can't legally hang you on the lease. And they can't sent you to England if you're a murderer. You know what they'll do – there are plenty of precedents for it – they'll sentence you to a flogging of five hundred lashes. And you'll die that way.' When he showed no reaction, Maskelyne added, 'Or Clive will hang. Is that what you want?'

'You'll not succeed, Edmund.'

'At what?'

'You're trying to sicken me, break my resolve.'

'Of course I am!'

'Then please stop it. I knew what I was doing when I accepted the challenge. And whatever you say, the fact remains, Clive has heaped insults on me. I know what he is about in that game better than you appear to do. You're mistaken if you believe he's trying to punish me for mistreating Arkali.'

'Isn't that his stated reason?'

'It's only what he says.'

Maskelyne's shoulders sagged. 'Then . . . I don't understand.'

'It's about destiny. Fortune.'

'It's a damned curious way to make his fortune!'

'I'm not talking about the making of a fortune.'

'Then what?'

Hayden Flint sighed, feeling the impossibility of conveying a self-evident truth. 'He's referring us to a higher authority.'

Maskelyne's exasperation spilled over now. 'Either you're a fool, or I am, for I cannot grasp what you're saying.'

'Listen: Hindostan has become a part of Robert Clive. He knows that here a man's destiny is already determined by the will of God. Don't you see what he's doing? He's deliberately setting his kismet against mine.'

Maskelyne shook his head. 'That's just Mussulman mumbo-jumbo! There's nothing at all to those ideas. It's like all those grotesque idols that help the Hindus spend their miserable lives in false worship. You can't believe any of that.'

'Can't I?'

'What about your cherished ideas of science? The new thought? Isn't all this – mysticism – contrary to those hard and rational views you once claimed to hold so dear? Hayden, what became of you out there?'

357

'I began to doubt pure rationality some time ago.'

Maskelyne's voice took on a keener edge as he saw the unshakeable conviction he was up against and he appealed to Hayden's conscience. 'You yourself brought us the news about Anwar-ud-Din. You, of all people, must appreciate how this puts St George in tremendous danger. Don't you think you have a duty to God and King, or to the Company, to preserve your life? This, this – *felo de se*, this suicide, is indefensible. And what of Clive – a man whom you declare a natural military genius? Don't you think it's your duty at least to refrain from slaughtering him before the coming struggle?'

'I do. But there are higher duties, and where they conflict I must follow the higher course. The Hindus have a saying: to accomplish any end, first you must set out along the path in the opposite direc – '

'Damn the Hindus!' Maskelyne scowled. 'You're moon-struck! Love-sick! You imagine your Moghul lady is dead, and therefore your life is not worth a fig. That's how you caught the fever. But it's all foolish thinking. You'll get over her, of course you will. And what if she's not dead? Have you thought about that?'

'I pray that Yasmin and I are destined to meet again,' he said, fighting now to keep his feelings under control. 'But you must see that not every future can be approached by marching straight there from the present.'

'Hayden, you're still not well. Let me go to Clive and tell him you are not able to proceed.'

'No. I must face him. This confrontation was meant. It cannot be avoided. Don't you feel that? Look around you, Edmund. The sky, the stars, the way their light is reflected in the lagoons. The way they stare down over the affairs of men from such a height. Don't you feel the magic of this place?'

Maskelyne kicked his boot in the dust. 'If you want it frankly, Hayden, no.'

He smiled. He felt the warmth of his friendship for Edmund Maskelyne flow from his heart and fill him. What a lucky man I am to have such an honest comrade, he thought. He goes to such lengths to save me from myself. I know I cannot make any explanation that will satisfy him. No good telling him about the certainty I feel, or why. No good explaining about the odds against my overhearing the Governor's message just as he reported the events at Ambur. Or that the timing of my arrival at the card table was exact to the moment to catch Clive in a mood to lay down this challenge. Last night's dream made it all clear at last. As clear as ice.

'It was meant. That's all.' He sighed at his newfound conviction and clapped Maskelyne on the back. 'Edmund, you label such things simple coincidences and leave it at that. You perceive only the determinate universe. You really believe that randomness exists, but that luck does not. That each man is no more in control of the events in which he finds himself than a cogwheel in a machine. You do not see the real truth of things.'

Maskelyne took out his watch and consulted it sulkily. 'I declare you are getting as bad as Robert Clive.'

'I should have thought Robert Clive's attempts at suicide would have convinced you. You might as well be a stone for all that Hindostan has penetrated you.'

'You're away with fever, Hayden.'

'Perhaps I am.'

'And a bloody fool!'

Hayden laughed, easing the tension between them. 'I thank you for your support and encouragement, Mr Maskelyne.'

'Well, that, at least, is something on which you can still rely.'

They came to a place near the lagoon where there was a stretch of hard-packed earth. Here the waters of the Triplicane stagnated in secluded creeks. He saw how English Madras merged with Hindostan in the pre-dawn quiet. The water-lilies spread their huge circular leaves out over the surface of the water, their flowers still tightly closed. A troop of Hanuman monkeys came down to drink thirty yards away, long tails cocked, their light fur covering them all over except for hands and feet and faces blue-black as Hindu gods.

The troup leader flinched and lost his dignity as something flew past his head.

Hayden Flint was shocked, angered. Maskelyne had thrown a stone.

'Shoo! Go on! Clear off!' He slapped the dust off his hands with satisfaction as the animals retreated warily into the vegetation. 'They're creeping vile things, those monkeys.'

'Why do you say that?'

Maskelyne shrugged and opened his watch again. 'Because they steal. Good God, it's almost half past five! Where's Clive?'

'I expect he'll be here soon.'

'Oh, yes, he'll be here. You can depend on that.'

As they kept a silent vigil he felt the anxiety in his belly quelled by Maskelyne's anxious pacing. There was no paradox; it was as if the man was drawing off the electric fluid from him like a spinner draws woollen thread. He heard Yasmin's voice telling him that fear was an illusion created in the mind, and just as easily uncreated. It was true that a man could not be overcome by two emotions simultaneously. He knew that as long as he concentrated on his love for her, there could be no place for hatred or fear in his heart. Even fever could be overcome by a sufficient effort of will.

Roosters railed at the light in the east. Clive and Anderson appeared with a third man a quarter of an hour later, Anderson with a box containing a duelling pair, pistols he had obtained from someone in the Company's pay. The third man wore a long boat-cloak and carried an instrument bag – a physician.

'To pronounce you dead,' Clive said. He had obviously not slept. His face was puffy, his eyes dark-ringed. He kept his back straight as if he dared not relax the muscles of his chest and abdomen. He tried to catch Hayden Flint's eye,

360

but Flint declined and offered his hand instead to the physician.

'How do you do, sir? I am the principal, and may I present Mr Edmund Maskelyne, Esquire, my second?'

The other shook his hand firmly. He was a stocky man, hatless, in his late forties, sandy-haired and heavily freckled like a Scot – which, by his accent, he was not. His manner was humourless, his appearance strict.

'James Nairn, surgeon, at your service.'

'You're a Royal Navy surgeon? Or of the Bombay Marine?'

'I am of His Britannic Majesty's ship, *Vengeance*. That's what this coat signifies.' He revealed a glimpse of the buttons under his boat-cloak. 'I have asked to be seconded to the Presidency, to give succour to the victims of the Madras fever.'

'A noble calling, sir. Only a humanitarian – '

'You must understand that I do not approve of duelling. My attendance here is strictly to render medical service, since I have no power to prevent you acting thusly, if it be your resolve. I must ask, on your oath, sir, if you are a willing party to this duel.'

'I am.'

'And you are sound in wind, limb and mind?'

Hayden Flint gave the surgeon a wan smile. 'I take it we are agreed that it is gross bad form for a less than completely healthy man to face death on the field of honour.'

'And you, sir?' Nairn turned stiffly to Clive.

'You may swear it!'

'I am informed that no servant of the Company, senior or junior, has been approached to supervise the proceedings.'

Clive nodded. 'That is correct.'

'The fewer who know about this matter the better,' Maskelyne said acidly.

Nairn's eyes flicked to him and away again. 'Then who is to officiate?'

A crooked smile appeared on Clive's face. 'I had hoped *you* might count us along, sir.'

'Me, sir?'

'I had hoped so.'

'You said nothing of this previously.'

'I had hoped – '

'Then, you hoped in vain!'

Clive's jaw clenched. He looked the ship's surgeon up and down, deliberating, then he said, 'As you've already heard, we're both determined to settle this affair here and now. We will do so whether you choose to oblige us or not. If you will not count us along then Mr Anderson will do it.' His tone grew conciliatory. 'However, if you agree to see justice done you will have rendered two gentlemen a great convenience.'

Nairn looked at Clive for a long moment, then he said, 'Are you by chance the same Company gentleman who saw off Lieutenant Keene of the *Eltham* some time ago down by Fort St David?'

Clive absorbed the remark stonily, then he said, 'That was the lieutenant's name, as I recall it.'

'Very well,' Nairn agreed. 'I'll make the count for you. But in any enquiry nothing will be said of this.'

'That is understood. Thank you, Doctor.'

Nairn put down the black leather bag and took out a canvas roll covered in dark stains. He undid the ties and rolled it out on the earth. It was sewn with tapes and small pockets containing iron instruments in the shape of hooks or blades. There were also jointed tools, somewhat like scissors, that appeared to be for opening wounds and retrieving objects from within.

'You are aware, are you not,' Nairn asked solemnly, 'that under the law the surviving participant will be held to have committed murder in the event of his opponent's death?'

'I know that,' Clive said. Hayden Flint nodded.

'And you, Mr Maskelyne and Mr Anderson, you also are aware that a man standing as second to a murderer will be held, under the provisions, to have abetted, thus making yourselves liable for execution?'

Maskelyne and Anderson stared. Maskelyne swallowed, then both men nodded hesitantly.

Nairn nodded at the ground. 'Mr Clive tells me the discharge is to be at twenty-six paces?'

'It is. Thirteen steps apiece, the better to tempt fate.'

'Then at such short range it's likely that all four of you will die as a result of this affair.' He cast an eye at Maskelyne. 'Most probably three of you will die, and the fourth, being the least willing accessory, will merely be ruined. I ask again, are you all still determined to proceed?'

Again they assented, each in their different ways.

'So be it. Then select your pieces.'

Hayden watched as the brass and mahogany pistol case was opened. The guns nestled together stock-to-muzzle, lock mechanisms uppermost, in the green baize interior. There were two dainty powder flasks, tools for reaming and cleaning the barrels and compartments to hold flint, wadding and ball.

He removed one pistol at random; Clive did likewise. Both men handled them to feel their weight and balance. They were of the finest quality. The triggers were adjustable so that the slightest pressure would trip them, the barrels were polished inside for accuracy and blued outside to prevent glare, and each gun had a checker pattern cut into the well-turned stock to improve the grip. They would be prepared by the respective seconds, with Nairn witnessing.

Hayden Flint looked critically down the barrel of the pistol. 'Excellent workmanship,' he said. 'Where did you get them?'

Clive turned to Anderson. 'Would you inform Mr Flint that they belong to Mr Trenwith.'

'I wonder Trenwith isn't here to count us along.'

Clive spoke to Anderson again. 'Would you inform Mr Flint that so far as communication with him is concerned, I desire none and will have none. For his information I have seen to it that all those who witnessed my challenge are sworn to secrecy. I would not jeopardize them for his sake. Please ask him to make his choice without further delay.'

'Mr Clive asks you to make your choice,' Anderson said lamely, his nerves betraying him.

He chose the pistol he had first lifted up; Anderson took the other and handed it to Clive.

Maskelyne knelt. The selection of flints was checked, each examined individually for edge and angle. The one he judged best he folded in a strip of leather and clamped securely in the jaws of the cock, testing the action until he was satisfied that it struck the frizzen squarely and could be relied on to shower sparks into the pan.

'Is that sufficient, Hayden?' he asked, unhappy with the responsibility.

'That's most satisfactory.'

Next, the pistol was loaded. A charge of black powder was put down the barrel and tamped hard, followed by a piece of wadding to hold the powder, then a tiny lead ball the size of a pea, as perfectly spherical and polished a shot as he had ever seen. Yet more wadding to prevent the ball falling out, then the priming-pan cover was opened, fine priming powder sprinkled into the pan from a second, small flask, and the pan closed with great care.

Exactly the same procedure was followed by Anderson, then the guns were formally given to Nairn, who handed them gravely to each of the principals.

'Please take off your coats and stand back to back,' Nairn told them. They complied, Clive facing the western hills, he facing due east, towards the sea. For the first time, it occurred to him that he was half a head taller than Clive. A bigger target, he thought fleetingly, then realized that at twenty-six paces' separation each would present an outline little bigger than an outstretched thumb.

By now the sky had brightened; the sun was rising up beyond the dominating bulk of Fort St George: Hindostan was fading, English Madras burgeoning, as the day came upon the land.

Poultry began to invade the flat space, watching them with stupid expectation. Hayden knew that soon Pedda Naik's Petta would be swarming with natives going about their morning ablutions, fetching water from the newly cleaned wells nearby. They had to get it over with. It would be unthinkable to continue with the duel before a gawping native audience.

He felt a flicker of disappointment as he understood the inevitability of the clash. The feeling threatened to grow huge inside him. Always it had been the same at moments of extreme peril: fear escaping, flooding him, panic rising, the knowledge that he would lose control – over his body, over his senses, over his thoughts, weakness robbing him of dignity, of the chance to be seen to be a man. Then the terror of fear itself overwhelming him . . .

He forced his mind to a pin-sharp focus. Yasmin, wherever you are, on this earth or in heaven, I love you. You are my world. My universe. Nothing exists but you and my love for you. Nothing can harm me now. Nothing matters. If I live I'll go on loving you. If I die I'll be with you. If I die . . .

Nairn's dogmatic voice was grit in his ear. 'Gentlemen. You'll stand still until I retire. I shall then ask you the question, "Are you ready?" to which you will reply "yes" or "no". If I receive affirmation from you both I will begin counting, otherwise the duel will be called off honourably. Do you understand?'

He heard Clive's voice saying smoothly, steadily, that he understood. It took all his will-power not to be intimidated by that voice.

'Mr Flint? Did you understand what I just told you?'

He tried to speak, to form the word, but he could not. His throat was useless, his mouth so dry he could not swallow or even breathe. His grip on the pistol was vicelike, its barrel vertical in front of his face. Then, as he was about to lower it, he heard himself whisper something and nod tightly.

It was enough for Nairn.

'Since the total distance is to be twenty-six paces, I shall count from one to thirteen. At each count you will step out a pace. On the thirteenth count you will halt and turn to face your opponent.' Nairn paused, watching the men in profile, studying their expectation. His tone held no contempt, but rather admiration for their courage, tempered with regret at the foolhardiness of their pride. 'Upon the command "aim" you will point your weapons. And upon the command "fire" you will discharge at your convenience. I'm sure that I have no need to remind you, gentlemen, that, according to the code of honour, if you should fire first, you will be obliged to stand, until your opponent has also availed himself of the chance to fire.'

Nairn stepped back. Hayden Flint half expected Maskelyne to rush forward and ask one last time if they still meant to go through with it. Part of him yearned for that to happen so that he could postpone the horror of the confrontation, but Maskelyne did not move.

'Gentlemen. Are you ready?'

'Yes.'

'Yes.'

Both raised their pistols in their right hands so that the barrels pointed directly upwards beside their cheeks.

'One. Two. Three. Four . . .'

They began to step out.

He felt the unevenness of the ground under his shoes.

'Five. Six. Seven . . .'

The spice of flowers and the smell of damp earth grew piquant on the air. Ahead and above, the dawn's vivid colours shot veins through the eastern sky.

'Eight. Nine. Ten . . .'

Nairn's gruff voice receded. He heard a dog bark. He tried to believe this was just a simple walk back to St George and the dark ramparts nestling under the new day. What if at the final count I just keep going? he thought. What then?

'Eleven. Twelve. Thirteen.'

He halted. Turned to find Clive already facing him.

'Take your aim!'

Up came his elbow first, then he laid the pistol over until he had his mark, matching Clive's actions. The pistol weighed heavier than lead in his hand, but he held it firm as Nairn drew breath. Then the noise of a tolling bell shattered the moment, and a flood of brilliant yellow light burst out at Hayden Flint's back and his long shadow stretched out to touch Clive.

'*Fire!*'

He heard the order but could not respond. Twenty-six paces away, Clive's free hand went up to his eyes to ward off the brilliance. An arc of sun had moved out from behind the walls of Fort St George, suddenly unsighting him.

A shot rang out. Maskelyne's head whipped round, turning towards the south-west walls. Major Lawrence himself was stepping out towards them across the Garden Bridge at the head of two dozen troopers. A sentry must have seen what was taking place, and called authority down on them.

Clive, determined to go on, tried to aim again, but it was already too late: Hayden Flint's pistol had been lowered. Clive lowered his pistol too, and waited. Then, after a long moment, Lawrence's troops descended on them, and they were forced to hand over their weapons to the sergeant.

Lawrence's fury was intense. He was a physically imposing man with a fragile temper.

'This is a duel!'

'Not a shot was fired.'

'Your intent alone is enough to have you flogged raw. Don't challenge me, Flint. I don't care who your father is, you'll not challenge me! Now, what have you to say?'

He stared sullenly back at Lawrence, not knowing whether he had been commanded to silence, or to speak.

'Nothing. To you, sir,' he said. 'This is a private matter between two gentlemen.'

The flippancy of the remark caused Lawrence to stripe his silver-knobbed stick menacingly down the front of Hayden Flint's shirt. 'Know this, laddie: it would be nothing to me if both you – gentlemen – had been blasted to hellfire. But you broke my law. And now you're going to pay for that.'

Governor Sawyer called for them at dusk three days later. They had spent the time in two stifling solitary cells built into the eastern wall, confined in sight of one another, the better to think their feud through. Throughout the period,

367

except for the occasions when water and a dish of oatmeal flummery had been brought down to them, Clive had lain on his back, hands clasped over his stomach, sweating and staring at the stone vault, and listening to the sound of boots treading the ramparts overhead. He had not spoken one word, nor had Hayden Flint.

Thomas Sawyer was a small man, direct in pursuit of official tasks but accustomed to bearing himself with poise. He was softly severe. 'I've heard Major Lawrence's report of the incident,' he told them, hardly looking up from his papers. 'I am disgusted by the matter. Mr Clive, it seems to me from your record that you have a character fitted for war, but unable to sustain a moment of peace. Your conduct has not been that of a gentleman, nor of an officer of the Honourable East India Company. You, of all people, should have been particularly aware that duelling is expressly forbidden in any Company lease. You chose to ignore the warning given you by a more lenient governor. Therefore you are hereby dismissed from the Company's service.'

Clive's eyes closed, and he swallowed as he accepted the sheet of paper handed him by the Governor. His filthy face was covered in sweat, his hair was plastered and uncombed. His shirt and breeches were stained and creased and stinking. He looked to Hayden Flint the picture of a man who had truly reached his nadir. Despite himself, he could not help feeling sympathy.

Sawyer looked up, a man in total control of affairs. 'Mr Flint, you have hitherto been tolerated on Company land only in so far as your behaviour accords with that expected of a guest. You have contravened that condition. In consequence, and by this order, you are required to leave the lease within the week.'

Hayden Flint took the sentence calmly. The fever had not returned. He still felt weak, and stubborn echoes of the malady ached in his limbs, but the events on Pedda Naik's Petta had raised his spirit up. He knew he had made another great stride towards the fulfilment of his destiny.

The Governor's imposition was great, almost as great as Sawyer could have made it. Why, then, did he feel no foreboding? The crime had been conspiracy to duel, not duelling itself, and that, Sawyer said, had saved their necks. But there was something not quite final about the look on Governor Sawyer's face. The tone of his words gave him away. He looked shrewdly, speaking to Clive.

'I have had words with Governor Covington at St David, and I know something of the circumstances of this extraordinary affair, but I would be interested to hear what in particular prompted this intense war between you.'

'The honour of a lady,' Clive said tightly.

'Indeed?'

Clive explained that Arkali Savage had been brutally treated, and that he had chosen to act as her protector.

The shrewdness in the Governor's manner intensified. 'But Miss Savage has long since moved back to her father's house at Triplicane, where she has not seen fit to bring any charge against Mr Flint, yet you have seen fit to maintain this grudge against your adversary.'

Clive stared back, defiant and wordless, an inch away from giving Sawyer a dose of abuse.

'And you, Mr Flint? What have you to say?'

As he began his explanation he felt Sawyer watching him closely. The man was waiting, assessing him, though to what purpose he could not imagine.

When he had finished his version of events he waited in silence for Sawyer to deliberate. The Governor took back the papers from both men and perused them distantly.

'That these reports are the ruin of you both cannot be denied.' They both stood like stones. 'However, it must be remembered that it is in my power to tear them into halves and thereby restore you.'

Clive was visibly jolted. Sawyer remained unsmiling. 'If I now offer to do that for you, you will agree to do something for me. You clearly know nothing of this, but a most extraordinary occurrence has taken place, an occurrence I consider must be laid before you without delay. You see the result of this futile warring? While you've been resting at your leisure, Miss Arkali Savage has been taken out of the lease.'

'Taken?' Clive asked. 'Sir, what do you mean?'

'Just that. Removed. Kidnapped. Along with the Gond woman who served as her maid.'

Hayden Flint was astonished. 'By whom?' Clive stared, confounded.

Sawyer got up and went to the window. 'Her father came here in haste and some great distress this morning to beg my assistance. He was badly bloodied. He had a deep sword wound in his head that made me wonder he could still stand. Mr Nairn has already taken three pieces of bone from it. At any rate, Savage swears his daughter has been abducted by a band of horse-soldiers. His only theory is that she might have been taken because of debts incurred by him on the Moghul authorities at Arcot.' His eyes followed something passing on the street below, then he added faintly, 'If it were so, it would not be an unprecedented act. Moghul royalty has been known to abduct European individuals. If the truth be known, they take rather more white women than they do tigers.'

'The Moghul authorities?' Clive said quickly. 'But who do you mean? Anwar-ud-Din is dead and his reign ended.'

'Quite so. Charles Savage says that he raised credit against capital, a quantity of specie buried under his house, but it was stolen by the French Admiral, La Bourdonnais, at the start of the occupation.' Sawyer paused but since no comment was forthcoming he continued. 'Since you have been so good as to have informed all Madras of the events that took place at Ambur, you will presumably also know that after the massacre the princeling Muhammad Ali Khan rode with a party of several hundred stalwarts to Arcot with the intention of emptying his father's treasury. He reached that place before news of the slaughter arrived there, and was able to convince those holding the walls that his father and brother were both dead.'

'Then he now possesses Anwar-ud-Din's capital wealth?' Hayden Flint asked.

'Most of it. Though we do not yet know where he has taken it.'

Clive's fists clenched. 'Trichinopoly! I'll swear to it!'

Hayden Flint nodded. 'I agree.'

'To raise the southern Carnatic to his green banner?' Sawyer said. 'That's a labour that will take every ounce of gold in his possession.'

Clive looked to the man he would have killed three days ago. Then he addressed him directly for the first time since the challenge. 'Do you suppose Muhammad Ali's men have stolen Arkali?'

'It's possible.' Hayden Flint began to calculate. Sawyer's words underlined his fears, but he hid his deepest suspicions. 'It's possible, but not for the purpose you suppose. It's my bet that she was not kidnapped for ransom, rather taken as hostage.'

Sawyer turned abruptly. 'Hostage? To what end?'

'If Muhammad Ali has taken her, it will not be for the simple reason of seeking to recover Charles Savage's debt. It's an ally he wants. The army of the Hon'ble Company to protect him from the French.'

'Yes!' Clive said. 'A political signal. I see that. By abducting her on this pretext he has certainly gained our attention.'

'It's a deuced strange way to do that,' Sawyer said, looking towards Hayden Flint. 'It seems you know the Moors?'

'Straight dealing – as we know it – is not their way.'

'If it was your intention to pardon us on condition we consented to find her,' Clive said to Sawyer suddenly, 'then you have been pushing at an open door. I would have volunteered, and do so now, freely.'

'I pledge myself likewise,' said Hayden Flint, feeling the responsibility for the whole flow of events seating itself on their shoulders. He looked to Clive. There was a bond yoking them now, a bond that had never existed before. Clive's black anger had been discharged without the need for a pistol shot.

Sawyer looked long and hard at them. He had noted Clive's presumption. 'Mr Clive, you read me well, but you appear to have grasped the kettle by the spout. It is true I had planned to offer a conditional pardon. I have vital work for you, work for which you are each particularly suited. If I have held the sword of Damocles over you, it is only to ensure that you apply yourselves to the task, for I am certain it will be less to your taste than you suppose.'

Clive's eyes narrowed. 'Sir, please state your offer.'

'Mr Clive, if you will agree to be bound by my terms, you are hereby recommissioned into the Company's army with the acting rank of Captain. You are to be associated with a special detachment of troops. My intention is that it will become the counterpart of Monsieur Dupleix's force now fighting in support of the puppet, Chanda Sahib. I want you to become Steward, to organize such provisions as may be necessary to satisfy the requirements of such a force.'

Clive looked crestfallen. 'What choice do I have?'

'The choice between possible glory and certain disgrace.'

'Then I must do as you say, and become a quarter-master.'

As soon as Clive retired Sawyer offered Hayden Flint a seat. 'Now,' the Governor said matter-of-factly, 'you will tell me what you really think.'

'Sir, I think there may be a more personal reason why Arkali Savage has been taken,' he said slowly. 'That reason is Muhammad Ali's jealousy. You see, he thinks I defiled his wife.'

'And did you?'

'I would not call it defilement.'

Sawyer considered, then he said, 'It is my belief that what has taken place after the Battle of Ambur may be as important as the defeat itself. Muzaffar Jang has proclaimed Chanda Sahib Nawab of the Carnatic, and the pair of them are, even now, riding to Pondicherry where they are to be received in state by Mr Dupleix. I need not tell you that these moves render Nasir Jang's authority null and void. I want you to return to Hyderabad, where you will act as official ambassador on behalf of the Company. The Nizam must be persuaded to gather his army, and to move it into the Carnatic as soon as possible. His aim must be the obliteration of Muzaffar Jang. And towards this essential enterprise you must thoroughly encourage him.'

FIFTEEN

The nine sowars went inland, following the Cheyyar River upstream as far as they dared, and as fast as their horses would go. They rode hard from the English settlement, fearing pursuit, but when young Lakshman's horse burst its heart, Zahir's temper blazed. He cut the young rider down with his sword in fury.

'We cannot take him, and we cannot let him remain. We must leave no clue,' he shouted. 'My Lord Muhammad Ali Khan has ordered it! It is the will of Allah!'

The old scout Mohan Das eyed the strong horse from which Zahir was now dismounting. He who is fated will survive, he repeated to himself, echoing Zahir's sacrilegious words scornfully. And I have not reached fifty-five summers by treating man and beast as you treat them. To drive us forty miles over rough country without halt is the work of one who is moonstruck. Abdul Masjid should have cut you when you were beardless, just as you cut Lakshman. As your God wills it, you will meet the same fate as that murdering Shatan in time! And I await your moment as I awaited Abdul Masjid's.

It will be Azad who kills you, he thought, stealing a glance at the solemn-faced rider. He has been looking to challenge you since the day we fled the Ambur Pass. Tonight there will be truth in the air.

They pressed on into the night, pausing neither for rest nor water until they reached the peepul tree. Even Zahir had to admit that further flight was impossible.

Mohan Das smiled as he recognized the tree. 'Do you still think the gora-log are on our tails?' he asked Zahir as the horses drank.

374

'Old fool! We have many enemies, not just the white men. Now we are strangers in our own land.'

'Verily!' Mohan Das was forced to speak his mind. 'We are surrounded by enemies. Muzaffar Jang's men hold Arcot, and detachments of Chanda Sahib's army will be at Arni and Gingee, for those places are on the main road from Arcot to the fort at Pondicherry. The feringhee, too, are abroad. The spoor of their marching columns is in the dust. Much better that we take the Volconda road.'

'Bind them both!' Zahir ordered angrily. 'And bind them tight, so that when they wake up they cannot run!'

Two bodies, covered in sacking, were pulled down from the horses and dragged five or six paces to the foot of the peepul tree.

Zahir growled. 'Take care! It is my Lord Muhammad Ali's work you do!'

'Your pardon, lord,' the one named Mahmoud said, touching his forehead with an insolence that Zahir missed.

You do not know the work you have done, Mohan Das thought. Harming women is evil work, and you will kill them if you continue like this. But take care, Zahir! I see Azad looking at you as he sharpens his knife! It is the tree's blessed influence!

Mohan Das drank from his goatskin, spat, got up and walked a little way from the encampment. He relieved himself over a thorn bush, peering into the night sky and shivering involuntarily as he tucked himself away. It was foolish to bring the Gond woman. How can the feringhee take them as servants? They are a dirty people, an ugly people. Until the Angrezi religious men catch them or buy them as children they wear nothing but tattoos and live in the jangal like animals. They worship the goddess of smallpox, and to appease her they leave the dirt of their dwellings on the road so that travellers will be stricken. That is the truth of the Gonds.

He climbed a little way up the hillside and squatted, feeling the comfort of the betel quid in his cheek. As always when overnighting in a strange place he settled his mind and cast a dispassionate eye over the land to assess the benefits of its lie. There was little merit in Zahir's choice: a blind valley, too close to the road, no immediate cover, except for the solitary peepul tree that was a local landmark, fit only to draw the eye of casual passers-by and to act as a rallying point for pursuers. They were close enough to the main roads to let their campfire be mistaken for that of genuine wayfarers, but Zahir had forbidden a fire. At least with Abdul Masjid, thought the old scout, we had a leader who was cunning and who liked his pleasures. Ah, but then we were fifty strong. Now we are just nine. Two of us have died on this dirty business already, and more will die soon.

Under the tree, where the darkness was greatest, there was a stirring.

Oh, they have cut off my hands and my feet! I cannot move them! I cannot feel them!

Mirah the servant girl's mind swam in and out of the nightmare like a river fish among the reeds. The aches that racked her body were so severe that she slipped in and out of consciousness. She dreamed that she was held tight by the many arms of Kali. She could feel the nails of the terrible goddess, white as lotus flowers, those demonic hands biting into her flesh until it was numb, until she cried out with fear, but the repeated blows against her ribs forced the breath from her and she fainted again. It seemed that she could hear her own pain-filled voice coming from a great distance, crying for the memsahib to come, but Miss Arkali was too busy to heed her, and the goddess's grip too tight for her to call louder.

She silently recited a little of the holy scriptures, then a passage from the *Gita*, without result. One of the bandits, a thin-faced man with sneaking eyes, came close, but his attention was on two of his fellow raiders. He lounged against a stone for a moment, watching the others gather tinder, then, when the flames began to crackle, he got up. 'Zahir Sahib!' he shouted. 'Azad is disobeying!'

'No fire!' Zahir shouted back, recalling his own order.

Warned that his authority was being flouted he could not endure it. He began kicking the flames out. 'A fire will betray us!'

'We want a fire. There is no risk!' The one called Azad dumped his armful of brushwood.

'I told you, no fire!'

There was a muttered curse, then Zahir faced the other down. Azad kicked out at the one with the sly eyes; there was punching and shouting. As the fight broke out the women were ignored. The men commanded by Zahir faced down the three rebels, and when the leader leapt at them they scattered into the night.

The old one spoke in the following silence. 'That was not clever, Zahir Sahib. You said it was Lord Muhammad Ali's orders to leave no trail.'

'They'll be back. And when they come I shall cut Azad!' Zahir swore, but those who surrounded him were less certain.

'How may we sleep?' one asked.

'Prayer is better than sleep!' Zahir told him. 'You are soldiers, and soldiers should sleep with their swords in hand. I will mount the first watch. If I should shout, you will come to my side at once. Mohan Das, you will guard the horses!'

Suddenly one of the bandits pointed to the ridge. 'Zahir Sahib! Look!' he hissed.

The scout staggered as Zahir's hand seized his shoulder with the strength of a vulture talon. '*Aiee!* The god-cursed Angrezi! I knew you had brought us in a circle, Mohan Das!'

'Quiet! Get down and lie like dead men!'

Mirah twisted and saw the line of figures coming over the ridge. Their moving silhouettes reminded her of the patterned back of a rat snake oozing from its hole.

When the sound of their feet reached the camp, Mirah knew that the horses would give them away by stamping and snorting, but the column came on, maybe a dozen men, roped together like slaves – but no, she thought not like slaves. Talking instead softly to one another.

They stepped very close to Mirah, terrifying her, for they were not Angrezi soldiers at all, or their sipahis. Unturbaned, their hair cropped close to their heads, they were dressed in tatters and their faces were the faces seen only on the skull necklace of the goddess, Kali. Leading them was one who carried a long staff like the crozier of the feringhee churchman. His head was tilted so that one flickering eye could grope straight ahead.

Their passing was eerie, a ghost dance, shuffling, listening, upturned faces scanning the sky for unseen stars. Nudges passed from one to another down the line. Mirah continued to watch until the sound of their feet had passed.

'The spirits of dead men!' someone whispered when he dared.

'Truly! Ghosts from hell!'

'Do you think they saw us?'

After a little while the old scout spat through the gap in his teeth. 'Blind men cannot see!'

'Blind men?'

'Who else may travel so surely in the cool of the night? They are beggars on a pilgrimage to Conjeeveram, to beseech the gods to give them back their sight. What better time for them to make their journey?'

'Then we are safe.'

'No.' The scout chuckled privately. 'We are discovered.'

'Uh?'

'Do you not know that the blind hear all, and taste the air as ably as dogs?'

The sly one said, 'I told them the fire would give us away.'

'They have certainly smelt the stench of horse.'

'You talk snake-talk, old man,' Zahir said. 'They passed us by, did they not?'

'Then you did not see the hand signals passing down their line?'

'What signals?'

'Private signals that only beggars know.'

'Then how do *you* know them, old man? Do as I told you and guard the horses!'

The scout scowled and spat again. Mirah heard him mumbling almost inaudibly: 'Yah. He shall be killed by fire, that same one who was cursed in his mother's womb . . .'

An hour passed while Mirah drowsed in aching discomfort, but then there was stirring. Azad had come back to the camp, and once more Mirah's eyes were open as the other horsemen jumped up.

'So you've come back?' Zahir said levelly. He was the only one not on his feet. 'Where are the others?'

'Gone. They say we should go to Arcot,' Azad told him. 'Mahmoud and Chetu both think that.'

Zahir stiffened. 'You came here to speak for those curs? Now you have done so, tell me what you think.'

Azad shrugged indolently and walked into the camp. The others watched him with intense wariness.

'Stay there!'

Azad paused as he saw Zahir's unsheathed sword. He shrugged again, but his movements betrayed the tension in him. 'Perhaps they are right. We could ransom the women ourselves at Arcot. Mahmoud says the Gond woman is only worth a dam or two, but the Angrezi would surely pay a lot.'

'That's treachery!' Zahir growled. 'My Lord Muhammad Ali's orders are clear – '

'Listen,' Azad said as if Zahir was missing an important point. 'Hear me out. These are difficult times. And in difficult times a man must choose his lord with care. Who is our leader? Once we were led by Abdul Masjid, and paid by whichever prince in Arcot paid the highest price. When Abdul Masjid was killed, we gave our allegiance to the feringhee, Flint. And when he gave us back to the service of Anwar-ud-Din it was you we allowed to lead us. On the nawab's death you chose to follow Muhammad Ali. Some of us do not think that was wise.'

'Your tongue is too long, Azad! It flaps like a garment on the washing stones!'

'I speak only of what I have seen.'

379

'You have seen too much,' Zahir got to his feet, 'and now you will pay for it with your blood!'

As he moved forward, one of Azad's accomplices burst into the camp, brandishing his sword. It was Mahmoud. His yells temporarily covered the din of hooves to all except Mirah whose ear was pressed to the earth.

For a moment she heard only screaming, and the slashing of a talwar through the air as the rider geed the horse towards Zahir's men. Then she was lifted up in strong arms and flung across a saddle. A voice called out, 'Get the other one!'

Mahmoud's smaller companion stumbled and was knocked to the ground by three others. Azad was fighting for his life against Zahir, but Mahmoud bearing down on horseback gave him his chance. In the confusion he broke away, and scrambled into the darkness, heading for the place where his horse was tethered.

'Treachery!' Zahir bellowed, throwing himself after them, but they had already escaped into the night.

Mohan Das's heart hammered as he jabbed his heels into the horse's flanks. The wind streamed in his face.

'*Kya khub! Yi sawar hoshiyar hai!*' Azad exulted, halting to take stock. '*Jey Azad!*'

'Ride! They are coming!' Mohan Das shouted.

'What do you mean? How can they?'

'I could not do as you asked – there would have been too much noise.'

Mohan Das had promised to hamstring the other mounts, disabling them permanently. But when he had gone to do it they had looked at him with such trust that he could not bring himself to make the cuts. Instead he had led them away and camel-hobbled them, looping ropes between their back legs and knotting them tight.

'Fool! Zahir will hunt us down! We must carry the women!'

'We have a start, Azad Sahib. And in the darkness we will surely lose them.'

Mohan Das guided them through the night for an hour or

more, until moonrise, leaving Zahir's men far behind. When they had gained the rocky slopes that led to the Arcot road, they climbed again, the horses toiling until they were high above the valley.

'Keep off the ridges,' Mohan Das warned. 'We must not show ourselves against the moon.'

'We must rest,' Mahmoud said.

They dismounted in a dry crevice under a shelving cliff which gave complete concealment from two directions yet provided a panorama to the south and east.

'It would be clever to free the Gond woman,' Mohan Das said. 'She is worthless. She will only slow us down.'

Mahmoud's eyes glittered. 'Maybe I will kill her.'

Mohan Das felt the cruel shock of the other's words. Out here beyond the writ of all authority, some men allowed themselves to become foully brutal. 'Is that why you brought her here? To kill her?'

The woman wriggled and whimpered in terror. 'Leave her,' Azad said. He had no stomach for murdering women.

Mahmoud pawed at Mirah's clenched form. Arkali began to pray, but then remembered that prayer was useless, that the God she believed in had turned His back on her every time. She felt utterly alone, at the mercy of these lawless slavers. Her only hope was that they would not want to spoil their merchandise.

Mirah wept, curled into a ball so that Mahmoud could not touch her. When he thrust his hand over her hip she yelped.

The leader, Azad, appeared. He said something to the tormentor, who paused, rose up, his expression that of a man who finds himself poised on the brink of a precipice, then he slunk away. Azad cut Mirah's bonds and moments later freed Arkali's hands too. Both women were given a skin to drink from.

Arkali gulped gratefully at the foul-tasting water. The leader took the skin away from her and spoke to her in his own language. When she stared back at him uncomprehendingly he told Mirah to translate his words, which she did efficiently, despite her trembling.

'My name is Azad,' she repeated in English. 'I am your protector.'

You're a foul slaver, Arkali thought, and one who has turned against even his friends now, but she said only, 'Thank you, Mr Azad.'

'This is for you,' he told her, giving her a blanket to wrap herself in. 'Be sure to tell them in Arcot what kindnesses I have done you.'

Later, the men sat apart in silence, eating with their right hands and afterward smoking pungent tobacco in carved wooden pipes. Arkali realized how hungry she was. She humbled herself to take what was offered: a little of the sun-dried meat and rice. It had been parcelled up in leaves, compressed by being packed in their shoulderbags.

'What did the leader say to make the big brute stop?' she whispered as soon as she felt it was safe.

Mirah looked down silently.

'Well? Answer me.'

'He was . . . persuasive, memsahib.'

'But what did he say?'

Again Mirah was slow to reply. 'It was . . . man talk.'

Arkali felt her exasperation rise. It could be important. 'Mirah, tell me! Now!'

'The leader, Azad, said to the other, Mahmoud, that he could choose to spend his seed once in the belly of a dirty Gond woman and die for it. Or, if he were wiser, he could take us to Arcot untouched, and live for a year and a day in a house of honey-skinned concubines on the reward.'

Mirah turned away, her shame burning.

So, Arkali thought coldly. It's just as I supposed: they're slave traders from Arcot. I've heard how they bring fresh blood into the harems of Moghul princes. But they will never imprison me. The prince who buys me buys a corpse!

Arkali woke as the first rays began lightening the east. She shook her maid anxiously. 'Mirah, wake up! What are they saying?'

The men, shocked from their slumber by Mohan Das,

listened to the old scout's warning. He had seen a group of riders, four or five, perhaps, moving steadily across the plain below.

'Come! We must make for the Arcot road by the shortest way,' Mahmoud said.

The scout argued with him. 'No! We must not cross the ridge. Manu and Sachal both possess eyes like eagles.'

'Stupid old man! We cannot stay here. Nor can we ride to meet them.'

Azad turned on him. 'Let the scout be the judge.'

'Why not leave the women, Azad Sahib?'

The suggestion triggered Azad's anger. 'Are you mad?'

'There's no time to bind them.'

'They will ride pillion.'

Mirah's translation broke off as the riders saddled up. She was forced to climb up behind Azad, and Arkali was pulled up behind Mohan Das, who was the smallest. They began to ride, faster than was safe, on the uneven and steepening slope. Arkali saw the sun rising, climbing up from behind the Eastern Ghats, sending its rays over the lip of the valley. Zahir's men were visible, no more than a mile distant, following their track unerringly. Any delay and we're certain to be overtaken, Arkali decided. She saw their plan clearly now: they wanted to get to the Arcot road and ride as fast as they could for the capital.

Mohan Das watched as Azad and Mahmoud cruelly whipped on their horses. Not clever, he thought. Terrify them on this ground and they will surely break a leg.

'Keep up, old fool!' Mahmoud shouted. 'Or must I take the woman with me?'

They reached the plateau and crossed it with all speed. Suddenly, there below them, was the Arcot road.

'Look!' cried Azad.

'Where do we go at the crossroads?'

'Follow Mohan Das. And pray to Allah that we meet with feringhees, or at least with Muzaffar Jang's soldiers!'

'And if we do not?' Mahmoud shouted back.

'Ride like you have never ridden!'

'But we cannot outride them on an open road.'

'Then pray, and pray again.'

When they reached the road, Zahir's men were out of sight. Mohan Das tried to decide which direction to take before they reached the crossroads. Ah, yes! The Cheyyar River. The lushest foliage marked the watercourse. The Angrezi woman squeezed the breath from his ribs; she rode with her body stiff and her knees bent at an awkward angle. She has no feeling for the animal, he cursed silently, no natural balance or sense of rhythm. She's a dead weight. *Bismillah*, let go of me!

Arkali hung on to him grimly. It's so far down, and so unsteady, she thought. The rocks are moving by at such a speed that my brains will be dashed from my head in a fall. Every time the horse takes a step, it pounds my spine. I'm being lifted a foot off the saddle and dropped back on it. Dropped, and dropped again! My God, I'm going to be sick.

Their shadows rippled over rocks and hummocks. Then they reached a level stretch and the going grew better on the hard-packed earth. The rhythm of the horse changed, its stride altered and its neck stretched out. Flecks of foam blew back from its mouth in the onrushing air. Arkali's legs chafed on the rough saddle cloth. Her petticoats were hitched high, her knees were bare, her stocking hose down around her ankles. Her legs were filthy and her shoes long gone, but an intense exhilaration rushed through her.

The crossroads loomed up ahead, and Mahmoud's horse, out in front, skidded to a halt.

'Which way?'

'There.' Mohan Das pointed down the northern fork that meandered towards the river. Tiny dark figures were at the ford, in hurried consultation. 'We must cross the Cheyyar.'

'Follow me!' Azad shouted. He began to lead them to midstream.

As the horse waded into the deepest part of the river, Arkali steeled herself. The moment was upon her so she took her chance, sliding over the horse's hindquarters and plunging waist-deep into the muddy water. The old scout shouted and tried to make his horse turn in pursuit. Wading was nightmarishly slow; she flailed at the surface with her hands, trying to paddle her encumbrance of skirts through the waters. He almost caught her so she launched herself forward and dived out of reach. But the dive took her headfirst into the water, going down and down, until her outstretched hands touched the bottom. The shock of going under made her gasp, and water entered her mouth and nose. Her lungs tried to cough it out, but she swallowed again and found that she could not draw breath. She heard and felt the horse's hooves stabbing into the water beside her.

Suddenly she found a footing, and then her head was above the surface and she was fighting to breathe, drenches of water pouring from her clothing. One of the slavers seized her hair and pulled her upright. She turned until the hand was twisted and her face was crushed against the horse's neck, but then her mouth was pulled against the rider's wrist. She bit. Hard. To the bone. Then the hand was gone, the horse bolting off downstream with the cursing rider.

Hope surged in her. She looked round and saw that she was closer to the bank than she had realized. Here the river was little more than knee-deep. She saw Mahmoud in midstream, and Azad returning from the far side, still carrying the passive bundle of Mirah behind him. There was shouting and frantic hand-waving. She tried to shout too, to Mirah, to make her jump down, but all that came out was a strangled fit of coughing. Then the old scout was splashing towards her again.

She tried once more to wade to the bank, but the huge weight of her sodden dress stuck to her and dragged her back. A hand gripped her bare arm like a deer-trap, the nails biting into flesh. Although he was old, Mohan Das was still surprisingly strong. She was lifted and pulled to the bank and dumped in the muddy margin where the bushes grew in luxuriant profusion.

Then an extraordinary thing happened: the old man put his hand across her mouth and held her down behind a big boulder. When he took his hand away she was panting hard, her eyes flickering to Azad and Mahmoud, who were paralysed by indecision in the middle of the river. She looked back at the old man, who bade her to be silent with urgent signals.

She heard little of the drumming thud of hoofbeats before the riders flashed into view at the ford. Zahir led them crashing straight into the Cheyyar with drawn sword. Mahmoud's horse reared, and his talwar glinted in the golden light. Then there was a furious confusion of vicious fighting, the slashing and hacking of rapid strokes.

'Mirah!' she shouted as her maid fell from Azad's horse and into the water. She saw no more. Her captor clamped his hand over her mouth again and shook his head. He began to pull her away using the cover of bushes and the big smooth rocks that had been carried down from the hills in the rainy season.

She went, not caring for the alternative. Better to be in the company of one slaver than five, she thought, turning. Look! The battle's already over, and Azad's and Mahmoud's saddles are empty. The others'll track us tirelessly, but this old man is as cunning a rogue as ever I saw.

Two of Zahir's riders were pulling a third man to the bank, the wound in his head grievous and bleeding. Zahir himself was bellowing, 'Now find the woman!'

Mohan Das chewed and spat as he scrutinized Zahir's men from the cover of a rock. One rider went upriver, splashing along the near bank, slashing at the bushes with his sword. Another took the far side, jumping down to examine the damp earth at the ford for hoofmarks. A third went downriver to gather the horses.

Zahir himself waited motionlessly at the ford, his dark eyes examining the scene meticulously, his ears listening to the sounds of morning birds and the water noises of the river. After a while, he consulted with Sachal, the man who had rounded up the horses. They were now no more than twenty paces away, attending to their wounded fellow.

'We will find them,' Zahir said.

'To find Mohan Das is no easy matter.'

'He is on foot now, and we are four. Only a magician could escape us.'

Mohan Das chewed faster. He saw them turn his way and hugged the boulder tight. The Angrezi woman was three paces away, crouching just beyond reach but in the safest place he could find, in the water, and sheltered from the searchers by a tree that had been pitched into the stream by a storm many seasons ago. It had continued to live, putting out a mesh of branches.

His heart hammered against his ribs. He knew there was still a narrow chance they would not be spotted, and that was a gamble worth taking. Then he cursed as he saw the torn hem of the woman's clothing snake out into the stream from behind the log, waving like a white flag in the current. She was beyond the reach of his outstretched arm. He made furious motions to her to gather it in, but she had buried her head in her hands, as if to conceal herself from the oncoming search party.

He signalled to her again as boldy as he dared, then froze. Now he could not afford to make a sound.

How could she be reached? There was no way to do it! They must be discovered.

Arkali kept her head down, until fear made her lift it. She saw the old man's signals, but made no sense of them and could only shake her head. The searchers had fanned out, under orders to find them. As the fanatical Zahir came closer she saw Mohan Das stiffen and stop chewing, then he launched himself at her and began to rave and jabber.

He took her by the hair and dragged her from the hiding place. She gasped in pain, screamed like an animal when he threw her down, howling at the old fool who had deliberately given them away.

Here she is, Zahir Sahib! I caught her skulking in the

broken lands. *Aou!*' He sucked his bloodied knuckle. 'She is wild like a civet cat when she desires to be.'

Zahir was astonished. He brandished his sword and bellowed, 'Lizard!'

'See – this is the one our Lord Muhammad Ali seeks! I have tracked her and brought her to you!'

'Agh! I shall kill you, Mohan Das!'

The old scout danced away across the boulders, red spittle bubbling at the corners of his mouth. 'Zahir Sahib, am I not faithful to you?'

'You rode with Azad!'

'Of course! It was I who misled him, Zahir Sahib. It was I who protected the Angrezi woman against crazy Mahmoud. Ask her! She will tell you! I am so pleased to see you, and give this vicious creature back to you unharmed.'

'Pray to your gods, Mohan Das. You are a dead man!'

He saw that Zahir was thus far a man of his word, that this was a moment where the ways forked: a moment of life or death. 'You would kill me? When I can give the one thing you desire.'

Zahir paused, mollified by the serpent words. 'What thing?'

'The route away from danger! Last night we saw men. The beggars of Conjeeveram will be spreading the news of our whereabouts even as we waste time standing up to our knees in this river. Only I know how to get us all safely away. Only I can deliver you to Trichinopoly. Choose, therefore. But know that both Allah and our lord share one desire.'

As the tip of Zahir's sword dropped, slow as the sinking of the crescent moon, Mohan Das knew he had won. Once more I have used my brain, he thought. And by avoiding the fight I live another day.

SIXTEEN

As Hayden Flint walked through the Nizam's palace in Hyderabad, six attendants entrained at his back, his mind was in turmoil. Wherever his eyes strayed he saw the gardens where he had walked with Yasmin, the pavilions where their illicit love had grown to full blossom, the marble bench where they had sat together, the apartments where they had consummated their desire and the steps upon which he had seen that eternal love burned to ashes by a cruel parting . . .

I will always love you, he thought, sickened by the bitterness of his destiny. No matter what happens, our love is great, and nothing can change that. Nothing.

'Your Excellency is unwell?' asked a voice. It was Osman, the footman whom Nasir Jang had provided. Osman the ever-present.

'It's nothing.'

Osman turned to his gaping subordinate. 'Fetch water!'

'No, no. Let's get on.'

He could feel their eyes boring through him. Their concern seemed to increase the pain eating at his soul. The task before me is impossible, he thought. How many times have I approached the untouchable hierarchy of Nasir Jang with recommendations of policy? A thousand times, it seems. And all my entreaties have been ignored or turned aside. It is like negotiating with a thorn bush. Why should Nasir Jang listen to me now? But he must. He must! And it's my duty to make him listen – and act.

He took out his kerchief and wiped away the sweat that spangled his face. As with Asaf Jah in his last months, the nobles of the court screen their master from me, and from everyone. Why? Letters are accepted, returned with smiles, unopened. In every negotiation I have been offered half-answers. Always I have seen that veil descend over their eyes, the veil that shows they are not convinced. And always, always, the word is: 'You must wait until tomorrow.'

He went over in his mind the forms he must observe if he were to approach the ruler's masnad without giving offence. The *gup* he had heard added a tantalizing uncertainty to the meeting. Rumours of Nasir Jang's dissoluteness worried him.

It was said that the heir of the great Asaf Jah had entered a decline shortly after his accession, had fallen to vice and 'vile practices', forfeiting the respect and esteem of his generals. What those vile practices were was the subject of great speculation, but the Moghul regime had sunk into so deep a mire of indolent luxury that any interpretation seemed plausible.

Hayden Flint had discreetly questioned his attendants, the loiterers in the palace gardens, the guards stationed outside his residence. Their impressions ranged from the wildly improbable to the all too credible, but one thread connected them all: the Talwar-i-Jang.

The thought made him uneasy. He had been the agent and bearer of a ruby whose value lay in its reported power to dim the lustre of the Koh-i-Noor diamond. Could it be that I am to blame? he asked himself. As much as a quack doctor peddling false preventatives while the patient sickens with the cholera?

Guilt wafted through him like a ghost. If the rumours are true, it's astonishing how closely the Nizam's decline has coincided with his accession. But is it the curse, or only his belief in the curse? Damn me, I'm beginning to believe their idiotic superstition myself!

They came to the appointed place. His way was barred by guards, and although their search was thorough, he was relieved of his silver-knobbed stick. His retinue were turned back.

He was led along yards of narrow, twisting passages, that might have been servants' ways, to a small door. The usher opened it, and held out a hand to show that the Angrezi should go ahead.

Inside, the decor was once more sumptuous. The light was low and filtered and the perfume as delicately sensual as the cool air. There were screens of gilded rosewood, and golden ewers with elegant spouts, and an elaborate hookah. The room was hung about with drapes of the finest transparent muslin, fine, like skeins of cobweb, and in the middle of it all a great mattress spread with silks.

He advanced into the room, pushing his way through the hangings, until he saw with astonishment that the huge couch contained Nasir Jang. He was face down, wearing only baggy pantaloons made of a light material that draped his legs loosely and revealed his buttocks. Two young light-skinned girls, their rouged nipples glistening rose pink, massaged his back.

The girls stopped their kneading and sat up dumbly. The moghul roused himself, adjusting his pagri turban as he did so. 'You seem surprised, Mr Flint,' he said, his voice soft, almost effeminate.

The Nizam was strikingly changed. Once handsome, he had lost much of his muscular weight to fat; his pale face was haggard, even in that gentle light, with something shocking behind his eyes, like the desperate pleading of a man who knows he is sinking into madness.

'Your Highness, I – I had expected to be received in the Great Hall,' Hayden Flint replied thickly in the courtly tongue, forgetting the formalities he had rehearsed. He straightened and stared bolt-straight ahead of him, trying desperately to avoid looking at Nasir Jang's slave-girls.

'I hope you will excuse the extraordinary surroundings, but I wanted us to meet in a place that I can be certain is free from the chatter of many tongues.'

'And the hearing of many ears,' said Flint, almost without thinking.

'Quite so. Please.'

The Nizam clapped his hands and the girls slid away from him and stepped off the couch to disappear silently. He pulled on a robe that was simple and without ornament; he glowed with fresh perfume as if he had just been doused in it. Sitting on the edge of the couch, he indicated that his guest should do likewise, and Hayden Flint complied stiffly. As they faced one another he saw that Nasir Jang had lost his eyebrows and that an attempt had been made to paint in new ones. His eyelids were lashless, their lower edges lined with black kohl. There was about him the ennui of decline. Something that made him instantly repellent.

'How long have you been here in my capital?' he asked.

'Seven weeks, Highness. And every day I sent a letter.'

'Seven weeks . . .' The Moghul repeated dreamily. He picked a candied sweet from a jade plate. 'An eternity.'

'It seemed so to me.'

'And so it is. You are a strange man, Mr Flint. Not like other men. Not at all.'

'I pass for ordinary amongst my own.'

'Oh, I think not. That is what the Jesuits who come to us from time to time always say, but invariably they are hand-picked to perform their particular missions.'

Hayden Flint bowed with difficulty from his perched position on the edge of the couch, accepting the comment as a compliment, hoping he was right to do so. An object on the carpets made contact with his foot. He looked down. It was something slender and solid, about three feet long, and bound loosely in a veil of plain white muslin. He knew at once what it must be.

A bead of sweat escaped from the band of his hat and rolled down on to his cheek. He wiped it away as if it was a tear and waited for the Nizam to speak, as custom demanded.

Nasir Jang's lips pursed. 'You are very silent for a man who has been obliged to wait so long for permission to speak with me.'

'My lord, I requested audience because I have an important message from the Governor of Madras. My silence does not diminish its importance. The long wait I have had to endure has, however, made it a matter of the greatest urgency.'

A lingering sigh. 'Then speak now.'

He swallowed and launched into his speech haltingly. 'I have been asked by the Governor of Madras once again to request your help in the Carnatic.'

'Again? Your Governor thinks I will change my decree?'

'The situation is not as it was. A wise man must move with events. Your army – '

'There are greater duties that call me. I am told that an Afghan army is moving on Delhi. That is where my army should go. North, not south.'

'There is a much more immediate threat. A wise man would come to terms with Raghoji Bhonsla, and enlist the support of his Marathas.'

'And what should an unwise man do?'

He immediately recognized his error and switched his attack. 'My lord, you must by now have debated with your advisers the reports about those in the Carnatic who are defying you. Surely you have been told of the smashing of Anwar-ud-Din's army, and of how that was accomplished? You must be aware that Anwar-ud-Din is dead, and that his son Muhammad Ali is either dead or in the rebels' control.'

Nasir Jang shrugged. 'I have heard there was a battle in my unimportant coastal province.' He stared at the finger-nails of his right hand for a long time, and began to polish them with his thumb. 'I know that Chanda Sahib has taken the masnad of that province. He has sent his embassy here to explain his actions.'

'You will remember that, at our last meeting, I prophesied these very events.'

'So, you are a prophet?' Nasir Jang's irony was luminous, but the flare died almost immediately. 'Perhaps that is why you seem unlike other men.'

'My lord, it is not prophecy so much as prediction. These wicked events have come to pass just as I said they would. I could foresee them only because I knew the forces that were

393

driving them into being. Now I know that Muzaffar Jang, your nephew, has joined forces with Chanda Sahib, and that the French are at the back of it. And that allows me to make a further prediction.'

Nasir Jang yawned and lay back languidly. 'What makes you suppose this manoeuvring has not been at my order?' he asked smoothly. 'Muzaffar Jang is my subject and my pawn; he only does my bidding. As for Anwar-ud-Din, he was appointed to rule the Carnatic by my father. I did not sanction his son to rule there after his death. I do not desire that the Carnatic should become an independent kingdom, ruled in perpetuity by a family whose members consider they have the right to appoint heirs. Why should I prevent his line of succession being upset by Chanda Sahib? He will pay tribute to me eventually. Or I will replace him also, and perhaps cut off his head for the marketplace dogs to feed on.'

Hayden Flint breathed deeply, trying to narrow his thoughts to a precise focus. His mind throbbed with horror to think that Nasir Jang might have summoned Chanda Sahib's representatives here in order to make an alliance with the French. Part of his mind knew that, even if it was not so, Nasir Jang might toy with the idea long enough to lose everything to Dupleix's strategems.

'My lord, Chanda Sahib is your enemy. He does not intend to pay you tribute, whatever his ambassadors may tell you. Muzaffar Jang wants your head. He has agreed to support Chanda Sahib in the Carnatic because in return Chanda Sahib has pledged to aid him in taking Hyderabad. Do not be deceived. This is the plan the French have long been hatching. You must move against them.'

'Ah, the French!' Nasir Jang smiled slackly. 'I asked myself how long it would be before you made mention of them.'

'The French are the devil's own spawn!'

He instantly regretted his angry words, realizing how severely he had been provoked by Nasir Jang's languid responses. By God, I begin to sound like my father, he thought, trying to calm himself. More levelly he said, 'The French are committed absolutely to your destruction, sir.'

Nasir Jang laughed abstractedly. ' "Sir", he says. A moment ago I was "lord". How fast have I fallen in your esteem already!' The Moghul's pride faltered just enough for him to reveal his loathing. 'I can see it in your eyes that you are like the rest after all. The French, Mr Flint, are exactly like the English: foreigners who are merely incidental to Hindostan. Come. Go. Stay for ever. Leave tomorrow. It is all the same to us. We can do without your trade, and the loss of the insignificant revenues you provide would not be missed. The private enrichment of a few minor subahdars on the fringes of my realm is of little consequence to me.'

'Highness, you are wrong. The world has shifted. Those trade revenues of which you speak have made the subahdars of the Carnatic into powerful and dangerous men. The issue is that their arms are – '

'Be silent.' Nasir Jang cut him short, his words still negligent and unconcerned. 'French or English, or whomsoever – I will tell you what you are – all of you: you are guests. Guests are welcome here only so long as they trade peaceably, only so long as they do not bring their petty European disputes into our country, and only so long as they leave our internal affairs alone!'

The Nizam's tone of voice remained light, but Hayden Flint recognized the warning it contained. He thought again of Yasmin's clever way of turning things on their head to see the truth in them. What would King George have done, he asked himself, if the coasts of England contained enclaves of various Oriental traders who brought with them armed ships and troops, who then began to foment sedition against him? Of that, there was no doubt. He would have used every device at his disposal to throw them back into the sea, and he would not have wasted time in drawing distinctions between one sort of Oriental and another.

A welcome breeze fluttered the diaphanous hangings.

Hayden Flint knew he had to accomplish his duty. He

wondered how he could disturb the Moghul's deep complacency. And once disturbed, how limit his violence to the French alone. In Hindostan, only the ways of Hindostan will work . . .

In his crispest voice he said: 'They say you are a rich man, Nasir Jang, but even you cannot afford to buy a passage home for Monsieur Dupleix. They say you are a wise man, but not so wise as to know that the Frenchman will not leave your affairs to you. The French are here to stay, as you correctly say, for ever. Their objective is to make a French empire of your domain. And although you are said to be rich, and said to be wise, they perceive you to be dissolute and weak, and I believe they will succeed in destroying you.'

An astonishing change came over Nasir Jang's face. His cheeks sagged, as a man who is confronted by truths he dare not face, but knows to be truths even so. His indifference seeped away, revealing raw fear. He put his hands to his turban and began to unwind the pagri. Beneath it his scalp was visible in patches, where fully half his hair had fallen out.

'You say I am weak. Do you know why I am as I am? Do you know why I prefer the pipe dreams of my hookah and the pleasures of my women to the truths of this world?'

Hayden Flint stared back as the Nizam leapt from the couch.

'This is what paralyses my spirit. This!'

Nasir Jang seized the muslin-bound object, holding it up. He snatched off the fabric and revealed what was inside. Hayden Flint remembered the Talwar-i-Jang, and when Nasir Jang slid it ringingly from its priceless sheath he saw the deadly curved blade glistering with koftgari of gold and Koranic inscriptions that almost obliterated the finely watered steel. He knew immediately that his suspicions were confirmed.

Nasir Jang grasped the hilt so tightly that the skin webbing his knuckles drew taut. The huge diamond they called the Mountain of Light lay embedded in the hilt, forming the disc-like finial. It was polished and smooth, and threw back the soft glow of the room with a flat opacity, as if the white fire within had burned low. And into Hayden Flint's mind there came a comparison with the legendary stone of the ka'bah, the stone that was whispered to lie at the heart of Islam in Mecca. He saw how fitting it was that such a diamond had been wedded to such a sword.

'Do you know what this is that I possess?' Nasir Jang demanded. His face was trancelike now, his stare fast on the evil diamond; he seemed transfixed by it.

'It is the Talwar.'

'Yes! It is the Talwar. It is the sword that proclaims my rule to all men.' Nasir Jang was cold now, his words thick as vomit. 'It must stay with me. Always.'

'You believe it is your death warrant.'

Nasir Jang's arm jerked back, but then, as if the sword had become suddenly white-hot, he released it, letting it fall to the carpet.

The Nizam began to sob. 'I can feel the evil in it! I have swallowed a slow poison and now I am waiting to die! I do not know how, or when, or by whose hand, but I know I must face the pain and terror of a thousand martyrs. I know it must come. Therefore each day I wait in terror, and each day is a hell for me. And so to relieve that hell I gorge myself at the table of life because tomorrow, or the day after, or the day after that, I know I shall have to pay!'

Hayden Flint felt compassion. Part of him wanted to wrap the sword and put it away from the Nizam, but he resisted the urge to touch it. If he could only undo some of the superstition that saturated the Moghul's thinking. He tried to calm the man who held the keys to all their futures.

'Highness, it is said there is nothing more deadly to a man than his own private terrors. Do you truly believe that this sword's gem will kill you?'

'It is written. The prophecy. The curse in the diamond. It is written that any man who possesses the stone is destined to die cruelly and prematurely.'

'How can you say that? Asaf Jah lived for nine years with

397

the Koh-i-Noor at his side. The curse never harmed him. Quite the opposite – '

'For nine years my father was protected!'

'Then surely you also are protected. If you are the rightful heir of Asaf Jah and you rule with Asaf Jah's blessing, there can be nothing to fear.'

But as he spoke, he saw that Nasir Jang was full of the terror that sprang from guilt. His head fell into his hands; he was shot through with despair.

'I am not protected!'

He watched the Nizam carefully, judging the precarious way forward, and whether he could take the next step. 'Your father died in old age. Quietly, in his bed. I was here in Hyderabad at that time.'

'You came with the embassy of Muhammad Ali Khan.'

'That is correct, Highness.' Nasir Jang's sidelong glance warned him that he must tread with extreme care. He said, 'I therefore know that you were with Asaf Jah when he died. And I must admit to being surprised that he did not impart the secret of his survival to you.'

'He told me nothing.'

When Nasir Jang looked up again his face was haunted. He seemed to have collapsed within himself, but the story came from him fervently.

'It was a terrible day. All day the palace had been in silence. The birds had stopped their singing, and the peasants had abandoned their fields. When the sun went down over the mountains I went to my father's side. I saw him lying on his deathbed, his breathing shallow, and I knew his spirit was slowly leaving his body. I remember thinking it was incredible how he had deteriorated in the space of only one month. His foremost wife had died during Ramzan, a very old and gracious lady, loved by all, and held in the highest esteem. She had always been his staff and without her spirit to support him he had declined so suddenly.

'I dismissed the servants and the guards, and knelt by him. You cannot imagine the fear and foreboding that swept through me in that moment. Until then, I had been avid to succeed my father. All my life I had wanted to become Nizam-ul-Mulk. But then I saw the Talwar lying at his head, unsheathed, and it was as if the diamond was watching him, sapping the strength from him. Each time his breathing faltered its light pulsed brighter. I looked at it, and I knew that, before midnight, this symbol of his power would fall to me. I had only to grasp it.'

Nasir Jang stopped. His back was bowed; his eyes stared down at the carpet; his hands were clasped in front of him in an attitude of prayer. The man hungered to make a difficult admission, so Hayden Flint held his silence.

'My elder brother, Ghazi-ud-Din, was in Delhi. He held a high ceremonial post at the Emperor's court, and he sent word that he absolutely refused to inherit. My father knew this, but still he favoured him, still he expected him to come. He had not returned for his mother's funeral – my father's foremost wife had been interred with magnificent ceremony at which he should have officiated – but even that had not tempted her son to return.

'I told my father, "Ghazi-ud-Din will not come. Proclaim me Nizam!" But he would not. I told him that unless he did so, Muzaffar would declare himself successor; that rivers of blood would flow in the palace, and a hundred pretenders would march their armies on Hyderabad from all the subahs of the realm to help claim the prize, or dismember it. He laughed at my words, saying that no man would be foolish enough to take the Talwar unprotected. The sound of that laugh will live with me for ever. Death rattled in his throat. I begged him to admit witnesses. To confer his power on me while he still could. To tell me the secret. Then I saw how this monstrous power had poisoned him. The Koh-i-Noor had twisted him, and he had become jealous of it. While he breathed he would never relinquish it freely . . .'

Hayden Flint watched as the Nizam's words trailed away. He held his silence still, encouraging the man to go on, but when no more came, he said, 'So you took it?'

Nasir Jang nodded his regret. 'Yes. I took it.'

Hayden Flint made no reply, and the Nizam drew himself up with a hint of his old imperiousness. 'I knew I had to act – for the good of the realm. You see that, don't you? I had to ensure the succession. There was no choice. The Talwar beckoned me. I closed my hand over the hilt and I felt the power flow into me. Such power! I had no concept of how it would feel. I had anticipated that moment for years, but still I was not ready for the sensation that flowed in me. It was like fire in my veins, heady like the peak of intoxication, with an oblivion of mind like the sex moment. I felt that with the Talwar in my hand I could conquer the whole of Hindostan, the whole of Asia!

'My father groaned and sat up. I don't know where his strength came from, but he began storming and babbling. I moved away from him, but he rose up, and laid his hands on me. A horrible stare was in his eyes. His hands were like wires, clawing back his greatest possession.

' "Thief!" he cried. "Thief! Murderer!" I thought the guards must hear him and come in. My order was that we were to be left alone, but I knew Asaf Jah's passionate screams would be too much for them to bear. I clapped my hand over his mouth, and pushed him back.'

Nasir Jang's face stared up in appeal, wan as the moon. He began to tremble. Whether it was remorse, or self-pity, or fear, or anger at his own impotence, Hayden Flint could not tell.

'And then?'

'And then I killed him.'

In that gaping silence the filtered light seemed to flicker. Hayden Flint's eyes were drawn to the baleful stone in the sword's hilt. It seemed as if the gem had become a source of light, casting a diffuse and gloating ambience. A shiver ran through him, but he resisted it, and it thrilled out of him, raising the hairs on his skin like needles.

What man could stand where I do, he asked himself with awe, and still disbelieve the power of the Koh-i-Noor? Who could deny the curse having once seen the way it crushes down those under its spell? The curse is very real! But it's real only because it has the power to release the fears that already lie locked in the hearts of men. To believe is to succumb utterly. Utterly.

In Hindostan, only the ways of Hindostan succeed . . .

Suddenly the strength of Stratford Flint seized him. Yes! And in our affairs, there can be only our solutions, by God! This man must be induced to back the Honourable Company's nominee for the Carnatic: Muhammad Ali Khan. That is my duty.

But how do I accomplish it? When he mentioned Muhammad Ali's name I could not perceive his mind on the man. Does he know and hate him for bringing a false amulet against the power of the Koh-i-Noor? Has despair driven him to believe in the Eye's power? Does he know Muhammad Ali possesses it still? Or does he really consider Muhammad Ali to be just an irrelevant princeling struggling to regain an unimportant coastal province?

Whichever way, I must broach the matter of the Eye soon. I must know whether he believes in it or not, whether he knows where it has gone. There must exist a precious alloy of East and West that can solve everything. There must be a way!

He closed his eyes and breathed deeply, knowing this must be a step into the unknown. His head filled with the piquant savour of the East, but the core of him was cold and calculating and he felt strong in his power.

He remembered the story of Excalibur, how it had been flung into a lake. How like the English to conceive such a legend. But this was no straight-edged English broadsword, and Nasir Jang was no Arthur. He opened his eyes and looked down. The sword lay at his feet, its curve and sheen as elegantly seductive to the eye as the line of a woman's body, a perfect breast, a perfect thigh. Like a bolt from the sky sudden inspiration came to him and he struck.

'Highness, do you remember the reason for Muhammad Ali's embassy to your father's capital?' Nasir Jang did not move, or make to answer, so Hayden Flint knew he must gamble. He said slowly, 'There is only one hope for you.'

Nasir Jang's misery would not be lifted. It lay upon him, consuming him. He groaned. 'There can be no hope!'

'I tell you, there is hope!'

Nasir Jang looked up angrily, his face clouding with ugly suspicion. 'I will not give it up! Do not ask that – it is impossible. Read the inscription: if I give the Talwar away the retribution of the curse will be multiplied tenfold. Why do you refuse to understand?'

'You are wrong, Nasir Jang. There must be a solution. You told me yourself that your father knew of one.'

'I told you also that the secret died with him!'

'Have you suspected that perhaps it did not?'

The sneer in the Nizam's voice was unexpected. 'I have thought that a thousand times, feringhee. I have thought that perhaps there never was any secret! Never any protection. Perhaps it was a great lie, and the great Asaf Jah bought his decade of worldly power from Shatan himself! Perhaps he sold his soul into hell for that, and once his span elapsed the curse reasserted itself. Now you know that he died at the hands of his son the meaning is clear. I strangled him! It took me an eternity to choke the life from him, and while I murdered him he looked up at me and the terror was there in his eyes. Oh, yes, have no doubt about it, feringhee, the curse killed Asaf Jah in the end. There is no escape.'

Hayden Flint stood unmoving as a rock. He had his answer. The strength of certainty had fortified him: Nasir Jang would believe in the Eye. He started to level an accusing finger; he longed to say, 'It was you who killed Asaf Jah. You, Nasir Jang, your greed, and your lust for power, and not any curse. And it is your guilt that terrifies you now.' But he did not say that. Instead he smiled as a man who is confident of victory smiles.

'I know the way of your escape.'

'There is none!'

'Believe me!'

'No!'

Nasir Jang's reluctance was huge. So strange, Hayden Flint marvelled, that when the door is opened on the dungeon of misery so few men have the courage to step through. He fears the sword as if its hilt contains an evil djinn who overhears him. He dare not test it in deed, word, or even in thought.

He stepped over the sword, interposing himself between it and the Nizam, then he drew Nasir Jang's attention to the shuttered window looking out over his private courtyard of fountains. He opened the screens so that the harsh light flooded in, and they went out on to a gold and marble balcony. Below, the waters whispered into an ornamental pool of green Chinese jade. Above, the sky was a rare clean blue. He lowered his voice.

'Nasir Jang, have you forgotten about the Eye? I myself brought it into Hindostan from the Isle of Lanka.'

'That was the fable spun to me. Instead I found a snake in a box.'

'It was a fable. And the snake was put there by those who wished both of us ill.'

He told again how he had brought the Eye to Anwar-ud-Din who planned to use it to gain the Nizamat. How he had struck the bargain in order to enlist the nawab's help in freeing Madras from the French, and as he spoke he saw that Nasir Jang was now moved to believe him.

'But Anwar-ud-Din's greater plans were ruined on the coast.'

'Yes. And so the Eye was offered at Hyderabad.'

'But I did not believe . . . Where is it, now that Anwar-ud-Din is dead?'

'It has passed to his son, Muhammad Ali, who is fled to Trichinopoly. Soon Chanda Sahib and your nephew will take their army there and lay siege to the fortress, and with French guns they will reduce it. When Muhammad Ali was here in this palace he dined many times with your nephew. You may rest assured that Muzaffar Jang knows of the Eye, and plans to make it his own.'

Nasir Jang's face betrayed him. Like a man who has languished in a dark place and is assaulted by daylight he rubbed at his face.

'Knowing this,' Hayden Flint continued, 'your advisers have sought to isolate you. They have kept the truth from you. They believe you are doomed, that their future lies with Muzaffar. They await your death and his coming. You must act now. You must raise your army and march south, on Trichinopoly. For there, and only there, lies your salvation.'

The banquet room blazed with candlelight. Joseph-François Dupleix put down his knife, and took in the gathering, smiling coolly to the members of his Council, to Louis d'Auteuil, and young Jacques Law, and the aristocratic Charles, Marquis de Bussy.

Such airs, he thought, looking round with approval. It should be clear to any man of intelligence and perception what is the true status of everyone here. Nevertheless, the reception afforded these Moghul lords is the most sumptuous I could devise.

It had all proceeded exactly according to plan. During the feasting at Ambur, after the great battle, Muzaffar Jang, self-appointed Nizam of the Deccan, had officially bestowed the title 'Nawab of the Carnatic' upon Chanda Sahib. Since the pretender, Anwar-ud-Din Khan, was dead it was only necessary for Dupleix to receive them in state, to recognize them, and confirm their alliance.

Now, as protocol demanded, the head of the table was occupied by Muzaffar Jang. Swathed in his finest robes and displaying a hauteur that eclipsed all around him, he wore a great and famous ruby in his turban. Then came Chanda Sahib, seated to his right, conservatively dressed. As host, Commander of Seven Thousand and holder of the six jagirs conferred on Sieur Dumas, Dupleix's great predecessor. In formal rank Dupleix superseded the other nobles of the Moghul establishment, and of course headed the officials of his own Council. They stretched far down the room, dressed in wigs and satin coats.

He had arranged that the seating was planned to an end other than pure protocol. Conversation would, so far as possible, be conducted in the court tongue, and where not, interpreters were standing by. The evening had been chosen to allow certain presentations, and to facilitate the discussion that had developed during the first nine courses of the banquet.

If my senses do not betray me, he told himself, the most difficult moment is now reaching its culmination. *Ah! Oui!* Chanda Sahib has just quietly fired the first volley. Here it comes, as I knew it must.

'Honourable Monsieur, we find ourselves in difficulties. We are men of title, but it is already being whispered amongst our men that we are like two beggars, the one calling out to the other "My Lord Nawab, where shall we sit today?" while the other replies, "Outside the house of the feringhee, My Lord Nizam."'

Dupleix smiled indulgently. 'Oh, but we need not fear the opinions of the common soldiery.'

Muzaffar shifted uncomfortably, his syrupy voice smoothing over the difficulty. 'Perhaps not, sir, but we approach the situation where we are no longer able to proceed. In Hindostan, armies will remain armies, they will fight, and they will march, only in so far as they are paid.'

Chanda laid aside his silver fork. 'They were promised much before the battle at Ambur.'

Dupleix stared back icily. A pathetic rabble, he wanted to say. Pardon, but I have read the reports in detail and I know how the Battle of Ambur was won. It was Captain Paradis and his men – French infantry and French-trained sipahis – whose discipline broke Anwar-ud-Din the first time at the Adiyar River; it was those same men, under Louis d'Auteuil, who were the steel that tipped the cane a second time at Ambur. French tactics! French discipline! And French power! That was what broke Anwar-ud-Din. Your rabble was there merely to make the operation legitimate, and loot the field. *Dieu!* The terms were fixed and agreed before we began, and I'm damned if I'll bow to extortion now.

He feinted. 'Ah, should we ask Monsieur d'Auteuil to describe for us events at Ambur? I believe he has a wonderful tale of how the jemadar of our sipahis sprang upon Anwar-ud-Din's bodyguard, vanquished them single-handedly, and then cut off the head of their master – is that not truly heroic?'

'Perhaps our present discussion is more important.'

'Perhaps yes, perhaps no. Are your promises no longer good? What do your men fear? Nothing that a few well-chosen words of leadership will not persuade out of them, I'm sure.'

Chanda stood his ground. 'So far, they have taken only what they could lift from the enemy's camp. A poor shadow of their expectations. It is customary for a nawab, even a vile usurper like Anwar-ud-Din Muhammad, to keep his treasures with him. If we had been able to stand before our people and scatter gold, it would have done much to underscore our status.' He lowered his eyes diplomatically. 'However, our army found little at Ambur. In consequence, there was unrest.'

Muzaffar lent him further support. 'It was then the words of leadership were spoken. I myself promised them the spoils of Arcot, but by the time we reached that place its treasuries had already been scoured.'

Chanda shrugged like a Frenchman. 'We are unable to pay our men. There have already been desertions. More will follow.'

Dupleix felt his frustration firm into anger. 'What do you suggest?' he asked. 'I have already explained most carefully – and several times – that it is imperative we invest Trichinopoly as soon as possible.'

'Out of the question now. The crushing of Muhammad Ali Khan will have to wait.' There was an edge to Muzaffar's voice and Dupleix turned quickly to him.

'It cannot wait. I cannot wait.'

Muzaffar drew out his pocketwatch and consulted it pointedly, mirroring Dupleix's own habit. 'Your urgency is incomprehensible. Anwar-ud-Din is vanquished, is he not?

His capital is in our hands. Therefore the struggle for the Carnatic is all but complete.'

'No! The south of the province is not secured. While Muhammad Ali lives he has the power to attract an army, and while that army stands you will not be the undisputed rulers here.'

Chanda sipped at the gilded rim of his coffee cup. 'Honourable Monsieur, since you are not seeing that place yourself, allow me to describe its character for you. The fortress of Trichinopoly is generally held to be unassailable, being a pagoda and fort built upon a pinnacle of rock that rises more than three hundred of your feet. There is a half-kos-long double wall – both walls rising more than twenty feet high, and separated by the same distance. It is protected on the outer side by a ditch thirty paces across, and half that amount in depth . . .'

As Chanda continued, Dupleix listened with particular interest. The spy network operated by his wife had already supplied a highly accurate survey of Trichinopoly's strength. He had committed the salient details of that description to memory and now compared them with Chanda's version.

He's correct in most points, he thought, *and in many other matters too. Trichinopoly is strong, and Chanda is a good soldier, with a good soldier's eye for detail. A pity I could not engineer affairs so that he was destined for Hyderabad instead of Muzaffar Jang. Muzaffar prefers manoeuvre to engagement; he is a tempered politician. I can already see from his manners that, in the coming struggle, he will make a poor general, and an even worse puppet afterwards.*

'. . . so it is my estimate that we should attempt to starve the usurper out of Trichinopoly. Thus we may succeed at our leisure.'

Dupleix shook his head. 'There is no time. The walls must be breached. Trichinopoly must be taken with all speed. We must march south without delay.'

Muzaffar looked to Chanda, then back at Dupleix;

407

mistrust laced his voice. 'Perhaps your ends are not the same as ours, monsieur? How if we choose to ignore Muhammad Ali? How if we decide that our best hope lies in consolidating the jagirs of the north? How if we forsake your foreign strategies and ignore your foreign orders?'

'In that case, Muzaffar Jang, you would not live up to your name, for you would be a cowardly fool. And you must know that I cannot allow a fool of any kind to become ruler at Hyderabad.'

Chanda saw his ally stiffen under Dupleix's words. It's not only a threat, it's an appalling insult, he thought. An unpardonable breach of etiquette. By exposing the fiction of Moghul power so openly Dupleix has humiliated Muzaffar, and is not Muzaffar notorious for the length of his memory when it comes to slights? I must speak, now, before it is too late.

He jumped in quickly, addressing Dupleix directly. 'Honourable sir, perhaps I may be permitted to suggest a compromise? Let us dwell upon those many matters in which we are agreeing.' He smiled, attempting with convivial gestures to ease the moment of friction. After a few inconsequential remarks, he moved smoothly to the heart of the issue. 'We are in accord that the fortress and town of Trichinopoly is our principal objective. Eventually, we must overcome Muhammad Ali Khan. To do so we must prise him from his shell. We are also agreeing that every day he remains in Trichinopoly is another day he is seen to defy our joint proclamations, those made at Arcot, naming myself Nawab of the Carnatic, and Muzaffar Jang Nizam of the Deccan. Every day he survives, his following swells while our own is depleted. But consider: to hold the fortress the usurper must also pay his men and feed them. Gold he has taken from Arcot, what little remained after Anwar-ud-Din's defeats, but he is gathering both food and tribute from the immediate district surrounding the fortress.'

Muzaffar made to speak, but Chanda succeeded in preventing him. 'That district is famed for its rice-growing.

The Cauvery River flows only one kos – perhaps two of your French miles, monsieur – from the northernmost part of the fortress. Another watercourse, the Coleroon, runs parallel several kos to the north-west. The strip of land between the rivers, called by the local people the Island of Srirangham, is low lying and waterlogged – ideal for rice: all because there is an earth dam midway between Trichinopoly and Tanjore to the east. This irrigated land is ruled by the Raja of Tanjore . . .'

Chanda paused again, but this time Muzaffar made no move to interrupt. Neither did the Frenchman, whose chin was resting on his hand in a thoughtful manner.

Dupleix was calculating. Some months ago, news had reached Pondicherry that the English had been entangled with the Raja of Tanjore in a dispute over the coastal town of Devicotta, situated at the mouth of the Coleroon River, twenty miles south of Fort St David. I see what Chanda is aiming at, he thought. After all, Chanda was the man who in the days of Dost Ali punished Tanjore severely for refusing to render prompt tribute to Arcot. He knows Tanjore of old. He knows it for a honeypot. It's true that old habits die hard.

He allowed his protégé to continue.

'Honourable Monsieur, the Tanjorines have gold and food. They have no means of protection from a European attack.'

'We should attack them?' Dupleix asked, as if suddenly taken by the plan. 'Is that what you want?'

'What we took from Tanjore we would keep from Muhammad Ali also.'

'And for this your men would march south?'

'The prospect of seeing what may be found in Tanjore will help persuade our warriors not to return to their own fields.'

Muzaffar laughed, and slapped his hands on his thighs. The great pigeon's-blood ruby on his turban stared glassily across the table. 'It seems Chanda has shown us the way! That is well, is it not?'

At a signal from Dupleix, a silver candlestick used as a gavel hushed the gathering and Muzaffar Jang was formally announced. He stood to a general toast. His speech was long and rambling; each paragraph was first read by him, then translated into French for the benefit of the Council.

Help rendered towards the smashing of Anwar-ud-Din's power had to be rewarded. The prize was to be the ceding of two areas to the French: Villanour and Valudavur. To these would now be added the port of Masulipatam, and the small territory of Bahur which was close enough to Fort St David to make it as important as the other three districts added together.

The announcement drew tremendous applause. Officers clapped and began to bang the tables with their hands until the candlelight shivered. Soon the Moghuls were doing likewise.

Dupleix applauded too, but he was still thinking. *We must make haste south. Soon they will learn what I already know: that Nasir Jang has begun to gather his enormous forces. The army of Hyderabad is 300,000 strong, and once that enters the Carnatic, no force on earth, European or otherwise, will be able to defeat it.*

Inside the Nizam's campaign tent, the air was dark and dusty. Twenty of Nasir Jang's nobles, three Marathas and six English sat round the French surveyor's map, while innumerable servants and guards stood in attendance in the opulent interior.

Hayden Flint looked towards Robert Clive. Their eyes met, and it was as if a spark passed between them, a spark like the man-made lightning of a Leyden jar. Both men felt the jolt; each knew the other had felt it.

Two hundred yards away English artillery were giving an intermittent barrage of defiance to the enemy. The cannonades were by induction, each piece fired giving the signal to the next down the line. As Hayden Flint listened a ragged volley ripped the air; half a minute later, a distant reply echoed.

'Sir, even this chart is evidence that Jack Frenchman has designs on your country.'

Stringer Lawrence's back straightened, his face florid in the suffocating heat. He squatted uncomfortably on a low stool, his great calves bursting at white silk hose; knees unaccustomed to bending more than a right angle cracked as he shifted his weight. He wore a new powdered wig, and an elaborately gold-laced red coat, with blue facings and deep cuffs. On Hayden Flint's recommendation he had come properly dressed to do battle with the military ignorance of his allies.

Hayden Flint winced as the Major spoke. He leaned towards him in as inconspicuous an aside as he could manage. 'Sir, you must address the Nizam as "Your Highness".'

'Hmmm?'

Lawrence will have to be guided carefully, he thought. Nasir Jang rules a land the size of France and England put together. Without due protocol our precarious alliance can still fall apart.

'I say it had better be this way, Y'Highness, or Jack Frenchman will eat you up. You'll expend the lives of your men needlessly, d'you see?'

Nasir Jang's languid, indifferent hand was all the reply offered. His eyes fell.

Instead, the fiery Nawab of Savanur spoke. 'I say that this craven manoeuvre is not in accord with the dignity of a Nizam! What honour may fall to his great name if he does as you say?'

Lawrence snorted into his handkerchief and tucked it into his vest pocket before tapping the knob of his stick onto the map. 'I cannot speak for that aspect of it, sir. However, if it is your aim to gain the day, it is plain to the veriest fool that you must interpose yourself here – leaving your present position, and taking up station closer to Pondicherry, as I tell you.'

The Nawab of Kurnool, a Pathan, gripped the hilt of his sword. 'It is better to attack! Our lord has seen fit to appoint you generalissimo of his armies. Our astrologers tell us the day is favoured. Why then do you not order our forces to the attack?'

'If I have command of them, then let them do as I say, sir!'

'I say you are escared of the French!'

Lawrence struggled to keep his temper intact. He leaned forward again, his silver-knobbed stick making sweeping arcs across the map. 'Let me make it plain t'you: Muzaffar Jang and Chanda Sahib have taken post within a few miles of us. Two thousand French have marched out of Pondicherry. They are under the command of one of the best French officers t'have set his foot in this country – Mr Daw-Tay. You can be sure he has not neglected to bring with him a sufficient train of artillery – thirty guns as you presently hear – and a consid'rable sepoy company. There is no doubt where your army must be drawn up.' He stabbed his stick into the map. 'Here, between Chanda Sahib and Pondicherry, so he loses his communications, and is cut off! That way p'raps you won't lose so many of your horse to their grapeshot!'

Morari Rao, the Maratha leader, his eyes alive with the prospect of battle, spoke out angrily. 'You do not understand our method of war. My men will not take orders from any European officer.'

Nasir Jang raised a hand and turned to Lawrence. 'My letters brought you here from Fort St George with six hundred men, Major Lawrence. You have not approached the enemy so far. Why are you still unwilling to join battle? Do their numbers intimidate you? If my army moves away from Chanda Sahib's troops as you suggest, it will seem that I am running from him.'

Hayden Flint whispered, 'You're angering him, Major.'

Lawrence's jowls quivered. 'Hmmm?'

'I advise you to invite Mr Westcott to speak.'

Lawrence grasped the knob of his stick and levered himself to his feet, his patience used up. 'Mr Westcott, a member of the Madras Council, carries the commission to treat with you,' he said wearily. 'He has the good offices of Captain Dalton here. Perhaps they can make my strategy clear to you since I certainly cannot.'

Foss Westcott coughed lightly. 'If Your Highness agrees, we might move on to item thirteen of our agenda . . .'

As the Council member's quiet diplomacy soothed the meeting, Hayden Flint's mood deepened. He felt his high hopes dull as the sea dulls when a cloud covers the sun.

He disengaged, turning his mind inward. Tiredness was making the world distant, making smoke of it, showing him the ultimate truth: that it was all insubstantial. But still the sound of the cannonade continued, soft and flat, then louder, then soft again. The roar of the French guns was deadened by distance and the material of the tent. The answering bangs from nearby eighteen-pounders were bassy thumps, felt rather than heard. Even the flies were drowsy as they landed on the chart to groom themselves.

Surely our fortunes are at their highest since these troubles began, he thought, forcing himself to consider the portents. The Nizam is camped here at Villanour, not ten miles from the gates of Pondicherry! With him is the greatest army in Hindostan, maybe half a million fighting men counting Morari Rao's Maratha horse, and most of his divisions as reasonably loyal to him as the sure prospect of victory can make them. Moreover, Nasir Jang has brought riches in proportion to his power, all the treasure of Aurangabad – forty chests of jewels and a crore of rupees in silver – ten million pieces! And now, to top it all, Stringer Lawrence is made commander-in-chief as a gesture by Nasir Jang!

What can Dupleix do? It would take inconceivable bad luck and stupidity combined for us to fail now.

But, damn me, it's not for want of trying! The honour that Nasir Jang's done the Major is being thrown back at him by Stringer's taking the title to command at face value. Can he be so naive as to think he's been given leave to dispose the Nizam's army as he wishes? Why doesn't he take the lead from Clive, keeping more of his own counsel, and speaking in the Eastern style when he must? At least Mr Westcott's doing as I suggested.

'. . . and thus, Highness, the Hon'ble Company's pledge of assistance is in no way dependent on any condition, least of all the matter of treaties.'

Hayden Flint was about to step in on Foss Westcott's political observations when the Nizam spoke. He mouthed the formalities like a man chewing dry dust, his voice weary, betraying the weight of his terrors. Hayden remembered that fruitless durbar with Muhammad Ali which had convinced the Nizam that his fate was already written, and that it was a devastating one.

The durbar, at which Hayden had first been present, had celebrated Nasir Jang's subjugation of the Arcot country three months ago. It had been specially staged, but for a different reason – to receive Muhammad Ali Khan officially.

The desperate nawab had ridden north a hundred and fifty miles with his bodyguard, a perilous journey – dangerous to leave Trichinopoly with his wealth unattended, with Pratap Singh, the Raja of neighbouring Tanjore, eyeing him with jealous ambition, and his own mercenaries less than trustworthy – but necessary to come up to Arni, not ten miles from Arcot, to bend the knee and prostrate himself before the glory of the Subahdar of the Deccan. Because, as surely as the sun and stars, Nasir Jang was the one man who could give him life and power in this land of death and dispossession.

Muhammad Ali's bodyguard had swept into the ford at Arni to be met by 500 of Morari Rao's riders. He must have thought himself betrayed. How unsettling to see those Hindu Marathas, the proud men of Raghoji Bhonsla's elite horse who had so often scourged Moghul lands, receiving him as a brother and conducting him to the limitless camp the Nizam had created.

It was a city in itself, a city bigger than any of the Carnatic. A million souls – scholars and sweepers, cooks and courtesans, as well as three to four lakhs of fighting men

– a city fifty miles around, erected, torn down and erected again as fast as the changing phases of the moon.

Hayden Flint had witnessed Muhammad Ali's astonishment. Not even his time in Hyderabad had prepared him for the scale of the Nizam's martial power. When fully assembled, the throng was an awe-inspiring sight, the whole directed by the will of one man. Had all things gone according to Muhammad Ali's plan, a snake's fangs would have stopped that man's heart, and the interfering Englishman would have been trampled in the killing pits of Hyderabad.

Ah, but unguessable fate . . . its snake writhings have shown all false prophets to be fools.

Despite the turning and turning again of the cosmic wheel, events had conspired to work to Muhammad Ali's advantage. That night in the heart of the Arcot country he had been pronounced Nawab of the Carnatic, and a strange night it had been.

The Nizam, ill-faced and haunted, full of wine and in an evil temper; Muhammad Ali falling down in obeisance, then coming forward to kiss the stone of power in the Talwar, looking starkly at the jaundiced face of his master as he was suffered to approach.

'Ask anything of me, O Great Lord Nizam.'

Nasir Jang had turned earnestly to his wazir, doubtless remembering the lessons he had learned as a boy at the knee of the great Asaf Jah, when he saw how his father wielded power and secured loyalty.

'Anything? A vast word. A capsule wherein lies infinity. Then should I test this promise and demand a part of him?' he said to his ministers.

The wazir made a formula reply as Muhammad Ali looked from face to face: 'As your magnificence wishes.'

'Which part shall we cut off?' he asked. 'His tongue or his penis? Mullah, what do you say?'

The greybeard came forward from the shadows, his devoutness a shield against the diamond's glassy stare. He said, 'Master, if you possess a man's tongue he can never again lie to you. Possess his penis and he is no longer a man.'

'Ah! Then choose, Muhammad Ali Khan. Which is it to be?'

The nawab's complexion blanched. 'Lord, you already own both parts – all parts – of me.'

Oh, yes, Muhammad Ali had been terrified, Hayden Flint recalled. Memories of the gift snake must have made him cold. Asaf Jah had always built up his victims to a height before slamming them down into the dust.

But Nasir Jang grunted and swayed, the conundrum clear enough to him: obedience – if the new nawab wishes to remain a man, he must also remain silent.

'Easy, Muhammad Ali Khan. I have other plans for what you must give me in return for your title.'

'Lord, name your gift!'

'Let us say . . . a ruby.'

'Master?'

'Muhammad Ali Khan!' Annoyance now, a man-trap set on the lightest of catches. 'Give me your famous ruby.'

And Muhammad Ali's face turned, aghast at the request, which was not a request but an order. He shook his head, shrugging and denying, but Nasir Jang's dreadful majesty held him.

'Lord, I have no ruby.'

'Yes, yes. The Eye. The Eye of the serpent Naga, whose constellation is in the heavens, the thirteenth sign of the zodiac . . . The same that Mr Flint brought into my domains!'

Muhammad Ali's glance was venomous and his anger as he looked towards Hayden Flint caused him to lose his humble bearing and reveal himself.

'Lord, I no longer possess that stone!'

Like lightning glaring from a monsoon sky Nasir Jang demanded, 'Then who does?'

Muhammad Ali thought furiously, his reddened eyes tracking back and forth, weighing what Nasir Jang must already know. He could not tell the truth. Not now.

'It is lost. Gone. Back to the hell from whence it came.'

'You lie. Muhammad Ali Khan!'

'No!'

'Then swear! Swear by the Mountain of Light that you speak truly!'

And Muhammad Ali knelt and kissed the stone once more and he told how the Eye had been lost in this selfsame River Cheyyar as he fled with his bodyguard south from Arcot, how his horse had stumbled in the ford, and the turbulent current, swollen by monsoon rains, had snatched it from him.

Liar!

Oh yes, Muhammad Ali Khan had lied, and fled the Nizam's presence as soon as he could, pleading the need to hold Trichinopoly and the South while the usurpers were at large. The rest of that night had been a gulf of silence; a clap of the lordly hands had dissolved the durbar, and Nasir Jang had retired inconsolable, to nurse his dead hopes alone.

But the consequences of that most extraordinary of nights were not brought to a conclusion by Hayden Flint taking to his bed. The blade of a knife had appeared over his head and slit open the fabric of his tent in the small hours. He had sprung awake and confronted the thief with two primed and cocked pieces.

'Stand, badmash!'

'I am no badmash, sahib.'

'Sweet Jesus! You!'

The betel-red smile was ghastly in the moonlight, weather-cracked and grinning. A face he delighted to see: the old scout once commanded by Abdul Masjid.

'Mohan Das? Or his very ghost!'

'Pssht, *baba*! You must be quiet! I come to tell the sahib much, and I would not be discovered during the telling.'

The old man revealed that Muhammad Ali had lied about the Eye. 'You should know that he sold it to Muzaffar Jang upon his father's orders. He was hoping to take Arcot from his father once Muzaffar became Nizam.' In the dark, Mohan Das's ironic cackles were oddly comforting.

'Why are you telling me this?'

'A good lord is worthy to know the truth. But listen! You have not yet heard it all.'

He listened as the scout told first of the trial, then of the horrific destruction at Ambur, and finally of the escape of Yasmin Begum.

'You are certain she's alive?'

'Sahib, she is reprieved and living in the zenana at Trichinopoly.'

Pure joy flooded him. He seized the old man's hand, unable to speak for a moment.

'I thank you for that,' he said eventually, meaning it more than he had ever meant anything. He took a gold mohur from his travelling chest. 'Mohan Das, this is a small token . . .'

The scout regarded the coin disdainfully. 'Not necessary, sahib. I am already paid. Here, in my heart.'

He grinned back, and the old man wagged his head with pleasure and cackled again.

Hayden Flint remembered his duty, and the pledge made with Clive. 'Mohan Das, I have a question I must ask you. This time I shall pay for your answer.'

Mohan Das relented and took the gold. 'That is fair.'

'You spoke of Muhammad Ali's zenana. Do you know if an Angrezi woman was taken there?'

The scout moved uneasily. 'I cannot speak of that.'

'Why, Mohan Das? Why can't you speak?'

But there was no answer. A distant sentry challenge made them pause. The sound of a struggle and shots fired as a dispute between the feuding elements of Nasir Jang's gigantic, turbulent camp erupted and was calmed. When it was over, he turned to Mohan Das, but the scout had gone, and the golden mohur had been left behind, gleaming on the carpet.

'Hmmm!'

The sound of Stringer Lawrence clearing his throat brought him back to the present. The Major had not given up an inch of ground.

'I say again: a soldier must be sure of victory wherever he fights. He must fight only once he has won.'

'He talks in impenetrable riddles!' the Nawab of Kurnool said.

'I'm talking about manoeuvre, sir!' Lawrence's gritty voice ploughed on. 'In this partic'lar instance a direct attack is sure to be attended with difficulty, and would cost the lives of many brave men. The enemy is strongly posted. He has with him a large train of artillery. But if you're pleased to move between him and Pondicherry you may, by cutting his communication, oblige him to fight at a great disadvantage.' He unbent a fraction towards cordiality. 'A certainty, eh? With honour, I assure you! Now, what do you say, Y'Highness?'

Nasir Jang's a man whose mind is consumed with the certainty of defeat, thought Hayden Flint as he looked on. His antique language, his conventions and forms, are utterly different to those of an ex-King's officer, but it's clear that Stringer despises him for another reason: because he has no faith in himself.

Nasir sighed. 'I say: God the Almighty gives prosperity to whom He wishes; dispossesses whom He wishes; honours whom He wishes and disgraces whom he wi – '

An ensign entered the tent, flushed and urgent. 'Sir, there's movement from the French!'

Immediately the meeting broke up. Orders were shouted. Lawrence growled about leading his redcoats back to Fort St David unless he was listened to. Then they were out into the eye-piercing brightness.

Outside, there stretched a panorama of war. The vast horse army made possible by this bounteous land stood arrayed below, drawn up and ready to fly at the enemy. Close by, the many standards of the Nizam's various divisions stirred in the breeze, overshadowing the heavy flag of the Honourable Company with its red and white bars and canton of the British Union carried by a red-coated soldier. The cross-belted infantrymen, fusiliers and grenadiers, carried their muskets upright, long spiked bayonets rising above the cocks of their hats. Beyond the Nizam's standardbearers a thousand panoplied elephants

419

waited patiently in the hot sun, the smell of their dung heavy on the air. At the sight of the Nizam, the elephants raised their right front legs for the near-naked drivers to spring up on to their heads.

The Nizam's party processed to their giant steeds with due ceremony, climbing the portable wooden stairs that had been brought for the purpose.

Hayden Flint got into his own howdah atop a ten-year-old bull. He called down to Robert Clive. 'Will you go along with the Major or ride with me? I'm an old hand at this transport. It's safer than it looks.'

Clive grunted. 'Nothing's safe in a battle!' But he followed all the same, dawdling carelessly in a way that gave him great dignity in the eyes of Lawrence's sepoys. He doffed his hat at the standard and walked up the steps as the line of native troops ported their arms. The jemadar's sword was smartly brought to the salute.

'A bit of theatre for the men?'

'Hurry up and wait! That's the motto of the Hon'ble Company's army.' Clive's insolent half-smile appeared again. 'What's the need to rush along?'

'What indeed? When you may use the time to make admirers.'

'Hah!'

'Look at you, puffed up and strutting like a pigeon. Hands thrust under your coat-tails, grinning and devil-may-care all in a damned show.'

'Thankee.'

'Next you'll tell me your excellent humour's real.'

'It puts heart in 'em. I say a smile forces good humour.' Clive shot him a steely glance, jabbing a thumb at his heart. 'Don't think our pledge has gone out of my mind. I carry the thought of freeing Arkali constantly.'

'I pray one day we might carry that forward.'

'Sooner than you think, once this day's business is over.'

Hayden Flint mentioned nothing of the hint he had taken from Mohan Das. That Arkali had been abducted by Muhammad Ali made sense. He would seek to use her, politically, and as an ornament to his repute, but most of all as a jagged edge with which to torment Yasmin. He would delight in keeping them penned together until they learned all.

Off came the cocked hat again as they passed by the red lines. Three huzzahs came back from the sepoys. Hayden Flint said wryly, '*Ave Caesar, morituri te salutant!*' Hail Caesar, those who are about to die salute you.

Clive sucked his tongue. 'Oh, I mean to lead these brave boys in this war. It's important they have some extra-ordinary impression of me, for without doubt I shall be demanding extraordinary things from them.'

'You're so sure of that?'

'Oh, yes, that's certain.'

The vanguard of Nasir Jang's army moved off pon-derously, raising a cloud of dust. Huge fringed parasols swayed, the gilded gear of the elephants catching the sun like brass mirrors. Clive extended his telescope and trained it on the distant lines where Chanda Sahib's and Muzaffar Jang's horse were drawn up in two distinct groupings. He knew they must clash soon, or sundown would end hostilities prematurely.

For an hour the prospect was filled with moving detail for as far as human eye could see. An ocean of coloured robes and turbans, the tan of horsehides, flashes of brightness from saddle blankets and spear-tips; colours made pastel by black-powder smoke, by dust and distance, and metal burnished to gold by the sun – lances, glinting shields, helmets and fish-scale armour, all shimmering like mercury in the haze of heat. And here and there in the sea of movement dark islands lumbering forward, bellowing as their mahouts goaded them to battle. There was a roar – screaming and yelping, shots fired, galloping hooves, the howdah creaking. Hayden Flint tasted burnt earth.

As the opposing armies approached one another on the plain the Maratha horsemen under Morari Rao shadowed the main army like a pack of jackals following a pride of hunting cats.

Clive gestured at them. 'The Hindu look a fierce mob, do they not? Good fighters these Confederacy people. A damned unlikely alliance between Raghoji Bhonsla and the Moghuls, eh?'

'Unlikely and unpredictable. I believe Nasir Jang has allowed the Peshwa's men to join us for wider political reasons. It was rumoured at Aurangabad that Asaf Jah did many deals with the Marathas, even that he invited them into the Carnatic in order to roast a wayward vassal for him a decade ago. That was when Dost Ali was nawab.'

'Chanda Sahib's father-in-law?'

'The same.'

Clive laughed abruptly. 'Who would have wagered on that?'

'As the Chinee curse says: May you live in interesting times.'

'Hah! I trust we do!'

'No, these are lost times. Who can look out there and not see Armageddon? What are we about but the slaying of one another?'

'I see a strong alliance, aye and glory! If glory should desert war it would become dirty butchery. But look at this: can't you see each man down there from the lowest to the most high charged with feeling? It's that flush a man gets when he gambles all against eternity.'

'It's madness and the frittering of lives.'

'Ah, but the purest essence of life is to be had just a blade-width from death.'

He wondered at that. Few could know the border between life and death and the risking of it more clearly than Robert Clive. He pushed the whole issue away from him. 'Well, these alliances can but make the fight more involved. Any alliance is difficult enough, but one that includes the Marathas is almost certainly doomed to fall apart.'

Clive watched them for a moment then shook his head. 'They're born freebooters, but magnificent for all that. They will not bow the knee to Moghul rule again. By God, look how they ride! Having smelt blood they're moving up for their share of the kill.'

'Until they meet with the French infantry.'

'That's unlikely. They're hidden from us. But they must be somewhere close. It's elementary that they move up soon in defence of the guns.'

'I can't see those, either.' Hayden Flint studied the main parties of the enemy alliance. Generals' messengers and runners of mercenary units were constantly galloping on fast horses to and from the two commanders' elephants. Camp informers and eavesdroppers ran to meet them, then they wheeled round Muzaffar Jang or Chanda Sahib, bargaining, haggling, upping the price of their continued suport before they carried away orders and ultimatums to their masters. Some divisions would stand idly when the call to engage came, others would desert or break away, or change sides. Before battle closed, many would join the enemy; with luck, more would leave.

Suddenly the waning afternoon came intensely alive. War trumpets brayed; the great kettledrums of the Moghuls beat out their orders to the squadrons of horse. The mahouts kicked their toes behind their huge beasts' ears as the line moved forward. Hayden Flint was astonished at his own feelings. Exhilaration at the prospect of battle consumed him, drowning his fear, but his rational mind knew the opponents were well balanced in strength: half a million of the Nizam's troops versus perhaps a fifth that number under the pretenders, but set against that were 2,000 French versus just 600 British. It had to be a bloody confrontation. Hundreds of thousands would die today.

His foreboding intensified as their pace quickened. It's a sense, he thought, feeling its compulsive magnetism, and absolutely sure of it now. It's the inner eye Yasmin believes we all possess. It says: 'You have nothing to fear. Nothing can harm you this day.' But there's no prescience of triumph with it. So what can that mean? That the French are to win?

He thought back to the Council of War, damning himself

for not somehow engineering a compromise. If he could have muzzled Lawrence he might have seen the Major's correct plan adopted. As it was, pride and protocol had locked them into this shapeless assault.

What was it Muhammad Ali said on the eve of battle a lifetime ago? 'In this world there are no would-have-beens or could-have-dones. There is only what is, and what is written. And that is the will of Allah.'

And now Clive was saying that everything was in the moment, that plans could never be adhered to, that a leader was a man who had learned to mould events in the present.

What Nasir Jang had started to say about honour and prosperity and disgrace was also true. If the ensign had not arrived at the tent the Nizam might have finished the quote: 'God the Almighty watches over the succession of day and night; out of life He makes death; and out of death, life; He bestows power without reckoning.'

Clive was scanning the enemy. Suddenly he turned, gripped by a new enthusiasm. 'Look! The French guns are moving!'

'That's impossible!'

'It's happening! They must be trying to make a flanking move!'

He took the telescope, saw the crews dragging their pieces out of the line, beginning to take them away eastward.

'No, by God, they're pulling back!'

It made no sense. The guns were able to sponge out and reload in fewer seconds than it took for a galloping horse to cover their range. While they stood, no frontal assault could succeed. Their grape would tear to pieces anything that ran inside three hundred yards of them.

'Without artillery they're at our mercy. What are they thinking about?'

'It must be a trade-off.'

'The French? No! They know war well enough. They don't trade and bicker like the Moghuls. Are you forgetting they're the deuced principals in this?'

424

'What then? A trap?'

'By God, no! Idiocy – or a mutiny! Where are their damned infantry?'

'Sweet Jesus, they're breaking!'

As they watched, almost half the opposing army began to follow their standards towards Pondicherry. A mass of horse started streaming away into their long shadows.

'See! They're Chanda Sahib's men! Running for the safety of the French lease!'

Clive took the telescope back and braced himself against the side of the rolling howdah, watching for long minutes as the opposing army dwindled. 'They're all retreating. Making for Pondicherry. And Muzaffar's following! No, he's standing. Surely he doesn't mean to fight now?'

As they advanced, there was a brief and bloody set-to. It was all Nasir Jang's commanders could do to restrain their men and prevent a massacre. It took almost an hour before Muzaffar Jang's colour party dared come forward to parley.

'Damn me! Robbed of action.' Clive's disappointment ran deep.

'You should thank God for it.'

'Last time I ride an elephant into battle.' Clive began to laugh.

'May I know the joke?'

'Look at them coming up to set terms, and not a hundred men killed.'

'Yes.'

'Come along, Mr Flint, we've done it! This is the pivotal event. It means the French are finished in Hindostan!'

Hayden Flint tried to smile back, but he knew it was a poor response to such a great moment. What Clive said made sense, but still the powerful feeling remained inside him that events had taken a terrible turn, and he could not make himself believe otherwise.

Chanda Sahib's white horse reared as he pulled back on the reins and jumped down. The grand streets of Pondicherry were packed with people. A thousand eyes were on them as

425

they dashed across the square to the gates of the Governor's residence.

His son, Raza, and his close bodyguard forced a way through. The atmosphere inside Fort Louis was tense and fearful, in contrast to the joyous excitement that had greeted them on their first arrival, or the confident expectation they had felt yesterday.

Chanda bore down on the gatehouse, his anger tremendous. Forty-eight hours ago, he had been facing the enemy's battle lines, praying to Almighty God for the victory that would restore him to his rightful place – astride the masnad of the Carnatic. Forty-eight hours ago it had seemed possible, even likely. Now, everything was in shreds.

European merchants and soldiers and servants of the French Company thronged the square, waiting for some reliable word of the disaster. Chanda heard his name shouted. Then ill-tempered jeering came at him from the crowd. It was almost as if they believed the débâcle was his fault.

News that Morari Rao had joined Nasir Jang's vast army had come as a crushing blow. After so long at Satara as a 'guest' of the Peshwa it would have been ironic but understandable if the Hindu horse-soldiers had sealed his final defeat. A revolt among his allies – that he could have borne; even a rift with Muzaffar's greedy generals. But never in his worst imaginings had he thought it would be the feringhees who would run.

Their infantry had mutinied, marching back to their fort like spoilt children. And over pay! Pay! After Dupleix's lecture on that subject! Then the precious guns had followed, after being stripped bare of the protection they relied on.

Now sentries challenged Chanda Sahib and his party at bayonet-point. They would have shed blood had it not been for the Marquis de Bussy who emerged, immaculate in blue coat and knee boots, and swept the muskets up to admit them.

'Where is Dupleix?' Chanda demanded.

'At his papers.' De Bussy's manner was suave.

'I will see him! Now!'

'Of course.' The Marquis snapped his fingers and a Tamil page in white gloves and wig bounded up the flight of stairs towards the Governor's apartments. 'I have informed His Excellency. Now – '

They tried as one to push past the urbane figure, their eyes following the pageboy along the upper gallery, but de Bussy danced nimbly ahead to bar them.

' – perhaps you would care to wait here, sirs.'

'Get out of my way!'

Chanda was shaking with anger. His son was at his side, his sword drawn now, alarming de Bussy. They got halfway up the stair before de Bussy was joined by d'Auteuil, Law and a number of other Council members.

Then Dupleix himself appeared on the gallery above them all, immaculate in white waistcoat and white silk breeches. He stared down, one hand pressed behind his back, the other holding a swan quill.

Chanda Sahib's party halted, all except Raza, who lifted his swordpoint to within an inch of the Frenchman's heart.

For a count of three Dupleix stared down at the Moghul, then he slowly brought the quill into contact with the heavy blade and pushed it irresistibly aside. He inclined his head a little, and a smile played at one corner of his mouth before he said to Chanda Sahib, 'Why do you let your son draw his sword in my house?' Then he turned and led them to the Council chamber.

When they were seated Chanda Sahib made his accusation. 'Your infantry ran!'

'*Si!*' Surely!

'And the guns followed them,' Raza said.

'*Si!* I admit it all.'

'Your mutinous forces have destroyed our last chance of victory!'

'Perhaps. But perhaps not.'

'Muzaffar has surrendered! His army has disbanded. We have barely twenty thousand men under our command, sheltering under the walls of your fort, hiding under the muzzles of your cannon, like . . . like dogs!'

'There is much that can still be done with twenty thousand men.'

'Against Nasir Jang? He outnumbers us twenty to one!'

'For the moment.'

'They will move against us!'

'I don't think so.' Dupleix's face shone, pale and luminous as the moon. He appeared completely unperturbed by the defeat as with the white quill he pointed out their errors. 'Nasir Jang has won a battle, no? He also has his heart's desire: the person of his nephew, no? He will fall back on Arcot to indulge in a junket, believing that the victory was won by the awe his name inspires. I have it that he is vain, and much given to his pleasures. He is not a pawn of the English. He will not attack Pondichery and the English cannot, since our countries are not at war.'

'But he cannot return to Aurangabad while I am here. He has declared Muhammad Ali Khan – '

'I said, he will go to Arcot. And once there, my letters will make explanation of the situation!' He indicated his inkwell and the scattered papers. 'You see. I have been hard at work, drafting letters. The Nizam will read them. I have declared an embassy to him. The Marquis de Bussy is an able negotiator. He will present the matter favourably.'

'How can you negotiate with the Nizam when you are protecting me?'

'What is the purpose of diplomacy other than to delay and to deflect?'

'You will do neither!'

'*Au contraire*. I will do both. The purpose of my letters is to propose gifts, to make flattery, and explain away the "misunderstandings" of late. After all, he saw Muzaffar Jang's army ranged against him. It seemed to you that my forces withdrew deliberately, leaving his nephew exposed, and with no alternative but to surrender. If it seemed that way to you, it will seem that way to him also.' He shrugged. 'I shall prevent him from moving.'

'How can you make him believe you?'

'I do not wish to make him believe me. It is enough that he retires to Hyderabad, or stays in Arcot. The bigger the army the more it costs to keep in the field. Every day we paralyse him is a day in which his army bleeds away.'

'I cannot share your optimism. They will fall on us and we shall be crushed.'

'No, it is quite simple.' Dupleix sighed, as if addressing a tiresomely obtuse schoolboy. 'If you were Nasir Jang, you would not wish to attack – you would not dare to attack – Fort Louis. This is because you would have to stoop to imploring the English to use their cannon to reduce our walls. You would perceive that the walls of Fort Louis are strong, and kept so by constant repair work. Therefore not only would the siege shame you, it would continuously shame you. For many months. Of course, your sense of grandeur would not permit that and you would, in preference, retire to Arcot.'

De Bussy watched the interview with admiration. It took almost a full hour for Monsieur le Gouverneur to placate Chanda Sahib, but his performance was magnificent. When Chanda Sahib's party had been led to their horses and sent back to their camp, the ignorant heathens had swallowed it all.

If only they had been able to hear his true thoughts, reflected de Bussy. If only I could hear them. But I suspect that would shatter everything. The mutiny of d'Auteuil's infantry was despicable, without parallel in the annals of French arms. Shameful the way Dupleix was obliged to cave in to them. And he redressed their grievances instead of hanging their most vociferous rogues! That shows how dangerous our true position is now.

The moment Chanda Sahib had vanished from sight, he turned to Dupleix. 'What are we really going to do?'

Dupleix cast him a nonplussed glance. 'As I told them, negotiate with whomsoever we can. Secretly. You will convey my respects to Nasir Jang's least partisan commanders – the Pathans and the Afghans. You will begin by wooing the Nawab of Kurnool.'

Dupleix must have had communication with some of Nasir Jang's people already, thought de Bussy, perhaps through his wife's intelligence network. 'You really think it can work?' he asked.

Dupleix shrugged. 'Of course. For the moment Lawrence will try to persuade Nasir Jang to blockade Pondicherry, but I believe the Nizam will retire to Arcot to enjoy his hunting and his women.'

'I am not convinced of that.'

'No?' Dupleix laid down his quill and laced his fingers behind his head. Leaning back in his chair he lifted one heel on to the edge of the table. 'Let me illuminate matters. There is one most important factor you are ignoring in this mathematical equation.'

'And that is?'

'The superstitions of the Moghul mind.'

'Sir, surely . . .'

'No, no, Charles. You forget we are dealing with a medieval people. They still believe that the stars and planets rule their fortunes. They have the most primitive comprehension of cause and effect.'

'It is simple. Nasir Jang has Muzaffar. He will stop at nothing to wring from him the location of the Eye and because Muzaffar is a coward, he will already have bargained it for his life, and certain assurances.'

'How can you be sure that – '

Dupleix brought his hands down across his lap and steepled his fingers. 'Charles, you may treat this supposition with confidence.'

'Perhaps that is so.' De Bussy could not keep silent any longer. 'I can imagine it was the substance of the parley between uncle and nephew. Your wife's sources must have been swift in their work.'

Dupleix ignored the remark. 'The only reason Nasir Jang came here was to obtain the Eye of Naga. Now he has it. Now he will relax. He will grow comfortable in his power, and therefore complaisant. He will return to his old beliefs, that we Europeans are merely irritating insects who infest his coast. He will tarry a while, then he will grow bored. And then he will go home – '

'Sir, I – '

'Leaving us, Charles, to destroy Muhammad Ali, for whom Nasir Jang has no particular love. And to take the fortress of Gingee.'

De Bussy baulked at Dupleix's seductive certainties. It was a trick of his rhetoric that he made 'predictions' about things he already knew to be facts. It was a trick that had worked on many of his more credulous subordinates. Already half the Council believed in Dupleix's genius, and the other half would not dare say they did not. Against this, de Bussy thought, there is only the stiletto question. So, I will ask it.

'You told Chanda Sahib I am to mount an embassy to Nasir Jang. Who is to be my prime objective?'

'You will open a dialogue with Shah Nawaz Khan, Nasir Jang's wazir.'

The Marquis caught his breath. He felt an unmistakable twinge of anger, but with it there was astonishment and disbelief and – yes – even grudging admiration, too.

It was still dark when the French sallied from the fortress of Gingee. They had captured it without loss several days ago. Dawn was breaking when they made their attack on the Moghul camp; they would do their work in the coolest part of the day.

The news came to the Nizam, rousing him. Immediately he had Muzaffar brought, then he called his nobles and generals to attend him in the open air amidst a great crowd.

Jeering broke out, as the pitiful prisoner was brought before Nasir Jang. The wayward nephew was manacled and fettered, and pleading like an Untouchable beggar. His rich robes had been torn from him by his guards, and the iron chain with links as thick as his fingers looped from ankle to wrist to collar and back, burdening him. Hayden Flint saw with disgust the scorch marks on his flesh, the weals where he had been flogged.

Since the battle at Villanour the Nizam, too, had changed greatly. His fear of the Koh-i-Noor had gone. He wore the Eye in his turban, just as his nephew had once done, proudly, in plain view, and over the seat of his mind. Yet it seemed that the Nizam's new confidence was an unhealthy thing.

The transformation became apparent in small ways. His manner became arrogant. He would not permit discussion within earshot. He had ordered his executioner to stand within a swordswing of Muzaffar at all times, to strike off his head in the event of any attempt to free him. Lately, the guard had been doubled. His three young half-brothers, the eldest of them a gawky youth called Salabat Jang, had been put in custody.

Later, there were stories of cruelties: to animals, and then, it was said, to his women. And when an aged and trusted servant had spoken to him kindly to ask why the Lord was behaving so badly, he had flown into a rage and had the retainer killed, though the man had served him, or Asaf Jah before him, all the years of his life.

Nor was his caprice confined to those close to him. Within a month he had welched on the promises he had made to Foss Westcott and the Madras Council. The army of the Nizamat had become bored with Arcot, and Arcot exhausted by the army. In the latter months, desertions had shrunk it to 60,000 men and a mere 700 elephants.

Muzaffar sprawled now before Nasir Jang's government, babbling in terror of his uncle's wrath, of the terrible vengeance he could no longer escape.

'Look at the dog!'

'See how he breakfasts on dirt at the foot of our rightful lord!'

'We see now why his own men deserted him! He is nothing.'

Another cry went up as a grey juggernaut climbed the low hill and pushed its towering bulk through the crowd. It was the Nizam's own beast, tusks gilded and jewelled, brought up for God only knew what purpose.

432

The ritual humiliation continued, forcing Hayden Flint to bury his gaze. It was a sport the Nizam had chosen to allow his nobles, but he, Hayden Flint, would have no part of it. To see an adversary broken and insulted, to have all his prestige and possessions stripped away, to have his cause ridiculed by the common soldiery: this was expected here. It was the reward of losers.

'Why do you not revile him, feringhee?' a lesser noble called out.

'He was promised safe passage.'

'He is no longer a man! Look at him!'

'By God, you know not right from wrong!'

He pushed his way out through the crowd, seeing the reproach in their eyes, suspicion that without the strength of Allah the Englishman did not have the moral courage to condemn a fallen traitor. He had held his peace too long. It was not enough to tell himself that the same fate would have befallen the tormentors had they lost and Muzaffar Jang triumphed.

He turned, and in so doing shouldered aside the man behind him. Osman, his attendant, called plaintively to him, worried the Nizam would take note and be angered by his show of weakness. If Nasir Jang did not see him now, there were many who would tell him later.

'Please, sahib! Stay and witness!'

'The beating of a tethered dog is no sport for gentlemen,' he stormed, angrier than he had supposed. 'It is the indulgence of uncivilized brutes.'

'But you must not leave! The insult!'

'And I cannot – I will not – stay to see some wretch trampled to death!'

'He is not a wretch, sahib. He is Muzaffar Jang.'

After a moment he saw that Osman had spoken expediently. This was no time to make moral demonstrations. Nasir Jang was becoming increasingly irritated by the presence of a lone Englishman in his camp.

For the greater good he allowed himself to be swayed, turning to walk back towards the hubbub. But Osman's delight at his apparent change of heart sickened him and he tore his arm from the man's grip.

Suddenly the noise abated. Nasir Jang mounted the howdah of his elephant and raised his arms. 'Muzaffar Jang,' he said portentously, 'you have opposed me and lost. The hour of judgment is come upon you. You must pay for the sins of the feringhee.'

Hayden Flint watched the cheering with disgust. The lesser generals were the most vicious in their insults – servile toad-eaters attempting to further their careers, demonstrating their love for Nasir Jang by expressing their hatred for his broken enemy. But he saw that the Nizam's major allies were unexpectedly reserved, and that Nasir Jang's wazir, Shah Nawaz Khan, was the quietest of them all.

Nasir Jang's rhetoric continued from the back of the elephant, aweing his poeple. He had seen no petitioners, had admitted to his presence only astrologers and food-tasters in his last thirty days at Arcot. He had been to great lengths to preserve himself against treachery, and since the battle he had appeared just this once before his people, impatient and full of fire to avenge the insults imagined against him.

He carried the Talwar unsheathed in his right hand at all times now. The gossipers said it was partly due to his jealous regard for it, partly because it was a killing weapon. And it was true, that the carrying of a naked blade in his hand suited his new mien. He had become completely unpredictable.

Hayden Flint watched Nasir Jang, and tried again to gauge him. How long will it be, he wondered, before he provokes a revolt?

Nasir Jang regarded his nephew with a piercing hatred. The cruel pantomime continued, but with a subtle shift: something unspecific, a gesture here, a smile there. What was it?

Hayden Flint's heart beat faster. A surge of panic rose in him as he heard the keen cracks of distant musketry. The piquant sound seemed to stir up Nasir Jang's wrath. He had issued an order to give no quarter to any who approached the camp, following it up with a threat to do as Nadir Shah, the Persian butcher, had done, and count heads.

They would take Gingee and smash the French, exterminating them to the last man. That was why he had ordered the Nawab of Cuddapah to lead a crushing advance on them.

'Spare no effort,' he had told the Pathan. 'I will have the liar's tongue cut out of his head by noon! The Marquis de Bussy has crossed me for the last time.'

Nasir Jang's face twisted as a messenger approached up the rise. Hayden Flint struggled to get through the mob of excited soldiers, too far away to hear the mahout's word of command but seeing the goad lifted to the Nizam's elephant. He felt the spirit within him gutter like a candle. It was impossible to ignore the sense of foreboding. He took hold of himself. In a matter of weeks, he thought, all our work has become foul – just as I always knew it would. By God, I know what it is . . . They've all been suborned: Shah Nawaz Khan and the generals have made a deal with Dupleix!

Damn them to hell! And Nasir Jang has no knowledge of it. He's in tremendous danger, and he hasn't the least idea! I must stop him!

But the bearer of the Talwar was already riding out at an elephant trot to see for himself why the French were not being destroyed as he had ordered.

Hayden Flint watched him go, telling Osman to find him a horse. Breathless, he followed on foot, shouting without effect. 'Nasir Jang! Highness! Listen to me!'

A dozen horsemen swirled across his path, cutting him off. He ran down the slope until his sides ached and his eyes watered, then halted, gasping for breath. Two hundred yards away the Nawab of Cuddapah's own elephant came to a halt in front of his immobile forces.

Why was Abdul Nabi Khan not engaging the French as the Nizam had ordered? There could be only one reason.

Nasir Jang approached the nawab in fury. A soldier in the howdah raised his jezail and took aim at him.

The soldier fired.

Nasir Jang was incredulous. He ignored the danger, unable to believe in it. His elephant continued its rush. The Nizam's shouts were full of rage now. He wielded the priceless sword in white-hot anger. How dare a soldier fire at him? How could any shot pierce him? He wore no plastron against death like lesser princes must. Was he not the Nizam, Subahdar of the South? The bearer of the Talwar? Charmed therefore? Twice charmed! By diamond and by ruby!

The next stab of fire was from the Pathan's own carbine. It blew Nasir Jang's heart out of his chest.

The Talwar spun from his hand. He pitched out of the howdah seat and fell heavily down on to the hard earth. The last breath groaned from him.

A sudden silence fell over the scene like a heavy blanket. The first rays of the rising sun, blazing like a red eye, shone over the land.

No one dared come forward. Then the Nawab of Cuddapah dismounted. He picked up the Talwar, and with it hacked off Nasir Jang's head. He grinned as he jammed it on to a lance-tip.

Hayden Flint found himself drawn along by the press of men who followed the nawab's grisly trophy back up the hill. He felt dazed and empty, bedazzled by the horror of the diamond's malign light. When they reached the cowering prisoner he cried out and flinched from the bloodied weapon, reciting, filling his last seconds on God's earth with the Fortieth Sura of the Koran: The Believer.

But to the astonishment of Muzaffar Jang his chains were stripped from him. He gaped as they threw a mantle about his shoulders, and the Pathan closed his nerveless hands around the hilt of the Talwar-i-Jang. Nasir's own turban was placed on his head, secured by the Eye which had lately been taken from him.

Those who had taunted him now fell down before him, while those who had designed his triumph rejoiced.

BOOK FOUR

SEVENTEEN

Arkali waited amid the carpets and cushions and allowed her gaze to escape through the stone lattice to where clouds gathered in the hazy sky to the west.

From the casement she looked out over an ancient and unchanging prospect. A heavily fortified town had been built from the living rock which rose up to a pinnacle hundreds of feet above the surrounding land. Steps wound upwards from the sacred tanks of the west side, up to choultries and colonnaded pavilions that were used for the comfort of Hindu pilgrims. At the summit was a pagoda, housing, so it was said, hundreds of pagan idols in their different denominations. Over it the nawab's huge green flag blazed, but still the Hindu made their ritual ascents. How many hours had she spent watching the devotees purify themselves in the tank and afterwards climb steadily up to do obeisance before their gods? Too many hours, while she herself salved the impotent rage that she could not express.

Soon. Today. It will have to be today. One brave act and the waiting will be over. But we all put away from us the things our minds dare not encompass, she thought. It took me weeks to realize what had happened to me. How foolish. I'd heard enough tales of European women being taken into the zenana of native princes. How was it I could not believe that had been my own fate? I have been taken not by slavers, nor as a hostage to bargain over, I have been collected – like a butterfly.

She sighed, heartsick. The thought that few such abducted women were ever seen again filled her with anger and then despair. What right had they to keep her here? What right?

But then what right did murderers need? They had murdered her father; they could just as soon murder her.

In her long captivity she had thought often about the blood that had streamed from the sword slash that cut her father down. She knew with a powerful certainty that the stroke had killed him.

When Arkali had first arrived at Trichinopoly she was terrified. Her clothes were filthy and torn; she was hurt and physically exhausted from the hard ride. They made her wear long black robes over her dress and Zahir tied and gagged her, and put into a palanquin to be carried up what seemed to be a mountain. But when the palanquin was opened and she was brought out she saw that the place was no horrid dungeon, rather a sort of palace peopled entirely by women.

Shocked and hardly able to stand, her perceptions were mingled with dreams and fancies. She was bathed and washed and her aches oiled away by naked attendants she thought must be dark angels. She did not know enough of their language to be able to make herself understood, and she slept long and deeply for what must have been the rest of the day and the night following. She awoke in the morning, in time to see the sun rising over misty hills many miles to the east, and to hear the moaning of Mussulman prayers giving thanks for a day that was already written but yet to be read.

It was a strange awakening, alone, in a palace that might have been Paradise, or a heathen's idea of Paradise. It's a mistake, she thought, awed, or else these Moors are right about God after all. But then again, what sort of Paradise would permit entry to a body that ached and was wounded? And what sort of Heaven was it that could not be freely renounced?

Now she shifted her weight uncomfortably. The native clothes in which they had dressed her since her arrival were unspeakable. The muslin material was so thin as to be near transparent. Each day girls had oiled and braided her hair, painted her eyes and lips and festooned her with golden jewellery, but the clothes hardly covered her, leaving her feet and arms bare and nothing to cover her midriff. She hardly dared move.

She sighed, her eyes dull. In the weeks and months since the kidnap it seemed that she had cried herself dry. She had tried everything, from attempting the walls to refusing food, all to no avail. Now the last thoughts of escape had left her.

Her captors' ways were beyond belief. Their shameless nakedness astonished her. They bathed incessantly, five times a day it seemed, which, she knew, must eventually affect the good health and sanity of any civilized person. It was horrifying that they expected her to do the same. The only thing that made such repeated dunkings tolerable was that the baths removed at least some of the pungent oils and overpowering perfumes which they rubbed into one another.

If her own education had been sudden and frightening, theirs had been equally so. They were fascinated by her, and dozens of them had surrounded her, gawping like children. She screamed and fought, but nothing she did had been the least use. She realized now that it was her colouring that made them stare. No one here had coppery hair, or skin so white, which seemed to be among them a sign of noble birth and therefore highly prized. They touched her, stared at her, and even scratched at the freckles on her arms as if they might be dislodged or washed away.

At first she had resisted at every turn, but it was not possible to fight like a cat for ever. After a while she had settled into stiff and obstinate sulking whenever her immersion was ordered. Now she merely accepted it.

There existed a strict social order. Servants performed all duties: there were sweepers and dressers, those who looked after the preparation of food and those whose sole task it was to pummel and knead the bodies of the others, and to decorate them after the country mode. There were young brasses who looked and acted like whores, others who took

441

comfort in solitude and yet others who spent their time in prayer or in pursuit of the constructive arts. Some senior matrons were deferred to as they marched their rounds, deciding this and that, accompanied by men the like of whom she had never seen before.

She had imagined eunuchs to be strapping soldiers set over the women to keep order, but these were not like true men, yet neither were they like the sort of men given over to effeminacy. They were quite different. When one was brought to restrain her after a particularly violent protest, and helped to forcibly strip her for the bath, she did not feel as violated as she had the terrible night of the bombardment at Fort St George.

It's hard to explain, she thought. But now the attention of eunuchs seems no greater indignity than to be searched over by the eyes of other women. These creatures are somehow like boys grown to full size, without a man's capacity, and without a man's sexual thoughts. Still, it's true they have natures as scheming as the powerful queen bee they serve, as if the loss of their sexual lusts is compensated by a delight in intricate politics.

Despite her attempt to blot it all out of her mind, there were discoveries to be made. She had learned that the prince of the country called himself 'Nabab', that the queen was his mother, and that in the Hindu tongue this place was named 'Tiruchirupalli'. She had searched for ways to escape, had explored the enclosed world carefully, and in so doing had found out its secrets. Some places were communal, others private. There were private baths and apartments; it was not permitted to visit certain areas of the garden. All life here was governed by a web of strict rules, rules that had the sanction of religion and long acceptance. They set out time and place and manner so precisely that, if she wished, a woman could surrender herself completely to them and never be without a duty. At every moment there was that insistent invitation to abandon her own will for the routine of the zenana.

There were less formal conventions too. She learned

442

there was a place under the gular tree where a woman could go if she wanted to be alone with her thoughts and remain undisturbed.

As she sat in the garden Arkali had begun to see how the women related to one another, often in subtle ways. There were cliques and power struggles, victims and victors; competition for royal favour drove the society as the will of a shepherd drives sheep. In private she used what few words she knew to learn gossip from the servants who had been assigned to her. She found out astonishing things: a curve of a servant's hand informed her that the woman who rocked in silent misery under the gular tree at each setting of the sun had lost her baby. The next day, Arkali discovered that the infant had been the child of the nawab's brother. And later, the same servant had tugged at her elbow, making fearful eyes at the queen bee, whose name, she learned, was Nadira. In her entourage was a striking creature they called Khair-un-Nissa, and the servant made it very clear what she was.

Arkali had put her hand to her mouth in revulsion: Khair-un-Nissa was an abortionist. There were preparations, her maid informed her, that could be drunk; powerful drugs that could end a pregnancy.

But if it had been a deliberate miscarriage, why did the girl remain inconsolable?

To find the answer she put everything she knew together. One of the young whores got with child by the prince . . . A struggle to gain favour . . . The skills of the creature who seemed to live as the queen bee's instrument . . . It made a horrible picture.

There would be great status to be gained as a royal favourite. To share the prince's brother's bed would surely raise a woman up, and to be delivered of a royal bastard would, in this society, doubtless consolidate that good fortune. Someone ruthless and jealous of their own power would not hesitate to use any weapon at their disposal to maintain their pre-eminence if it came under threat. Slipping drugs into the girl's food would not have been difficult . . .

With Arkali's realization had come the first stirrings of understanding of her own status within the hierarchy. She had, after all, been kidnapped: a deliberate abduction, certainly sanctioned by the prince himself. And now this nonsensical, interminable, will-destroying waiting. She must have been brought here and held in this limbo for a reason. What if that reason also made her a threat to someone important? It was clear by the way Nadira behaved that she found Arkali's presence unsatisfactory. The rest of the zenana viewed her with suspicion, or transmitted the fear they felt at Nadira's disapproval. Only one of the principal women had shown her any particular kindness, giving her the book whose margins had become her sanity. She scribbled a form of journal in it, using kohl and a fine nib cut from straw.

She remembered the first time she had felt her heart contract at a revolting thought: surely, sooner or later, the owner of this seraglio must intend to put her to the use for which he had obtained her.

It was then that she had formed the idea of her one deadly consolation: a secret steel pin. It was four inches long and bright as tin, with a little silver butterfly to ornament the end. Her mother had given it to her, and of all her former possessions it was the sole survivor. As she turned it over in her hand it sparkled, reminding her of the day she had hidden the pin in a hem against the moment of bitter last resort.

Until then she had been powerless in this timeless prison. The pin that had once secured her bonnet might, if thrust deep into her own heart, stop it beating. And that grim knowledge was a comfort, albeit a distant one.

Nevertheless, the idea of the pin haunted her in her blackest moments. Did she possess the strength of mind to use it? She suspected not. She felt that no terror imaginable would give her the will to drive it in deep enough to kill.

In the worst days she had thought about the butterfly pin time and again. But when nothing more painful than indignity had befallen her, her terrors began to recede. Yet for how much longer would the warfare continue? And how long before Nabab returned?

Then, the day before yesterday, she had heard the commotion. There were shouts and the women had flown to their high windows. Hoofbeats sounded below, and a warbling went up from the women, an eerie and unearthly sound, like nothing she had ever heard before. She realized that Nabab had arrived. Pale and shaking, she understood that it might only be a matter of hours before his eunuchs came for her . . .

She was mocked by the only reminder left to her of England. That despairing diary, written in a volume of Theobald's *Shakespeare* that now lay discarded on the table, the only book here, looted no doubt from a Company baggage train in some despicable ambush. It had been given to her out of kindness perhaps, but there was little comfort to be had in her own writings, or in the story of the Moor of Venice, and the open book lay face down on a low table beside a glass of coffee dregs.

Thoughts of the butterfly pin flitted through her mind again. Perhaps there was still some way to use it. But now a more certain means had come to her. She had spoken to her maid and the maid had spoken to the maid of the queen bee, and the word had come back that the queen bee had agreed . . .

Waiting. Waiting. Why did no one keep their word here? How cruelly they use time to taunt a body. They said tomorrow and they meant a week from now. They said certainly and they meant perhaps . . .

Then, as if summoned by her thoughts, there was a sound in the passageway, bare feet on the tiled floor, the tinkle of bells. Not daring to hope, Arkali slipped the pin back into the sleeve of her choli bodice.

The painted woman appeared, the one they called Khair-un-Nissa dressed in a gold and sky-blue sari. She was graceful, beautiful even, but there was a whiff of evil about her. Her perfume recalled orchids; she moved like a flame. As she approached, her haughty face remained fixed,

445

without any change of expression except the furtive glances she flashed at the screen and the recesses of the room.

'Do you have it?' Arkali asked. Knowing the woman spoke no English, she gestured as if to drink. 'Do you? Do you?'

Khair-un-Nissa made no reply. She knelt beside Arkali and reached slender fingers between her breasts to produce a paper doubled into a small envelope. Then she unfolded the paper.

Trapped in the crease was a white powder, crystalline, gritty, like powdered diamond. It smelt bitter.

Khair-un-Nissa met Arkali's eye. Her hand made a stirring motion.

'In water?' Arkali asked anxiously. 'Do you mean mix it with water? Oh, what's your word for it – *pahnee*?'

The woman cocked her head in that maddening, ambiguous way, then rocked back and stood up. A quick glance round and she was gone.

Yasmin had taken pity on the Angrezi woman, but had not spoken to her for fear their conversations would be reported by Nadira's spies. Any suspicion of a plot would bring down Nadira's wrath upon the unfortunate one and herself alike. And the Angrezi woman was unfortunate. It was distressing to see how confinement had sent her into decline, her spirit drawn off little by little, and the light of madness growing in her eyes. An English book of printed words was all Yasmin could offer by way of comfort and so she had made a present of it.

After their escape from Ambur, Muhammad had showed his gratitude to her, publicly cancelling the charges he had heaped upon her two days before. A wicked plot, he had called it. Lies put out by the serpent tongues of Chanda Sahib's *gup*-mongers – Chanda Sahib who was the mother of all crocodiles, the Shatan from whom flowed all injustice and godlessness.

When Muhammad granted her her life she had promised to obey him henceforth in all things and live peaceably

446

within the zenana at Trichinopoly. Now Yasmin laid down her needlework and felt the crushing weight of that promise. She was lonely, Gilahri, her little squirrel, had not escaped from Ambur, and she had given up her love, pinched out the flame of its memory. She had agreed at last to be the wife Muhammad had always wanted her to be.

But he had not changed. Before the bandages were lifted from his eyes he had twisted their bargain by taking an Angrezi woman into the zenana. It was a skilfully cruel ploy, ensuring that a white woman would be a constant reminder to her of Hayden . . .

'Why do you not take this woman to you?' Muhammad had asked her. 'I am told that you shun her. Remember your promise to uphold the peace of my zenana.'

'I have not harmed her, lord.'

'Neither have you helped her.'

'Why should I?'

'You are the one who speaks her language. Why do you resist me, when you have promised to obey?'

'I have not resisted you.'

'Then take this woman to you, introduce her to our ways and prepare her for my pleasure. So that one day, when this war permits, I may enjoy her as a civilized human being.'

She heard the unspoken words 'as I have never enjoyed you' hanging in the air.

'Lord, who is she? Why did you bring an Angrezi among us?'

'Go now. And if you have questions, ask them of her. I do not want to hear that she is refusing her food.'

She lowered her eyes and acquiesced to that command. And so the first approach was made.

'Are not these roses wonderful in the cool of the evening?'

'You speak English?'

'After my poor fashion.'

'Oh, thank God! Thank God!'

And the Englishwoman sank to her knees and cried out, but later they spoke again and the woman was bitterly hostile, as if it was Yasmin's fault she had been brought here.

447

'I can bring you food. Name whatever it is that pleases you.'

'I will not eat it, whatever it is.'

'What is your name?'

'That is none of your business!'

'I understand your anger, but anger will not help you in the Walled World.'

'I must get out of this cathouse. I must. Or I shall go mad!'

'It is not a cathouse. We call this our zenana. It means "protected". In it we are protected. It is our home.'

'But you are all prisoners!'

'We are . . . sheltered. How do you say it – sanctuaried?'

'Oh, yes, from all but the one who rules your lives!'

Yasmin asked quietly, wanting to know, 'What is your Christian marriage if not surrender to one man?'

'I will not debate that with you. Except to say your foul way makes animals of women. You are taken for cattle, yet you do not protest.'

'How can we protest God's laws?'

'How can you say they are His laws? If they were His we would follow them in England.'

Ah, England, she thought. How Hayden wanted to go there. His words had made an image of it for her: an England of the mind.

'I know England is a land of green and plenty where pomegranates fall from the bough and the sheep fatten upon asking.'

'You plainly don't know anything of it!'

'I know that God's true laws were revealed elsewhere. In a hard, dry land, in a warlike time, long ago.'

'Is that how you excuse your barbarism?'

She pursed her lips and held back her temper, remembering that this woman had suffered. 'In the days of the Prophet Muhammad, Peace Be Upon Him, many men were killed on the field of battle. Therefore was it not right that a man should take more than one wife? So that no woman be denied motherhood and the fulfilment of her life? This is why we delight in the boy child, for a boy grows to be a soldier and in warlike times, such as we have again, soldiers are needed. This is why God's law is wise.'

'You talk of wives when you mean whores. Nabab keeps his whores here. It would be an affront to any wife to be made to live with her husband's whores.'

Yasmin smothered her own fury at that, and forced herself to reply calmly. 'I think you mean courtesans.'

'I mean whores. Like yourself!'

'I beg your pardon, but I am the wife of whom you speak. You were brought as the whore!'

They faced each other then, rage meeting rage, and Arkali slapped her face, so Yasmin slapped her back and left her weeping.

Later she came back to the Englishwoman with a banana leaf loaded with delicacies. 'I am sorry I hit you,' she said stiffly in the silence. 'But you deserved it. For your own good you must learn to bend in the wind like a reed. Life here can be good – '

'*Good?*'

The bitterness and anger in that single word was immeasurable.

'Yes, good. But you must open yourself to its possibilities. You must understand that this is a world made for women's pleasures as well as for the pleasures of our lord. You must soften a little and you will see.'

'Soften?' It was a shriek.

'Relax a little.'

'I am a prisoner here!'

Yasmin felt shame at her own hypocrisy, knowing exactly how the Englishwoman was feeling.

I have given up all my dreams, and it almost makes the words catch in my throat to tread down the dreams of another. But it has to be said all the same, if this stubborn Englishwoman is to be helped . . .

'We are all prisoners of something. You, I, our lord. English soldiers and traders. Everyone. Even the Subahdar of the Deccan, Nasir Jang – Fierce in War, Great is His

Name – even he is a thrall to his state. Tell me who is truly free?'

The Englishwoman said nothing, but within the hour she took one of the sweet morsels from the leaf-plate.

Good, Yasmin thought. That at least is a start. First you must give a little. Then you must open your mind to our ways.

It was not the thought of Nabab's return that had induced Arkali to obtain the poison. It's quite simple, she thought. A person who is used to making things turn out as she wants cannot be narrowly confined. The longer it goes on the worse the torture becomes. My nature is what it is, and that's why I must have the crystals. They're power.

She took a long-sprouted water jug and went casually outside. There were noises in the precinct below, laughing and squeals, mindless games to amuse the younger women, pulling the tails of donkeys.

Down in the flower garden there was one secret place where women and girls could look out of their world. Years ago a family of mongooses had burrowed into the soil, leaving the foundations networked with runs. A crack had opened in the wall. The wall itself was twenty feet high, made of stone blocks an arm's length thick, but the repair to the old masonry had dried and crumbled. There was no way to escape, but it was possible to press an eye to the crevice and catch a glimpse of the outside. Arkali had sat there dozens of times, looking out across the narrow slice of roadway, watching people coming and going – pilgrims on their way up the rock, traders, labourers, porters plodding under huge loads.

She unwrapped the crystals and looked at them, feeling the self-destructive urge swirl through her. It turned her stomach over as the compelling temptation gripped her. She shut her eyes.

Surely it would be painless? There would be honour in death, and an end to suffering. At last the anguish would stop. It remained only to tip the crystals on to her tongue, to swallow and think pleasing thoughts. And when they came for her they would find nothing but a cold body. Her soul would be gone.

But then there would be no hope of salvation. God did not permit into His heaven those who took their own lives. There would be an eternity of torment . . .

Surely God will make an exception for me, she thought. He knows my suffering. He understands.

She opened her eyes and lifted the brass ewer to her lips, drinking deeply. The water was cool and tasted of metal. The colours of the enamel flowers were suddenly vivid to her – reds of a shade she had never seen before. The jerking movements of a jewel wasp stabbed around her; she felt a slight breeze against her skin. The moment lasted a thousand years. And she knew she could never do it in reality.

She looked down. The glittering crystals lay in their fold of paper. She could not take the irrevocable step.

The ewer sang on the stones where she dropped it, water spilling from its trumpet mouth as it rolled. The buzz coming from the zenana was distant. Gradually she became aware of a rhythmic beat. It sounded like marching . . .

As she listened, the noise grew louder, echoing off the high stonework. She stared round at the walls, trying to decide where the sound was coming from.

'Look to yer dressing, that man!'

She heard it clearly. The accent was Irish. Irish!

'Stand!'

The marching stopped. Then came the order to rest easy.

She put her eye to the crack in the wall. And there they were! Soldiers, red-coated Europeans. Men in Company uniforms, dozens upon dozens of them, propping up their muskets, slumping down beside them in the street and drinking thirstily from canteens as if after an exhausting march. There was an officer in a tricorn hat. She recognized him at once from Madras as Captain Cope and cried out his name as he moved out of view.

He did not hear her. She craned to the widest angle

possible in the crevice, where the thinnest sliver of red jacket was visible. It seemed he was talking to his sergeant. She shouted again.

Captain Cope reappeared and looked about uncertainly, then turned away again.

She shouted a third time. 'John Cope! I'm here! I'm here!' This time he stepped up to the crevice.

'Who's there?'

She saw his long, mournful face, his eyes searching. 'It's me, Captain. Arkali Savage.' He stared at her through the crack in the wall, but seemed less than surprised, looking about anxiously to see if anyone was in earshot. 'Miss Savage? I've been warned you might be here. Wait for me if you can. I'll come back as soon as may be. Before midnight if I can.'

She begged him to stay. Begged. But he would not.

'Wait for me.'

Hours passed. Feverish thoughts passed through her mind. Relief that the soldiers had come to save her. They had known, after all! They had found her and come, in their hundreds, to take her back. To show the barbaric Moor that he could not do just as he pleased. Now he would rue his crime. It was sweet. So sweet.

Dusk fell and two young women came down arm in arm to take the perfume of the night flowers. She raged at them to go away, bending to pick up handfuls of pebbles and fling them until they retreated. They were used to her unpredictable violence and took themselves off. They would not come near the mad Angrezi woman.

But what about John Cope's words? *Warned* . . . That was the word he had used. What did he mean by it? And why had there been no fighting?

Cope returned as promised, as the moon was setting over the western plain. 'This is very dangerous,' he whispered. 'It has cost me a damned fortune in bribes to make the sentries look the other way for five minutes, but I wanted to explain things to you.'

'When can you get me out?'

'Miss Savage . . . I have not seen you,' he said stiffly. 'Please do not say anything of my coming here to talk to you, or there'll be awkward questions. Our delicate position here may be put in jeopardy, and I shall be forced to deny everything.'

'What are you talking about?'

'We have come here to reinforce the nawab's army. You probably do not know that Nasir Jang's been killed and in consequence Muhammad Ali's fallen back on this bastion. The fact is, Miss Savage, Madurai has declared for Chanda Sahib now, and I cannot tell you how much worse that makes the situation. There's certain to be a siege. Food is already running low and so is morale. That's why we're here. We cannot trust Muhammad Ali's mercenaries. In lieu of silver he's trying to keep them from mutiny with promises. I'm charged with keeping order here and making sure he holds this rock.'

Arkali could not believe her ears. How could he be talking this way? 'But what about me? You must get me out!'

There was a delicate cough. 'First we have a military problem to solve. I feel certain you can see our difficulty. The garrison – '

'Get me out! Immediately! Or the Governor will know of it! It's your duty as a soldier. As a gentleman. Your duty, I tell you!'

'Please lower your voice, Miss Savage. Rest assured the Governor knows of your plight.'

'Then why do you not rescue me immediately?'

Cope's face was hard and pale in the moonlight. 'I thought I had made it quite plain. At this moment the Moghul ruler is very important to us. His word is law, and there is no way an English Governor at Madras can risk jeopardizing our position by interfering with his prerogatives.'

'His prerogatives?'

'That is to say . . . dammit, Miss Savage, keep y'voice down. You can see the difficulty I'm in.'

'I am betrayed!' Her soul shrieked, but what came out was barely a whisper.

'It is as I have told you.'

She began to shake. Out of fear, or anger, or both, she did not know. 'But they've kidnapped me! You must get me out of here!'

'I'm sorry, Miss Savage. I have a job to do. Perhaps in a few months, when this business is at an end . . .'

'Months? Don't you see? The monster's here. I'm to be used by him! Do I have to spell it to you letter by letter?'

Cope wetted his lips. 'I do understand what you say, but there is nothing to be done about it. Wait, I pray you. In six months' time perhaps . . .'

'I'll pay you well, Captain. Name your sum. Name it! You must know that I'm heir to a remarkable fortune. My father was Charles Savage – '

Again that delicate cough, a pause. 'I . . . believe your father is quite well. Of course, he wants you safe and well, but he agrees with the Governor that – '

'My father? Alive?' she said, her voice suddenly hollow. 'Will you at least pass a message to him?'

'I cannot do that.'

'Then – to Robert Clive?'

'I . . . fear that Captain Clive has fallen to a sickness. And in any case – '

She saw the world spinning. 'Sickness? Is he dead?'

'No, no. Gone to Calcutta, I b'lieve.' There was the sound of an owl hooting. He listened, and when he spoke again his voice had hardened. 'My signal. I must go.'

The Captain's long, regretful face creased in annoyance, then vanished. She stared around, unable to move, or to think. Then there was the sound of running feet, maids and eunuchs coming into the garden to find her.

EIGHTEEN

The elephants moved onward through the heat of the day, heading a column that stretched behind until it was lost to sight. The remnants of the new Nizam's army were moving north, returning to Hyderabad, where they would yield up the city to the French before being disbanded.

De Bussy had triumphed: Dupleix's plan had succeeded, and French ambitions had won the day. For his part, Hayden Flint was a prisoner of three months' standing. Thoughts of his absurd position annoyed him like flies. It's a charade, a mime within a mime, but the hard truth at its centre is real enough: I'm a make-believe envoi to a leader who is himself the puppet of an enemy power. I'm tolerated by de Bussy only because I convinced him that my continuing presence serves Dupleix. But at least I'm alive and, while that's so, I'll fight their designs to the limit of my power.

On the day that Nasir Jang was murdered he had argued with the Marquis at pistol-point: 'M'sieur, it seems to me that any fool may see it easily enough. If the Nizam keeps an English ambassador what more perfect screen to Muzaffar's true and subordinate condition can there be? Surely no better proof of his independence can possibly be shown to the world.'

'You are far too much trouble, insolent Englishman.'

'In the past, perhaps. But what trouble could I be to you now?' He smiled poisonously at the Frenchman.

'Be careful, monsieur,' de Bussy said, glorying in his power. 'As official ambassador to the Nizam, on behalf of the English Company, you may think yourself immune to arrest against the Nizam's wishes.'

455

'Oh, I have no illusions about you, sir.'

'I merely wished to make myself clear. Hindostan is a difficult country and it is ever possible that a man may meet with a fatal accident.'

He faced down the suave condescension head-on. 'You admit you would kill a hostage in cold blood?'

'You misunderstand! You are – our guest.' De Bussy put up the pistol, icy humour breaking across his mouth. 'Whether you like it or not.'

'I agree to no parole. You'll have no promises from me, and I will not be made diplomatically impotent.'

The Frenchman's smile vanished. 'That sounds as if you are resolved to leave us.'

'You may take it how you will.'

De Bussy turned to the Nizam. 'What shall it be, Highness? Will you keep him? Or will you let him go?'

Muzaffar Jang waved the entire matter away from him.

'So, there it is. Since you have no permission to go, you must stay – and observe.'

Observe your victory, he thought, churning with cold fury. And risk anonymous assassination. Sweet Jesus, to think that only yesterday I was set on so different a course. It seems impossible that a bare twenty-four hours ago I had the managing of them all!

Osman sat beside him now as they rode, absorbed in eating a picnic of his own devising, some fruits, balls of rice, a little dried mutton. Osman's jaw moved slowly in time to the elephant's step, his head going back with enjoyment as he swallowed. He was more relaxed and less formal than he had been. Cleansed by prayer and uncomplicated by his surrender to Allah, he had neatly escaped the settling of scores that had followed upon Nasir Jang's murder.

He's counting blessings, as we might call it, Hayden Flint thought, glancing at Osman's unreadable features with a new respect. Perhaps you never were Nasir Jang's man, but Muzaffar's? I shouldn't be surprised if you had contrived to be paid by both sides. But then you're probably only accountable to yourself when all is said and done. And therefore good luck to you.

He recalled the first day of his captivity. The death of Nasir Jang was so sudden and so unexpected that the event had shocked through the army of the Nizamat like a typhoon. Each commander of horse was forced to consider himself, and the ecstatic de Bussy had moved at once to quell doubts, advising the dazed Muzaffar Jang to issue a proclamation of amnesty.

'To demonstrate your largesse, Highness. And your power. You are Nizam. You own the palaces of Aurangabad and the wealth of Hyderabad both. You are the master of the Deccan and holder of the Talwar-i-Jang, just as you always wanted to be. Just as Monsieur Dupleix has always promised you you would be.'

Muzaffar sat there, open-mouthed. The degradations of his ordeal had not yet left him, and he had found it impossible to rejoice. Hayden Flint had felt the guilt bite into him then as Muzaffar had suddenly dropped the Talwar and its priceless diamond to examine the bloodied turban of his uncle. Even through the fog of his torment he had been ready to remove the Eye of Naga from it and clasp it to his heart.

The Eye! How was it Muzaffar still believed in its power? He had asked Osman that question, certain it was now obvious to everyone that the ruby had no power against the diamond's horrendous curse.

Osman inclined his head. 'Lord Muzaffar Jang, Prince of the Fortunate Conjunction, has his wish. He is become Nizam. So, sir, how else would you have him believe?'

Now, three months later, he shook his head at the memory. The present Nizam's ambitions had been fulfilled in all respects.

He watched the ragged fingers of the Eastern Ghats slide by on their left. The slopes were misty and beautiful and set his mind to meditating on wider vistas. The elephant that headed the column of the royal van was Muzaffar's; de Bussy's walked a pace or two behind. But it was the dozen ranged between the head and his own elephant he studied now. Of these, two in particular carried dangerous men: Abdul Nabi Khan and the Nawab of Kurnool – the two men who more than any had given Muzaffar Jang the Nizamat. Their boundless greed had shown itself in Fort Louis, but only he had noted its full significance.

Eighteen chests of jewels and a crore of rupees in specie and bullion – ten million rupees – had been looted from the hoard of Asaf Jah. On the death of Nasir Jang they were taken into Pondicherry to be shared out.

I wonder how much of it Abdul Nabi Khan got for his treachery, he had thought at the time. Not enough by the look of him.

As he regarded the Pathan he felt the hairs rise on his neck. Last night he had spoken with the man, another made of the same clay as Abdul Masjid. A devil in him had prompted him to tell the ferocious nawab that the man's liege lord had promised the French the region of Kurnool as a gift, once he was safely installed at Hyderabad. It had been a dirty piece of politicking, a nasty, peevish deceit playing on the vilest preoccupations of a most foul person.

As he reflected on what he had done he began to sweat. Clouds boiled up dark and grey over the distant hills, flashing them with dry lightning and turning the day ominous. He imagined Yasmin beside him, and wished the daydream was real. She would have brightened the sickly light of the sky, but without her its jaundice deepened. He could have asked her about his suspicions, he could have admitted what he had done, but she was not here.

He roused himself as the temperature fell twenty degrees in as many elephant paces. Out in the fields, peasants began streaming back to their villages in droves. It was astonishing to see their fear. Lightning was a terrifying mystery to them. They could know nothing of the experiments of Mr Stephen Gray and John Desaguliers in Oxford that proved the nature of the electric fluid. And had not the estimable Dr Franklin written that earth, and the thunderclouds that rolled above it, could be considered as merely the two

458

halves of a Leyden jar, and that the phenomenon of lightning was but the spark that leapt between? For the Hindu, lightning was the wrath of a monstrous god that struck fire into their sacred treetops, raised the hairs on their dogs' backs, made their babies cry and curdled precious milk. It awed them, and drove them to prayer.

Perhaps they were right: a new cycle was beginning. The shifting of power. A new Dance of the Cosmos. The Lord Shiva's footfalls could be heard in the echo of men's laughter. The great width of his god-blue back could be seen stirring in those purple hills. A storm was breaking the like of which the world had never seen . . .

Patterns of chaos boiled in the sky of his imagination. Ghost visions swirled out of the hills with the rain, haunting him as the first drops squalled across the road and moistened his face. He closed his eyes and saw French troops burning London on the hundredth anniversary of its Great Fire. A great red glare lit the sky over St Paul's, over the Octagon on Greenwich Hill. He saw the East India fleet at Bow Creek taken by French naval vessels. And the people overwhelmed by terror, reduced by starvation, unaware that a great turning point in history had been passed – irretrievably – somewhere beyond their ken, on the other side of the world. How could they know that the smiting off of a Moghul viceroy's head would lead inexorably to the same fate for King George? But wasn't that the true, crooked way of human affairs?

He pulled his cloak about him, Osman fussing with the baggage.

'Drink, sir.'

'Take it away.'

The cold gripped him. Thoughts coursed in his head, suddenly making sense. With the capture of Hyderabad and the installation of Muzaffar at the nominal capital of Aurangabad, there would be an end to the conflict. The British would have to leave Madras and probably Bombay too. The French would control half of Hindostan and, within a few years, all of it. As they tightened their grip on its wealth there would be a vast and increasing outpouring of revenue to France, which would tilt the balance between the two Great Powers and start another world-spanning war.

But this time, he thought, it'll be a war France'll win. Hindostan's saltpetre and teak-built ships will ensure that French sea power will dominate. The American colonies will be taken. Ultimately, England herself'll be invaded and made Louis's plaything. All stemming from a killing I witnessed less than a hundred days ago.

The jubilation attending Muzaffar Jang's amazing turn-about echoed in his mind. He felt the utter desolation of that moment; the gleaming sword held aloft by a man too shocked to know what he was doing.

And now?

No difference. Now Muzaffar had begun to strut and preen in exactly the same peacock way as his predecessor, Nasir Jang.

The waves of ill-fortune were rising, getting up like ocean waves, but these waves were growing under no earthly gale. It was clear why the Hindu revered the Koh-i-Noor diamond. It was without doubt a real focus of evil in the world, and no false magic could contend with it.

Muzaffar had changed and changed again since his fated day. The new possessor of the Talwar had been obliged to take his army to Pondicherry to accept the congratulations of the French Council. He entered the citadel to be received by Dupleix himself. Te Deums were rung in the Chapel of the Sisters of Cluny and in the great church, and in the Governor's palace the honours and feasting were extravagant.

Hayden Flint had not been excluded from any part of it. He had expected a repeat of the moment at Hyderabad when he had been humiliated by de Bussy, but this time he was offered no indignities. Dupleix wanted to show his high degree of civilization. Magnanimity to the defeated, the man who was a silent witness to the fact that the English were no longer a threat.

The ferocious-looking Nawab of Kurnool had stared at Hayden Flint thoughtfully throughout the entire ceremonial. Muzaffar said little. A disagreeable mood had settled over him, dyspeptic, like a man ulcerated in the stomach who dined on pickles and rough wine. After the public enthronement, Dupleix breached his own etiquette, asking if this was indeed the sword that was revered by the Mussulman second only to the Prophet's own?

Muzaffar Jang tolerated the candied remarks darkly, allowing the Frenchman to study the milky depths of the great uncut diamond which was the largest the planet had yet disgorged.

Dupleix admired it to Muzaffar's face, but in a vinegary aside caught moments later, leaned to de Bussy and said, 'It's disappointing, no? It seems far less than its repute.'

But still Muzaffar brought out his French watch and flourished it, resetting the hands as he had been shown on the stroke of midnight by the chimes of Notre-Dame des Anges. Then, as arranged, the climax of the night's extravagances took place. Dupleix was made Muzaffar Jang's 'deputy', and given control of all territory south of the Kistna River. Not simply the Carnatic, but an area bigger than the whole of France and containing a population of three crore.

Of course, the honour was refused – or rather, transferred. Henceforth, the Marquis de Bussy would be the Nizam's deputy, but for his part, Dupleix promised the founding of a new capital, to be built on the place of Nasir Jang's death. The city would be called Dupleix-Fatehabad, and the erection at its centre of a victory column to outshine that of the Roman emperor, Trajan, was to be begun immediately.

They had departed in state for this march to Aurangabad two days later. Three hundred French and 2,000 sepoys, accompanying the fifty thousand remaining of the vast horde that had come out of Hyderabad under his prompting almost a year ago . . .

The rain stopped as suddenly as it had started. The sky

brightened and the intense beams of the sun warmed Hayden Flint, driving wisps of steam from his clothing.

He became conscious of raised voices at the head of the column. When he looked up he saw others staring towards the Nizam.

A shot rang out, then another and another. Musket-fire!

An elephant trumpeted with pain and bolted. Osman craned over the side of the howdah, pointing into the undergrowth at the side of the road. There were figures there – ambushers. Pathetically few, but their fusillade had sent the lead elephants stumbling in confusion.

Less than fifty yards away Muzaffar Jang's elephant was brought under control in a sea of pushing, shouting men. The enigmatic Eye stood out, a red spot in his turban, his body jolting as the beast pirouetted comically. It was all over and done. The ragged adventurers who had made the ludicrous ambush were running like antelope for their lives. Some of de Bussy's sepoys were unwrapping the rags from their musket locks, but few succeeded in getting off a shot, and by the time the horses plunged after them the assailants had made the cover of a dense thicket.

He saw the Nawab of Kurnool's elephant moving closer to the Nizam's own. There seemed to be a dangerous premeditation in the man's movements as his lance was lifted. Then Hayden Flint gasped as the nawab drew back the weapon and thrust its steel tip through Muzaffar Jang's temple.

Muzaffar crumpled, and the victor raised his arms in self-acclaim, throwing huzzahs at the crowd, seeming to believe that the army would have no choice now but to follow him.

Hayden Flint watched powerless as the killer was engulfed. How can any man have so misjudged the mood of an army? he asked, revulsion rising in his throat.

The nawab was shouting to God, his eyes mad, every sinew in his body taut. But his cries of 'God is great!' would not halt them; his charisma had failed. He howled despairingly as they fell on him, then he was grabbed, hauled down from the howdah and sucked into the boiling morass of men.

The mussoolah boat crashed through the surf, landing Robert Clive under the shadow of the walls of St George. He slapped the powdered sand from his breeches and told the bearer to take his baggage to his accommodation. The day was waning but he felt refreshed by the sea spray, and this topsy-turvy ride from the Company ship had enlivened him. It was sweet as honey, yet bitter as bile, to be back at Madras.

His stay in Calcutta had been many things. He had been sent north by Sawyer, officially on business, ostensibly to convalesce, privately, he suspected, to be got out of the way. Once, decades ago, the post of Steward had been limited to the duties of procuring for the Governor's table those provisions that suited the dignity of his office. Now, it was a senior appointment: Quartermaster to the Company's staff and Commissary to its forces. He was in charge of large amounts of specie, and he began to use his position to advantage.

On arrival in Fort William he had presented his card at Stratford Flint's godown, meaning to set him to rights over the duel with Hayden. They met and dined together, but in the conviviality of the meeting he had forgotten to mention the duel. Instead he had confined himself to informing Stratford Flint of the situation in the Carnatic and discussing general conditions of trade. As the night wore on, however, he allowed himself to be importuned into paying interest on the trader's debts, saving him, so he said, from the usurers with whom he was entangled.

'It's simple, lad,' Flint said. 'At the top of the market are raw silk and opium, muslins and chintzes, at the bottom, coarse cotton, dyewoods, ghee and saltpetre. In a little while, ye'll come t'have faith in me judgment. So come to me when ye will, and I'll draw up a contract. There's numberless ways to spend the Company's money here, ye'll see, investing illicitly and in quantity under me good advice. We'll trade salt, betel-nut and indigo, and if ye're clever ye'll accept a half-cut in the resulting profit as I'm offering ye.'

But there had been transactions other than pure business between them. Like a father initiating a son in the mysteries of life, Stratford filled him with wine one velvet night and led him to the house at Kali Ghat where the black-eyed beauties were hidden behind tatties and screens of chick bamboo. Urged there under intoxication and false pretences, he was drawn inside by his physical desire. But the shaven girl had revolted him and he left her two bits of silver and staggered away hatless. In the street he was accosted by men who turned out to be palanquin bearers and took him to Flint's riverside house where he vomited on the steps and hung on to the white columns, wanting only to stop the world spinning.

Stratford was waiting for him. He walked him to the Hooghly's shore, plied him with strong Mocha coffee and Flint philosophy as the sobering sun rose. And in return he told Flint how thoughts of Arkali in the harem of a Moor was surely killing him inside.

'I lost me own wife who I dearly loved,' Flint said, looking across the sluggish waters. 'Fer a while I was out of my right mind, too. But time heals, and like the Hindu say, a man can dwell upon but one thought at one time. I say: fix one gigantic thought in yer mind, blot her memory out, and ye'll be helped.'

'There is no thought gigantic enough to do that, sir.'

'Ah, but there is!' Stratford's scrutiny intensified. 'There's two obsessions, and one I can see behind yer eyes at this instant. A melancholy tending towards death – am I right? Ah, ye're a strange one – ye'd throw yerself into oblivion as soon as snap yer fingers. But if ye'll take my advice, ye'll think on what I said to ye. There's just two obsessions are big enough to combat a loss of love. Two remedies as can bring relief to a man who's afflicted like yerself.'

'The whores of Kali Ghat do not interest me.'

'I'm not talking of them!'

'Then why in hell's name did you direct me there?'

A glitter of humour entered Stratford's eye. 'Call it an adventure to bring ye to the right condition fer unburdening yerself. The surest way to deal with any pain is a razor drawn from ear to ear, and I'm certain there's plenty would offer their services to ye in that. But I judge it too severe a resort in this case.'

'Then what is the other way, Mr Flint?'

'Avarice, by God!'

'I don't see – '

'It's straightforward. Yer preferred, radical way of changing yerself is to do as I did.'

'Which was?'

'Throw yerself body and soul into amassing. That'll make a new man of ye. A new man. D'ye see?'

'I don't think I do – '

Flint clapped a big hand across his shoulders. 'Ah, ye'll be surprised. I've seen it. Been there. Done it. Be told by me, lad, that's the way of men's lives. We think we quest for happiness, when the truth of it is we're seeking after woman, then once we have her, it's wealth we must have, then once we have that, it's power. Y'see? But if one quest is fruitless, then ye must just skip to the next!'

'I cannot.'

Flint sighed, and withdrew his arm. 'Well, that's candid enough of ye. And now perhaps ye'll be as candid about the causes of yer duel.'

That was a slap in the face. 'You know about that?'

Flint snorted, lit up his stogie. 'Of course I do.'

'But how? All the way to Calcutta? It was a secret transaction. Even Governor Sawyer swore blind – '

'Thomas Edwardes, Captain, Royal Navy, is an akwaintance of mine of great long standing.'

'I have no recollection of Captain Edwardes.'

'His ship's HMS *Vengeance*. An appropriate name, considering.'

'I am certain I don't know him.'

465

'No, but ye know his surgeon, Mr Nairn.' Flint was suddenly hard as mahogany. Unmoving, unsmiling, all conviviality gone. 'I know ye, Robert Clive. I know ye wouldn't have been in any duel without the will to send Hayden to his grave. And I remember telling ye flat I had no wish t'see him dead. What were ye thinking on by defying me?'

Clive bowed his head and mumbled something. And Flint held him with a stare until he felt his will crumble and he told everything, except that the duel was postponed instead of cancelled. He made an apology, and even a promise he supposed he could not keep, since there was already a prior promise to meet Hayden Flint on the field of honour, and settle their respective fates once and for ever.

Stratford Flint had accepted the promise that he would do nothing to harm Hayden, then the easiness had struck up again between them and they had talked of their expected profits.

There were already plenty of those coming back: Flint's first ship with ten thousand pieces of made-up silk-and-cotton mix, fifteen hundred maunds of raw silk – alone worth two and a half lakh rupees, iron balasore from Orissa, sugar, ginger and benjamin bound for Surat. A substantial profit could be anticipated.

As the sun rose over the rich flat delta across which Hindostan poured out its sacred heart, he learned that Bengal was twice the goldfield of trade the South could ever be, and that the firm control exercised by the Moghul ruler of Bengal prohibited Anglo–French conflict there, promoting trade as never before.

Now, Robert Clive dusted his hands and wiped the salt spray from his face, before climbing up to the Water Gate of Fort St George. As he passed the soldiers standing sentry-go on the gate and accepted their salutes, he was amazed to see Hayden Flint. He hailed him.

The other seemed tired and careworn. The initial reluctance he saw in the man's bearing took the hostility from his voice.

'So, you're here again? I hope we can still speak in a civil way,' he offered cautiously.

'If it's letters from Calcutta you bear, I doubt that. Otherwise, I see no reason to break our agreement.'

'No. No letters.' He saw the expression that flitted across Hayden Flint's face. Disappointment? I-thought-as-much? Anger? 'But I did speak to your father. He's very well, and renewing his fortune steadily.'

'Are you back here for good?'

'Well, let us say for a while at least. My duties for the Hon'ble Company have brought me back sooner than I'd planned. And you?'

'Likewise.'

Brushed out of the Nizam's establishment like a flea from a pelt, I dare say, Clive thought. 'So, what news?' he asked, ravenous to know what had passed off and wondering if Hayden Flint would now play square with him. 'Anything more?'

'Nothing cogent to our purpose. But what do you know of great events?'

'Only so much as I knew when I left: Nasir Jang murdered; Muzaffar Jang lording it at Arcot; Chanda Sahib's people looting the country around with impunity; and Muhammad Ali and his army trapped like a bug in a bottle at Trichy. Dupleix must think himself very clever. Any word from Cope?'

Hayden Flint's coolness began to melt as they walked. 'The man's failed at Madurai against a town declared for Chanda Sahib.'

'A bloody misnomer, Captain Cope! He might have better been called Captain Incompetent. By God, we're in a bad position now.'

'It's worse by far. You're behind the times when it comes to great affairs. Muzaffar Jang is murdered too, and the Deccan has fallen to Salabat Jang – which means Charles de Bussy.'

'God's teeth! And he let you go? Just like that?'

'De Bussy said he had thought better of allowing me to

spy on his affairs at Hyderabad. It's my conjecture that he thought to send me back to kill hope with the truth of what has happened. Maybe he was thinking I'd scotch all stories that Muzaffar lived, or that his boy successor might be more amenable to Englishmen. Maybe it was to bring back news of an altogether more amazing thing.'

Clive listened as Hayden Flint told how Muzaffar's brainpan had been opened by a spike; how the Frenchman had set up the adolescent Salabat Jang in his place; how the youth had accepted the nomination but refused the Talwar.

'Refused it? Never in this world!'

'It's the truth. I saw it with these eyes. As masterful a stroke of sure-timed statesmanship as I've seen, and from one so young in so sharp a crisis. I fair near choked as de Bussy took the sword himself. He was obliged to, you see.

'How's that?'

'A gift of recognition, made by a prince to his master. Impossible for him to refuse.'

'So that brute of a diamond's gone to de Bussy? Jesus God, no wonder the man wants it boasted about!'

'No. It was accepted by him – but on behalf of Dupleix.'

Clive stopped in his tracks. 'They say there's an uncommon powerful curse on the stone. Did you ever believe in that? If Dupleix has it – '

'Ah, but does he believe in it?'

'I doubt that he disbelieves its worth in terms of the power and gold he could exchange against it once he took it into France. As for the curse . . . I am left wondering.'

They cut a diagonal across the parade square.

Clive said, 'I don't believe Dupleix would leave Hindostan for any amount of gold. His ambition is in empire.'

'Agreed, but think of the influence such a potential gift would give him with his monarch. Do you remember the Pitt diamond? It transformed Thomas Pitt from impoverished rector's son to Member of Parliament and politically influential landed gentlemen. When he sold it, it was to the Régent Orléans, just so that prince could say the biggest diamond in Europe was the centrepiece of the French crown jewels. Who'd bet that King Louis could resist the opportunity to top that?'

As they passed the flagpole, Clive checked him, asking his opinion on the immediate position.

'If you want to consider tangibles, only Trichinopoly remains to us. For how long that may be, I can't say. Muhammad Ali has offered to accept Chanda Sahib as Nawab of the Carnatic – '

'No!'

'– so long as he is permitted to keep Trichinopoly.'

'Chanda Sahib must have declined that offer?'

'Who in his position would not? His son is obliterating Tanjore even as we speak.'

Clive snorted, his mind working over the complex pattern of forces that were tensioning the situation affecting Trichinopoly. The loyalty of the surrounding areas is crucial, he thought, coming quickly to the kernel of the matter. Tanjore again. It's adjacent to Trichy. The raja there is a Hindu and may dislike Muhammad Ali's Muslim rhetoric, but there's common cause between them. Or there could be, with a little persuasion. He certainly has no love for Chanda, who crossed him years ago, whose men have ruined his harvests and extorted what they could from him once before. We may suppose that his people are now unwilling hosts to Raza Sahib's rabble . . .

'Damn them,' he said. 'What's Sawyer's view?'

'Shortly you may be able to ask him that yourself – he's up from St David to inspect the outworks here. But before you think it through, you ought to know the rest of it.'

Clive listened intently and without interruption as he was told that the Company's European Battalion, 600 strong and supported by 3,000 sepoys, had been sent south under Captain de Gingens, a Swiss officer in the Company's pay.

'The plan is to underscore Muhammad Ali's authority at the fortress city of Valikondapuram, but de Gingens's force was shadowed on its march there by five hundred French grenadiers and some thousands of horse from Chanda

Sahib's army. The killadar of Valikondapuram feared for his own position. He declared neutrality and shut the gates of the city to both armies, leaving de Gingens to face superior numbers. By all accounts a fiasco followed. An ensign and six men were killed. There's been a shameful retreat by the rest of them, prompted, I imagine, by confusion among the officers. The result had been the withdrawal of the whole army to save its skin.'

'How they do mismanage things with the men,' was Clive's only comment. He asked, 'Where did they land up?'

'Chanda pursued them to Trichinopoly itself. They're there still.'

'Then it's a bloody mess! What's needed is a firm lead. A relief force must be got to them, and when that's done and they're resupplied, they must be roused and got up to fight as I know they can!'

'Chanda Sahib's army has them all trapped. There's no one here to lead a relief.'

'I'll do it, if the Governor allows it.' Clive tossed his head like an angered bull. 'What alternative is there? Who else would undertake it?'

Hayden Flint felt the brittleness of their truce and the fragility of Clive's state of mind. The news had not pleased the man; he hungered body and soul to throw himself into the fray. There was a certain canniness about him now, but it barely concealed the wild aggressor within. The whole notion of getting himself to Trichy stank of self-indulgence, but it also made a kind of rude sense.

He wondered at the determination of the man, while debating whether or not to open wounds by mentioning what little more he had learned of Arkali. Clive was looking stronger. The sojourn in Calcutta had fortified his spirit, but his root feelings ran deep, and he was still a dangerous man to deal with. Even so, the agreement between them had been solemn. He decided he must speak.

'It's well for all of us, Robert, that you've come back

now. I assume you've not forgotten our pact to release Miss Savage, but you'll agree there's not much can be done about it with the worsening of the general position?'

Clive's expression darkened as he had expected. 'I've forgotten nothing. Thoughts of Arkali are never far from me. On the passage here I'd worked up a proposal to put to Sawyer. Your news has perhaps made it workable. I've a mind to see the Governor and plead with him. Will you support me?'

'That depends.'

They found Sawyer in an iron mood. He had risen late and was without his wig. Cope's letters and now de Gingens's had made disquieting reading for him, and he heard out the plan with a vinegary smile.

'Gentlemen, Trichinopoly, for all its strength as a fortress, is beset with weaknesses. To be specific, a lack of money and victuals. As ever, princely armies depend on silver and gold to keep their commanders loyal. It must be the limit of what the nawab's people can endure to see their allies – allies upon whom they depend – made fools of by the enemy. Now it is all de Gingens can do to prevent a rebellion in the city. Men are deserting. It seems that the sands are running out of the glass for Muhammad Ali.'

'Then, sir, we shall have to move with all speed.'

Sawyer fixed Clive with a cold eye. 'You may think yourself well informed, Captain Clive, as to my intentions. You are mistaken. I'll not throw good men after bad. I have already anticipated matters in the South and my mind is made up. There can be no relief attempted on Trichinopoly. Our people marched themselves there – fled is the more accurate description. I cannot send more men into the place. We have hardly enough to defend our own walls.'

'Sir, we cannot allow Trichinopoly to fall!'

Sawyer spread his hands. Without his wig he had lost some of his judicial air. 'This is the time to put our faith in words. We shall do as Dupleix himself did after the triumph of Nasir Jang. We shall resort to diplomacy.'

'Diplomacy?' The word exploded from Clive.

'Captain, we must tread with care, and consider the legality of what we do at every step. France and Britain are no longer at war. The veneer we have applied to the situation here is thin, but it is intact. We must not breach that delicate understanding, or there will be severe consequences in Europe. If I act in haste, or without sufficient seeming cause, any gains we make may be nullified by the stroke of a pen by the Court of Directors.'

'Governor, the fact is that Monsieur Dupleix never trusted solely to diplomacy. While he amused us all with his letters he was plotting Nasir Jang's murder!'

Hayden Flint saw the cords standing out on Clive's neck, his face flushed red with the effort of making a fool understand. He decided to step in.

'Suppose the Company's force comes out from Trichy,' he said. 'Then what? Muhammad Ali's establishment will desert him immediately, and his head will be separated from his body within the hour. Our legitimacy to make any move whatsoever against the French will be forfeited.'

By his tone, Sawyer's patience was almost exhausted. 'We are bound at hand and foot as it is,' he said. 'When de Gingens's force was assembled ready for dispatch south, I had to wait until detachments of Muhammad Ali's army could rendezvous with it before ordering it to move.'

'Which may be the reason why de Gingens could not reach Valikondapuram in time to avail himself of that fort's protection.' Clive crossed the line of respect a captain in the Company's service ought not to cross when addressing his commander-in-chief. 'Look at the facts of it! Sir, you must allow me to mount a relief of Trichinopoly!'

'I have told you no, sir.'

'Then at the very least give me leave to take a baggage train there! Let me run supplies to them. With speed and surprise we can come through. Damn me, I know it can be done!'

'Do not raise your voice to me, Captain. Do you think yourself one of the country traders? Be told, or I shall reconsider your position here.'

The Governor's sharpness seemed to bring Clive to his senses and he drew back. 'I ask your pardon, sir.'

'Well, then, you may have it, but do not tax me. I have no doubt your motives for visiting Trichinopoly are manifold. I have no doubt you believe you could cut your way through a hundred of Chanda Sahib's men to reach your goal, but I am ultimately responsible for our people and I cannot allow it.'

Hayden Flint saw the way Clive fought to control his face. It's uncanny, he thought. Robert's behaving like a man who already knows what consequences must flow from each course of action open to Sawyer. Does he know? How could he? But it's certain he believes it – see his frustration at his inability to convey that certainty! That he cannot persuade his seniors to trust him wholly, enrages him.

'Governor, I must say that I believe Captain Clive is capable of winning through,' he said on impulse. 'The real position may not be as you believe. Much the better part of the Company's forces are at Trichinopoly. We must know their condition, and how thing stand with Muhammad Ali and his people.'

'I understand your feelings, Mr Flint – ' Sawyer started to say.

'Perhaps you do. But perhaps you are leaping from unsafe assumptions. I pledge you my word that the greater good of the Company is uppermost in my mind – in both our minds. And I believe Captain Clive is able to offer reasoned arguments for each detail of his recommendations, if you will but open your opinions to alteration.'

Sawyer got up, paced the room, his hand smoothing his lips. Then he stopped, turned suddenly, his eyes dwelling a moment on Clive's sun-faded red uniform jacket.

'Well,' he said eventually, 'I know of no reason why a Governor of the Madras Presidency may not alter his opinions after hearing reasoned argument. If I cannot, then no one can.'

Clive would report to Sawyer the moment he arrived back

473

here at St David. The Governor had come to the southern fort once again to get a closer view of events than Madras could afford him.

The guard had come out, given prior warning by the piquets. The whole fort was in an uproar of expectation to hear the news. Apart from the arrival, two days ago, of Stratford Flint's ship, the *Wager*, with much-needed supplies from Calcutta, they had been without news or succour. It had been a hard month's wait.

Against all odds Clive was returning with his mission accomplished. Hayden Flint, now attached informally to the Governor's staff, felt a surge of triumph at first sight of him as they met in the shadow of the main gate.

Clive climbed down from the saddle and looked instantly to Hayden Flint, a look of breathless urgency on his face.

'My dear fellow,' Sawyer said, pumping Clive's hand.

'You are a worker of miracles. I would not have believed it possible!'

'You did not, as I recall, sir.' Clive took a bottle of water, supped, leaned forward and scrubbed the remains into his scalp. 'But it's no miracle when every man in a red coat accounts himself the equal of fifty sowars.'

Clive had departed at the beginning of the month of July, collected his supplies together at St David and marched a convoy to Devicotta. From there he had thrust directly to Trichinopoly. With astonishing good fortune he had managed to evade Chanda Sahib's six thousand men, and make a final dash for the fortress town's walls before d'Auteuil's grenadiers could prevent him.

'As for the French, I ran the standards of two companies past them, and that was enough to dissuade any attack on us, as few as we were.'

'Genius!' Sawyer shouted, raising cheers from the gathering.

'I consider myself flattered by that remark, sir. But tricks will not work twice. We lost too many men getting out of Trichy. My sepoys were cut about.'

'An heroic effort, Mr Clive. As no one could deny.'

474

Sawyer rubbed his chin. His face lost some of its jubilation. 'And the Trichinopoly garrison?'

'By God, they're in a sorry condition – as I supposed,' Clive said. 'But we have no option other than to keep the army at Trichinopoly.'

'And that is your opinion?'

'Sir, it is. Unless you would leave Muhammad Ali to the crows.' Clive hungered to have agreement from Sawyer. Some of the briskness left him. 'I spoke with the nawab at length. The truth is, he's aware that we need him. He calls us his protectors. He's a worthless man, cruel because he's eaten up with fear at the core, and without principle. I'd just as soon see him begging – '

'We do need him, Captain.'

Clive recovered himself, the flame inside him subsiding again. 'Yes. The fact is, we do.'

Sawyer took his elbow and murmured, 'I sympathize with your personal feelings. I trust they were not communicated to the nawab.'

'I was discreet and . . . businesslike, sir.'

'Good. We'll talk of that later. Now, your report.'

Still Clive did not move. He drew out a sealed letter. 'Sir, if I may draw your attention to this communiqué from the nawab?'

Sawyer opened the parchment and quickly read through the flowery formulas that prefaced the contents. 'What the devil is this?' he said, and looked up before quoting scathingly, ' "If an audacious officer and five hundred men could be sent to raise a disturbance in the Arcot country, it would serve to confuse the enemy . . ." Is this your notion of humour, Captain?'

'The letter is Muhammad Ali's. It has his seal, and look there, his signature.'

'It seems to have gained somewhat in the translation.'

Clive stared back, unabashed.

'Well, sir?'

'I have no opinion about that, Mr Sawyer.'

'Do you not? Well, I do, sir!'

Clive's unblinking eyes remained on Sawyer. 'Since we cannot afford to let de Gingens starve, and nor can we bring him away, it's clear that an alternative plan must be employed.'

'An alternative, yes – but to march on Arcot!'

'I find myself in accord with the nawab. If Mohamet may not go to the mountain, then the mountain must be enticed to visit Mohamet. It may seem an audacious plan, but I am at a loss to think what else would draw Chanda away from Trichinopoly.'

'And Muhammad Ali thinks five hundred men would be sufficient for the seizure of his capital?'

Clive nodded. 'Sir, it's almost a case of the fewer the better.'

'Clive, confound you! I do not follow you at all. Either you are a genius or you are a madman.'

'I shall agree with the nawab, then. Five hundred men, if properly led – and if two hundred of them be Europeans.'

'No, sir! That would leave St David guarded by a bare fifty! And no more than a hundred here at Madras. Are you seriously suggesting that I should agree to that?'

'Sir, it's plain enough. French troops cannot attack St George or St David directly. To do so would be a *causus belli*. It would force the French Company to recall Dupleix and I judge him too wily for that. Failing bombardment, either fort could hold out against any number of irregular horse such as Chanda has for an indefinite time.'

'With so few defenders?'

'According to my assessment, that is so.'

'Sir, resupply from Calcutta would not be difficult.' Hayden Flint judged it right to add his weight to the argument. 'The worst outcome would be a full siege by Chanda Sahib's entire army. But both St George and St David have, in the past, withstood comparable Maratha attacks. And remember, we have the sea.'

'And Chanda's army have no interest in our forts. They will be too busy marching on Arcot.'

Sawyer drummed his fingers. 'Chanda Sahib would only

release his stranglehold on Trichinopoly – and your plan could only succeed – if you took Arcot. Suppose you failed.'

Clive shook his head vigorously, the thing inside him igniting once more. 'No. Suppose I can take Arcot, imagine what must happen then. Think of it! Chanda Sahib, newly proclaimed Nawab of the Carnatic, become a great laughing stock. Ridicule is something the Moors detest more than death. They will say, "Here is a prince who cannot sit his own masnad because a feringhee is upon it." And I shall taunt him, sir, have no fear of that! Do you see the sport of it? The killadars of all the lands about will be watching: those nursing ambition; those wavering; those bearing grudges; the men who wait to see how the wind blows – all of them will think again concerning Chanda Sahib and his claims.'

Hayden Flint said, 'And Muhammad Ali's own allies will think again too. How better to dissuade the rebellious element among his following?'

'Enough to permit Captain de Gingens to bring out his force?'

'It may be.'

Sawyer was on the brink of the idea. He said, 'If you will indulge me for a moment, Captain Clive. How much of this great battle plan is of the nawab's own devising?'

Hayden Flint saw the look on Clive's face. He's judging him, he thought. Judging the moment, too. Like a tiger about to leap.

'Mine. All of it.'

Sawyer regarded him for a long moment, then he said very evenly, 'Your presumption is astounding, sir.'

Clive's compelling grin broke through, provoking Sawyer further. 'At first, when I thought on the problem, I understood it like this: Muhammad Ali needs gold and food to maintain himself. So, I thought it might do to scour the fortified towns – Vellore, Arni, Cauveripak, Conjeeveram – all are within twenty miles or so of Arcot. I thought to a raise little money for our cause, or at least to prevent

Chanda getting it as revenue. Then I saw the answer, shining like the deuced sun, d'ye see?'

Hayden Flint watched Sawyer shake his head, clearly angered, before the Governor's own genius for cool dispassionate decision-making came to the fore.

'Audacious,' Sawyer said at last, meeting Clive's eye directly. 'You called it that yourself. It may be that such audacity will set the balance down on our side. I shall consult with Mr Prince.'

'You intend to champion my plan at Council?'

'I'll lay the nawab's letter before an extraordinary session. With my recommendations.'

Sawyer began to turn, but Clive was not finished with him. 'When, sir?'

'When what, Captain Clive?'

'The session.'

'As soon as possible. As soon as a messenger may be mounted up. My memorandum will go to George Pigot at Madras to tell him to make ready a corps of eighty. You'll have to content yourself with a bare hundred and thirty men from here. The lowest sweepings of London's gutters I ever saw, some of them, but there's nothing else for it. As for the Council, we shall meet as soon as the members may be got together. First thing tomorrow morning.'

'But, sir, that's too late! By the day after tomorrow Dupleix's spies will have the plan all over the Carnatic!'

'Are you suggesting that my Council – '

Clive was impatiently racking his brains. 'Sir, tomorrow is too late! The moment we march out of the fort we'll advertise our intent and invite interception. If we move now, we might force the route overnight and rendezvous with the Madras contingent along the way. We might still evade Chanda's horse, given luck!'

'Have you forgotten? The new men have not been in this clime long. You'd march them too hard, and what use would they be in a fight after that?'

Clive's face fell. It seemed to Hayden Flint that he was

unable to accept that mere human weakness could thwart his plan.

'You may be right, sir,' he said slowly, 'but I feel certain in my bones that we can do it.'

'How? Tell me that.'

'I . . .'

'Damn me, you believe everyone is like yourself,' Sawyer said. 'One day that belief will rear up and bite you.'

Clive stood like a man at a burial, mourning the loss of his plan, then Hayden Flint seized his arm. 'I can think of a way you can go without your movements being followed.'

Both men looked up at him.

'Think of it – your men going at a goodly trotting pace, carrying all your gear and ordnance, and still fresh as fountains when they reach St George twelve hours hence.'

'How?'

'We shall commandeer my father's vessel.'

'By God! Yes!'

'The *Wager*, gentlemen. By the look of her she's readying canvas to sail for Calcutta as we speak.'

Sawyer's letter went with them, for Cully had been prepared to fight them to keep them off his quarterdeck.

'No dispossessed bastard'll come aboard this fucken ship,' he roared down at them. His pistols were cocked and his lascars carried long creese knives. They hung in the shrouds or looked over the bulwarks, peering down into the Governor's gig in which Hayden Flint stood.

The Company's soldiers formed up under the walls of Fort St David were a shimmering smear of red on a white beach two cables distant across glittering blue water. The braid on Hayden Flint's formal coat was lavish.

'I'm boarding your vessel, *na-khuda*.'

'Lay one hand on my gunnels, Hayden Flint, and I'll strike you dead, Christ help me!'

'That's the same song you were singing last time I saw you, Cully,' he said. 'Remember?'

'I'm warning you! There's no Old Man here to bid me put up my guns this time!'

Hayden Flint spoke to the man at the tiller, his face a purposeful blank. 'Bring her alongside.'

'Up sweeps!'

'God damn you, boy!'

He judged the swell then leapt for the forechains and swung up easily. Below, the master's mate waited with a coiled rope. The old shipboard tang of hemp and tar and spices wrenched his guts.

None of the lascars moved to lay hold of him. Their dilemma was plainly agonizing: their captain had spoken, but the tale of the son of Flint Sahib was already an epic in Bengal. Cully might be *na-khuda*, but this was the true Prince of the House of Flint.

Cully stuck both pistols in his face. 'McBride!'

A redheaded youth came up. He had a narrow face that the tropical sun had blasted full of freckles. He carried a krenging hook taken off a whaler.

Hayden Flint stopped them both dead with a formal bark, and produced a paper. 'Captain Joyce McCulloch, it is my duty to inform you the merchant ship *Wager* is hereby commandeered by authority of the Honourable East India Company, the Governor of the Madras Presidency, and the garrison commander of Fort St David, in whose name and with whose powers I now take control of this ship. Now step aside.'

The effect of the words on Cully was mortifying. He had buried the name of Joyce McCulloch half a lifetime before when quitting the Royal Navy. He had thought and hoped the name had passed from the world for ever, but to hear it spoken by a uniformed man in a public declaration came close to his most hideous nightmare. He lowered his guns a fraction, and Hayden Flint took them from him smoothly, barrels first, so that everyone aboard gasped at his courage.

Orders were issued to make sail. The men of Robert Clive's improbable army came aboard, twenty at a time, and the strongest were put to work, leaning their breasts into the bars of the windlass to raise up the anchor.

An hour after weighing, they were sailing large on the starboard tack, on a course that would bring them to Madras, the helmsman coaxing the benefit from a moderate land breeze. Clive's redcoats were settled between decks in lieu of a more sweet-smelling cargo.

Hayden Flint went forward up the lee side in a quiet moment and asked McBride, 'How is my father?'

'Quite well, what I seen.'

'And his finances?'

McBride cocked back his head and shot a quid of spittle expertly through the gap in his teeth and into the foaming water. 'Doan know.' A look of secret delight spread over his face. 'Joyce! That really the capt'n's name?'

'Yes.'

McBride sniggered. 'That pole-axed him, right enough. First time I seen him rooted like that.'

'It's common enough for a man to bear his mother's maiden name.'

'Aye, but Joyce! Wait while we reach Fort William!'

'I wouldn't advise that,' he said quietly.

McBride scrutinized him suspiciously. 'Why would that be, then?'

'Seems to me a lad like you might be thinking about setting up as a trader himself one day.'

'One day.' McBride digested the remark further. 'What if I am?'

Hayden Flint shrugged casually. 'It's a hard world. No point in making enemies without need. A trader wants all the help he can get.'

'I see what you're saying, Mr Flint, you being something at St David now.'

'Who knows what might happen there, eh? About my father . . .'

McBride slid round against the heel of the deck and rested his back against the rail. He ran his eye along the distant horizon to windward. 'His Honour's prospering.'

'I had it he even cleared his debts with Omi Chand.'

'That happened a long time since.'

He grunted. 'Must be the first one ever to get out of that usurer's coils.'

'Could be.'

'How did he do it, do you think?'

The youth shrugged. 'Bengal's a bounteous land. The Moorish king, Aliverdi Khan by name, he keeps it tight and tidy. His Honour says strong government be trade's best friend.'

'And here? Do you think he'll rebuild the Madras godown?'

'It may be he will. He has dealings with Charles Savage and others.'

'Still?'

'Aye. It's a fact that Mr Savage only just got out of ruin by the greatest of efforts during his time at Calcutta. Whereas once your father was nothing beside him, that ain't true now.'

'You know, McBride, they had almost grown to be equals the year before the French war started.'

'Aye. Your father says Mr Savage never dealt with him square once before the war. Always thought himself the master and your father the man. But the Carnatic wars has changed all that. It has meant good trade at Madras. Nothing ventured has come out half so well as Flint's supply to the Company's forces since old St George came back to us. Your father, he's got Savage where he wants him now.'

'He always told me war was no good for trade.'

'Not in general, but this one is – on a special account.'

'Is that so?'

McBride leaned forward like a conspirator. 'Comp'ny rations.'

'Company rations are profitable, then?'

'Aye. Since your Captain Clive's appointment as Commissary.'

He nodded slowly at that, looked up at the masthead and strolled back amidships.

So that's it, he thought. Clive's been fixing it exclusively with the Flint concern! How much did he get Sawyer to agree to it? Three fanams per man per day. Four? That's riches! Fever, by God? Convalescence? He's been at Calcutta trading. They've been dragging it out of the Company and splitting it. Sweet Jesus, is nothing sacred!

George Pigot met them at Madras. Solid and fleshy and sweating, with a straw hat he always wore to keep his slit-eyes in shadow. Cynical and world-weary himself, he was surrounded by a throng of keen young volunteers.

'I heard Sawyer's Council tried to persuade de Gingens to move on Arcot,' Pigot said, frowning over the letter.

'How did you get hold of that?' Clive asked. 'Arcot was only so much as mentioned yesterday.'

'Damned Council chambers are sieves. No country for a secret. You should know that.'

'De Gingens is a shroff-brained Swiss. Not the kind of man to make himself opportunities – of any kind.'

'Whereas Captain Clive is, I take it? With a strength less than a battalion of infantry?'

Clive's chest swelled. He pinched the broadcloth of his jacket. 'Success is a fabric you weave, Mr Pigot. Warp of efforts, weft of good fortune.'

'Yes, and you'll need good fortune aplenty.'

'That's as may be. We're marching out a company of two hundred regulars and three hundred sepoys. That's a start.'

Pigot threw up his hands like man brought suddenly to understanding. 'Is this any way to conduct business? When I think on the tenuous thread we've dangled on for so long, I tell myself we ought to quit this place. Yes, pack up the lot of what we have, and get aboard the homeward passage.'

'But we don't, do we, eh, Mr Pigot? Ne'er a coin turned back in old England without a deal more effort. That's the truth, isn't it?'

'You're a madman, Robert Clive.'

'You've said so before, Mr Pigot.'

'And doubtless will again – if I live to see you more.' He

lowered his voice. 'You realize that of your eight so-called officers only two have issued an order to soldiers afore? They're young lads. Clerks!'

'That's no matter.'

'You've have three small field guns, and you've left St David with a bare hundred defenders, and ourselves with fifty. This is . . . lunacy!'

Clive turned to those who were to become his officers. They shook firm-handedly and made introductions, even those he knew well.

'Symonds, sir!'

'Revel.'

'Trenwith, at your service, sir.'

'Harry Wilkes.'

'And I'm Billy Glass, sir.'

Hayden Flint saw how the rest followed, clustering somewhat shyly and laughingly in the way willing lads do in front of those they account men of substance. He watched the way Clive manipulated their opinions. His exploits had already put him on a pedestal, out of reach of dissent. Now he set about inspiring them. It was a magnetic talent to watch in operation.

As he stood back Hayden Flint tried to see beyond their present keenness, to what they really were. Their eagerness to be among the killing troubled him. They seemed so young; they stood about with motley weapons and bits of kit, and ate up everything Clive said. His ride to Trichinopoly had lifted his reputation. He was their hero.

'So,' Clive asked them. 'It's war for you, then, is it?'

'Yessir!'

'If you'll have us, sir.'

'We'll show Jack Frenchman British play, sir!'

'That's good enough. And you know the first three rules of soldiering, don't you, gentlemen?' A crooked smile played over Clive's mouth. 'Drill. Drill. And yet more drill. So let's get to it, if you please.'

'What? Now, sir?'

'Yes, Lieutenant Revel. Now, sir.'

Three days' marching would bring them through steamy heat to Conjeeveram. From there it was still thirty miles to Arcot.

Hayden Flint found his thoughts returning to the time when Mohan Das had led the Moghul column here; the scout had found a route that skirted the pagodas because the press of pilgrims had been too dense to pass through. He remembered Yasmin's words about the magical sacred tank whose waters rose when the multitudes came to bathe there . . . and smiled at the memory, a bittersweet smile that jagged him inside. Conjeeveram, the teeming holy city with its treasures of gold and its famous stone chain. Ah yes, Yasmin's lesson had been patience. Perhaps we'll need to remember that anew.

As night fell he counselled caution. They halted by the road, lit small fires, took off their coats and hats, but pickets were put out on the approaches. Ensign Glass was sent ahead with a dozen men to reconnoitre. He was back five hours later, grinning like a demon as he found the huddle of officers. A horse patrol had been discovered, the light of campfires giving them away.

'They were twice our number and more, sir. But we had the dark and surprise. So we upped and at them, sent them running like rabbits! They have no idea of our main strength, nor where it lies, of that I took care!'

Clive watched the young ensign's brow furrow. 'But, Billy, by tomorrow they'll know at Arcot that we're coming for them, and will have time to shut their gates.'

Groans went round.

'Is that the essence of your report?'

'I . . . yes, sir. I didn't think. I'm sorry, sir.'

'Mmmm, but don't be sorry. Perhaps you did well, after all, Billy-boy. Surprise was never ours. We couldn't have kept our approach secret long, if secret it ever was. What you showed them was a dose of terror.' He winked at Glass affirmatively. 'If they must know we're coming, it's best they be good and scared of us, eh?'

'Yes, sir. Th-thank you, sir! That's what I thought, sir.'

Clive got up and spoke briefly to his commissioned officers. Then Sergeant Burton's voice was ringing down the lines: 'Night march! Let's see you formed up in good order!'

For the next six hours they marched along the north bank of the Palar, manhandling their guns laboriously across difficult country. The full moon shivered like ice on the paddies until a wraith's mist began to well from the damp earth and obscure everything. It was in the midst of a tropical sunrise that they first saw the black spires of the Conjeeveram pagoda.

They found a scene of desolation, no one to be seen on the streets or in the marketplace. All the signs were of a hurried abandonment.

From the temple itself there came a trembling deputation with a call for parley. *Gup* about what demonic European soldiers could do had run rife through the Carnatic. Stories of massacres on the Coast, tales of supernatural proportions, magnified by the vast numbers of deserters who had melted from the Nizam's army and streamed through the land on their various ways home.

Hayden Flint wiped his face and went forward with Clive to meet long-haired sages with the stripes of Vishnu on their brows. They requested the foreigners to halt, to prevent their polluting the sanctity of the temple.

Hayden Flint said from the corner of his mouth, 'Like everything else in this country even fighting's become a damned ritual.'

Robert Clive smiled and doffed his hat in a stately fashion to the Brahmins. He said in an aside, 'Explain to them we have no designs on their people, or their city.'

He did as Clive had told him.

'The venerable one offers you his compliments but regrets that you must leave now.'

Clive forced an overripe smile. 'Tell him we have no wish to interrupt the commerce hereabouts, or to molest anyone so long as they are peaceable towards us.'

'You know they don't care a damn about the town. Or the people. They're terrified you'll defile their precincts.'

Clive growled, clapping his hat on his head. 'Tell them that a soldier's art is to avoid fighting by showing the enemy the inevitable. Best done here, I think, by maintaining a reputation for never adding an insult to an injury. It is a place of worship, after all.'

When that was accepted Clive said, 'And add this: I only want to boil the eyes of whomsoever I might find in Arcot. I see no profit in breaking plaster images. I have no need of that kind of terror, being capable of enough devastation of a real kind.'

Yes, Hayden Flint thought. It's already as if a great red dragon has descended on the land. As soon as the Brahmins spread your repute abroad, something gigantic will precede you. You're right to want to put awe and not anger in the people. It will load Chanda Sahib's garrison with anxieties like nothing else.

The dragon stamped into town. Leaden breakers of cloud rolled overhead in breathless heat, intensified by streaming humidity. Clive had spoken to them all as they filled a vacant street. 'Any man crossing a threshold for whatever reason will be flogged. The man who touches a single chicken feather will be strung up for it. Tell them what I say, Jemadar. I won't tolerate stealing. That is the law. Now, Winslowe, fetch the scout, Balram. I want a message to go to Madras this instant, a request for two eighteen-pounders.'

All day and the next they marched in darkness. No one opposed them. They pitched canvas and settled down to rest in the main heat of the day, saving the least acclimatized skins from a killing agony. Necessities of speed had cut their baggage to what they could bring without oxen. A European could barely tramp through such oppression with the weight of a musket and sufficient food and water to sustain himself. There was little respite; even at night their stumbling and the annoyance of insects added to their discomforts, and the ghostly howling of forest animals spoke out warnings like the spirits of the reincarnated.

487

When they halted on the third morning the dawn was as red as a butcher's block in the east. The air was dense and the heaviest dew he had ever known had soaked them through, the air still thick with moisture. The skies were scarcely lighter than before sunrise, eerie as an eclipse. The ominous mood intensified the superstitions of the sepoys, who were anxious to pitch their tents and get under cover.

Hayden Flint sensed the electricity in the air. Currents of wind were stirring, drifting the smoke of campfires.

Their scout brought in a significant report. He had found what he had been sent out to find: lamp lights on the towers of Arcot. It was no more than twenty miles away, and he had counted a hundred glimmerings.

'Now's the business we came here to finish, I think,' Clive said. He pulled his boots back on and took his jacket from the tentpost. 'Rouse the men up again, we'll break camp and march on Arcot instantly. It will be perfect if we can be there by tomorrow. I'll give them a first and last chance to surrender.'

Flint scoffed at Clive's brisk optimism. 'You've not so much as seen Arcot yet, and your eighteen-pounders have still to arrive – that's if ever they're sent.'

'So? We have three smaller pieces.'

He persevered. 'They're a full garrison. Despite my very best efforts, it doesn't seem I've given you an accurate impression of the strength of the place. If you believe they'll come out on demand – '

'How many do you say there are in Arcot?' Clive asked, not listening to him, gesturing with his cane at the west. 'How many?'

A sudden perverse wish to sport with Clive's dignity came over him. 'You propose a wager on it?'

Clive looked askance at him. 'If you want to. What? Say, a hundred silver rupees?'

'That's good enough.'

'And the wager shall be: How many men are inside Arcot's walls at this present instant? Lieutenant Winslowe's impartial count or estimate to apply.'

'Agreed.'

'I say a thousand, a hundred or so either way. Since that was the estimate of the Hindu at Conjeeveram.'

Hayden Flint leaned back, his foot still up on the rock that was serving as their table. 'Well, I say . . .' He narrowed his eyes and sucked on his teeth. 'Oh . . . a figure between ten and twenty thousand.'

Clive looked at him as he would a madman. 'Be serious, now, if you want a proper wager.'

'I mean what I say. Between ten and twenty thousand of them.'

'Ridiculous! In that case they'd be wedged tighter than dunnage in a Comp'ny ship's hold. Come, they don't have that many people and well you know it.'

'Then discount what I say entirely. I am after all only a plenipotentiary.'

Clive stared long and hard at him. 'Damn you, sir! Straight, now. Do you want to make the bet or not?'

'Did I not just say so?'

Clive scoffed. 'If you mean to insist I'll set a year's pay on your being wrong.'

'How much is that?'

'Let's say fifty pounds in Sterling!'

He recalled what the McBride lad had told him aboard the *Wager* about Clive's dealings as Commissary. A pure profit of four fanams per man per day, each and every day, for each and every man in the entire Presidency . . . but Clive had never given a hint of the fortune he was amassing. He said, 'A year's income to you is a nominal captaincy in the Company's pay. How can you go to fifty pounds?'

'My income's my own affair. A private matter. If I say fifty then that is my pledge!'

'In that case I'll believe your willingness to risk fifty pounds, but can you raise it?'

'Talk yourself deeper, then. I don't have a care about it. I'll show you how to raise a stake, sir! I now say a hundred in Sterling! Will you take that?'

It was so easy to rouse him. 'No, I will not. But I'll take five hundred.'

'Damn you! A thousand, sir, if you wish it!'

'Done!'

'Aye, done! And devil take you, sir! Ten thousand men, indeed!'

They wrote out promissory notes to one another and gave them to Lieutenant Winslowe. Then they shook hands violently, and Clive simmered in the steaming air as the columns formed up again. 'Ten to twenty thousand, by God! The man's affected!'

They marched through the morning and the skies grew no lighter. The winds blew up enough to make the palms and plantains roar and shred. Driven ripples chopped up on stretches of flat water and leaf litter and dust skeltered along the road ahead of them. Lightning flickered livid all round. The fields were deserted.

The white ostrich trim of Clive's tricorn boiled and flew as he gestured broadly around the horizon. 'The vaisyas – they're all hiding away.'

'They're peasants, and they know it's about to break.'

'It'll be a right downpour when it does.'

'But it's more than that,' he told Clive. 'They deify nature and believe storms to be heavenly warfare. Lightning is the scourge of the gods, so to stay out under the sky is counted open defiance.'

'Damned superstitions!'

'There aren't many in England who'll curse God in his own parish church – especially in a storm.'

Thunder rumbled continuously round the circuit of the sky as they pushed on, then a curtain of warm rain lashed in suddenly from behind them, hissing. It pelted hard on their backs, a coarse deluge, so that they were soaked in seconds. The dirt road became a boiling ochre soup. Water buffalo stared up mournfully from their wallows, haloed in spray. As he walked he saw that young rice shoots were beginning to submerge under the livid flashes of the reflected sky. He also saw that the sepoys were in agony of mind.

The column approached a village of thatched huts that straddled the road. It was Clive's intention to ignore it completely. His mind was made up: they were marching to Arcot; they must be there tomorrow. And what was a little rain?

Black openings yawned in each dwelling, but these were not abandoned houses; faces huddled in the darknesses within, the fear showing in the wide eyes and the tightness with which the women held their babies. Their terror could not have been more abject if the column had been a real dragon come down from the moon.

Hayden Flint felt a strange prickling on his skin. Then, at the end of the line of huts, a searing light flashed purple and a terrific clap rocked him in the same instant. The column halted involuntarily. He shook his head, blinded by the persistence of the image in his eyes, wiped the rain from his face and stared.

The electric bolt had hit a large tree no more than a hundred yards away, engulfing it in a fire that smoked white and guttered in the rain. Shouting broke out. He looked back and saw numbers of sepoys breaking ranks and heading for the houses as their NCOs tried to prevent them. A few were unconcerned, some torn, but most were desperate to get under cover.

As muskets clattered down and packs were thrown off, Clive's anger boiled up. 'Get them back into line, Jemadar!'

'No! Let them go,' Hayden Flint warned. 'Give them orders to billet here. Wait for the storm to pass, or you'll force them to defy you!'

'We must be at Arcot by tomorrow! Before Chanda Sahib can reinforce. Before he gets a true picture of our strength. We can't sleep in a storm, so we must march! They can rest later!'

'If you insist you'll have a rebellion!'

'Out of my way, sir!'

Hayden Flint saw the whole enterprise dissolving, like pillars of salt melting in the rain. There was nothing he could do.

When he stood aside, Clive ordered his men to drag the runaways out of the houses and into the open, but as fast as they were thrown back into the street they scrambled away again. Swirling rain continued to drench and blind them.

The undignified farce persisted for long minutes, even Clive himself bundling men out into the open, shaking the limp figures furiously. Hayden Flint stared around, helpless and angry. No musket'll fire in these conditions, he thought, and it's a horror I dare not contemplate to see the Company's soldiers fall on their comrades with bare steel. Thank God no one had yet drawn a blade. Suddenly, Clive seemed to recognize the futility of the struggle. He ordered all into line who would go, and made the column retire at attention some way off. Hayden Flint went with it. Still the village huts bulged with panic-stricken sepoys. Clive stood in the centre of the street, looking around for a moment. His shoulders sagged and he turned about, his hands open to them in appeal. The clamour inside the huts stilled as they began to watch him.

He took off his hat, walked the street slowly from end to end. Dozens of muskets and packs lay discarded in a forlorn heap. There was not a sound save the hissing of rain and the thunderous sky. Hundreds of eyes flinched each time a violent streak of light threw Clive's shadow off his body like a discarded life. But with each stroke of heavenly light the insane Englishman grew bolder and more nonchalant. A jauntiness entered his step and he looked about his cowering people like a showman at an audience, casting out comments and smiling. He captivated them with little nods of the head and a name mentioned here and there. He did a swaggering dance that was full of humour, a mime that was one part hornpipe and one part nautch girl and three parts pure Robert Clive. Every little movement he made said, 'Look you!' and 'Do you see fear?' and 'It's nothing to me!'

Hayden Flint heard a remark passed through the men at his back. 'God love 'im, will yer look at that!'

In the centre of the street again, Clive was wagging a finger at the sky, holding a dialogue with the clouds. A huge flash and bang was all he got in reply, and at that he swept a low bow and put his hat back on his head. Then he went back to the column and joined Hayden Flint at its head.

'Have the men fix bayonets, Lieutenant,' he said.

Revel saluted. 'Yes, sir.'

'The slow march, in good order, with fifes and drums, if you please. Unfurl the colours, Ensign Glass.'

'Sir!'

Sergeants' orders were bawled to march on. The men dressed six abreast on their right hand, all their pride in drill brimming over as they stepped out in the peculiar halting way of an infantry rank ordered to march off in slow time.

Extraordinary, Hayden Flint told himself, keeping as strict a step as he could to them in the heaviest rain he had ever seen. He began to laugh. Extraordinary and bizarre! A clockwork army marching ankle-deep through the flood! Thatched hovels to either side! The sky a tumult of light and noise! It's like something acted from a damned nursery rhyme, by God!

Several men broke from the huts, picked up their muskets and packs and fell in on the back of the column. Others joined them, and then the rest, anxious not to be left alone and shamed. The storm swirled up raw and angry as they left the confines of the village, but their terror of it was broken, and the road to Arcot was theirs.

NINETEEN

Yasmin approached the casement. Her heart was battered by what she had learned, and she felt the anger that had been forming like fist inside her all day.

Nearby, a tiny yellow bird fluttered in its golden cage, hopping from perch to perch. Unrest was in the air. Over the Old Town smoke and the red glow of fire had blemished the purity of the sky. Trouble smouldered in the hours of daylight and flared in the hours of darkness, and a looming, inescapable fear hung over the whole country.

Last night she had heard the sounds of riot. There had been musket shots, and many voices. Perhaps English soldiers had been used for keeping order. Whether they had or not, there was turbulence among the lower castes. Food was growing scarce and expensive, and beyond the palace even water was rationed.

She sighed. There were other, more pressing, matters demanding attention. She watched Nadira and Khair-un-Nissa from the enclosed balcony, knowing that if she did not intervene soon the Englishwoman must fall victim to their schemes.

Outside in the garden a dented goblet had been found on the path. On the marble bench where Arkali had sat there were traces of white powder, like ground sugar, but not sugar because it had burned the eunuch's mouth when he had tried to taste it . . .

It was a poison made from zerumbet and cobra venom. Few knew the secrets of the ritual with which it was prepared. Despite the growing easiness between them, Arkali had never confided anything important of her feelings to Yasmin, and she refused to disclose who had given her the powder – or to admit whether she still possessed any of it.

She's so distrustful, so hard to talk to, Yasmin thought. And just as I thought we were closing the chasm between us.

'You must accept kismet,' Yasmin had counselled her.

The green eyes glinted like emeralds. 'After being kidnapped, and brought here a slave? For the gratification of some fat and loathsome old man?'

'What are you saying?'

'You know very well!'

'Be at peace here. Enjoy the luxuries afforded you. Open your heart a little to your new sisters.'

'Sisters? I will not convert to Islam. I shall never master your language. And I want nothing to do with the witchcraft that is practised here.'

'Oh! Fortune-telling is not witchcraft.'

'Your people are always looking for ways to predict the future.'

'Whereas your people seek to make the future in the image of your desires. You are none of you content with the lot God has given you.'

'Ugh! You have no faith in achievement. Your people will not strive for improvement.'

'Your people try to falsely shape all creation as you would have it.'

Arkali stared at the far horizon. 'And we succeed. I am accustomed to my own world. I would never have left it, but for . . .'

Tears filled her eyes, and Yasmin took pity on her. 'You are so sad, so full of despair.'

'Yasmin Begum, I would do anything to be free of this place!'

She said as kindly as she could, 'Put aside your thoughts of freedom. I, better than anyone, have come to know they are illusions. Neither be restless in your mind. Some day you will awaken and feel accustomed to this world.'

'I do not think I shall ever feel that way within your walls.'

'Truly we are behind these walls, but what is beyond? The citadel is locked against the town, and the town secured against a sea of enemies. The whole land is stalked by lawlessness and banditry. No one is free. There is fear and grief for all. So, take the moment in which you dwell. Here and now there is peace, and a refuge. Open your heart to it, for our lives are but a brief blooming. And such peace as we now have will not always be ours.'

'Do you call this peace?'

'Perhaps peace is state of the soul, not a state of the world.'

'Foolishness!'

'Not so. Oh, you are as selfish as a newborn baby! You believe you are the centre of all Creation, but you are not. Think rather that you are a little soul bearing about a corpse wherever you go. That way you will see your true importance in the world, and you will learn humility.'

Arkali fell sulky again at that until she glimpsed a plump young woman walking in the garden beside the fountains, a living gift who had been presented to the nawab by a minor prince to seal some territorial matter. The girl stopped and looked around, but failed to see them observing her. She continued down to the place where the crack opened in the walls.

Arkali pointed. 'Look – '

Yasmin touched her finger to her lips. 'Shhh!'

'But isn't that Umm-Kulsum? What is she doing?'

'Risking her life.'

'You mean . . . an affair?'

'An assignation. She meets at the wall with a man.'

'A man? Oh, who is he?'

'A soldier. Of a northern jagir.'

'Oh?' Arkali scrutinized with hungry eyes, but what was to be seen except a lilac veil? The girl's eyebrows met in the middle, she had a twisted tooth and a faint moustache; she was not a great beauty – her name meant Mother of Plumpness.

'How does she know him, this soldier?'

'It's rumoured he was her lover before she was presented to our lord.'

'Isn't she taking a great risk?'

'Oh, yes. What she is doing is strictly forbidden.'

'But surely to risk her life for a man is folly?'

'She has not been with us very long. The pain must be keen still.'

Arkali watched for a while, then she turned, as if prompted by a sudden thought. 'So. I think now you must admit there are others here besides myself who have not yet learned to master the art of surrender?'

Something dissolved in Yasmin then. It was as if the practical spiritual advice she had given the Englishwoman to help her survive had clashed with her own personal beliefs. 'No,' she said, 'you are not the only one to feel imprisoned.'

'What? An admission that this is not paradise? From you, the grand advocate of submission?'

'You have misjudged me.'

'Oh? Have I indeed?'

There was such haughty disregard in the Englishwoman's tone that Yasmin said, 'There was once a man in this world for whom I almost gave my life – for whom I would gladly give my life now, if I could see him once more.'

'You speak of the nawab?'

'Oh, no. Not he.'

Arkali's emerald eyes lit. 'What's that? You've had an affair? I don't believe it. When? Tell me.'

Yasmin felt weak, and in that moment she dropped her defences. 'Oh, but it is an old scandal now, and not worth the telling.'

Arkali lifted a small honey pastry to her lips. 'Please, why not tell me? It will pass the time nicely, and show me the side of yourself that you have tried to hide away.'

Yasmin hesitated. This was wrong. Too close to her heart. To speak of Hayden to this silly, weak, shallow woman would not be right. Instead, she turned to lore, to tell and yet not to tell. 'You know, the zenana at Arcot was artfully made. There were many secret ways within. Such secrets were guarded fiercely. Venerable grandmothers used to tell a story of days long past, of Dost Ali and his favourite concubine, Ayisha, who was Hindu. The nawab was then in his failing years, but Ayisha was in her fullest flowering. When Dost Ali discovered she was in love with a young man he became deranged.

'One night he waited for them to meet. His soldiers rushed into the gardens and surrounded her chamber so that there could be no escape. The nawab threw himself at the doors. His veteran sword was drawn in his hand – he was ready to kill. He had vowed to have the youth cast from a high tower so that Ayisha would be forced to see the beauty she had destroyed by her faithlessness.

'Dost Ali would have killed them both, but when he broke down the door of the bedchamber there was no one within, save two blood-red butterflies on the bedpost.'

Perhaps the story had not run as Arkali expected. She gave a little grunt of dismissal, but she continued to listen.

'Amazed by this miracle, Dost Ali laid down his sword, gathered up the butterflies and released them at the window. Afterwards he made the bedchamber into a shrine.'

'A nursery story. And one, if I may say, that has little point to it.'

'No, this is not a story for children. Tales of women who defy the law and live are not common. We do not tell such stories often.'

And despite herself, Arkali saw there was a point to the story, because she said, 'What you're saying is this: it is the secret dream of some women to defy the law. No matter what the penalties, they will always, in their hearts, long for the outside world, and some will go so far as to seek it.' She looked slyly at Yasmin. 'And I thought no one here understood me. Really understood. Now I see you do. What does your story say happened to the butterflies?'

'The story says nothing of that.' Yasmin's mood had

clouded. 'Maybe the gods forced one to stay for ever in Dost Ali's garden . . . while the other flew away over the walls. Who can say?'

There was a space of silence. The fragrance of spices wafted on the warm air. Then Arkali said, 'Who was he? Your lost butterfly?'

Yasmin sighed emptily, then felt her smile become rich in regret. 'It was in Hyderabad. You will not believe me when I say to you, he was Angrezi.'

'An Englishman?' There was a wealth of expression in her response: surprise, amusement, disbelief, perhaps ridicule.

'I said, you would not believe me.'

'Why should I doubt what you say? It's just so unlikely that I – '

Yasmin looked up as the Englishwoman broke off. For a moment it seemed she was in pain because her hand went to her throat. Then she began to stare, as if she had seen a demon enter the garden.

'What was his name, this Englishman?' Her voice was barely louder than a whisper.

Then Yasmin knew it had gone too far. 'That is of no consequence.'

'Tell me. You must tell me!'

Their eyes met. There was a desperate need to know in the Englishwoman, and Yasmin decided she must tell her no more.

'What was his name?'

'Captain John Smith,' she said very deliberately. 'An officer of the Company who went long ago to Bengal.'

Arkali got to her feet, scattering the food tray perched on her lap. She looked down for a moment, piercing the lie with a look of such deadly unforgiving that Yasmin flinched to see it. Then she ran away, her maid staring after her, aghast.

Yasmin's emotions simmered now at the memory. It's strange, she thought. For a long time I didn't understand what had happened. Perhaps I didn't want to know. I lied to her without knowing why I was lying. Captain John Smith! – a foolish name to invent. Of course it was an easy lie for her to see through. There was only one explanation, and it had to be avoided.

For her part, Arkali had said nothing more of the outburst. Since then the Englishwoman had given her nothing but cold politeness, and that was more difficult to accept than her fiercest rages. What a terrible thing to feel sexual jealousy so strongly. How crippling to the spirit! And how despicable of Muhammad to do what he did. I can forgive anything, she thought, feeling the fist of anger begin to tighten inside her again, anything except malice.

Below, Nadira and Khair-un-Nissa passed out of view, and once more the gardens were silent.

Yasmin stood stiffly at the window, her hands at her sides, feeling the breezes of dusk ruffle her veil. I bear Arkali no ill-will, she thought. On the contrary, I'm sorry for her. She is surely the greatest victim of my husband's vicious games.

Why do I feel responsible for her misfortunes? Now she has learned a little of our language, she's less dependent on me. She gives my advice too little consideration, but she is learning. Since she is not yet fully fledged in our way of life, she does not see the dangers that surround her. She cannot survive without allies. If Nadira wants her dead she will be killed, unless someone protects her. I must continue to do so, whether she wants my help or not.

Yasmin turned and stepped back from the casement. The hard knot of rage was forming faster in her now, the fist clenching tight inside her chest, and inside the fist was the vow she had made to Muhammad. There was no doubt that Muhammad had conceived this kidnapping as an intricate torment.

An Englishwoman . . .

At first she had believed it was simply his sexual curiosity. That would have been understandable, for men were infinitely curious about women's bodies. Later, it seemed that Arkali had been abducted because her father owed gold to the sarafs of Arcot, and later still that she had been taken hostage as part of a piece of gutless political manoeuvring. But no.

Muhammad had not ordered his men to steal just any pretty Englishwoman, nor to imprison a bankrupt's daughter or take a suitable hostage – he had sent them to collect the particular woman betrothed to Hayden Flint Sahib.

Could it then have been done to punish Hayden Flint? No!

Muhammad had chosen cruelty. He had abused his power and his promise, he had given orders designed to cause Yasmin pain for one reason alone: because he liked to cause her pain.

She felt the fist inside her tightening and tightening until it was unbearable. It was done to torture me! He believed it would stab me deeper than any knife. And all this while I humbly and diligently tried to keep my vows . . . I even agreed to help subdue Arkali for him.

He said I must be her mentor, told me to be her friend. But he did not tell me who she was. Oh, wicked man! He did not tell me because he wanted me to find out in time – like this. He wanted me to see her green eyes, her copper hair and pale skin, her strange beauty, and therefore be plunged into a hell of jealousy! Oh, stupid man! Stupid, worthless, malicious fool! What have you done?

She looked at the pathetic little bird behind its golden bars and opened the cage on an impulse. As she stepped back, the bird hopped through the opening and darted for a star-shaped hole in the window. There was a brief flutter of yellow and it was gone.

Suddenly the unbearable pressure inside the fist burst, and she felt the tension inside her run free. No, she thought. I am not jealous of Arkali Savage's pale skin. She is a pitiful creature, selfish and immature and inconsiderate. But, Muhammad, you have roused me to hatred. You have gone far, far beyond our agreement. You have deliberately mistreated your only wife, and the vows I made to you are hereby broken.

Arkali grunted as the air was forced from her lungs, the pressure on her bare skin almost intolerable. Fragrant oil was trickled into the small of her back and the kneading of the masseuse's fingers drove the stiffness from her muscles, making her skin silk-smooth.

They had bathed her and shaved her, combed out her hair and plaited it into a tress. Soon they would return to make up her face like a Moghul princess, with black kohl for her eyes, sindoor to mark her brow and beeswax to redden her lips. They would trace intricate henna designs on her palms and the soles of her feet to complete the Rituals of Adornment.

Ten days ago a female astrologer had come to interview her. The questions had been despicable, indelicate, horrid. The crone had left her pronouncing the day when the phase of the moon would be correct for her to be received by her lord.

Two weeks had passed since the last time she had spoken with the nawab's wife: plenty of time to think over what had been said.

'How she tried to lie,' she whispered through clenched teeth. Her attendants nodded and smiled like good-natured nurses. They had been warned of the Angrezi woman's strangeness, but knowing nothing of English they had grown used to ignoring her words. 'Your sister lied to me. But she could not hide it from her eyes. She stole Hayden. At the court of Hyderabad she bewitched him, and damn the bitch to hell for what she's done!'

She thought of the deadly powder. The remaining portion was safe among her private things, alongside the bonnet pin with the metal butterfly and the special gold ring with the chips of sky-blue in it.

Yesterday, so many jewels had been laid out for her to inspect in the rosy-pale glow of dawn. While the dew lingered on the grass they showed her complex pendant earrings of pearl and ruby, a casket of finger rings, all pure gold and finely worked. There were long strings of pearls, brooches and hair clasps of solid gold, and a diamond stud to fit the nose from which three fine chains looped to an ear stud.

They had brought ornaments for the rest of the body, too: bands for the upper arms from which tassels hung, bracelets, anklets – circlets for all parts of the limbs, it seemed – and a zaraband girdle to loop across her hips.

At last she had lifted up the choker of fine gold links, an inch deep, and trimmed with alternating red and green squares of emerald and ruby, edged in tiny seed pearls, clasped so artfully that, when closed, it was impossible to see how it could be opened.

A flush of tremendous power had passed through her as she fingered the object, heating her face and chest. It was like looking at a tinsel travesty of the finery of her own cancelled marriage. To imagine herself dressed like a slave in these things – only these things – before a man made full of desire by them . . . and by her.

In that moment she let the casket fall, and as the appalled maids scurried to pick up the contents, she saw that a big ring had been left on the cushion beside her. She picked it up and examined it: chased gold and chips of turquoise drew her eye. Then she saw the concealed hinge, and had understood what it was. How could it have got here? A ring like this? An object of such lethal purpose? She had snapped shut the secret compartment and added the ring to her selection.

Now a steamy humidity hung in the air of the bathhouse. The masseuse finished her work, and Arkali was lightly towelled so that the sheen of her skin was buffed to a glow. They brought her muslins so fine they might have been spun by spiders. The chest in which they had been kept was strongly scented with camphor and other essences, incenses to complement the colours and textures of these most erotic garments.

They had taught her that to resist was useless. She put her arms into the short-sleeved choli, a fine bodice shot with gold thread that transparently clothed her breasts. As she breathed the musk, she experienced the stifling closeness of an orchid house. The confining inevitability of what was happening to her pressed in all around, and there welled up in her a desire to run screaming for the walls, to hammer upon the studded doors until they broke open.

Only the thought of the butterfly pin prevented her, and she fixed her mind on it. The ring would do her bidding, and the bonnet pin would be her insurance. When Muhammad Ali reached out to touch her, she would embrace him with death. The pin would slide from her hem, and its tip would enter his heart, stopping it. She would do that. Yes, she would do it without remorse. To pay him back for what he had done to her.

The gossiping in the chambers beyond frothed louder. She listened, heard Yasmin Begum's voice, then broke away from her attendants, demanding to know what was being said. They would tell her nothing, but Yasmin came – the creature who had stolen her husband-to-be, the woman who had twisted her life so cruelly, and who by so doing had destroyed her future. Yasmin, the chief architect of her fate.

'Arkali? What troubles you?'

'I want to know what they're saying.'

Yasmin's dark eyes ran quickly over her apparel. 'Why are you dressed in those jewels?'

She felt a pang of bitter triumph. 'You should know the answer to that, since it has been done at your husband's command.'

Yasmin Begum's voice was no more than a whisper. 'The jewels are mine.'

'No longer, it seems.'

The other turned away swiftly. Then one of the gossiping girls ran up, her face lit with the desperate eagerness of a news-bringer. The excitement dropped from her when she saw the nawab's only wife and the expression on her face.

'Oh! Please excuse me, Begum.'

That much of the language Arkali knew well enough. There was a short exchange, little of which made any sense, except the words 'Angrezi' and 'Kohp Sahib'. Arkali's patience left her.

'What is she saying?'

'Nothing to concern you.'

'How dare you decide what might or might not concern me? Tell me!'

'Very well. There has been another riot in the town. It seems it has been quelled.'

'A riot? Over what?'

'This time trouble between Hindu and Muslim, mistrust sparked by hunger. Captain Cope and Captain de Gingens have barely enough men to keep order among the palace guard. If more violence breaks out in the town they will not be able to control it.'

Arkali felt a pang of hope and fear combined, but it was quickly overwhelmed by the knowledge that even if a riot broke out this instant it would be too late to change anything for her.

'We must hope the Captain has sent for reinforcements.'

'We must hope.'

One of the older sisters raised her hands to heaven, wailing.

'What is she saying?'

'She says we must not hope, we must pray. She says the Prophet taught that Allah is the master of all Creation. His way is merciful. In Him there is a sure haven in times of trouble. There must be no murmurings at His decrees.'

'No murmurings? Why, then you deserve all that comes to you!'

'Perhaps,' Yasmin said, turning to leave. 'I think it is as the English say: "The Lord best helps those who strive on their own behalf." As for you, I warn you to help yourself also. Beware Nadira Begum, for she means you harm.'

And she was gone.

Arkali felt the woman's briskness sober her. It was undeniably satisfying to think that Yasmin had seen her like this. She stole Hayden from me, she thought. Now it's my turn to rob her.

The moment for her presentation to the nawab had come. A chamber had been prepared. There was a bed of many cushions spread with silk and hung with velvet. He would be there, even now. Ready. Waiting for her to be brought.

There was little time left. 'I must compose myself,' she told the women. 'I would like some wine. Red wine. Then I would like to be alone.'

The senior attendant nodded to the youngest maid and she left the chamber. Arkali went quietly to her belongings and slipped the gold and turquoise ring on to her finger. The pin she used to secure her veil in such a way that its deadly length was not obvious.

When the wine was brought and poured, she held it up to look at its colour: deep and old and peppered with sediment. Perfect. She took a sip, then a longer draught, and stared out at the garden, turning her back on her women. It was not difficult to open the secret compartment of the ring and let the white crystals fall in. They disappeared instantly into the rich, ruby-red liquid.

When she turned back, Nadira's eunuch had opened the doors. Nadira herself emerged from behind his bulk like an ancient procuress. 'It is time for you to come,' she said. She took the wine glass from Arkali's hand and examined her face critically, with cruel eyes. 'Just a moment,' she said, taking the corner of a handkerchief. Moistening it, she began to dab delicately at the corners of Arkali's mouth, the way a mother might treat a child who had been eating messily. The red wine must have stained her lips.

Yasmin's words boiled furiously in Arkali's mind: Beware Nadira Begum . . . How the old queen despises me, she thought. They say Nadira tries to control everything her son does. To her I must be a symbol of his independence. Khair-un-Nissa is her means of controlling him, but what if he begins to desire me instead?

She reached out to recover the glass, but Nadira moved away. Arkali's heart pounded: she must get to the wine glass, she must have it. As she moved towards Nadira she saw the jealous evil in the old woman's face, then she remembered the pin, and forced herself to smile.

Nadira returned the courtesy, her own smile a grimace. She had only come here to gloat, knowing that for Arkali the prospect of obligatory sex was repellent, that this was a moment to feed upon.

Still smiling, Nadira watched the inner doors close on the Englishwoman, then she raised the glass and toasted the moment gleefully.

The wailing began in the early morning as the dew spangled the turf of the zenana's manicured lawns. The older sister who discovered Nadira saw she was beyond all help.

There was foaming blood on the begum's lips; stomach cramps had bent her double, starving her of breath or the capacity to cry out. The death of the queen was monstrous to behold.

The servants cowered with staring eyes. Khair-un-Nissa was summoned to the begum's rooms. She arrived accompanied by her sinister shampooer, who glanced at the unmistakable mask of death and back at her mistress for a moment before she spoke.

'Well?'

'There is no hope.'

Khair-un-Nissa's eyes dwelt for moments on her ruined future before her poise deserted her and she rained blows on her shampooer's head. Fear turned the courtesan's slim elegance into the angular violence of a feral cat.

By now the whole zenana was awake. Yasmin pulled on her shawl and started towards the uproar. It's begun, she thought, still groggy. Only a revolt could shatter the peace as completely as this.

Suddenly her arm was wrenched hard and she staggered sideways into a niche. She felt a big hand pressing over her mouth, and was horrified that a man had breached the security of this forbidden place so soon. She struggled, suspecting the next shock would come against her ribs, the punch of a knife being thrust into her, then tensed, scratching blindly at the air, knowing there was nothing she could do against so strong an assassin.

Is this the way it ends? a voice asked.

It was the calm, disappointed voice of her soul. In that dilated interval of time she was amazed at her inner composure. The overwhelming emotion was not fear, but annoyance that death had caught her unprepared.

Then a hard voice hissed in her ear and time moved forward again. 'Keep still, Begum. I will not harm you. Please do not cry out or I will be discovered!'

She gasped as his hand was taken away. 'How dare you touch me, scoundrel? How dare you presume to enter the zenana of your master?'

'I come with tidings for you, Begum.'

It was Umar, once Anwar-ud-Din's news-gatherer. She composed herself indignantly. 'You risk death.'

'I know it, Begum.'

'What miracle made you invisible? The eunuchs who guard our world have sharp eyes.'

'But my mission is well starred, and gold has the power to blind men for a little while.'

'Speak quickly. You must be gone, or we will both die.'

'My informants come with news – of Flint Sahib.'

'*Allah ke kudrat!*' God's power!

'His Angrezi soldiers have captured Arcot.'

The news paralysed her mind. 'But how? Why? What you say makes no sense. The Englishman, Clive, promised that an English army would be sent to relieve us here . . .'

Umar's eyes stared solemnly at her confusion. 'It is surely that same English army which was sent instead to Arcot.'

'Then we are destroyed!'

'No, Begum, all is not lost. It was a most clever initiative. The Angrezi army camped in the Brown Hills outside the city of Arcot. All night the sky was full of such lights and noise as you have never seen! As the Europeans came to the gates Chanda Sahib's peons ran away. Most of his people have not seen such red coats and big black hats and of course they took them for devils. Or worse, an army that has fought with devils – and won.'

She put her hand over her mouth, then drew it away and begged, 'Tell me of Flint Sahib.'

'He is very well.'

'Allah is merciful!' The shock of Umar's sudden appearance made her come back at him. 'But who may trust the dispossessed? Who may trust a man who has scorned his new master?'

'Do not say that, Begum. I remain an honest man, though my love for your husband is not the love I had for his father.'

'I need proof of your words, scoundrel.'

'Then surely this is it.'

She took the cloth he pulled from his pouch and unwrapped it. A letter in the English style, its envelope bearing her name in sloping script, caused memories of Hayden to thrill through her, as strong as ever.

She thought furiously. 'If their army has marched to Arcot, we are forsaken. We are relying on the English to drive away Chanda Sahib's armies from these gates.'

'They cannot come here – they are so few. But now Chanda Sahib is enraged. He has sent his son, Raza, with five thousand horse to Arcot!'

'So leaving five thousand here? Then we are still doomed. Unless the siege can be lifted and supplies brought in soon we will all begin to starve.'

Umar spread his big hands. 'It will not come to that.'

She heard a sound and hushed him, looking around fearfully. 'Be careful, Umar. Something terrible has happened. Tonight the sisters and their servants have been especially tense and watchful because of the Englishwoman.'

'Do you not know that Nadira Begum is dying?' He marvelled at her ignorance. 'That is why I have come here now, risking my life. Because it is urgent, and because you are now our only hope.'

Yasmin's mind reeled. 'I, Umar?'

'Yes, Begum. When Nadira is dead the last trace of the old days will be gone, and also the last rein holding back Lord Muhammad Ali's zeal. You will be the first lady of the zenana. It will be your responsibility to prevent this disaster.'

'What are you telling me?'

'That the Hindu of the Old Town are about to rise up.'

'They are hungry, they fear for their families. But how do you imagine I can deliver them?'

'It is not the want of food that stirs them. They have known famine, and their gods have always given them the strength to suffer.'

She felt her frustration growing. Umar's keen mind leapt and bounded, making those who heard his arguments think themselves slow and dull, but sometimes he seemed to delight deliberately in obscurity. She remembered Anwar-ud-Din and coolly commanded him, 'Explain yourself simply.'

Umar's Adam's apple bobbed as he swallowed, and his large hands moved in explanation. 'There are tales circulating among the pilgrims at Conjeeveram that our lord wants to pollute their tank. Even here the people have begun to believe his Islamic faith will drive him to destroy their choultries. You must beseech him to allay those fears, or this citadel will surely revolt. The Angrezi soldiers will be murdered even as they sleep.'

'The gates will be thrown open to the Raja of Tanjore,' she said, seeing it clearly. 'They will kill Muhammad.'

'No, Begum.' Umar's eyes were polished steel in the darkness of the alcove. 'Worse. They will give him to the French.'

A cold hand gripped her heart. She thought about Umar's words, then made a decision based on expediency alone.

'French, you say?'

'Yes, Begum.'

'In that case it must be prevented.'

*

Muhammad, the fool! Muhammad will kill us all with his intolerance!

She strained to listen at the closed curtain of the palanquin. The cries of the Untouchables in the street could be heard, making her heart heavy, calling out their tireless warnings in case a Brahmin should step on their shadow and be defiled.

The tank invited her. She went there veiled, humbly, to the sacred temple, to offer respect to the gods of the Hindu. At the threshold they stopped her because of her outer clothing. But she threw it off and they saw that the tucks of her sari were those of a devout person.

'But is this not the wife of the nawab?' they asked. 'How can this be?'

'Since I married I never once sought the help of the gods of my childhood. But last night, at the moment of Nadira Begum's death, a powerful feeling led me to my garden, to the tree that is special.'

'Special?'

'It is said that at Desera, and at the festival of Holi, garlands of orange flowers appear in its branches. So it stood last night. At the sight of those flower chains words from my past came drifting to me.'

And they marvelled as she sang to them a verse the cowherds and Gopis sang to their cattle in the noon heats of a late springtime long ago. They fell back before her, bidding her come into the shrine. She knelt before the image of Ganesh, Lord of Obstacles, god of scribes and merchants, elephant-headed son of Shiva and Parvati. There she offered an honest prayer for the safety of her true love who was in peril and far away. And as they watched her they knew her heart was open and pure, and when she rose she was admitted to talk with those greybeards who were the will of the city.

TWENTY

Throughout the day some ten thousand of the enemy had pushed up to occupy the outlying town of Arcot. Now, as Hayden Flint watched through his glass from the fortress walls, he could see horses grazing on the far side of the maidan and along the banks of the Palar River. Tails flicked lazily, white-swathed figures strolled among them, squatted at campfires, while kites wheeled above on the last rising airs of the day.

They might as well be vultures, he thought. To look at the mass of the enemy it's almost beyond imagining we can get out of this place alive. But Governor Sawyer said we must hold it.

The citadel of Arcot was more than a mile in circumference, but the walls were in many places ruinous, the rampart too narrow to permit the firing of artillery, the parapet low and slightly built. Several of the towers were decayed; none of them were capable of receiving more than one piece of cannon. The ditch of still green water was neglected, at its best parts probably fordable, at its worst choked up and dry. Between the foot of the walls and the ditch there was a space about ten foot broad, intended for a fausse-braye, but there was no parapet at the scarp of the ditch. Clive had pointed out the fort's two gatehouses, one to the north-west, the other to the east. Both were massively built and projected forty feet beyond the walls, but the huge wooden gates were thrown wide. No matter that the ancient masonry was thick enough to withstand days of pounding. Not a single soul of the eleven hundred men Chanda Sahib had left to guard it had awaited the coming of so awesome an army.

The wager he had sealed with Clive had come to nought. Clive had claimed a win, but Hayden Flint had denied him as Lieutenant Winslowe looked on.

'I said a thousand men, and you said between ten and twenty thousand,' Clive said.

'Arcot was deserted.'

'So I was closer.'

'Not so.'

Clive had been instantly suspicious. 'How do you figure that?'

'A dozen men would have been between ten and twenty thousand.'

'You obviously meant ten *thousand* and twenty thousand.'

'No. That is what you assumed I meant.'

Clive had looked hard at him then, and said finally, 'You are surely the son of your father, Hayden Flint.'

The forces of the Honourable East India Company had entered the fortress unopposed, taking it over lock, stock and barrel. It had taken only three days to make good the most urgent flaws in Arcot's defences. They found that the store of provisions in the fort was sufficient for only sixty days.

On the tenth day Hayden Flint awoke to see the grizzled face of Mohan Das grinning down at him.

'Sorry, sir. But he says he won't talk with no other.'

He dismissed the flustered corporal and put his hands together. 'Mohan Das, *Bahee Salam!*'

'*Ram*, Flint Sahib!' The old scout proffered a letter under the Company seal.

'I thought you were at Trichinopoly, my friend.'

'I was. Now I am here. Howareyou, sahib?'

Hayden Flint grinned back. 'And in the English too! All the better for seeing you is the answer to that question.'

The scout reverted to his own vernacular. 'I am going Trichinopoly Madras with papers from my lord nawab. In that place the Angrezi Governor is saying me: are you knowing a way for getting inside the fort of Arcot?' His heavy eyebrows lifted and his head shook. 'Not a clever question, sahib.'

'Nor better man could the Angrezi Governor have trusted to be his messenger.'

'You are too kind to a poor old beggarman, sahib!'

He took the satchel from Mohan Das, opened it, digested the contents, threw on his shirt and went to find Clive.

'Sahib, there is also better news!'

'Tell me on the way, Mohan Das.'

Clive was in his bed. His personal servant jumped up from the foot of it with a pistol in his hand as Hayden Flint shoved past the sentry.

'Oh, it's you, is it?' Clive waved the servant from the room.

'I have a letter here from Richard Prince. Governor Sawyer has sent out a relieving force. A hundred and thirty regulars with Lieutenant Innes in command.'

Clive shook the sleep from his head. 'And?'

'According to my source they have been found by Chanda Sahib's men, and have fought with some loss. Innes's force are now themselves besieged at Poonamallee.'

The news shafted Clive so that he winced. 'The fools!'

'With his last people, and anyone he can scour from the ships in the Roads, Mr Prince is looking to assemble a further force to relieve them. If and when he succeeds, he plans to put Captain Killpatrick in charge.'

Clive erupted. 'Killpatrick is a mutineer! I charged him myself! He's in jail, waiting to be shipped back to England to face – '

'What else do you suggest? He is the last remaining officer who has any understanding of how to lead a column here.'

Clive began to pace about. 'When will they realize? I don't want any damned relief!'

Hayden Flint sat down heavily, watched Clive pace. He offered a careful contribution. 'So far you've done well. I see your plan. You've built an admirable confidence in the

514

men, in their own abilities and in yours too. But you can't hope to hold Arcot for more than a week.'

Clive turned on him hotly. 'I told you that in coming time I would lead an army to great victories, and so I shall! We don't want relief. It would mean the upset of everything!'

'What do you mean?'

'I have thrown a stone into a still pond, and now I'm watching to see the ripples spread out.'

'Take care, Robert. It is a natural law of the universe that every action has an equal and opposite reaction.'

'That is as may be. But such waves as I make will excite whomsoever they touch. You told me yourself that the Regent of Mysore, for one, does not care to have a feringhee ruling the Deccan. Still less a malevolence such as Dupleix directing all the South as he pleases from Pondicherry. I want that man to call the viceroy's whole army down here!'

Hayden Flint snorted at the ludicrous hubris. He said, 'Rest assured that Salabat Jang will not come again to the Carnatic. He has his own pretenders to watch. The whole damned empire's breaking up. The Great Moghul of Delhi himself is teetering. Therefore we may take it that M'sieur de Bussy and his two thousand sepoys are not suddenly going to appear below us on the glacis.'

'Listen! You know that if we fail at Arcot, the whole house will fall! It will be the end for us in Hindostan?'

'That is in the nature of a gamble. We set out to stake all, win or lose. That was very clear.'

'Yes, to George Pigot, and Richard Prince, and the rest of them.' Clive seemed suddenly to relax. 'But you and I know quite well that the outcome is waiting to be born.' He flicked a silver rupee so that it spun on its edge across the table. 'If we can only win . . .'

'Yes, if we can win, then every tiny kingdom south of the Kistna will lose their fear of the French, knowing that the English are a match for them in arms, and that there is a remedy to be found.' Yes, he thought, watching the coin track along the grain of the tabletop. And then the great Robert Clive would make himself indispensable. As indispensable as de Bussy is to the Nizamat, and perhaps as rich. 'But are you a match for the French?'

'I told you,' said Clive, with a crooked smile. He snatched up the rupee and spun it again. 'It is already written. More, it is graven in marble tablets: I am a match for anyone.'

Hayden Flint stared back at him, slamming his hand suddenly down over the coin. 'You're talking to me, now! To the man who faced you one-to-one on the field of honour. Aye, and who saw you show yourself plainly at the vital moment. I should not need to remind you that I'm not one of your damned boys! Now tell me straight. What chance do we have of holding here?'

Clive stared back dangerously for a second, then he scratched his chin as if chastened. 'None, without faith. With faith . . . anything is possible.'

'And what about Trichinopoly?' asked Flint, meaning Arkali Savage and the solemn promise they had made.

An ugly laugh escaped Clive. 'That damned Swiss is almost wholly unserviceable, but even de Gingens may sit still adequately. Whatever happens, Muhammad Ali will never allow him to do otherwise. De Gingens's men are the only reason our nawab's head remains upon his shoulders.'

'I have little doubt that your idea of marching here is far from Rudolph de Gingens's conception of how to wage a war. Do you think Madras may make another gesture?'

'Madras has no more ordnance. Without guns infantry will never reach us here.'

'Robert, how long are we provisioned for?'

'Not long. It depends how many of us carry over from one day to the next.'

'Then it's clear we cannot wait for another ship to anchor at Madras. And since no one will come chasing up-country, we're on our own . . . There's little consolation to be had from these,' he added, putting the satchel on Clive's table. 'Read them.'

The Chevalier Mouhy and 300 men had left Pondicherry for Arcot. Neither the Regent of Mysore nor Morari Rao had ridden to bolster Muhammad Ali.

He watched Clive put down the papers and then continued to stare into space. His mind turned over the narrowing alternatives.

It's straightforward enough, he thought. I'm seeing Clive face the greatest decision of his life, but I'm unwilling to offer him any advice. It's as Governor Sawyer said, once the siege begins there'll be no prospect of a relief. But to withdraw now'll be suicide to the Company's interests. The top two layers of government have been wiped away in this province. The Carnatic's now a patchwork of hundreds of local killadars and landowners, all of them faced with the choice of offering their loyalty to one or other of the European powers. How many of them will declare for us if we're seen running from the French?

Clive picked up the papers again and spoke Richard Prince's words: 'He says, "I always thought the King of Mysore was not in earnest, or he would have sent his troops long ago . . . We don't know what turn the expedition may have given affairs, nor what prejudice a sudden retreat may be, but you are the best judge of the situation." He's put it in writing. Handing it down to me, bless his white liver.'

'And?'

'And I say – we fight.'

He left Clive and almost walked into Lieutenant Revel.

'What's happening?' Revel asked.

Hayden Flint shrugged. 'I watched two thousand more men join Chanda Sahib from Vellore. There are three hundred and twenty-two of us inside, ten thousand outside. In term of Europeans, there are seven Frenchmen to every Englishman.'

'The five and twentieth day of September,' Revel said ominously.

Hayden Flint watched the horizon, saying nothing to Revel about the small movement that had caught his eye. 'Or the fourth of October, by French reckoning.'

'However that's squared up, I think we'll never see Christmastide.'

517

'With small rations we may stretch our food for a month. Who knows what may happen in a month?'

'I would gladly ream another hole in my belt – if I thought it would be needed. I predict we shall all be in our graves a week from now.'

'You should not say such things, not even in jest.' Hayden Flint peered closely at the place beyond the glacis where someone from the enemy camp waved a white rag. It's a signal, he thought. Someone wants to talk. What else could it be? A ruse? He looked at the lieutenant. Coming on the death of his close friend, Trenwith, the enemy's ultimatum had knocked much of the spirit out of him. Hayden Flint offered him a pinch from his snuffbox.

'No, thank you.'

'Look at those birds circling there.'

'Vultures,' Revel said morosely. 'Ugly birds, but they know their business. Look at me, Mr Flint. You know, I thought I could be something in this world. Before ever coming to this shore I had planned to be something grand one day.'

'Sweet Jesus, Lieutenant, you are not the Delphic oracle! You cannot possibly say what will happen in something so complex as a siege.'

'It seems simple enough now, Mr Flint. We surrender today, and march back to Madras under escort, or they will overwhelm us, cut out our eyes and tongues . . . and worse.'

'It's the standard form hereabouts to offer all manner of privileges to those who will meekly surrender, and to promise perdition to those who will not. Don't think on it too hard.'

'We're trapped with no hope of relief. What else may I think?'

Hayden Flint tapped a little snuff on to his hand and sniffed it up. 'The longer I live the more I believe that prophecies will oftentimes fulfil themselves. The best armament against bad luck is optimism.'

'That's not a view I would expect from a Natural Philosopher such as you, Mr Flint.'

He wiped his nostrils with his handkerchief and felt the powdered tobacco burn up into the space behind his eyes. 'Suffice to say I have no understanding of the mechanism, but the empirical evidence has persuaded me. What the mystics of Hindostan call karma, and the Mussulmen call kismet, is no more than the science of cause and effect. Our European system of thought has yet to tackle causation and prediction, except in very simple, mechanical ways.'

Revel thought about that, then said, 'I understand a weight hanging, making a pendulum swing, thereby regulating the clock. We may say that if this time is noon, then one hour hence will be one of the clock, and the angles of the hands will at that time be disposed so and so. Is it not science to suppose it is thus with everything?'

'Perhaps that is European science.'

'But you think things proceed otherwise?'

'I have been forced to that opinion.' He shrugged.

Yasmin put her hand to her mouth, stifling a gasp of recognition.

In the furnace heat of the day dust stirred and twisted across the flagged courtyard below. Its stone was exposed to the merciless noonday sun, but the soughing of trees destroyed the usual silence of this, the Hour of Small Shadows.

In the cool interior, the fountains hissed into the pool and everyone dozed. Without wine she had been unable to sleep, and instead had gone to the balcony window to read, but a movement had caught her eye. Through the pierced screen of white marble she watched the blue flame of Khair-un-Nissa's diaphanous garments trailing in the hot breath of the day. The courtesan was heading towards the nawab's apartments.

A heaviness gathered in the pit of her stomach. Foreboding. Something was not quite right.

She knew what the beautiful, immoral animal that was Khair-un-Nissa offered to a man of power like Muhammad. It was something he could not have from the wives and concubines of his zenana. Exquisite manners, the highest proficiency in the sexual arts, astounding physical beauty – Khair-un-Nissa possessed all these things, but there was something else.

For when all was said and done, a prostitute acted a role. She could never be more than an exciting physical vessel into which men spilled their seed. No matter what she did, Muhammad could never believe in her affections so long as he could imagine her giving the same faultless performance to other men of rank. Khair-un-Nissa was the most accomplished kind of prostitute, but she was a prostitute nevertheless. And a continuing danger, for she was also an intriguer, and there was no longer a place for her.

A contract bought and paid for by Nadira, Yasmin thought, suddenly realizing what had unsettled her. Of course! Khair-un-Nissa's contract is ended, therefore another must be negotiated. I refuse to play the foul games of suspicion and murder that Nadira played. I have said publicly: God grant that I am able to govern through kindness, for I will not stoop to cruelty and abhorrent deeds, and to be without those weapons a nawab's foremost wife must be both wise and strong, and well respected.

But how long may such high ideals survive in the face of evil? Only God can know what powers He has wrought in me.

She gathered the hem of her veil, drew it across her face and put on her slippers.

'Where are you going, Begum?' her maid asked, rousing herself, acute now to her every move.

One look was enough to hush her: be at peace, little one, I have important business I must attend to. Private business. Quiet business.

The eunuch guard parted to allow the nawab's wife to pass. The sound of bolts being slipped back on a heavy wooden door opened dozens of eyes behind her, but they were used to her excursions, and her exit roused no one.

As she passed along the echoing cloister of shade her

mind turned over the source of her worries. If they had but one name, then that name was Arkali Savage.

Since the Englishwoman had gone to his bed a week ago, Muhammad had made no attempt to see his wife, or anyone else of his zenana. When the Englishwoman reappeared among them after being presented for the first time, she had said nothing at all.

Since then, Arkali had been called back daily. And each time she had gone to Muhammad without a flicker of emotion on her face, guarding her feelings from her sisters so nothing could be read.

I told her that such selfishness cannot work in the zenana, Yasmin thought, as she turned the corner. Here we are all sisters. We must share all, all joys and all sorrows, as the bees share all in their lives. For is there not strength in sharing?

She bit her lip and looked carefully inside herself for jealousy, but found, to her relief, only urgent concern.

Coming to the entrance that led to the nawab's private apartments, she saw it was barred with a silken cordon. The two guards sweltered in their niches beyond, young and grave-faced, swords drawn in eloquent intent, nervous about the responsibility they had been given.

Umar stood before the cordon, unable to gain admission. She breathed his name. 'Umar!'

He turned, his face troubled. Neither felt they could raise their voice above a sacred whisper. 'Lady?'

'Is she *still* with him?'

He eyed her with evident anxiety. 'Yes, Begum. She is still with him.'

His answer was rendered superfluous by the groans that could just be heard from the depths of the apartment.

'She makes so much noise!'

'Perhaps that is the English way, Begum?'

'Do you think so?'

Umar rocked his head, uncertain, then he examined her with eyes that looked deep into her soul, until she shrugged off his candid inspection of her mind.

'It is not jealousy, I promise you,' she said, her voice sounding flat even in her own ears.

'Are you sure of that?'

'I'm thinking of the state, Umar. What's best for the governance of the Carnatic.' She straightened. 'You were good enough to point out my new responsibilities. Do not be surprised if I am taking them seriously.'

'I am not surprised at that, Begum.'

It was maddening yet magnificent how Umar backed so adroitly away from confrontation. No wonder he had been Anwar-ud-Din's indispensable servant for so many years. He stood now with his palm pressed to his heart, his shoulders stooped in a respectful half-bow. A challenging, irritating intelligence, however, twinkled in his eyes.

'What, then?'

'You are . . .' He paused. 'You are rightly concerned. He is spending too much time with the Englishwoman. They are like . . .'

He half turned from the guards, and his voice trailed away, but she finished for him what he had been too delicate to say '. . . like two dogs in the street.'

'. . . like young lovers. Your husband remains the Lord of the Carnatic, Begum.'

She felt her anger rising. 'Yes. And he has affairs of state to attend to. We are embroiled in a desperate war, Umar! And all he can do is lock himself away with . . . with that – stupid woman!'

'Therefore: wherein the lord will not, his servants must do in his stead. So have I done.'

She eyed him coolly. 'Then – you have moved without consulting me.'

An evasion lurked in his eye. 'Not . . . as such, Begum. I have just worked out a preliminary accommodation with Murtaza Ali. You see, his men are at Arcot, camped alongside the army of Raza Sahib, and . . .'

Yasmin felt the stab of betrayal, and the tiny hairs rose on the nape of her neck. 'Umar, not you too? I believed I could count on you.'

'It is merely a small practical matter.'

'No! Umar, you have overstepped yourself! You have been beside the fountainhead of power long enough to have learned what is policy-making and what is the execution of practicalities. In my husband's stead I make the policy, Umar. I, not you. I will not tolerate any trespass on my authority.' She watched him closely for his reaction, and when she was sure of his contrition she salved his pride. 'You invited me into this . . . this regency. You know me well enough to know I will do what I have agreed to do. I trusted you, as you trusted me. We must have each other's trust still, or all is lost.'

'Sweet are the waters that emanate from the fountains of power. It is true that I have tasted them a little too long.' He would not look directly at her. 'You are right to humble me, Begum.'

'Umar, you have humbled yourself. Now, tell me quickly, what is the proposal you have put to Murtaza Ali?'

He seemed to awake from a morose reverie. 'Simply that he turns on Raza Sahib, and thereby relieves Arcot.'

'In exchange for what?'

'Vellore. Promised to him and his heirs in perpetuity. And certain jagirs thereabouts that would secure his position.'

She threw back her head. 'Umar, this was foolishness. Have you forgotten that Murtaza murdered Safdar Ali in order to claim the nawabship of the Carnatic for himself? He cannot be trusted.'

'Then who, Begum? Tell me. We are at the end of our tether. Who can we trust now? You know, Begum, the beggarman must make his bed with pariah dogs.'

'And he who deigns to sleep with curs is taken for a beggarman. I will not lie down with a dog like Murtaza. I say better the thief than the murderer.'

Umar's eyes lit. 'I hear what you are saying: better the Marathas than Murtaza Ali.'

'We shall send an emissary to the Marathas. I know just the man. A most experienced scout who rode with Anwar-ud-Din's bodyguard . . .'

She looked up to see a blue flame burning in the darkness. Khair-un-Nissa materialized from the shadows, her surprise at seeing Yasmin hastily concealed by a haughty stiffness that did not go unnoticed by Umar. Yasmin put aside the conversation instantly.

The courtesan offered the obeisance of greeting.

'And may peace go with you, also, Khair-un-Nissa,' Yasmin replied, 'though you deserve it not.'

The courtesan strove to control her face as she ignored the remark.

She's walked into a completely impossible position, Yasmin thought, all charity gone from her mind. Why should I make it easy for the murdering bitch? She obviously hoped to approach Muhammad unnoticed, to be accepted into his apartments, and to apply her charms to the confirmation of a new contract. But now she's realized she can't get to him, and instead she has me to deal with.

'What is your business here, Khair-un-Nissa? Clearly my husband has not summoned you. She gestured towards the source of the ecstatic sounds. 'As we can all hear.'

Khair-un-Nissa saw the trap closing on her. Where once she might have tried bluff, now she hesitated. She began to back away. 'It was nothing. A petition. A small matter. Excuse me, Begum.'

'A petition? Then let me see it.'

'It is nothing.'

'I said, let me see it.' She put out her hand and waited.

'You must do as the begum says,' Umar murmured.

Khair-un-Nissa produced the contract, and surrendered it.

'Three years?' Yasmin said, looking up from the vellum. 'You want a three years' renewal? But at such an increased cost! My dear, as you have doubtless realized, I am not at all like Nadira. I have always thought your price was excessive.'

Pride hardened the courtesan's eyes. 'Oh, no, Begum. I earn my gold. My skills are very fine, and my range far greater than you could know.'

'But you must admit, you are not as young as you were. I imagine that in the time you have spent with my husband you have been through your entire repertoire several times.'

Avoiding a direct clash, Khair-un-Nissa raised an eyebrow in the direction of the nawab's chamber. 'As for my age, any man will tell you that the juice that may be sucked from the unripe fruit of a young girl is as nothing compared with the succulence of a woman of experience.'

The sounds from the apartments crescendoed higher.

'It sounds to me as if my husband has found himself a most satisfactory passion fruit.' Yasmin handed the contract back. 'I think you shall leave Trichinopoly now. Before nightfall. Perhaps Chanda Sahib's soldiers may offer to employ you.'

The courtesan offered no ground. 'I have come to speak with my lord, not with you, Begum.'

'Since the expiry of your contract you have no right to be here. Therefore you will leave now. Directly. You will not discuss anything with my husband. That is my command.'

Khair-un-Nissa was mortified. Her poise collapsed and the beauty left her face. 'You cannot do this! I insist on seeing the nawab!'

'The nawab is seeing no one. Not even me.'

The courtesan pushed towards the entrance, but the guards stepped forward and drew their swords on her, so that she halted.

She turned, her eyes wide now. 'He must see me! I have something to tell him.'

'What? Say.'

A tremor passed through the blue flame as she tried to decide whether to tell was the correct move. 'Nothing.'

Yasmin remained adamant. 'Good. Then you may leave now. If you are found within the walls after sunset I will order that you be trampled.'

Seeing the blind alley, Khair-un-Nissa blurted out, 'You cannot have me trampled, lady. For I am with child! The lord's bastard! Your husband's bastard!'

'You're lying!'

'No, Begum, I am not lying. And I will see the nawab tomorrow.' She turned, knowing better than any horse-soldier when the time was right to withdraw.

Yasmin felt anger flood her mind, but allowed Umar to stay her. Muhammad's guards would not desert their posts, and there was no other seemly way to prevent the courtesan leaving.

'Umar, she's lying!'

'I know it, Begum. But until that can be shown, she will remain inviolate.'

'I want her sent out of here, Umar.'

'Leave her to me.'

She looked up at his gaunt face. Shadows hid in his eye sockets. For the time being, the sounds from the apartments had stopped.

It was the dark of the moon. They were seated in Clive's den: half a dozen young men in red coats, watching the grizzled minister of the Lord of Vellore with mistrust. The envoi had brought two dumb accomplices with him to give him dignity. Everyone had been told to keep their eyes skinned for whatever they could learn.

Coffee had been served, as yet unsipped. Hayden Flint considered the situation. Five days had passed since the first tentative parley with a frightened and fervent man who claimed to be the agent for Raza Sahib's chief ally. An approach had been made, paving the way for a visit by none other than Murtaza Ali's cousin. At first Clive disdained the approach, but was persuaded otherwise by good arguments.

'You should speak to him.'

'Why?'

'Why not?'

'Because, Mr Flint, his master is a treacherous man. What good can come of talking with him?'

'Tell him to beg the envoi to come here at the dark of the moon. That's five days from now. If he asks why the dark of the moon, say because you know there are strong influences at work on that night, and add that this is the time his master will be best protected from prying eyes and wagging tongues.'

Clive had smiled for the first time in several days. The needling attrition of sniper fire back and forth across the walls was inglorious and unappealing to him. It had taken a steady toll on his people: a sergeant standing beside him on his daily rounds shot down and killed; this morning, a second man hit in identical fashion. Among the men a renewed awe had sprung up at their leader's extraordinary good fortune, but under the outward show Robert Clive was turning dangerously melancholic. He needed fresh distractions to take his mind away from the worry that threatened to eat him up.

Now Hayden Flint watched the eyes of the men who had entered the fortress by way of a long bamboo ladder, eyes that, until five minutes ago, had been blindfolded at Clive's order for the sake of the garrison's security. That was the measure of trust Clive had vested in this fleshy little envoi who sat here swathed in gold-embroidered kincob, looking rich as Croesus.

After prolonged ceremonial Clive's crucial question was finally loosed. 'Tell me this: why should your master be disposed to help us?'

'My – cousin – makes this offer to help restore the rightful nawab.'

A careful answer, but syrupy, and rendered by a man whose cousin and master was infamous throughout the Carnatic as a child murderer. What trust could be placed there? Hayden Flint purposely kept his face a blank, thinking the Company's young officers showed their suspicions too easily. They were looking on with barely veiled disgust as the negotiations proceeded.

Clive was more judicious. He inclined his head, tapping his fly swat against his boot. 'To summarize then, you propose we should make a sally, and you will undertake to attack Raza Sahib's army in the rear? Interesting. A tactical curiosity if I may say.'

A cautious smile broke over the envoi's mouth. Clive's nuances of deadly humour were lost on him. The English lieutenants to right and left gasped in disapproval, horrified that Clive would even consider such a bald artifice. Revel went so far as to utter the start of a cynical laugh. It drew a deadly glance from Clive, and formality suddenly froze over the juniors.

'And what does Mr Flint think?' Clive asked, turning.

Hayden Flint cleared his throat. He said slowly, 'A remarkable plan. One that must be fully explored.'

Indignation almost boiled at that; each lieutenant would have kicked the envoi back over the wall rather than listen to more.

Fresh fruit perfumed the air, ostentatiously set about the room in teak bowls to demonstrate their plenty. As the last of their precious coffee was drunk down they went through the details minutely. It was agreed that Murtaza Ali's men would stand off from Arcot pending 'further negotiations'.

As they watched the trio descend the wildly swaying ladder, Revel murmured, 'The insolence of him! He wanted to lure us into a bloody trap.'

'Hold your tongue, Lieutenant.'

'But, sir! I – '

'I said, hold your tongue.' Clive watched the envoi disappear into the streets of Arcot, then allowed himself a smile. He jabbed a finger at the town. 'What that man wanted, Mr Revel, was a firm answer. What he got was no answer whatsoever. And what I had from him was time – which to us is more than gold.'

As Hayden Flint took his leave, he speculated on Robert Clive's state of mind. It's astonishing how his mood has turned around again, he thought. Times of slackness oppress him, turn him into a stone. But the prospect of action – oh, how that lifts him! Right up from black melancholy to blazing white conviction! Who would count this man the same sullen and listless wretch who was able to contemplate self-killing with such ease? Well – he'll have his action soon enough. Of that there's no doubt.

When would it be? How long would Murtaza stand his men off? A week? Two? Hayden pictured the Killadar of Vellore and Chanda Sahib's pensive son growing ever more impatient with the plan, becoming furious with one another, their hopes fuelled up every two days by Clive's letters of assurance, then fading away by degrees.

He settled down on the weakest part of the ramparts, looking out over an inky land made more impenetrable by the light cast from pitch flares burning nearby. They had been set up to distract sharpshooters from the place where teams of men were digging trenches behind the fausse-braye to augment the outer defences. He felt an itch in his back, between the shoulder blades, as if a musket was trained on it. He moved, ducked down, and felt it subside.

Nearby, three sepoys were talking in their difficult southern tongue. It sounded as if they were making fun of something, and he picked out the northern word *bahadur*, then there was laughter. Laughing and play-acting in the direst of circumstances.

'What was that?' he enquired.

The nearest man grinned betel-black in the gloom, then he remembered his formality and straightened.

'There was no disrespect, sah.'

'No, no. But you said "*bahadur*". What do you mean by that?'

'It mean brave as lion, sah.'

He nodded thoughtfully. The spirit of the translation was right enough. 'Brave as a lion. And that is your name for Captain Clive, is it not?'

'Yes, sah.'

He eyed the man whose grin had disappeared. Uncertainty had begun to trouble him.

'That's very good.'

The sepoy relaxed a little as he saw Hayden Flint smile. The man's naik spoke up on his behalf, wearing his rank of corporal as proudly as his extravagant moustaches. 'This man only say Bahadur Sahib is lit by the fires of Agni, Son of Brahma.'

'Indeed?' he said, knowing they meant that Clive's great energy had been born of heavenly fire. Privately, he thought, judging by your hand actions you suggested the Bahadur Sahib has been shocked up the rear by a bolt of lightning. But I'd say that was an astute observation rather than an insult.

He grinned again and said, 'Yes, perhaps he is possessed by Agni, at that.' And for a while the brooding silence was broken by the comfort of laughter.

The assault began at first light. From the moment he first set eyes on Arcot's fortress Clive had realized that the western wall was the most easily defensible. From the east and south Chanda Sahib's men had lower walls to scale; at one or two places they stood hardly more than six feet above the top of the revetment.

He stood on the western side, commanding the best eighteen-pounder, the one that was now depressed twenty degrees, double-quoined, chocked up and lashed to fire straight down in front of the main gates to deter a direct assault. The gates were huge slabs of iron-studded wood, reinforced at every point by timber props footed diagonally into the earth.

'Why's he attacking here when he's seen what I've laid up for him?' Clive asked, as if nonplussed by Raza Sahib's decision.

'Sir, he's attacking from all quarters!'

Down below, the enemy swarmed across the open ground towards the ditch. It was now possible to pick out the white-swathed warriors individually. Clive surveyed them calmly. The tide might overrun the outer defences, but without the benefit of breaches in the citadel's walls Chanda Sahib's attack would be thrown back easily. The wars against the French fifty years ago had turned the conduct of a siege into an almost exact science. Stringer Lawrence had been their avid student, and Clive had listened to the debates between Lawrence and Admiral Boscawen when the latter invested Pondicherry, and he had learned. The reasons for the failure of that enterprise had rooted themselves in his mind.

'Fire!'

There was a moment of doubt, perhaps half a second in duration, as the priming powder fizzed in the vent, then the cannon jerked up and crashed down again. The area below the walls was obliterated by a white cloud which swirled and thinned to reveal the ruined spearhead of the attack.

'Fast as you can, my lads!'

The practised gunners were already unlashing the heavily chocked carriage and dragging the piece away from the wall; the man with the wet-sponge leaned far out to insert the sopping head and push it down, hand-over-hand with a twisting motion to douse any smouldering wadding that might remain in the barrel.

Clive looked a hundred feet along the ramparts where men were firing their muskets down on parties of men who had reached the walls with scaling ladders. An appalling yelping behind him spun him around: another victim of the sniper fire, running in circles, one of the tribe of skinny ginger mongrels that prowled the citadel. A musket ball had buried itself in the creature's hindquarters and it was whirling like a dervish, snapping at the bald patch on its hide as if at a giant fleabite.

'Have a care for sharpshooters!' he yelled.

A non-commissioned man roared the command along the wall. On the top of the tower one of Sergeant Burton's boys was patiently ignoring the battle, his musket aimed on the suspect houses.

Clive turned back to the battle and grinned. They were still trying to shoot him dead. Like the company flag that flew from the tower he drew fire but defied it. They'll never succeed, he thought, because I'm destined to remain unscathed. I know that. I'm destined to leave this place so loaded with honour I'll hardly be able to move.

Seeing the cannon reloaded he ordered it to fire once more. Again, a mass of swarming insects below was brushed away from the walls by the fiery cloud. As it cleared, he saw a long bamboo ladder, snapped into a useless wreck by the grapeshot, entangling half a dozen attackers.

He shook his head. Ladders could not work against fully manned walls. By the time the assault was over there would be hundreds of the enemy dead, and nothing would have been gained by it. It was heart-killing to see such tremendous courage wasted so. He took off his hat and swept it wide to salute and acknowledge the sacrifice of his foe, and such of his people that saw it delighted in the extravagance of the gesture and cheered it loudly.

Clive indulged them. 'Because Raza Sahib knows nothing of the science of war,' he shouted, 'he will have to learn by his mistakes. He will have to think again.'

Hayden Flint took a sip of water from the pewter cannikin and set it down on the upturned barrel that served as a writing desk. All was quiet now. The curtain screening his quarters was lit by candles. His bed was comfortable, a straw palliasse set up on a string charpoy. He lay back on it, feeling the glowing ache in all his muscles. The morning's attack had lasted almost two hours. It had been a pointless gesture by the enemy. Hundreds had died, but they meant nothing: they were the enemy and part of an inexhaustible supply of peasant warriors.

'Yes, it will make Raza think again,' he told Clive. 'But perhaps this time he will arrive at the correct answer.'

Clive had been brim-full of himself. 'Ha! He cannot winkle us out by diplomacy. While we maintain two hundred men on the walls, he cannot carry us by main force – not without rushing ten thousand men upon us at the same time through at least two breaches. And if he does nothing, and tries to starve us out, he'll make us the talk of all Hindostan – to the greatest embarrassment of his father! Every day we remain here our prestige mounts at Chanda's expense. Whatever way things fall out, we cannot lose. We may all die, but we cannot lose!'

Hayden Flint snorted at that, astonished by the man's

outrageous optimism and the way he had reinfected his people so easily in the wake of the attack. 'If I were Chanda Sahib I would try to wear down the defence, thinning it as best I could until fewer than two hundred men manned the walls. Then I would mount a massive attack. I would blow the main gates, burn them down. I would have my French friends use their siege guns to make breaches in both east and south-west walls.' He sighed. 'How many are now fit for duty?'

'Two hundred and forty.'

'Well, then. Ten days of sharpshooting will see us weeded thin enough for such an assault, even if our losses are no more than we've seen so far. And if there is disease . . .'

He lay back; his body was stiffening after the exertions of the morning. The more he thought soberly upon it, the worse it seemed. The men responded to Clive's devil-may-care, they thought him a hero, but no one here knew the inner pain that drove him. An enigma lay at the heart of his bravado. Part of his soul had been burned away, destroyed by an intense love. It must have been like a furnace to have consumed him so. Some men could not quite erect the mental barriers needed to protect themselves. Hayden's mind turned away from it, swatting instead at a small and nagging matter.

The letter Mohan Das had brought him from his father remained unopened among his possessions. This, I can say, is perfectly clear: I know the foolishness of pride, he thought. Why do we feel the need to cleanse ourselves when we think it likely we are going to die? If it's to make a good showing to stand before God, it's a futile gesture. Respectful, yes, but who better than He knows what we've done in this life? Well, there it is, and if pride's a fault of mine I'll have done with that at least.

He fetched the letter, tore open the seal and pulled out the enclosed page. His mystified eye ran back and forth over the sheet, trying to fathom some signficance in the meticulous copperplate and faded ink of the Bengali clerk. The carefully ruled sheet gave no clue,

4 dye pillows . . . seven pounds and eight shillings; 24 gallon bottles with white glass ground stoppers . . . nine pounds; 1 cask fine new currants . . . one pound; 2 pieces brown Holland . . . three pounds fourteen shillings and one half-penny . . .

Old transactions. The page was torn from an accounts book from five years ago. His heart began to sink – perhaps this was some idiot's idea of a joke.

He turned the sheet over and saw impressed in large crude pencil letters that could only have come from his father's hand: TRUST THE MARATHAS.

He put his hand to his face, as if to assuage a sudden flush of emotion, then he got up and sent Revel's orderly to fetch Mohan Das.

Maratha armies had been making raids on the viceroys' lands since the time of Aurangzeb, when Shivaji's Hindu horsemen had swept down from Poona and Gwalior to antagonize the South. In the beginning, like the Moghuls before them, they were bandits. Mobile. Unpredictable. As destructive as locusts. Now their leaders were warlords riding at the head of huge squadrons of cavalry. When they fell upon the land, it was ravaged; when they left, it was empty. Lately, with their own centres of power established and the great Asaf Jah dead they had become a complicating element in the internal conflicts of the Moghul powers of the South.

According to Mohan Das, the army of Morari Rao was already in the Carnatic, 4,000 strong and watching the conduct of the siege with absorbed interest.

'For God's sake, why didn't you tell me?'

Mohan Das rocked his head maddeningly. He reeked of hashish. 'Oh, sahib, they will not come here.'

'Why not?'

Red-eyed, the scout looked about him dreamily. 'Because they are busy watching the south. The Regent of Mysore is said to be mustering his soldiers, sahib. He has provided silver for my master.'

534

'Mysore is a Hindu country, not part of the Moghul's domain.'

Again that careless rock of the head. 'Wery true.'

'What I mean to say is: the regent can have little love for Muhammad Ali. So why is he sending him silver?'

'How the monkey rubs his hands in glee to see two tigers fight.'

Hayden Flint nodded in understanding. 'And would doubtless prolong that fight . . .' It's not impossible, he thought. The Marathas owe allegiance to no Muslim ruler. If they're here to profit from the feud, then they can be swayed – at the right price. 'You think Morari Rao's eyes are on Mysorean silver?'

'Whocansay, sahib?'

He bent to his makeshift desk and penned a dozen pages, then he called again on the scout, where he slept in the corner. 'Is it possible you can get this letter through to Morari Rao?'

Mohan Das inclined his head, grinning bloodily. 'Sahib, do dogs have fleas?'

Arkali held her hands under the stone spigot, letting the cool water trickle down over her neck and back. Her maid hovered dutifully nearby, as her mistress used a big ocean sponge to clean away the staleness. Arkali glanced challengingly at the maid, and the girl's eyes darted away from contact.

Since she had been spending unprecedented amounts of time with the lord, no one wanted to talk to her, no one was willing to be caught even looking at her. And that was how she wanted it, how it should be. That way a certain due propriety was restored. Only one woman dared meet her eye now. Only the wife: Yasmin. And from Yasmin's eye she found she always had to look away.

She slid into the bathing pool, swimming under the water so that the birdsong and noise was cut off and the world became a green-tinted cavern. She held her breath, pulsing her limbs, for that long moment of freedom, touching the mosaic that decorated the bottom, then floating up slowly to the crystal surface, a world of light and air and madness.

It's their fault, she thought before reaching that world: my father's, for bringing me here; Hayden's, for rejecting my love; Captain Clive, for pestering me; the Governor's, for abandoning me. What could they expect of me after such ill-treatment? They can all go to hell. That was my old life, of which there is nothing left and this is my new.

She broke the surface, remembering the moment she had passed inside Muhammad's chamber for the first time. At the memory a burn of embarrassment at her own foolishness dried the breath in her throat. I know what made me think that way, she thought, I imagined he would be like the Portuguese soldier, drunk and slavering and insane with lust, wanting to rip me and hurt me. How could I have been so foolish?

She put her face in her hands and took the burn from her cheeks, splaying her fingers as she combed them back over her head to drive the water from her hair.

How different it had been. And how different was the act of sex from the way she had always imagined it must be. How was it that nobody ever thought to tell her the truth about the astonishing pleasure that lies in the act? Why had nobody explained?

A tingle passed over her, sending a frisson through her skin that made her shiver. And what a pleasure it was! There was nothing like it at all. Nothing so intense, or so shocking to discover. It was indescribable, better than food, better than drink, better than any activity, like all the pleasures of the world rolled into one.

She put her hand to herself in remembrance of that abandoned state of mind as an echo of her latest orgasm reverberated within her. The itch and the heat were still in her flesh, even after the cooling water, or perhaps these were anticipatory stirrings. How could she wait? But she must. Soon Muhammad would call her back, and they would lie together, for the fifth time that day, and that would be Paradise again.

A persistent doubt came back to haunt her, now, as it had time and again, that it was not surely possible for a lady to love a gentleman without the convenience of a common language, for without any possible conversation between them everyone must realize their time was spent in physical union. That meant it was lust she was admitting to. The sin of lust.

Then she remembered the poison and the butterfly pin, her means of escaping the pain and the horror she had been expecting. But when she had seen Muhammad for the first time, sitting alone on his cushions, his hands clasping his arms, and his eyes filled with such quiet sadness, she had forgotten all about them.

She had found her nawab fascinating: his dark complexion, black oiled hair and clipped beard, were the features of an ogre, but it was his eyes that gave him away. Without those eyes his appearance would have terrified her, looking as he did so dangerous and cruel and tigerish.

He stared back at me, she thought, with that wholly forsaken gaze, the gaze of a lost soul. Then he gave an involuntary toss of his head, and his eyes fell. I was right about that toss being a symptom of the pain trapped inside him. I knew at once that I could cure it. Perhaps I was the only woman in all the world who could do that. Certainly the only woman within the walls of Trichinopoly.

And how did I know that? Because I saw what a scheming, dominating mother had done to a son who had not the strength to escape her coils. And I saw that his wife, whom he once loved so hopelessly, had rejected him – just as Hayden rejected me. That's why I could understand the sort of pain that makes a man toss his head twice every minute.

No, it's not possible to feel terror in a circumstance like that, and so empowered was I that I approached him, and it seemed inappropriate to kneel and kowtow in the way I had been instructed, because the two of us were alone in his room, just this tiger and I, and I knew I had it in my power to salve his hurts, and after so many weeks and months without seeing a man the sight of him intrigued me so very greatly.

I came to him, and I stood before him, and he looked up and saw me for the first time, and I thought to put out my hand to him, and he looked at it strangely, but then took it, so lightly. And, though I was still scared, it was as if I was leading him, and not him leading me . . .

She swam to the steps and left the bath, towelling herself dry and putting on a light garment of pantaloons and choli bodice. She felt hungry, but as usual she would spurn the communal meal and instead eat alone. Then she saw Yasmin.

Arkali looked away, instinctively seeking to cover her emotions. She knew that Yasmin was the most important woman in the zenana now that Muhammad's mother was dead. It would not be wise to carry on their quarrel. This time Yasmin was not to be so easily shrugged off.

'You are blushing,' she said.

Arkali detected no guile in the remark. She registered faintly that her maid had disappeared. 'Am I?'

'Yes. Perhaps you were thinking of something . . . secret.'

'Perhaps I was.'

Yasmin smiled, and there was still no trace of guile. 'Tell me, how is my . . . how is Muhammad?'

Arkali gathered up her mirror and comb and oil bottle briskly from the marble bench. 'I don't think I should talk with you.'

But Yasmin touched her arm. 'Please. Do not imagine I am ill-disposed towards you. I ask this because affairs of state are affected by this period of mourning.' Her tone softened. 'Also, I know how great a part of his soul was affected by his mother. I have wondered how easily he has taken Nadira's death. If he has been . . . exactly himself.'

'Why not ask him?'

'Because he does not call for me.' She lowered her eyes. 'And he will not answer my requests to be received by him.'

Arkali turned, and for the first time their eyes met for a

count of three. She felt the emotion rising in her chest. 'Yasmin, don't you see how hard I find it to talk to you?'

'Yes. But . . . there is no need.'

'Yes, there is. You are his wife!' Suddenly Arkali felt her carefully gathered reserve dissolving. She put her hand to her mouth and blinked back the moisture forming in her eyes. 'And I love him.'

Yasmin's arm enclosed her and they sank down together on the bench seat as the sobbing came over her. She pulled away, feeling foolish and undermined. 'I'm sorry.'

'Do not be sorry. It is your soul that speaks.'

'Oh, how I need it to speak!'

Then the words came pouring from her. How she had not known Muhammad sexually that first time. How she had been recalled to him the following day, and how he had blanched and broken down on receiving the news of his mother's death. She had somehow known to cradle his head in her lap, and rock him like a baby to comfort him. But she recovered herself when she thought of the amazing love-making that had ensued two days later, and the flow of words began to dry. How could she talk of that, even though it had been such an astonishing revelation?

Yasmin left a silence for her, so she smoothed the fabric of her choli and took a deep breath. 'It took a little while for him to shake away his melancholia. But now he is, I think, free of it.'

'Does he give you presents?'

'He has given me this silver comb. A token, rather than a present.'

'That is good.'

After a moment Arkali chose to say, 'I will tell you, Yasmin Begum: he is no longer unhappy.'

Amazingly Yasmin said, 'I think you are correct. I have heard the sounds of his new happiness echoing all over the palace. But such happiness – is it possible? He seems to be indulging himself four and five times a day. That is very good for a man. But all with one woman? Doesn't he overtax you?'

'No,' she said, amazed at herself. 'He doesn't overtax me. In fact, I . . . I enjoy everything he can give me.'

There! It was said, she had declared it! She did enjoy it, and what reason was there to feel guilt any more? Still, she blushed. It was a vast adjustment of mind for her to accommodate. To have discovered what intense and un-imagined pleasure Muhammad was able to give with his tongue before using his manhood on her, then to admit to herself that she liked it, to give in wholeheartedly to liking it, and now to admit it all, and to his wife.

'Excellent. I am pleased for you both.' Yasmin's eyes regarded her more closely. 'But you must tell me: does he enjoy you . . . completely?'

She did not understand, but saw that the question was in earnest. 'Completely?'

Arkali hunted a blur of memories. The first sex had come about quite unexpectedly. She and Muhammad were talking stiltedly. Nadira had been dead and buried for two days, and after much wine she had cradled his head in her lap and he had dozed. The wine had relaxed them both, and she felt confident with him until he began to have a bad dream, and she watched his hands form into fists and the sweat stand out on him. She felt the rigidity in his muscles and then saw the stiffness under his jama, and thought that something vile must happen if he awakened. She stared at him, petrified at the prospect, but he did not wake, he only turned on his side and buried his face in her lap, and the nature of his dream seemed to change, because he calmed then.

Still the stiffness remained in his jama, and no wonder because his mouth was so close to her pubis, and for many minutes she felt his hot breath penetrate the muslin there, and her heart began to beat faster, and her breath came in gasps, because of the incredible feeling that had begun to mount in her lower belly. Then her thighs slipped irresistibly apart, and she felt the wetness growing, and then, astoundingly, without waking, he had begun to suckle her . . .

Yasmin's voice blew the reverie away like cobwebs. 'Yes, completely. I must know if he – what is the word – produces. Does his manhood flow white at the Moment of Unbeing?'

The question gave Arkali a sense of unreality. It was hard to believe she was having so intimate a conversation with the wife of her lover.

'Yes, it does.'

Yasmin's eyes flashed. 'Truly? Are you sure?'

'Yes. Yes, I'm sure.' She paused, biting her lip. 'I did not know that was what happened to men, and it surprised me. But you're right, it is white and . . . quite salty. Sometimes he makes a lot, sometimes only a little.'

Yasmin fell silent. She seemed to be calculating, and Arkali began to suspect she had told her too much, when the other said, 'That is very good.'

'Thank you.'

'I will tell you: he was never able to produce a single drop for me.'

'No? You mean – never?'

'Never one single drop. Though, as Allah is my witness, he tried like a demon.'

Arkali considered that, and the knowledge gave her a secret delight. It was true that Muhammad had showed great joy in the event. Such . . . gratitude. She ventured to say, 'I think perhaps it was his first time.'

'Yes.' Yasmin's eyes gazed far away. 'That would explain his extraordinary appetite just lately. Do you know, even I did not suspect how deep Nadira's influence lay in him.'

'What do you mean?'

'It is no mere coincidence that Nadira Begum's spell over her son failed on the third day after her death. As soon as her soul had completely departed this world, he was free of her.'

With that, Yasmin excused herself and left. Others began to arrive in the bathing area, and soon afterwards the chief eunuch brought Arkali's summons.

It was not until she was lying in his strong arms, panting,

her mind drifting and spinning, that she thought to wonder how Yasmin could know about what a man produces in lovemaking when her husband had never done so. Then she thought of Hayden Flint, and saw him in her mind's eye, but it was only a fleeting glimpse, as if through a pierced marble screen.

Day by day Hayden Flint looked for the return of Mohan Das, feeling the scout might still attempt to find some way to slip into the fort. He made his circuits of the walls, speaking to soldier and sepoy alike, describing the white-bearded messenger and warning that this man must not be shot at.

Now he sipped cinnamon tea in the hot, singing darkness. A lull in the cannonade against the walls and a pause in the firing of the mortars had allowed the magic of Hindostan to close in on them again. Night gave the garrison some physical respite, but there were times when, under the ghastly illumination of flares, the scenes he glimpsed would work upon his imagination fourfold.

He watched as a crazed figure chopped with an iron spade at the bedrock that underlay the citadel's founds. The place was outside the 'hospital' walls – where the dead had lain. Hayden Flint watched as the task was carried out with the relentless rhythm of maniacal obsession, and the sight moved him deeply.

A third sergeant had died beside Clive as he walked the walls. It was now November – the third day in England's calendar, the fourteenth by French reckoning – and the breaches in the south-western and north-western walls were beginning to gape. Their remaining eighteen-pounder was hit, and thrown from its carriage, so that Clive had ordered it taken down from the walls to reinforce the wide breach.

They had all come to know what sustaining a long siege must entail. The hundreds killed in the assault lay unattended on the dust of the outer defences, their corpses drying like soft fruit under the blazing heavens. No parley had been agreed to clear away the dead. The wide ditch with its foul water stank, green and motionless, dotted with more bloated bodies.

Disease victims from inside the citadel had been sewn into sheets and tipped from stretchers over the northern perimeter. For several days they lay among the rubble made by the French cannonade like so many grey larvae.

A very bad idea, he thought, hardened to the crisp brutality of his own sentiments. The dead should have been dumped downwind.

The stench of corruption had mounted in the garrison's throats as the days passed. It filled them with fear and threatened to send another wave of disease through them, for was it not proved to the satisfaction of all modern physicians that illnesses invade the body severally through the digestion, the pores of the skin, and the lungs?

Hayden Flint allowed his eyes to dwell on the far horizon, and the domes of the palace where he had been received by Anwar-ud-Din so long ago. The devastation that had been visited on his lost capital was very great. What suffering necessarily attends the fall of empires, he thought. Terrible to witness good government and civilization turned to dust, and hard not to think it a consequence of the death of great men. Anwar-ud-Din and Asaf Jah both – no matter if they were despots or wise guarantors of peace – they are now merely the kind of rotting meat that decorates the outer-works of this ruin. Terrible to think that we all must go that way, sooner or later. Terrible to think that we are all doomed.

Ah, what even of the Nizams and the nawabs now? What of their manifest destiny, and their auguries? The huge diamond glowed coldly in his memory. Where is that evil gem now? Gone north to Aurangabad with Salabat Jang? How long would that young man control it? How long would he survive before it changed and controlled him? Though its baleful light was gone from this land, still the place was made as ruinous as an outer ring of hell.

As he looked about he saw men with faces veiled like devout Muslim women, or rather, highwaymen. Disease perfumed the air, so that the men who patrolled the walls were obliged to tie rags soaked in vinegar over their noses and mouths to keep out the miasma.

The immediate reason for their torment was easy to explain. At first the vultures and crows had picked the dead bodies apart, until there was little left of their feasts except scattered bones. Those monstrous birds were so greedy they had barely been able to fly. The first night after the assault jackals and dogs had gathered in snarling barking hordes to tear at the mountains of provender that lay for the taking. But since then few carrion feeders had returned, so gorged were they.

No such limit of appetite affected the flies. Looking through his telescope over the parched earth and its festering heaps he had fancied the seething motion of heated air was the convulsions of bug-fly grubs within the bodies. The amazing vitality of tropical maggots could only be attributed to the temperature. He had had to turn away from the sight.

Now he flinched at the maniac chip-chipping of iron on stone. The annoyance of the sound had become suddenly intolerable.

Lieutenant Revel had spent two nights trying to dig himself a grave. Hayden Flint went to him, his lips tight. 'What are you doing, Revel?'

The lieutenant continued striking the spade into rock. And as he chipped, he muttered. Hayden Flint spoke to him again, but still Revel paid him no heed.

'You must stop that.'

Revel's single-mindedness shocked him, and he stared, watching the spade conjuring sparks from the bones of the land. Disease, starvation and all their hardships had come upon them by slow degrees, allowing them to adjust gradually to the changes. Now, seeing Revel, the full desperation of their situation was borne in on him. Raza Sahib had offered again to discuss terms, this time making it clear he wanted the siege to finish. Still Clive refused to contemplate surrender. The mile-long perimeter had no more than two hundred men to defend it. They had run out of shot and had started tearing the citadel apart, melting down the lead on the dome, using nails and then stones in their muskets. But Clive continued to hold out.

'Stop it and save your strength. Go to your bed!'

Revel's own anger snapped back, and he raised the spade against the interruption. 'Take your hands off me!'

'For God's sake, the men are watching you!'

Revel gave no answer.

'You are to go to bed, Lieutenant. That is an order.'

Again no answer as Revel went back to his chip-chipping.

Hayden Flint launched himself at the man, took him in an unbreakable grip as he wrestled him down. 'Revel! You will get a hold of yourself! If you're suffering, bear it. If you're afraid, hide it. If you feel despair right through to your marrow, then fight it! D'you hear me?'

With a howl Revel burst free and scrambled to his feet. He was in a screaming rage that stiffened his entire body. 'Leave me be! Leave me, or I'll – '

Hayden Flint killed the hysteria with a blow that burst Revel's nose, showering him with blood. The lieutenant sat down, stared a moment, holding his face. He moaned softly when his hat was clapped on his head and he was lifted up.

'Now go and do as you're bid.' He watched Revel shamble away, then was aware of a figure looming darkly behind him. It was Clive.

'Taking liberties with my officers, Mr Flint?'

He shrugged. 'Perhaps saving his sanity. Though I don't know what for.'

'What you call knocking sense into a man, is it?' Clive showed his teeth and chuckled. 'Quite a turnabout, eh? For the lad who once fetched his father a crack on the sconce – and hated him famously too – in payment for the same discipline you just gave out.'

He snorted. 'How do you know about that?'

'From your father's own lips.' Clive became suddenly earnest. 'He's proud of you for standing up to him. Do you know that?'

'If that's pride then he has a strange way of showing it.'

'It may happen he has other prides to maintain, as befits a man of his standing and many talents.'

'When it comes to prides, he's a seething morass of them. Just like I am – given five minutes in his company.'

Clive grinned again, crookedly. 'Well, don't we become wiser in our years?'

'Don't we just.'

The bloodied full moon rose, marking the middle of the last month of the Mussulman year, and in the sweating dark they stood a while in silence. Then Hayden Flint asked, 'What will you do should they overrun us?'

'Arcot will not fail.'

'That's no answer.'

'Then I cannot give you an answer.'

'Why?'

'Because I do not countenance your hypothesis.'

Flint massaged the knuckles of his right hand, which were bleeding. 'Then pray indulge me this once.'

'Ha!' Clive's face was part beatific, part demonic in the gruesome light. 'Did you never read your scriptures? It's in the nature of perfect faith to admit of no doubts. Don't you yet believe in the power of faith?'

'I merely ask because I want to know what to do if you're killed. Trenwith is dead, Revel in no condition to lead. I expect I'll be called on to take over. How would you want it finished?'

He had already decided what he would do if they were engulfed. If driven from the last remaining cannon he would draw his pistols and his sword. If they failed him, he would fight with whatever he could lift, and at the last with bare hands. And if death came it would in all likelihood be over suddenly. That would be the cost of losing.

The siege had already lasted too long, with only the sharpshooters successful. Apart from the first assault there had been no attempt at a storm. Why was Raza Sahib content to watch the breaches grow wider? Was it because the nawab's son had no stomach for an attack? Twice now he had called on Clive to yield; his last offer had made promise of a vast quantity of gold.

'So, Robert, how is it to end?'

'Honourably.'

'Then you will negotiate? Lead our brave men from here alive? While they live and breathe?' He sighed mightily, a man bone-tired. 'Robert, the job is done. Leave it now. And let us see bodies spared.'

Something groaned in Clive's breast then, an annoyance perhaps at those who lacked his own indomitable energy. 'Is this to be the new spirit of our age? Are you this kind of man? Is this what science brings us to? So that we may esteem only what we may measure? Bodies? Is that your rational principle? What about their spirit?'

'Forgive me if I urge you to examine your own principles.'

'There'll be no surrender,' Clive said triumphantly. 'That's my only principle.'

'Very well. Having come so far . . .'

He brightened at Hayden Flint's doubt. 'Courage, my good friend. Why do you think I've had every man jack making cartridges for all he's worth these two weeks? The fact is, I have a new plan to show the enemy defiance! I'll demonstrate to all Hindostan what little regard I have for Chanda Sahib's offers of clemency, or his bribes!'

'Rations have been halved again yet still you can say that?'

Clive stared into the heavens for a long moment, then he turned his full gaze on Hayden Flint. 'It's not what *I* say. Do you know what our noble sepoys are saying?'

'No.'

'They are saying that since the English soldiers have more need of food than they, they will give over their rice and content themselves with the water in which the rice has been boiled.' He shook his head, his eyes now seemingly on the point of filling with tears of pride and admiration. 'What kind of courage is that? Our cause is just, but even if it were not, what power on earth could withstand spirit of that kind? I will not betray them with a surrender.'

He was humbled by that. 'No.'

'Now, come and see this.'

As the French cannon boomed again Clive led him down to one of the ancient storerooms where rice sacks had once been piled from floor to rafters. Now the chamber echoed emptily, and a great and ornamented verdigris cylinder, concealed for two generations, was revealed. It was almost as long as the room, and had a bore a dog could have lain in.

'What is it?'

Clive's eyes glowed. 'A vast piece of cannon.'

'What? That big?' And suddenly he recalled the vaunting of Anwar-ud-Din so long ago. The smells and sounds of that time in the great tent haunted him, when the old nawab had boasted of his Lord Champion Conqueror of Armies.

'Aye. Sent, according to the tradition of the fort, from Delhi by the Emperor Aurangzeb.'

'His reign ended half a century ago.'

'As you see, it has been forgotten at least that long. It is said to have been drawn here by a thousand yoke of oxen.' He polished the great green cannon with a piece of sacking. 'See? Bronze. It's like something that hastened the fall of Constantinople. And we found a dozen iron balls. They weight seventy-two pounds apiece. It'll take a deal of powder.'

'Sweet Jesus! You don't mean to fire it?'

'Yes! If you will calculate the elevations.'

'But – how?'

'From the top of the west tower. From there it may be possible to reach the palace. I've seen the young Chanda meet with his father's generals each day at noon.'

'You want to strike at Raza himself?'

'Why not? At present he luxuriates in the knowledge he cannot be harmed by us. I will disabuse him of that idea.'

It had become a ritual. The bronze monster was set up on an earth and rubble mound built atop the chosen tower, a place from which the palace could be seen. 'There'll be one firing per day,' Clive had announced. 'Based on the finest calculations Mr Flint's mathematics can provide.'

548

The trajectory had been difficult to calculate; so much was uncertain about the huge gun. He had scaled up the figures for an eighteen-pounder, and made certain obvious corrections, but he had little confidence in the outcome. Even so, he thought, to land a ball creditably close to Raza Sahib's headquarters would be a triumph, and the damage inflicted on the enemy by the ball would be the least of its advantages.

He told Clive just before the firing, 'It's certainly been the most well-anticipated occasion.'

'Aye, everyone's been made alert by it.'

'Perhaps because they know the damned thing is much more likely to kill us all than any one of Raza Sahib's soldiery.'

Clive smiled. 'But there's no denying it has raised up their spirits, eh?'

And so it had. He knew it was a dangerous amusement. The country casting was bound to be faulted. The proportions of the piece were visibly wrong – too much decorative reliefwork and an insufficient thickness of metal for the bore.

'The Moghuls have always relied on the reputation of their gigantic guns to terrify and disperse their enemies,' he said. 'Imagine the *gup* that would have run ahead of such a weapon! What a sight! Huge trains of draught animals dragging the thing clear across the Deccan . . .'

Clive nodded. 'You can bet that among our enemy there will be great marvelling.'

'What must have been the impact on the Hindu mind,' he asked softly, 'to see such a thing borne onward by so many holy cows? No wonder they feared Aurangzeb's power.'

But Clive addressed a more practical aspect. 'You realize it's likely never been fired before, except with a blank charge?'

Their first attempt to hit the palace had been attended with great ceremony. A carefully weighed charge of powder was measured out and the roundest ball selected. Six men handled a specially made rammer. Breaching ropes were lashed across the barrel, holding it tight to its angled bed of earth on top of the tower. A trail of powder snaked from the vent, giving the gunner time to retire. The shot had gone soaring over Arcot town, but landed short of the palace. It was attended by cheers, so the next day they added a pound more to the charge. Some swore they saw the shot punch a hole through the wall of the old zenana. There were corrections for windage to make; measurements were taken with protractor and plumbline, and he made further calculations. The third attempt had almost certainly hit the eastern tower, and sent Raza Sahib's officers diving.

Now they watched as the generous charge was ladled and rammed home, and wadded, and rammed again. Two men lifted the great iron orb, as big as a man's head, and rolled it into the muzzle.

'Another wager, then?' Clive asked. 'You said my cannon could not stand it three times, and I've had six hundred rupees off you. D'you care to stake the same on this firing? Double or bust?'

'Done!'

'I hope you've science on your side, this time, Mr Flint,' Sergeant Burton murmured when Clive had moved on.

Flint lowered his voice. 'It's a fact that when England cast her own cannon in bronze back in the times of King Hal they were thin as pipes because they needed only be eighty times the weight of shot fired. Now the Royal Navy's best guns are of iron, forty-two-pounders, yet the barrel weighs three hundred times what the ball does. And why?'

'I'm sure I don't know how to answer that, sir.'

'Because the quality of refined powder has improved in the intervening time, Sergeant. Don't you know that England's best hope of future greatness lies in the quantity of fine ingredients for black powder to be had in Hindostan? Purest nitre and sulphur. That and good teak for ships. This is why we are fighting, you and I – to keep French hands off those particulars.'

Burton scratched his chin. 'With such a deal of science on it, sir, I think I'll keep my lads' heads well down.'

'You had better. The barrel looked a mite bulged to me when I inspected it this morning.'

Clive awaited noon with his foot on a stone, his back against a wall; his heavy pocketwatch was in his hand, cracked open like a golden oyster. When he gave the signal the powder fizzed and flared along its track as the watchers crouched down. The gunner threw down his portfire and fled down the tower steps three at a time. Then, with an ear-tearing roar, Aurangzeb's great piece blew itself apart.

The forty-eighth day of the siege was coming up fast out of the eastern plain as Hayden Flint lay in his favoured spot on the eastern wall, his glass trained, as usual, on the dim movements a mile away. He has chosen his corner carefully, a place safe from Chanda Sahib's marksmen. From it he had noted the positions of the four French mortars with which the fort was constantly annoyed. They were beyond the range of all but the eighteen-pounders, and those guns were needed below the ramparts.

Four days ago excitement had flooded through the fort when a band of Maratha horsemen were sighted in the vicinity of the town. They had looted one outlying district, but had probed too far, coming upon a group of Raza Sahib's troops. They beat a hasty retreat, but hopes were raised when one of their number broke away and approached the ramparts waving his hands in what was recognized as an agreed signal.

The news Mohan Das brought had encouraged them further. A body of six thousand of Morari Rao's Marathas were encamped at the foot of the western mountains, no more than thirty miles from Arcot. Mohan Das told the English that the Marathas had been hired by the King of Mysore to assist Muhammad Ali. That prince's retreat to Trichinopoly had made them cautious.

Hayden Flint immediately read the letter Morari Rao had penned in reply to this own. The Maratha chief said he would not delay a moment to send a detachment of his troops to the assistance of the brave defenders of

Arcot – they had convinced him the English could fight after all.

'What do you think Morari Rao will do, my friend?' Hayden Flint asked, feeling light-headed. Whether it was from elation or want of food in his belly he could not tell.

Mohan Das rocked his head. 'Who can say what will happen? Marathas might come. Or they might not come.'

'There's no arguing with that, my friend. But when it becomes known the Marathas are approaching, Raza Sahib will be forced to a decision. I think he can afford to wait no longer.'

'Remember, Flint Sahib, the tenth day of Mohurram approaches.'

'Yes, Mohan Das,' he replied, made thoughtful by the remark. 'Yes, indeed it does.'

The warning had plagued him worse than the flies until he had come to his decision. Now it was made he went down to see Clive. The man's chin jutted in the air as a sepoy barber delicately stretched his jowls between spidery brown fingers. The occasional bombs from coehorn mortars had not deterred him from placing his chair square out in the open.

'Ah, Mr Flint. Good morning.'

'Robert. How is our strength today?'

'Four score Europeans and six score sepoys.' Sun-fire glinted on the razor as it did the last of its work.

'So, two hundred men in all, your minimum number to hold the walls against an assault.'

'What of that?'

'Only that we are hungry and exhausted, and that the French guns have now completed their two ways into our stronghold. The one gap is presently fifty feet wide, the other is thirty yards, so that hardly a stone stands between the two towers, and – '

Clive pulled the cloth from his neck and rinsed his face with a handful of water from the pail. 'I know the extent of the breaches. I have good counterworks behind them, and well-fortified buildings command each with a crossfire.

Today I'll order a new trench dug under the ramparts. Maybe behind that a second, both scattered with iron crow's-feet. The wall of the house behind can be torn to the height of a breastwork, from whence a row of palisadoes can be planted up the rampart to the parapet. That should hold any assault.'

'I advise you to make sure you finish all your preparations by tonight.'

'Yes, I pity the poor sons of parish dogs who'll be sent to storm us . . .' He looked up suddenly, his hard eyes searching Hayden Flint's face. 'What is it? Have you heard something new?'

'Not precisely. But Mohan Das's words on the Moghul faith set me to thinking. In our calendar today is the thirteenth day of November, but in the style of Islam this is their first month: Mohurram.'

Clive's eyes were slits. 'So?'

'You do not know what falls out at this time?'

'Tell me.'

'I'd better. At Hyderabad it was explained to me that Islam has a schism much as does Christianity, between Catholic and Protestant. The Muslims divide into Shias and Sunnis. It is the Shias – which are the kind we have in Hindostan – who celebrate the festival of the brothers Hosain and Hasan. It is for them a great time of religious fervour.' He paused, gauging Clive's appreciation of his words. 'It is when the devout, as it were, bewail the catastrophe of Ali's family – some arouse themselves so fanatically they die of their devotions . . .'

He recalled to Clive Yasmin's instruction as best he could. How Ali, cousin and son-in-law of the Prophet, became caliph, but was then murdered. How his eldest son, Hasan, had allowed power to pass to his father's rival, and how Hosain, Ali's youngest son, had been invited to become caliph.

'Hosain left Mecca with his nearest relations to join his adherents on the River Euphrates, but upon the plain of Kerbela his party was surrounded and destroyed – only one of Hosain's twelve children escaped the massacre. His is the story recounted by the mullahs on the tenth day.'

'I see. And you think we should be on special guard?'

'They are utterly persuaded that whoever falls in battle against Unbelievers during the holiest days shall instantly be translated into the higher Paradise, without pause at any of the intermediate purgatories.' Hayden Flint ran a hand over his day-old growth of beard, feeling the bone of his jaw, the flesh of an Unbeliever. 'You know they will use bhang to excite their courage even more. If I were commanding, I would ensure that every musket was loaded and well provided for by the break of dawn tomorrow.'

It was like balancing on a knife's edge.

Yasmin knew her decision was vital. Umar had told her that neighbouring Mysore, a Hindu kingdom, was considering the opportunity to profit by the struggle in the Carnatic, and that even more armies could be sent against them. Umar could offer advice, but the decision, as she had told him, was hers alone: should she send a letter to the Regent of Mysore or not?

Today is a day of great portent, she thought, taking a deep breath. Already several knotted problems have been undone.

And it was true. The morning's events had been startling. Yasmin, veiled and swathed in black, had watched with satisfaction as the servants stripped the courtesan's rooms bare. Guards stood by an unhinged door, eyeing three anxious maids who had refused to admit them into their mistress's apartments, while the owner of the house, a short, rotund man with sweat-bespangled face and thinning hair, argued his innocence to the officer.

Three large chests of clothing and jewellery and other trinkets stood outside, surrounded by a gaggle of porters. Townsfolk were starting to gather at the end of the street by the time Khair-un-Nissa appeared.

Sapphire light flashed from the courtesan's eyes, but

otherwise she kept her composure, sure of herself in the face of harassment.

'I'm certainly hoping you will be able to explain the meaning of this intrusion to me, Begum.'

Yasmin marvelled at the woman's effrontery as she made ironic obeisance. 'It is fortunate that unblushing insolence becomes you like no other expression. As to your question, I should have thought that a Hyderabad sophisticate such as yourself must have arrived at some conclusion as to the meaning by now.'

She knows perfectly well, Yasmin thought, piercing the audacity of the courtesan. I can see exactly what is going through her mind. She is sure I have come here to turn her things out into the street so they may be combed through for evidence of the poison that killed Nadira. She is also quite secure in her mind that my precipitate search will be futile, and that I shall be shown up as a fool.

'Where is your foul creature Jemdani the Shampooer? Doubtless she is in some disgusting cellar shopping for more scorpion venom.'

Khair-un-Nissa laughed. 'Your jokes are most amusing, Begum. Tell me what you are looking for and perhaps I can assist you in your search.'

Yasmin plunged in her knife. 'Search? Oh, this is not a search. It is an eviction.'

'On what grounds?'

'On the grounds that you are an uncontracted whore who has insulted the nawab and his zenana with false claims. I told you that you must leave Trichinopoly. Therefore you will now take your maids, and the revolting creature you call a shampooer, and you will go back to Hyderabad from whence you came.'

Khair-un-Nissa's voice gritted with anger. 'High and mighty lady, you may not evict one who is with child. I have already declared it: I am with child!' She glanced at those listening and thrust her face close to Yasmin's. 'And a child, as you very well know, of excellent blood. Before Muhammad, I intend to apply to be taken into the zenana.'

555

'Oh, no, Excellent Among Women, you will certainly not be accepted into our zenana. You are not with child. And even if you were, it could not have been sired by my husband.'

'You cannot prove that before the nawab. You have no evidence. Whereas I have only to show the testimony of my maids that I have not bled throughout two new moons. Jemdani, who was once a midwife, will also testify that it is so. You cannot offer your husband any evidence to the contrary.'

'Fortunately, I can.'

Khair-un-Nissa smiled triumphantly. 'Really? I do not recall permitting an examination of my body by your physicians, Begum. Nor do I intend to give permission. You may only force such a thing through the court. By all means have it convened at your expense, but, since Muhammad must preside, my case will be heard by him and every other witness at court. All will know I carry his child, and that is an embarrassment he would prefer to remain within his own walls.'

'I repeat: you are not with child.'

'I repeat: I am.'

'Curious. Because it is a rare woman who can conceive a child without a man's seed.'

Khair-un-Nissa was rocked by that, but she made a quick reply. 'I know little of your experiences, Begum, but he always produced copiously with me. I told you that my skills are most consummate. And my maids, who were often present, will confirm what I say.'

'Then they will be lying, just as you are lying, Khair-un-Nissa, because I have the evidence of the Englishwoman that Muhammad produces seed only with her. You see, Nadira had her son under a spell, but now she is dead, and Muhammad and the Englishwoman have unlocked one other. Since the first time for him was after the death of his mother, you could not possibly be with his child.'

'How do you know all this?'

'Muhammad admitted everything to the Englishwoman,

and she told me. It is now a cause of great joy in our zenana, and a matter of common knowledge among the sisters. I have no idea whose bastard you are carrying, if you are carrying any whatsoever, but the argument is no longer of any interest. You are leaving.'

The courtesan began to tremble, then she collapsed at Yasmin's feet, begging contritely not to be sent out to cross a hostile land without an escort, but Yasmin denied her curtly.

'Your entreaties are but an act. Your soul is as hard as old bones. In any case we have no men to spare for a whore's honour guard. If I were you I would walk to Chanda Sahib's camp and offer your consummate services to his men. If you are lucky they may pay you afterwards.'

And Khair-un-Nissa had picked herself up, brazen-faced once more, and the guard had taken her to the main gate and opened it just wide enough to expel the courtesan, her maids, her shampooer and three chests of fripperies.

Yasmin opened her eyes and shook the vision of that scene away, knowing she must dispel all distractions and concentrate her mind. She looked at Umar. 'Unless the words I dictate to you now are clever enough to convince the Regent of Mysore, this letter will bear no fruit. And we shall all die . . .'

Umar turned to her as she paused. He was ready to take down her words, and his mournful eyes regarded her discomfort and agitation with sympathy. 'Together we shall write a masterpiece, Begum. This will be a diplomatic letter the like of which has never been seen.'

'You misunderstand,' she said. 'It must be anything but a masterpiece. This letter must be thoroughly of my husband. It must be bigoted and brusque and . . . and hollowly imperious, and yet it must be the letter of a supplicant, persuasive and, and . . . oh, it is impossible to devise such a letter!'

Umar said slowly, 'Perhaps the regent knows more of what has passed in this place than you suppose.'

'You think he has spies in Trichinopoly?'

557

'Undoubtedly. Even in the palace.'

'Truly? How so?' She seemed perturbed by the revelation.

'Because *gup* is a remarkable thing, Begum, it knows no walls. It was your late father-in-law's judgment that a diplomatic letter should never attempt to take its reader for a fool.'

She looked back at him, her dark eyes momentarily reflecting her approval of his advice. 'Then the letter shall be styled and sealed "Muhammad Ali Khan", but it shall be transparently written by . . . the one who holds power.'

'That is very wise, Begum.'

She instructed him to set down the formal rubric as he would, then she closed her eyes again, and began.

'Say: Know, neighbour, that I, Muhammad Ali Khan, son of Anwar-ud-Din, have due claim to power in the empire of Hindostan as rightful Nawab of the Carnatic. At this moment, however, according to the unknowable design of Allah, I am playing the part of the worthless killadar of a certain Rock that is sacred to no one but the Hindu. Even so, on account of this Rock's most fortunate position, not one of the armies of these turbulent times has yet shown itself able to interfere in my affairs.'

She paused, allowing Umar to write the words in his meticulous hand.

'Now, if a powerful man like Your Majesty is determined on opposing this insignficant person, I invite you to array your armies against me. But consider: that action alone would be discreditable to the dignity and greatness of the prince whose affairs you presently oversee, and should your army so much as assemble before me that would surely speak of the elevation of my position in your estimation. More than anything else, Your Majesty, it would be a matter of pride for my humble self.'

Umar rocked his head approvingly. 'That is very good!'

She smiled, warming to her task. 'The world would say that the ancient Kingdom of Mysore had, out of extreme fear, marched armies upon a mere killadar of the Moghul line. These words alone would be a matter of great shame for Your Majesty, the bestower of crowns.

'Moreover, the ultimate result is not altogether free from uncertainty. If, with all this power and equipage, you succeed in destroying a weakling like myself, what credit will there be gained? About me they will only say, "What power and position had that poor man?" But if by divine decree, which is not known to anyone, the affair takes a different turn, what will it lead to? All this power and military superiority brought about in Mysore by Your Majesty's government during so careful a reign will vanish in a moment.'

Umar looked up as she sought inspiration. The concentration of her mind caused her to put restless fingers to her lips, and he knew some part of her mind was thinking of the man Flint again.

'Say: As to the threatening and violent order issued for the slaughter and devastation of myself and my country by certain pretenders, my warriors have no fear on that score. It is well known that no intelligent man has any faith in this transient life. As for myself, I have already crossed most of the bridges of life and know all about those that remain. There shall be no greater blessing than that I should drink the draught of martyrdom, that has to be taken sooner or later by warriors. If I take the field of battle with my valiant soldiers, and leave my name, and that of my ancestors, on the pages of the Book of the Age, it will only be remembered that a powerless one breathed equality with such a great and powerful king as yourself. According to the One True Religion, those who fall in the battle against Unbelievers have a clear path to Paradise. As for myself, I, Muhammad Ali Khan, want nothing so much as the opportunity to die in battle, and the same virtuous intention lies at the heart of my many faithful followers and companions.'

She breathed deeply and laced her fingers, seeing the way the argument must end.

'Say: As for the other course, even if I wished to make up my mind to attend at the threshold of your angelic court, the honour of my subjects does not permit me to do so. Under such circumstances, if Your Majesty – the Fountain of Justice – accommodates me, who bears you no ill, and turns instead your attention to expeditions against pretenders, peace may reign between us, and no harm shall come to your dignity or glory.'

'Excellent, Begum!' said Umar, marvelling at how quickly and skilfully she had taken to statecraft. 'Excellent. But how to deflect Mysore's claim on Trichinopoly?'

She ran her finger along the marble sill and thoughtfully rubbed the thin grit adhering there against her thumb. A wind from the interior had blown fine dust in from the Kingdom of Mysore.

'We cannot deflect such a desire,' she said, 'any more than a stalk of grass can deflect the wind. But as any leader knows, there is a time to take and there is a time to give. In closing, say: The truth about this fortress belonging to me is this: It is the object of your wrath, which has been regarded by Your Majesty's sycophants as weak as a spider's web, but if it was yours it would be in their mouths as invincible as Gwalior's ramparts.

'These walls need not be painted with the blood of courage. For Arcot is the proper place for a Nawab of the Carnatic, and I would go there in preference, leaving Mysore to enjoy certain freedoms in the South.'

Umar regarded her judiciously. 'You are offering to cede him Trichinopoly?'

'Yes. What man in his right mind would try to take at such cost what he believes is coming to him for nothing?'

Umar rocked his head, delighting in the stratagem, then he said, 'But how will you seal it, Begum? Such a protocol requires the nawab's signature.'

'He will sign. And I will take that task upon myself.'

When three mortar bombs exploded in the night sky in fast succession Hayden Flint knew the signal to attack must have been given by the French. Before the light of the flares died in the ditch his mind had already begun to flit from weakness to weakness along the ramparts, probing his misgivings, magnifying them.

It's too late now,' he whispered. 'Much too late.'

However he looked at it, there was no escaping the truth. They've been pushed to it, he thought, by the Marathas sitting across their lines of supply. Raza Sahib's twelve thousand must move; he can't wait the few days more it'd take to starve us out. Therefore he must swing down his most fearsome hammerblows now. And we don't know for a certainty where they will land.

He began to feel a deep grumbling in his belly, a twinge of nausea – the symptom of hunger gone far past the point of desire for food. He touched the cold iron of a musket barrel and fancied he could feel the electric fluid drain out from the nerves of his hand into the receptive metal. Then a sense of power stole over him as he realized how easily he had quelled his fears. It seemed to him in that euphoric moment that he had come upon a stunningly simple truth: a man could endure anything, achieve anything, if only he could first take control of himself.

Jackals howled on the glacis, their night's work almost done, and he stared into the dim labyrinth of Arcot town, imagining the mood of Raza Sahib's men. The town contained a seething mass of warriors, all drawn up in readiness. Their fears would be blunted by religious fervour and hashish, but they would have little real confidence in victory.

Why haven't they come at the signal? Why haven't they stormed the fortress in darkness? Has there been a wrangle? Has Murtaza Ali bethought himself? It must be less than an hour to sun-up. Perhaps the last I will see, he thought distantly, making a note to indulge himself. Yes, a reward. A glorious view of the sun's disc rising up out of the eastern plain – if there's opportunity.

There was a sound of retching, followed by an outbreak of coughing. Those sick and wounded who could lend any assistance had been brought to the walls. Even so, he thought, we who must repulse the attack are but eighty

Europeans and one hundred and twenty sepoys. We have only five serving pieces of cannon . . .

Another noise close by alerted him. 'Sergeant Burton? Is that you?'

The reply was gruff and cracked. 'Yes, sir. Shall I awaken the Captain, sir?'

'Is that what he ordered?'

'He didn't say nothing of it, sir. Only a joking word last night to his servant about what time be breakfast.'

He grunted at Clive's grim humour, wondering what his orderly could have made of the quip since there was no breakfast to be had. 'By all means inform him. If you think he could be sleeping at a time such as this.'

'He's sound asleep, sir.'

A few minutes later a figure crept back along the parapet towards him.

'Did you tell him?'

'I did, sir.'

'And?'

The sergeant shifted. 'He weren't to be roused, sir. Says he trusts you've got all particulars in neat preparation, and to waken him when the attack proper begins.'

'I see.'

When Burton had moved away again Hayden Flint allowed himself a small snort of appreciation. He said out loud, 'That piece of hocus-pocus'll be in every part of the fort in two minutes, and well he knows it.'

He deliberately set his mind to reviewing the work of the past twenty-four hours. It was Clive's hope they would be able to keep up a raking fire across the breaches, a fire heavy enough to repel the forlorn hopes that would surely be thrown against them. To keep the walls manned for the past few nights no one had slept more than four hours. They had spent slack time making cartridges. Every man had been given the task of assembling a hundred little tubes of paper, each with a measured ounce of powder, enough to charge a musket barrel and prime the pan, enough to fire a round lead shot through an enemy.

The paper used to contain the powder would serve as necessary wadding when rammed down on top of the ball. On the ramparts, where muskets would be pointed steeply down, it was important to stop the shot rolling out before it was fired. Clive had told him to find whatever he could to serve, so he had used baggage account books, and when they ran out he had torn the pages from Lieutenant Trenwith's Bible, and after that he had sacrificed his own notebooks.

He had searched out every musket in the fort, those weapons they had brought with them, as well as those they had found on their arrival and those assiduously collected on the sallies made since. He distributed new flints and as much matchcord as could be afforded for the discharging of captured jezails. The defence he conceived was a series of concentric rings. 'If one circuit should be overwhelmed,' he told Clive, 'then survivors can fall back on an inner line, then on this group of central buildings, then on our final stronghold. At each position fresh weapons and ammunition will be waiting. That seems best to me.'

'No! It's faint thinking. Put everything on the ramparts and the counterworks. Make sure the walls have sufficient for their wants, especially above the gates. That's where the battle will be won.'

'You seem very certain of that.'

'I am quite certain.'

A supply of primed pieces was now stacked up beside each man on the ramparts, three guns to a man, which with the supply of cartridges would allow an average of less than two shots to be taken at every enemy sent against them. After that, their powder would be exhausted. He prayed it would be sufficient for the task.

A distant, quavering cry carried across the dewy air. Against the purple light of dawn he saw a turbaned figure standing on a housetop with outstretched hands, exhorting those below to surrender to Allah.

Prayer is better than sleep . . .

An answering howl broke from the army of Raza Sahib,

563

and almost immediately the beating of drums, as bodies of men were established in position.

All the time as he watched, the sky was running up through a scale of fathomless colours, brightening, driving away the pools of shadow from the defensive ground of the glacis. Then he saw them begin their advance. Dozens of men carrying ladders emerged from the streets and alleys of Arcot. He dispatched a sepoy down to wake Clive, and opened his glass on the enemy. As he watched the straggle swelled to a multitude that began to scream and flood towards every part of the walls not protected by the ditch.

His eye was deceived by the apparent formlessness of the attack, so it was not until moments later that he saw four distinct concentrations drawing forward behind the first wave. I can see their purpose, he thought with sudden shock.

The two greatest bodies of men began to manoeuvre towards the breaches for a mass assault. The other two were advancing on the gates. Then a musket was touched off prematurely along the rampart. He turned on the man immediately, his face showing intense anger.

'Hold your fire, damn you! I told you to make every shot count!'

He succeeded in forestalling a useless volley, then he saw Clive's red-coated figure on a salient of the gatehouse twenty yards away; he made an acknowledgement, doffing his black tricorn, then turned to study the advancing enemy, his head pushing down on his sword hilt as if he was a statue on a plinth of ruined masonry.

Hayden Flint returned the compliment unnoticed. Fine hairs stood like needles on his neck as the screaming howl of Raza Sahib's army rose in his ears. Other sounds intermingled, bestial groans of anguish and complaint, as of huge ogres driven from a forest. The source of the noise, he saw, was the battering parties that stormed from the cover of the town and launched their attack on the gate.

A dozen large elephants lumbered forward at a trot, followed and flanked by a morass of hundreds of running infantry coming up the road to the main gate. The beasts were goaded on to the bridge across the ditch, and he saw the large iron plates fixed to their heads like armour.

But it was not armour.

They mean to use them to break the gates down, he thought, willing the realization to reach Robert Clive. On the gatehouse Clive's sword was suddenly raised and the muskets of thirty men waited, poised for his downswing. When the volley came, the air below the top of the gatehouse filled with white smoke. Two or three hangfires peppered the aftershock of sound, and Flint heard elephants, shot through by the musketry, trumpeting their fear and pain. They were turning and trampling their close-packed escorts, driving men off the bridge into the stinking green water of the ditch, and running amok among the advancing ranks.

Scaling parties had crossed the shallow ditch below Hayden Flint's position without trouble. The clatter of wood against stone alerted him that a ladder had been set against the rampart top. He drew his hanger and ran to the two spines of wood that cleared the battlement, ready to hack at anything that appeared. As if conjured by his thoughts a white turban came up, and a waving shamshir sabre.

He slammed the blade down with his full strength towards the man's head, but the stroke was parried by the shamshir. He struck again, this time square on to the cushion of twisted cotton. He saw his mistake as the attacker's bearded face roared a paralysing shout, enraged rather than hurt by the blow. The man was about to leap on to the rampart when a sepoy advanced with a ramrod from one of the eighteen-pounders and shoved it hard against the assailant's chest.

As he was pushed back, the man let go his sword, catching at the ramrod with one hand and the battlement with the other. When the sepoy pushed again he let go the ramrod and dangled from the stonework by his right hand, then swung up his left and began to haul himself up.

In an agony of indecision over how to counter such obstinate courage, Hayden Flint cursed himself for a fool. Then he wrested the ramrod from the sepoy's grip and prepared to swipe it across the attacker's temple so that he was knocked back into a fall. But as he raised the ramrod he saw the man blasted apart by a blunderbuss fired from just two yards away.

Sergeant Burton was at his side. 'This is hot and bloody war, sir!' he shouted with venom. 'Ain't no blame to it when it's do or die! Forget your notions of honour and cut the bastards before they bloody well cut you!'

He gasped at the veteran's words. Together they grabbed hold of the top of the ladder and tried to prise it away from the wall, but found it lodged up at an angle of thirty degrees. The weight of four more men climbing up was too much to shift. When they let go the ladder snapped back against the wall with two hundred pounds of force. The leading man was almost at the top. Horrified, Hayden Flint tried to push again, and felt the wind of a sword-cut that barely missed his face. Lead shot whistled up at him from sharpshooters kneeling on the far bank of the ditch. It chipped into the wall or zinged about his head.

A surge of anger-strength helped him to heave the ladder sideways, so that it slipped and collapsed, Burton's curses following it down. He looked around. Another ladder and another were slammed up, but his men were learning how to counter the threat. They discharged their pieces down the rungs, then threw the ladder down, or lassoed the tops with ropes and dragged them aside until they toppled.

As soon as it was clear the enemy would not gain entry here, Hayden Flint turned his attention to the north-west breach. The ditch had been forded there too and the walls were under ferocious attack. Hundreds of men were swarming up the heaps of rubble in the breach, mounting it with a single-minded courage, while a second wave negotiated the ditch behind them. As he vaulted down the steps with two sepoys he saw a dozen of the leading attackers charging through the breach. The defenders waited behind a low wall, making no reply. He joined them, awaiting the order from the jemadar, Gopal Rao, to give fire, picking the man he would have as target. Some of Raza Sahib's men had crossed the trench and were bare yards from the wall. Gopal Rao was screaming, '*Banduk mat chalao!*' Hold your fire! to stay them, then the order came.

The volley did grim execution. Before a dozen more attackers had reached the trench fresh muskets were passed forward by those behind. Another volley blasted out, then another. And so it went on until maybe a hundred assailants lay dead in the breach.

There was a short respite while the men frantically reloaded muskets. Then a new din came from below: swordsmen charging forward, throwing themselves on. The first shock had filled the air with dust, which with the powder smoke had bleached reality from the scene beyond the breach. Misty figures appeared, stormed across the rubble heap, their outlines growing sharper with every step, then died. But as one died two more materialized from the smoke. The weight of numbers was beginning to tell. Two thousand men were converging on the breach, urged on by a Moghul officer in a turmeric-yellow turban. There were so many they must soon be overwhelmed by the tide. He knew he could not move from his position now he had chosen it. He gasped for breath in the acrid backdraught of powder-laden air. Men's eyes challenged his own for any sign that his resolve was failing. In reply he thrust his sword into the air, and showed his teeth in a war-cry.

'Stand firm! Do or die, boys! Do or die!'

'*Sangin charhao!*'

Gopal Rao had ordered his men to fix bayonets, and Hayden Flint's guts churned as he realized they would soon be at close quarters. Then he heard volley fire from the ramparts to right and left above his position, and saw that a reinforcement had come to their aid.

Hundreds more of Raza Sahib's men were fording the ditch now. He saw Lieutenant Revel standing out on the rampart, careless of his own safety, exchanging empty muskets for loaded ones from his helpers, discharging piece after piece into the mêlée below.

The insane charge broke through, and for a moment it looked as if the tide must overwhelm them, then shrouds of dust and smoke engulfed the field. A concussing explosion hurt his ears, making his head ring. The howling grew muffled. Only the cries of the injured rose up, piercing and shrill.

The men who guarded the breach craned their necks and clawed at the air, blinded now to what was coming at them across the broken-toothed opening. As the breeze caught it the dust curtain thinned in wisps. Hayden Flint steeled himself, not wanting to see what would soon be revealed.

Two pieces of cannon emplaced on a housetop had fired on the breach, blasting it with langridge – grapeshot made from nails, pieces of horseshoe, coins, all kinds of sharp iron. Incredibly the survivors continued to come on. They were caught by more musketry before the next body who had crossed the ditch advanced, to be swept away by another storm of grape.

The gunners had reloaded the cannon ready to meet the onslaught before it reached the counterworks. He stayed Gopal Rao, fearing his sepoys might fire too soon, and peered into the murk, nerves taut as violin strings. A single figure appeared, a dreadful wraith who stumbled from the smoke six or seven steps away and stopped, seeing them at the instant they saw him. The sword fell from his hand and he collapsed as the lifting curtain revealed what the langridge shot had done to the hundreds of men who had been converging on the breach.

He saw Clive himself manhandling the spokes of the guncarriage wheels as they rolled it back out of sight. Bombs with short fuses were thrown down from the rampart, exploding in the fausse-braye, driving those who had crossed the ditch ready to attack the breach back from it. The momentum of the assault had been halted; as it bled away, the attackers turned and fled back through the breach.

He was reloading muskets with shaking heads when a naik came to him with a message from Clive to reinforce the south-west breach, which was protected by the best part of the ditch. Here the water was so deep it could not be forded by an armed man. The barest skeleton crew had been assigned to defend it, and fearing the worst he detached two sepoys to appraise the danger.

One returned and said the enemy had brought a great raft, and that perhaps seventy men had formed a vanguard to cross the ditch.

'A raft?'

'Yes, Flint Sahib. They are pushing it across with long poles.'

He sent word up to Clive for one of the field pieces to be brought up and turned on the raft, then he climbed up the shattered stone of the closest bastion and watched the perilous craft edge nearer to the bank.

'Come on, come on!' he whispered, urging the eighteen-pounder to appear. He saw that if the enemy succeeded in landing everyone on the raft they would easily overwhelm the dozen men who tried to cover the sixty-foot gap in the wall.

Desperate musketry was aimed on to the raft. Some men fell from it into the filthy water, but the rest clung on, and still the long poles propelled it onward. The muzzle of the cannon appeared as the raft came within jumping distance of the bank. The first discharge flung the attackers into a panic; so many lost their balance and were forced to swim for their lives. The second shot capsized the raft completely, sending men spinning into the putrid water. On the far bank a thousand men waited uselessly, deprived of their only means of gaining access to the breach, but without orders to go elsewhere.

The enemy had no clear plan now. Fire from the walls had taken a heavy toll of their officers and continued to snipe at the leaderless men who wandered the glacis aimlessly. Hayden Flint felt the sun suddenly hot and bright on his face. He sat down hard, searching out his canteen of water, gulping a mouthful to clear the powder from his mouth. He wiped his face against his sleeve. Sweat had carried so much salt into his eyes they stung. How had the sun climbed so high in so short a time?

He got up again, realizing with astonishment that over an hour had passed. Musket cracks resounded from the walls in isolated firings, but despite the lack of a formal truce the first attack had effectively ended. He looked down over the scarred glacis to see hundreds of dead. More were lying in the grim throat of the north-western breach, pairs of men braving the hazards to carry off the casualties. An expensively attired officer in a turmeric-yellow turban had fallen in the fausse-braye. Hayden Flint remembered the man urging forward the attack. Now one of his people waded across the ditch, picked up his body in the face of fire from forty muskets, and withdrew with it.

The defenders saluted his tremendous courage, but no one stopped firing. It's dangerous to permit an enemy to recover dead before the terms of a truce have been arranged for that purpose, he thought, staring at the carnage. But there are hundreds clogging the breaches. It won't take long for this hot sun to make the stench intolerable. If Raza lost five hundred, he's still got twenty times that number to come again. If this fight goes on, as it surely must, we'll be in hell three days from now.

'Aye,' Clive said, coming up beside him and indicating the mass of dead. 'We've done good work today, but have you seen how many of them are French?'

'Not a one.' He snorted at the irony of it. 'And how many have we lost?'

'So far this day, four Europeans killed and two sepoys wounded.'

'So far? Do you think they'll come again today?'

'That depends on how long your diplomacy may forestall them.'

They watched Raza Sahib's forces regroup. The respite was welcome, but within two hours the French had renewed their siege fire against the fort. Their batteries began to pound at the walls and a steady drizzle of musketry came in from the nearest houses, seeking those too jaunty or too jaded to bother to give themselves cover.

Hayden Flint judged the annoyance no more severe than what they had endured for more than a month, and said so to his people. They were in high spirits to have driven off so concerted an attack. Just to be alive seemed cause for celebration. They took a little boiled water infused with what tea leaves remained and used the rest of the brew to boil out their musket barrels in readiness for the afternoon's onslaught.

After a couple of hours the cannonade ceased. Clive told Hayden Flint he expected a truce flag, and began to prepare a reception. It came out at two o'clock in the afternoon, a solemn delegation of six, headed by an officer who passed on Raza Sahib's compliments. His offer was, in the interests of hastening the inevitable and avoiding unnecessary sacrifice, to allow the garrison unhindered passage from the fort to the coast. Clive declined so favourable a set of terms with exquisite politeness.

'Tell him that in our tradition it is the victors who set terms at a parley. Tell him that, Mr Flint. And tell him also that I will be pleased to have Raza Sahib's army drawn up here within the hour to lay down their arms in a general surrender to me.'

The officer took the answer with such gravity that Hayden Flint supposed he had been charged with making a success of negotiations. He took refuge in formulas worthy of a carpet-seller, then mentioned a sum of bullion that was to be made over to Clive personally.

Still Clive rejected the terms, this time with visible disdain. When the sum was doubled, he walked away. The delegation also withdrew, but returned a few minutes later, their chief's face sickly pale, demanding leave to recover their dead, which permission Hayden Flint was pleased to hear granted.

The grisly work went on until four o'clock, when the burial parties withdrew and the cannonade commenced again. Hayden Flint sat in solitude to watch the sun go down, and remembered his broken pledge to himself to watch it rise. Sunrise, sunset, he thought. These now are the measures of my life. May it please God I see the next. He was so exhausted that he fell asleep propped against a wall, despite the reverberations groaning through the old stone.

He came to with a start: to darkness and silence.

A mosaic of dream and waking disorientated him, so that he momentarily thought himself back in Hyderabad, discovered while lying with Yasmin. The guilt within him crystallized, stark against the anger that such things as princes and politics could have forced them apart. The sudden explosion of lucid clarity faded. He asked the nearest man when the French guns had ceased.

'Just now, Mr Flint, sir.'

'And do you know the time?'

'I'd say it were likely two or three of the clock by the heavens, sir.'

He stood up to stare into the starry wastes of the south, in the direction he had stared with longing so many times before. A shooting star streaked briefly across Argo Navis, the great constellation of the ship, then a lone gun flashed out, a few random shots pocked the air, and there was silence.

He went down to relieve himself and take a drink of water. He found his belt had need of a new hole, so set about it with an awl. A while later he remembered with delight half a sweet biscuit he had been saving in his waistcoat pocket. It was smashed to crumbs, but he emptied them carefully on to a skillet and roasted them over the fire until they were caramelized, then poured boiling water over them and waited until they dissolved.

'Care to toast the new dawn with a sip of mariner's coffee, Sergeant?' he asked as Burton came by.

'No thank you, sir. I got coffee of my own. Made of black beetles, it is, and not quite so evil as what it sounds.'

The silence continued unbroken until cockcrow. In passing it seemed strange to him that there could be fowls strutting and advertising themselves in the streets of Arcot with so many hungry men about. If only they could be tempted here, he thought. The vision of succulent chicken flesh carved from the bone assailed him, and he breathed deep to dispel it.

Above what remained of the fort a magnificent Hindostan dawn began stretching fingers across the sky in impenetrable pastels. The stars of night were dying in their spheres. The horizon became intricately fretted with palms and the angular buildings of Arcot. As the sun was about to slide up inexorably into the eastern haze, he knew, suddenly and crushingly, that they must face another burning day of thirst and flies, and the stench of death all round.

So, he thought, after fifty days, we have forty-five Europeans and thirty sepoys dead. How many more are wounded or full of disease? And all to what end? Who yet can say?

A sepoy, newly woken up at his side, rubbed at his eyes, stared, rubbed them again.

'It can't be true!' he said in his own language. 'It can't be true, but it is! *Jeh Sabat Jang Bahadur!*'

'*Yih kya hai? Tumko kya hua hai?*' What is it? What's wrong with you?

'*Bismillah!* Look at the town,' the man said. 'The army of Raza Sahib. It is gone!'

TWENTY-ONE

Yasmin watched Muhammad, still expecting his calm to snap into rage. Instead he picked up the quill and poised the nib in readiness. Arkali had persuaded him to meet his wife, though he had not wanted to do so.

'I am told it is of great importance. What is it?' he asked, looking at the curled sheet as she weighted it down for him with a silver-hilted dagger.

She held her breath, her pulse beating in her ears. How like Muhammad to become suspicious as a wolf after so many days as a lamb. How like him to find some reason to delay and resist at this crucial moment. Umar would be astonished if he signed.

'It is a letter of acknowledgement to the Regent of Mysore,' she said, smoothly circumventing his question.

He looked up at her, his eyes clear and open. Amazingly, the torture she had seen there so often was absent. 'What does it acknowledge?'

She faltered; a tremor of heat passed through her and she felt her composure begin to fail. She knew she must remain calm, or appear so at least. The treaty under Muhammad's hand was vital. Nadira Begum would never have allowed such a letter to come under his consideration. It made concessions, but sacrifice was the only way.

'His recognition of you, lord, as Nawab of the Carnatic,' she lied.

'That is as it should be.'

He barely glanced at the wording, Two-thirds down the page, buried beneath the complicated rubric, was a clause that would sign away the fortress of Trichinopoly. Instead of reading it Muhammad began the involved calligraphy that was the signature of his title.

What had happened to him? An astonishing change had transformed him. He was unadorned, dressed only in a long mustard jama, open at the chest, and without his pagri. His hair was untended; he had allowed it to grow out a finger's length longer than normal. Once his haunted glances had never ceased to follow her wherever she went; now she found it hard to keep his attention. The nakedness she felt whenever she was in his presence had disappeared. It was as if the source of a bad smell had been cleaned away, as if the demon possessing him had suddenly left.

He stood up, stretched the tiredness from his bones; there was no sign of the stiffness in his arm that he sometimes unconsciously massaged in her presence; he no longer tossed his head. He went to stand by the pierced stone lattice of the window so that the fresh greenness carried on the breeze, stirring his thin hair. He breathed deeply.

'Thank you, Yasmin.' He turned back absently. 'Is there another matter you wish to raise?'

'Not for the moment, lord,' she said, trying to keep the wonderment from her voice. It's amazing, she thought, he is completely altered. So it was a spell after all!

The shocking thought came to her that she was married to someone she no longer knew. What if I grow to love this new husband? she wondered. How strange that would be.

'That is well.' His eyes dwelt longingly on the far horizon and his voice sighed. 'Then you may go, if you wish.'

'Thank you.'

She bowed to him and took three paces back before turning. It was more than modesty that made her cover her face before passing the guards. She did it to hide her expression of glee from them. Now the treaty was signed and sealed, it remained only to have it delivered to Mysore. Umar would be ecstatic.

On the way back to the Hall of Audiences her thoughts ranged over the sudden change in her fortunes. The men appointed by Muhammad to superintend his government were weak. That had been a deliberate policy, for it had been Nadira's notion that without strong, intelligent men close by him, her son would seem to be all the more a nawab. Men like Umar had been kept at a distance, deemed too clever; men like the bodyguard leader, Zahir Zamani, had been strangled on a pretext because they inspired fear, but without men of vision there was no one to see the way, and without men of steel there was no one to shape the future as it must be shaped. Only Nadira herself. But now Nadira was dead.

Ah, she thought, it was ever thus. When men are found wanting it is a woman's lot to do their work for them. How many unsung heroines have avenged their fathers and brothers? How many have taken the burden from their husbands when difficult times demanded it?

Since her visit to the temple, Muhammad's government had stood in awe of her. Some zealots had recoiled at the idea of a woman conducting policy, but in the days of crisis they understood that their only chance was to listen to what she told them, and to act on it. She had prevented the rebellion. She had delivered to them the accord of the city. The temple visit had been made on her own initiative – hers alone. She had saved them, therefore they were prepared to pay her tribute, though the price she demanded was high. For a few months, before the truth trickled out, she would have power. Real power.

The *gup* in the zenana had already turned to speculation, respectful when spoken within earshot, less so when whispered behind her back and reported to her by servants.

'What a change we have seen in the lord since he took the Angrezi woman to his bed.'

'The foreign devil has bewitched him!'

'He has certainly become a dreamer since the death of his mother.'

'He has all but retired from affairs of state.'

'And left the management of the city to his wife.'

'But who is his wife?'

'We know who is the wife. But who is nawab?'

She sighed, thinking of Hayden. The news from Arcot had been terrifying, and, after a month, terrifying again. There had been rumours of disaster, then reports to make her hope, and finally, something beyond hope. Mohan Das had brought her a second letter. She had read it over and over with ridiculous tears, and a heavy ache growing in her heart. She saw his hand in the curving letters of the script, his particular faults in grammar and his curious way with the language. Without a copyist to help him he had written the courtly tongue in an archaic form, which was not at all the way to do it, but it had affected her heart more intensely than the most magnificent love poem.

In the weeks since the letter's arrival she had taken it out many times in secret, just to smell the paper, to see if his scent was there. Merely to breathe it filled her with longing.

His letter said: 'Chanda Sahib to Vellore is retreated, whereat Murtaza Ali doth succour give. The rebel many desertions has suffered; he fifty thousand still commands . . .' Then, later, with his quaint embarrassment: 'Lady, in the halls of the old palace yesterday did I walk. Thoughts of rosebuds and lilac sunsets and great times long ago to me came. I do not know whether my heart such memories can accommodate.'

'What of the Angrezi army?' she asked Umar, anxious for Hayden.

'They have moved on from Arcot, leaving some of their number to guard the fortress. The one they call "Valiant in War" has marched his men out to Timeri. The killadar there has welcomed him, but the Marathas have refused to close on Vellore to help extinguish Chanda Sahib.' He threw up his big hands. 'Those bandits want nothing more than to plunder our lord's lands. Morari Rao does not want to finish this anarchy. It suits his purposes exactly. But how different it would have been for him in the heyday of my lord, Anwar-ud-Din!'

'Be thankful the Marathas intervened on our behalf at all,' she told him sharply. 'It may be that we shall need them again.'

Since her visit to the temple, the city had been calmer. 'That,' she told the men of Muhammad's government, 'is more than any zealous Muslim should expect. The South is a wounded land, bleeding and resentful. Trichinopoly is a citadel built round a Hindu shrine, in a land of many Hindu and bordered by the lands of the Hindu Rajas of Mysore and Tanjore. The siege has heightened uncertainty, and uncertainty is the nest of mistrust. Do what you can to pour balm on these wounds, or they will become infected and the poison will kill us all.'

I had no choice but to take on my shoulders the task of quelling the troubles, she thought now. For it is certain the foolish Angrezi captain, de Gingens, had no idea of the danger about to overwhelm him. He believed his soldiers were the arbiters of peace within the city, and he believes so still. But maybe it's more than that. De Gingens is a reluctant leader, without enthusiasm for, or understanding of, his job. I don't like him.

Because the warfare at distant Arcot has stripped most of Chanda Sahib's men from our walls, de Gingens has decided to venture his troops outside. I know that only a directive from Madras ordering him on to the offensive has persuaded him that far. Further, I think, he will not go anywhere near the enemy.

She met Umar unexpectedly, ascending the stair, his secretary in his wake. The young man was beautiful: grey-eyed and fair-complexioned, much to the taste of Umar. His eyes bulged when he saw her. His big feet slapped his leather sandals down on the stone treads, sending a flat echo from the hem of his jama. He addressed her anxiously.

'Salaam, Begum.'

'Salaam, Umar. I have good news.'

'Does it seem he will agree to sign?'

She produced the scroll, smiling under her veil. 'He has done so!'

'*Auh!*' So soon?' He took the treaty as if it was red-hot gold, satisfaction breaking over his bony face. 'This is excellent work.' He gave the scroll into the keeping of the youth with directions to take it straight to the messengers. 'Begum, you may have saved us.'

'Yes. But at what price?' Already the regrets had begun to eat at her. 'Whether he knows it or not, Muhammad has agreed to cede Trichinopoly to the Regent of Mysore. What kind of rescuer is it that robs while giving succour?'

'Most physicians, Begum, and all rulers.' He smiled regretfully, readying himself to depart. 'Have we not talked it threadbare, and agreed there was no other way? Without Mysore we are destroyed. With Mysore, there is still a chance Muhammad Ali Khan may again rule at Arcot one day. You are right, Begum: if Trichinopoly must be lost, then so be it.'

'Where are you going?' she asked him.

'Each day at noon I climb to the summit of the rock to sit beneath the prayer flags. The people see me, and they know you are watching over them too. From that place I may also watch the disposition of the foreign armies. The smoke of their musket practice and the dust rising from their marching tells me much. I can see more clearly from my peak than the Angrezi general can from his camp beneath the walls. Do you know that he makes his men sleep on their weapons?'

'Captain de Gingens is a very – cautious – man, do you not agree?'

'Perhaps another might call him a coward, Begum.'

Her eyebrows arched. 'Then may we not shame him into moving?'

'Shame is not a strong motivator in the breast of a coward. And who knows how Angrezi minds may think?'

She smiled at that. 'What if you tell him there are more Angrezi here than the feringhee ranged against him outside? Which is surely the truth now.'

Umar made a gesture of uncertainty. 'He intends to send a part of his army with Captain Cope to dispute an unimportant fortress. It is my belief he may use this to plead lack of numbers to his superiors.'

'God knows, he is lacking in spirit.'

'The guns of the French are still firing at the limit of their range. We must thank Allah that the feringhee commander has no more will to attack than the Angrezi has inclination to put him to flight. I warn you it is soon to change, Begum, but thanks to your persuasiveness we may have help from Mysore, if it can arrive in time.'

She considered his words. Chanda Sahib's armies had crossed the Coleroon River on their arrival and overrun Srirangam Island, giving the French artillery a place from which to bombard the walls. Each day the guns had fired on the city, but there had been little damage and no assault.

Umar touched his forehead and took one pace back. 'The game of static patterns continues. I must have leave to observe it.'

She let him go, then called after him, 'Soon to change, you said.'

Umar's Adam's apple bobbed. 'Since we last met, Begum, I have received disturbing news. I cannot yet be certain, but I shall tell you what I already know. It seems the French commander has been ordered back to the coast. They have sent a more ferocious man in his stead. According to my man in Chanda Sahib's camp, the new commander has orders to lead an attack on us once his reinforcements arrive. That is why the treaty is so important. Without the help of Mysore, and perhaps Tanjore too, we cannot stand long.'

Hayden Flint's return to their camp from Madras lifted the spirits of Clive's veterans. There was excitement about the camp, he thought, and a pride of bearing in all. They were greatly pleased to see him back among them.

These were men content. They had braved hell with all defiance and faced down the devils in their own souls. They were resolved to live or die as chance befell, but they would do so as soldiers, and as brothers.

Clive was sitting at the heart of the camp, in a bamboo chair. A vast eye-dazzling silk carpet was spread outside his tent like a Moghul's garden. The space was cleverly fenced, hung with arms and trophies, warnings of hazard and might. Clive's personality dominated the area around him like a radiant blaze. Determined to have the news first, he sent his officers out of earshot on whimsical duties, so they were alone.

By God, Hayden Flint thought, how they obey him perfectly! It's a show that fits any of the warrior kings who have ridden through Hindostan in the last thousand years. But this land somehow lends itself to men of extraordinary clay, and that's one secret of its magic.

There was so much to say it was difficult to know where to begin. Hayden Flint tapped the letter from the Governor, reading it aloud as they sat in the ornate surroundings.

'Listen to it! Governor Sawyer's own words: "I am informed the mullahs are writing a history of the wars of Arcot wherein the name of Robert Clive will be delivered down to future ages . . ." '

Beside him Clive rocked back on his bamboo chair and said nothing. The languid flick of a small cane fan brought scant relief from the streaming heat.

'And this, from Muhammad Ali: "By God Almighty's grace you are most fortunate in all engagements. You have met with an incomparable success in all your expeditions. I am assured that you are star-favoured . . ." '

'Hmmm.'

'Robert, all over the Carnatic they are calling you *Sabat Jang Bahadur* – the Valiant in War. Your acclaim is universal. Does that not please you?'

'For a certainty it pleases me.' Clive put down his fan. 'Because it makes my task that much easier.'

'St David's now has two hundred men from Bengal, arrived on my father's best ship, and there's better: Stringer Lawrence is back.'

That jolted Clive. The obstinate major had been in dispute with the Honourable Company. Incredibly, the fools at Leadenhall had allowed him to resign his post and sail to England before they had seen sense enough to give in to his conditions.

Clive said, 'At last the Company's listening to their people? Amazing, because Stringer's easily the best soldier in India. That news pleases me greatly!'

Hayden nodded. 'In perfect time to deal with the South. Stringer stepped out of the *Durrington* like an apparition, without fanfare or theatre, just as you might suppose. It seems the Court of Directors saw the better of their decision. Offered him back his powers of court martial, made him commander-in-chief of Company forces, a full colonel, on double pay. We are ordered to march to a rendezvous with him. I'd call that justice for a deserving man.'

Clive listened in silence, hearing how Lawrence had already duelled with the French in the southern part of the province, then he began to examine his fingernails. 'Did I tell you that I met Raza Sahib at Arni?'

Hayden Flint sat up. 'Met him?'

'That is, I crushed him. I took his army off him, d'you see?'

'And the French?'

'Fed to my artillerymen.' A crooked smile lit Clive's face.

'Oh, you have a way with war, Robert!'

'If so, it's a knack I've been at pains to learn.' He drew himself up. 'I lost eight men. But they took six Frenchmen apiece, and above two hundred of the enemy died in all.'

As they sat quietly, Hayden Flint thought of the loss of life and felt himself far from the grief of it. Once, the terror of pain that lived in his mind would have blinded him to the truth. The war had cost many lives, but death came to everyone in time. Few lived out a full span in such a climate. It was one thing to rot alive with some filthy disease, but for a man to give of his life swiftly in a glorious cause, and in the full flush of youth, was an assertion of the spirit, a kind of martyrdom. In Hindostan, courage was a virtue. And glory came to men who kept faith with their cause. He could see that now.

The news of what had passed at Arni relieved his mind. If French power has been shocked by Arcot, he thought, then the seven hundred French sepoys who fell down like worshippers before this astonishing man in the paddy fields of Arni must make the beginnings of a legend in this land of tales.

'You realize we cannot go south as Stringer wants?' Clive said. His voice was level and very quiet.

'Colonel Lawrence's letters are orders.'

'We're not finished here yet.'

'You say you beat Raza Sahib comprehensively at Arni. Why – '

'I beat him, but I did not destroy him.'

Ensign Symonds appeared a little way off, a tall dark-haired young man with a humourless air, looking around as if something eluded him. A servant hovered close by, hidden from Symonds's view, standing in the subtly annoying way that his caste status had perfected in him. Without looking round, Clive said, 'What is it?'

'A boon, lord,' the servant said.

'Boon?'

'*Aam*, lord. This man, he wery poor, wery sick man.'

He led an old man out from behind the tent. He was swathed in a blanket from head to foot. When he allowed the veil down they saw he was blind, his face and hands blunted by a mass of stinking sores. He tottered forward pitiably with elaborate salaams.

The servant knelt and put his hands together in an attitude of extreme respect.

'Sweet Jesus . . .'

Symonds stepped purposefully towards the servant, then recoiled as he saw the wretched figure. 'Good God! He's a leper!'

'He is my . . . my father.'

The pleading in the servant's voice enraged Symonds. 'God damn you, man! He is diseased. How dare you bring him here? Don't you realize the panic you'll cause? Take him away.'

The servant stood. The leper trembled.

'Go on,' Symonds hissed furiously. 'Do as I say! There's nothing for him here. Get him out!'

Hayden Flint winced. Symonds was screeching like a parrot. Doesn't he yet know that in Hindostan everything is watched at all times by a hundred eyes? He's blundered up and ignited a situation.

Heads swayed like poppy flowers in a breeze. A whisper went about. Eyes were shaded from the sun shamelessly. Sepoys gathered from nowhere in knots to sop up the *gup* before their havildars got a grip on them.

'Wait!'

Clive had spoken. He sat in silence for a moment, then stood up, stretched out his hand to the leper and laid it on his head. The leper cringed under the contact, then Clive slowly took his hand away, turning to the servant to say, 'Now go.'

The servant swathed the leper in his blanket and led him stumbling through the camp. A bugle ordered two companies of sepoys to their weapons for practice, and the incident faded quietly away.

When they were alone again, Hayden Flint shook his head. 'That was unwise.'

'You think so?'

The moment had passed but it had left a bad taste in his mouth. 'You toyed with that man.'

Clive dusted his hand casually against his knee. 'Symonds told the leper there was nothing here for him. But he was wrong – there was hope. And I gave it to him.'

Hayden Flint thought about that, wanting to say that Robert Clive had no right, that he was dealing in false belief, but he recalled the Eye, and the way he himself had behaved, and instead he muttered, 'You should not have encouraged him. Already they think you're a demi-god. What more do you want?'

Clive stared at him for a long moment. 'Perhaps I am a god,' he said, and he laughed.

The laughter angered Hayden Flint. 'No, Robert.

You're a man. You have courage, and talent, and something for which there is no name in any living language, but you're still a man.'

After a pause Clive said, 'I see your real thoughts. I read you well enough to know what angers you. You think me puffed up by my successes. Arrogant.' He threw his hands wide. 'Certain of myself, yes. That I will allow. But it is not arrogance that proves itself a third time.'

'A third time?'

An eerie light came into Clive's eyes. 'Sometimes I lie abed at nights and I can feel the workings of my opponents' minds. I know Dupleix is a haunted soul. He will certainly try to throw good men after bad. Equally I know Raza Sahib will try to take Arcot back. So there must be more. It has not yet happened, but who can deny it will?'

Not only a god, Hayden Flint thought, feeling the shiver run up his spine, but his own prophet too.

He had brooded long on Clive's reasons for turning back north and declining to meet up with Lawrence. To speed the march Clive had ordered a party of wounded and sick back to Madras with Lieutenant Revel and Ensign Glass among them. A detachment of sepoys was sent south with the captured guns. They made two more rendezvous, meeting up with the Bengal reinforcements. Then they had marched into Conjeeveram, finding the holy city deserted and the pagoda occupied by the French.

Four days had passed in waiting. On the fifth day teams of bullocks were brought up and guns emplaced in redoubts that could readily be seen from the walls. The watch went on, greatly intensified. By six o'clock in the evening, Hayden Flint felt doubt beginning to eat at him. He knew the investing of a fort was a game; there was a set form to be observed. Investing a pagoda was much more delicate.

A sentry cried out. He had seen what they were waiting for: a man coming up from the guns.

'Now the business we came here to accomplish, I think,'

Clive said. He pulled on his boots, took his jacket from the back of his chair and went to meet his gunners.

Hayden Flint smiled wryly, following Clive down for lack of anything else to do. 'Like everything else in this country, even fighting's become a ritual.'

'A soldier's art is to avoid fighting by showing the enemy the inevitability of defeat.'

'What about maintaining a reputation for never adding an insult to an injury? It is a pagoda, after all.'

Clive grinned, clapping his hat on his head. 'I only want to win. As I have said before, I have no interest in insulting their religion. No one must lose face, but I will have them out of there.'

The bombardment lasted three days. They smashed a breach in the pagoda walls. Inside they found the fragments of a stone chain, an astonishing, ancient, holy thing made from one piece of rock, now broken to bits.

A breathless corporal reported: 'Our people's all here, sir! Tied up but otherwise without harm, and that's a blessing. Of the Frogs there ain't no sign.'

The French had decamped on the final night, their threats proven hollow, and it had turned out for the good, but now as they rode Hayden Flint thought of Yasmin and her conviction that in Hindostan all things must come to pass in a Hindostan way. Since leaving Conjeeveram the sepoys had been subdued, like men thinking over a tremendous insult. If a test should come now, as it seems to be coming, he thought, how will they behave?

In the late afternoon they had come across the bodies of four peasant refugees lying in the dry nullah that paralleled the road, their arms and legs akimbo, their throats cut. One of Gopal Rao's naiks had pronounced them freshly dead, evidence of the terror that stalked the land. Since Raza Sahib's withdrawal from Arcot, uncontrolled bands had swept through the countryside, looting and spreading chaos.

Our strength is near 400 Company troopers, he thought, feeling uneasy, 300 sepoys, and six guns. Even so, it's nothing to compare with the force we're seeking to engage. Clive says he must scorn hesitation, but we're like a dog hunting down a tiger. It'll be something to sleep easy tonight in such a difficult place.

He stretched the stiffness from his shoulders, wondering when they would have the order to make camp. Despite the foot-blistering pace of their forced march, the men were unsettled. There was an unbearable tension in the column that manifested itself in low voices and watchful glances. No man was willing to give in to his exhaustion. An hour ago their scouts had encountered Raza Sahib. They confirmed the devastating rumour that he had been joined by another force of 400 French and 2,000 sepoys. Latest reports said he was camped close to the village of Cauveripak. They had continued up that road, Clive's conviction that the enemy were striking for Arcot still holding firm.

Hayden Flint watched the pastels of the western sky deepen. It was as if the sky had sucked the colour from the land, leaving it heavy and grey. In the half-light of this bloodstained dusk they were entering a sweet-scented place. The air was heavy with the perfume of a mango grove standing a cable's length to the right of the road.

The jemadar, Gopal Rao, came up and reported to Clive. The whites of his eyes were a brilliant red and he wore a magnificent moustache perfumed with patchouli. 'Sir, my scouts say some horse from Raza Sahib's army have begun to move towards Conjee – '

The jemadar's words were cut off by a tremendous roar. Cannon fire had blasted across the head of the column, many pieces, perhaps six, perhaps seven, lighting up the grove with deadly fire and scattering men like skittles. For a moment there was silence and uncertainty. Then grape-blasted fusiliers began to pick themselves up, stumbling out of the carnage. There was no time to consider.

'Take cover!' Clive's voice rose above the hail of musket cracks, ordering them into the dry nullah that ran beside the road. He drew his sword, and shouted again for his ensign. 'They're in the damned orchard! Six! – *Aarru!* – Seven! – *Aezhu!* – Count the seconds! – Eight! – *Addu* – Nine! – *Onpathu!*'

As the column dissolved into the overgrown watercourse, those measured numbers marched through each man's mind. Precisely sung out as Clive had taught them at drill, the minimum time passing before the guns could roar again after firing.

'Get down!'

Hayden Flint slammed down on his belly, losing his hat. This time he counted nine big guns in the salvo, their muzzle flashes searing into the gathering gloom. He crawled a little way, recovered his hat, then started as he looked across the open ground to the left. The counting had started again under every man's breath.

'Sweet Jesus – look there!'

Clive's eyes followed where he pointed. His face was grim. Away to the left, there were dark shapes – hundreds of horsemen moving on the nullah.

'Lieutenant Collins, take one gun and five and fifty men, go and guard the baggage! Move yourself!'

'Yes, sir!'

'Ensign, go with Gopal Rao. Take your men and form them up in line to protect our left. I want it straight as a lance. Just there. And I'll have a gun guarding each of your flanks, if you please.' He turned to Hayden Flint. 'If we'd made ten minutes better time on the march we'd have had their cavalry falling on us. In this light they are unable to charge.'

We're in some luck, after all, he thought, drawing his sword. Boots crunched by as two men dragged a dying corporal back along the road. As they passed within a yard of him he saw thick blood darkening the ground in a trail behind them. Two rags of bloody flesh trailed out where the man's legs should have been.

Clive called the Portuguese half-caste sergeant to him, a trusted man. 'Double round quietly, over there. D'you see where I mean? Find if there's a way into the orchard for us. Then come back to me. Go!'

The sergeant grabbed six men and took them off.

Hayden Flint wondered at Clive's self-possession at the centre of chaos. It's awesome to behold, he thought. The way he makes men believe instantly that if they do exactly as they are bid, everything must come out right. He looked round and gasped. A file of French infantrymen was advancing along the gut of the nullah just two abreast but fifty in number, their bayonets fixed. He got to his feet, and was aware of half a dozen men rising with him. He was at the fore, momentarily uncertain what he should do. It was the narrowest of fronts, man-to-man and hardly wider, a defile the depth of a grave, a hellish snare into which to step.

'Lead them on, Mr Flint!'

It was Clive's voice, daring him.

He grasped the future in both fists and began to walk forward along the trench, forcing a show of confidence.

He shouted, 'No quarter!' and felt the blood-lust of those that followed behind him. Their courage was far greater than his own, yet he must lead them. That was the paradox.

Bright fire blasted again from the grove, but now the French guns were trained on the rear of the column. His men crouched involuntarily, and he halted. But he knew he must be first to move on. For a moment he was night-blind, then he saw white facings and silver buttons closing with him, and the enemy's dark face: an officer, a man much like himself in build and stature, wielding a slim épée, the light leaden on his crescent gorgette; and then they were in contact, each fighting for his life.

He hacked at the man with his hanger, chopping furiously, but the Frenchman's agile blade turned his strength aside. He could hear the grunts of concentration as each of his five frenzied blows rang down the steel, and were parried.

By God, he's so skilled, he thought, amazed that his own strength was so competently used against him, then, as he hesitated, the épée flashed up, and the point of it parted his cheek below the eye. He slammed his own sword down, but its arc ended against the épée's delicate hilt, knocking it away, but not out of his opponent's grip. They spun back from each other a pace, then steadied. He immediately drew his first pistol in his left hand, and cocked it by jamming the hanger's handguard against the dog-head until it clicked back.

A bloody mêlée had sprung up on the road above as a hundred men from each side lunged and thrust. Men climbed up out of the nullah and engaged with a line of French sepoys. Bayonets and clubbing musket stocks were all that remained at close quarters. A ragged fusillade flashed out from the fringes of the fight, taking a dozen men down, then screams and yelling fury erupted as a knot of Frenchmen drove forward close by. A figure fell back off the bank, doubled up with pain, and crashed down at his feet. He disregarded the man, unsure if he was friend or foe.

Now the shock of his own injury came home and he could feel his cheekbone open to the night; the lips of the wound hung apart and a deal of blood gouted from it. He tasted the keen tang of powder smoke on the air, and a tremendous anger welled up in him.

The French officer came forward again, his eyes fast on the pistol that faced him. Dozens of men massed behind him, and Flint felt men at his own back, ready to carry the task through when he fell. The thought strengthened him, focused him.

'I'll do for you, you bastard!' he shouted. His hand shook tremendously as he squeezed the pistol trigger. Still his opponent was crabbing forward at point-blank range, demonstrating astonishing courage. Sparks flew from the frizzen and the priming guttered, but the weapon had been primed many hours ago, and the moisture in the air had ruined the powder.

There was no time to pull and cock his other pistol before the épée flashed again, the officer stepping low and long into his lunge. In that terrible moment he was aware of the accuracy of the thrust, knew that he could not avoid it. He tensed as the point lanced true into his navel, then the punching pressure like a lusty thump as the sword was driven home.

The horror of the movement froze him. He felt the slender strip of steel penetrate, saw it arch up with the force of the drive, then, miraculously, the blade snapped at the midpoint, canting the officer forward on to his hands and knees.

Hayden Flint saw the last nine inches of the Frenchman's sword projecting from his belly. He slammed his boot into the man's face, making him curl into a tight ball. Immediately a bayonet stabbed forward over the body, but he had enough balance to reel away from the point and slash at the extended musket, so that his sword bit into the French trooper's wrist. Then he threw himself into the wounded man, staggering him back, and tensed as his own men rammed into him one after another, churning the steel in his guts but hammering the French advance back.

He felt his belly convulse in a moment of extreme danger as the bayonet points of those who followed him thrust into the ribs of the struggling mass. Something sharp and hard passed between his arm and ribs and jabbed into his thigh. Then the points of his own men were pushing them back, and he had time to look up as another blast from the battery hidden in the grove shook the ground.

A crew under Ensign Barclay, running a heavy gun forward along the road, were caught in the hail. They were stripped from the gun and left in heaps like butcher's meat. A shattered ramrod and wet-sponge showered into the trench, followed by a blasted corpse on to which he was forced to step as the mass of men wheeled.

He struggled to free himself. In the roadway the gun rumbled on untended, its big spoked wheels turning with the camber, bouncing it over the grassy lip of the nullah. For a moment it teetered, then tipped on to its side and plunged down on to the scrimmage.

He felt the immense weight of the gun carry past him, tearing the man with whom he had been wrestling from his grip. Something whacked into the top of his head and he staggered; lay against the slope among trampled weeds, his thoughts momentarily scattered to the four winds.

A glutinous warmth spread across his belly: blood trickling through his pubic hair. There was not much pain – how much more would there be if he pulled the sword-shard free? Once, in Calcutta, he had been told by a man affecting to be a duellist that a weapon often plugged its own wound; that only when it was withdrawn was there a great flow of blood, and then unconsciousness. He could not afford that . . . The thought drifted away. He had lost his tricorn and the ribbon had slipped from his queue, allowing his hair to fan out like a maniac's; his right hand was wet with the blood seeping through the front of his breeches, and his cheek was on fire, but the crushing impact of the gun had kept him alive, which was more than could be said for half a dozen men around him.

Suddenly he became aware of a wider concern: the concussion had in some way interfered with his eyesight. In the darkness he had lost his direction, but the bloated orbs of a double rising moon reorientated him. Men were filing past him with all the speed they could make and he saw that the enemy had turned and were running back the way they had come.

He saw the danger and jumped up to physically bar his men from following, shouting the rest back. Light-headed and short of breath, he found it hard to put the necessary authority into his voice, but he made an effort.

A cable's length away along the road, no more than two hundred paces, the other guns were blasting back at the mango grove. There were three of them, but the duel was very unequal. They were pinned down and the position was quickly crumbling.

He stumbled back up the nullah as fast as he could. Prone figures littered the ground, some corpses, but mostly men gasping for breath. This was a vale of purgatory, colourless and dark, made otherworldly by the waning moon. He fell twice, unable to pick his feet over obstacles, but on both occasions he was able to twist and fall on his side. After what seemed an age he heard Clive, and made for what seemed to be his silhouette.

Lieutenant Hume's voice was loud. 'Sir, what can we do? If their guns're not silenced soon my men'll be cut to pieces.' He pointed to a second nullah that cut between the road and the black shape that was the mango grove. A slight rise of earth fronted it.

'I will not attack across open ground,' Clive said. 'Remember Arni.'

Hume's voice was brittle. 'You must do something.'

The Portuguese sergeant had crept back. A powder flash limned his expectant face with lightning. 'Sir, there is a path. And they have no guard on their left flank.'

'That's good. It means we can work round the rear of the orchard and rush them. That's what you must do, Hume. Take your whole command and follow Sergeant de Sa. It's dark enough now for the manoeuvre to escape notice. I'll come along with you a way.' He turned and peered into the blackness. 'Flint, is that you?'

'It's me,' he said tightly.

'You know that your advance saved us? They followed you well and did you credit to a man. By God, are you hurt?'

'I'm . . . serviceable.'

'Hold them here until we've dealt with the guns. Then bring them up.'

Four companies of sepoys and Hume's command of 200 Company troopers moved out. As they pulled back along the nullah, the remaining men kept up a covering fusillade. Their three guns kept up a steady fire, but the necessity to move them after every discharge meant the gun-layers lost their marks on the enemy.

A gun was hit. The keg of powder burned and fizzed beside the carriage, sending up a dense pall of white smoke as it popped a knot and spewed flame from the hole, straight up like a Roman Candle.

Flint got up and began to survey the remaining force. Of necessity they were strung out thinly in holding the line of the nullah. He set the wounded to reloading the muskets of fitter men. Those who were able to get up to the top were sent to fire them.

For a while they performed well, but then the remarks that began to float through the blackness started to worry him.

'Wouldn't have thought so many'd've been pulled out to make a diversion.'

'Where's the Captain gawn to?'

'We're too stinking thin to fight this rearguard for him.'

'Where's Hume's people?'

'Ah, they've pissed away off and left us to it, so they have!'

For hours he sat through the stalemate, the nightmare of his belly wound forced away from his unanchored consciousness by great effort. It was essential to act as if it had not happened. Instead he willed the men to await the strategy, but their numbers were thinning. He went among them, with words to lift them, the gash on his face a badge to shame them and the sword blade sticking from his belly hidden from them.

All the while the pitiful lament of dying men underlay the cracks of distant muskets and the intermittent bellowing of the field guns. After each salvo a storm of French grape raked the corpses on the causeway, sending horrifying offal spattering into the nullah. To die here, after everything? It seemed so unfitting. The spasms that gripped his guts were increasing in severity; they could no longer be ignored.

Where is the goddamned attack? he wondered savagely. In the darkness, unsure of their own numbers and the numbers of the enemy, the men were fast losing their will to fight. Even Clive would have had difficulty holding them here. The fear of mutiny, or a treacherous giving of ground, loomed.

As the exchange continued, he eased the watch from his pocket and looked at the white dial in the sallow moonlight. After a while he forced the hands into a drunken focus. Gone ten o'clock. No wonder the men were thinking the worst.

A file of six men pushed past him. He called after them, 'You! Where're you going?'

But there was no reply, and they did not stop but melted into the shadows. They were the new men drafted in from Calcutta. He turned back on Sergeant Burton. Faintly he said, 'Keep your rate of fire up, Sergeant. We want them thinking we're all here still.'

'Aye, sir.'

Burton started as he saw the sword blade sticking out of him. 'Christ, sir!'

'If they get wind we're short of powder they'll be upon us like the plague.'

A voice came from behind. 'Aye, and they'll be 'pon us anyhow, soon enough.'

He reeled forward, grabbed the man close to him and hissed in his ear, 'Pack up that talk! We've got to hold here for the Captain's sake.'

He saw a couple of fusiliers slide away from their positions and into the shadows; the terror of night fighting had worked upon their minds. Unseen enemies were magnified as the hours passed; allies out of sight were counted lost or deserted. The desperateness of the position seethed in his mind. He shouted, 'Remember Arcot!'

Those who had been at the siege murmured replies.

He shouted again to give them heart, and this time they shouted back. 'What are we?' he roared. 'Soldiers! – What do we do? – Fight!'

Then something swiped him on to his back. The pain in his head bloomed, pressure on his throat made him gag, and he flailed out against something yielding. He was pushed down heavily and fell back against the slope. Two sepoys were on him instantly, gripping his arms.

'Hold him, lads! That's the way.'

Then Burton was above him, a dark shape, just a hole in the starry sky. His face lit up like Satan in the red glow as he blew on an end of slow-match. Bright sparks fled from the end.

'Burton?' he panted, concerned that the light would draw fire. 'What are you doing?'

'It's the only way. Just you be still, sir.'

'Let go of me!'

'I can't do that, sir.'

Burton fed the ember on to the wick of a tin lantern until it caught. He seemed to be winding a rag round his fist as he stooped. A sepoy began to heat a knife over the smoky flame. The sergeant put his boot on Hayden Flint's belly and wrenched the sword point out.

At first there was resistance, then it came away all at once. 'Well, I'll be buggered,' Burton said, bringing the lantern close to investigate the metal.

'Shut down that lantern!'

'Captain!'

'By God, what're they doing to you, Flint?'

It was Clive. His colour party had returned. Burton held up the blade. 'We thought he – that is, I took this out of him, sir.' He turned back. 'But you're a lucky man, Mr Flint. Thought it felt wrong when I pulled it. Looks like the sword got jammed tight in your belt buckle. Point didn't go into you more'n an inch. There's plenty of blood, but it's not hardly worth searing shut.'

He sat upright. 'What's happened? What about the attack?'

'That's in the hands of Mr Hume and his people.'

'You left him?'

'A methodical man, is Hume. He'll move in once he's got to where he wants to be. You did well to hold them together here. I cannot be everywhere at once.'

They waited. The moon rose higher, its course across the heavens now seemingly a third part done. He looked at it, seeing its double aspect converge as he willed strength back into himself. Clive strode up and down the nullah, encouraging and chivvying. The musket fire went on, and the French field guns continued to blast out from the mango grove, but they kept up enough reply to dissuade an attack. Hayden Flint's slit cheek began to pulse angrily and the bump on the top of his head had swelled up like a knuckle.

He walked the length of the nullah as he had almost three hours ago. At last he met with Clive again. They crept up the bank to look on the dark stand of trees. It was impossible to see anything except the flash of muskets, like fireflies in the grove.

'What's the hour?' Clive asked.

'Gone eleven, by the moon. He's taking his time.'

'It's as I told you: Hume's methodical.'

Moments later the grove exploded in light and sound. From not more than thirty yards five hundred muskets fired into the unprotected French positions. Hume's companies screamed down on the French emplacements. Within ten seconds all their guns had been overrun.

As they watched, they saw the enemy bolting from their positions. There was yelling, and some attempt at a regrouping, but nothing came of it as the French infantrymen were rudely routed from their lines. It was as if they thought a huge army was lurking in their rear, and had burst upon them. Hume's men gorged their bayonets mercilessly. Packs of men burst from the copse and headed for the road, then realized they were running into the enemy they had been firing on moments before.

In panic they dashed for the horse lines, where Raza Sahib's cavalry waited. The haemorrhage of Frenchmen became a flood; those who did not run were killed. Then Hayden Flint saw the loss of the French guns had had its effect on the cavalry squadrons: unprotected now, and fearing the guns being turned on them, they began to pull back.

Clive ordered his last remaining company up and out of the nullah. They cheered as they charged, until they closed with the hapless French who were trapped in the middle, upon whom they took a bloody revenge.

When the light of morning broke over the land Hayden Flint saw crows and vultures gathering to feast on the carnage. Occasional musket reports banged, scattering them for brief moments before they winged down again on to their lifeless prey. Despite the efforts of the parties detailed to gather the bodies, there were still many dead strewn around the main sites of the battle.

The French battery stood silent now, nine big guns, all intact. Heaps of French-pattern muskets were being stacked, and once Lieutenant Collins brought up the baggage train they would be loaded up as booty.

Hayden Flint sat down, bodily exhausted and more than a little hungry. His middle was tightly bound up and his flaming red cheek so swollen that his left eye was almost closed. The livid wound had congealed dark purple, and Clive's servant had smeared it with a decoction of ghee and herb extract to help it heal, and – the man promised – to drive the flies away. He felt a confusion of emotions. Paramount was the gratitude he felt for the slightness of his hurts, but eating at that was a kind of guilt that he had led men to their deaths under his orders. It recalled to him his feelings over Daniel Quinn's drowning, and that made him realize that that sort of guilt was false, a spectre thrown up by an improper understanding of the true working of fate. A peculiar melancholy had followed on the vast elation he had felt at midnight when the victory had been secured. Then this morning he had been humbled by the astonishing sight of a naik, both his leg stumps bound up in white bulbs of cotton at the knee, sitting placidly and smoking. Most of the badly wounded had by now been taken by raw opium into a painless waking dream.

He looked away to the roadside where the bodies of seventy servants of the Company lay side by side, some almost whole, others mutilated. He had walked among them half an hour ago, to pay his private respects to their courage. In another place a more terrible total awaited the consuming fires of the cremators, or the pits of Christian graves. Fifty-three Frenchmen and 327 French-trained sepoys had been slaughtered in the final clash. These he had forborne to walk past, not through any bitterness, but lest he saw among their number a French officer with white coat-facings, silver buttons and a shattered sword.

A group of four dozen Frenchmen sulked in the shade of a mango tree. Their sullen lieutenant stood a little way off, hands thrust under his coat-tails in an attitude of great thoughtfulness. They had been surrounded in a nearby glade and had surrendered before first light. Now they seemed to be wishing themselves with their comrades who had escaped with Raza Sahib's horse.

An inspection had found among them six Englishmen who had broken from the nullah in the hour of greatest despair. These were tied at wrist and ankle now, and lay trussed to the wheels of the field guns.

A little before noon, the little army was drawn up to witness punishment. Clive stood beside him, and two junior officers came up also, standing a little away.

'This done, may we attempt to link up with Colonel Lawrence directly?' he asked drily.

Clive looked up and said, 'No . . . not directly.'

Impatience made his tone sour. 'D'you mean to prove yourself a fourth time?'

Clive's warning was deadly calm. 'Don't mock me, Hayden. There's still important business to finish.'

'By God, you'll run short of enemies soon. And, I may say, allies. We must go south now! If you will not respect Colonel Lawrence's orders then think of our pact.'

Clive murmured. 'I do think of it. Every day. And we shall march south. But there's one more transaction to be completed. Something I'm told is standing in a place you've been to before.'

The drummers produced a final roll, and fell silent. Lieutenant Hume read the formulas. The deserters already knew their fate. In fear of their lives they had chosen to discard their honour; they had failed their comrades and the Company's law was clear. They were brought forward, hands bound behind their backs. Six ropes had already been thrown over the strongest bough of a sacred mango. The nooses were put round their necks, their heels were lifted clear of the ground, and the life coldly strangled out of them.

The next day they crossed the Palar and marched eastwards, then south, during a long afternoon. That night a warm gale tore at the canvas of their tents and sent the sparks dancing up from their campfires. Hayden Flint fancied it was the passing of the spirit of war from the land. In the morning, they forded the Cheyyar and continued south, and late in the day came to a desolate plain where the earth was pitted as if shallow graves had been scraped up by wild animals. There was a stink lying over it and it had the appearance of a place people shunned.

Clive took the air deeply. 'This is it. Hereabouts is a pretty milestone to mark the start of the South – a country under Chanda Sahib still, but new to us and continuing dangerous.'

A delicate matter lay heavier on Hayden Flint's mind as they rode. So far he had hesitated to broach it.

'You've made no comment about Stringer,' he said, opening what must be opened. 'The latest is that he's camped three hours' march away from Trichinopoly with four hundred Company infantry and twice as many sepoys.'

'It's good that Stringer's back. He's a fine tactician.'

'He allows you liberties, you mean. But there's an important point to consider, something I guess you have overlooked.'

'Oh?'

'It will be no mere detail to drive Jacques Law's people from Trichinopoly. You forget that you will be obliged to cooperate with Rudolph de Gingens and John Cope, in fact half a dozen captains more senior than yourself in the Company's service.'

Clive grunted, his face glowering. 'By God, that's no worry to me. After what I have achieved? They will respect that.'

'If you believe that, Robert, you are deluding yourself. I have tested the mood at St David, and I say it will not take a week for the rejoicing to decay into envy. Bare lieutenants will consider you thrust over their heads by the Council if you do not take the greatest care of your hubris.'

'Look at my achievement! Who knows better how to crush an enemy?'

'Achievement is nothing to do with it. If anything your

600

victories have made that particular situation worse. You have, by your example, shown them up as bumblers.' He sighed. 'You know the Company well. In a strait of desperation they will give you your head, but have you forgotten the rigidity that sets in whenever the Council finds itself in a position of strength? And have you forgotten the capacity of commissioned officers to allow their jealousies to pinch out the flame of their judgment? Beware. I think you must not seek to command the expedition against Trichinopoly, nor allow Stringer to give it to you. Be humble, Robert. For once, be humble.'

'I'll do what it's in me to do. Look around you, and feast your eyes. Do you know where we've got to now? Have you no recollection of this place?'

The fetid air gusted. 'Did you bring us out of our way just to pass through here?'

'I did.' Clive looked around, imperious as a general. 'Do you know it?'

'It's a foul place. Spiritually moribund.'

'Nothing is worse than the scene of calamity. Did you ever visit a battlefield a year afterwards? In the middle time, when all the glory has drained away but before the crust of legend has set over it? It's somewhat like this. See there.'

He turned and saw an impossible sight. A single stone pillar rising thirty feet. It was white and Roman and extravagantly carved with laurels and vine leaves. On its base was an inscription cut in Latin, proclaiming this the site of a future capital, a great city to be called Dupleix-Fatehabad, first city of the new empire.

'Don't it say all?'

With a sudden shock, Hayden Flint realized that they had come to the place where fate had dealt against them. This was the rise on which a Nizam had been murdered. A frisson of horror passed along his spine as he remembered the slow insanity that had crept over Nasir Jang's personality. He relived the moment when Muzaffar Jang, despite his astonishment at the sudden fulfilment of all his ambitions, had clutched the Eye to him in terror.

I wonder how Salabat Jang fares at Aurangabad, he thought, shuddering. What use now the Talwar-i-Jang? It has become the obsolete sceptre of a counterfeit power. But still I wonder about that melancholy youth who refused to bear it. He so wise above his years. How would he have fared under the burden of the Mountain of Light?

It took a half-hour for Clive's gunners to pack Dupleix's megalomaniac monument with captured powder. Then, giving delighted cheers, they watched as it was blown into a thousand pieces.

Yasmin gazed in wonder at the sights revealed by the telescope. News of the approaching English army had excited Umar, and she had wanted to look on it herself as it approached. Three hours ago, she had seen puffs of white smoke coming from Coiladi. Now the same were appearing at Elmiseram, only half as far away. Cannon fire.

She clamped the edge of her veil between her lips as she used both hands to lift the heavy brass tube again. From the noonday peak of Trichinopoly's rock the lines of troops could be clearly seen, their encampments and supplies, and all their movements, laid out as if on a map. The whole of Srirangam Island was spread from horizon to horizon, distinct and detailed under the bright sun, a morning's walk in length and one third that wide. The panorama faded in the distance, but everything else was revealed to the all-seeing eye. To the north-west was the silver ribbon of the Cauvery where it split to form the Coleroon.

'Umar, the river is quite beautiful when the sun shines upon it.'

'Its waters are always high at the spring season, Begum.'

'Difficult to ford,' she said.

'Therefore easier for Chanda Sahib to defend.'

She considered. 'But also harder for the French to retreat from.'

She picked out the pagodas on the island that Umar had shown her: Lalgudi with its grain store, and the spire of Pichondah where the French had stocked up their munitions. Tremendous excitement flashed through her. 'Did I not say, Umar, that the English would come from the east?'

'I prayed you were correct.'

'The French will have need of prayers,' she said, 'if it is true what they say about the deeds of Sabat Jang Bahadur.'

She continued to scan the landscape. To the east was the rocky eminence of Elmiseram, now occupied by the French, and in the far haze the fort of Coiladi. Umar's spies had spoken last night of an English army of fifteen hundred, with eight big-wheeled cannon, coming down the north road from Arcot. Perhaps the French guns were firing on the English, but there, raising dust, were thousands of Maratha horse.

Below in their camp about half Captain de Gingens's troops were going about their duties. The rest, six hundred of them, had marched away at dawn in response to the news. Their aim was to join the approaching army, strengthening them just as the French attempted to meet them.

As she watched throughout the afternoon, she saw French infantry come streaming from their camp across the plains halfway to Elmiseram, forming up in long lines to bar the English approach. They had with them at least twenty guns. North of them Chanda Sahib's horse massed, a dark shape, boiling like chaos, sending a pall of dust high into the air. Then the English infantry came forward and attacked the deserted buildings that stood on the plain.

Her eye sweated at the lens. Gunfire rippled the air with distant deep drumbeats. She saw the French cannonade, and recalled the lesson Hayden had taught her about thunder and lightning. She counted the seconds between what she saw and what she heard. 'Two English miles,' she whispered. And when Umar, ever attentive to her, showed his puzzlement, she said, 'Nothing. Only English thoughts.'

A light breeze stirred the prayer flags overhead, but down on the plain the still air smouldered in heat-haze. The guns filled the air with brilliant smoke that thinned but never quite cleared. Through it she saw glimpses of the French and English guns disputing like street hawkers, while the horse armies manoeuvred restlessly on the edges of the fight.

From here it was obvious why the cavalry charges, no matter how brave and thrusting, were never enough against well-trained foot-soldiers whose flanks were protected by cannon. Whenever the horsemen approached, the infantry lines halted, closed up and concentrated their gunfire on the attackers, breaking the charge and causing it to swerve away uselessly. A broken rabble of foot-soldiers was easy prey for cavalry, but so long as order was maintained these soldiers were impossible to defeat. Vigilance and discipline were all that was necessary on an open plain. Their spiked muskets did the rest.

Her arms ached. She handed the telescope to Umar, wanting to see the wider vista. Steady progress was being made by the marching columns of infantry. Because of the baggage trains, and the need to protect them, they could only come forward at the speed of oxen. But because of the guns, the French lines could not engage.

Then Umar reeled as if he had been shot. '*Alhumd-ul-Illah!* One of Chanda Sahib's generals has fallen to the cannons! It is Allum Khan, he of the white horse and black plume. They are dropping back, Begum! Look!'

She watched as the long afternoon declined and the sun reddened. After an hour, the French guns ceased fire, the lines of infantry and wheeling squadrons of horse withdrew towards the river and their encampments on Srirangam. She saw the striped flag of the English Company and the coloured standard of their soldiers ported in salute, their long shadows cast slantwise across the country. The strangeness of their drums and high-pitched whistling pipes struck her as music began to warble in victory. It was settled. The English had forced a way with hardly any loss. Soon they would be at the gates of the citadel.

She lowered the telescope as the head of the first column

reached the outer walls, pushed the smooth brass tubes inside one another, looking again at the name engraved on the side. A pang of longing wounded her, and she quickly suppressed it with a sigh.

'We had better go down.'

'I am thinking the same thought, Begum.'

Why will the wound not heal? she wondered, sighing again. Has not an age of time passed since it opened? Why then will this hurt not pass from sore to scar?

Umar was looking at her with a soft, sensitive intelligent gaze. 'What troubles you, Begum?' he asked knowingly.

She smiled at him quickly, then turned away. 'I am full of passions today.'

'Because he is coming?'

She turned back to him, biting her lip. 'He is there with Sabat Jang Bahadur. I know it.'

Hayden Flint sat at the open window, feeling the night air teasing his freshly washed hair. He was on the point of a decision. It would mean defying Lawrence, but he held no army rank so it would be no mutiny.

He held up a looking glass to catch the light. The bandage had come off his face an hour ago and he examined the wound thoughtfully. The swelling had subsided; the burning had turned to itching; the flesh had knit somewhat. There would certainly be a scar.

He was about to call for his orderly, but remembered that the man was no longer with him. After marching with the army for so long it was strange to be without comrades. To have been left high and dry along with the wounded and diseased was one thing, but to be left in Trichinopoly with no demands on his time was another entirely. The closeness of the air made him restless; the knowledge that she was near tormented him mercilessly.

He poured a generous glass of Shiraz and inspected its ruby depths before returning to the window. After the rejoicing of the past three days all was quiet again. The arrival of the relief force had hit the city like a typhoon, but now the troops had left again a hole had opened up in the life of the population. The storm might have moved away, but an active enemy was still encamped within five miles; few refugees had found the confidence to return.

After the smashing of Dupleix's monument they had marched to Madras, then to St David for the briefest possible time to replenish supplies and gather news. Clive had been tireless, insisting they head south; they had joined up with Stringer Lawrence's relief force.

When he was certain the column was close enough to Trichinopoly, Rudolph de Gingens had sent a reception force under John Dalton to meet them and conduct them back into the fortress city. Twenty French guns had fired on them, the French infantry had formed up and marched in the burning heat, protected by four thousand of Chanda's horse, but they had been impotent to prevent the reinforcement. Eleven hundred sepoys, 400 Company infantry and eight guns had run the gauntlet, with a loss of seven men, all of them to heat exhaustion.

Tonight, inside the citadel, he was unable to ignore the mounting excitement of knowing he was close to Yasmin. The walls of the zenana were high and blank; from the beaded shutters that covered the windows of the palace seeped a dusky orange light that invited him. He thought wildly of throwing off his sword and coat and trying to scale the wall. But then what? A vision of holding Yasmin, looking on her again, feeling her touch. It was a piece of madness, but its power to compel frightened him.

No, it can never be. But just to see her would be something, maybe that much is possible. I've waited so long. Why must I wait any longer?

Despite his warring emotions he had been called to do his duty in council. He had met the emissaries of Tanjore and Mysore, whose men were encamped a respectful distance from the French, and talked with the envoy of Morari Rao. Muhammad Ali had sent his wazir to greet the relief, but had not deigned to come down from his seclusion in person. De Gingens had welcomed them, but they had been greeted somewhat coolly by Lawrence, unimpressed by the un-enterprising disposition of the Company's troops.

The Colonel had told de Gingens, 'You have permitted M'sieur Law to sit on Srirangam Island for too long. He's doubtless hoping the river will protect him. Tomorrow he'll awaken from that fantasy and we'll have at him in Captain Clive's way. That is, most rudely!'

Beneath the obligatory laughter, Hayden Flint had detected green jealousy: de Gingens trying to control his face as he tasted the bitterness of Lawrence's sarcasm, Cope cold as ice towards the newcomer, many of the junior men offering Clive congratulations with muted enthusiasm, and Lawrence himself blithe to it all. Only one officer, Captain Dalton, had been man enough to mean it when he offered himself to go as volunteer under Clive's command.

Lawrence had laid it out for them on the campaign map. 'It's clear enough. Law and Chanda Sahib are ensconced on this eye-shaped tract of land, so-called here Srirangam Island since it is bounded to the north by the River Coleroon, and the Cauvery to the south. Two forces are best used to destroy the enemy on Srirangam. I will command the southern. Clive, you will take your people north.'

De Gingens had bristled, but held his peace. The humiliation's obvious. Hayden Flint thought, even to our noble allies. What's more, it's a plan with Clive's signature written all over it.

As they left, he took Clive by the arm. 'Remember what I told you, Sabat Jang Bahadur. Humility in your victory.' But Clive had swept past him.

The next day Hayden Flint had visited Lawrence at his camp outside the walls, wanting to know his part in the final confrontation, but the Colonel had judged it more important that he stay.

'Colonel, are you ordering me to remain here?'

'No, sir. It's the Governor who expects that,' Lawrence said, brisker and stiffer than a man of his girth could properly be. 'You're the ambassador of our President, Flint. You know these Moghuls, you've played their style of chess. You're to build for us a satisfactory relationship with the man who will soon – by our efforts – be Prince of the Carnatic once more. D'you see what I'm telling you, Flint?'

He gave a short and bitter laugh in reply. If only Lawrence knew what he was actually asking of me, he thought, savouring the irony. 'If I should tell you all that stands between me and Muhammad Ali Khan, you would sooner not entrust me with the Company's checkmates.'

Lawrence tossed it off lightly. 'Well, there it is.'

'Yes. And Robert Clive? Will he be allowed a respite? We have a matter to conclude. A delicate matter concerning which Governor Sawyer will have doubtless spoken. It is time we had it out with our pet nawab. I speak of kidnap. Abduction. Charles Savage's daughter. We know it was Muhammad Ali's people who took her. Discreet enquiry has revealed that she's held here.'

There was a pause, then de Gingens spoke. 'Governor Sawyer believed it was some impulse to take a hostage against our abandoning his cause. Richard Prince says it's on account of her father's debts.'

'It's neither.'

'I know you were once promised Miss Savage, but . . .'

Hayden Flint's anger showed. 'But what, sir?'

'Clive's – genius – is needed on the field,' de Gingens said, insincerity oiling his tone.

Lawrence was more direct. 'We cannot give Clive a respite for that would mean a respite for the French. Remember they hold the field still.'

'And after Jacques Law and the Marquis d'Auteuil are driven from it?'

'Ah, then the game will have changed.' Lawrence looked up at the dark, pitted walls of Trichinopoly, his fleshy features hardening. 'But until then, on my orders, Captain Clive'll be kept from this poxy acropolis at all cost.'

'Why?' Hayden Flint was at the very limit of his patience.

'Tshch! You know fine well why, sir. I've spent my life among men of war, and I know a driven individual when I

608

see one. He has moved mountains to bring himself here. He has one more to move, then he will have moved the whole earth. For her sake he will move earth and heaven both, and I shan't have him disappointed until we are the victors.'

'Disappointed?' There was something ominous in the word.

'Robert will not find the heaven he is looking for.' Lawrence turned to de Gingens. 'Tell him what you told me about the damned Savage woman.'

The echo of de Gingens's words heated him now as he recalled them.

At first he had refused to believe the man. Had he not been captain of the English garrison here under less than glorious circumstances? Judging his character, de Gingens would likely say whatever Lawrence told him to say in order to reingratiate himself and save a flagging career. But as the explanation emerged, the man had offered such a wealth of proof that it was put beyond doubt. There was nothing else but to agree with him. What had happened to Arkali was kismet. Nothing more. Nothing less.

He downed the rest of the Shiraz in a sour toast: 'Good luck to you, Arkali. And to you, Robert.'

He had made his decision. He would join Clive for the final battle, await his moment with care, and then break the news personally.

Chanda Sahib's red-rimmed eyes looked up as he ducked from under the flap of his tent. His meeting with Jacques Law had been a counsel of despair. The Frenchman had returned to his own part of the encampment with no firm agreement. It had been plain that he was more than ready to negotiate a separate deal with the enemy.

In move after move the Angrezi had shown themselves the better soldiers. The French had been outmarched and outwitted. At Volconda and Utatoor, at Lalgudi and Pichondah, Sabat Jang Bahadur had lived up to his name. Now that d'Auteuil had surrendered, Law was like a man in paralysis. He had lost his dignity.

Chanda Sahib stood up as straight as his guards. The commotion that had pulled him from his prayers stilled as he appeared. Three men were dragged before him, keening pitifully, crawling on their hands and knees, their wrists and ankles hobbled together with rope. Raza and the men of his son's bodyguard crowded round in the circle of firelight to watch the whipping.

'We caught these dogs trying to sneak away!'

'They are deserters, lord. They must be flayed.'

The pretender's eyes dwelt on them, then moved over the group of zealots who had sworn allegiance to him at his zenith. They were nobles, men of honour, soldiers. But much fewer in number now, and every one of their faces was worn with exhaustion. For two days he had seen a madness glinting in their eyes and had recognized it as desperation. He looked sadly from one to the next, feeling the silence of his prayers cold in the pit of his stomach, knowing how much these men wanted to cut the living skin from the wretches before him as an atonement for their own failure.

'It will achieve nothing,' he said flatly. 'Let them go.'

The guards stood uncomprehendingly, so he repeated himself in the same toneless words.

Nadir Zaman, one of his closest allies, complained and spat, but choked into silence as Chanda Sahib laid a heavy hand on his shoulder.

'It is over, Nadir. I know it – and you know it. We have fought and we have lost. It was the will of Allah.'

One of the captives grunted as he was cut free. Two bolted for life, plunging into the darkness, but the third fell at his master's feet, tears burning his eyes.

Chanda Sahib bent and raised up the deserter. He looked into the man's war-burned features and clasped him to his breast. 'Thank you, friend,' he said. 'You have served me well. Now I release you from your promises. You are free to go if you wish.'

He smiled at his son, who had also fought and lost. Poor headstrong Raza! The retreat from Arcot had killed the spirit of his army. The débâcle at Cauveripak had seen their final crushing. An ambush! How stupid! Had he not told his son to harass the Angrezi, but not to bring them to battle, no matter what his superiority in numbers, and no matter what the French said?

Oh, yes, he thought, numb and angerless as he regarded his son. Looking back with wiser eyes, it is easy to see that Sabat Jang Bahadur made sure of the Carnatic at that moment. After that defeat you took your bodyguard to Pondicherry, but the great Dupleix could not forgive your stupidity as I can. Farewell, my son. May God nourish you.

He called in his allies and the men who had stood by their fealty to him. In durbar he divided between them all that remained to him in this world, saying that it was little enough, but that no amount could have sufficed to repay their sacrifices.

'No lord has been served so well by his people. You came to me freely. Freely you may depart. My time has come and gone. Should it come again I shall be long in your debt.'

As he dissolved his power, their wailing rose like the tongues of flame that leapt from the campfires.

That night, knowing the French were watching them, Raza and Nadir Zaman headed a truce party to negotiate with Muhammad Ali's generals for papers of permit, allowing Chanda Sahib's erstwhile allies to pass through the ring of death unharmed.

Returning just before dawn, Raza came to his father's tent. With him was Nadir Zaman and another, who held his peace. This man remained a little way off, swathed in a blanket so that only his chin showed.

The embers of a fire glowed red outside Chanda Sahib's tent, and the man who had come within a hair's-breadth of gaining the Carnatic stood alone under the stars, contemplating the charred wood and drinking cold water from a French soldier's canteen. Raza's report was like poison in his mouth as he spoke.

'They want your head so much they have set a thousand horse patrolling! They are catching and killing anyone who seeks to slip through their lines without surrendering! Father, they are looking for you!'

'Compose yourself. Now tell me what happened.'

Raza hid his despair as best he could. 'Your pardon, esteemed Father.' He paused, imposing his will on his fear and began again formally. 'Muhammad Ali Khan's generals spoke against free passage, but the Angrezi commander, Colonel Lawrence, had more honour.'

Honour, my son? he thought. Lawrence merely allows a cool mind to rule him.

Raza went on. 'They have now issued passes and those who choose to leave must line up at the first sight of the sun, to be conveyed through the lines.' His face became indignant. 'About two hours after midnight there came a letter from Monsieur Law. They showed it openly to me, saying, "The better to convince these diehards who still cling to Chanda Sahib." But I knew they just wanted to sow seeds of vengeance in our hearts, so that we would fall upon the French curs and do their work for them!'

'What did Monsieur Law offer?'

'He has said he will retreat from Srirangam to Pondicherry and leave the choicest of his cannon for Muhammad Ali.'

'And the reply?' He poured the remaining water over the fire, extinguishing it.

'Muhammad Ali's generals told the messenger that only unconditional surrender would prevent their annihilation. Lawrence did not object.'

'The Angrezi are not fools.'

'But I bring hope also, lord,' Nadir Zaman said. 'May we speak in private?' He signalled the stranger to approach. Chanda considered a moment, wrestling mightily. The inner peace he had struggled to gain depended on his acceptance of death. Tonight he had read of the Book; he had found the suras to calm his soul. He was ready. Nevertheless, what harm could there be in hearing about hope?

Once inside the tent, the swathed man revealed himself.

He was Monaji, commander of a squadron of Maratha horse. 'I see you love life,' he said in a western lisp, looking around at the tent's decorations. 'But you must know that Muhammad Ali Khan will not suffer you to enjoy it more.'

Chanda inclined his head in understanding almost imperceptibly, but a smile broke over the Hindu's lips.

'The incense, the fine food, the wine, the women . . . ah, such is the joy of life . . .'

Chanda's anger focused to a cold needle's point. 'Say what brings you, weasel.'

'If you fall into the hands of the English, they will give you to Muhammad Ali, who is merciless.'

'Say!'

The smile dropped from Monaji's face. 'I have come to offer you life. I can ensure your escape to Karikal.'

Raza broke in. 'I demanded a hostage of rank to set against my father's security.'

'I myself am come here at your invitation. Without security.' Monaji drew himself up. 'Do you think I am unconcerned for my own safety? But we are all men of honour and rank. Our promises are trustworthy.' His eyes flashed to Chanda. 'Or am I mistaken?'

'How if we choose to kill you now?' Raza asked, angered by the Maratha's arrogance.

The Hindu inclined his head guilefully. 'If you decided to break your word, how could I prevent it? But kill me and you kill your esteemed father. I do not think you will jeopardize his escape. Or your own.'

Chanda Sahib smiled inwardly. The bitterest irony of his life was before him. Amazing that Morari Rao's Marathas should be such constant persecutors of my cause, he thought; that they should have imprisoned me during my prime, that they should have appeared magically at every toss of my coin. At every crucial moment they have turned the outcome against me. That is kismet, and the reason is unknowable. But how beautiful the symmetry of it. How like a rose the pattern of my life!

'And the price?'

'Your son pledged all the gold you possess.'

'All of it?' he asked, a glitter of wry humour veining his words.

'That was the bargain on which both our oaths were given.'

'I have little enough to offer you, Monaji,' he said, emptying a small pouch of golden mohurs before him. 'With luck, there may be fifty there.'

The Maratha began to examine the coins methodically. Chanda Sahib watched him. It's like watching a baker bake or a sweeper sweep. These men are bandits through and through, born to plunder. How they love their work.

He said in a faraway voice, 'I came to Trichinopoly at the bidding of Dost Ali twelve years ago for fear of Maratha attacks. I warred on Tanjore and its raja to try to save that kingdom from the depredations of your horsemen. I took Trichinopoly by strategy for my lord's sake, and held it three months under a siege that Morari Rao pressed. It was from that rock that his men took me in chains to Satara. There I learned well the love you people have for gold. Since my release you have appeared at every battle I have fought, yet always opposing me. I ask myself how this can be when your one impartial motive is self-enrichment?'

Monaji made a gesture suggesting something that passed understanding. 'Karma,' he said.

'It is as unlikely as tossing a coin to heads fifty times in a row. Whoever heard of that? How strange the world we inhabit.'

'This gold is good,' Monaji said blithely. 'It augurs well for you. Where is the rest?'

'Rest? You are welcome to search the whole camp for it, and you may keep all you find.'

'I promised you all there is,' Raza said. 'This is all there is!'

'But fifty mohurs? For the life of a great man?'

'I am great no more. And fifty mohurs is better than nothing.'

The Maratha's disappointment was grievous. 'But I thought . . .'

'I did not promise an amount,' Raza said triumphantly. 'I have kept my side of the bargain. Now you must do the same.'

Chanda Sahib closed his eyes, gigantic questions still plaguing him. And now, he thought, this Maratha weasel comes to offer me my life if I will go with him. All because my son has made a shabby bargain unworthy of the lowest pedlar. What would my astrologer say to that?

'Come, then, Hindu. Let us have done with it. Lead me through their lines to freedom.'

He laughed aloud, and felt the void within him tremble.

They rode into the city of Arcot six abreast at the head of their column, colours proud, the drums and fifes playing 'Lillibulero'. Captain Dalton was still talking about the French capitulation.

'. . . and at Pondicherry, they say Dupleix was so distraught he could not eat for ten days!'

Captain Rookewood grinned. 'Shouldn't be surprised if the loss of an empire occasioned an equivalent loss of appetite, eh?'

'Look at the crowds of them. They've emptied the fields for miles around to welcome us.'

'Palm fronds strewn on the road, by God!'

Hayden Flint was phlegmatic, detesting the sort of rigid ceremonial they were soon to encounter. He was uneasy because he had not spoken to Clive in a personal way as he had planned. Last night there had been a celebration meal under the walls of the city, and it had not been appropriate. Umar had attended. Thoughts of what the man had said of Chanda Sahib's fate still lingered painfully.

'A valiant and honourable enemy,' Robert Clive had proclaimed when the news broke. 'But his was not to have power. A tragic destiny.'

Perhaps it's true, he thought. Some may roll the die and win the pot with far greater regularity than natural

615

philosophy predicts. Others, Chanda Sahib for one, must bear loss upon loss. His army has been smashed and scattered, and its leader most sadly ill-used. I would have taken him up and pensioned him, but he could not have known that. As Sawyer's man and the Company's political representative, I had that course in my power . . . a tragedy indeed.

He had heard it all last night from Umar, who had himself gathered the story from a Tanjorean soldier, a porter and the wife of an onion seller. Umar passed it on a morsel at a time between courses, serving up the ironies and pathos of Chanda Sahib's end with great skill. He patiently plucked out the splendid embroidery from the tale and told it elegantly in the form of several ever-decreasing spirals, in deference, he said, to the dialects of Trichinopoly.

'I heard it thus, Flint: Chanda Sahib with those faithless Marathas a bargain made – a fool to trust them, but surrender to the Angrezi he feared would mean certain delivery into the hands of my lord, concerning whom was it said by slanderers that eyes and tongue and all else in slow stages would he have taken. And this Chanda Sahib feared.'

After hors d'oeuvres Umar added more. 'Chanda Sahib's hopes were to flee to Karikal, which place is a nest of Frenchmen – and has been for many years – they who would not help when their ally could no longer help them. But such with the motherless enemy is always the way.'

And one sweltering course later: 'Chanda Sahib was led by a false guide. A man upon whom his last remaining wealth he had endowed – a great sword which surpasses all others and has the power to command lightning. In its hilt the bright star of Golconda – you know that of which I speak, Flint Sahib. From the Nizam Salabat Jang had it come, who had refused to inherit, but who had made a present of it to the King of all Frenchmen in Hindostan, a man who knew little of its power and cared still less, who thought to use it, so accursed ambitious was he.'

Hayden Flint had sat up with unconcealed astonishment at that. The Talwar in the hands of Chanda Sahib? Could it be?

Umar's knowing look confirmed it. He was whispering now, to enhance the horror of it.

'My lord demanded the person of his enemy. But the Maratha's word was given to the Raja of Tanjore. So Chanda Sahib was taken to the very place where, by deceits, he had won Trichinopoly for himself so many years ago, and in that choultry they divided him: his body for the raja, his head for my lord.'

Hayden Flint recalled now how the revelation had shocked him yet also delighted his mind. How else could Chanda Sahib have failed, but by the working out of the diamond's curse?

Because of the narrowness of the arch they passed inside the city two by two, and the crush of people was swept away before them. As they rose through the citadel the way became steep and the walls of the stone buildings that flanked the street seemed to lean in on them. Their escort left them. The tumult of the town fell away. They dismounted in a hot and dusty place where rosewater had been sprinkled to perfume the air and carpets were laid along the path. He and Lawrence led them, Clive and Dalton following, then the others following de Gingens, ranked in seniority, down an aisle of fierce mailed men, armed with round shields and matchlocks, like a hybrid of past and present ages. He smiled inwardly at the newfound loyalty the honour guard displayed towards their master.

The carpeted way led into a courtyard containing several hundred turbaned men, and as the gates opened he saw Muhammad Ali Khan in his finery, camped under an awning, fully composed and attended by servants with plume fans and a descending establishment of officers in gorgeously braided jamas. He was standing, an attitude which struck Hayden Flint as inexplicable until he realized this was a coronation in all but name.

He watched in silence. The moment the nawab lowered himself on to the jewel-crusted masnad, a unique rule would commence in Hindostan: the only uncontested native official to be sponsored by the Honourable

Company. Who can doubt, he thought, that there will be more like him? Perhaps unto the limit of French and English competition. A partition. A divided rule, as the old empire is gobbled up by us piecemeal.

As Muhammad Ali's people began their interminable ceremonial preambles, he looked at the prince and saw a changed man. Gone was the obsidian stare, the hard-set jaw, the stiffness of bearing. He seemed relaxed now, even majestic, inclining his head slightly as he caught first Lawrence's eye and then his own without rancour.

For a moment Hayden Flint was perplexed. At Arcot of old such acknowledgement would never have been given. And neither the victory over the French nor his assumption of official rank had anything to do with it. Muhammad was a man now touched by a new understanding. What could have unlocked his heart? He saw the nawab look away and up, and involuntarily his own eyes followed to a small balcony with a widely spaced lattice and a beaded screen set around it.

Shafts of raw sunlight speared the gallery, bursting on to the eye from shawls of every colour, chrome yellow and tangerine, lime and emerald blue. But it was the woman in the red veil whose gaze pierced him. As he watched, he saw her hand lift, falter, and then fall.

Yasmin . . .

It was as if an electric spark had jumped between them. And in that slightest gesture, a million words were told, and he knew her heart exactly.

Beside him Robert Clive looked up too, his face momentarily that of a man in trance.

In the front row of the balcony the sun projected the beaded pattern of the screen on to an emerald bodice, on to pale arms that bore golden bangles, and a paler face framed in braided skeins of coppery hair and adorned by a jewelled nose-ring.

Clive continued to stare for several seconds, then turned away, his eyes glassy, his mouth compressed into a line. There had been not a single sign of recognition from the

618

pregnant woman Muhammad Ali Khan had lately made his foremost wife.

Hayden Flint saw understanding transform Clive's face like a death. He felt for the man, knowing that in his hour of triumph he had lost everything he had hoped for.

Robert Clive left Arcot the next day. At news of his going, Hayden Flint came down to hold his bridle and squeeze his hand in friendship.

'Where is it to be? St David's? Or Madras?'

'Madras. And you?'

'I'll stay here another day.'

'Then you're a braver man than I.'

'That's a great compliment to receive from "the Valient in War", Robert.'

'To that they might also add the title: "The Hopeless in Love".' Clive smiled at the bitterness of his admission. 'I should have expected as much. It's a trick of kismet. Win at war, lose at love. No sane God would dare invest both talents in a single body. For an instance look at the French!'

There's joking that conceals an agony, Hayden thought. He loves her, and he was able to bear it only so long as the war went on.

'Now Dupleix is all but beat, what will you do?'

Robert Clive met his eye. 'Shake the pagoda tree as hard as may be until another fight comes my way. There'll be more from the French before this decade's done, I think. In particular I am indebted to you for the letters you brought out.' He patted his breast pocket. 'That from Edmund Maskelyne especially. I'm invited to enjoy Madras in the company of his sister, Margaret.'

'You're a man of some means now.'

Clive raised his eyebrows. 'Of course, I have my gift of thanks from the nawab's government. If I accounted all my funds together I believe I might find several lakhs of silver to make an investment. I'll carry on trade with your father.'

'If you find him, tell him I think of him.'

Clive seemed to consider, then decide against, saying

something most confidential. Instead he said, 'Your father's the only man who really knew me. We are somewhat alike, he and I.'

'More alike than father and son. That much is a certainty!'

Their conversation petered out, until Clive asked, 'So? What will you do?'

'I don't know. Go to England, perhaps, if the Company will accept a resignation. I have long had a yearning to see the great city.'

Clive's lop-sided grin bloomed bittersweet. 'Take care, then. And I'll wish our paths may twine again, there or here.'

'Yes. Wish that. And I'll hope for it, too.'

He slapped the horse's haunch and watched until his friend's figure had boiled away in the heat-haze of the plain.

When he returned to his private quarters he sat a while, in semi-darkness, his eyes closed, his head in his hand. A torture of sighs attended the closing of this era. He felt the unburdening with some pain, but also with a measure of relief. Strange how the work of years comes abruptly to a conclusion, he thought. Why does the heart ache so when we step back to take the long view over our doings? Perhaps it is how a Hindu soul feels when transmigrating from one body to another. Perhaps it is the universal emotion that comes when one time has ended and another is yet to be.

A small movement caught his eye. A blood-red butterfly had landed on the corner of his marble bench seat. He stood up, wanting to approach it, but its wings flexed and it took to the air, zigzagging out of the half-shuttered window. He stared at the milky stone of the bench, and saw standing upon it a carved rosewood box he had never seen before. A sudden irrational fancy touched him that the butterfly had left it as a gift. As he reached down to pick it up another sensation thrilled through him. The box was not unlike the one he had handed to Nasir Jang, the one that had contained a krait snake.

Under the box was a paper. He broke the seal and found

the rubric of the nawab. Beneath it were written two verses, penned in the language of Aurangzeb's court, in Muhammad Ali's own hand.

Praise to God, Lord of the Worlds, The
Compassionate, the Merciful, King of the Day of
Judgment, Thee we do worship; Thee we beseech!

Guide us on the Straight Path, The Path of those
whom Thou has favoured, Not the Path of those who anger
Thee, Nor of those who be Prodigal.

Now, Flint, for the sake of Honour, in gratitude
and acknowledgement, we bestow a rare scarlet jewel
upon thee.

The hairs lifted on his neck as he read. He felt a giant presence fill the doorway behind him, and had to exert all his will to prevent himself from turning.

'Well? Why don't ye open the box?'

He turned, and felt his soul close up like a clamshell.

'When did you come here?'

'Ah, in the night. Now the filth be controlled, as I allus knew they would be, their trade's loose for them as dares take it up. Fer them as can be first to it, see? And before ye aks, young Robert Clive knew I was here.'

'He said nothing to me.'

'Ay. Becos I told him to keep silent. Why don't ye open the damned box?'

Hayden Flint cracked it open and saw the gem inside glow dully. It was the Eye of Naga. He lifted it out and weighed it in his palm, then tossed it at his father, who caught it deftly in his right hand.

'Yours, I believe.'

'Aye. Mine.'

'That's payment in full.'

'Aye.' Stratford Flint held the jewel up in a shaft of sunlight. 'Found in Chanda Sahib's mouth, so the *gup* has it. I'd say it's payment in full. Well then, I'll be attending to business and I'll let ye get along with yours – son.'

As his father turned to leave Hayden felt something like a physical pain go through him, but he took care not to show his intense joy at his father's final word. He knew there would be no handshaking or hugging or holding. There would be no displays of sentiment. In private, as in public, Stratford Flint would remain true to himself.

His father had reached the doorway before he paused with the mildly puzzled look he always assumed when delivering a parting shaft that turned a deal on its head.

'I nearly forgot t'say: that note of Muhammad Ali Khan don't make clear what rare scarlet jewel he means. Nor what Flint. I suggest ye get packed up t'leave Arcot just as soon as ye can.'

In the silence that followed the echoing away of his father's boots he reread the words Muhammad Ali Khan had written, but without further enlightenment. Then slowly he became aware of noises in the courtyard below his window. Horses were snorting and stamping. He opened the shutters and looked down.

There were many bearers, soldiers of the nawab's honour guard, his own horse, saddled and in readiness, and now a noblewoman's palanquin, swaying on the shoulders of eight men.

All its curtains were scarlet.

EPILOGUE

EPILOGUE

Robert Clive reached Madras and there met Edmund Maskelyne's sister, Margaret; they married within days, embarking for England early in 1753. When Clive returned to Hindostan, this time to Calcutta, he paid his respects at the grave of a certain trader, a friend who had died in the infamous Black Hole.

Almost exactly a year afterwards Clive met the ruler responsible for that tragedy on the field of Plassey. He commanded 1,000 European infantry and 2,000 sepoys against 40,000 enemy infantry, 15,000 cavalry and fifty guns. His complete victory won the country of Bengal for the Honourable Company.

In 1762 Robert Clive was created Baron Clive of Plassey, was elected Member of Parliament for Shrewsbury and made a Knight of the Order of the Bath.

He left the shores of Hindostan for the last time in 1766, returning to suffer the attacks of politicians who were jealous of the great renown and the greater riches he had won for himself. He died, by his own hand, on 22 November 1774, in his fiftieth year.

His son Edward governed Madras from 1798 to 1802.

Joseph-François Dupleix, bearer of the Talwar for just three days, continued his private war against the English. His visions of Oriental empire burned undimmed until August 1754, when Monsieur Godeheu, an official of the *Compagnie*, stepped ashore at Pondicherry to present papers relieving him of his governorship.

Dupleix, one of France's greatest patriots, was ordered to return to Paris, there to be reprimanded, dismissed and shamed. He died a pauper in a Parisian garret some years later, embittered and friendless.

Muhammad Ali Khan, known as Nawab Walajah, ruled the Carnatic until 1795, when the nawabship passed to his son, Umdut-ul-Umara, a fair-skinned man who proved to be a great friend to the British.

Nizam Asaf-ud-Dawlah, Salabat Jang, continued as Nizam of Hyderabad until 1762. He endured the influence of Charles Castelnau de Bussy until 1758, when the English succeeded in replacing him with an influence of their own. The man who arrived was reputed to be the son of a country trader, a man who had had the good fortune to marry a divorced Moghul lady.

History does not satisfactorily record what became of the Mountain of Light during the latter half of the eighteenth century. What is certain is that it moved north and left a bloody wake across the entire subcontinent. It came at last into the hands of Dhulip Singh Bahadur, Maharaja of the Punjab. In 1849, following the Sikh wars, a treaty was drawn up whereby the Punjab was incorporated into the territories of the East India Company, and the world's largest diamond was surrendered to Queen Victoria. It travelled to England in darkness, locked inside two iron-bound chests, aboard the paddle steamer HMS *Medea*. In 1852 the stone was rose-cut and polished by a Dutch diamond-cutter so terrified by his task that he fainted immediately after making the cleavage. In 1937 the Mountain was set into the State Crown of Her Majesty Queen Elizabeth, the Queen Mother, who remains its guardian.

Science cannot determine whether a jewel carries a curse or not. Suffice it to say that the Koh-i-Noor's ownership is only allowed to descend from woman to woman in the British royal family.

The diamond's magnificent light may be seen today by

anyone curious enough to visit the Crown Jewels in the Tower of London. Its brilliance is filtered by a great thickness of armoured glass, but it still exerts a hold of fascination over those who choose to look for more than a few moments into its depths.

INDIAN NAMES AND WORDS

Mention must be made of Moghul names, honorifics and titles. There were no Indian family names as such, so in the interests of clarity I have used the titles of the politically important and the names of those less so – which would have been the case among the English of the time when in conversation.

The provincial ruler known as a 'nawab' was often mispronounced 'nabob', but more often this name was used by Englishmen in England to refer to those of their countrymen who had grown rich in India and returned home. Today, by the same token, we might call a business magnate a 'moghul'.

The suffix '-ul-Mulk' means 'of the Empire', '-ud-Daula' or '-ud-Din' 'of the State', so that 'Fakhr-ud-Din' would translate approximately as 'Pride of the State'. 'Jang' refers to prowess in battle, so that 'Nasir Jang' means something like: 'He who succours in battle' and 'Muzaffar Jang', 'the Triumphant in War'. The addition of 'Ali Khan' (high ruler) to a name was an honorific that implied no family connection.

A living language changes much in the course of two hundred years, and the Indian languages are no exception. Agrarian natives of the Carnatic, in the south, spoke Tamil, a Dravidian language completely unrelated to the languages spoken in the north. But trade flourished along the Malabar and Coromandel coasts, and the trading centres would have heard a dozen different tongues spoken, along with a unifying lingua franca. The Moghuls came from Persia, so the official language of the Muslim courts was Persian.

From it developed a form of Persian which was the soldiers' language. This was Urdu.

Urdu has always been written in a modified Arabic script, but the sounds of any spoken language may be reproduced by using Roman letters along with a consistent convention of pronunciation. Unfortunately for lovers of uniformity this feat of scholarship was only undertaken in the mid-nineteenth century.

Before this there was no convention, so the English simply wrote down what they heard and hoped for the best. (Bengal's head of state, Siraj-ud-Daula, was cheerfully known to the English as Sir Roger Dowler.)

One source of confusion arose from the fact that Arabic script has two *a*'s, one short, sounding a lot like the *u* in 'but', the other long as in 'car'. To complicate matters further, mid-eighteenth-century English was not its modern offspring, and the long *a* was often spelled *au* or *aw* as in the old spelling 'Cawnpore', (Kanpur) and the short *a* by *u* as in 'bungalow'.

Also the English tended to write diphthongs like *kh* and *gh* to approximate to sounds that do not appear in English. This probably led to *h*'s being inserted at will in words, thus the researcher will find 'Moghul', 'Mogul', 'Mugal' and 'Mughal', to give just a few variants.

The older form *oo* has now given way to *u*, so that 'Hindoo' has become 'Hindu', and 'Goorka' has become 'Gurkha', and as a result almost everyone mispronounces it: 'Gerker'.